MADISON

HOUSE

A Novel

PETER DONAHUE

 HAWTHORNE BOOKS & LITERARY ARTS | *Portland, Oregon* | MMV

Hawthorne Books
& Literary Arts

1410 NW Kearney St.
Suite 909
Portland, OR 97209
hawthornebooks.com

Form:
Pinch,
Portland, Oregon

Editorial Services:
Michelle Piranio

Printed in China
through
Print Vision, Inc.

Set in DTL Albertina.

First Edition

9
8
7
6
5
4
3
2
1

Library of Congress
Cataloging-in-
Publication Data

Donahue, Peter, 1943–
Madison House: a novel /
Peter Donahue. – 1st ed.
p. cm.
Includes bibliographical
references and index.

ISBN 0-9766311-0-5
(alk. paper)

1. Seattle (Wash.) – Fiction.
2. Boardinghouses –
Fiction.
I. Title.

PS3604.O533M33 2005
813'.6 – dc22
2005021180

For my parents, Burke Archie Donahue and Gladys Irene Donahue, and for Susan, Elizabeth, and Tana

Contents

MADISON HOUSE

Who hath measured the waters in the hollow of his hand, and meted out heaven with the span, and comprehended the dust of the earth in a measure, and weighed the mountains in scales, and the hills in a balance?

— *Isaiah 40:12*

Above upon thrice seven hills,
A strong young city stands,
Prophetic in her main
And outstretched welcoming hand.

—AUTHOR UNKNOWN

Prologue

Arrest (1908)

CLYDE BOUGHT A DOZEN HOT DOUGHNUTS FROM THE Armenian and ate them straight from the greasy paper bag. He meandered past the farmers' stalls, enjoying his leisure on this warm September morning, forgetting the events of the past two days, glad he'd accompanied his father to the market where the old man peddled the fruits and vegetables he grew back at his Lake Union homestead.

He was biting into his third doughnut when two grim-faced men materialized before him and brought him up short. He nearly collided with the larger of the two, then fell back and looked both men straight on. Like a wall dropped from the sky, the two men stood shoulder to shoulder, looking imperiously at him as they obstructed his way.

"I said, are you Clyde Hunssler?" the smaller one asked.

Clyde hadn't heard him the first time, his hearing still dulled from the explosion two days earlier. The man's tone made Clyde wary of their intentions. He figured they were thugs from one of the regrade work crews out to harass him, as they'd done repeatedly over the past year. Yet both men were clean-shaven and dressed in plain dark Kuppenheimer suits, too slick for regraders. Clyde noted the sleek imperial hat with a silk band on the smaller man, and the stiff, well-brushed bowler on the other. The smaller man, in the imperial hat, had a cleft in the middle of his knobby chin and seemed to be sucking on his cheeks. The larger, in the bowler, stared out from beneath a brow that overhung his eyes like a rock ledge.

Clyde tried to pass around them, ignoring the question, but the one in the bowler commanded, "Answer the question," and stepped sideways to block his way.

Clyde relented and answered, said he was.

"Try to cooperate," the one in the bowler ordered.

"If you don't mind," said the imperial hat, tempering his partner's tone, "we have a few questions for you."

They practiced their back-and-forth to perfection, Clyde thought. "What's it about?" he asked, thinking that whoever they were, they had him pegged to the explosion at the regrading site. "You two Wells Fargo men? Pinkerton?"

They stared Clyde down, unwavering in their demeanor, until finally the good cop, the one in the imperial hat, replied, "We're detectives, Mr. Hunssler. Seattle Police. You were present at Third and Battery two days ago. Five men were killed, you know."

Clyde didn't respond. In the near distance, he heard a boy bark out the price of squash, rhubarb, and beets. He looked down at the greasy bag of doughnuts in his hand, past the people inspecting the farmers' produce on display on the back of wagon beds or in the open-air stalls, and searched for his father's familiar rice-farmer's hat.

"Mr. James Carney told us you made threats that day," the bad cop, the one in the bowler, added. "You reside at Madison House on Blanchard and Fourth, that right?"

"I was at the regrading site," Clyde said. "But I don't know what this Carney fella is talking about. I'd never seen him before. He was ranting on about finding gold beneath Denny Hill. You dicks oughta question your sources better."

Clyde grew both annoyed and anxious over the direction this exchange was headed. He knew it wouldn't likely end well, that the devastation visited upon the Denny Hill neighborhood by the massive regrading over the past several years – and not just the disaster he'd witnessed two days ago – was about to bear down on him full force. He should have kept his vow to Maddie and stayed clear of the regrading site the other day. He really couldn't say what impatience had led him down to the site. He didn't know. Perhaps he was a hot-headed half-breed after all. Perhaps the same defect that blanched his skin and made him more pallid than a winter's fog also made him so damn restive that he had to go see the worst for himself.

"Why didn't you go to the police?"

He didn't have a ready answer for this. To say he'd been afraid wasn't adequate. There was more to it than that. His reluctance involved all the harassment he'd endured over the past many months. It had to do with the workmen at the main regrading site, and at least one supervisor, having already accused him of sabotaging their equipment. It had to do with the fact, too, that he had a solid hunch who the real saboteur was – and being sympathetic to his efforts, he wasn't about to snitch on him.

"Maybe we should have this talk elsewhere," the one in the bowler said, and with a single step forward crowded Clyde toward his partner.

"What talk?" Clyde said. "The damn boiler blew and that was that."

As if on cue, the two men scowled. The big one's granite brow grew a fissure right down the middle between his two eyes, and the small one's cheeks drew even more taut, revealing a sharp jawline. They looked at each other, and it was obvious to Clyde that they were thinking *This one's not going to cooperate.*

"No," the imperial hat said. "We better have a sit-down talk at the station. We need to know what you were doing down at Joe's Bay. We already have your friend Russell Bowles, but he's not being very helpful either."

Clyde looked again at the bag of doughnuts in his hand and then at the crowd of people swirling about the market and the two detectives standing with him in the middle of the road. He wondered how they knew about his trip to Home Colony, the syndicalist-communitarian homestead in South Puget Sound. He wondered why they'd spoken to Russ, and what Russ might say if pressed by these two well-dressed bulls with badges.

"I'm not leaving my father here by himself," he told them.

"Then that's it," the bowler announced, and before Clyde could react, he seized Clyde's left arm and wrenched it behind his back, kicked him behind the knees, and pressed him down to the ground.

In an instant, Clyde rolled onto his back and swung his fist squarely into the side of the detective's head, knocking his bowler off. The detective released Clyde's arm and stumbled back. Clyde leapt to his feet, but before he could run, the other detective pistol-whipped him across the back of the head, and he collapsed to his knees again. The large detective recovered and gave Clyde a vicious kick square in the back between the shoulder blades. Clyde went down hard, face first, his forehead hitting a large paving stone. He felt both arms being twisted behind him and handcuffs being clamped onto his wrists. His head throbbed, and he felt faint. When the two detectives lifted him up by his elbows and began to drag him down the road, clearing a path through the gathered crowd of onlookers, he raised his head hoping to catch sight of his father, and a warm trickle of blood ran down his forehead and stung his right eye.

When they reached the detectives' black Studebaker sedan, one of the detectives – he couldn't tell them apart anymore – rammed Clyde's chest against the rear fender while the other opened the back door. Then one of them grabbed his hair, yanked his head back, and looked him in the face. It was the one he'd slugged.

"I'll give you anarchy," he said, and walloped Clyde in the stomach. Clyde doubled up and heaved for air as the two bulls lifted him off his feet and tossed him into the backseat of the automobile like a bundle of kindling.

One

1. Returning (1899)

THE STEAMSHIP'S SECOND-TO-LAST STOP ON ITS TWELVE-
day passage from Alaska to Seattle was Mukilteo, nothing more than a
skinny dock extending from the shore, a heavily wooded bluff, and atop
the bluff, a weathered-gray shack with smoke rising from its chimney.
From the ship's foredeck, Maddie watched a man lead a bridled mule
weighted with his outfit down the gangplank. The man's felt hat had lost
its shape, the wide brim flopping down over his sunken, bearded face.
He was wet and dirty and carried a stick for balance as he yanked the
mule's reins. He resembled every other luckless, weather-worn prospector beginning to flee the Northland for points south, or else making a
run for Nome in a last desperate venture for gold, as her husband, Chester, had foolishly done.

Maddie recognized this spirit-beaten fellow, something in the way he
clucked at his mule and coaxed it onto the dock. He was the wagoner who
had transported their outfit – Chester's and hers and Morris and Laurette's,
the four of them having teamed up in Seattle for the voyage north two
years ago – from the dock in Skagway to the base of White Pass when
they first landed in Alaska. His other mule had probably grown weak and
been abandoned along the trailside to perish there, and he had probably
sold his wagon to pay for his steerage home. Though the man reminded
her of Chester, which made her angry, and of every other dejected gold
grubber she'd crossed paths with, Maddie felt sorry for the man as she
watched him standing beside his beast of burden on the rock-strewn
shore while the steamship pulled away from the dock. Unlike so many
others, at least he had survived. Who knew even if Chester were still alive?
She almost wished – secretly, abashedly, yet justifiably, she well knew – that
he wasn't, that his frozen corpse was rotting on the bank of some rocky
creek bed in the Alaska wilderness. At least the old wagoner could now
resume his farm life or woodsman's life or whatever kind of life he led
prior to catching the gold fever. Just as Maddie now hoped to resume –
rather, make anew – her own life in Seattle.

As the steamship left the dock behind, the wagoner peered after it as if watching his dream of riches sail from view. Maddie knew that he, perhaps more than she, should be carrying home the pouches of gold. She regretted the man's poor luck, yet she in no way rued her own good fortune. The gold had been her only deliverance once Chester had deserted her in Dawson City. A blessing upon her really, for all her suffering and loneliness these past many years with him. And now she could hardly wait for the steamship's final docking and her longed-for return to the city she had been so captivated by before her husband lured her away from it, just as he'd lured her away from her home in New Jersey more than a decade earlier. Over the past two years, in the Yukon, as she had seen less and less of Chester and yet each day had dreamed persistently of returning to Seattle, the young city had gradually replaced him in her heart. Now the lingering wrench of having been abandoned by her husband receded as her eagerness in approaching her new home and her new life mounted.

Maddie leaned along the port-side rail wondering how she would proceed once the steamship reached Seattle. She simply would, she told herself, as she spotted a locomotive with a line of freight cars snaking its way along tracks that ran parallel to the shoreline. Many more commercial buildings than she remembered this far north of the city appeared along the shore, most made of clapboard, some of brick, as well as clusters of large and small frame houses. The city was expanding outward. At a large scoop in the shoreline where a signboard at the end of a long pier read *Shilshole Bay*, fishing boats, yawls, dories, and various other small craft crowded the marina. The steamship made its way around a large peninsula with steep sandy bluffs rising from the shore. On the rise above the bluffs, Maddie could see a compound of white-washed military barracks at the center of which stood a flagpole with the Stars and Stripes ripping against the wind. At the base of the bluffs, she saw a couple walking slowly along the beach, their heads down, the man carrying a shovel and the woman a bucket. The sight made her ache inside and secretly long for such ordinary companionship. Then a lighthouse appeared at the end of the long spit, tall and white, its bright beacon rotating slowly in the mid-afternoon haze. She could not recall the lighthouse being there when her party had sailed out of Seattle for Alaska. But then again, she had paid little mind to anything other than keeping her wits about her, and keeping track of her distracted husband, their trunks, and her new friend Laurette, who had seemed even more fragile and frightened than she.

Maddie watched the lighthouse, a buoyancy coming over her, and when she looked past the ship's bow and southward along the shore, the city suddenly opened up before her. Even from this distance, it seemed so much larger than she remembered it. A great sprawl of buildings extended the full length of the ram's horn curve that was the shoreline of Elliott Bay. As the ship passed the Smith Cove inlet, she could make out the familiar piers and wharves along the waterfront, including the round clock tower at the end of Colman Dock. Behind these, in the city's central business district, larger buildings crowded one another, and among them tall stacks bellowing white vaporous steam or black sulphurous smoke, creating a haze over the downtown. Beyond the business district and farther up the hill, Maddie could see the start of neighborhoods, narrow row houses to the north and splendid mansions to the south. At this moment, she felt she would take any one of them as her new domicile and be equally happy.

As other passengers began to press to the ship's port side to take in the view, she thought she could hear the clamor of the city as the steamship pushed its way toward the line of wharves. There was Schwabacher's Dock, where the S.S. *Portland* had tied up in July of '97, carrying the "ton of gold" that Chester had exclaimed over before hurrying down to meet the ship. And even though Maddie, being so nearly impoverished as she and Chester had been back then, had never entered Schwabacher's, which was undisputedly the city's finest department store, the sight of its dock made her muse momentarily on the gold stored away in the leather pouches at the bottom of her trunks – her very own gold poke – and on the many opportunities that lay before her.

Just north of the downtown, the Denny Hotel rose above the congestion and commotion of the city like the most grand chalet, proud in its prominence and aglow with its own grandeur. Maddie spotted the small tram that ascended the steep slope leading up to the hotel's ornate entrance and thought she might even take a room there while figuring out what next to do. She began to picture herself in one of the many houses that spread out along the broad hill on which the hotel stood – Denny Hill, as she recalled from the day she'd hiked to its crown by herself before departing for Alaska – with its splendid view of the city and bay. Denny Hill was one of many hills in the city that, like a series of waves, reached inland from the bay in rolling undulations. With the grand hotel atop its southern knoll, the hill seemed to Maddie a kind of gateway to the entire Great Northwest that lay beyond.

Sailing down through Puget Sound earlier in the day, the steamship had occasionally passed a purse seiner trolling the waters for salmon, but here in Elliott Bay the fishing boats had almost entirely disappeared. In their place, steamships, paddleboats, scow schooners, tugboats, and ferries plied the waters, coming and going from the waterfront and making the bay a very busy place. Among the larger craft could be seen small sloop boats, punts and dories, and even an occasional canoe riding the swell. Maddie's steamship wended its way through all this traffic until its piercing steam whistle blew and the ship's steward paced the deck calling everyone to prepare to dock.

"Seattle," he shouted over and over again. "Last port of call."

Yet while the other passengers scurried back to their cabins, Maddie remained leaning against the rail enthralled by the sight of the city growing more detailed, more real, more animated as the steamship approached the dock and brought her back to Seattle. She also, strangely, felt a thin veil of loneliness fall over her. She thought of Chester again and remembered their enthusiasm upon entering the city by train for the first time, Chester attired in his checkered suit, she dressed in layers of chiffon like the sophisticated Phoebe Snow in the famous Erie Lackawanna advertisements. She remembered how as they pulled into the train station Chester had begun elaborating on his plans to make money – he would open a tavern, get to know the right people, invest in a streetcar or ferry company, and eventually become a real player in the city – without ever a word about how she, his wife, would fit into or benefit from his business schemes.

The recollection made her grateful to be entering the city this time on her own terms.

Several dockworkers secured the ship to the dock while others milled about smoking and talking, waiting for the gangplank to be lowered. As soon as it was, passengers began to disembark along one side of the gangplank while the dockworkers pushed their handcarts up the other side and onto the ship's deck. In general, the waterfront seemed less frenzied than it had just two years ago, at the height of the gold fever. The city had changed since then, had become both busier and yet more settled, more sure of itself. Maddie could see the change simply by looking about. The waterfront was more built-up and more congested with railcars, wagons, carts, and even a few whirring motorcars. There was a steady ebb and flow of people along Railroad Avenue running directly in front of the wharves: workmen in heavy boots and work gloves, wearing corduroy or duck coats, driving teams and pushing handcarts, loading and unloading freight, while an entirely different class of men, in polished calf-leather shoes and cotton summer suits, casually strolled up and down the waterfront as if it were a grand promenade. There were also a number of women on the waterfront, some in worn housedresses and long coats selling clam broth and sandwiches from pushcarts, others in shirtwaist suits, outing jackets, and hats stacked with milliner's mull, silk flowers, and assorted plumage. The women strolled arm in arm in pairs or else accompanied the well-dressed men. These handsome men and women had successfully made their way in the city, just as Maddie had once fancied she and Chester would. Yet for all this new bustle, something also seemed more routine, more organized, more efficient about the city than she remembered from those frenzied days surrounding the arrival of the S.S. *Portland*. The city seemed to have come into its own. It was both getting down to work and stepping out, ready to shed its frontier past and declare itself a metropolis for the new century. Maddie instantly appreciated this new aspect of the city, and wanted to be a part of it.

She promptly hired a dockhand to help her with her luggage – the two trunks she had kept with her since leaving Trenton twelve years ago, and her friend Laurette's straight-back chair, which she'd salvaged from the fire that had destroyed their home and dressmaking business in Dawson City and that had taken her young friend's life. Maddie knew she didn't want to return to the seedy area south of Pioneer Place where Chester had made them lodge when they'd first arrived in Seattle – the area known variously as Whitechapel, Blackchapel, the Tenderloin, the Lava Beds, and, most commonly, the Deadline – so she bought a copy of the *Post-Intelligencer* from a boy hawking newspapers at the end of the dock and sat down on one of her trunks to look for notices for respectable boardinghouses in other neighborhoods. When she came across one called Billings House on Fourth Avenue and Blanchard Street, she asked the dockhand waiting on her what neighborhood this was in and he told her it was up on Denny Hill. "Just a few blocks north of the hotel, ma'am."

"The Denny Hotel?"

"Yes, ma'am, the large one atop the hill. They call it the Washington Hotel now. Finest hotel west of the Mississippi, or so they say. I've never been inside it myself."

"I imagine the neighborhood must be a pleasant one then."

"Respectable enough, ma'am. Though it's no First Hill."

Maddie liked the idea of being up on a hill overlooking the city and bay, and decided she would look the neighborhood over. On the chance there would be a vacancy at Billings House, she ordered a small spring wagon from among the many lined in front of the wharves, had the dockhand load her two trunks and Laurette's chair onto the open flatbed, and after climbing up onto the narrow wooden bench beside the driver, asked him to please take her to the corner of Fourth Avenue and Blanchard Street on Denny Hill.

The sun by now had burned away the morning mist, and the day began to turn into a warm, Indian summer afternoon. Tired and content, her brief spate of loneliness and regret behind her, Maddie sat perched on the wagon bench and looked about excitedly as the driver snapped the harness lines and with a jerk from the dray horse turned the wagon away from the wharves and straight up the incline of Spring Street and into the city. On Third Avenue, the wagon turned left, and straight ahead in the distance appeared the Washington Hotel, monumental in its broad and well-trimmed facade, its fancy turrets, cupolas, window boxes, balconies, and verandas. It was like the Acropolis rising high above the rabble-filled city that sprawled below it.

Bouncing along in the spring wagon, Maddie felt as privileged as any high-society lady in a private, silk-lined coach-and-four. As the wagon continued north, they passed the Plymouth Congregational Church, which had the tallest and most graceful spire Maddie had ever seen, and she thought that if everything worked out, she might attend a service there some day, though she'd never counted herself among the particularly religious. She thought it would be the neighborly thing to do. Meanwhile, just behind the church, according to the driver, were the former grounds of the state university, which had recently relocated to a site north of the city. Third Avenue was lined with homes and businesses, with poplar and pear trees turning yellow, and spindly telegraph and electrical poles that looked like so many orthodox crucifixes crisscrossed by wires. A streetcar descended Denny Hill, heading southward on Third Avenue, and clanged its bells as it approached them. Clapping along on the plank road, the wagon sidled to the right to avoid the advancing streetcar. As it passed, Maddie studied the passengers, ordinary people like herself, seated inside, and envied them briefly before realizing she would now be able to board a streetcar anytime she wished. The very thought pleased her so much she nearly laughed out loud at the simple joy of it.

It was such a fine day that Maddie considered asking the driver to stop the wagon so she could get down and walk the remaining distance, especially since the sidewalks were so dry and clean – which differed markedly from the pocked and muddy streets and sidewalks she remembered from the last time she was in the city. As the wagon moved farther up Third Avenue, Maddie became more taken by the neighborhood. After having endured two years in the Yukon, first living in a tent alongside the lakes and rivers as their party made its way to the gold fields, then crammed into two rooms above an outfitting store in raucous Dawson City, after persevering through all this, she felt a sense of ease and security, inspired by the modest, genteel quality of lower Denny Hill, that she had not felt since childhood and the modest comforts of her parents' home. Before the wagon had even reached Blanchard Street, she knew she would remain in Seattle and never return to New Jersey. Her parents had both passed on more than four years ago, while she and Chester were still residing in Cleveland, and after losing them she no longer had ties there. Chester, who had worked on the railroad with her father, had always scorned Trenton, saying it would never amount to what Philly or even Allentown had become. Yet Trenton was where Maddie's family had made their home, where she'd gone to school, and where, until she fell in love with Chester, with his footloose ways, she had believed she would always stay. If she were honest with herself now – as she always tried to be – then she knew she owed Chester at least this: that his contempt for New Jersey had compelled them across the continent and eventually to Seattle, the one place where she now felt she truly belonged. She would make her new home right here in this neighborhood in fact, on this very hill. The decision was that simple – and it was hers alone to make.

At the base of Denny Hill, a small tram carried well-tailored guests to the entrance of the Washington Hotel. The wagon driver turned right and began circumventing the steepest part of the hill, eventually turning up Sixth Avenue where the slope was not so sharp. The horse lowered its head and steadily pulled them up the hill, the driver snapping the reins and clicking his tongue, while Maddie turned about in the wagon seat to look at the city as it came into view below them. At the top of the hill, the driver turned right on Blanchard Street, letting the horse amble at its own pace until they reached Fourth Avenue.

Billings House was a three-story frame house, rectangular in shape, on a large corner lot. In the front, a pair of wide bay windows arched out from two second-floor rooms while two third-floor dormers extended up from the pitched roof. A covered porch stretched across the front of the house, which faced onto Fourth Avenue and looked west over the rooftops of the houses and apartment buildings on the hillside below. Beyond that, the view took in the open blue expanse of Elliott Bay, the thin dark shoreline of Bainbridge Island across the bay, and toward the northwest, the jagged, white ridgeline of the Olympic Mountains. The boardinghouse was large, twice as large as the simple house Maddie had grown up in beside the railroad tracks in Trenton. It appeared to be one of the largest houses in that part of the hillside neighborhood, although clearly in greater need of repair and maintenance than any of the other houses in the vicinity.

Maddie stepped down from the wagon and looked about as the driver struggled to unload the trunks that were weighted with gold and her limited worldly possessions. Directly across the street two houses stood side by side, smaller and narrower than the Billings House, each a modest single-family home, but each well cared for. Farther down the hill, there were a number of similar homes, with a series of row houses mixed in. Yet on the block where she stood, there was only one other house, at the corner of Lenora Street. She could plainly see, two blocks south of this corner, on the first hump of Denny Hill – which, with its two humps, resembled a camel's back – the back of the Washington Hotel. Past the massive hotel, the entire city extended out all the way to the mudflats where the Duwamish River flowed into the bay. A wooded hill with a scattering of houses on it rose above the mudflats, and then, in the far distance, floating over the horizon like the city's frozen white crown, Mount Rainier appeared.

Not until the wagon driver announced that her trunks and chair were waiting for her on the front porch did Maddie draw her eyes away from the mountain. The driver took the four bits she handed him from her handbag and with a quizzical look asked, "Why just the one chair, ma'am? Did ya lose the other?"

"It belonged to my dearest friend," Maddie replied, and looked at the driver. "All that remains from the fire that took her life." She wanted to tell the driver how Laurette had died senselessly, had been murdered really, but restrained herself from saying any more. She would not allow the events in the Yukon to detract from an occasion that, to her, felt like a new gathering of herself, a renewal of sorts ... this moment that, for whatever reasons, had taken on the aura of a homecoming for her. She handed the wagon driver a generous tip instead.

"I'm most sorry to hear that, ma'am," he commented, and nodded as he took the tip from her. "Good day and good luck to you, ma'am." He climbed back onto the wagon and was off, heading straight down the hill and leaving Maddie standing in front of the boardinghouse.

A wooden signboard with hand-painted red lettering hung from the front eave of the porch:

Billings House
Rooms 50 Cents per Night
$3.00 per Week.

Maddie considered the sign for a moment, then looked about one more time at the view, and as she turned up the walkway, climbed the steps to the large front porch, and knocked at the front door, all seemed good and right to her.

2. Clyde About (1903)

CLYDE WALKED INTO THE CITY EVERY DAY LOOKING FOR odd jobs to support himself and, when possible, to help his father out with a few dollars. The shingle mill his father had once owned and operated on his twenty-acre lot on the eastern shore of Lake Union was now defunct, the machinery sold off, the mill shed crumbling. What remained of the shed gave shelter now to a creaky old apple press that Herman Hunssler used to squeeze cider from the apples he gathered each autumn from the dozen or so trees on his property. He sold several gallons of the cider to his neighbors and fermented the rest to stay drunk on through the wet winter months.

Clyde wasn't much interested in this new enterprise and tried to stay away from his father's place as much as possible of late. He preferred ambling about the city, only half-heartedly looking for employment. These days he liked to let the work find him, since for the past six years, from age fourteen when he started working at the coal mine to right before his twentieth birthday last June when he was fired from the salmon cannery, he had worked twelve-hour days, seventy-two-hour weeks, all year long without relief. And where did it get him?

Despite himself, for several weeks now he had been shoveling coal every Monday and Thursday at the Washington Hotel when the coal wagon made its twice-weekly delivery. He knew the wagoner from his two years at the Cle Elum mines, right after his father fetched him back from the Makah, his mother's people, out at Neah Bay on the Olympic Peninsula, and sent him to work at the mines as a coal picker. This was before the cannery, when he made $1.50 a day sorting anthracite from slate with twenty other boys lined up before the picking tables as the coal tumbled off the conveyor belts that the hoist boys loaded far down in the mine shafts. His wagoner friend used to work in the mines, too, but had recently set himself up in town distributing coal instead. He'd initially wanted Clyde to shovel for him at all his stops around the city, but Clyde said he'd help with the hotel, the biggest weekly delivery, and that was all.

Already this morning Clyde had walked from his father's house on Lake Union up and over Denny Hill and down to the waterfront and had eaten an egg sandwich at one of the food stands where the stevedores took their breakfast. When he'd been fired from the cannery last year, he'd tried getting work on the docks, where work was always plentiful and where he knew his way around from loading ships one full summer, working block and tackle, when he was seventeen. Yet when he spoke to one of the dock supervisors on this particular occasion last year, the man had looked him over long and hard and asked, "What're you anyway?"

It was a question Clyde had confronted often enough. Aside from his being albino, which confused most people already, his features drew equally from both his Makah mother and his German father: a wide jowly face, strong chin, and high forehead. He was average height – perhaps tall for a Makah and short for a Kraut – but was broad in the shoulders and strong-limbed from his steady years of manual labor. Of course, what was most striking about his appearance, what really set him apart, was his chalk-white skin with the pink hue just below the surface that, when he got angry or embarrassed and his blood ran strong, could give his skin a rippled marble look. Otherwise, he simply looked opaque, like limestone, and most of the time kept himself fairly well covered by keeping his sleeves rolled down and tying a blue neckerchief about his throat. His face and hands, though, remained in plain view, and that's what got people's attention. And if he ever took off his wool newsboy cap, which he rarely did, his long, straight hair fell to his shoulders like fine white filigree – the color of a spark, his mother once told him. His eyes, a mixture of brown like his mother's and mottled blue like his father's, were the only part of his face that retained any color. So when speaking to someone, especially someone like this ignorant dock supervisor, he kept his sights on that person and held the fellow's attention with his eyes.

When faced with the question about what he was, Clyde knew exactly what was being asked, and more often than not replied that he was German. "My name's Hunssler," he would say. Most people would then take his paleness as a Nordic strain in his lineage – no matter that he retained his mother's flat nose, wide cheeks, and, as he liked to believe, her sense of humor, which could range from utter derision to giddy approval, depending on the situation. And this one called for derision.

"I'm ready to work, that's what I am," Clyde answered, and waited for the supervisor's response. And when the man paused a moment to glower at him and then said abruptly, "Well, we're not hiring," Clyde glowered back at him and walked off, wanting nothing to do with the lunkhead supervisor.

Despite this incident a year ago, Clyde still liked to come down to the waterfront to watch the activity along the docks, even though this morning he was almost struck by a train as he stepped past one line of cars at a standstill just as another line barreled through on the adjacent set of tracks. Railroad Avenue ran the length of the waterfront, always the busiest part of the city, and someone was killed on the tracks at least once a month; as Clyde ate his egg sandwich, he was just glad it hadn't been him this time.

He tarried about the waterfront until heading back up Denny Hill, where he needed to meet his friend's coal wagon at eleven. Yet when he reached the Washington Hotel, the wagon was still not there. This gave Clyde the chance to poke around the vast hotel, which had opened its doors to guests four years earlier when the wealthy speculator James A. Moore rescued it from the financial woes it had run into after its initial construction by the legendary pioneer Arthur Denny. For this reason, among others, many people regarded Mr. Moore as the city's greatest booster, and even though Clyde was more skeptical, figuring Moore was angling to become Seattle's next mayor, he had to admit that the newly refurbished hotel was something to behold. He wandered about the six-acre grounds – the terraced lawns and walkways edged by beds of roses and carnations – admiring the view of the city from the wide verandas. He remained discreet, knowing he would be chased away if discovered, and kept out of view of the hotel guests and liveried bellhops. At one of the side entrances, he slipped into the hotel and wound his way through the glorious main rotunda, which was decked out in redwood paneling, with copper trim and the mounted heads of several big game animals, including a large elk above the wide central staircase, and then began

exploring the adjacent sitting parlors, writing rooms, smoking and bil-
liard rooms, and the three separate dining rooms until finally he found
himself climbing the central staircase and strolling down the carpeted
second-floor hall to a door that led out to a lounging deck, where he halted
at the ornate railing to take in the view of the downtown. When he spotted a bellhop turning the corner, he slipped back into the hallway, entered
a back stairwell, and descended into the basement kitchen with its white
floor-to-ceiling tiles and white marble tabletops, where he felt that with
his translucent white skin he might very easily disappear.

As he sidestepped his way past the preoccupied kitchen staff, he passed
a young woman in a white body-length apron standing at a cutting table
with a wood bin stacked high with silvery Coho salmon. Holding a filleting knife, she slowly and with considerable uncertainty worked at scaling,
trimming, gutting, and filleting the fish. Clyde saw at once that the poor
girl had never been taught how to properly gut and clean a salmon. Not
only did she take too long on each fish but she wasted far too much of the
valuable, rosy-orange meat.

Having spent two years with the Makah when he was still a young
boy and three seasons working for the Colson Fish Company on Shilshole
Bay, Clyde knew how to handle salmon. After his stint working as a picker
at the Cle Elum mines, his father had found work for him closer to home
in the Colson cannery. The recent Exclusion Act had cut down on the
number of Chinese working in the canneries around Puget Sound, and
since the Chinese had been the only ones willing to do such low-paying,
backbreaking work, the canneries were desperate for labor. So when
Clyde made his application and the cannery manager saw him step up to
the sliming table and clean six 30-pound salmon in under a minute without wasting a single ounce of meat, he was hired on the spot. It was seasonal work, which suited Clyde just fine, and he would have stayed at it
if the bosses hadn't eventually brought in the big red iron machine that
in the blink of an eye seized the fish, chopped off its head-tail-fins, split
the body down the middle, removed the entrails, scraped the blood from
the backbone, and washed the meat clean and made it ready for canning
at the rate of sixty salmon per minute, ten times faster than any human

could do the job. The Chinese who hadn't already lost their jobs because of the anti-Chinese riots, lost them to the machine that the bosses soon dubbed the "Iron Chink." And when the new season rolled around, Clyde found out he wouldn't be hired back either.

Clyde came up to the young woman and said, "Let me help you." He took the filleting knife she was using and put it aside, and then reached across the table for the large gang knife and proceeded to show her the correct way to trim, gut, and fillet a salmon. When he saw that she had some three dozen fish in her bin, he said, "Do you mind … ?" and started cleaning one after another in rapid succession until the bin was empty, the slum bucket below the table overflowing with discarded fish heads, tails, and guts, and the cleaned and filleted salmon piled to the side ready for the hotel chef to prepare for that evening's guests.

"Thank you," she said, and then wrapped one of the cleaned salmon in a sheet of parchment paper and handed it to Clyde. "Come back tomorrow same time, if you want to do more," she said, appearing both impressed by Clyde's fish-cleaning skill and relieved to have been spared the task herself. "I'm sure the kitchen manager won't mind."

Clyde left the kitchen with his wrapped salmon and out back of the hotel found the coal wagon pulled up to the coal shed and the wagoner angrily shoveling the load of coal himself.

"Where the hell you been?" he shouted at Clyde, and threw the shovel at his feet. "You finish here. I'm going to drink this bottle of beer as I should've been doing all along," and with that he took a brown quart bottle with a cork plug in its top from beneath the wagon seat and disappeared around the opposite side of the coal shed.

Clyde laid his salmon on the wagon seat, picked up the shovel, climbed onto the wagon box, and began shoveling the coal into the shed. The wagon carried over 5,000 pounds, and it took him a lot longer to unload the coal than it had taken him to clean the three dozen salmon in the kitchen. By the time he had the last of the load out of the wagon box, his back ached and his fingers and palms were swollen with fresh blisters. He could feel the gritty black coal dust coating his sweaty face and could see how it turned his hands and forearms gray.

Just as he jumped down from the wagon, the wagoner appeared in front of the team of horses. He fed each horse a crabapple and cooed to them in a slurry voice, then came up to Clyde and slapped him on the shoulder, sending a cloud of coal dust up from Clyde's shirt and causing him to wince. "You're a good man, Clyde," he said. "Here's your dollar. And no hard feelings."

Clyde pocketed the coin, tipped his cap, and told his old acquaintance from the mines that he would see him back there at the hotel for next Monday's delivery. "Maybe I'll be on time, too," he said and grinned at his friend. He retrieved his salmon from the wagon seat and began the long walk back to his father's place on Lake Union.

As he cut north across Denny Hill, making his way toward Westlake Avenue, which would take him straight down to the lake's south shore, he caught sight of something very curious indeed: a woman climbing a ladder in front of a large, run-down house four blocks north of the Washington Hotel. With one hand she gripped one side of the ladder and with the other hand she hiked up the petticoats of her billowing housedress. She also appeared to have on a bib and apron over her dress, though Clyde couldn't get a very good look at her front. He sauntered along the plank sidewalk and watched her for a moment, mostly out of amusement at her balancing act, yet also mildly taken by the slender, black-stockinged ankles she revealed beneath her skirts. When she began to wobble, he quickly put his amusement aside and ran up the short berm from the sidewalk and onto the lawn. "Excuse me," he called up to her. "May I hold that ladder for you?"

The woman jerked her head and torso about, wobbled again and caught herself, then looked down at the person speaking to her from the lawn. Rather than respond, she turned back around, hiked her petticoats up again, and came down the ladder. Once back on solid ground, she brushed her hands on the front of her apron and straightaway approached Clyde, who watched her now with some concern.

"Perhaps you know someone who could do a small job in my stead," she said, and crossed her arms over her chest. "Seeing how clumsy I am at climbing ladders."

The woman at first appeared frustrated, but she then smiled more pleasantly at Clyde. She seemed several years older than he, perhaps in her thirties. She had a full, welcoming face, rather oval in shape, and a very direct gaze. Her russet-tinted hair wound into a bun on the back of her head and was held in place by a do-rag. Clyde imagined that her tresses were very long and fine when set free from their bun. Although her frame was rather thin, she did not in the least appear slight. Rather, in both posture and manner she came across as physically strong, even muscular – if that could be said of a woman – as if she were accustomed to a good deal of physical exertion. She was clearly not a lady of leisure, and certainly not afraid of being caught climbing a ladder in full view of the public on a late afternoon. There was determination in the way in which she planted herself squarely before Clyde and looked him straight on. They were nearly the same height and their eyes met at a level. Nothing in her countenance expressed surprise or unease at his sudden appearance in her yard or how he looked – all of which inclined Clyde to respond in the only way that seemed appropriate.

"I might help you," he said, and added, "I hate to see a lady in distress."

"A lady, maybe," replied the woman. "*In distress*, hardly. I only require assistance. Not rescue."

"I meant only... "

"I've seen you before," she went on, "walking about to and fro."

"*To*, maybe," Clyde retorted, recovering himself. "But *fro*, hardly."

The woman laughed at this. "You walk about a lot, don't you?"

"It's my preferred mode of conveyance, yes ma'am." Clyde was enjoying this bit of badinage, uncertain if he was speaking to a schoolmarm or a showgirl – she seemed to possess a little of both – and wished it to continue.

"Please," she said, "you don't have to *ma'am* me. My christened name is Madison Ingram, though most people just call me Maddie." She extended her hand and Clyde took it in his, still somewhat uncertain, and they shook. Her grip, like her gaze, was firm.

"If you tell me what the task is you're attempting, I'll be happy to complete it for you," he said.

She looked at him, seemingly bemused by his confident offer. "Well," she said, "I was *attempting*, as you say, to clean the eaves." She turned to look at the front of the large house and with a note of resignation, added, "It's a lot of house to manage on my own."

"Why on your own?" Clyde asked, recognizing as he did just how much they were parroting each other's words. "Is it your house?"

"It is," Maddie said, and continued to stare up at the front of the house as if trying to comprehend the reality of what she'd just said. "As of six months ago, when I purchased it." She seemed to wait for Clyde to say something, and then, unsolicited, explained how she had been a lodger in the house since she returned from the Yukon almost two years ago. The previous owner had been an old man named Harold Billings, who let rooms to two or three ladies – and only ladies – at a discount rate in exchange for making his meals and doing his laundry. When he died eight months later, the man's son came up from Portland to bury his father and sell the house, and that's when she decided to buy it, and at a very good price too, since the son wanted to be free and clear of the property and also because Maddie could pay cash with what she'd banked from her ventures in the Yukon. One lodger moved out right after the old man died, but the other, a young woman named Chiridah Simpson, from Tacoma, who was enrolled at the Egan Dramatic and Operatic School, remained on as Maddie took over as proprietress of Billings House – though she hadn't yet decided whether to take in new boarders.

"So it's a boardinghouse," said Clyde. The thought crossed his mind that Maddie might be a madame and her boardinghouse actually a whore-house.

"Eventually," Maddie said. "If I ever can get it back into working order."

She seemed genuinely daunted by this task, her brow furrowed as she reexamined the front of the house, and Clyde was genuinely sympathetic. "I'll start on the eaves," was his response, and without even negotiating a price for his labor, as was typically his first order of business, he stepped across the walkway and proceeded up the ladder. Maddie, meanwhile, stepped out onto the sidewalk and watched as Clyde scooped debris from the eaves, including an abandoned starling's nest, and dropped it all to the ground. At one point he called down to her that several of the fascia boards were rotted through and should be replaced before the seepage reached the support beams.

"Can you replace them?" she called up to him, her hand held at the side of her face to shield her eyes from the glare of the sun setting behind the Olympic Mountains.

From atop the ladder, Clyde felt as if he might be standing higher than any person in Seattle at that moment. He looked down at Maddie, then across the Sound to the mountains, and came down the ladder. Maddie met him half way up the walkway.

"I can bring my tools tomorrow," he told her. "I can probably find the right size boards back at my father's place ... unless, that is, you want me to go to the lumberyard for new ones."

She answered that his father's boards would do just fine, and thanked him again for helping her.

"It's a beautiful house," he said, looking back up at it. "And it's in a good neighborhood."

"I'll pay you for your work, of course. Just let me know how much."

Clyde shrugged and said that whatever she thought was appropriate would be fine by him. He was between jobs, he told her, and was in no hurry to reestablish himself in full employment. "I like to think I specialize in odd jobs these days." After some more talk about the eaves and fascia boards and a few other tasks that needed to be done, they agreed that Clyde would help Maddie over the next several weeks get the house ready for taking in new boarders.

Clyde admired the woman's initiative, yet he wondered where her family was, her husband, parents, and children, if there were any. She seemed to be undertaking this project entirely on her own, and yet at the same time she seemed perfectly capable of doing so – that is, with his helping hand. "And what will you call your boardinghouse?"

"I'm not sure," she said. "I haven't really thought that far." She seemed to ponder the question a moment, her eyes on Clyde. "The obvious name would be Ingram House," she said at last.

"Or Madison House," he said.

She looked surprised at this. She looked at the house, then back at Clyde, then again at the house. "Madison House," she said. "I like that."

"It's a pleasant name," he replied.

BY THE END OF OCTOBER, CLYDE HAD DONE A NUMBER OF fix-it jobs about the house. He replaced the fascia boards straight off and then the roof's tar shingles with cedar shingles he recovered from several perfectly good houses that had been razed recently as part of the regrading project farther downtown on Jackson Street – for reasons he didn't comprehend, except that the city seemed lately to be undertaking such big, senseless projects every few months or so; maybe people just needed the work, he thought, or maybe the city just didn't know how to leave well enough alone. He also rehung or straightened all the shutters over the windows and then painted the entire front porch white and the porch and window trim a dark green. He painted the front door white as well and reset the door's three glass panes. On the inside, he secured the linoleum to the kitchen floor where it had begun to peel away along the edges and in the corners. He replaced several dowels in the railing on the front stairs and painted the banister black. Toward the end of the month, he removed the musty old wallpaper from the front parlor and den and pasted up a new floral pattern that Maddie selected and had delivered from the Coastal Paint & Housewares Company on Spring Street. On matters of decorating, to which he was generally indifferent, she routinely consulted him and he readily accepted her choice of color or pattern. In all, Maddie seemed delighted with the progress being made on the house, and Clyde was glad to see her so pleased. When she would express her gratitude for all his efforts, as she did frequently, he would accept her thanks and move on to the next job at hand.

It was in the first week of November, with so many projects completed and so many still to be done, that she suggested Clyde might stay in one of the two attic rooms rather than walk all the way back to his father's place on Lake Union each day. Both rooms were spacious, splitting the length of the house between them and running its full width, but were unfinished, situated as they were directly beneath the sloped and exposed rafters of the pitched roof. Each room had one of the two dormers that jutted out from the roof on the front of the house and a smaller window on either end of the house. The rooms were reached by the back staircase that led up from the kitchen. Clyde had been up there frequently to clamber out onto the roof from the dormers and had wondered what Maddie's plans for the rooms were. There was already an iron bedstead and hand-sewn mattress in one of the rooms. The idea of being closer in to town, having his own place to sleep each night, and getting out of his father's shack on Lake Union (even though it was where he'd been born and reared) appealed to Clyde, and he told Maddie he liked the idea and would take her up on it. And for her part, she seemed not a wit concerned that an albino half-breed was crawling around on her roof, scaling the front of the house, traipsing through the front door, trimming shrubs and cutting grass in her yard ... so why should she mind if he was sleeping in her attic? And although he didn't bother to ask, he certainly viewed the arrangement as temporary – at least until the house was ready to admit boarders.

Maddie told him she wanted to begin letting rooms by Thanksgiving and seemed content that the list of tasks the two of them came up with was being completed on schedule. She didn't seem to feel the need to make any formal inquiries about Clyde's character other than what she'd gathered in their conversations when she brought him coffee and biscuits on the front porch in the morning or invited him into the kitchen for a sandwich and cold bottle of ginger beer in the afternoon. And Clyde didn't feel any need to volunteer information about himself other than what came up in these conversations. It seemed that from their very first meeting that September afternoon at the front of the house, they trusted each other. Even more than this, it seemed to him that they actually enjoyed each other's company. As a grown man of twenty, Clyde had never had such a casual, friendly acquaintance with a woman. Although he knew he could become fretful about it if he gave it much thought, he avoided doing so by keeping as busy as possible about the house.

Most evenings, up until Maddie offered him the attic room, Clyde would walk back to the lake and more often than not find his father drunk and hungry and downright ornery. He gave his father some of the money

Maddie paid him, told his father not to spend it on hooch, and then made the two of them dinner – usually the salmon he brought back regularly now from the Washington Hotel kitchen where he cleaned fish twice a week before shoveling coal.

Then one day, after he had been staying at Madison House for a few weeks, he trudged back to the old homestead and his father was off to the side of the house turning over dirt with a spade. He didn't notice Clyde as he walked up. The old man, only fifty but stooped and grizzled and wearing a straw hat with a brim that extended nearly to his shoulders, was bent over his spade, pressing it into the sod, and yanking out large clumps and flopping them over like gigantic flapjacks, exposing the dark brown soil beneath. He had dug several rows about ten yards long – several hours' work at least, Clyde figured. When Clyde coughed to get his father's attention, his father just kept digging. Then without looking up from his work, the old man said, "I'm going to have the best damn garden in Seattle, damn that Robert Patten," and stabbed his spade into the earth.

"It's November," Clyde said. "What're you going to grow in the dead of winter?" He didn't know what to make of this burst of mistimed industry on his father's part, or of his father's curse upon Robert Patten, his old friend and lakeside neighbor just to the north who lived in one of the few houseboats on the lake.

"Everything," came his father's reply. "I'm going to put in some plum trees too. Should have done it years ago."

Of course, Clyde thought. Plum wine. Mr. Patten's specialty. The two drinking buddies must have had some kind of spat.

"Where've you been these past weeks?" his father asked him without a pause in his work, continuing to hurl his spade at the ground with a vengeance.

The question baffled Clyde. He'd told his father more than once about Maddie and her boardinghouse. Yet the old man never paid him any mind.

"It's not trouble you're getting into, is it?" He pitched his spade into the ground, leaned against the handle, and looked at Clyde across the rows of overturned dirt. This was the voice of Herr Hunssler, the stern father, the disciplinarian, the son of the Lutheran minister in Hamburg, Germany.

"I've been helping a lady repair her house, to get it ready for boarders," Clyde replied. Perhaps this was the first time his father had not been drunk when he told him this. "She lets me stay in the attic while I'm working there." Clyde thought his father might accuse him of abandoning him, of leaving an old man alone to fend for himself. But he was mistaken. His father simply wiped his brow and said it was very gentlemanly of his son to help the lady out like that.

"Is she a good cook?"

"She can cook…" was all Clyde could say, and thought of Maddie's salmon biscuits, something she told him she'd learned to make along the trail in Alaska. Their taste and texture, unfortunately, never quite matched the degree of pride Maddie took in making them. "She gets by," he added.

"I'll sell her some of my fruits and vegetables once I get this garden going," his father declared. "Did I tell you it's going to be the best damn garden in the city? Back in the Fatherland, I used to garden all the time."

Clyde thought Maddie would welcome buying her vegetables from his father, although he doubted he would still be at Madison House by the time his father brought in his first harvest. He certainly wasn't going to say anything to Maddie about his father's offer. "I'll mention it to her," he lied, and then seeing how his father slumped over the spade handle, told him to go sit down and he would bring him some water. And for the next hour and a half Clyde turned the ground while his father rested.

He ate dinner that evening with his father, who had earlier in the day shot a wood duck and had already plucked, boiled, and roasted it that afternoon. It was a fat greasy bird, which allowed for good sopping with the half loaf of stale bread he had left over, followed by apple slices and some stiff cider. Clyde asked his father if he had seen Mr. Patten lately, and his father just grumbled and said something about Mr. Patten's getting high-and-mighty about his garden and how a man living on a houseboat should be careful his big head didn't sink it. Clyde figured it was just another one of their many fallings-out, which occurred about once a month, and that by next week harmony would be restored to the lakeshore.

After this brief exchange, Clyde didn't bother trying to engage his father in any more conversation – even though his belly was full of warm duck and cold cider and he was feeling kindly toward the old man, and at one point even thought of inviting him to Maddie's house to see the work he'd done there. Yet he refrained from making the invitation, not wanting to risk the good working relationship he'd established with Maddie. Apart from his mother and father (his father's faults aside), Maddie treated Clyde with about as much respect and kindness as anyone ever had. Even during his two years with the Makah, he had endured repeated ridicule from the other, much darker boys on account of his stark white skin. They said he was paler than whale blubber. They said if he were in their house at night their families could save on lamp oil, he was so bright. But of course these were just children. The adults in the tribe, unlike adults elsewhere, accepted him without comment. As did Maddie. Never had she drawn attention to his albinism—except perhaps once, on a warm afternoon at the end of September when she noticed he wasn't wearing his neckerchief and that the back of his neck had been burned red from the sun. She went into the house, found an old calico cloth, and tied it into an ascot-like scarf about his neck. From then on, he wore the cloth regularly.

Only after Clyde drank a third cup of cider did he break the silence between himself and his father and start to speak more about the kinds of jobs he'd been doing for Maddie, about her cooking, and about the kind of person she was. "She's a Klondiker," he revealed to his father, whose eyelids had begun to droop as his work overturning sod all day caught up with him.

"Is that so," he said, rousing himself enough to swallow the pulpy swill at the bottom of his glass.

"Her husband went to Nome, and since then she hasn't heard hide or hair from him. She figures he's dead."

"You sure she didn't kill him?" His father looked up at Clyde with a mischievous, watery glint in his eyes, which in the dim light of the fireplace made him seem perfectly sinister. Clyde was reminded of Fagin from *Oliver Twist*, which his father had read to him as a child.

"He's probably frozen up north somewhere. Like so many of those damn fools who went chasing the gold," Clyde said, taking the turn in his father's mood as a signal to end the conversation.

"I was never that foolish," his father came back, "although I wish I had been."

"You'd be rich or dead," Clyde told him. "One or the other – and probably not rich."

"You don't know that," his father shot back.

Clyde stood up from the table. Now that his father was turning cantankerous, he wanted to be back at Maddie's, in the quiet of his attic room, reading on his bed by lamplight or sitting in the dormer box and watching the lights of the ships at anchor in the bay, and wondered if it were too late for him to walk back up the hill. "That's a fine garden you're going to have come spring, Pa."

"The best in the whole damn city," his father mumbled, settling back down now.

Clyde cleared the table and stepped outside into the dark lakeside night. South of the lake a yellowish glow rose up from Denny Hill and the city that lay beyond it, a glow that hadn't been there a decade ago, before all the electricity. Just last week Maddie had asked him if he could figure out a way to wire the house, and he said he would certainly try. Unlike his father's three-room shack, Maddie's house also had running water and two separate water closets with flush tanks. And after the electricity, she informed him, she wanted him to try to put in a telephone. As he began walking back toward the hill, which he was beginning to regard as home, he figured that if he and Maddie kept working at this pace, Madison House would eventually be the finest boardinghouse in the whole damn city.

3. Upon the Hill (1904)

MADDIE WALKED UP THE HILL SLOWLY, STEADILY. IT WAS a strenuous walk, yet she knew if she paced herself there was no need to stop and rest. The walk up Denny Hill could never compare to crossing White Pass, as she'd done seven years ago. Her time in Alaska and the Yukon made her strong physically and secure financially – in other words, well prepared to run a boardinghouse. Nevertheless, she knew she could not manage it all without the help of Clyde – who, as far as she was concerned, had been God-sent – or without the weekly rent of five dollars she collected from each of her three boarders. This strenuous walk up the hill was, really, her reward for that Northland trek that seemed a part of some remote past, a life that hardly belonged to her anymore. And good riddance to it, too. The happiness she enjoyed now made her realize just how much she had endured, and not just during those two years in the Yukon but throughout her arduous twelve-year marriage to Chester. What she had now, including her neighborhood, her house, her boarders, and even the uncomplicated companionship she enjoyed with Clyde, was as good as she'd ever had. She especially took pleasure in the routine of it all. She made the walk everyday from her house on the highest point of Denny Hill to the greengrocer's, the dry goods store, the butcher's (or fish monger's, depending on the day's menu), then back up the hill to the boardinghouse, which her more waggish boarders had recently dubbed – good naturedly, of course – "The Mad House."

She loved living perched atop Denny Hill. After the many years of unsettlement while Chester scoured the country for his fortune with her in tow, she knew that she had found something even more valuable than riches – a home, a place where the daily struggle had a purpose, where she felt thoroughly at ease, where, despite the occasional loneliness that tinged her routine, she would remain. She'd felt a similar attachment long ago to her girlhood home in Trenton; but as with her stint in Alaska and the Yukon, her years growing up in New Jersey seemed to her little more than something she once read about in a not-so-memorable novel. She was content in her present; the past hardly registered with her any longer.

Seattle suited her, in temperament and climate, and with her parents gone, and with Chester certain never to reenter her life, and with the title to the old Billings House now in her name, she could declare the city her true and final home, the place where she would build her life.

With a cloth satchel in each hand to carry her purchases, she made her way around the wide girth of the Washington Hotel, the elaborate square-block edifice on the south hump of Denny Hill. When the *S.S. Rosalie* had pulled away from the dock, taking her and Chester to Alaska, she had looked back at the hotel and dreamed of one day staying in one of the third-story suites with a balcony overlooking the city, the harbor, and Mount Rainier in the distance. What could be more splendid? What hotel on the grand tour of Europe, in Paris or Rome or Budapest, could compare? And now as she walked past the great hotel she realized how very close she had come to fulfilling this dream. The front porch of Madison House had as magnificent a view – or very nearly so. Thinking back on that fanciful daydream, she flattered herself now with the fact of her own achievement.

Being so elevated above the city on such a late, lazy morning seemed like a fabulous luxury to Maddie. Although the neighborhood could not lay claim to being Seattle's most exclusive – that distinction belonged to First Hill, where the Burkes and McGilvras had built their immaculate mansions and, increasingly, to Capitol Hill, where the city's newly minted rich were beginning to settle – Denny Hill nevertheless was a good and stable neighborhood consisting of mostly single-family homes owned by shopkeepers and office managers; several boardinghouses, such as her own, where mechanics, dockworkers, office workers, and the occasional student lodged; and a few small brick apartment buildings that mostly housed merchant marines who stayed in Seattle for short layovers while waiting to ship out. A few small businesses occupied the storefronts of corner buildings along the main avenues on the hill – a laundry, a bakery, a tavern, a stationary story, a barbershop – and a few modest-sized churches were tucked into the neighborhood here and there, including Bethel Methodist, Nativity Roman Catholic, and Second Baptist. And, of course, there was the Washington Hotel, behind which the rest of the

Denny Hill neighborhood lay. The hotel stood on the south side of the hill, on the first hump, like a sovereign's castle guarding his hilltop fiefdom. Many people who lived on the hill worked at the hotel as chambermaids, kitchen staff, bellhops, and porters. Last year, two of Maddie's boarders were working there when President Theodore Roosevelt, mustachioed and bespectacled, arrived in Seattle on his tour of the West and stayed three nights at the hotel. She herself had been at the base of the hill when the president boarded the small tram that trundled up to the hotel's entrance, and she was surprised that the man who had declared himself as strong as a bull moose had not insisted on climbing the hill under his own steam. Those three days during which the President of the United States resided at the Washington Hotel had probably been the three busiest days ever seen on Denny Hill.

Maddie walked past the front of Madison House on the plank sidewalk, turned the corner on Blanchard Street, and came up the side path that led to the carriage house and the back entrance of the main house. She went up the back steps, entered the mudroom, and set her two satchels down. She removed her covert-cloth jacket and knobby Oxford walking boots, and entered the kitchen. The house, as it sometimes did during the long midday hours, seemed empty and hollow. Her plan was to make clam chowder for the evening dinner, and she needed to get started right away if it was to be ready by six o'clock. She retrieved her satchels from the mudroom and laid them on the table, then walked out through the swinging kitchen door, through the dining room, and into the front parlor. She knew that the empty house, as much as her husbandless state (with few prospects of a suitor any time soon), accounted for the lonesomeness that sometimes crept over her otherwise hardy spirits.

"Ada," she called out through the house. "Ada, where are you?" From all appearances, her young housegirl had at least done her cleaning. The davenport and sofa pillows looked plumped, the side tables and credenza dusted, and the oak floor and Oriental rug swept. Thankfully, Ada could usually be counted on to carry out her chores even when her mistress was off running errands, which made her an excellent helper indeed. Besides this, Ada was simply a darling young child. Though Maddie tried to regard her as the hired help, try as she might, she could not keep from doting on Ada in her own motherly fashion. Nor, when occasion demanded, could she keep from gently admonishing the child, as any good parent now and then must.

Maddie heard scurrying footsteps, like heavy mice, above her head and knew at once why Ada had not answered her summons. She had forbidden the ten-year-old from going upstairs ever since she caught Ada prying into the boarders' closets. Maddie went to the foot of the stairs and, squinting up into the dark stairwell, shouted, "Ada Brock, come down from up there this instant!" She knew the girl was probably too frightened now to stir an inch. "I just walked up the hill and I don't want to have to walk up these stairs. Please don't make me," Maddie went on, but she knew her tone would probably scare the young thing even more, and so she softened it by saying, "Ada dear, I need your help in the kitchen. So please come down now." She took a deep breath and added, "I'll be in the kitchen when you're ready to help me make the chowder," and with that she walked back through the front parlor and the dining room and returned to the kitchen.

Maddie decided not to waste her time waiting on Ada – like a cat in a tree, the girl would come down when she was ready. She began unwrapping the newspaper from around the five dozen littleneck clams she'd purchased, dropped the rock-sized creatures into a large steaming pot, poured water into the pot from the double-basin sink, and placed the pot on the cast-iron cookstove. With an ear turned toward the second floor as she did all this, Maddie at last detected light footsteps shuffling across the upstairs floor and then softly descending the front staircase. Maddie took the bag of black peppercorns from one of her satchels and poured half of the contents into the wood grinder and turned the crank until a coarse powder filled the bottom tray. She poured the ground pepper into a small blue bowl and set it on the counter. She was about to return to the mudroom to retrieve the potatoes and onions when the swinging door opened from the dining room and Ada sidled into the kitchen, her feet scuffing along the linoleum, her chin pinned to her chest. Maddie decided the best punishment was to pay her no mind and let her stew a few minutes. She went into the mudroom and selected a dozen russet potatoes and half a dozen Walla Walla onions from the copper bins beneath the bottom shelf and, cradling the potatoes and onions in the skirt of her housedress, carried them to the table.

"I'm sorry, Miss Maddie," said Ada, addressing the kitchen floor as Maddie let the potatoes and onions tumble onto the tabletop. "Miss Chiridah's dresses are so lovely – and soft. I just wanted to look at them this once. I won't do it again, I promise."

Maddie stood beside the table and looked at Ada, her pale face with its shy expression, her thin frame, her soft brown hair in two plain ponytails. How could she not feel sympathy for such a dear being? Ada lived with her mother and father in an old farm-style house down the hill on Second Avenue. They were poor. According to the mother, doctors had told them that Ada had suffered brain shrinkage in her infancy due to malnutrition and that this accounted for her being so slow to speak as a child. Not long after this diagnosis, school officials told the parents that these mental deficiencies made Ada incapable of making adequate progress and therefore she could no longer attend classes with the other schoolchildren. So when Ada turned nine, her parents, instead of leaving her at home all day, tried to find work for her. The mother went door to door with her daughter, mostly in the Denny Hill neighborhood, offering Ada's services as kitchen help or a housegirl. Since Maddie was taking in more boarders now and needed an extra hand cleaning the rooms and preparing meals, she invited the mother and her daughter into the kitchen on the day they came to the backdoor, and after hearing their story, she agreed to take Ada on.

"You can ask Chiridah when she gets back to show you her dresses," Maddie said. "I'm sure she would be more than happy to. In the meanwhile, don't let me catch you sneaking up there again, do you hear?"

"Yes ma'am." Ada darted a glance at Maddie, as if checking to see that her remorse had been acknowledged. "I won't," she added.

"Okay, then," Maddie said, and smiled at the girl. She had to admit, she enjoyed the little sprite's company, and even admired her streak of mischievousness. Still, there was work to be done. "I want you to peel these potatoes and onions and then cut the potatoes into chunks and dice all the onions into small bits."

"Yes, ma'am," Ada said once more, but instead of sitting down at the table where Maddie had placed a peeling knife and a bucket to gather the peels, the girl surprised Maddie by hurrying out of the kitchen. She returned in a flash carrying the morning *Post-Intelligencer*. One of Ada's first duties since coming to work for Maddie five months ago was to walk the two blocks to the Washington Hotel with a nickel that Maddie handed to her each morning when she arrived at the backdoor, buy the morning newspaper, and return to the house and place it on the letter stand in the front foyer. She ran this errand while Maddie walked down the hill to do her shopping. Her bringing the newspaper to Maddie in such a determined fashion right now was a testimony to the fact that, despite her transgression in going upstairs, she had fulfilled this important duty.

"Thank you, Ada," said Maddie. "You can come tell me when you're finished in here. You also did a fine job dusting the parlor." Maddie took the newspaper and retired to the front parlor where she liked to sit each morning and read about the previous day's doings. Though everything was right again with Ada, she wondered sometimes whether taking the child on had been the proper thing to do. She gave her three dollars a week for her work at Madison House and in return received endless expressions of gratitude from the child's mother. Yet when the mother had suggested that Ada might stay at the house permanently, Maddie made it clear to her that this was not an option. Fond as Maddie was of Ada, it seemed to her that the mother was trying to unload the poor child on her – and that simply wasn't right. Maddie sympathized with the mother's plight, but she also recognized a mother's duty to tend to and care for her own children. In addition, she knew in her heart that the heavy responsibility of raising a child was one she did not feel adequately prepared for. The very notion of motherhood unsettled her, which was one reason (of many) she was relieved never to have borne Chester any children.

Maddie's favorite chair to read her newspaper in was a curve-backed wing chair she had purchased brand new from the Standard Furniture Company on Second Avenue downtown. Upholstered in a fine maroon chintz that she'd picked out herself, the chair was one of the few new pieces she'd allowed herself to buy. The rest of the household furnishings – in the front parlor: the davenport and sofa, the two floor lamps, the matching coffee tables, the upright piano in the opposite corner, and the letter stand and coatrack near the front entrance; in the back den: the two additional (yet smaller) reading chairs with matching ottomans, two side tables, and the small rolltop desk with its saddle-shaped office chair; and finally, in the dining room: the extension table with eight solid oak chairs, sideboard, and china cabinet – all this she came by either as part and parcel of the purchase of the house or she bought secondhand after scouring the newspaper for notices of estate sales or enlisting Clyde's vigilance in his rounds throughout the city to snag whatever was no longer wanted by its owner that he thought she might like, and hence the letter stand and, remarkably, the upright piano. Finally, the oval rag rug in the center of the parlor was one Maddie had woven herself from the toss-offs of Chester's wardrobe and assorted rags and remnants she had accumulated over the years.

Maddie enjoyed this moment in the late morning, early afternoon, after she had run her errands and set Ada to some task or another. Since she regarded herself as a good citizen, she liked to think of this as her time to catch up on the city's and the nation's news. If women ever received the vote, she liked to think she would be among the first to exercise that right. (Indeed, women in Washington State had once possessed the vote, yet for reasons that escaped her, the right had been rescinded not long ago.) In the meanwhile, she made her way by hard work and perseverance. And when necessity dictated, she wasn't averse to circumventing the rules – such as purchasing Madison House under Chester's name to get around the laws limiting sales of property to women, and one year later filing to have her husband declared officially dead and the property title reissued in her name as his legal heir.

To allow more light into the room, Maddie pulled the lace curtains back from the front windows. Having started out clear and cold, the day was turning overcast as usual. During daylight hours, Maddie tried to avoid lighting the gas lamps to save on fuel costs and keep the gas fumes from stinking up the house. She pulled her sweater about her – since pulling the curtain back had allowed a small draft into the room – and unfolded the paper and scanned the front page. The United States government was sending more teachers to the Philippines in an effort to educate, in President Roosevelt's words, "our little brown brothers who will one day wish to assume the responsibility of self-rule under a democratic constitution." Work on the Panama Canal continued, even as Americans continued to perish from malaria and yellow fever. Mr. Olds and Mr. Ford had both passed the 5,000 sales mark with their motorcars – which did not surprise Maddie at all since every week there seemed to be more of the contraptions on the streets of downtown Seattle, endangering life and limb of every ordinary citizen who chose to use their God-given legs to get about. Fortunately, the steep grade of Denny Hill kept the neighborhood relatively free from the noisy intrusion of most of these vehicles, though this same steep grade had also stirred protest recently among many business leaders who saw the hill as an obstacle to progress in the new automotive century. Such clamoring baffled Maddie, who saw the hill as one of the city's finest features and wondered why Seattle residents didn't seem to cherish their hills in the same manner San Franciscans did theirs.

She considered getting up to check on Ada, but decided to let her be. Yet then, remembering that the pot of clams was still on the stove, she laid the paper down on the floor and returned to the kitchen, where Ada sat at the kitchen table contentedly peeling potatoes, a bowl of water filled with chopped potatoes in front of her and a pile of peeled potato skins beside it. The child paid no mind, however, to the lid dancing and rattling on the big metal pot on the stove. Maddie grabbed two dishrags and seizing the pot by its handles slid it off the stove round and onto the top of the reservoir casing. She pulled out the tray of steaming clams, their shells sprung wide open, and set it in the sink. She turned to Ada and said, "We'll just let those cool a while."

Ada looked up at her – "Yes, ma'am" – and resumed peeling the potatoes.

For the life of her, Maddie could not persuade the girl to stop calling her "ma'am" and to address her by her first name as everyone else in the house did, even though she had insisted on it since the first week Ada came to work for her. Rather than call her "Maddie," the girl would simply not address her at all, or worse yet, would call her "Miss Maddie." Finally, when Maddie relented, Ada reverted to using "ma'am." It occurred to Maddie one day, when the mother, Mrs. Brock, also called her "ma'am," that the formal address was merely parental training, and that it mattered little to Ada what Maddie wanted as long as her mother was telling her otherwise.

She returned to the front parlor and resumed reading the newspaper. After scanning the front page, she flipped ahead to the *City News* section where, in the very first column, the headline in bold, uppercase letters read, "TO LOWER GRADE OF TWO AVENUES." Of course, regrading activity throughout the city was nothing new. Such work had been going on for the past several years, confined to areas downtown around Fifth and Sixth Avenues, and south of Pioneer Place along Jackson Street and Dearborn Avenue. As she understood it, the projects were all part of the master plan of City Engineer Reginald H. Thomson to make Seattle the premier West Coast metropolis. In earlier civic projects – to Mr. Thomson's credit – he had laid claim to the Cedar River and its watershed on behalf of the city, securing a permanent supply of fresh water for Seattle, and had brought about a modern sewage system that people said would serve the city for the next century and beyond. Only during the past two or three years had Thomson undertaken the various regrading projects, having deemed Seattle's hills a barrier to the city's commercial expansion. Contractors had recently lowered several blocks downtown along James Street to make the grade from the waterfront less precipitous, and they were now working on Jackson Street to facilitate access to Rainier Valley, which lay southeast of the city on the way to Renton, a major coal distribution center on Lake Washington's south shore. Maddie had even heard talk that the maverick city engineer might propose regrading portions of Denny Hill to facilitate businesses moving northward from downtown, which would allow more ready access to Queen Anne Hill and Magnolia Bluff and open routes to the Interbay and into Ballard, one of the city's outlying industrial communities. But when Maddie heard this talk of regrading portions of Denny Hill – a topic that would come up occasionally among boarders, neighbors, and local merchants – the scale of such an undertaking seemed inconceivable to her. How could such a thing be done? And even if it could be, wouldn't the good citizens of Seattle, and especially the residents of the Denny Hill neighborhood, promptly point out the city engineer's wrong-headedness in proposing such a thing and bring his foolhardy plan to an abrupt stop?

That's what she had always believed at least – until she read further along in the backpage article in the *P-I*, where the next two subheadlines read, "Level First and Second from Pike to Denny" and "Cut Down Present Hill." She looked up from the paper, heard Ada moving about the kitchen, and then read the two headlines again. As she did so she could feel the blood drain from her face, her breath become shorter, and her stomach begin to tighten. A sudden pressure at her temples made her raise her fingers to her head and knead her brow. The headlines didn't make sense. They were misworded, surely. *Cut Down Present Hill.* Which hill, she wondered, like someone who failed to recognize her own name when hearing it called forth in a crowd. In days gone by, people sometimes spoke of Seattle's Seven Hills, comparing their grandeur to the hills of Rome, yet far more than seven hills rippled the city if all the knolls, humps, rises, and bluffs were taken into account. Could the headline actually be referring to Denny Hill? *Level First and Second from Pike to Denny.* How could that be? Perhaps there was a Pike and Denny on Beacon Hill, a far less established neighborhood than Denny Hill. Parts of Beacon Hill, in fact, had already been sluiced into the mudflats as landfill at the south-most end of town. Then she read the third and final subheadline – "Might Remove Washington Hotel" – and with her pulse already racing, she felt her breath catch as if a weight had been dropped on her chest. It was Denny Hill the article spoke of – *her* hill, as she commonly thought of it. And yet it was much more than that. The article, she realized, was talking about nothing less than taking her home from her.

She understood instinctively that if the city could tear down the Washington Hotel, the crown jewel of Denny Hill, then what was to stop such movers and shakers as Reginald H. Thomson from tearing down the hill on which it stood? Maddie tried to remain calm, forcing a deep breath and reassuring herself that common sense would prevail among the city leaders. According to the article, when City Councilman Marvin Reinhold first proposed paving First and Second Avenues, in the area generally known as Belltown after the pioneer William Bell, Councilman W. J. Muldour objected on the grounds that such an endeavor would be a needless expenditure unless the thoroughfares were first leveled. The entire city council eventually came to a consensus that property values would be augmented five-fold by virtue of the comprehensive regrading and paving of First and Second Avenues and the subsequent expansion of the business district north of Pike Street. "It may seem like a Herculean venture at first," Councilman Muldour was reported as saying, "but it is safe to estimate that the advance in property values will be sufficient to warrant the loss of the property holders' structures."

Maddie had to reread this confounding quotation three times before she could finish the article, which went on to say that the city council had agreed in the end that a petition would be gotten up and circulated among property owners granting the city a mandate to proceed with the regrading project. In closing the meeting, Councilman Akron Lewis reported that the esteemed City Engineer Reginald H. Thomson, who had been unable to attend the meeting, was known to lend his wholehearted support to the project and that he would deem the city council exemplary of the "Seattle Spirit" in giving the project its approval.

Maddie let the paper fall to her lap. ... *loss of the property holders' structures.* The phrase repeated itself in her mind, yet she could not quite decipher it. The phrase seemed like the familiar yet ultimately dense and incomprehensible language of a nighttime delusion. She would have to ask Ray, her newest boarder, who was reading for the law, what it all meant ... what the legal ramifications of such a plan as the city council's might be. What she really wanted to know was, did it mean she could lose her house? She was, after all, a property holder – of the very sort referred to in the article. Everything she had worked so hard for, had risked her life in Alaska and the Yukon for, had invested her take of gold in ... was all this in jeopardy? In no other neighborhood in the city, except perhaps the tatty sections below the Deadline or else far beyond the reach of the trolleys, beyond Ballard, could she afford anything other than the flimsiest pasteboard house. She had been fortunate that her take from her gold claim had been enough to buy the Billings House outright, fix it up, and for now at least maintain it from month to month. As the city rapidly grew, its population expanding tenfold since she and Chester had first arrived in 1896, every other neighborhood but Denny Hill had become very nearly prohibitive in cost for regular working folks. It seemed the city's divide between rich and poor was increasingly pronounced, to the point where one lived either in shameless luxury or in shameful poverty, in a First Hill mansion or a Blackchapel flophouse. In this increasing divide, Denny Hill was an island of working- and middle-class respectability. And now, if her apprehensions over what she had just read in the morning *P-I* were legitimate, the hill was being threatened by the business ambitions of a powerful city engineer and the do-nothing compliance of a weak-kneed city council.

"Ma'am, the potatoes and onions are ready." Ada stood in the entry between the dining room and parlor. Distracted by the alarm and apprehension stirred up in her by the newspaper article, Maddie had forgotten all about the clam chowder. Ada looked at her shyly, almost solicitously, when she did not respond to her announcement about the potatoes and onions. Maddie gazed back at Ada, then smiled at the child and thanked her. She told her she would come in just a moment, and watched Ada quietly retreat back into the kitchen.

Maddie then slumped low in the reading chair and let her head roll to one side. *Seattle Spirit*, Reginald H. Thomson had said, in endorsing a project that in all likelihood had been his doing from the get-go. Maddie had heard the slogan often since her return to Seattle from the Yukon four years ago. She had always appreciated it, felt as if she shared in this spirit, embraced it as her *carte d'entrée* to the city she confidently called home. When she purchased Madison House, her Seattle Spirit had soared. It was legitimated by her capital investment in the neighborhood and the sweat equity of the labor she put into the house. Yet at times – and this was most certainly one of them – it seemed that on the lips of politicians and in the pages of the city dailies the Seattle Spirit slogan was too often used to rally support for whatever boondoggle project city business leaders wished to tax the public for. Judge Thomas Burke used the slogan in his war of words with former mayor Eugene Semple over where the Lake Washington canal should be located: south through Beacon Hill and into the tideflats, as Semple wanted, or north through Salmon Bay and Lake Union, as Burke insisted. With this latest invocation of the Seattle Spirit by Thomson, whose goals for the city sometimes seemed indistinguishable from his private ambitions and who dictated city policy more than the mayor and the city council combined, the slogan had achieved its most crass, most venal usage.

Growing angrier by the moment, Maddie pushed herself out of the reading chair and stepped onto the front porch to clear her head. The sky above the city had become inconsistently overcast, patches of blue still peeking through here and there. Across the Sound, along the lowest steppes of the Olympic range, a dark blue cloud, rain in all likelihood, appeared like a wide curtain. The cloud seemed to progress across the water, darkening everything in its path, while the city, in contrast, bending around the rim of the harbor shoreline, seemed to become more illuminated with its approach. The cloud both absorbed and reflected the day's remaining light. This vivid contrast, imposed onto the full breadth of Maddie's view from the front porch of her house, wrenched her heart with its sheer and stunning beauty. She leaned against one of the support posts on the porch and gazed southward over the city of wood-framed houses and brick buildings, churches and schools, hotels and department stores, offices and warehouses, all unfolding like a three-dimensional map toward the tideflats and the shadow-green hills beyond.

She had never paid much attention to the regrading projects being undertaken elsewhere in the city, had never really believed they would advance this far north. And still she felt certain that Denny Hill residents would rally to prevent the worst, that James A. Moore, owner of the Washington Hotel, the grandest hotel in all the West, would make his opposition known, and the hillside residents would ultimately prevail. The city seemed to have contracted regrading fever, just as it had suffered through gold fever less than a decade ago, as if city leaders had determined that regrading could cure all the city's growing pains that had come about since that last great boom. Right or wrong, it was how the city believed it would remake itself and shed its frontier past once and for all.

Maddie felt a wind come up as the rain cloud approached. She knew she needed to make sure the windows in the upstairs bedrooms were closed and shuttered, that there was enough coal in the scuttle to keep the stove going and the house warm through the night, and that the clam chowder, salmon biscuits, and apple crisp made it onto the dinner table on time. So after taking one more lingering gaze out over the city – and realizing there could be no shining city on the hill without there first and forever being a hill for that city to shine on – she went back into the house.

4. Finding Home (1905)

CLYDE ROSE BEFORE DAWN. HE DIDN'T LIKE TO LINGER about the house, even though Maddie told him he should wait and eat the breakfast she served her four other boarders between six and seven every morning. He preferred to be up and about the city as it rousted itself for the new day. He also didn't want to intrude on Maddie's boarders, suspecting that some of them would object to someone like him sitting across the table from them. She tried to persuade him otherwise, but as he reminded her, he wasn't officially a boarder. When he'd moved into the attic room almost two years ago, they had agreed that he would pay half the weekly rate for the room in lieu of the chores he did to keep the house up, and so according to this arrangement, he told her, he wasn't a real boarder and, therefore, had no meal privileges. Besides, this morning as on every Thursday morning, he had papers to deliver for James Colter, the publisher of the *Seattle Sentry*, the Negro newspaper that James printed twice each week from the carriage house in back of Madison House.

After dressing, Clyde put on his corduroy jacket, scarf, and wool cap in the dark attic room and quietly made his way down the back stairs, past the kitchen, through the mudroom, and out the back door. Through a window of the carriage house he could see two kerosene lamps burning brightly inside. James kept his press on the first floor and a bed, a washstand, an old armoire, and two writing desks on the second floor. When James had first come, around six months ago, proposing to Maddie that he could rent the carriage house for his press and live in the room above, she balked. While no law expressly prohibited a white woman from providing lodging to a Negro man, such an arrangement could have unforeseen consequences, she'd told Clyde that evening. Several houses on the hill rented rooms to Negroes and Orientals, but they were lower-end establishments. Was that what she wanted for Madison House? She discussed the matter thoroughly with Clyde, reviewing her worries aloud to him, and Clyde told her that James was a good man, that he'd known him since he'd first started his printing press in a warehouse down below the Deadline several years ago. "He may very well be the most honest newspaperman in the city," he told

Maddie. "At any rate, he won't actually be boarding *in* the house," he added. "As I am." Maddie seemed to be listening, so he went on. "And unlike me, he'll pay the full rate."

"Clyde," Maddie said at last, "you make a good case for my throwing you out." In time, though, she persuaded herself that having James at the boardinghouse would be to her advantage. She remarked how making genuine use of the carriage house for more than just storage had never occurred to her, how the prospect of gaining a small weekly income from it was appealing, and how, Lord knows, the extra money would come in handy. Clyde was absolutely right, she told him later that week. James was indeed a gentleman, as she could readily tell from just their first meeting. And if there were any repercussions from her neighbors on the hill, she would deal with them as they arose. Clyde listened, and when she was done speaking her mind, he commended her for her good sense.

He was crossing the short alley between the back of the main house and the carriage house when the side door of the carriage house opened and James stepped out. In the predawn dimness he didn't notice Clyde right away. He rubbed his hands with an inky-black rag and wiped his shirt sleeve across his forehead. He leaned against the door frame and lit a cigar stub before seeing Clyde standing directly in front of him.

"Just in time," James said. "The Thursday, November 3, 1905, edition of the *Seattle Sentry* is hot off the press." James was about Clyde's height and weight, yet unlike Clyde, he was long-limbed and lanky. His well-trimmed beard and mustache gave him a distinguished appearance. Though he was obviously tired from having worked all night, his eyes were keen and alert, his speech clear. Clyde didn't know James's exact age, but he figured him to be in his thirties, probably his early thirties.

"It's a cold one this morning," Clyde said.

"You're right there." James took the cigar stub from his mouth and blew his breath out to see the vapor. He remained leaning against the door frame, and for the next several moments the two men – a black and white transposition of each other – stood in the soft, fading dark, appreciating the cold morning air.

Then James stood up straight and waved Clyde forward. "Come inside and have some coffee."

To get the Thursday edition out and onto the streets by morning, James stayed up all of Wednesday night setting type and running the large and outdated Linotype press. The days prior to bringing the paper to press, he wrote stories and edited copy that came in from his two or three sometime reporters. The *Sentry* was one of two newspapers in Seattle owned by black men. The other was the larger, more renowned *Seattle Republican*, which often deflected attention from the *Sentry*, allowing James to take more polemical positions on the issues that mattered most to him, issues such as the rampant lynchings in the Southern states or the rise in racial discrimination among Seattle businesses. Because of the *Sentry*'s lag time in publication, it could also run more in-depth human interest stories, such as last week's feature on the legacy of one of Seattle's first Negro pioneers, William Grose, who had owned Our House, a hotel and restaurant downtown that served Negro and non-Negro clientele alike throughout the late 1800s.

Along with *Seattle Republican* publisher Horace Cayton, who owned a large house in the most affluent section of Capitol Hill, James was one of only a handful of blacks who lived north of Madison Street, the demarcation line above which only Caucasian people generally lived. Black people, such as those who worked in the factories and on the wharves, lived mostly down around Chinatown, near the railroad tracks, or, if they were merchants rather than laborers, south of Madison Street in the area becoming known as the Central District, which used to be predominantly Jewish but was steadily changing. Denny Hill remained one of the few (though limited) exceptions to this geographic segregation. Maddie was one of the few property owners on the hill who rented to non-Caucasians. For Maddie and for James, the arrangement worked out just fine. With the press occupying the carriage house in back (where James re-mained mostly out of sight, or if seen by neighbors, regarded as Maddie's hired help), he could run his newspaper in relative seclusion, which, he told Clyde, inclined him to be even bolder editorially.

Clyde liked James as a person, but he also liked working for him. He earned one dollar for the Monday and Thursday morning route, which took less than three hours and left him plenty of time to get to his other jobs about the city, from cleaning fish and shoveling coal at the Washington Hotel to whatever house maintenance duties Maddie had lined up for him on those two days.

He followed James into the warm carriage house-turned-printshop. The space was wide enough to fit two brougham carriages side by side. In the middle of the hard-packed dirt floor sat the large printing press, oddly resembling the "Iron Chink" with its wrought-iron frame and multiple moving parts. The two wide doors that faced onto Blanchard Street and through which the carriages would enter remained closed. The last day the doors had been open was when James drove up in a buckboard wagon with the printing press on the back bed, the whole load pulled by a four-horse team to get it up the hill. He and two other Negro men and Clyde had rolled the behemoth piece of machinery off the wagon and into the carriage house, and then James had closed the doors and in three days had printed the next edition of the *Sentry*.

In the corner sat a small pig-iron box stove with a blackened tin pot resting on one of the stove's two rounds. Beside the stove were several slabs of wood. James took up the pot using his ink rag and poured them each a mug of coffee. Clyde swirled the thick sludge around in his mug to settle the grounds to the bottom, then took his first taste and shook his head. "That's some potent brew, James," he crowed, peering down into the mug.

"It's deadline brew," James replied, and stepped over to the press with an oil can, inserted its narrow spigot into the machinery, and turned a side lever. The tabloid-size paper was bundled and stacked on a wooden palette beside the door. James only did a run of 2,000 each issue, which was about a thousand under the total number of Negroes living in the state of Washington. He usually sold a thousand in Seattle and shipped the rest to Tacoma, Olympia, Bellingham, and Spokane. After paper and ink costs, postage, and paying his three reporters, four newsboys, and distributor (Clyde), James made just enough at a nickel a paper to put out the next issue, pay Maddie his room and board, and put some aside for unexpected expenditures such as parts for the press or an increase in the cost of newsprint.

"Someday, Clyde, you're going to have to start writing for me."

James was always saying this, and Clyde didn't discourage him. He already served as a stringer of sorts, keeping James apprised of goings-on about the city. During the week he would recount to James events he witnessed or heard about – someone hit by a train along the water-front, a new business opening downtown, a bear wandering into the city from the foothills – and more than likely his accounts would appear almost verbatim in the next edition of the *Sentry*. He liked to think that someday he might write something down for James, just for the byline, for something to show his father and Maddie. Given how well he knew the city, he figured he could be as good a beat reporter as the next fellow.

"Maybe I should start carrying a pad and pencil with me," he said back to James, "and maybe someday I'll make city desk editor." This was a joke, since they both knew the paper had only one editor and that was James, who was also publisher and chief staff writer.

"Did you hear about the regrading?" Clyde asked him as he began loading bundles of paper into the wire basket he'd rigged on top of a handcart with a rope handle so he could wheel the papers about town to the designated drop-off points.

"I saw something about it in the *P–I.*," James said. "You don't think they'll push it this far up the hill, do you?"

"I wouldn't be surprised if they wanted to take the whole damn hill," Clyde came back, tossing the coffee grounds from his mug out the open door. "First and Second Avenues are just the start. Maddie says they'll be sending a petition around to tell the city to go ahead on it. I knew a fellow on Jackson Street lost his house to the regrading. He didn't get anything for it, and after they widened the street he didn't even have space enough to rebuild. He's living in a flophouse down below the line now." Clyde put his mug on the window ledge above the stove and took hold of the rope on the makeshift handcart.

Though the *Seattle Sentry* tried to cover the entire city, it couldn't compete with the half dozen dailies in Seattle, so James focused on the city's neighborhoods rather than the big news events – he liked to say his was a community paper – and he examined issues of special concern to Negro inhabitants of the city and state. Since he'd arrived on Denny Hill, the hillside neighborhood had become one of his main beats, which is why Clyde pressed him about the regrading news.

"I've heard, too, that there's been some sabotaging of equipment down at the Jackson Street site – some of the hoses slashed and chutes busted up. It didn't slow 'em down any, but I imagine it made a few people pipin' mad."

"We'll keep tabs on it," James said, looking at Clyde in the doorway, listening to what he had to say. "It could be big, but we'll just have to see," which was the response Clyde expected to hear, and he wished James would express a little more alarm at the threat he believed the regrading really posed.

"You know," Clyde said, noting that James seemed eager for him to leave on his rounds, "Maddie, owning this house, could be caught in the middle of it all and end up like that fellow on Jackson Street." Then he looked James straight in the eye. "That could mean you and me too."

James nodded his recognition of this point, and Clyde, saying nothing more, satisfied that he'd made his point for now, pulled the cart loaded with papers into the alley.

The dark night sky was now washed out by the dim foggy glow of dawn. Across the alley, the gas lamp burned in the kitchen where Maddie was probably preparing breakfast for her boarders. The thought of the regrading driving Maddie from her house, scattering the boarders, and forcing James to find new quarters for his press infuriated Clyde. As for himself, he wouldn't move back to his father's place on Lake Union, so he didn't know what he would do if it came to that. He might go back to his mother's people, back to Neah Bay. But mostly, it was Maddie he was worried about. He wanted to stay with her in the house, making it better, maintaining the boiler in the shed, wiring more rooms for electricity, finishing off the second attic room – he wanted to keep doing these sorts of things for her.

Suddenly, as if his thoughts of her had invoked her very shape, Maddie appeared standing before the kitchen window, leaning over the sink, her thick reddish-brown hair falling down about her shoulders, framing her face. She looked up, but apparently could not see beyond her own reflection in the glass. She pulled her hair off her shoulders and began to tie it up with a kerchief. As she did so, Clyde admired her long neck and the lift in her bosom as she held her arms above her shoulders. The impression he took of her at this moment, and its effect on him, startled him, and he averted his eyes.

He then turned away and pulled the handcart to the front of the house, diverting his attention to the hard-packed dirt on Fourth Avenue that was just wet enough to be slippery and potentially cause a fall. Because he was pulling the handcart loaded with papers, he walked in the middle of the road rather than on the wood-plank sidewalks. He gave the image of Maddie's neck one last glance in his mind and turned his sights on the city below. He felt good as he began lopping down the broad street. In no time he arrived at his first stop, a shoeshine stand at the corner of Pike and Third. Yet as he continued from there, his thoughts once more strayed back to the soft, sleepy image of Maddie tying up her hair.

CLYDE FINISHED HIS ROUNDS JUST PAST NINE AT THE billiards hall on Occidental Avenue near the manufacturing district. He bought a roll and a cup of coffee from a pushcart near the King Street station and sat on a concrete wall to watch the morning hubbub: the railroad workers readying train cars (Maddie once told him her father had worked for the railroads), newsboys hawking the morning papers (Jerome, a small Negro boy, loudly waved the *Seattle Sentry* above his head), deliverymen with their wagons and peddlers with their pushcarts (including an Italian with a large copper contraption that oozed a thick black paste, on top of which he spooned dollops of white foamy stuff for the Italian dockworkers lined up at his cart), and lust-driven businessmen already making their way down below the Deadline to the saloons and variety theaters where they could be serviced by the showgirls in their private assignation boxes (Clyde wondered at their early start).

Clyde also watched two squat Suquamish women at the other end of the concrete wall sitting side by side on a twined-woven blanket that had diagonal designs in yellow, blue, and black. Around their slumped shoulders, they wore mallard-down robes, the soft, warm kind interwoven with cedar bark that Clyde remembered his mother being buried in. In front of them, the two women had spread several blankets similar to the one they sat on, and on the blankets lay a collection of wood carvings that included several small potlatch boxes, rattles, and miniature poles with figures of Eagle, Raven, Bear, and Salmon. These reminded Clyde of the carver in Neah Bay everyone called Young Doctor who sold his elaborate carvings to sailors and merchants passing through the straits and stopping at Neah Bay for supplies.

Clyde wrapped the remaining half of his roll in wax paper, put it in his coat pocket, and approached the two Suquamish women. Standing before their blanket and looking down at the carved totems they were selling, he decided to address them in the Chinook jargon, which most Indians still readily conversed in, though most white people (his father the exception) no longer could speak it. He asked how much they wanted for the *Pa-see-sie*, the blankets. Without at first answering, the two women stared at him, making Clyde suspect they hadn't understood him. Then one pulled her robe about her shoulders and said, *Mimaloose Tamahnous Siwash.*" Clyde understood this to mean "ghost Indian." He shook his head no, and said, "*Wake, Naika t'kope Siwash, wake mimaloose*" – no, he was a white Indian, but not dead, not a ghost. The two women looked at him for several moments longer and then seemed to accept his word that he was not among the dead. The first one said, "*Nika kumtux*" – she understood. Then the one who had not yet spoken took one of the folded blankets and handed it to Clyde and said, "*Naika potlatch okoke paseesie, Naika ow.*" Clyde thanked her for the gift of the blanket, and since she had addressed him as "my little brother," he returned the courtesy by addressing her as "*skoo'-kum Ahts*," strong sister. He would give the blanket to Maddie, he thought, as he again thanked the two Suquamish women and walked away. He planned to return tomorrow to give the two women something in return, as was customary.

He placed the blanket in the empty basket of the handcart and began walking back uptown. Encountering the two Suquamish women – so few Indians remained in Seattle compared to ten or fifteen years ago –

made Clyde miss his mother. He wondered if she, who had been as dark brown as the mallard-down blanket, had the same response to him when he was born – believing he was some kind of ghost baby. He was born at the mill house on Lake Union, and as he recalled his father once telling him, he had come out pink, not white, his transparent skin like a film through which his parents could view his entire circulatory system. Only after the first few weeks, as he put on weight, as all healthy babies do, did he become fully void of color – "and as round and opaque as a full moon on a foggy night" was how his mother told the story to him. He also recalled his mother telling him when he was only eleven and she was taking him back to Neah Bay, how "In certain light, you were like light itself." At one time on that long trek she confessed to him that his father and she had at first wondered to themselves if such an odd and rare child were a curse on their marriage, punishment for the white man and red woman lying together, even in marriage. "But then you had my sea-depth eyes," she told him, "and I knew different."

Clyde's father was never so forthcoming with him as his mother had been. Herr Herman Hunssler, as Clyde himself sometimes thought of his father, had emigrated from Germany via England, where he spent almost five years, adopted the language along with many British mannerisms, and befriended his son's eventual namesake, an Englishman named Cloudsley Kittridge, with whom he traversed the Atlantic before parting ways with Cloudsley in New York when Clyde's father decided to cross the continent for the Pacific Northwest. It wasn't long after his birth that young Cloudsley Hunssler, as Clyde was christened, with his fine white hair and smooth blue-brown eyes, was renamed simply Cloud by his mother.

Kathy Markishtum, short and stout but, like a woman twice her own size in posture and comportment, spoke to her son in her native Makah tongue, one of the three Nootka dialects. Herr Hunssler, who had adopted the Chinook jargon to facilitate trading with the Indians during his years on the Olympic Peninsula, would use various Chinook words and phrases with his son. So Cloudsley grew up conversant in a stew of English, German, Makah, and the Chinook jargon. Back then his father still traded furs with the local Indians – the Duwamish, Suquamish, and Mukilteo near Seattle, and farther north the Swinomish and Lummi – and would bring Cloud-sley with him on his excursions into the Skagit Valley and as far north as Whatcom County. When his mother accompanied them, they would sometimes stay with Indian families in their longhouses, jawing in the Chinook jargon, eating the smoked salmon and dried elk offered them, and leaving in the morning with a wagon cart full of elk and deer hides, bear furs, and beaver pelts, which Herr Hunssler would later fashion into hats and gloves and sell on commission at the Seattle outfitting stores.

During these same excursions, Clyde's father would read to his family from the English novelists he had become enamored of during Cloudsley Kittridge's tutoring of him in England. Clyde could recall listening to the adventures of Nicholas Nickleby as he curled up inside a soft deer skin on his mother's lap while the family camped beside the Salish River. Awful Arthur Gride and mean Ralph Nickleby, ridiculous Messieurs Pike and Pluck, sweet Kate and saintly Mrs. Nickleby. Clyde's father brought the characters to life by reading the fanciful prose with an alternation of German exuberance and English reserve. His father also read to his wife and child at home, usually from the Bible, though frequently substituting the Old Testament prophets and New Testament apostles with the Brit-ish poets and novelists that Clyde had little doubt his father preferred.

His mother, meanwhile, told him stories of life among the Makah in the village of Neaah, which eventually came to be called Neah Bay, far out on the northwest tip of the Olympic Peninsula – of how she learned to make tightly twined baskets and mats from grasses, roots, and cattail reeds, and of watching the men launch their sea canoes loaded with spears with mussel-shell heads, harpoons made of yew, seal-skin floats, and ropes, and then paddling out into the open ocean to hunt the hump-back whale. And later, on the same day of the hunt, the scurrying and shouting throughout the village as the men returned with their kill and thanks were offered for the bounty of meat, oil, and bone that the sea once more provided the Makah. Then, after the whale was hauled to the beach, the men cutting away the layered flesh from the massive animal (the harpooner keeping the back fin and later decorating it to honor the whale's spirit) and the women carving the slabs of meat into strips and hanging them to cure in the smokehouse, boiling down the blubber to make pure, clarified oil for burning, and later cleaning and bleaching the bones for carving. If the whales were not running, the men might return with several seals or a porpoise. The night of the hunt the entire village would feast, even though the men who had been out in the canoes would be weary from contending with the rough waters off Cape Flattery and would fall asleep shortly after they had eaten. Whenever she told him about her childhood in Neah Bay, Cloud's mother would also promise that one day soon she would take him back to her village so that he could be welcomed into the tribe and initiated into Klukwali as the young man he was quickly becoming.

When he was old enough for school, Cloudsley's parents sent him to the schoolhouse in Seattle that would eventually be replaced by the large Denny School, on Denny Hill, not far from Maddie's boardinghouse. It was there that his teachers began calling him Clyde rather than Cloud or Cloudsley, either mistaking the pronunciation of his mother's nickname for him for the more Germanic first name or else wishing simply to Americanize him and thereby draw less attention to his immigrant background and half-breed status. Whatever the teachers' reasons, the new name caught on with his classmates and stuck, so that before long he was even introducing himself as Clyde – even though his mother and father rejected the new name and continued to call him Cloud and Cloudsley.

Clyde remained in the school for four years, until he turned eleven, when his mother came down with cholera. Rather than walk the two miles to school and back each day, he stayed at home and took her place in helping his father in the mill, separating out the split and un-sellable shingles for firewood, shoveling saw dust away from the planing saw twice a day, and helping to tie the good shingles into bundles of thirty and load the bundles onto the wagon to be hauled into town.

Soon after his mother's health had seemed to improve, she informed Cloud that it was time to take him back to her village. Promising her husband to return within two months, she packed clothes for herself and her son and purchased them each passage on the sidepaddle boat that made a daily run between Seattle and Port Townsend. From there she and Cloud walked (and occasionally rode on the back of a stranger's wagon) to Port Angeles, where she met up with a tribesman, a Makah whaler known as Lighthouse Joe, who offered to take them in his sea canoe the remaining distance to Neeah.

In all, the trip from Seattle to the village took them ten days. It was an arduous trip, yet Clyde could remember his relief in escaping the mill-work his father enlisted him to do. The trip, unfortunately, proved much harder on his mother, and four days after they arrived, she again fell ill. The village women were called together to tend to her. She was sweated and made to drink bark tea. An *Ucta'kyu*, or disease-curer, was even led to her side in the longhouse and a Tsayak ceremony was held. But after ten days, Kathy Markishtum succumbed to the fever, and Cloud was left motherless. A canoe filled with offerings to *Cha-batt-a Ha-tartstl* (a mask, a bird feather blanket, a beaver pelt, a grass mat, and a wooden bowl) was hung in the longhouse where she died, after which Cloud's mother was buried not in the frayed housedress she had worn from Seattle but in the traditional cedar-bark fringed skirt, sea otter mantle, and dentalia shell necklace.

Clyde remembered how curious he thought it was to bury her like this, although he also knew that she would have approved. Only a few elders still wore the traditional garments. Mostly they were used for cer-emonies. Most of the women in Neeah simply wore trade cloth dresses and store-bought blankets, while the men wore trousers and flannel shirts like working men everywhere. It was one week after his mother's burial when Lighthouse Joe and several other men came for Cloud and brought him out in one of their sea canoes to hunt, teaching him the canoe song – *He ya ha'o-ha, 'eya ha'o-ho, 'eya ha 'eya ho, he ta sa da qo, he ta sa da qo* – and adopting him as a tribal son. Though Cloud was too young to hunt whale, he was allowed to spear a seal on his first outing. Over the course of his two years with the Makah, he also learned to fish for cod by casting nets from the canoes and to catch salmon by building weirs in the streams when the salmon runs returned from the ocean. He learned how to har-vest crabs, clams, mussels, cockles, barnacles, limpets, and sea urchins from the tide pools, and salal, elderberries, salmonberries, blackberries, and wild currants from the forest undergrowth. He also returned to school, this time with the Methodist missionaries who had been in the village since his mother was a child. This whole time he lived with the family of the brother of Lighthouse Joe, which included a boy one year younger than Cloud with whom he went to school, played, and hunted squirrels.

It would be two years before his father came to the reservation to retrieve Clyde. When his father appeared one day in the village, heavier and sadder than Clyde remembered him, his father's first words to his son were, "You've been away too long. I'm bringing you home." His father also called him by the name his schoolteachers had tagged him with – Clyde – which surprised him. Herr Hunssler met with several of the Makah elders in the longhouse in the center of the village, and when he came out he told his son, who was now thirteen, to say his good-byes and prepare to leave. Within the hour the two of them, the stern German father and his pallid-skinned son, each mounted one of the two horses Clyde's father had borrowed in Port Townsend and together rode away from the village.

Clyde still remembered that day as one of the most confusing, saddest days of his life, as if at that moment of leaving the village and the people who had adopted him he was forced to fully reckon with the loss of his mother. This, and the fact that his father had changed. Riding the horses back to Port Townsend and then boarding the sidepaddle boat to Seattle, his father barely spoke to Clyde except to say how hard things had been at the mill. He never mentioned Clyde's mother. Instead, he smoked his pipe incessantly and drank more heavily than Clyde ever remembered his father drinking. He also continued to call him "Clyde" – rather than Cloudsley, the only name his father had ever used for him – which troubled Clyde until finally, with other passengers on the boat soon calling him by the name, he accepted it as his own, once and for all, and became Clyde.

AFTER ENCOUNTERING THE TWO SUQUAMISH WOMEN, CLYDE felt out of sorts and drifted about the city the rest of the morning and into the afternoon. He eventually made his way to the Washington Hotel where he cleaned three dozen salmon in the kitchen and shoveled a wagonload of coal into the coal shed, and then returned to Madison House. When he brought the handcart back to the carriage house, he found James consorting with two of his colleagues, beat reporters for the *Seattle Argus* and *Seattle Star*, white men whom James had befriended over the years within that fraternity of newspapermen. Under pseudonyms, Clyde knew, the same two men sometimes wrote for James as well. The group sat on two rickety chairs and a stool around the stove. As was custom within the fraternal order of newspapermen, the three men were also drinking cheap whiskey, presumably in recognition of James having put out another edition of the *Sentry* that morning. And to Clyde's surprise, they were discussing the recent regrading of portions of Denny Hill and the news of a proposal before the city council to regrade even more of the hill. One of the men, the *Star* reporter, also boarded somewhere on the hill and was worried.

"Nothing will come of it," the *Argus* reporter said. "James, Roger, you have nothing to worry about. It's too big an undertaking. It will cost the city millions."

"What Lord Thomson wants, Lord Thomson receives," said Roger, the *Star* reporter.

"The city will go ahead with it just to show itself and the world that it can," offered James. "It's can-do-ism run amok. You just wait and see." He then took up the whiskey bottle and poured his friends each another drink and asked Clyde if he wanted a taste.

Normally, Clyde would have taken James up on the drink and would have tarried in the carriage house to gab with the three men. But he was tired, and his encounter with the two Suquamish women had stayed with him, making him feel more withdrawn than usual. So he waved off James's offer, shook hands with all three men, and left the convivial carriage house.

He crossed the alley and entered the main house through the mudroom. In the kitchen, he found Ada at the table playing with a wind-up tin toy of a ringmaster and four circus horses. According to Ada, when questioned by Clyde, Maddie had taken the streetcar down to the bank on James Street. Clyde put the wrapped salmon he always carried back with him from the hotel in the refrigerator – and checked the ice in the ice chamber to see if he needed to retrieve another block – and placed the Salish blanket in the mudroom for Maddie to find later. He then washed the salmon juice and coal dust off his hands, forearms, and face at the hose at the back of the house and went up the back staircase to his attic room. He came down the stairs a few moments later with a clean shirt on beneath his corduroy jacket.

The memories that had seized him earlier in the day still lingered, and he wished Maddie were around to help dispel them. Talking with Maddie always brightened his spirits. Yet without Maddie in the house, and with Ada making a racket with her clacking wind-up toy, he remained restless. So snagging an apple from a bowl on the kitchen sideboard, he went back out, heard the three newspapermen still yammering away in the carriage house, and headed over the hill in the direction of Lake Union.

When he reached the old mill house on the lake's east shore, his father was nowhere to be found either. People, it seemed, were disappearing on him. It was nearly dark now, so he went inside and sat in the only good chair there was in the three-room house. He decided he would wait for his father, but soon dozed off. Sometime later, when he woke in the dark, the clock on the stone mantel read nine o'clock. His father, he figured, must have taken one of his trapping jaunts, which meant he might be gone for four or five days. Or else he was just up the lakeshore a ways with Robert Patten drinking plum wine or blackberry brandy or applejack on the roof of Mr. Patten's houseboat.

Clyde felt restless, groggy, and hungry. He didn't want to return to Maddie's and he didn't want to loiter about his father's shack any longer. He found some onions his father stored in a bin, peeled one and bit into it. It was sharp and sweet and instantly staved off his hunger. He stepped outside and, with no idea where he was headed, angled up the northwest side of Capitol Hill rising up directly behind the Lake Union house. He trudged straight up the steep ridge, bushwhacking through waist-high ferns and young cedar saplings. A few small houses, little more than shacks, had been built onto the hillside, but as he neared the top of the ridge larger family homes with yards began to appear, even though all of the side streets were still just dirt tracks. Across the top of the hill, lots had been cleared for future building sites – this north portion of Capitol Hill becoming the newest enclave for the city's rich and powerful. As of this month in this year, though, November 1905, not all the tall cedar, fir, and ash trees had been cleared from the hilltop. Portions of the hill could still remind Clyde of his childhood, when the entire hill was nothing but thick forest.

At the crestline, he was able to look out in three directions: west across Lake Union to Queen Anne Hill and beyond it to the dark expanse of Puget Sound; north to the scattering of neighborhoods that stretched to Green Lake and the grounds of the State University; and east across Lake Washington to its uninhabited eastern shore. Soon he came upon the large clearing that had been platted several years ago for Lakeview Cemetery, where Chief Sealth's daughter, Princess Angeline, had been laid to rest in a full Christian burial. Just south of the cemetery he came to the Volunteer Park Reservoir, which had been dug and cemented several years earlier to supply water to Capitol Hill. He walked back to Broadway, the avenue that stretched the north-south length of the hill, and passed Columbia School, which he would have attended had he remained in school.

The exertion of climbing the hill helped ease his restlessness, yet he still didn't want to return to his father's or go back to Maddie's. Something about the way he had looked at her that morning and had so much anticipated seeing her when he returned to the house that afternoon made him uncertain and nervous ... mostly about himself, but also about what she might say if she knew he had been thinking of her that way. By his best estimation, it was well past midnight by now and he had been walking (and thinking of Maddie) almost continuously since six in the morning. Yet he wanted to go on. Rather than continue down Broadway, which would be the quickest way back to the boardinghouse, he started down the eastern slope of Capitol Hill. Near Nineteenth Avenue, he crossed a large clearing where the stumps still rose from the ragged ground. Along the western edge of this clearing, a neighborhood was forming. Along its eastern edge, trees still stood tall and dense. It was as if, by standing in this single clearing, he could see into the city's future on one side and into its past on the other. Neighborhoods expanding and forest disappearing. He found a path leading into the trees and followed it. At turns the path became steep and twisting and barely wide enough for him to see where he was going. It was a path he had walked once or twice before in daylight, but in the dark he could barely remember the course it wound through the woods. He believed that eventually it would intersect with a dirt track and angle down to Union Bay, off of Lake Washington. Yet as he entered a steep ravine, the woods became more dense and he began to doubt himself. Twice he stumbled over tree roots and nearly fell. A night owl screeched, and he thought he could even hear the death-throe squeals of a wood mouse caught in the owl's talons. Since his days among the Makah, he never felt fearful in the woods at night, even though his maneuvering skills were no longer as acute as they once had been out on the peninsula. He heard the owl's wings flapping through the trees, the predator returning to its roost. Then the woods turned quiet again and he listened to the soft rustle of the wind in the branches. At last the trail met up with the dirt track that he remembered, and after another half mile or so he could make out a small boathouse and dock that extended into Union Bay. Afraid of being shot for trespassing, he cut into the woods again and bushwhacked the rest of the way to the shore, putting a safe distance between himself and the boathouse.

When he emerged from the trees at the head of the bay, where it opened out into the lake, the water's surface lay still and undisturbed, quietly resting against the rock-strewn shore. The moon hung low on the horizon, giving the lake a faint glow. As he walked the shoreline, the margin between the water and the treeline varied in width, and at certain sections he had to climb back into the woods to circumvent a small inlet or marsh. Yet for the most part he strolled along the shoreline with ease. On the opposite shore, which he could view clearly, Webster Point created a kind of gate between the bay and the lake. Past this gate, farther out on the lake, he could see a small steamboat plying the open waters, lanterns strung from its bow to the top of the steampipe and then down to the stern. The pleasure craft's rhythmic chug echoed off the shore, and as Clyde rounded the bend, the faint ripple of its wake pulsed against the shore with a quiet washing.

Farther up the shoreline, he made out the lights of Madison Park. The resort consisted of a large boathouse, a pavilion, a band pagoda, dressing cabins, and concession stands – the companion resort to the more raucous Leschi Park two miles south on the lake. He watched the sparkle of the resort's electric lights and then could hear an orchestra band playing, followed by singing and laughing and shouts for an encore. Clyde knew he needed to steer clear of the revelries. Most of the resort people – Seattle's sporting set, college kids roughly his own age – would be cavorting about, drinking, showing off to one another, and he knew that his spectral presence coming down the shoreline, if detected, would only cause a commotion.

With this in mind he backtracked until he could no longer see or hear the revelries at the resort. When he came to a portion of shoreline where the moss grew thick along an eroded slope that slid gently toward the water's edge, he sat down and leaned back in the soft green stuff and watched the moon descend below the horizon and out of view. Almost immediately upon the moon's setting and the darkness in the woods deepening around him, his fatigue hit him. He pulled his jacket tightly about his chest and lying all the way down, let his body sink into the soft moss, and within moments of closing his eyes, he was fast asleep.

5. The Photographer (1905)

RAY WAS TIRED OF LIVING IN THE YMCA. "A GRUHLKI CAN do better than that," asserted his older brother Thomas, a sales manager at Schwabacher's Department Store who was working his way through the ranks and had recently built a bungalow-style house for himself and his family on First Hill. "When are you going to make something of yourself?" Thomas asked Ray every time they saw each other.

The thing was, Ray thought he *was* making something of himself. He sat nightly at the small desk (or in the small reading chair) in his cramped room at the Y and read for the law, as he'd been doing for the past year and a half. Several years ago, when Thomas refused to grubstake him so he could go to the Yukon to make his fortune, Ray had decided to become a lawyer. He read Oliver Wendell Holmes's *Common Law*, and then the great justice's autobiography, and was won over by his clear-sightedness, his sympathetic sensibility, his plain old common sense. The notion that the law was only as good as it was practical was a notion a young man could set his watch by. Idealism could not be divorced from day-to-day practices. So Ray had begun working as a law clerk during the day (for Edward Holton James, nephew of the novelist Henry James) and at night he read the law, both state and federal. However, as he quickly came to realize, the law was far more mired in tedious minutia than the great Oliver Wendell Holmes ever let on, and Ray soon grew weary of it.

The Washington State Criminal Code lay on his lap as he looked at the numerous photographs he had taken and posted about his small room. He knew Thomas would throw a fit when he announced to him that he now wanted to become a professional photographer and not a lawyer. He could hear Thomas clearly: "You just don't become a professional photographer overnight. Have you thought of the competition you would face? This city is crowded with photography studios. Do you know how much really good photography equipment costs? Hell, the world always needs more lawyers. It doesn't need more photographers."

As these fraternal objections echoed in Ray's head, he admired the photos he had taken with his handy one-dollar Kodak Brownie. His efforts rejected the routine family photographs that everyone who owned one of these popular cameras took. It didn't matter that the prints came back from the Kodak plant in Rochester, New York, in the same round format (to compensate for tilt) as his sister-in-law's photos of Thomas and their children. His photos transcended such quotidian usage. He had purchased the Kodak Brownie a short while after stopping into the Curtis Studios one day and perusing the walls of the front gallery. He was especially taken with the live-scene photographs by Asahel Curtis, preferred them to the more set-up photographs by Edward Curtis, Asahel's brother. They expressed an immediacy that Ray admired, and they seemed to express the essence and truth of the moment rather than the photographer's staging of it. It was after this that he mailed away for the Kodak Brownie and as soon as it arrived began prowling the streets of Seattle looking for shots of people going about their business, people who were not likely to walk into a photographer's studio and pay to have their portrait taken. Later that year, when he read about the Photo Secessionist exhibition in New York organized by Alfred Stieglitz and Edward Steichen (whose eerie and evocative photograph *The Flatiron* he had seen in a magazine), Ray realized that he, too, in his own modest way, had already recognized that the camera was merely an extension of his own artistic sensibilities. Yet because he had to send his film (the entire camera, in fact) back to Rochester, to be developed, he was not able to manipulate his prints as the Photo-Secessionists were wont to do. Instead, he relied solely on his own visual apprehension of his subjects. His photograph of a small girl playing in the muddy Lake Washington canal, of a longshoreman smoking a cigarette in a transit shed on the waterfront, of the big Sicilian Vincent Amato cutting hair in his barbershop on Union Street ... all of these emphasized his own aesthetic sensibility, which was closely allied with ordinary subjects and everyday scenes. With showing the city back to itself. That he didn't have a more sophisticated camera than the Kodak Brownie, little more than a leather box with a viewfinder on top that you held at your solar plexus and aimed ... well, it didn't get any more ordinary or everyday than that.

Just thinking about all this made him want to toss aside the law book on his lap and take up his camera. The resolve he had been waiting for, he sensed, was near at hand. By God, why not? He would find a new place to live *and* he would pursue his photography. He would still clerk for Edward Holton (Ned) James to pay his bills. But he would be making a fresh start. He would no longer be pretending. He would now be the artist he was meant to be. Indeed, he thought, he would commence this very instant.

He stood up and let the law book fall to the floor. He donned his white plaited shirt, a fresh collar, a silk band neck tie, and his best alpaca pants, vest, and coat. It was Ray's position that while one might have the artistic inclinations of a bohemian, one need not dress like one. Ray was all too happy to allow Thomas to provide him with sizable discounts in acquiring a wardrobe for himself down at Schwabacher's. At six feet and some change, Ray often required custom fitting, which made the discounts especially handy. He liked to dress well, that's all there was to it. Doing so made an impression on his employer, on the ladies, and on himself. Looking at himself in the mirror above his dressing table, he wondered if he should remain clean-shaven or grow a moustache to mark his new course in life. He flipped his stiff bowler hat off the hook on the door and pressed it down onto his head of wavy brown curls. He then draped his cielette rainproof coat over his arm (just in case) and palmed his camera from the bedside table where it lay. From now on, even if just stepping out to search for new lodging, he would not go anywhere without his camera.

RAY DISCOVERED MADISON HOUSE BY FIRST SPOTTING THE albino on a ladder hanging a signboard from the front porch:

MADISON HOUSE
Rooms for Let – $3, With Board – $5
Mrs. Madison Ingram, Proprietress

When Ray asked if he could take a photograph, the albino man, who looked almost blue beneath the overcast sky, turned around on the ladder and brusquely asked, "Of what?"

"Of you, of course," Ray replied. This aspect of photographing the common man, of being a street photographer, that is, of having to ask permission of his subjects to take their picture (or else snapping the photo on the sly) did not come easily to Ray. If he took the photo on the sly, he felt sneaky, like a voyeur leering about, almost as if he were stealing something from someone. Yet if he spoke up and asked permission, he felt as though he were imposing himself on someone, putting that man or woman out, and making a scene. He knew if he was going to succeed as a photographer he would have to overcome these scruples and become more comfortable and more adept at both approaches to getting the shot he wanted. It was just part of the territory he was determined to inhabit.

"What if I don't take to being the object of your curiosity?" the albino said, and returned to adjusting the signboard on the two chains that hung from the porch. Ray had half-expected the man to be an idiot or dumb mute, and was surprised at how well he expressed his objection. When it came right down to it, he looked as intelligent as he sounded. Ray could tell he was no ordinary laborer.

"No, no, sir," Ray remonstrated. "It's not that at all. You see, I intend … well…" – he paused – "yes, I suppose you're right. You're a curious sight on that ladder and I thought it would make for an interesting photograph. After all, that's what I do … or what I try to do … take interesting photographs."

The albino came down the ladder, having successfully hung the signboard, and then laid the ladder on the grass and came up to where Ray stood on the wood-plank sidewalk. Although he stood two or three inches taller than the albino, Ray thought the man might accost him, and he tried not to look too frightened.

"You can take my photograph," the albino said. "I'll stand beneath the new sign." The man appeared quite jaunty in his calico neckerchief and wool newsboy cap, his tan collarless shirt unbuttoned at the neck and revealing a white hairless chest, his shirt sleeves rolled half way up to his thick pale forearms, his black vest buttoned snugly about his trim midsection.

Ray let out the breath he'd been holding in waiting for the first blow. "Thank you," he said, "thank you for your cooperation," and readied his camera.

The albino stood directly beneath the signboard, crossed his arms over his chest, tucked his chin down, and looking straight ahead with a stoical expression on his face waited for Ray to take the picture. Although this wasn't the candid photograph Ray had originally wanted – the one of the albino on the ladder, engaged in his task, unaware of the camera – as he peered through the viewfinder, he figured it would nevertheless make for a very intriguing portrait. After all, how many albinos had he ever encountered in all his walks about the city? After taking the first shot, he asked the fellow to sit on the front steps leading up to the porch, and when he obliged (and this time he looked a little more at ease), Ray shot a second photograph.

Ray rolled the film and thanked the man. He was about to move on when the albino hurried up to him and asked about the camera slung around his neck. Pleased at the fellow's interest, Ray gladly explained how it was a simple box camera, a No. 2 Brownie that used No. 120 roll film. "One of the first cameras to use roll film," he added, and went on to explain how the camera operated, how release of the shutter exposed the light-sensitive film, and so forth. He appreciated the opportunity to show off his limited mechanical expertise.

"Well," the albino said, after listening attentively to Ray's detailed explanation, "I hope you'll bring that picture by and show it to me sometime."

"I'll do that," Ray replied, and thinking he ought to reciprocate the interest the fellow had shown in his camera, he asked about Madison House and the albino recounted a short history of the boardinghouse. When he was done, he reached out his hand and introduced himself as Clyde Hunssler. "I help out around the place," he said. Ray shook his hand and introduced himself as well, and then mentioned how he himself was seeking new lodging. The next thing he knew Clyde Hunssler was escorting him up the porch and in through the front door of the boardinghouse in order to introduce him to Mrs. Madison Ingram, the proprietress.

IN THE MONTHS THAT FOLLOWED, RESIDENCE AT THE BOARD-inghouse on Denny Hill proved far more pleasant to Ray than his barebones existence at the YMCA. The cost was only marginally more, and, as a dedicated agnostic, he no longer had to endure the prayer sessions before each evening's meal. The day Ray moved into Madison House, Clyde had him take a photograph of Maddie in front of the house, beneath the signboard Clyde had hung the previous week. And then, upon Maddie's insistence (and with Clyde demurring) he took a photograph of the two of them together – Maddie smiling, her hands on her back hips, and Clyde looking nervous, his arms locked straight at his side.

Ray liked both of them immediately. Maddie, he thought, was an attractive woman for her age, which he guessed to be about thirty-five. Crow's feet spread out from her eyes when she smiled or frowned, yet this sign of age and experience was offset by a freshness in the rest of her complexion that seemed particularly youthful. While her manner was usually jovial and smart, there also seemed to be something hardened deep within her, as if she had come through a set of circumstances that had left her shaken yet stronger, as if her mettle had been tested and been proved worthy of whatever the world could strike it with. At the same time, oddly, she came across as both good-humored and mildly withdrawn. She dressed rather plainly, even though, as Ray thought, she plainly had a good figure. In all, he thought she would be a very good landlady.

Having successfully found new lodging, Ray continued to work for Edward Holton James, Esq., writing legal briefs and memos for the attorney, researching past cases and current statutes, making filings at the King County courthouse (which locals called Katzenjammer because of the many cockeyed additions made to the old wood-frame building over the years), and running menial errands to assorted offices about town (mostly banks, title companies, and other attorneys' offices). He actually preferred his duties as a runner for the office since he would always bring his camera with him and take half a dozen photographs between James's office in the Colman Building on First Avenue and the Katzenjammer all the way up at the corner of Seventh Avenue and Terrace Street.

It was a happy day, six months after his arrival at Madison House, when he went downtown to the Rhodes Company department store in the Arcade Building to buy the new Graflex Double Extension camera that he'd been saving up for. (Schwabacher's had the exact same model, but he didn't want his brother to discover that he was dropping $23 on the new camera.) The camera's automatic shutter and F8 three-focus convertible lens, he explained to Clyde that afternoon in his room adjacent to Clyde's in the attic of the boardinghouse, would allow him to control exposure and depth of field in a manner never possible with his simple old Brownie box camera.

"This is where the artist meets the technician," he declared to Clyde, who simply said that he would have to take Ray's word for it. Clyde had wanted Ray to buy a stereoscopic camera so that the whole house could have stereoscopic images to ogle at through the viewmaster. "We could keep them in the den," he'd said. But Ray, setting him straight on the matter, told him such gimmicky images would be obsolete in ten years. Nonetheless, Clyde seemed mildly disappointed that Ray had purchased the Graflex and not the stereoscopic camera.

Ray handled his new camera with all the care and tenderness of a father taking his new-born babe into his hands for the first time. With this, he thought, as he extended the red leather bellows to its full length, he will transform the art of photography. He placed the camera on the wooden tripod he had also purchased at the Rhodes Company and screwed it securely into place. He stepped behind the camera, draped the focus cloth over his shoulders, and slid a loaded plateholder into the back of the camera. He asked Clyde to step in front of the camera and then spotted him through the viewfinder and adjusted the lens and shutter and, on the count of three, squeezed the bulb. This, he thought to himself, was the inaugural shoot of his new photographic career – a new era in photography!

"Isn't it rather dark up here for picture-taking?" Clyde asked.

"Yes, but you're not," Ray said confidently as he removed the plateholder and loaded it with a new developing plate, ecstatic at his own adeptness in handling the new camera. "You're positively radiant," he added, kidding Clyde, though he suspected his friend might be right about the insufficient lighting in the attic room.

"What will you do with your old camera?"

In all his excitement over his new camera, Ray hadn't given this a single thought. The simple Kodak Brownie camera had served him well, and he loved it still, yet everyone and his second cousin owned a Brownie box these days. The scores of photos he had taken with it remained taped to the bare wood slats of the wall above his desk, pinched into the frame of the mirror on his dresser, and crammed into the two shoe boxes beneath his bed. Some were good, others showed promise, but most, he could admit to himself now, were all too ordinary.

He looked at Clyde. "Would you like to have it?"

Clyde thanked him for the offer but without even a pause said no, one photographer in the house was enough. "Keep it," he told Ray. "You never know, you might need it again."

Clyde was right, of course. The Brownie had its limitations, but it was reliable. A good standby. Every professional photographer had several cameras – different tools for different occasions – so he would do as Clyde advised and hold onto the Kodak Brownie. But for now, he only wanted to get outside with his exciting new Graflex.

Since the new camera was quite a bit heavier than the Brownie, he asked Clyde to carry the tripod for him, and the two made their way down the back staircase and out the back door. Since he would no longer be sending his roll film off to Rochester, he knew he would need to go back downtown to inquire into the rates the different studios charged for use of their darkroom, as well as for instruction on how to develop his own film and make his own prints. He had studied several photography manuals from the library but was nervous all the same about making his first foray into a bona fide photography lab.

Before worrying about any of that, though, he would take his new camera on its inaugural tour of the neighborhood. The afternoon light was muted, which meant minimal contrast yet also minimal glare, and his faithful friend and temporary assistant, Clyde, was reliably at his side. The world – or Denny Hill at least – awaited his panoptic eye.

6. To Alaska (1897)

MADDIE WASN'T ON THE WHARF WHEN THE *S.S. PORTLAND* docked in Seattle that summer of 1897. Chester was, though. He joined the throngs that gathered at Schwabacher's Dock to greet the newly wealthy passengers aboard the steamship from the Northland. He even hired on with one of the prospectors to carry his bags of gold to the Scandinavian American Bank – the federal assaying office having not yet opened in Seattle – and received payment of five dollars for his efforts. Which was good solid money, Chester told Maddie later that day, and not just some featherbrained pipe dream, but good solid money! Maddie replied that she supposed it was.

The riches aboard the *S.S. Portland*, which heralded new bounty for Seattle, instilled in Maddie the exact opposite reaction they inspired in Chester. She believed she and Chester should stay in Seattle and set up shop supplying the stampede of gold-fevered prospectors racing north that was certain to follow – most of whom would stop first in Seattle to stock up on provisions. She had a hunch that that's where the best business sense lay, and not in risking everything they had (scarce little at that) for a chance to pan a few ounces of yellow dust (if they were lucky) from an ice-clogged stream in the frigid and barren north. Besides, she had grown fond of Seattle in the short time they'd been there, even if they did reside far below the Deadline, in one of the city's most notorious districts. She occasionally sauntered into the other neighborhoods, where she could imagine a better life for them eventually, if they just stayed on and worked hard.

To seek their fortune, however, was why they'd ventured out to Seattle in the first place, Chester reminded her. Indeed, well before the headlines spread across the nation with news of the *S.S. Portland's* "ton of gold," Chester had already contracted gold fever. They'd gone to Cleveland from Trenton because he had heard that all the good manufacturing jobs were there and that a man could rise to floor manager in no time and, keeping his wits about him and having plenty of drive, even become company president. But in those depression years of the mid-1890s, every city in America was struck hard, including Cleveland, and the manufacturing plants weren't hiring. Any work at all, even street sweeping, was scarce. So after just one year on the shores of Lake Erie, they packed up and came to Seattle on James J. Hill's Great Northern Railroad, all because Chester had heard there might be gold in the region, even as close as fifty miles north of the city, in the foothills of the North Cascades. Looking back on that time in her marriage to Chester, Maddie realized she couldn't have guessed just how desperate her young husband was becoming, and probably had been all along. She'd fallen in love with him because he seemed like the stable, hardworking type that her father was—her father even helped bring Chester along with his railroad job—and because, well, he was darned good-looking and knew how to sweet-talk a girl, which she did not discourage. Losing her innocence to Chester just weeks before they were married convinced her she was in love with him.

For two years after their departure from Trenton, they lived off the small inheritance and insurance claim from her parents—both of whom died in a train crash only a year after Maddie and Chester wed—yet by their fourth month in Seattle, this modest fund was nearly all gone. They moved out of the Providence Hotel and into a $7-a-month flophouse five blocks below the Deadline, which was approximately parallel to Yesler Street straight through Pioneer Place. It was a despicable clapboard tenement made up of a dozen flyblown rooms with paper-thin walls, dirt-smeared hallway commodes, scurrying baseboard rats, drunken vomiting boarders, and a savage proprietor who let rooms to anyone who could pay and booted out anyone who could not. The prospect of vacating this sorry excuse for lodging after six intolerable months was the one upside of her husband's determination to head north to the gold fields.

The day the *S.S. Portland* made dock, Chester was already busy packing their few remaining household belongings into their steamer trunks when Maddie returned to the flophouse from one of her walks, bolted past the leering old man in the foyer holding a bottle in his lap, and rushed up to their room on the third floor.

"Look," Chester said, the instant she opened the door and entered. He held something up between his thumb and index finger for her to see. Whatever it was, it was too minuscule for her to make out in the room's dim light. She unlaced the tie on her bonnet and set it carefully on top of the battered dresser drawers. She had been out looking for housecleaning work, inquiring door-to-door. Her knees ached and her ankles were swollen, and she was tired to the bone.

"What is it?" Then, looking about the room and seeing their trunks out and open, she stared at Chester and said, "What are you doing? Have you been packing?"

"It's gold," her husband declared, and brought it up to her face for closer inspection. "Put out your hand."

Maddie laid open her hand and Chester placed a thin yellowish sliver with roseate tints and rough, uneven edges in her palm. Despite its coarse and tarnished appearance, the object was soft and seemed almost iridescent. As she held it, Chester told her how it was the very same stuff, just in the raw, that the delicate chain and locket her mother had bestowed on her on their wedding day was made of. (The same chain and locket, Maddie recalled looking back on that moment, that they'd pawned two months earlier, a detail that slipped Chester's mind in his fascination with the gold sliver.) Maddie handed the piece of gold back to Chester without comment.

"One of the men off the boat gave it to me," he explained, almost whispering in his excitement, perhaps afraid one of their neighbors would hear him and try to steal his treasure, "along with five dollars for helping him carry the rest of his gold to the bank." He turned and motioned toward the four open trunks in the room, then put the gold sliver in his shirt pocket, buttoned it, and took hold of both of Maddie's wrists. "We're going to the Klondike, Maddie. That's where all the gold is. We're going to be rich, Maddie, just like that man I helped off the boat today." He produced a copy of the *Post-Intelligencer*. "Here, you can read it all for yourself. This is what we've been waiting for."

Maddie didn't know what to think – of the little sliver of precious metal, of Chester's fervency, of her wretched life in the Seattle flophouse, of their decision to leave Trenton for Cleveland, Cleveland for Seattle... any of it. She didn't respond to her husband, but just let him go on telling her how wonderful their life would be from now on.

During the next several days, she watched as the city worked itself into a frenzy to get to Alaska and the Yukon. Chester would have left that very afternoon if they could have afforded it, but they didn't have enough money to book passage on one of the many steamships now heading north, much less buy all the provisions people said were required for the overland trek to the Yukon gold fields once you reached Alaska by sea. For the next several weeks, they had to work – Maddie cleaning rich folks' houses on First Hill, Chester down on the docks as a stevedore – and then they had to sell the last few items of furniture and jewelry that Maddie held onto from her family's home in Trenton, and finally, within seven weeks, working almost eighteen hours every day, they had almost enough money – by which time Maddie's initial doubts about the entire enterprise had grown into grave apprehension for their personal safety and welfare, as well as for their marriage.

It did not take a clairvoyant to see that not all the desperate souls pouring into Seattle ravenous to get rich up north would achieve this goal. Most would not. Most would likely come back more destitute, more physically ravaged and morally disillusioned than they had ever been before the gold rush news broke. Already, just one month after the *S.S. Portland's* fanfare arrival in Seattle, there was evidence of this – families split, marriages ruined, men begging on the streets, broken by their own misguided ambitions. Chester was simply too determined, and was going to have his way.

The three hundred dollars they scraped together in this seven weeks could have bought them a small (but pleasant) house north of the downtown. It was plain to see that the people profiting from the gold rush were the Seattle merchants. When she wasn't cleaning houses, Maddie was stitching tent canvas for Cooper and Levy, Pioneer Outfitters, at their warehouse several blocks south of their store on First Avenue. Outfitters throughout the city were finding it difficult to maintain their stocks. When Maddie first broached the notion with Chester of their staying in Seattle and setting themselves up in business, he scoffed at her. When she mentioned it again the next week, he shouted her down for even suggesting such an idea, said she was a fool for not seeing the

opportunity that lay before them plain as day, and accused her of dis-
loyalty to her wedding vows to abide by her husband's word. Then, after
she tried to placate him, he seemed to plead with her. "This is our one
big chance, Mads, dontcha see? Dontcha want to be rich and wear fine
dresses like those ladies you clean house for? Try to understand, Mads.
It's now or never."

She wasn't persuaded. Yet she gave up trying to change his mind.
Chester's intransigence on every consideration she raised made Maddie
increasingly ill about the whole undertaking. At one point she even
hinted that perhaps he should go alone, that she would only be a hin-
drance to him and would be better off waiting for him in Seattle. But he
insisted on needing her with him in Alaska, and promised her they would
be back in Seattle within a year. This was the one time she ever regretted
not being able to bear them a child. If they had had a child, she knew, she
would never have gone north with him.

After selling the last of their few belongings to outfit themselves with
the necessary equipment and provisions – a Klondike stove, blankets,
parkas, knee-high boots, wool-lined mittens, a red Union suit each,
beaver hats, and then (by way of food stuffs), 50 pounds of flour, 20
pounds of dried beans, 10 pounds of lard, sacks loaded with potatoes,
cabbages, and acorn squash, and 10 pounds of cured beef (although
Chester swore he would provide them with fresh meat – "You don't mind
caribou, do ya, Mads?" – with the secondhand Remington rifle he bought) –
they still came short of the year's worth of supplies the Canadian Mounted
Police required of prospectors crossing the border from Alaska into the
Yukon. In lieu of all her work sewing canvas for them, the proprietors
of Cooper and Levy, the two Jewish merchants Aaron Levy and his son-
in-law Isaac Cooper, let Maddie have a large tent, complete with poles
and stakes, on top of her regular wages. This savings left her and Chester
barely enough to book steerage aboard the steamship *Rosalie*, due to
depart for Skagway on August 29.

That morning, Chester hired a horse-drawn wagon and, along with
another man and his wife who had recently moved into their same flophouse and were also Alaska-bound, they transported all their provisions

down to the wharf. It was just before dawn, still dark. The waterfront was as chaotic as the day the *Portland* arrived – and perhaps more so, since with each passing day and the quickening approach of winter, people became more desperate to depart for the gold fields and claim the fortune they deemed rightfully theirs. The wagon driver hurried them through Pioneer Place and across the Great Northern railroad tracks and north along Railroad Avenue to Atkinson's Dock where the *S.S. Rosalie* waited. As they approached the dock – with Maddie and Laurette sitting on the back of the open wagon holding onto the trunks and twined bundles of canvas, bedding, and tools, while Chester and Morris rode up front on the bench with the driver – Maddie listened to the cacophony of waterfront noise ... ships' steam whistles piercing the morning fog, seagulls screeching, mast lines clacking, davits groaning, pylons creaking, the shouting of men and whinnying of horses. It was a relatively calm morning, so each noise became that much more distinct. For the first time since Chester placed the gold sliver in her palm on the day the *Portland* docked in Seattle, Maddie physically feared what lay ahead for them. For the first time since leaving New Jersey, then Ohio, she held deep in her chest an anxiousness toward her husband, the man she married at age twenty-two, when her parents warned her to marry and bear children or else become a lonesome old maid – a fate that seemed comforting compared to current perilous circumstances and how little she dared place her faith in Chester in confronting these circumstances.

She raised her head and looked over the top of their provisions at Laurette, whose bonneted face seemed leaden in its hard stare at the road passing beneath them. Only when the wagon hit a bump, jolting everything and everyone in it, did she reveal the slightest grimace across her set lips. The younger woman, only nineteen, must have sensed Maddie watching her because she turned her head and forced a wane smile upon making eye contact with her.

"I pray the boat provides a smoother ride," Laurette said loudly over the rattle of wagon wheels.

"Let's hope so," Maddie shouted back, and gripped the sideboard as another deep rut sent the wagon jarring forward.

The two women resumed their silent endurance of the wagon ride until at last they reached the dock. As Chester and Morris unloaded their supplies, Maddie looked eastward and observed the dawn lighting the sky above the cluster of brick, stone, and wood buildings climbing the hill from the waterfront. To the south, on what she had heard derisively called "Profanity Hill," there rose the large center cupola of the County Courthouse, while to the north, atop Denny Hill, like something out of a fairy tale, appeared the eminent and ornate Denny Hotel. Since their arrival in Seattle she had begged Chester to take her up to the hotel, just to see it up close, but he repeatedly told her he'd been up there and that the hotel was nothing but a big, empty shell, nothing to see at all. "I'd like to go anyway," she said, "for the view." She thought how when they returned to Seattle wealthy with gold – should they be lucky enough return at all – she would persuade Chester to buy a house on Denny Hill near the hotel that so majestically overlooked the city.

As it turned out, Chester had arranged to team up with Morris not only on the transfer of their provisions from the flophouse to the dock, but all the way to Dawson City. From there, according to his plan, they would be partners in staking a claim. To Maddie's surprise, Chester had already arranged with the ticket office for Morris and Laurette Robertson to share a rear cabin with them, a space smaller than a rail car compartment, with only two bunks that the four of them would have to share and through which billowed the sooty coal furnace exhaust from the flue at the center of the ship. It was agreed the women would share one bunk and the men would take turns sleeping in the other. The provisions, which Maddie learned they would also be combining with the Robertsons' to help disguise to the Mounties the deficiencies in both, were stored mostly on the forward decks.

By the time of its scheduled 8:00 a.m. departure, the S.S. Rosalie was overrun with humanity. Yet it seemed to Maddie that she and Laurette were the only two women aboard. As the whistle blew a long, sustained blast and the ship pulled away from the crowded dock, Maddie, already separated from her husband, who stood jawing with a group of men near the bow, leaned against the railing at the stern and watched the city's horizon widen. Noting the bustle of the streets as the business day commenced, watching the large houses atop First Hill and Capitol Hill come into panoramic view, she hated having to leave, and as the ship moved into the harbor and proceeded north through Elliott Bay, she edged her way around the deck's railing, keeping sight of the city until the very last. Then, at that moment, having also lost track of her husband and not having yet truly befriended Laurette, Maddie felt about as alone and displaced as a person could.

FOR THE NEXT TWO WEEKS, THE *ROSALIE* STEAMED NORTH-ward through the coastal passages of British Columbia and Alaska. On board, Maddie and Laurette became fast friends, preparing meals, playing cards, reading to each other from Anthony Trollope's novels (which Laurette had packed into one of her trunks), and generally keeping each other company. Maddie also made the acquaintance of a clean-shaven man (one of the few aboard the ship) who was about her age and who had the peculiar first name of Asahel. Asahel Curtis, or Mr. Curtis, as she addressed him, was traveling to Alaska not solely to prospect for gold but also to document the life and adventures of the prospectors with his camera, a large wooden box-shaped apparatus propped atop long, stilt-like wooden legs. With the help of his assistant, a rugged, bearded man named Lyle, who was approximately Laurette's age, he took a picture of the two women aboard the ship as it stood in dock at Prince George, British Columbia, to load coal. He showed them the negative of their image on the glass plate and promised to give them each a copy of the photograph once they had all returned to Seattle. He explained how he would be sending all his plates back to his brother Edward at their studio in Seattle for developing, and how one day his photographic chronicle of the great historic event of the gold rush would be renowned.

Maddie was impressed by his clear purpose and quiet confidence. She and Asahel Curtis continued to converse as the *Rosalie* resumed its voyage through the coastal passages, between the craggy and densely forested islands and farther into the northern cold and wilderness. Maddie expressed genuine interest in his vocation, so popular of late but still, according to Asahel, in its infancy. He explained how he wished to be out among his subjects, not distancing himself from them as so many studio photographers did – which was why he was venturing north.

"I want to experience what they experience, first-hand and for myself. Or you might even say, I want the camera to experience what they experience."

Based on her only two occasions of being photographed, this simple comment made sense to Maddie. The first time was in Cleveland, when Chester wanted to have a man-and-wife portrait made by a professional photographer – a project that cost them nearly a full day's wages, only to have the photographer endlessly arranging their attire and scolding them about not holding their pose; and the second time, aboard the steamship the previous day, when Asahel Curtis engaged the two ladies in conversation as he adjusted his equipment, made them feel at ease, told them to relax and be themselves, and then with only a second's warning, without any chance for them to get into position or become self-conscious (or "unsincere," as he phrased it), he squeezed the rubber shutter bulb and took their picture. Maddie tried to protest that her hat had been in disarray and Laurette worried aloud that she had been slouching and might have blinked, but Asahel reassured them they had both looked splendid.

For the remainder of the passage north, Maddie would see Asahel on deck every day. In his wool cap he seemed very boyish. He would sit quietly on deck and watch the men discussing their plans for reaching Dawson City once the boat arrived in Skagway, where best to seek a claim to stake, how best to spend their new-found riches. He also wrote in a small notebook with a pencil that he would periodically sharpen with his penknife. If not for the fact that his assistant Lyle was accompanying Asahel Curtis, Maddie would have feared for his fate in Alaska and the Yukon. Like the prospectors themselves, he seemed too preoccupied by matters apart from merely surviving. Yet, unlike the prospectors, he didn't strike her as a man driven by his ambition for easy wealth. Rather, he seemed content to merely observe and to take his many photographs, immune to the gold fever that gripped the other men. Maddie estimated he took two dozen photos or more every day.

She saw little of Chester during these two weeks aboard the *Rosalie.* Chester and Morris let Maddie and Laurette set up house in their steerage cabin and most nights took their bedrolls and bunked on deck in the open air with the other men, smoking cheap cigars and drinking rotgut through the extended dusk and well into the night. One morning just past dawn, while Maddie strolled along the ship's foredeck, she saw Chester sprawled out asleep between a pile of mooring ropes and another man, a stranger. The stranger was wrapped in the fine wool blanket that Maddie's grandmother had spun and woven as a young woman in Scotland and that Maddie's mother had handed down to her as part of her marriage dowry. Maddie wanted to kick her husband for his disregard for her and yank the blanket away from the stranger lying next to him … yet she restrained herself, and when she looked away from the horrid sight of the two men and toward the shore, she saw for the first time the coastal mountains pitching straight up from the white-misted shoreline, so high and steep she had to lean her head back to see their peaks. The sight startled her. She wanted to rush to the cabin and draw Laurette out to show her, then find Asahel Curtis and help him carry his camera to the deck to take a picture. But then, as she continued to stare at the frighteningly beautiful mountains, she also remembered the warnings she had overheard about the passes, Chilkoot Pass and White Pass, and understood what those warnings portended.

When she looked back across the foredeck of the boat, the provisions piled high, the sleeping men strewn about, she spotted Asahel, seated quietly on one of the capstans, his legs crossed, his cap pulled down low on his forehead, and an arm resting across the ship's metal gunwale. His camera was set up beside him, not aimed at the mountains in the short distance, as Maddie would have expected, but on the men sprawled across the deck.

"A good morning to you," he said from across the deck after she spotted him.

"Good morning to you, too, Mr. Curtis," she answered.

"Some of these men won't make it," he said offhandedly, as she stepped over and around the bodies to reach where he sat.

"It appears that some of them already may not have made it," she returned. "My husband perhaps among those unfortunates." Maddie pulled her light wrap tighter about her shoulders. When she reached the port side of the ship, Asahel stood and offered her his seat on the capstan.

"I have to check the light," he said, and stepped behind his camera and tossed the black drapery hanging from its back end over his head. Maddie heard the shutter snap, and when he emerged he slid the plate from the side of the camera and set it in a large leather case next to the camera. "The roll of the ship may be a problem," he said, "but we'll just have to wait and see." And then, coming from behind the camera to stand beside Maddie, he added, "Don't worry about your husband. He'll make it. And so shall you."

Solely on the basis of Asahel Curtis's own calm, even-measured sense of the world, Maddie accepted this reassurance, groundless as it might have seemed to her right then. Indeed, she was grateful for it, and in return she wished him success in his endeavors as well, and resumed gazing at the mountains.

FOG OBSCURED THE NARROW INLET AS THE *ROSALIE* STEAMED toward the Skagway docks. Two other steamships and a paddlewheel boat were already at dock in the small harbor. Through the fog, the surrounding mountains faintly appeared, snow already whitening their sharp peaks. White Pass, she could plainly assume, cut straight up the middle between the two parallel ridges receding northeastward, away from the town. The inlet was like an arrowhead pointing through the town laid out on the edge of the tideflats, to the base of the mountains, and straight through the pass.

The commotion among the men on board that had been stirred up as they realized they were coming into Skagway subsided as the *Rosalie* slid through the chill fog and eased up to the dock of rough-hewn timbers. Maddie and Laurette stood next to each other at the boat's stern and when it lurched upon first bumping into the dock, Laurette grasped Maddie's arm. Maddie knew Laurette's alarm extended far beyond her temporary loss of balance. Throughout the entire voyage Laurette had maintained a longanimity that Maddie could not help but admire, and felt lacking in herself. Rather than complain even once, Laurette spoke repeatedly of Morris's skills as a craftsman and outdoorsman, and of his unflagging determination, fortitude, and devotion to her.

"It's all right," Maddie whispered to her now as she pressed her hand on top of Laurette's.

Laurette looked at Maddie and then removed her hand from her arm and bravely leaned over the railing to watch the men on the dock tying down the mooring ropes. Suddenly, as the ship settled itself against the dock, a cheer went up from the men standing three or four deep along the starboard side where the gangplank would be let down. Maddie looked up and saw Morris coming toward them.

"Where's Chester?" she called to him, as he pushed past the men to reach them. Without answering her, he took Laurette by the arm and led her back to the cabin. "Where's Chester?" Maddie asked him again, following.

Morris looked over his shoulder and nodded toward the bow, where the mass of men was crowding its way toward the gangplank just then being lowered to the dock. Picking her husband out from the crowd was impossible. Most of the men wore either a bowler or some variety of wide-brim felt hat, though a few were smart enough to have fur caps on their head. Maddie finally just shouted out his name, once, twice, three times, and each time waited for his reply. Only after the third call did she see an arm rise from the crowd and was able to follow it down to Chester's familiar face. When she waved back, he signaled to her to stay where she was. "I'm going ashore," she heard him shout back to her. "Stay on board till I come for you."

She lowered her arm and watched as Chester inched forward toward the ship's railing and eventually descended the gangplank. Once he set foot on the dock, she quickly lost sight of him.

A moment later, Morris and Laurette returned, he carrying one of their trunks and she with a valise in each hand.

"Chester's gone ashore," Maddie told them.

"He's probably gone to get a handcart and wagon," Morris told her, and guided Laurette forward down the ship's side. "We'll find him," he added, leaving Maddie frustrated that Chester had not consulted with her on how they would proceed once the ship docked.

She looked up again at the mountains looming over the small, hastily built former mission town, and returned to her cabin to wait.

It took half a day to unload the *Rosalie*. Two more steamships entered the inlet and docked adjacent to the *Rosalie* during the successive hours that Maddie, having eventually made her way by herself down the gangplank and onto the dock, waited for the ship's crew to unload the hold and deliver her and Chester's provisions to them. Chester and Morris paid a wagoner by the hour to wait with them, at the ready, while Maddie and Laurette sat patiently on their steamer trunks watching the commotion along the dock. Dozens of Indian men, Chilkats, accompanied by their women in headcloths and toting children, worked the docks, haggling with prospectors in an effort to contract with them to haul their gear through the pass. Maddie watched from a distance as Chester, growing more frustrated with the delays by the ship's crew to unload the hold and itching to start the long trek to the gold fields, pushed away an Indian man who pressed his services on him. A scuffle ensued. Two more Chilkats – short, compact, powerful men – came to their fellow's aid, shouting in their language at Chester, who now began peering anxiously about the dock as if seeking a weapon to seize hold of, someone to back him up, or else an escape route. Morris quickly interceded, placating the men by offering each a generous plug cut of his tobacco. Yet when the Indian men accepted his offer and moved on down the dock, Maddie could hear Chester still cussing them.

"Damn Injuns," he fumed as he came up to her, shooed her off the trunk where she sat, and after opening it began rummaging through its contents. "Damn animals get right in your face ... What's a fellow to do? Where's my Bowie knife ... ?" When he found the long-handled knife in its leather sheath, he tucked it inside the front waist of his pants and pulled his canvas jacket over it. He closed the trunk lid and, without another word to Maddie, returned to where Morris and the wagoner sat on the back of the buckboard wagon.

Later that day, Maddie asked him if they ought not to go into town to find lodging, and Chester said no, that from now on, or at least until they reached Dawson City, they would be sleeping outdoors. "That's why we have to get a move on before the lakes and rivers freeze," he told her. "That's why we can't be standing around waiting like this, dammit."

Maddie hadn't heard anything about the lakes and rivers, just the mountain passes, and wondered what her husband was talking about. It wouldn't surprise her, though, if he had kept from her some vital piece of information about their journey. Since the day the *S.S. Portland* arrived in Seattle and he came back to their room at the flophouse with his sliver of gold, Chester had become increasingly distracted and uncommunicative. Sometimes, when he looked at Maddie, she had to wonder if he even recognized her. The change in his behavior at first did not fully register with her, but before long it seemed to take over the man who, back in New Jersey, could so readily charm her.

When their gear and supplies were finally unloaded from the ship and piled onto the wagon, their foursome made its way into town, the edge of which was just a few hundred yards from the docks. From what Maddie could gather, the plan was to have the wagon haul their gear to the trailhead outside of town, where they would make camp, and then from there begin the successive trips required to pack their gear and supplies over the pass to the first of what she now understood would be a series of lakes they would have to cross.

As they entered Skagway, the town throbbed with activity, offering a scene like nothing Maddie had ever witnessed or could have imagined. It seemed as if all the taverns, gambling houses, flophouses, floozy hotels, cheap eateries, and overpriced outfitting stores that made up the area below Seattle's Deadline were compressed into Skagway's four-block thoroughfare. The street was planked, yet the boards had long ago sunk below the surface of the ankle-deep mud and horse manure. With no room on the wagon bed and the team of two mules struggling just to pull the weight of their provisions, the four of them trudged alongside the wagon as best they could while the wagoner held his mules by their bridles and pulled them forward. Maddie was relieved that she had taken the time to pin up her skirts during the long morning wait, allowing her knickers to serve as mud spats. She was helpless, however, against the wet that had already soaked through both shoes and stockings to her feet and ankles, chilling them to the bone. She and Laurette clung to each other's forearms for balance and slogged on as best they could.

The progression of everyone else through this slough of mud and manure, especially those people right off the boats, whether on foot or with hired wagons, tended north through town toward the trailhead leading up through the mountain pass. The more Maddie saw of the town, the greater her relief that they would not be stopping there for the night. It presented a reckless, dangerous appearance, men and horses everywhere, a din of drunken, angry, riled-up shouting punctuated by frequent and apparently random gunfire. For the first time since leaving New Jersey, Maddie had a severe pang of longing for her Trenton homeplace. It all seemed so distant and so long ago ... her childhood, her parents, her simple home beside the railroad tracks. She knew it could never be regained. She would instead, if she had her wish, be content simply to return to Seattle. If she could only make it back to Seattle, she thought, knowing that the most arduous leg of this journey still lay ahead ... *if she could only make it back.*

Toward the middle of town, Chester and Morris called to the wagoner, a grizzled old-timer with a torn and soggy cigar stub stuck in the corner of his mouth, to stop and wait for them while they entered an outfitting store. The store was the last in a row of three storefronts that were part of a two-story wood-plank structure, the Red Onion Cafe and Pay Streak Saloon being the other two. As Maddie and Laurette waited for their husbands to return, Maddie spotted Asahel Curtis and his rough-bearded assistant, Lyle, exiting the Red Onion Cafe. She wanted to call out and greet them, but she knew such forward behavior, even here on the streets of Skagway, was unbecoming a lady. Yet to her delight, when Asahel Curtis turned from Lyle and saw her and Laurette standing there beside the wagon, he hopped down from the raised boardwalk and came forward to greet them.

Maddie nodded to Asahel and Lyle as they approached, and said, "I'll have to insist, Mr. Curtis, that no photographs be taken while we're in this compromised condition," and indicated their muddy shins and then the mules' rear ends behind them.

"I wouldn't dare," said Asahel, "though you two ladies present the most dignified and charming aspect of this mulish town," and then looking about added, "Welcome to Alaska, ladies. We'll no doubt be crossing paths again in the course of our mutual portage inland."

Barely had he finished speaking when Chester and Morris came around the side of the building where the outfitting store was, pulling three sleds behind them through the mud. They heaved each sled atop the tottering wagon and then turned to face the two men speaking to their wives. Maddie made the introductions, surprised that her husband and Asahel Curtis had not once met during the entire two-week sailing from Seattle. Upon being introduced, Asahel extended his hand, but Chester, instead of shaking hands with him, turned and tossed a rope over the top of the sleds stacked on the wagon.

"You're that picturetaker, aren't you?" Chester said, and fastened his end of the rope to a hook on the wagon's sideboard.

"Yes," Asahel replied. "Maybe I can take a photograph of you all sometime."

"I don't think so," Chester answered him. "We're here to find gold and that don't leave time for posing for pictures. That goes for my wife and me alike."

"I'm here to find gold, too," Asahel said, "*and* to take pictures."

"Well, good luck to you," said Morris, stepping in, again filling the role of conciliator.

"Good luck to you, too," said Asahel, and stepped back from the wagon, tipping his newsboy cap to Maddie and Laurette as Chester signaled the wagoner to get a move on.

Disgusted at her husband's behavior, Maddie nodded to Asahel and Lyle, took Laurette's arm again, and followed behind the wagon in its tracks. They quickly left the town behind and joined the tattered line of people trudging along the wagon trail that gradually inclined toward the encampment at the base of White Pass. The entire way, she didn't speak a word. It seemed that the ugliest aspects of Chester's character had come to the fore since their docking in Skagway. She had seen this side of him before, off and on, rarely in Trenton, but more frequently in Cleveland and then Seattle – his irritability, his short-temperedness, his ill manner toward others – and she didn't care for it. He complained incessantly about their money and grumbled that everyone else had an unfair advantage over them in the rush to the gold fields. She repeatedly told him aboard the *Rosalie* – that is, when she saw him – that if this undertaking was beyond their means or too strenuous for them, then they ought to do the smart thing and turn back. Which only made him lash out at her for making such a proposal.

"Then stop complaining," she told him the last time this exchange occurred, leading him to push past her out of the ship's cabin, not to be seen or heard from again until they reached Skagway.

About four miles out of town the wagon tracks they followed narrowed and grew more steep. The air turned colder as they advanced into the mountains and night came on. They passed a waterfall that seemed to pour straight from a rift in the mountainside, sending up a cloud of mist as the water crashed onto the mossy rocks below. The leaves on the trees had already turned – mostly brown and yellow, some red – and were beginning to drop to the forest floor. When a breeze blew, a shower of leaves fluttered across the path of the wagon track. Finally, along with a caravan of a dozen or so other groups, some on foot with their gear on their backs, others with handcarts, and still others with hired wagons, they arrived at an open pasture beside a wide stream flowing directly from the mouth of the mountain pass that receded northward and eastward before them.

Prospectors overran the pasture. It was as if a whole new town was forming at this very spot to rival the one they had left behind just hours earlier. Dozens of tents were pitched about the grounds. Dogs roamed between the tents or were tied to posts. Men chopped wood, smoked, and played cards on overturned fruit crates while at various fire pits women stirred long wooden spoons in pots and skillets. There was even a scattering of children – which broke Maddie's heart, to think of the hardship these babes would be made to endure. The scene resembled a

vast army camp or field hospital, similar to Matthew Brady's daguerre-
otypes of the war between the states, which made her understand all
the more why Asahel Curtis had come here. Maddie guessed there were
over a thousand people crammed into the pasture, all waiting their turn
to traverse White Pass.

Their wagon slowed to a stop at the edge of the encampment and the
wagoner looked down at Chester from the driver's bench and growled
to him, "Pick your spot, mister."

"All these people come looking for gold?" Chester asked him.

The wagoner pulled back the brake on the wagon and laughed. "Them,
you, me, my two mules here, even the right honorable mayor of Seattle.
It ain't the scenery we're here for, mister."

Even before leaving Seattle, Maddie had heard the story about the
city's mayor, how after hearing about the gold while visiting San Francisco he had cabled in his resignation and hired a team of men to take
him straightaway to Alaska. It was just one more sign that something
was wrong with all this gold fever. People were acting crazy. And looking now over the hordes of gold seekers spread out across this streamside
pasture, their faces haggard and their tents and flannel shirts mud-caked
just a day or two after they'd disembarked from the boats that brought
them here, Maddie knew her ill sense of this venture was well founded.
But it was too late now, for her or all the others alike. They would all be
going forward. Even from where she stood at the pasture's edge, she
could see men moving up the pass, their backs burdened with loads piled
a yard high over their heads, while other men loped wearily back down
the trail without packs, returning to fetch the next load. Maddie vowed
to herself then and there – a moment she would remember for years to
come – that, riches or no, she would survive the ordeal that lay ahead
for her. Scared as she was, she wouldn't let it defeat her.

When the wagoner asked again where to, Chester pointed to a spot
between two tents near the trailhead, and the three men, because the
wagon could not advance any farther, began carrying their combined
outfit to that spot. As they did so, Maddie and Laurette set about clearing
the ground for the tent, finding wood for the pit fire, and unpacking the

food provisions so they could prepare their first meal in the Alaskan wilderness.

Later that night, shortly after Maddie and Laurette finished scrubbing the skillet and washing the coffee pot in the stream, snow began to fall from the pale night sky. People in the camp stopped talking, suspended their chores, and looked up as the first white flakes drifted down. The scene seemed to signal both wonderment and dread – the soft air so quiet and still, the prospect of a heavy downfall so ill-boding.

Maddie and Laurette returned to their tent area from the stream and found Chester and Morris strapping portions of their outfit to the sleds they had bought in town.

"We'll pack out tomorrow," Morris said, speaking to Laurette.

Chester pulled hard on a rope from one side of the sled. "Get on top and push that down," he told Maddie, and following his orders she climbed atop the load piled high on the sled and pushed down on it so the rope would slacken enough for Chester to tie it down.

"How many trips do you suppose it will take?" she asked him.

"People are saying at least twelve, maybe as many as twenty. But with you two pulling a sled between you" – he raised his chin to indicate Laurette – "we can cut that down." He took his Bowie knife out and cut the rope above the knot he'd just made.

The snow was becoming a steady swirl through the air, clinging to the creases in the tent, gathering in the creases of the oilskin canvas covering the sleds, and dusting the ground where there wasn't yet mud.

"This will be our only night here," Chester added, and put his knife away. "So do what you need to do and turn in."

It was still dark when, a mere four or five hours later, Maddie heard stirrings outside the tent and woke up. She climbed out from beneath the blankets where she lay next to Laurette, put on her coat, mittens, earmuffs, and hat, and stepped out of the tent to discover that several inches of snow covered the ground – and that it was still coming down. Morris saw Maddie emerge from the tent and told her to wake Laurette.

"We'll need breakfast 'fore starting out," he said.

Maddie ducked back inside the tent, roused Laurette, and then set about mixing biscuits and grinding coffee. She didn't know what time it was and didn't much care. She had gotten some sleep, but not nearly enough to keep her from feeling groggy almost to the point of nausea. She also thought that maybe her woman issues were coming upon her sooner than usual. Laurette eventually joined her in preparing the breakfast, and by the time the food was cooked and they were all eating it, the sky was turning less dark and the snow was easing up.

As they brought the plates, cups, and skillet back to the stream to clean them, Maddie and Laurette again encountered Asahel and Lyle. The two men had an entire sled loaded with photographic equipment and supplies. The camera, propped on its three-legged stand, stood before their tent. They all four greeted one another in passing but didn't stop to chat. When Laurette stumbled and dropped the plates she was carrying, Lyle quickly stepped to her aid. He was about to tip his hat to her, but when he realized he was hatless, he just smiled at her instead. Laurette smiled back and continued on her way to the stream.

When they returned to their campsite, Chester told them which sled they would be pulling and showed them the best way to do it – in tandem, holding in front of them a yard-long pole to which a pull-rope to the sled was tied, and then walking steadily forward. He and Morris, who would each be pulling his own sled, then picked up the pull-ropes for their sleds and showed them how.

"We'll go slow," he said, and repeated, "but steady," and then with a tug began pulling his sled out of camp, followed next by Maddie and Laurette, with Morris taking up the rear.

Less than fifty yards past the encampment, the trail turned far more narrow and steep. It was also slippery, and Maddie and Laurette had to wedge their boots into the snowy slush for traction. Fortunately, one advantage of the snow was that the sled pulled more smoothly than it would have over mud. They had been pulling for about twenty minutes when just ahead of them a large outcropping of rocks forced the trail to curve to the left and out of view. Seeing this obstacle, Maddie and Laurette paused long enough to let Morris pass. Maddie turned to look back at the encampment that now lay below them, and at its edge she saw Asahel

Curtis with his camera aimed directly at them. She nudged Laurette with her elbow, and again the two of them put their combined weight and strength into pulling their sled up the trail.

It took their group two trips back to the encampment that day to advance all their gear just five miles into the wilderness. At one point along the trail they passed the treacherous ravine where a dozen horses had already fallen or been thrown when they became too exhausted to go any farther and now lay dead, their carcasses rotting. To Maddie, it felt at times as if Chester were pushing them in a manner not unlike the owners of those dead horses, fearful as he was of not reaching Lake Bennett before it froze and having to wait out the harsh winter on its shores.

By the end of the day, Maddie's boots were again wet through to her skin and her skirt black with mud nearly to her waist. In several places, usually along the steepest passages along the trail, ice had already begun to form. Every once in a while Maddie, and sometimes Laurette, would lose her footing and fall. Twice the men had to backtrack to help the women haul their sled past the next cutback in the trail, which only frustrated Chester, who started to blame Maddie for delaying them.

"Do you want to end up like one of those packhorses back there, your carcass at the bottom of a gulch?" he said to her at one point. "Is that what you want? Because if you do, that's what you'll get. Or better yet, we'll all freeze to death with you when we can't reach Dawson by winter."

Maddie refused to respond to these outbursts. She knew better. Hadn't she always heard that, worse even than being unprepared in the wilderness, was losing one's head and panicking? Well, she wasn't about to lose her head or panic, even if her husband did. She took the pull-rope from him and continued hauling her and Laurette's sled up the trail.

ONE WEEK LATER THEY REACHED LAKE BENNETT, A LONG icy-blue stretch of water high in the Yukon mountains. The encampment along the shore of the lake appeared nearly as large as the one just outside of Skagway at White Pass. Men were busy felling trees and burning and carving them out for canoes, or planing them to tie together into flatboats, or generally constructing any manner of craft that would float them the remaining 500 miles to Dawson City. There were also boats for hire, including a small paddlesteamer. To Chester's credit, the reason he had refused to hire Indian packers, he now told their party, was to hold back enough money to book them passage on a boat. Yet as they soon discovered, the paddlesteamer was beyond even their combined means and they would have to settle for hiring a common flatboat instead. The boatman they eventually found to take them had already made seven trips that summer and boisterously assured them that he could get them safely to Dawson City.

They stayed shoreside for two nights in order to rest the first day and load the boat the second day. Then on their third morning at Lake Bennett, they pushed off with all their provisions aboard what seemed to Maddie little more than a floating wagon, and began their long drift even farther northward. Though still short-tempered with Maddie, Chester seemed satisfied: they had outrun the hard freeze that would have trapped them on the lake's shore until spring.

The first several days aboard the flatboat went by smoothly as they traversed the four connected lakes—Bennett, Lindemann, Tagish, and Marsh. By the fifth day, after Lake Marsh, as they entered the headwaters of the Yukon River flowing from the lake, the passage narrowed and turned more turbulent. Before they entered Squaw Rapids, their boatman brought the craft ashore and battened everything down with extra ropes, and then warned his passengers that the next bit of river might turn a bit rough and that the men would need to work the oars exactly as he told them to.

The warning frightened Maddie, and, as it turned out, rightfully so. As they made their way into the rapids, the roiling waters churned brown and tossed the flatboat about like a child's float toy. Maddie and Laurette clung to their battened-down outfit while the men plied the oars in the water and the boatman worked the rudder to guide them through the treacherous whitewater. A constant spray soaked their clothes and chilled them. Finally, they seemed to have made it through the worst section of Squaw Rapids, yet a short while later the boatman informed them that they were approaching Whitehorse Rapids and shouldn't bother to dry off.

Along this next series of rapids, which were fiercer than the last, Maddie could make out the wreckage of boats that had broken up and been scattered along the river's boulder-strewn shore. At one point, when the front of their boat rose nearly vertical into the air and came down with a loud slap, she feared their boat might be next, that it would just disintegrate with the next series of rapids. Yet the small flatboat remained intact, and soon the waters smoothed out again, and that night they made camp at the northern-most end of Lake Laberge, where the boatman declared that they were halfway to Dawson City.

Over the next several days, they passed the confluence of the Teslin River and the Big and Little Salmon Rivers, and, in fulfillment of these rivers' names, every night the men caught sockeye salmon as big as a baby and laid them between two grill racks to be turned over the open fire until the tender reddish meat just flaked away from the oily skin. Maddie caught much of the salmon grease and mixed it in with the cornmeal and flour and made cornpone that everyone said tasted good and soon began referring to as Maddie's famous salmon biscuits. One night Morris shot a deer that wandered right down to the river's edge, and they skinned and gutted it and ate venison steaks that night and for the remainder of the trip.

At night the temperature dropped, occasionally bringing more snow, and in the morning they had to chop away at the ice along the shore to free the boat. At Five Fingers Rapids, when they hit a particularly violent sequence of rapids, the boatman slipped and lost control of the rudder, which sent the boat into a spin as Chester and Morris desperately tried to straighten it. They collided with several rapids, backwards and sideways, and it seemed they wouldn't be able to regain control of the boat when, by skill or good fortune or some of both, the three men managed to guide the boat through the last of the rapids and pull it ashore. When the boatman plunged his arm down into the frigid water and reached below the boat to feel for damage, he found the rudder had snapped in half, so for the rest of the afternoon they had to work to fashion a new rudder from the debris they found from less-fortunate craft – the same debris Maddie had begun to notice a few days earlier.

When at last they glided past the Klondike River, where it met the Yukon River and floated into Dawson City, the boatman congratulated them all on a successful voyage, dropped their outfit onto a short rickety dock, collected the second installment of his fee from Chester, and pushed off for farther downriver where, he said, he had a little shack where he stayed.

The four of them – Maddie and Chester, Laurette and Morris – stood on the dock and looked at the sprawl of hastily built two-room houses and two-story buildings and large and small tents that spread out from the river and right up to the hillside behind the booming city. No one, not even Chester, who had spurred them on to get to Dawson City as fast as they could, knew what they would do next or where they should go. Supposedly Morris knew of an agent who contracted men to work the valley around Eldorado Camp on Bonanza Creek, but he couldn't remember the man's name right now. Chester counted their money and proposed that the men keep guard of their outfit on the dock while the women take a room in one of the clapboard hotels on Front Street, which stretched from one end of the riverfront to the other. In the morning, Chester told them, they would find Morris's man and hire a wagon to take them to the gold fields.

Two

7. Up from Tacoma (1905)

LOYE CAUGHT THE 8:30 A.M. TRAIN FROM TACOMA TO Seattle and arrived at the King Street Station an hour later. She had made the trip three times previously, after deciding to attend the University of Washington in the fall and, in anticipation of her enrollment, to relocate to Seattle in the summer. She carried an overnight bag containing extra undergarments, an extra blouse, a jacket for the evenings when it turned chilly, a gymnasium suit, tennis shoes, a couple of books (a volume of Aeschylus and a biology textbook), and her diary. In a paper sack she carried the lunch her mother had packed for her: a roast beef sandwich with horseradish sauce, two cold, boiled new potatoes, and a cored and sliced apple.

As on her previous visits – the first time to meet with university administrators and Coach McDonald of the women's basketball team, the second to confer with her future professors and get a head start on the readings for her fall courses (hence Aeschylus and biology) – then as now, the contrast between Seattle and Tacoma struck Loye the moment she stepped through the station's heavy brass doors and onto the street. The more northern Puget Sound metropolis was larger and more congested. It was noisier and flashier, and also more intimidating. Something was happening here, something was taking hold – something that clearly wasn't taking hold in Tacoma. And whatever this something was, it proved both exhilarating and unnerving, and was a marked contrast to Tacoma's reliable yet uninspired operations as a modern city. She was familiar with the rivalry between the two cities – over the naming of the 14,000-foot mountain to the east, the location of the railroad terminus, the vying for the central seaport – all disputes which Seattle had won, making it clear that this city would prevail, had perhaps already prevailed, in becoming the region's preeminent metropolis.

Loye found the frenetic activity in the Seattle streets daunting, yet also enticing. She had graduated from Stadium High School in Tacoma two years ago and her twentieth birthday was just two months away. In Tacoma, she had already begun to feel like an old maid, as familiar with the city and its customs and the routines of her life within Tacoma's limited social sphere as someone three times her age. Which is why she had resolved to leave it. Leave her secure job in her father's bank, her comfortable room in her mother's well-kept house, her charming and reliable circle of friends, and move to Seattle. She knew her apprehensiveness about the city derived as much from her own parochial views of the world as it did from the big brash city now shouting at her as she stood on the sidewalk in front of the train station. Nevertheless, when, one after another, men approached her the instant she stepped out of the station (*accosted,* her mother would have said) and begged her to let them carry her valise, to take her arm and escort her to the nearest lodging ("Only the most respectable") or the nearest hansom stand or omnibus stop, and she had to insist, *No,* she could manage for herself, thank you, and at one point even had to pull her bag back from a young cad so brazen as to attempt to seize it from her hands ... then she knew that Seattle would present her with a host of challenges for which Tacoma had not, and never could, prepare her.

Her father had given her enough money to take a hansom cab to her destination, but choosing to exercise her independence and save the expense, Loye decided to take the streetcar. After shooing away the pestering swarm of men loitering near the King Street Station, just waiting it seemed for young callow prey such as herself, she walked from the train station, across the hazardously busy Western Avenue, two blocks over to Pioneer Place, and from there boarded a First Avenue streetcar, which the conductor assured her would take her all the way to Denny Hill.

"I wish to get off near the Washington Hotel," she told him.

"Visiting, are you?" he asked, and clanged the bells once to signal the car was moving on.

"Not at the hotel. Goodness, no," Loye said. "Do you know the Madison House? I expect to be rooming there."

"'Fraid not," the driver said. "But if it's near the hotel, you shouldn't have any trouble finding it."

Loye had hoped the conductor would have a good word to say about Madison House and was disappointed when he didn't even know of it. The boardinghouse had been recommended to her by a friend in Tacoma who knew a young actress, also from Tacoma, named Chiridah Simpson, who let a room at the house and had reported that it suited her fine, that it was affordable and clean and that the proprietress was a woman of character. On this recommendation, Loye had telephoned the boardinghouse several days ago and had spoken to Madison Ingram, the proprietress, and the two had agreed that Loye would visit on this day to look the house over and inspect the room she would be assigned, should she decide to move in. The woman had sounded quite pleasant on the telephone, and Loye was confident it would all work out. She wished to live in town rather than on the university campus in the dormitory because, first, she was two years older than the other girls starting that fall, and second, she planned to supplement the monthly allowance from her father with substitute teaching in the local schools and would need to be more centrally located.

Loye enjoyed the long, inclining ride up First Avenue, past several hotels, some more well-appointed than others, numerous store fronts with fashionable ladies' and men's attire displayed in the windows, past the post office and the YMCA, until eventually the streetcar reached a juncture at Virginia Street. The driver told her that from here he would loop around the wide girth of Denny Hill, eventually coming up the hill right behind the Washington Hotel, which would take another twenty minutes. Or if she preferred, and which might be faster, she could walk up the hill from this point, though he had to warn her it was not so easy a hike to the top.

Thanking him for this information (and caution), Loye said she didn't mind the walk and asked to be let off right there at the base of the hill. She stepped down from the streetcar and began vigorously walking up the slope of Virginia Street. As the driver had warned, the climb proved strenuous, and to give her legs a rest, catch her breath, and keep herself from perspiring too much, she paused at each corner before attacking the next block. She could tell that if she refrained from riding the streetcar and made this same walk everyday, she would doubtless be in superb conditioning for basketball by the time the season rolled around in November.

When she crested the top of Denny Hill and had walked past the monumental Washington Hotel, she readily located the boardinghouse at the corner of Fourth and Blanchard. It was a large well-maintained three-story house, with a columned front porch on the first floor that ran the length of the house, two large bay windows on the second floor that likely belonged to bedrooms, and two dormer windows extending from the long, sloped roof on the third floor that probably belonged to additional bedrooms. The house seemed well cared for, painted white with dark green trim. The appearance of a young man with opalescent skin and luminescent white hair on the roof of the house startled her somewhat. He looked like a strange bird perched up there, the rare and elusive white raven, which she had only recently read about in preparing for her fall philosophy class, of William James's gnostic quest made manifest. Preoccupied with applying mortar to the chimney, the curious-looking man did not see her approach up the sidewalk, and without ever being noticed by him she came up the walk, stepped onto the porch, and knocked at the front door.

An instant later a young girl about eleven years old opened the door and stared vacantly at Loye. Already, with the presentation of these two figures, the milk-white man on the roof and the vacant-eyed girl at the door, doubts cast a shadow over Loye's mind and she wondered if it might not be too late for her to reserve a room in the women's dormitory for the fall term.

Then, from deeper inside the house, she heard a woman's voice tell the girl to invite whoever it was at the door into the parlor and she would be there in a moment. The girl stepped aside, opening wide the large wood door. "You can come in, miss," she said to Loye in such a sweet, demure manner that Loye realized the girl was probably only shy.

"Thank you," Loye replied, and stepped across the threshold and into the front foyer.

"Are you a friend of Miss Chiridah's?" the girl asked, as Loye entered the house.

Loye set her valise down next to the coat rack and after extracting a pin from her straw hat carefully removed it from her head and patted her hair into place. "I haven't had the pleasure of her acquaintance yet," Loye answered the girl. "Although I do look forward to meeting her."

As Loye stood facing the young girl, who held out her hand to take

Loye's hat, the lady of the house came through the parlor wiping her hands on her apron and smiling warmly at Loye. In the full yet well-defined features of her face, in the brightness of her eyes, in her direct stride across the room toward Loye, even in her calico skirt and billowy yellow blouse, the woman impressed Loye as an earnest and well-meaning individual, despite her being in somewhat of a fluster over whatever she'd been doing in the kitchen. Though her hair was tied behind her long neck, a halo of loose strands floated about her head. The woman's appearance fit with Loye's sense already of the general peculiarity of the house – yet a peculiarity not without its appeal. She guessed that the woman was closer in age to her mother than to herself, and certainly – and Loye was ashamed to have such a thought – the woman seemed far more animated than her dear old mams. Loye's family life in Tacoma was as staid and ordinary as any banker's family could be. Their modest social circle comprised half a dozen similarly staid families with whom they shared occasional winter evenings of dinner followed by cribbage or in the summer an outing to the beach for a swim or to the Point Defiance Park for a picnic. Eccentricity was anathema. All the more reason, Loye was convinced, for refusing to allow her mother to accompany her on this outing to inspect her new lodgings.

"You must be Loye Atchinson," the woman said to her and took her hand. "Welcome, I'm Maddie Ingram, proprietress of Madison House, and, as you can see…," casting an eye down at her apron, "head chef."

"I understand perfectly," Loye said, returning Maddie's smile and shaking her hand. "It's nice to meet you." She suddenly felt nervous, yet also slightly exhilarated, to think she might actually reside in this odd house with these unusual people.

"Let me show you around," Maddie said, and then turned to the girl. "Ada, put the young lady's hat on the table and go stir the stew."

Loye had noticed the warm, comforting smell of the stew the instant she'd stepped into the house. It added to the homey atmosphere of the interior, which appeared neat and tidy, a fact that would please her mother, even if it were a bit more modest in its furnishings than what she was accustomed to (though probably no less comfortable). The parlor presented a somewhat bricolage look in its unmatched (or rather eclectic) furnishings. Her mother, in that tone of voice just short of dispersion that she used whenever describing a home other than her own, would have characterized it as "bohemian".

Maddie placed her hand on Loye's elbow and led her first into the parlor and then through all of the downstairs rooms. In the dining room, she explained the schedule of meals: breakfast between six and seven, lunch (if she chose to eat it there, which most boarders did not) at noon, and dinner at six. She showed her the kitchen and let her know that boarders were welcome to partake of anything they found in the refrigerator, cupboards, or cookie jar. In the den, she explained how the men occasionally liked to retire there in the evening for an after-dinner cigar. Then, back in the front parlor, standing beside the small upright piano, she asked Loye if she played, and Loye answered that she did. "Or at least I try to," she said.

However, it was the mention of men boarders that preoccupied her thoughts now. She had taken for granted that the house would be occupied exclusively by women. She turned to Maddie. "So you have gentlemen boarders as well?"

Maddie looked at her, apparently noting the tone of surprise and uncertainty in her question. "Yes," she said, "three. Two occupy the two dormer rooms in the attic, which I should add has a separate staircase, and the third gentleman has possession of the carriage house out back. He runs a small newspaper from there, if you can believe it. The ladies, meanwhile … and right now that would include only Chiridah and myself … occupy the second floor rooms exclusively and we use the main staircase." Maddie continued to look at Loye, apparently watching to see how she would respond to this detailed information. "I hope this arrangement is not unsatisfactory to you."

Loye was reluctant to affirm either that it was or was not. She could not imagine what her mother and father would say if they learned she was residing under the same roof as, well, at least two male boarders. They would most certainly fear for her reputation. Perhaps her safety, too. After all, how could she be sure what kind of men these were. They were total strangers. And no doubt bachelors, to boot.

As if sensing Loye's quandary, Maddie said, "They're all three fine young men. James in back runs his own newspaper, as I said, and then Ray is a law clerk who, as he recently told me, plans to open his own photographic studio one day, and then Clyde, whom you might have seen on the roof outside, he's our jack-of-all-trades around here. He's been with me from the start and I'll dare say I couldn't run the house without him."

Loye was not sure if she was reassured by this statement or not. Instead of responding, she said simply, "May I see the upstairs," and Maddie, agreeing that this was an excellent idea, led her up the front staircase to the second floor.

Maddie proceeded to show Loye three of the four upstairs rooms, including her own on the back side of the house, the one next to it that remained vacant, and then the spacious (but also currently vacant) front room with toile curtains pulled back from its two bay windows that looked out over Fourth Avenue and had a lovely view of Elliott Bay and the Olympic Mountains, a windowseat with storage, an iron bed with brass trim, a dresser with mirror and beside it a wash stand, a small reading chair with a linen covering, and in the middle of the floor an oval rag rug, a smaller version of the one in the downstairs parlor. Loye was positively captivated by the large, lovely room, which was undoubtedly superior to any dormitory room. As Maddie explained that the adjacent front room, which was identical, was occupied by Chiridah Simpson, Loye forgot all about the matter of the male boarders.

Maddie said that she believed Chiridah was auditioning for a show that morning and that, if she won the part, rehearsals would start that very same day. "Do you enjoy the theater?" she asked Loye.

Loye, who had only ever been to her high school drama productions, never to real theater, replied that she had not had much occasion to attend so couldn't honestly say. "I think I would probably enjoy it," she said.

"Well," Maddie went on, "I know you and Chiridah will get along just fine. She's one of the sweetest girls I've ever known. If anything – and mind you I'm speaking as a coarsened old Klondiker now – Chiridah, I sometimes think, may be too delicate a soul for the hardships of the stage."

Ignorant of what kind of hardships life in the theater imposed on one,

Loye had nothing to say, except that she certainly looked forward to meeting Chiridah. She took one more glance about the room, pictured herself contentedly reading her school books in the window seat, and then followed Maddie back downstairs.

In the parlor Maddie gestured to Loye to take a seat in the large armchair and told Ada, who waited for them at the bottom of the stairs, to bring them tea with the hot water that was on the stove. "And be careful," she added. "Don't scald yourself." Then she sat on the sofa facing Loye. "I believe you said over the telephone that you're going to be a schoolteacher."

"Substitute teacher," Loye said. "Or at least I hope to be, once classes at the university start."

"Yes, of course ... I remember you saying you'll be attending the university in September."

"Yes, ma'am."

"Please," Maddie said, "call me Maddie."

Loye liked Maddie, her direct and unpretentious manner. A Klondiker, she'd called herself. That would account for her independent demeanor. Maddie seemed like a person in charge of her own destiny, as Loye's father would have said if Maddie were a man. According to Loye's father, who was as kind and paternal a man as could be, men needed to take charge of their destinies as certainly as they took charge of their education, their bank accounts, or their wardrobe. Women, on the other hand, had the luxury of having their destinies prescribed to them (by men, Loye had always assumed he meant) – a philosophy that accounted for her father's original disapprobation of Loye's plan to move to Seattle and enroll in the university. Fortunately, he had eventually convinced himself, through no suasion on Loye's part, that the university would be a good place for her to find a suitable, well-educated, self-directed young man who, through the institution of marriage, would prescribe his daughter's destiny to her. Loye's father would almost certainly be perturbed by Maddie's independence and self-reliance, and no doubt outraged by his daughter's association with such an example of womanhood.

Loye felt confident, nonetheless, that Maddie, personable as she was, could win over even her father. As she laid out for Maddie her plans to play basketball, and then had to backtrack to explain exactly what the game of basketball was, she felt herself embracing the idea that Madison House would be her new home.

When Ada brought in the tea, the young girl continued to stare at Loye as if she were an exotic curio. When Loye asked the girl how old she was, Ada lowered her head and said nothing until Maddie gently prodded her to answer the young lady.

"Eleven," the girl said. "And three-twelfths," she added. "That's one-quarter."

"Pardon ...," Loye looked at the girl somewhat befuddled.

"Three-twelfths is the same as one-quarter. You have to divide down. It's nine months to my birthday, or three-quarters of a year."

"Very good," said Loye. "You're quite the mathematician."

"Thank you, Ada," Maddie said then, and with that Ada curtsied to Loye and retreated to the kitchen. When she was gone Maddie explained how it was a shame that school officials had deemed Ada too slow to attend school. "And in some matters she may be," Maddie said, "like any one of us. But in other matters, why, she's as sharp as a whip."

Loye's heart went out to the girl, and before the notion had even fully registered in her thoughts, she found herself saying, "Perhaps I could tutor her."

"You would be too kind," said Maddie, her hands in her lap, appearing genuinely pleased by the proposal.

And then, just as unexpectedly, Loye found herself asking, "How much did you say the room and board were?"

Maddie regarded Loye pleasantly across the short space between the sofa and the armchair. She leaned over and poured them each a cup of tea. "I believe over the telephone we said five dollars per week, which includes your meals. Please correct me if I'm mistaken. Unlike sweet little Ada, figures are not my strong suit."

"I believe that's correct," Loye confirmed, and on that Maddie handed Loye her tea and they agreed that Loye would stay the night at Madison House to meet her fellow boarders and then the following week, on Saturday, she would move in.

"I'm sure you'll be happy here," Maddie said.

"I think I will be too," Loye replied.

They finished their tea, and when Maddie said she had better get back to making supper and invited Loye to join them for the evening meal at six, Loye said she would be happy to and returned upstairs to put her overnight bag in her new room. She lingered a moment, taking it all in again, and when she came back downstairs carrying only her day satchel and retrieved her straw hat from the coatrack, she already felt right at home.

SHE WALKED STRAIGHT OUT ONTO THE FRONT PORCH AND immediately spotted a tall, curly-haired young man in the front yard positioning a camera on a tripod and aiming it toward the roof.

"Now look this way when I tell you to, Clyde," he called up to the albino whom Loye had seen earlier working on the chimney. "Now," he exclaimed, and then, "Got it! Great!" and removed a plateholder from the camera and set the photographic plate in a leather case at his feet. "That's a good one," he called back up to the roof, and in the same instant looked forward and saw Loye standing on the porch watching him.

Loye stepped down from the porch and into the yard and introduced herself to her two new fellow boarders. Clyde Hunssler, who leaned over the roof to speak to her, seemed like a perfectly nice fellow ... all she could think of was her parents' flabbergasted cry upon learning their daughter was living under the same roof as an albino. Ray Gruhlki, however, struck Loye as a moderately confused young man. In the brief repartee they exchanged about his picture-taking, just enough to leave her curious about him, he came across as both nervous and brash. The whole situation with these male boarders made her wonder what kind of surprise the man living in the carriage house had in store for her. Whatever it was, it would all be part of the great enterprise of her venture into independence.

She reiterated to Ray and Clyde how nice it was to make their acquaintance, bid them each a good afternoon, and took off back down Denny Hill with a new sense of exhilaration about being in the big city. Banished was the apprehensiveness stirred up inside her when she'd stepped out of the train station earlier that morning. She began loping down the hill and several times caught her skirt beneath her feet and nearly went tumbling down, like Jill gone to fetch her pail of water. Yet each time she recovered herself, as if too light and too dexterous to actually fall, as if her anticipation of the new life that awaited her buoyed her up and let her virtually float on the soft summer air.

She reached the bottom of the hill and like an omen from above, a portent of good fortune to come, the first streetcar to approach was bound for her very destination, the University District. The streetcar came gradually to a stop and she boarded and paid her nickel fare and after taking one of the middle seats on the nearly empty car pushed up the glass window so she could lean out and enjoy the warm midday breeze on her face and arms. As she held her straw hat down with her hand, the streetcar rattled up Pike Street, ascending Capitol Hill, and then headed north on Broadway Avenue. The streets seemed to widen the farther from downtown the streetcar traveled. Large square houses with expansive yards and wrought-iron fences soon appeared. Past the quaint villagelike district forming along Broadway, the streetcar's route entered less developed areas where the houses were far and few between and clumps of tall firs and cedar remained standing. Then, as the streetcar descended the hill and picked up speed, Loye removed her hat and held it in her lap, then leaned even farther out the window, letting the wind push her hair back from her brow and over her ears and feeling it all coming undone from the tidy bun she'd placed it in that morning before leaving her house in Tacoma. She could see the Cascade Mountains to her right and between the trees spy patches of brilliant blue, which had to be Lake Washington. Straight ahead and across Portage Bay, she could see the university grounds – a large, open clearing with only a few buildings scattered along connecting paths. Loye thrilled to see this panoramic view of the university she would attend in the fall. She knew she was fortunate indeed to have such an opportunity to advance her education and eventually become a superior schoolteacher. At times she fancied herself attempting a graduate degree, the master's or perhaps even the doctorate of philosophy, once she completed her undergraduate course work. She knew she loved learning enough to achieve such a goal.

She loved athletics, too, and with opportunities ever increasing for women, such as the new ladies basketball team on which she'd won a place for herself during tryouts last May, she sometimes fancied herself becoming a coach once her own playing days were over. In fact, since she had already met all her professors, she wouldn't waste time going to their offices again once she reached the campus. Instead she would go straight to the gymnasium.

The streetcar slowed as it approached the wooden bridge that spanned the narrow channel between Lake Union and Portage Bay. As the car crept over the bridge and the wood pilings creaked and groaned, Loye wondered about the bridge's sturdiness, if it would hold, not just now but in the future when she would ride over it nearly every day to get to her classes. Below the bridge, she saw several structures built on floats at the water's edge: small, closed-in huts with narrow walkways around their perimeter. Smoke came up from the stovepipe in the roof of one of these huts. The floating structures made her think of the lairs of bridge ogres waiting to devour the passengers of the hapless streetcar when it finally plummeted off the rickety old bridge. Yet when the streetcar at last made it across the bridge, Loye recognized that in all likelihood she would probably become bored with this daily trip from Denny Hill to the university over the course of the next several years. Yet right now, simply imagining that such an experience could eventually become commonplace thrilled her.

The streetcar went up University Avenue, which was lined with numerous small businesses, with the new university grounds on the right and to the left a residential area of modest bungalow and two-story frame houses. About half way up University Avenue, Loye reached up and pulled the bell rope to signal the conductor to let her off at the next stop. Although the district was clearly expanding, this section of Seattle seemed like an altogether autonomous little hamlet, separate from the commercial hubbub of the downtown, or the older and mixed residential streets of Denny Hill, or the expanding blocks of more luxurious homes along Capitol Hill.

Glad once more to be walking, Loye made her way onto the university grounds, which seemed more like a large, recently cleared pasture in certain areas than the well-groomed college campuses of popular imagination. There were few lawns in sight and almost no ivy. Instead, thick woods bordered the open grounds on which a scattering of sycamore, birch, and spruce saplings had recently been planted along with rhododendron and mountain laurel shrubs. A couple of hard-packed roads intersected the campus, and narrow dirt paths, like deer trails, connected the assortment of university buildings that were generously spaced across the grounds.

Loye passed the large rust-red women's dormitory and felt relieved to know her lodgings at Madison House were secure. At the massive Administration Building, she had to pause and just gaze up at its cream-colored brick, terra-cotta trim, and pitched and dormered roof that was crowned by an impressive copper cupola, all of which combined to make the building look like an elegant French chateau. The building housed all the administrative offices, most of the professors' offices, and a good many classrooms as well. True to her intentions, she walked right past the Administration Building and down the sloping path in the direction of the field house, which had been set a fair distance from the academic buildings. The path eventually came upon the long, wooden structure where Loye had tried out for the ladies' basketball team. The building was painted white and had a bowed roof like a train station's and a series of long and narrow arched windows at either end.

Loye entered at the main doors and looked up into the curved wood rafters. A running track suspended from roof trusses encircled the full interior of the building like a waist belt. At either end of the scuffed hardwood floor, she found what she was looking for: the two iron rims, with a cotton net hanging from each, nailed to square backboards marking each end of the basketball court. Past the basketball court, gymnastic equipment, including ropes, parallel bars, a hobby horse, and a set of rings, was arranged around padded mats. Several doors along one side of the building, opposite the bleachers, led to the equipment locker, the men's and ladies' locker rooms, and the coaches' offices.

Since she seemed to be the only person in the building, Loye removed her hat and set it on one of the benches. She took several safety pins from her day satchel and pinned up her skirt just below the knees and removed her walking shoes and put on the canvas tennis shoes she had brought with her. She walked over to the wire-enclosed equipment locker and, feeling a trace sheepish knowing she probably shouldn't be snooping around like this, opened the metal door, stepped inside, and retrieved one of the pebbled-leather basketballs from a rack that hung next to the field hockey sticks, boxing gloves, jump ropes, and assorted wands and clubs. Her nerves settled down as soon as she dribbled the ball on the hardwood floor and started trotting down the court toward the far basket. Near the top of the penalty key, she came to a stop, planted her feet (ten inches apart, right foot slightly forward), held the ball in both hands (right hand slightly higher than the left, fingertips lightly cradling the leather orb), and eyeing the rim of the basket, shot the ball from her chest in a high arc. When the ball sailed straight through the iron rim and dropped out the bottom of the cotton net, she knew she'd received another good omen.

8. Council Adjourned (1905)

BY THAT AUTUMN, MADDIE HAD BEEN OPERATING MAD-
ison House for more than two years. She found Loye, her newest boarder,
a charming girl, a gift really. In many ways, Loye's life recalled for Maddie
the life she'd once imagined for herself in her youth, an ambitious future
filled with college and career and eventually love, marriage, and children,
long before she married Chester too young and they began roaming the
country like a pair of stray mutts. With Loye Atchinson, her young university student and future schoolteacher, Maddie now had a full slate of
boarders in the house – which included Loye, whom she knew she was
going to like; Chiridah Simpson, her beautiful, struggling actress; Ray
Gruhlki, her tall drink-of-water law clerk and soon-to-be-famous photographer (she felt certain); James Colter, her Negro newspaper publisher;
and Clyde Hunssler, her albino handyman and, as she so often thought
of him now, her co-proprietor, business partner, boardinghouse consort,
and all-around unassuming companion, since without him Madison
House would not be the well-tended, smoothly running establishment
that it was and she ... well, she didn't know what she would be without
Clyde as part of her day-to-day, month-to-month life. She had grown so
accustomed to his presence that to imagine him not there was to imagine
a different life altogether. In general, Maddie liked to think of all of her
boarders as *hers*, as more than just boarders. To Maddie they were her
family, her charges, the people she provided with a safe and clean home,
nourished with her food, and looked after. This was likely her mothering
instinct, which had so far remained unexpended on offspring of her own.
Yet when it came to Clyde, the instinct was not a mothering one at all, it
was something more, an urge, and impulse even, which she most certainly
felt yet which she did not dare acknowledge openly, much less pursue.

By September, the regrading of the twelve-block stretch of First and
Second Avenues from Pike Street to Denny Way, along the west side
of Denny Hill, was well under way. The streetcar line that ran up First
Avenue was discontinued north of Pike Street and on the very same rail
tracks, donkey engines with shovel buckets and rows of dump cars were

brought in to gnaw away at the hillside and carry away the enormous volume of dirt.

Around the breakfast and supper table, Maddie said nothing about the regrading project that would eventually, everyone knew, come within just two blocks of the corner where Madison House sat. She regarded the Washington Hotel as the threshold to Denny Hill, the security gate, past which the regrading would never proceed, ultimately preserving the hilltop neighborhood in the main from the devastation that had been wrought upon districts farther south by past and current regrading projects – all of which, just like the current First and Second Avenue regrading, had been undertaken by authorization of the city council, the city attorney, and the city engineer under the irrefutable banner of civic progress. To all of these city leaders progress equated to improvement. And yet, as she knew in her heart, this was not always the case. When Maddie sat down each Saturday morning to update her accounts ledger for Madison House and balance her checkbook, a duty that served regularly to remind her of the modest financial margin by which she operated the boardinghouse (her Klondike windfall having been expended in "capital investments," that is, the costs of purchasing, repairing, and properly furnishing the house), it was then that Maddie understood that for city leaders – elected officials and the city boosters within the chamber of commerce – progress more accurately equated to profits, not improvements. When Reginald H. Thomson had been quoted in the *Seattle Herald* proclaiming that Seattle's hills were "an obstruction to the natural northerly expansion of the city" – a statement with implications that made Maddie fume – did he have any understanding of what constituted the Denny Hill neighborhood? Did he recognize the *natural* contribution it made to the city's well-being? Did he understand (and she feared he did not) that the success of Seattle as the preeminent city of the region, the Queen City of the Pacific Northwest, was not solely contingent upon expansion of the downtown business district but on the preservation of its vital neighborhoods as well? Of the family homes, boardinghouses, and apartment buildings where the people who really ran the city lived. The shops, cafes, and small manufacturers interspersed throughout these residences. The churches, lodges, and, yes, even the taverns where these people publicly gathered. The big business interests were important, certainly. Railroad, coal, lumber, canning. She was not opposed to these. Though reform-minded, she wasn't one to advocate a Socialist redistribution of the nation's wealth (even though she supported Theodore Roosevelt in his vows to check the country's most aggressive monopolies and, similarly, supported the Populist-Democrat George Cotterill, who wished to do the same locally). But equally important were the interests of regular people, people like herself and everyone else living at Madison House (and on Denny Hill for that matter) who didn't wield the city's business might, but who nonetheless shared in the Seattle Spirit as fully as every single dues-paying member of the chamber of commerce.

It was a mild Indian summer day in late September, when the foliage of the few deciduous trees scattered in among the evergreens on the hills surrounding Seattle had begun to turn yellow and russet, when a six-day stretch of sunshine and relative warmth had dried out the yet unplanked or unpaved roads about the city, when anticipation of the lingering autumn rains was foremost in everyone's minds, that representatives from the city attorney's office began canvassing Denny Hill with peti-tions seeking residents' endorsement for the extended regrading project, to take it beyond First and Second Avenues. The petition would then be formally presented to the city's corporate counsel at a mid-October meet-ing as part of the procedures for achieving final approval of the city engi-neer's plans to regrade *all* of Denny Hill.

It was mid-afternoon in the middle of the week when a young man, his face clean-shaven and his eyes wide with intent, his worsted-wool suit tidy and trim, a black bowler set squarely atop his head (a headwear fash-ion that always impressed Maddie as both cocksure and obtuse, even though her boarder Ray wore one), stood on the front porch of the boardinghouse and, smiling at Maddie as soon as she opened the front door – sneering almost, she later felt, despite his puppy-dog visage – presented her with a clipboard that held the petition. Maddie took it from him and began exam-ining it carefully. The first page was a statement of endorsement for the regrading project, and beneath it lay a half dozen pages for signatures.

The young assistant to the city attorney voluntarily summarized the endorsement statement as Maddie reread it for a third time. "In sum," he said, "it states that Denny Hill residents concur with the city engineer's unofficial assessment of the ten-fold increase in property values to be had from the appropriate, *and necessary*, regrading of select portions of Denny Hill, and that they support proceedings to duly compensate residents in light of said assessment for any damages incurred during the project." He then held out his fountain pen to Maddie.

"I might add," he went on, after she simply glanced up and then resumed her scrutiny of the statement, "that so far we have had 100 percent cooperation from your friends and neighbors, that there is unanimous support for the project."

Yet when Maddie flipped up the statement page and looked at the signature sheets and saw that only two of the six sheets had signatures on them, she became even more skeptical. "Really?" she said.

The young man seemed to become impatient. "Smart people know a good deal when they see one," he remarked. "This venture will ensure that our fine city continues to thrive, that it progresses unhindered into the twentieth century. We all want to do our part, *as citizens*, to see that this effort succeeds. Don't we?"

Maddie wanted to ask him, *Unhindered by what?* The hill? The people living on the hill? What exactly? Instead, she stood with him in the doorway, parting from her customary practice of inviting any and all visitors into the front parlor, and asked plainly, "Where does it stop?"

The good-humored smile was gone from his face now, and he looked on Maddie rather sternly. "Where does *what* stop, ma'am?"

"The regrading," she said. "After Second Avenue, will Third Avenue go? Then Fourth?"

"Mrs. Ingram, ma'am, I'm afraid I can't answer your questions specifically. But if you care about the city of Seattle at all, if you care about its future, nay, if you have the self-interest to guard your own property values and the investment you and your husband have made, then you'll endorse the city engineer's initiative. Just think of how South Jackson Street has prospered since its leveling."

Prospered indeed, Maddie thought, and wondered how this young turk in his sleek bowler knew her name was Ingram. If by prospered he meant dislocated, then she knew exactly what he meant. She was acquainted with a merchant, a small stationer and stamp man, who had lost his store to the Jackson Street regrading and was never able to rebuild or find a storefront affordable enough to recoup his losses and reestablish himself in his modest business. He now worked as a floor clerk in the large Standard Furniture store downtown. That's how he'd prospered by the regrading of Jackson Street.

Clearly growing more frustrated at this point, the city attorney's brash assistant abandoned his sales pitch and told Maddie that she ought to attend the city council meeting three weeks hence, at which time the matter of the north-end regradings – "Do you mean Denny Hill?" Maddie asked him, and he said, "Yes" – would be discussed in meticulous detail.

"I believe I will do that," she replied.

"And in the meanwhile," he tried one last time, "signing the petition will ensure the swiftest completion of the project."

Maddie glared up at him to let him know she did not favor his tactics with her. He had the audacity of the Northland che-cah-quas, she thought, those reckless young men who ventured into the Yukon on a fancy of finding their fortune, only to discover white death, their bodies becoming wolf meat in the spring thaw. There was also something raffish about the young man, perhaps even depraved, that incited Maddie's ire.

"Excuse me now," she said to him, and stepped back into the house.

Yet before she could close the door – having never closed the door on anyone in her entire life – he placed his patent-leather shoe across the threshold.

"Ma'am," he said, "all your neighbors are in favor of this initiative."

"Sir," Maddie replied, and gave him the look of white death, "I am not," and with that she thrust the door into his insole and heard him curse as he pulled his foot away.

FOUR WEEKS LATER, MADDIE SET OFF DOWN THE HILL FOR city hall to attend the city council meeting at which the petition for the regrading of Denny Hill would be presented and both the city engineer,

Reginald H. Thomson, and the city attorney, Scott Calhoun, were expected to speak to the issue. She had asked Clyde if he wished to accompany her, yet, with regrets, he told her he had to run several errands for James and then had to check in on his father. Maddie was a little crestfallen, knowing that Clyde's support could bolster her spirits on such an outing as this.

In the weeks preceding the city council meeting, Maddie had tried her best to guard her boarders from worrisome discussions of the regrading project, believing still that the worst would be averted. But the implications of such potentially momentous events proved impossible to ignore. James, her newspaperman, asked her outright for her views of the situation not long after word broke that "the regraders," as they were being called, were targeting Denny Hill. She told him that she believed they would no sooner regrade Denny Hill than they would Mount Rainier. Ray, her photographer, said he wanted to take as many photographs of Denny Hill residents standing next to their homes as he could before it was too late. Maddie found herself offended by this offhand remark, and when Loye, who was in the room at the time, saw the effect Ray's words had upon Maddie, she quickly reassured her that everything would be all right, that Ray – "the camera-happy lout" – had meant the houses down on First and Second Avenues, many of which had already been vacated by their owners. Chiridah, the dear, the one who had lived longer than anyone else at the boardinghouse, longer even than Maddie, said only that she loved living at Madison House and had no intention of moving. Only Clyde, among all her boarders, refrained from saying anything to her about the regrading, and the one time when the opportunity arose in the company of the others, he changed the subject by asking who would be interested in walking with him down to the nickelodeon at the Unique Theater later that evening. Chiridah immediately said she would, proclaiming to everyone how moving pictures were the next big thing and someday she hoped to act in one. Maddie took note of Clyde's discretion and appreciated him all the more for it.

On the morning she set out for the city council meeting, a clear, brisk October day, she could hear the hiss and chug of the donkey engines from the front porch of the boardinghouse. The sound very nearly made her cringe. The dirt was supposedly being sluiced through flumes down to the waterfront where it was loaded onto barges and towed out into the bay to be dumped. She wondered if they planned to fill in Elliott Bay just as they were filling in the tideflats with the earth from Jackson Street and the other south-end regradings. To Maddie, the incessant noise from the steam engines that ran on the narrow-gauged tracks down on First and Second Avenues was a frightening, ominous sound, and ever since the regradings had begun down there she strictly avoided that side of the hill and opted instead to remain on the Fourth or Fifth Avenue side when coming up or going down the hill on her errands.

For the occasion of the city council meeting, she wore her best shirt-waist suit (dark-brown with white trim along the collar and cuffs), her gray coat (old and somewhat worn, but still warm and sturdy – like a good man, she liked to think), and her modest turban hat (purchased last year at the Bon Marché). She figured that the meeting called for at least some measure of formality. She walked down Fourth Avenue, past the well-trimmed east lawn of the Washington Hotel, and at Pike Street caught a streetcar that would take her straight to City Hall.

By the time she arrived, the meeting hall was already crowded and over-heated. Maddie took one of the few unoccupied chairs at the back of the room and removed her hat and coat and set them on her lap. At the front of the room sat the eight city councilmen behind a long bench on a foot-high raised platform, looking like a row of judges except that none of them wore robes. Nonetheless, all eight men looked stiff and formal in their long coats and beards, plainly suffering from the room's stifling heat and no doubt wishing for the meeting to convene, the sooner to bring it to adjourn-ment. At two long tables facing the austere city councilmen, three other men sat waiting for the meeting to convene, their backs to the people crowd-ing into the room. Maddie thought she recognized the man on the right from newspaper photographs as Reginald H. Thomson: of mid-height, a somewhat slender build, ashen brown hair and a pointed beard, sterling white collar and cuffs beneath a well-tailored suit, and a posture with the perpendicularity of freshly milled lumber. She had read somewhere that he was a teetotaler and an ardent churchgoer – two habits which she, personally, could not abide by. Indeed, he seemed like a self-composed and rather closed-mouth man, someone who in his physical reserve was accustomed to having his way in most matters – if not upon demand, because he didn't seem to be the demanding sort either, then certainly in due time. He faced forward, his hands folded before him on the table, and calmly watched the councilmen grow agitated with their overheated waiting as the crowd settled into the meeting hall.

To Thomson's right at the adjacent table, a less fit and far more fidgety man of about the same age – fifty or so, Maddie guessed – leaned on his elbows, his forehead supported by the scaffolding of his fingers. Maddie took this man, who was rather rotund and looser in his attire, to be the city attorney, Mr. Scott Calhoun, since in the chair right beside him, prim and proper, sat the young, insolent assistant who had come to the door of Madison House with his clipboard and petition several weeks earlier and had left with a sore foot.

Maddie recognized several faces throughout the meeting hall, people she had become acquainted with over the years going into stores or riding the streetcar or just strolling about the neighborhood. This familiarity with her neighbors, even if not always a speaking familiarity, was one of the aspects of living on Denny Hill that she most cherished. Before the room had fully settled down, the chairman of the city council, a large-nosed man with a tight collar from which his florid neck squeezed out, began harrumphing loudly and hammering a gavel onto a wood block. People took their seats as he called the room to order, and in no time the room was very nearly still. He laid the gavel down and cleared his throat.

"We will call to order this meeting of the City Council of the City of Seattle. Our business today is to hold a public hearing upon the necessity of the continued and further regrading of the area north of Pike Street and the efficaciousness of proceeding thereupon." He paused in this pronouncement to look to either side of him at his fellow councilmen, who in near unison nodded their concurrence.

"We have with us today by way of witnesses, the city attorney, Mr. Scott Calhoun" – the chairman nodded his acknowledgment to Mr. Calhoun, who solemnly returned the nod – "and the city engineer, Mr. Reginald Thomson." The chairman did not make a similar acknowledging nod to the city engineer, but rather pointed to him with his gavel. Thomson, meanwhile, remained as still as a statue, content seemingly to let the hearing unfold at its own pace and to minimize his own presence as much as possible.

"Counselor," the chairman said, addressing the stout Mr. Calhoun, "I'm given to understand that you wish to make the first statement."

Scott Calhoun pushed his chair back from the table and, pressing his hands down upon it, pushed himself up and stood to face the row of city councilmen. "Yes, Mr. Chairman, thank you, I would," he said, and immediately sat back down.

"Proceed then."

Once more Calhoun rose from his chair. He took a moment to adjust his jacket and shuffle through several papers lying in front of him on the table. His assistant then handed him what he seemed to be looking for.

"Mr. Chairman –," and he turned to Reginald H. Thomson, "and Mr. Thomson. The City of Seattle hereby agrees, upon the filing of a 75-percent majority petition" – and held the petition up for all to see – "to introduce and duly pass an ordinance providing for the establishment of an improvement district as herein described . . ." He then described an area that, to Maddie, seemed to include the entire circumference of Denny Hill: from Pike Street to Denny Way, between First Avenue to Sixth Avenue.

Maddie was not prepared for this, not by the newspaper stories she had tried to keep track of, not by the statement on the petition that the city attorney's despicable assistant had brought to her door, not by anything. Calhoun was proposing, in effect, the leveling of Denny Hill in its entirety, in one fell swoop – a project of incomprehensible enormity, exceeding in magnitude anything carried out so far in any other part of the city. A project that would undoubtedly devastate the neighborhood and visit upon it such destruction as to, in all likelihood, lay it permanently to waste. A project that would mean the loss of her boardinghouse, her livelihood, her dream, and her passion – her home and everything it stood for. Where would her boarders go, where would Clyde go (certainly without her), and where would she go? She had come to this meeting expecting to hear both opposition and support of a much less ambitious project, to partake of the careful and civil deliberation that such a serious matter demanded ... and yet, by the manner in which Calhoun was addressing the city council, the project was essentially a sealed deal.

The city attorney went on to outline for the city council the establishment of an official "improvement district." Then he had his assistant rise from his chair and place on an easel a large poster that had been designed to promote the project. Beneath an illustration of steam shovels gauging out one side of a hill while hoses attacked the hill from another side, the poster declared, "Dumping Seattle's Hills Into the Sea". The image was appalling. Oddly, Maddie quickly noticed in her regard of the illustration that there were no buildings on the hill – no houses, no businesses, no Washington Hotel. The steam shovels and hoses were simply removing a large barren mound of dirt. Just as suddenly as she'd noticed this telling detail about the poster, Maddie also realized that she must be part of the 25-percent minority not represented on the petition.

Calhoun brought the petition forward and handed it to the gavel-wielding city councilman, then returned to stand behind his table. "It must be borne in mind that several thousand pieces of property are involved in these proceedings," he continued, "and as to each piece of property, every person interested therein, either by fee title, by lease hold, as mortgagee or lien claimant, is made a party to the proceeding. Each of the second parties hereto are permitted, at their own cost and expense, to remove the dirt necessary to be moved in making the said regrade at the earliest possible time, and to avoid delay necessarily attendant upon such a large public improvement."

Maddie could hardly follow the legal claptrap that Calhoun was spouting. From the general tenor of it, she gathered that, for the city attorney at least, the removal of Denny Hill was a *fait accompli*, and that Madison House was one of the thousands of pieces of property referred to, and furthermore – had she heard this correctly? – that residents, whether they owned or leased their property, would be required to pay for the regrading of their property out of their own pockets. Such an outrageous notion!

Just then a man she recognized from the neighborhood, although she couldn't say if he lived on Denny Hill or just worked in the area, a middle-aged man more stooped and haggard than his apparent age should allow, who had an unkempt beard and bright pale rings around eyes set deep into a dusky, coarsened face, stepped out from one of the back rows and into the center aisle of the meeting hall and walked forward shouting out that Calhoun was a dirty thief, a greedy cheat, and a no-good liar. "You're stealing people's homes right out from under them is what you and yours are up to," he railed, and still came forward. When he reached the city attorney's table, he turned to face the entire room. "A dollar. That's all they're plannin' to give you. One dollar. Are you going to rebuild with that? Are you? What will you do when they take away your business and tear down your house?" He caught the eye of Maddie and pointed to her. "I know you," he said. "Will you rebuild your house for one dollar? Will you?"

Stunned by his recognition of her, Maddie stared back at the man. Was he mad? His eyes shined with eerie light and his arms gestured and swung in a wild, sweeping motion. As with Calhoun's talk moments earlier, Maddie could hardly fathom what he was saying. Was his tirade about one dollar and rebuilding the rantings of a lunatic? Somehow she didn't think so. Somehow both his appearance and his words seemed to express the very outrage she herself was beginning to feel at that moment. She watched as the city attorney's assistant stood up from his chair and moved toward the man at the same instant that two uniformed policemen advanced from the other side of the room toward him.

"Ask them about Jackson Street ... ," he railed on. "I had a house there. But they razed it, they did. Now they want to do the same to my roominghouse on Lenora Street." He jerked his body around when the attorney's assistant tried to grab his arm. Then the policemen stepped up and each seized one of his arms, and the assistant stepped back. The man tried to tug free of the policemen, but realizing they had him pinned and that they were both much larger and stronger than he, the man ceased protesting, relented to their superior force, and let them drag him back down the aisle and out of the meeting hall.

Maddie watched the policemen remove the man and then, looking forward again, she noticed that throughout the entire disruption, Reginald H. Thomson had remained quietly composed at his table, just feet from the ranting man, never once appearing fazed or even so much as concerned by the man's outburst. The whole while, Thomson simply remained facing forward, calmly waiting for the hearing to resume.

By contrast, the city attorney was thoroughly flustered by the man's outburst. He raised his hand to get the attention of the city council chairman, who had been fitfully hammering the table with his gavel for the past several minutes.

"Sir, if I may… , " shouted Calhoun. "I will explain."

The chairman acknowledged the city attorney, granting him the floor, and laid his gavel down. At this, Calhoun breathlessly apologized to those in attendance for the offensive display of incivility they had all just been made witness to. He then wiped his brow with a handkerchief he pulled from his vest pocket and, addressing the city councilmen, proceeded to explain how a commission had been formed by the city attorney's office, made up of building inspectors and real estate assessors, appointed jointly by the counsel's office and the city engineer's office, to fix the compensation for each property due to be condemned within the designated improvement district. It was indeed determined that the compensation to be awarded in most cases would amount to the sum of one dollar.

"Granted, sir, it is a token sum," the city attorney declared. "However, it is posited against the inevitable augmentation of each owner's property value once he levels said property to the proposed street grade. For those wishing to cede their property to the city, the commission is prepared to make a full and equitable assessment. There is no question, after all – ," and here Calhoun pulled himself up straight, chest out, prepared to make an irrefutable point, "that the eminent domain act does so provide."

"Thank you, Mr. Calhoun," the city council chairman said. "You have rendered your explanation quite satisfactorily," and here he paused a moment while the city attorney acknowledged the compliment with a nod and took his seat. "I would now like to solicit the opinion of the city engineer, Mr. Reginald Thomson."

Maddie was not sure she was able to follow all that was going on. She did understand that the city attorney had to some degree confirmed what the irate man who'd disrupted the meeting had accused him of. Recognizing the severe import of what was transpiring before her, she tried her best to follow. She sat straight and still in her hard chair, her heart thudding in her chest with unnamed distress, and waited for Reginald H. Thomson to speak. The appearance of the staid and self-possessed city engineer seemed almost to reassure her. After all, he had always done right by the city, and why should now be any different?

Thomson rose from his chair and thanked the city council and all in attendance in the meeting hall for their interest and patience in this hearing. "With the city council's approval of the petition before it," he then said, his voice clear and distinct, "this ordinance, Number 13515, will make the great Denny Hill regrade possible."

There it was.

Reginald H. Thomson had said it himself.

Very nearly gasping from the horrific realization that Thomson's words brought, Maddie covered her mouth with her hand, and although she thought she might break out in sobs at any moment, she realized she was too much in shock to respond in any way other than to look on in stunned disbelief. *They're going to cut down the hill* was all she could think, repeating the statement to herself several times before her mind could clear enough to again hear what the city engineer was saying.

Confidence resonated in Thomson's voice. "Property values will be augmented tenfold," he testified. "Businesses from the central downtown area will extend northward, bringing commerce to the area and affording an unobstructed path for expansion. I endorse the ordinance without hesitation. It befits the true Seattle Spirit." And without saying anything further, he sat down and again folded his hands before him on the table.

Maddie felt dazed. She didn't understand. How would all this come about? Would they evict every person from every home and boardinghouse and apartment building on Denny Hill? From every shop, cafe, and tavern? This commission of appointed experts sounded shady at best – a group of strangers passing down verdicts on the worth of someone else's property, their home and livelihood. How could these so-called experts know what it had cost Maddie, really cost her, to buy her house? How could they place a value on what was home to her and every one of her boarders? They couldn't. They couldn't understand the hardship and fear she'd endured on her trek north to the Yukon with Chester, or the anguish of his abandonment of her, or the risks she took as a woman staking her own claim. Nor could they comprehend her miraculous and unfathomable good fortune when she had done just that. Nor her relief when she could at last return to Seattle, the city she knew she would never again leave, the city she claimed as her own and dedicated herself to. Damn the city councilmen, city attorney, and city engineer. Curse them all. Seattle was as much her city as theirs. Even though the newspapers declared them the men who held the unequaled vision for Seattle, the men who would lead it through the twentieth century to become one of America's great metropolises. At what cost, Maddie wanted to know. Who would pay most dearly?

She looked about the room as the meeting seemed to enter a lull after Reginald H. Thomson sat down. The walls were lined with dark fluted wainscoting, pipes ran the length of the ceiling, the wood floor was worn dull. The room was filled with sixty to eighty people. She couldn't decipher who these people were any longer. A few were probably reporters – the men jotting down with their pencil stubs everything that was said. A number of those in attendance were undoubtedly interested businessmen, well attired and keenly attentive to the proceedings. A few, the minority probably, were Denny Hill residents and business owners. She wondered how well the hearing had been advertised, because, except for the tip from the city attorney's assistant the day he came to her front door, she had seen no public notices of it. Surely if all Denny Hill residents knew what was afoot, they would have overrun city hall.

When she looked to the front again, the city attorney's assistant had stood up and was preparing to address the row of city councilmen. He began explaining the procedures by which the commission would make verdicts on the several thousand pieces of property that the city attorney had referred to earlier. The procedure entailed a complicated ratio involving tax rates and the current assessed property value against the projected property value once a property had been regraded. The assistant seemed so well versed in the legal technicalities of this procedure, his explanation so thoroughly rehearsed, that Maddie now understood that the issues being discussed at this hearing had gone well beyond the proposal phase. They were policy. She heard him use the term "eminent domain" again. It seemed to be the term that was used to trump any anticipated opposition to the regrading. The assistant – addressed by one of the councilmen as Mr. Williams – was explaining how individuals who had not signed the petition for the improvements ordinance would be dealt with on an individual basis.

"Your honor," he said, "the city reserves the right to invoke its claim of eminent domain for the good of the municipality in respect to those who did not sign the petition." At this point he turned, ever so slightly, and, it seemed to Maddie, cast his gaze all the way to the back of the room to look directly at her. "There are individuals who refuse to recognize how their property would benefit from the improvements and how it would unquestionably be assessed at a rate far greater than any amount awarded in a just and equitable verdict upon the property by the commission, should the property owner force the commission into taking such action."

The implication of the look he gave her, that she was one of those recalcitrant few who had refused to support the improvement plan and who would force the commission's hand, riled Maddie to no end, and she had to restrain herself from jumping up and cussing him down much as the stooped little man had done earlier with Scott Calhoun.

"The unreasonable – nay, *rash* – opposition to this forward-looking project is best embodied by the outburst we witnessed earlier in this very room," the arrogant assistant to the city attorney proclaimed.

Maddie could stand it no more. She worked hard to run a respectable boardinghouse and thereby contribute to the improvement of her neighborhood and her city every day. She paid her taxes and voted for every levy put forward on the ballot for new schools and paved roads. She was in every way a model citizen and would no longer sit by and listen to this despicable man misrepresent her opposition, or the opposition of the man who had dared speak out earlier, to this blind and boondoggle plan to regrade Denny Hill.

She stood up. "Gentlemen," she called out from the back. "Pardon my interruption." She laid her coat and hat on her seat and stepped into the aisle. "I am a homeowner on Denny Hill, and when this man came to my door with his petition, he thoroughly misrepresented its purpose to me. He said it was for improvements to the streets, for electrical street lamps, for better streetcar service. He failed to mention the intended regrading at all ... and never said a word about assessments or verdicts or people losing their homes and businesses."

The room had turned its full attention on Maddie as she spoke. The assistant spun about to look at the city councilmen lined up behind their bench and then, turning back toward Maddie, dismissively gestured toward her with his hand as if to say here was a prime example of the unreasonableness he had just spoken of. The room stirred, and the city council chairman was about to seize his gavel and bark the room back to order when Reginald H. Thomas again rose from his chair.

"Sir," he said, addressing the chairman, "if I may," and turned to face Maddie. "Miss ..."

"Ingram," Maddie said.

"Miss Ingram," Thomson spoke, "you indeed have a worthy point." He stepped into the aisle and stood directly facing Maddie at a distance of about twenty paces. "The city must seek the support of all its citizens for such a momentous civic undertaking. This project, if allowed to proceed, will be on a scale unlike any undertaken in the entire United States thus far. It will be on a scale, dare I say, comparable to the Panama Canal. Seattle will be recognized worldwide for being a city that seized an opportunity to advance its future – much as we have done with the Cedar River water supply and the Point Roberts sewage plant – and we will be commended and much emulated for it. Arthur Denny, a pioneer and one of the most esteemed founders of this great city, and on whose original plot the hill stands, would himself have backed this project wholeheartedly as evidenced by the pledged support of his posterity. Yet it is the citizenry at large that most needs to give its unequivocal sanctioning to this project.

Or else it will indeed fail, and with it, a part of Seattle's future will surely fail." Saying no more, and clearly not expecting nor inviting any response to his statement, Thomson returned to his table and sat back down.

Maddie listened to this speech and was more than a little awed by it. His initial recognition of her seemed encouraging, but then she became confounded and even frightened by what he was saying – and how he was saying it. While he seemed to offer a concession, it was delivered like Scripture, with the gravitas of Gospel. "For the mountains shall depart, and the hills be removed; but my kindness shall not depart from thee . . ." Yet his words failed, Maddie realized, to acknowledge her complaint or the fervent concern – the loss of her home – that lay behind it.

"Sir," the city council chairman said forthrightly from behind his bench, "thank you for your moving words. Nonetheless, while I remain in charge of this hearing, we will have no more such interruptions. I insist that this hearing be conducted in a manner consistent with the rules of order." He then pointed his gavel at Maddie. "Ma'am, you will please be seated."

Upon hearing this rebuke, Maddie almost laughed out loud. It embodied so perfectly the buffoonery of the entire meeting. She decided she had heard enough. She would not let herself be talked down to, or patronized, or chastised by these unconscionable city officials a moment longer. So rather than sitting back down as commanded to do, she snatched up her coat and hat and without a single glance back charged out of the meeting hall.

MADDIE EXITED THE CITY HALL REELING. SHE WALKED DOWN Yesler Way unaware of anything going on about her, her attention set, but unseeing, on the sidewalk five feet in front of her. Her mind was locked on the stern figure and domineering presence of Reginald H. Thomson, the city engineer. He was like Caesar, an emperor bent on shaping the city to his own will and purpose. She could readily imagine herself playing the part of Brutus, thrusting the knife point into his worsted-chest as he exited the meeting hall with his coterie of city councilmen. She knew she had the anger for such an act, just not the disposition. She also knew that despite her anger, Denny Hill was likely to be leveled. If Reginald H. Thomson wanted the hill to come down, it would come down!

Maddie walked back toward Denny Hill as if she were in an air-tight barrel, as if the city around her had been sealed off from her senses. Typically on her jaunts this far downtown, she would linger before store windows, maybe enter a shop to inquire about the price of a dress or a hat. She would observe the pedestrian traffic – Seattle residents like herself – so many faces of varied composition and so many bodies hurrying down the sidewalk and across intersections, entering and exiting buildings, boarding and disembarking from streetcars, riding in cabriolets and driving wagons, generally making the city hum. Yet right now she was oblivious to it all. It no longer seemed to belong to her; no longer could she embrace it as hers ... since, the certainty now loomed, it would inevitably be taken from her.

She made her way to Pioneer Place and remembered the joy she felt last year attending the city's potlatch celebration with Clyde, eating warm caramel popcorn with him, watching the parade wend its way down crowded First Avenue with one of the city's founding pioneers in his gray beard, long coat, and top hot serving as Grand Marshal. (She was sure it had been Arthur Denny, older brother of David Denny!) She crossed the square now and heard someone shout at her to watch where she stepped, a wagoner (when she looked up) hauling barrel-sized kegs of beer. Directly in front of her stood the totem pole that reputedly had been pilfered from a Kwaitl village on the Alaskan coast and brought to Seattle for display. She looked up at the thick faces and squat figures carved into the fifty-foot pole and recalled her encounters with the Tagish and Tlingit from her years in the Yukon – especially Shaaw Kla'a, or Aage, one of Skookum Jim Mason's sisters (the other being Kate, George Cormack's wife), the woman who revealed to her where to stake her claim, the one that would allow her to buy Madison House. She also thought of Seattle's Indian War, which drove the Duwamish people from their settlements along the river and tideflats – the same area that was now being filled in with earth from the south-end regradings.

They're going to cut down the hill ... The refrain persisted in her head like a dull thud, though she could not pierce its true meaning. All she could do was keep walking. Past the totem pole, she made her way up First

Avenue. When a streetcar clattered past her, she hardly noticed it. Out in the harbor a foghorn blew and she looked up and saw passenger ferries and cargo steamers coming and going from the wharves. Train whistles sounded down along Railroad Avenue, adjacent to the waterfront. She put her head down and let her stride carry her forward, twice bumping into people walking in the opposite direction.

It wasn't until she passed the main business district, which for years had been steadily extending northward and now wanted to claim Denny Hill, that she stopped at a corner to get her bearings. She remembered that she'd left the house that morning planning to buy canned salmon and baking flour to make her salmon biscuits for supper, but that task seemed to belong to another time and another world right now, and she decided to abandon it. When she looked up, she hardly recognized where she was. Straight ahead of her, First Avenue ended abruptly and a scene of devastation spread out before her. A gash in the west slope of Denny Hill extended northward along the hillside for as far as she could see. Rail tracks were laid at the base of this gash, while down these tracks a row of waste cars were being loaded by two steam shovels taking turns tearing into the hill with their large, clawed buckets. Water and sewage pipes shot out from the exposed ground, and houses at the top of the gash appeared ready to collapse at any moment. The whole scene seemed like a terrible wound upon the earth, as if the city were eating itself alive.

Maddie knew this had been going on down here but had been too afraid to walk the six blocks from her house to witness it for herself. Here was the first phase of the Denny Hill regrading. It was supposed to have stopped at Second Avenue, at least that was the original plan, but it was evident from the sharpness of the cut into the hillside, a direct incision with no effort at gradation, that the long-range plan was to remove the hill entirely, block by block.

Maddie thought she recognized the modest farmhouse where Ada and her parents lived, set back from the gash by about half a block. Two of the second-floor windows were busted out, jagged shards still lodged in the molding, while one entire corner of the front porch sagged forward. The house looked abandoned, but as far as Maddie knew, Ada and her mother and father still lived there. Several times in the past year she had walked Ada back to the house in the late afternoon, after it had gotten dark. Yet everything in the surrounding vicinity had changed so much recently that she could hardly be sure it was the same house. If it was the same house, did Ada's family still occupy it? And if not, where had they gone? Ada was always so quiet, so reliable, never demanding anything of Maddie, that Maddie sometimes took her for granted, and too infrequently asked after her mother or father anymore. She felt ashamed of herself suddenly for having neglected the child so.

Maddie wanted to try to get closer to the farmhouse for a better look or even to knock at the front door, but there was no clear route around the cut in the hillside by which she could reach it. Deciding to make her way home then as quickly as possible, she backtracked two blocks and headed up Pine Street, bypassing the First and Second Avenue regrading altogether. Her boarders would have to make do with leftovers for supper, she thought, as she climbed up the hill and passed the Washington Hotel. It would be the first meal she had missed preparing for them in more than a year...in fact, since Ada had come into her employ. Yet when Maddie finally arrived back at the boardinghouse, Ada was nowhere to be found. She was supposed to stay until after supper was served to help clear the table and put away the dishes. But the house was strangely quiet. Maddie looked upstairs, thinking the child might have gone into Chiridah's or Loye's room to look at the dresses hanging in their closets. She even went up to the attic to see if she might be snooping about in Ray's or Clyde's room. But she wasn't there either.

Maddie returned to the kitchen, telling herself she was unduly worrying, that the girl's mother had probably come for her or else she had gone on an errand for one of the boarders. She then set to patching together a supper, dicing cold chicken from the refrigerator and mixing it with chopped onions, carrots, and peas. She then began the gravy that she would pour over the chicken and vegetables on top of toast. Her concern for Ada had at least distracted her from thinking about the city council meeting, and the kitchen work now distracted her from worrying about Ada.

It was a relief when she heard James whistling to himself in the carriage house and knew she was no longer the only one on the premises. She removed the gravy pot from the stove, set the chicken and vegetables back in the refrigerator, and with her apron still on over the dress she had worn to the city council meeting, she went out back for some company.

The side door of the carriage house was open, and after knocking lightly on it, she stepped inside. The person she'd heard whistling, though, was not James at all, but Clyde. He sat in the corner on a work stool with a copy of the *Seattle Sentry* open on his lap. When Maddie came in, he folded the paper and stood up. She was embarrassed by his unexpected presence and wished she'd remained in the kitchen.

"Are you taking up James's whistling habit?" Maddie asked nervously. "I thought you were him."

"Was I whistling?" Clyde answered. "I didn't notice."

"Let me guess," said Maddie, trying to josh her way through her nervousness. "'Bunch of Blackberries.' Isn't that one of your favorite songs?"

"I suppose it is, yes. Come to think of it."

"Well," Maddie said, "you were whistling to beat the band." She tried to say this cheerfully, but it came out forced. There was a long pause as they both stood next to the large printing press in the relative darkness of the carriage house. Maddie's nervousness subsided, and she began to feel the weight of the day press upon her again.

Finally Clyde came up to Maddie and asked, "Is something the matter?" When she didn't answer but simply hung her head and raised a hand to her brow from the strain that was focusing itself at her temples, he said, "You look pale," and then trying to josh with her in return, added, "And I know what pale looks like. Here, come sit down."

As soon as he said this, the entire burden of the day's traumatic events seemed to bear down on her and she tottered against the printing press. Clyde stepped forward and grasped her forearms to help steady her. With one arm about her shoulders, he guided her to the stool where he'd been sitting and continued to support her as she sat down.

Once her dizzy spell had passed, Maddie became embarrassed again and apologized to Clyde for her silly weakness. Yet she was glad he was there with her. Clyde stood beside her with one hand on her shoulder and asked again if she were all right. Maddie realized that, on top of everything else, she hadn't eaten all day, and asked Clyde if he would bring her a glass of water from the house. He ran out of the carriage house, and while he was gone, she tried to compose herself. A moment later Clyde returned with a glass of cold water and handed it to her. She took several sips and thanked him. He really was very caring toward her, she thought.

"Thank you, Clyde," she said again, "for everything," and then, as he crouched down to one knee beside her and looked up at her, she placed her hand on his cheek and looked into his face. She wanted to tell him about the fracas that had occurred at the city council meeting, the ruination she had witnessed at the regrading site, and her worry about Ada. Yet even the notion of trying to express all of this made her dizzy again.

"What's the matter, Maddie?"

It was such a simple question. And he asked it with such compassion. Then he took her hand from his cheek and held it in both of his hands. He watched her, his gentle brown-blue eyes unveering. The look of deep concern on his face made Maddie soften, and then begin to cry, and as the tears came down her face, he took the glass of water from her and set it down on the dirt floor.

"Maddie," he whispered, "what's wrong?"

She wiped at her tears, sniffled, then looked at him and said, "They're going to cut down the hill, Clyde. We're going to lose our house," and with the source of her distress finally out, she bent forward and wept.

Clyde leaned in to her and, putting his arms around her, gently pulled her to him. She laid her head against his chest as he rested his chin on the top of her head, patted her shoulder and then, with the most tender, lightest touch, began stroking her hair. She could not imagine there being a tenderness equal to her anguish, yet here it was, this is what it felt like … Clyde holding her, gently stroking her hair.

"It'll be all right, Maddie. It will. You'll see."

Maddie stayed in Clyde's arms, comforted by his soft touch, the steady beat of his heart, his reassuring words, and let his calm persuade her.

9. Reading (1905–1906)

WHAT HAPPENED BETWEEN HIM AND MADDIE IN THE carriage house took Clyde many days to reckon with. Replaying the scene to himself that night, he could not sleep. Maddie had been distraught and he had tried to comfort her. After holding her for several moments, until her crying subsided and she could breathe more easily, he took her back into the house. A series of events that had taken no more than twenty minutes he now rehearsed in his mind into the small hours of the nights, wondering if he were remembering every detail correctly and, if so, what each detail meant. How would this singular event affect his regard for Maddie – and, more important, hers for him?

In the parlor, he had sat her on the davenport and pulled one of the smaller armchairs closer and had then let her recount, very slowly, what she had been through that day. She seemed relieved to tell someone of the traumatic developments. Most pressing of all, she began, she was worried about Ada after seeing the house where she thought she and her parents still lived. Clyde assured her that for the present Ada was safe, that she was with Loye and that they had gone to the stationer's shop to buy Ada a writing tablet and some pencils. Maddie was glad to hear this. Then, when it came to telling him about the city council meeting and the indomitable manner of Reginald H. Thomson and the reprehensible behavior of Calhoun and Williams, Maddie turned livid. Clyde tried to bolster her spirits by recounting what he'd heard from one of the reporters for the *Seattle Sentry*, that James Moore, the owner of the Washington Hotel, was insisting that the city leave the area around Second Avenue and Virginia Street, along the first hump of Denny Hill, untouched in order to preserve a carriage route to the hotel.

"It doesn't matter how many buffoons signed that petition," he said. "As long as James Moore says the hill stays so he can run his hotel, it stays." He was happy to be able to deliver this tidbit of information to Maddie, and added, "Thomson, Calhoun, this Williams fella, and the whole damn city council can go to hell."

Seeming to regain her spirits, Maddie thanked him for this all-inclusive condemnation and said that, surprisingly, no one had mentioned Mr. Moore and his hotel prior to her walking out of the hearing. She then asked Clyde if he would check with Ray about this "eminent domain" that Calhoun and Williams kept referring to. "Maybe he can look it up in one of his law books," she said.

"Whatever it is," Clyde said, glad to see Maddie looking less distraught and confident in his reassurances to her, "it won't bring down the Washington Hotel."

When Maddie thanked him again for all his support, he sensed she might be feeling abashed by what had transpired in the carriage house. He felt the same way, yet all he could think to do was to offer to help her with supper since Ada still hadn't returned. But Maddie told him that wouldn't be necessary. "It's nearly ready," she said, and patted the back of his hand. "And besides, Loye and Ada should be back shortly."

It was well into evening, after the supper dishes were cleared, after Ray and Loye went out for a walk, after Chiridah went off to rehearsal for a play in which she had a small part, and after Ada had been taken home — Clyde escorting her and learning that the family indeed was still living in the house on the edge of the regrading – when Clyde and Maddie sat down in the parlor, the two gas lamps flickering overhead, casting wavering shadows throughout the room, and Clyde asked Maddie if she would like him to read to her.

"My father used to read to me and my mother all the time," he said. "I would look over his shoulder, and that's basically how I learned to read."

"Read what?" Maddie asked.

"Novels mostly. English novels."

Maddie looked at him quizzically. "All right then," she said at last. "I think I would like you to read to me, Mr. Hunssler."

Having planned all day for this moment, Clyde now came to it well prepared. That afternoon he'd stopped at Beatty Booksellers on Third and Pine and browsed the shelves looking for the most appropriate title with which to make his offer to Maddie. The work most certainly had to be fiction, to provide amusement and diversion, but also a measure of feeling and perceptiveness. For this purposes, clearly no average writer would do, no dimestore novelist, not even Seattle's own Elizabeth W. Champney with her best-selling historical romances of imperial Rome, feudal France, and ancient Japan. It could not be overly sentimental, or maudlin, or brimming with pathos. It had to be just right. His father had read to him from Thackeray, Scott, and Eliot – but his favorite, always, had been Dickens. *The Pickwick Papers, Nicholas Nickleby,* and *Oliver Twist.* His father had read *The Pickwick Papers* to him in its entirety, then half of *Nicholas Nickleby.* The second half of *Nicholas Nickleby,* and all of *Great Expectations,* he had read on his own. After he expressed his interest in Dickens to Mr. and Mrs. Beatty, the gray-haired, slightly stooped booksmiths showed him a complete illustrated edition of Charles Dickens's works, which, since it was secondhand, was marked down considerably. Clyde was instantly taken by the twelve-volume set bound in green cloth and embossed on each front cover with a goldleaf profile of the writer, and, as deferentially as possible, asked if he might purchase it on an installment plan – "At, perhaps, one book per month, for the next twelve months" – since this would be the only way he could afford to buy the complete set. Mr. and Mrs. Beatty, kind people that they were, looked at each other and jointly consented. The volume from the set that he chose to purchase first, the one he would read to Maddie if all went right, he selected solely on the basis of its length – *Our Mutual Friend* – because he wanted a novel that would last. He wasn't familiar with the story, but trusted Dickens to deliver a good one, and the title, he thought, had its own appeal.

Clyde held up the thick volume for Maddie to see and said, "Do you like Charles Dickens?"

"I don't know," Maddie answered honestly. "I do know that my dearest friend Laurette used to read to me from Anthony Trollope when we were on the boat to Alaska and that I could do without him. So sonorous."

The tone of this assessment worried Clyde. Perhaps Maddie's literary tastes didn't incline toward English letters, perhaps he should have picked an alternative to Dickens, an American novelist, even Elizabeth W. Champney. Clyde replied that he didn't know Trollope's novels, but that of the handful of British novelists he had read, Dickens was incomparable.

"Your word is good enough for me," said Maddie, and reclined on the davenport and with a leisurely, exaggerated wave of her hand, said, "Read on, sir."

Clyde opened the front cover and began, "*Our Mutual Friend*," by Charles Dickens. In four books ... "

"Oh my," Maddie let out and laughed.

"Book the First," Clyde went on, determined to succeed, "The Cup and the Lip'"

"I like it already."

"'In these times of ours, though concerning the exact year there is no need to be precise, a boat of dirty and disreputable appearance, with two figures in it, floated on the Thames, between Southward Bridge which is of iron, and London Bridge which is of stone, as an autumn evening was closing in . . .'"

For the next hour and a half, Clyde read slowly and deliberating, looking up only with each new chapter to see that Maddie, who watched him carefully the whole while he read, continued to listen and, as best he could tell, enjoyed what she heard.

From that night on, he read to her (and occasionally she to him) nearly every evening in the sitting room after supper. Several times Maddie commented on how reading aloud to each other like this was the perfect way to pass the lengthening Northwest evenings, which now began around four o'clock. She asked Clyde if reading by gaslight strained his eyes, and he told her that it was no strain at all, that he had his mother's keen eyesight. He also apologized for not having yet installed electrical wires in the parlor, and vowed to put that task at the top of his list. The whole notion of reading to Maddie turned out so much better than he'd ever imagined that he refused to let tired eyes, or anything else, interrupt their nightly sessions. He knew, too, that reading aloud from *Our Mutual Friend* had quickly become the best diversion he and Maddie had from their mutual worries about the Denny Hill regrading.

IN JANUARY, CLYDE READ IN THE *SUN HERALD* THAT CON-trary to his reassurances to Maddie the great Gothic structure that was the Washington Hotel was going to be razed. Its owner, James Moore, had reached a settlement with the city that granted him an undisclosed amount for his losses plus untold tax breaks to rebuild a modern New Washington Hotel on Second Avenue and Virginia Street once the site was fully regraded. Clyde didn't know if he could face Maddie with this news. What could he say to her? He was ashamed of having induced her to trust to the indominability of the great hotel – from the veranda of which, just a few short years ago, President Roosevelt had predicted that within his lifetime Washington would be the third most important state in the union after New York and Pennsylvania. Clyde had led her to believe that, because of the hotel, Madison House would be spared the steam shovels and sluicing hoses of the regraders. Even worse, he had done so when Maddie was most vulnerable. Didn't his deception, uncalculated though it was, nonetheless make him responsible for whatever fate might now befall the boardinghouse?

When he finally worked up the courage to tell Maddie about the Washington Hotel, he genuinely feared what the news might do to her. He stood in the corner of the kitchen, studying the molded tin ceiling, the shadows the gas lamps made in its contours, as Maddie and Ada cleared the supper table and placed the dishes in the sink as it filled with hot soapy water. Maddie would wash and Ada would dry, as they did every evening. The kitchen had a warm, dim, after-supper aspect to it. The peculiar straightback chair with barley twist legs that Maddie refused to let anyone sit in was in its usual place beside the large cast-iron stove. A drying rack, consisting of eight thin wooden rods for hanging wet clothes on, was on the other side of the stove. On the opposite wall hung several copper molds: a pineapple, a lobster, and a rooster. Clyde studied these as he waited for Maddie and Ada to finish clearing the supper table. Ray had invited him to smoke a cigar with him in the den, but he had declined. Finally, when Maddie saw that he was lingering in the kitchen, she said he looked like he had something on his mind and asked if anything was the matter. Clyde answered that there was, and asked if he might speak to her in the sitting room.

Maddie looked at him with concern, and then turned away as the kitchen door swung open. "You just let those be, sweetie," she said to Ada, who was placing the last of the dishes in the sink. "I'll do them later. You run home now."

Ada wasted no time in doing as she was told. As soon as she had slipped out the back door, Maddie pulled her apron up over her head and draped it over the back of one of the kitchen table chairs. She then followed Clyde into the front parlor. When she was finally seated in one of the reading chairs, Clyde stood before her, feeling as if he were bearing the news of a family death, and explained to Maddie what he had recently learned about the Washington Hotel.

As Clyde spoke, Maddie sat perfectly silent, unblinking, looking at him, but also looking away, as if glancing at something over his shoulder. As he came to the end of what he had to tell her, he observed her take a deep breath and let it out. She then sat up in her chair, her forearms and hands squarely on the armrests, and said clearly and unequivocally, "I don't care. I'm not abandoning my house or my boarders."

She looked almost serene as she said this, Clyde thought. Serene yet undeterred. A smudge of flour was on her earlobe and he wanted to wipe it away for her – kiss it away, if he could. Instead, he just remained standing before her, without saying a thing.

Then Maddie stood up, gave him a gentle hug, touching her cheek to his, and said, "If that's all, sir, I think you should dry tonight in Ada's stead."

Clyde was dumbfounded by this response. It seemed so casual. All he could say was, "That's only fair," and admire Maddie's poise.

"Then we'll read more about this crazy Wilfer family that Mr. Dickens has us all embroiled in." She looked at him resolutely, as if to confirm her determination to carry on, and returned to the kitchen.

A few minutes later, after Clyde had followed Maddie back into the kitchen and they stood side by side at the sink washing and drying the evening dishes, Maddie confessed to Clyde that his news about the Washington Hotel did not entirely come as a surprise to her. It only confirmed what she'd been suspecting for several days, ever since the *Post-Intelligencer* had begun hinting that something was up between James Moore and the city attorney's office, though never stating exactly what. Without recognizing the fact – that is, until now – she realized that she had long ago resolved within herself that no matter how the Denny Hill regrading played out, she would hold onto Madison House for as long as she could.

"Maybe you could rebuild like James Moore," Clyde said offhandedly, to which Maddie replied with a silence that made him realize he should think more carefully before he spoke.

"Not everyone wants the regrading to go ahead," Maddie said eventually. "There *are* some of us … folks who don't want to lose their homes and businesses." She handed Clyde a dripping serving platter. "There's even talk …You know George Wessells on Bell Street? He's one … of suing the city."

This came as news to Clyde – and proof that Maddie was more current on things than he'd acknowledged. It was also very encouraging news, to know that Maddie's neighbors might have some fight in them. He made a note to himself to talk to Ray about arranging a consultation with Edward Holton James, the attorney Ray worked for, to see if they might solicit some legal counsel for this group of holdouts and resisters that seemed to be coalescing in opposition to the regrading of Denny Hill. It was the least he could do, he reckoned, and took a handful of forks and knives from Maddie.

LATER THAT WEEK, IN LIEU OF HELPING RAY WITH HIS PHO-tography – carrying his tripod, keeping track of his glass plates, and essentially serving as his man-about-town since he (not Ray) knew the best places and most curious people in the city to photograph – Ray agreed to introduce Clyde to his employer, Edward Holton James. Mr. James – or "Ned," as Ray referred to him outside the office – practiced law from a suite of offices in the Colman Building on First Avenue near Pioneer Place. It was an elegant building of large mullioned windows and cast-iron trim and an ornate glass and steel overhang along the sidewalk that had recently been added to the building. For the occasion of the introduction, Clyde polished his brogans and wore the only matching pants and jacket suit he owned. Ray, who almost always dressed to the nines, loaned him a collar and necktie.

When Ray escorted Clyde into the offices on the second floor, Mr. James was in his private office at the rear of the suite. The front office was subdivided by three-quarter walls that were half panel, half frosted glass, and that created separate cubicles where Ray (the senior law clerk), Erasmo (the junior law clerk from the Philippines), and Mrs. Clark (the secretary, an older, squint-eyed woman) each worked. Ray greeted his officemates – first Mrs. Clark, then Erasmo – yet received only a nod from the one and a "How do" from the other. Without bothering to introduce Clyde to either person, Ray put his hand on Clyde's shoulder and guided him to the frosted glass door that led into Mr. James's private office. He knocked and waited for a reply. When he knocked a second time, this time much louder, Clyde heard a man from inside the office say curtly, "What is it?" At this Ray opened the door and shoved Clyde into the office ahead of him.

Mr. James sat in a leather chair and peered across his large oak desk at Ray and Clyde as they entered. He was a relatively young man, in his mid-thirties Clyde guessed, of slight build and long limbs, thinning hair and a narrow forehead, full lips and a tapered chin. He was dressed in a dark pin-striped suit, rather nondescript except that his coat was open and his vest unbuttoned, revealing his shirt buttons and the fact that his bowtie was slightly askew.

"Mr. James?" Ray said, approaching his desk.

"What is it, Raymond," the lawyer snapped back at his clerk.

"I want to introduce you to someone," and with this Ray put his hand on Clyde's shoulder and presented him to his employer. "This is Clyde Hunssler. We board together at a house on Denny Hill. Clyde here would like to have a word with you, if he may, about the regradings that have been going on in the city."

"Greetings," Ned James said to Clyde from behind his desk, not bothering to stand or offer his hand. In his disheveled attire and with his wispy uncombed hair, he seemed caught out, and in turn acted somewhat put upon by the intrusion into his office. "What is it you want to know, Mr. Hunssler? Is it a legal matter? I can't say I'm familiar with this regrading business or have kept close tabs on it. Why don't you go to the city engineer's office? That man Thomson is the one in charge. He's the one you should be talking to."

"I know about Mr. Thomson," Clyde said. "I won't take but a few minutes of your time, Mr. James, if you'll just hear me out." When Ned James nodded, Clyde proceeded to brief him on the matter of the Denny Hill regrading and Madison House and the hearing that Maddie had recently attended with a quick summary of what she'd told him about the verdicts and awards, and then asked him finally if he would explain the significance of the term *eminent domain*.

"Eminent domain," Mr. James said sonorously, leaning across his desk, "means essentially that the government can confiscate anyone's property for its own purposes if it deems that doing so is in the public's best interests. It's very simple, and once invoked, non-negotiable. As for any action your landlady might take to guard her property interests, I'm afraid I can't help you. I recommend that she find an attorney more expert in property law than I." He looked to Ray and then back to Clyde. "Is there anything else then?"

Clyde was neither disappointed nor surprised by Mr. James's rather brusque lawyerly manner, and replied no, that was all. He thanked him for his time and began to back out of the office when Ray put his arm out, halting his retreat, and said, "My friend Clyde here, Mr. James, sir, is always looking for work, in case you should ever need to hire a runner. I'll tell you this, he knows the city like no one else's business."

"I appreciate that, Mr. Gruhlki," Edward Holton James said, and seemed ready to leave it at that. Yet, half a moment later, to Clyde's surprise, the lawyer stood up from his chair and coming around his desk put his hand out to Clyde. "As a matter of fact," he said, as Clyde shook his hand, "come to think of it I may very well need someone to run all sorts of errands for me in the near future. Let's sit down and talk, shall we?" He then led Clyde and Ray to a foursome of chairs encircling a coffee table in the front corner of the office.

As he sat down, Clyde felt himself irked at Ray for his forwardness in offering Clyde's services to Mr. James just like that, without even consulting him. Sure, he had mentioned to Ray the other day that he was thinking he should start paying Maddie the full $5-a-week rate for his room and board because he knew she could use it ... the only hitch being he would need to find more reliable income than the odd jobs he did week to week about town. But still ... sitting now across the table from Ray and Edward Holton James, he wished Ray had given him some kind of warning. He decided the least he could do, before he gave Ray a good piece of his mind once they were back outside, was to hear Mr. James out.

"You're an albino, right?" was the first question out of the lawyer's mouth once they were seated.

Clyde looked at Ray, then at Mr. James, and said, "That's right."

"That's settled then," he went on. "I just wanted to get that out of the way. Now, let me tell you a little about myself and what our office is going to be up to in the coming months, which also happens to be the start of the next electoral season."

Mr. James leaned back in his chair, crossed his right leg over his left knee, and commenced to speak at length on how his father was Robertson James, who was the brother of William, Henry, Alice, and Wilkes James, in a word, the James of New York and Boston. "My father, being a successful businessman, has not achieved the celebrity of my more literary uncles, mind you ... You are familiar with William James, the philosopher, and Henry James, the author, are you not, Mr. Hunssler?"

Clyde said he was ... although, he added, he hadn't had the opportunity of acquainting himself with any of their works.

"That's of no account," Mr. James assured him, and then went on to inform Clyde and Ray that his uncle Henry would be paying a visit to Seattle in the near future. "As part of his extended American tour."

Clyde thought he detected a note of sarcasm in the way Ned James spoke of his famous uncles, but he let it pass and made a mental note to himself to stop by Beatty Booksellers later in the day and ask Mr. and Mrs. Beatty if they had any titles by Henry James.

Ned James went on to say that he himself, unfortunately, had scarce little time for reading given his occupation and – here he seemed to pause for effect – given his plans to run for the state senate as the Democratic candidate from the 36th District. "I have absolute faith in my cause," he announced to Clyde and Ray. "The measures and principles which I advocate are my politics and my religion, and when carried out they will mark the dawn of a new moral and spiritual life for the American people." He was going to conduct an aggressive campaign, he informed them, apparently on the political stump already, based on reform of the state's labor laws and enactment of new vice laws aimed at making Seattle a sin-free city, the kind of city its more morality-minded citizens could be proud of ... in place of, in his words, "the torrid unscrupulosity" that existed here today. "Especially below the Deadline," he remarked, "though in other wards as well." While he believed with all his moral fiber in temperance and drank three eight-ounce glasses of wholesome milk a day in lieu of beer, wine, or spirits of any kind, he would not make statewide prohibition part of his platform. Rather, he aimed to propose selective prohibition within the city limits and, more important, a city-wide ban on the pernicious practice of whoremongering that existed in theaters and saloons throughout the city – but as ever, especially below the Deadline. "Seattle is not the frontier outpost it once was," he declared, as if rehearsing his stump speech on Clyde and Ray. "It is a modern metropolis that has the opportunity before it to attain civilization's highest standards of moral decency and human progress."

As Ned James paused to take a breath, Clyde did not know if or how he should respond to this screed of political hoo-ha, and could only hope that Ray would be able to. But Ray said nothing either, and eventually Ned James broke his own silence.

"Mr. Hunssler," he said, leaning forward toward Clyde, "on top of the daily office tasks I'll ask you do, I'll need you to run the endless and myriad errands that will arise during my campaign for the state senate. What do you say?"

Clyde was struck dumb. He muttered that he was interested, yet, being mindful of keeping himself available in case Maddie needed him for chores around the house, he asked Ned James what the hours and pay would be. When Mr. James replied that he would pay him three dollars a day, for four hours work each day, Monday through Saturday, Clyde readily consented. They then agreed that he would start next Monday, and after rising from their seats, they all three shook hands to make the deal final.

Minutes later, after leaving the office and again standing outside the

Colman Building, Clyde thanked Ray for butting into his business and landing him a new job. When he offered to buy his friend a bucket of beer, Ray pointed up the block to Beck's Cafe where he said he felt certain based on past investigations that they served Tannhaeuser beer, his favorite local brew. As they headed up the street, Clyde said that right now that sounded a lot better than any ol' glass of milk, no matter how wholesome.

10. Excursion (1906)

LOYE AND CHIRIDAH HAD BEEN PLANNING THEIR BICYCLE ride to Lake Washington all winter, and with spring's daylong sunlight and mild breezes finally here, the day to pull the bicycles out of the shed on the side of the boardinghouse had arrived. The plan was to ride down Denny Hill, straight up Capitol Hill, and then down Madison Street to Madison Park, from which point they would follow the Lake Washington cycling path that meandered through the woods along the lake's shoreline.

It was Chiridah's only day off from the vaudeville skit she was performing at the Seattle Theatre's second stage, hoping as she did to some day land one of the coveted slots on the theatre's first stage, from whence girls frequently went on to San Francisco, Chicago, and even New York. As she told Loye, since it was her only day off, she wanted to get out of the city and enjoy some fresh air and exercise. For Loye, the outing was a good chance to spend time with her friend and fellow boarder as well as maintain her own fitness now that the basketball season had ended and her days, devoted exclusively to studying for her classes, had become more sedentary. Loye loved physical exertion, she longed for it, and men today were certainly more lenient in allowing women to explore their physical natures – within limits. As for herself, she would not flinch from an opportunity to demonstrate her body's strength and endurance, and trusted that doing so would only enhance, rather than diminish, her femininity. This was one reason Loye owned her own bicycle, which she had brought with her from Tacoma. For Chiridah, she arranged to borrow Maddie's bicycle, which their landlady never used.

These days Loye was feeling more comfortable than ever in her residence at Madison House, due in great part to Maddie's genuine warmth and hospitality. It had been almost two years since she came to the boardinghouse, and even though the threat of scandal surrounding her living under the same roof as men boarders (one a half-breed albino) and sharing daily meals with them (including a Negro) continued to worry her parents, she herself had long ago accepted the arrangements as entirely innocuous and, if anything, socially quite engaging.

"That's nothing," Chiridah told her last week when Loye had mentioned her parents' fears for her reputation. "Actresses are always fighting an uphill battle for respectability. It just goes with the territory. The secret's not to give much account to what other people think."

"Well," Loye said, "if worst comes to worst, we'll guard each other's reputation. How's that?"

Even though it sometimes seemed they had little in common, Loye was certainly glad to have Chiridah for a friend. Pleased by the memory of this brief exchange last week, Loye pulled the bicycles from the storage shed. Fog still covered most of the bay and obscured both mountain ranges, but it appeared to be the thin, wispy kind of fog that would burn off by noon, leaving a clear, bright day. Until then, the low fog cover would keep them cool as they rode their bicycles (or pushed them, as it were) up Capitol Hill.

Loye unbuttoned the sleeves of her waistshirt and rolled them up over her elbows. She pulled out Maddie's bicycle first, then her own, a Columbia Classic for ladies, which her parents had bought her for her birthday three years ago. She checked the tires on each and leaned both bicycles against the side of the house. The two bicycles both had the new pneumatic tires, curvy handlebars, and wide, spring-cushioned seats. The center bar on the frames sloped down to allow a lady to discreetly seat herself, rather than immodestly having to swing one leg up and over the frame. The issue of such discretion mattered little to Loye, but the convenience of not having to hike her skirts and hoist the fabric around like a sail was much appreciated. She hopped on her bicycle, stood up on the pedals, and spun around the yard. The seat was the right height, and as soon as Chiridah appeared, she would adjust her seat for her. Chiridah had done three afternoon shows the day before and so was still soundly asleep when Loye got out of bed, dressed, and went downstairs a little more than an hour ago. After she had taken her morning coffee and bowl of corn flakes – despite Maddie's insistence that she eat a full breakfast of eggs, Canadian bacon, and buttered toast with jam – she climbed the stairs again to find Chiridah beginning to rouse herself.

"I won't be long," Chiridah had said, with droopy eyes and her bed covers pulled around her chin.

Yet here Loye was, a full thirty minutes later and ready to go, wondering if she should go back upstairs and fetch her friend. She was just about to reenter the house when, from around the corner, Chiridah appeared, still looking groggy but smiling benignly. She had taken Loye's advice and had dispensed with her corset for the day. She was a large girl, big boned, though she maintained an excellent figure, which, she often told Loye, was as essential to a successful stage career as dramatic training and God-given talent.

"Brava, Chiridah," Loye exclaimed, applauding her friend's corsetless figure. "You're a liberated woman. Go ahead, take a deep breath. You may never strap on a corset again."

Chiridah curtsied. "If I had your figure, Loye, I would never have to." Like Loye, she wore her ready-to-wears: a billowy white shirtwaist buttoned smartly at the neck and tucked tightly into a durable cotton skirt. As for the tailored toque with satin bow that adorned her head, Loye could only laugh.

"I suppose you're going hatless," Chiridah said, in response to Loye's amusement.

"No," Loye said. She touched her hair, which she'd pinned into a tight bun. "A simple straw hat will do." She then ran into the house and a moment later came back with Maddie's straw hat and handed it to her friend.

Chiridah removed the toque and replaced it with the straw hat and seemed pleased. "How sporting," she said, and kissed Loye on the cheek. "We look like sisters now."

Loye stood Maddie's bicycle in front of Chiridah and said, "Here, get on so we can measure the seat. Maddie's about your same height, so it might be all right."

As Loye held the bicycle steady, Chiridah looped her leg over the cross bar and hopped onto the seat. Loye held the bicycle steady as Chiridah wobbled, got her balance, then sat up straight and proud and looked about like a queen on her royal post-chaise.

"Well?" Chiridah asked. "Does it fit?"

"How does it feel?"

"It feels fine, I suppose."

Loye let go and Chiridah hopped to her feet to keep from tumbling over. "Then off we go," Loye said.

"*You!*" Chiridah squealed, regaining her balance. "That was not nice."

They walked their bicycles to the Blanchard Street side of the house and then set off down the eastern slope of Denny Hill. From the top of the hill they could see the fish-shaped parameter of Lake Union and the lumber mill located in the lake's southern cove. To the south and behind them, the built-up and congested streets of the city's business and entertainment districts spread all the way to the tideflats, which were now mostly filled in and being prepared for development. For today, at any rate, they were leaving all that behind them to enjoy a day in the country. Loye let herself fly down Denny Hill and straight across Westlake Avenue. With less experience riding a bicycle, Chiridah displayed more caution and held back, stopping at the intersection to allow a wagon and streetcar to pass before she crossed.

Loye was well ahead of her, climbing the next knoll, standing up on her pedals and pushing down with her full weight, seeing how far she could make it on her own steam. Finally, about half way up, she dismounted and looked behind her to find her friend slowly but surely walking her bicycle up the sharp incline. Loye waited for her, catching her breath, and from that point on they both walked their bicycles up the steep grade of Capitol Hill, pausing occasionally to turn about and take in the widening view of Lake Union, Elliott Bay, and the downtown. As they reached the top of the hill, the residences became larger and fancier, far newer and better maintained than the houses on Denny Hill. Loye imagined herself some day moving to Capitol Hill, after Denny Hill had succumbed to the regraders, as Maddie increasingly seemed to fear it would.

It was true, Loye thought ... she wanted to settle down in due time and have a family, perhaps even with Ray Gruhlki. *Even*, she said to herself, and almost laughed aloud. She admired Maddie's independence and Chiridah's professional ambition – and she thoroughly enjoyed her own freedoms – yet she also thought that perhaps family life had its own virtues as well, that it didn't have to mean enslavement to a husband, imprisonment in the kitchen, becoming a household drudge whose only diversion came from flipping through the pages of the Sears, Roebuck catalog and creating a nice place setting. She could imagine other advantages, too, such as a yard to tend with begonias and hydrangeas and rhododendrons, a sitting room in which she could lounge beside her husband as they read to each other in the evening (as Clyde and Maddie did), and little children to nurture and rear, the boy strong and clear-headed, the girl also strong and clear-headed, and both as smart and good-looking as their parents. She would walk them to school in the morning, and when they were old enough they would both attend the Broadway High School, a fine institution ... the roof of which she could now glance as she and Chiridah topped the hill and turned onto Broadway Avenue.

"Look, Loye," Chiridah exclaimed, breathless from the hike, "I've made it to Broadway!"

"I always knew you would," Loye answered, and glanced down the length of the main thoroughfare.

"Now which way?" asked Chiridah.

Loye looked about her. Lincoln Park reservoir was to the right. To the left were assorted neighborhood businesses: a barbershop, a tailor, a bakery, stationery store, a couple of cafes. It was a dry ward so no taverns or saloons were permitted in the neighborhood.

"Straight over the top," Loye announced. "And down!"

Chiridah unpinned her hat, wiped her brow with a kerchief, and reset her hat on her head. The sun had finally appeared and the morning fog was nearly all burned away.

"Don't get me lost," Chiridah warned her. "You told me you knew your way around this side of town."

"I do," Loye said, and tried to remember the route she and Ray had taken when he invited her on this same outing last fall. "I think we may have to ride one of the counterbalance cars back into town," she added. "To spare us all these hills a second time."

"I couldn't agree more," Chiridah said.

Loye then pushed off across Broadway with Chiridah following. They had another small ridge to mount and then they began zigzagging their way down into the valley, at one point stopping to take in the view of Lake

Washington and the Cascade Mountains extending north to Mount Baker and south to the hulking mound of Mount Rainier. Chiridah turned bold suddenly and soared past Loye as they swooped down Madison Street. Their momentum enabled them to coast half way up the next ridge, and as Loye caught up to her friend, Chiridah's flushed face, with her hat pushed back by the wind and barely clinging to her head, expressed pure exhilaration.

"I'm thoroughly wind-swept."

"You could be a bird."

"I would like to be a bird. Perhaps a sparrow," Chiridah said, "small and unobtrusive, a delicate flyer through the trees. As our dear Hamlet says, 'There's a special providence in the fall of a sparrow.' What kind of bird would you be, Loye?"

Loye and Chiridah pushed their bicycles side by side. Wooded lots now bordered either side of the road, creating a kind of buffer between the city and the lake. There were also several grand, elegant houses set back from the road with long, winding drives leading to the front entrance.

"I'm not sure," she answered.

"Would you be a bird of prey? Perhaps an eagle?"

"No, no," Loye said. "Maybe I'd be a whitsit."

"What's that?"

"It's a special bird that nests near the sea, then flies to the mountains for its food. It can also live in the city, though, on the cornices and eaves of tall buildings."

"Oh," Chiridah said, "you're just playing with me now."

"Come on, sparrow." Loye climbed back on her bicycle for the final ride down to the lake. "Fly like the wind." She took a deep breath of the woodland-scented air and pushed off. Chiridah did so too and stayed even with her, the two looking across at each other and shrieking with joy as they swooshed down the hill toward the lake.

They soon reached the head of the bicycle path that followed the shoreline. The smooth packed dirt, wide enough for two and nearly all level, made for easy pedaling. The path wound around grassy curves that gave onto splendid views of the lake and eventually led into a densely wooded area thick with ferns that encroached onto the path. The woods were dark with shade and cool. From out of nowhere, as if in a fairy tale, a miniature chalet-like building suddenly appeared alongside the path, with a signboard above the door that read Corabelle's Tea Room. Loye coasted to a stop and Chiridah pulled up beside her.

"What's a tearoom doing in the middle of the woods?"

Chiridah looked a little bewildered. "Maybe a wicked witch lives there and lures young maidens like us in and feeds them poison-laced treats."

Loye scowled at her. "Look, there's a couple out on the deck."

An ordinary-looking man and woman were seated at one of several tables on the wooden deck that extended from the tearoom's entrance; their bicycles lay against a tree near the stairs leading up to the deck.

"Let's go in," Loye said.

They laid their bicycles against a tree, climbed the stairs, politely nodded to the man and woman, and entered the quaint tearoom. The interior was decorated in a country English style with flowered wallpaper and small round tables draped with white lace over pink cloth. A large balsamwood birdcage was hung in the corner and inside it four blue, red, and yellow finches chirped and twitted about. A woman in an apron who instantly reminded Loye of Maddie invited the young women to be seated at one of the tables and brought them each a glass of ice water and a menu card.

"Have you ladies been out cycling?" she asked.

"Yes," Loye answered. "And it's very pleasant to come upon your establishment here in the middle of the wilds."

"Thank you," the woman replied. "Though it's hardly the wilds. The bicycle path meets the road just a little farther along and we have a sign at the trailhead, so folks will often take the short walk down the path. It works out nicely."

"It's charming," said Loye, and took up the menu card. "I think I'll just have a cup of tea and a scone."

"And for you, miss?"

Chiridah paused a moment to study the menu, then said she would have the same. "Do you have cream for the scone?"

"We do," the woman said. "I can put it on top if you like."

"Yes, please," Chiridah replied, and when the woman had left, she said to Loye, "I really ought'n to, but this is a special occasion," and then leaned across the table and kissed Loye on the cheek.

After their tea and scones at the tearoom, they returned to their bicycles and continued the rest of the way down the path to where it intersected with the road. Even though there were several carriages and even motorcar traffic on the road, they decided to take the road rather than the path since it ran directly adjacent to the lake.

EVENTUALLY THEY NEARED LESCHI PARK. THE ROAD TURNED more congested with bicyclists, pedestrians, horse-drawn carriages, and motorcars as they approached the resort. A festive atmosphere seemed to prevail. It almost seemed as if the day were a holiday rather than an ordinary Saturday afternoon in April. People crowded the docks and waited in line at the boathouse to take out rowboats and canoes. From the docks, boaters fanned out upon the lake, with those closer in struggling to maintain their balance in their canoes or to coordinate the two oars of their rowboats. Farther down the shore, at a larger dock, a midsized steamboat with red, white, and blue buntings strung along its sides waited for the next load of passengers to board for a cruise about the lake. Chiridah saw the boat and instantly turned to Loye. "I know we said we wanted to take out a canoe, but now that I see them, they look awfully dangerous. Let's go on the steamer instead and tour the lake, do you mind? We'll be able to see so much more."

"But what about our exercise? I thought it would be fun to paddle ourselves about."

Chiridah looked at Loye as if she wanted to paddle her right then and there. "You're the athlete, dear Loye. Not me. The bicycle ride has been plenty of exercise for me for one day. Please don't make me endure anymore." And Chiridah, the actress, put on such a pleading, wounded appearance – worthy of Ophelia or Cordelia – that Loye could not resist.

"You know the steamboat costs more money."

"That's all right," Chiridah said. "I'll be happy to pay anything not to have to pedal or paddle or push or row another inch."

They walked their bicycles onto the dock where the tour boat awaited and after asking the dock attendant if it would be all right for them to set their bicycles behind the ticket booth – "For two such beautiful ladies," he said, "anything" – they purchased their tickets and stepped gingerly up the gangplank and onto the deck of the steamboat.

They stood along the railing at the stern end of the boat and watched the swarm of people along the shore. Everyone seemed so well dressed, the men in cotton outing suits, sporting straw or haircloth hats, the women in jumper suits or petticoats, many carrying parasols. There was a beer garden set back from the boathouse crowded mostly with men, each with a glass mug in his hand, nearly all standing, while in a roped-off area to the side women sat at white tables with bunches of yellow daffodils set in the center. On the opposite side of the boathouse stood the large resort house. It housed a restaurant, a dance hall, and (or so Loye had once heard Ray say) gambling tables. There had recently been talk in the newspapers that when Isadora Duncan visited Seattle later in the year she would visit the Leschi resort and give a performance. And who knew, she might even ride on the very same tour boat that Loye and Chiridah were on right now. This thought was too tempting not to share with her actress friend Chiridah.

"Imagine," Chiridah said. "What if she were on the boat right now with us ... in disguise."

"Surely, don't you think they would arrange a specially reserved excursion for Isadora Duncan? By invitation only?"

"I suppose," Chiridah replied, clearly not interested in Loye's fussy stipulations. "I only hope someday I can perform half as well as Miss Duncan."

Chiridah looked down wistfully at the water as she said this, and Loye put her arm around her friend's shoulder. "You do already, dear. You're a fine actress." Loye had seen Chiridah in only two performances, and though she was certainly no theater critic, on both occasions she thought Chiridah had performed superbly. She was most impressed by her role as Piolo in *King Dodo* at the Lyceum Theater last year, which had been her biggest role to date, and for which a publicity photo of Chiridah had appeared in the *Seattle Mail and Herald*. Since then, however, her friend had been repeatedly frustrated in her auditions for dramatic roles of the same quality, and was forced to take parts in variety shows which, as Chiridah explained to her once, could stigmatize a girl to the point where eventually even the most classically trained actress was viewed by stage directors and theater managers as no longer fit to perform in high-class dramatic stock. Lately Chiridah feared this was the direction in which her career was headed.

Just then the steamboat let go a blast of its piercing steam whistle and both Loye and Chiridah grasped each other's arms in exaggerated fright. Passengers crowded the railings as the boat backed away from the dock. As it steamed out into the lake, the wind picked up and Loye and Chiridah had to pin down their straw hats extra tight. It had become a warm, sunny day, with Mount Rainier in full view, rising large and white above the lake to the south of them. Loye and Chiridah lounged along the outside of the main cabin enjoying the sunshine and fresh air, despite the wind that tried to snatch their hats and tussle their skirts.

The boat headed toward the middle of the lake and turned south toward Mercer Island. A few adventuresome souls had bought lots on the island and were building houses there – which Ray last autumn had told Loye was something he fancied doing someday – even though the island residents were required to take boats anytime they wanted to go somewhere. There was also the lavish Hotel Calkins, a resort hotel, on the western side of the island, which could be seen from the tour boat. Mostly, though, the large island that some people now called East Seattle remained largely uninhabited; it was mostly woods except for a small area of its northern tip that had been cleared for a park that included a lunchstand, a dozen picnic tables, and a dock where the tour boat now prepared to dock. As Loye and Chiridah leaned against the forerail and watched one of the crewmen throw a rope to a boy standing on the narrow pier, someone came up from behind them and cleared his throat loudly enough to draw their attention. When they turned to face the middle-aged man with the trimmed mustache and mildly amused smile, he tipped his black felt bowler and bowed to them.

"Excuse me, ladies, for interrupting your idyll," he said. "I know it's not prudent to allow strangers to address one. However—," and here he turned ever so slightly toward Chiridah, "correct me if I'm wrong, but I believe I saw you last week performing at the Park Theater. There was the minstrel number, 'The Ham Tree,' then the whistler, then you came on in a scene from 'Hip Hip Hooray.' Am I correct?"

Chiridah tried not to look astounded at the exactness of the gentleman's recall and his recognition of her, even though she had worn heavy rouge and eye liner for the part in "Hip Hip Hooray." She raised her hand to her neck and tried to suppress her smile.

"Yes, that's right," she said, "That was me. How astonishing that you should recognize me."

"Well," the man went on, appearing pleased to have his hunch confirmed, "even from the other side of the boat, I thought to myself, 'Those are the very same unmistakable features as that girl from the Park Theater.' You're performance, I thought, was astonishing."

"Thank you," Chiridah replied, her full, soft cheeks turning pink as she blushed.

"Please," the man said, looking mildly abashed, "let me introduce myself. I'm Lewis Pittman, an associate of the Considine-Sullivan theaters—a talent scout of sorts, if you will. You've heard of John Considine, no doubt. I also manage several small theaters of my own here in the city." He paused, smiled demurely down at the deck boards, and corrected himself by pointing back across the lake toward Seattle, "Of course I mean over there—in the city." He then chuckled to himself.

"Indeed," said Loye, the first words out of her mouth since the encounter with the stranger began. She was generally wary of such forwardness by strange men, yet this Pittman fellow made her especially wary. While it pleased her to see her friend Chiridah acknowledged for her work on the stage, Loye suspected Pittman's compliments had little to do with his appreciation for her acting abilities and more to do with some secret and salacious intent. She had heard of John Considine as the man who, along with his rival Alexander Pantages, ran nearly all the theaters and moving-picture houses in Seattle. There was a scandal some years ago, which people still spoke of today, in which Considine had gotten one of his showgirls pregnant and, in some bizarre twist of events, ended up shooting to death a former Seattle policeman, though he was later acquitted of the murder charge. These days, according to Chiridah, John Considine was an honest theater owner who paid his actors and actresses the best rate in town.

Chiridah's face lit up with recognition at Pittman's mention of the name. "Of course I know of Mr. Considine. Everyone does. It's an honor to make your acquaintance, Mr. Pittman."

"Please, call me Lew."

Chiridah curtsied. "Sir … I mean, Lew … this is my friend Loye. We board together at the same house."

Lewis Pittman tipped his hat to Loye for a second time. "Pleased to meet you." Loye nodded, and he turned his attention back to Chiridah. "You two ladies would be doing me a great honor if you would permit me to buy you lunch at the lunchstand on shore. I would very much like to discuss your stage career, if we may, and maybe even future prospects for working for myself or Mr. Considine."

Chiridah turned to Loye as if to plead for her consent in accepting this invitation. Loye looked at all the people shuttling off the boat and up to the lunchstand located on the other side of the lawn sloping up from the landing dock.

"How could we refuse," she said.

"You're so right, Loye," Chiridah chirped in, and turned back to Pittman. "We accept your kind offer, sir … but please, only if you'll tell me all about your own life in the theater and what it's like to work for Mr. Considine. You must see so many wonderful performers."

"I would be delighted to," Pittman replied, and gestured for Chiridah and Loye to precede him down the gangplank and onto the dock.

The line at the lunchstand was considerable given that nearly every passenger from the tour boat waited to be served. Loye and Chiridah sat at a picnic table while Pittman stood in line. Chiridah grasped Loye's hand the instant they were out of his company and suppressing her excitement with a squeal told Loye how this could be her big break, that she had wanted to work in one of John Considine's theaters since she started attending the Egan Dramatic and Operatic School five years ago. She knew of any number of girls who had moved on from one of the Considine theaters to bigger theaters and more successful careers in places like San Francisco, Chicago, and New York. Loye then reassured her friend that she would no doubt achieve her success based on her exceptional talents and not on whom she knew or worked for. But then, seeing how her comment seemed to dampen her friend's spirits, she added that if Mr. Considine, or Mr. Pittman for that matter, could assist her along the way, then she was certainly deserving of that assistance. She then reached her arms around Chiridah and embraced her.

From therein Loye kept her reservations about Lewis Pittman to herself. For whatever reason, in her unbiased estimation, Loye found him less than trustworthy. While he was courteous, well groomed, and apparently successful, perhaps it was the simple fact that Loye didn't trust men who approached women out of the blue, without an introduction, and were then so openly flattering to them. Though in no way wanting to begrudge Chiridah the attention she deserved, she wished the encounter had never happened and that the two of them could go on enjoying their little outing together as planned. Rather than sitting at a picnic table waiting for a stranger to bring them their lunch, they could be exploring the island's woods and shoreline and making the most of this fine spring day.

Eventually, Pittman carried a tray of sandwiches and drinks over to the picnic table where they sat, and as they ate he inquired into Chiridah's stage history, and happily, though somewhat deferentially, she enumerated the many plays, musicals, and variety shows that she'd either played a role in or been an understudy in, from high school in Tacoma right up to the present in Seattle. Pittman, who was already rather short and now seated across the table from Chiridah seemed even more diminutive, nodded steadily the whole while Chiridah spoke, intently chewing his sandwich and occasionally remarking on some show or another that she would name.

Loye finished her sandwich and seeing that the conversation was going to remain exclusively between the two of them, she asked to be excused and set off down to the park's shoreline where several children and men, with their mothers and wives standing behind them, were skipping stones across the water. She admired the wholesome family activity and thought of Ray, whether he might be the one for her, or perhaps the young botany student from the university who had lately taken such a keen interest in her – and with whom she'd recently gone "queening," as the *Pacific Wave*, the campus newspaper, had termed the cuddling activity that had become so popular among the students. After that single episode with the botany student, she had been moderately embarrassed for herself, though secretly excited too, and for the next week or more she had avoided Ray.

As people slowly returned to the dock to board the tour boat again, she strolled back toward the picnic table and watched as Pittman reached across the table and placed his hand on Chiridah's forearm. Chiridah beamed back at him, and then he stood from his bench, came around the table, and offered her his arm. When he saw Loye approaching them, he smiled at her, a smile that she immediately distrusted.

"I was just telling Miss Simpson – "

"Please," Chiridah interrupted him, "call me Chiridah."

He laughed as if to say of course, and went on, " – that I could put your bicycles on the rear of my auto and you could ride back over the hill with me if you like."

Loye quickly thanked him for his offer and replied that they could not accept it, informing him how she and Chiridah had ventured forth on the day's outing for exercise and the mutual enjoyment of each other's company and that they wished to continue in this purpose. Yet even as she said these words she could tell from the look on Chiridah's face that her response did not sit well with her friend and that in all likelihood she was spoiling all of Chiridah's fun. Nonetheless, she held her ground. Chiridah or no, she was not going to ride with Pittman in his auto.

"I understand perfectly," Pittman said. "And should you change your minds, I won't be far." He pointed to the boat. "Right now, however, we had better get aboard if we don't wish to spend the night as island castaways."

The three of them hurried down the dock and were among the last few stragglers up the gangplank before the steam whistle blew and the gangplank was raised. For the duration of the ride back to Leschi Park, Pittman sat inside the deckhouse reading a newspaper while Chiridah and Loye sat in two deck chairs at the boat's stern. Despite her initial disappointment with Loye for not allowing them to ride in Pittman's car back to the city, Chiridah was now nearly beside herself as she recounted her conversation with the theater manager.

"He wants me to audition next Thursday for a new show, a musical. It's not the lead, but it's a major part. Oh Loye, thank you so much for taking this boat ride with me."

"I want to be in the first row on opening night," replied Loye, glad for Chiridah, but also concerned for her. Chiridah no doubt sensed Loye's tempered enthusiasm because, for the rest of the ride back to Leschi, they both looked out over the clear lake waters and kept their thoughts to themselves.

At the Leschi Park dock, a new group of people waited to board the boat for Mercer Island, and as the current passengers disembarked, Pittman tipped his hat to Chiridah and Loye once more and said what a pleasure it was to meet them both, and then said to Chiridah that he looked forward to seeing her Thursday morning backstage at the Auburn Theater for auditions for his new musical. He then went off in the direction of the main resort building while they walked over to the ticket booth and found their bicycles just where they had left them.

They rode for several blocks to reach Yesler Way, yet once they did the hill quickly grew more steep and they were both soon winded. When they saw a cable car approaching them from farther down the hill, they stopped, conferred briefly, and decided to wait for it.

"I believe there's a bicycle rack attached to the front," said Loye.

"Thank God," Chiridah let out, and dropped her bicycle to the ground.

11. Alleys (1906)

RAY BROUGHT HIS CAMERA WITH HIM EVERY DAY. HE
took it down to Ned James's office in the morning, leaving Madison House
two hours before he needed to be at the Colman Building, and shot a
dozen or more photographs as he meandered through the downtown
streets on his way to work. He had begun to pursue one series in particular in the months since acquiring his new camera, a motif of sorts, that
involved photographing the miles of alleys that stretched from the far
north end of the city to the far south end, from Denny Way to King Street.
Something about the filth and narrowness and general sense of seques-
tration made alleys attractive locales to Ray. His eye appreciated their
vanishing, one-point perspective, like railroad tracks, and the sharp con-
trasting values of light and dark that their confined spaces created even
in broad daylight. He also knew that here was an area of the city that no
one else had ever imagined worthy of photographing, a space (public or
private, it hardly mattered) that constituted a good third of the city's
thoroughfares. Other than by trash collectors and deliverymen and the
occasional derelict or vagabond, the alleys went unnoticed by the great
majority of Seattle citizens. Alleys were neither here nor there, but always
behind and between the other places people frequented. They presented
an interior frontier that no one seemed willing to acknowledge, much
less venture into. Of course, they were putrid, damp, shadowy places that,
understandably, were not inviting to the average pedestrian who wished
to remain out of harm's way and breathe unfetid air. At times Ray himself
hesitated before turning down an alley, knowing he was deliberately
removing himself from the notice and protection of the street traffic.
Similarly, he would have to swallow a tinge of shame when he emerged
from the alley and tried to blend again with the general citizenry.

So far, fortunately, he had only had one threatening encounter in a
Seattle alley. Three hoodlums—the type an editorialist for the *Mail and Herald*
had recently characterized as "a cross between a coyote and a boiler factory,
for the disgusting habits and sneaky proclivities of the prairie scavenger
and the ear-cracking tumult of the rivet house"—these three hoodlums

approached Ray from the north end of a downtown alley as he was setting up his tripod and camera one late afternoon to capture the lucent glow and deep shadow on the upper and lower portions of the three-story brick buildings that lined the alley. At first he thought their black silhouettes in the distance would give the shot scale, and even a subtle sense of human effacement. But as the three gents swaggered down the alley, yammering to one another in a drunken, boisterous manner, their attention locked on Ray, and he realized that his presence directly in their path might very well precipitate an incident. As the three hoodlums came up to him, the group split at his tripod, one stepping to his right, another shuffling a few feet to his left, and the third remaining directly in front on him.

"What have we here," the one in the center declared. He wore a stained slouch hat, a dirty canvas jacket, and brown corduroy pants, and by his size and demeanor, Ray could tell he was the gang's leader. "What's that you're up to?" he said, and pointed to Ray's set-up.

"It's just a camera," Ray said, a squeakiness in his voice, though he didn't fear so much for his own flesh-and-bone body as he did for his camera. The Graflex contained all his dreams, it had cost him months of savings. In all it was far too important for him to allow a group of thugs to steal it from him or so much as touch it without his putting up a good fight. For an instant he thought he might snatch the camera and tripod and flee down the alley and back onto the street before they could catch him, but he knew the equipment was too heavy and too bulky for such a fleet-footed escape. So he steeled himself and awaited the assault.

One of the adjutant hoodlums, who wore an oversized newsboy cap that hung down over one half of his face, snorted and spat an oyster-sized loogie onto the alley's macadam. The other one, a sullen, emaciated fellow whose jacket and pants hung on him like tent canvas, inspected Ray head to toe as if sizing him up and estimating how much fight he had in him.

"You're a newspaperman, are ya," the leader said. "And ya thought ya could go ahead and take our picture and we wouldn't care no how?" He planted his fists high on his hips and seemed to await an answer from Ray. Then he added, "What if we was wanted by the law, did ya think of that? Like Slim here – " and he slapped at the shoulder of the emaciated fellow with the droopy clothes, "who's wanted for armed burglary, or maybe Lucius over here – " and he poked at the cap of the snorter, "who could be wanted for murder as far as you know. Did ya think of that before ya pointed that thing at us?"

"I had no intention ... ," Ray stammered, "I didn't see you fellas down there, in the shadows and all."

"What's intention got do with anything?" the leader said.

Ray thought that whatever was going to happen to him would happen now.

But then, without his even thinking about what he was saying, but just coming out with it, he asked, "Well, sir, would you mind if I photographed you ... I mean the three of you?" He looked the leader straight in the eye.

The leader squinted at Ray as if taken off guard by the proposition, then scrunched up his chin as if intrigued by the idea, crossed his arms, and said, "Well, sure, why not. I've never had my picture taken before. Have you boys?"

The one in the cap shrugged and mumbled something to the effect that he didn't think so, and the emaciated one, Slim, didn't respond at all, either in word or gesture. The leader then reached out with both his arms and yanked his two cohorts by their jacket sleeves to his side and in direct view of the camera lens. "Alrighty then," he declared, "you can take our picture now."

Ray hurried to make the necessary adjustments on his camera, opening the lens wide and slowing the shutter speed since the light had faded considerably in the past few minutes and then spotting the threesome through the viewfinder. The leader grinned broadly with his arms proudly around his cohorts' shoulders, the one in the cap smirked, and Slim looked a bit scared, as if he might actually be wanted for murder. Then Ray called out to them to keep very still, squeezed the rubber shutter bulb, heard the shutter snap open and close, and shouted, "*Voilá*. It's done!"

The head hoodlum released his two cohort hoodlums, and they all three took turns shaking Ray's hand. "We'll look for our picture in the newspaper then," the leader announced. "Which one did you say it was?"

Ray, not daring to correct him by telling him he was not a newspaper photographer – or worse, disappoint him – told him that their picture would appear in next week's *Mail and Herald*, and trusted the big lug was not the kind of fellow to pick up a newspaper, and that, what's more, by next week he would have forgotten all about it. "Thank you, gentlemen," Ray added, as they walked around him and his tripod and continued on their saunter down the alley.

Two days later Ray developed the shot, and while the photograph turned out a mite dark overall (and blurred where the fellow on the right tried to pull his cap down and created a wave motion across the negative), it was one of the few respectable portrait shots Ray had ever taken. And because it was of three hoodlums in an alley (and because he didn't lose either his camera or his life in taking the photo), it instantly became one of his favorites. He even matted it, something he rarely bothered to do, being too cheap and too lazy usually to go to the trouble.

MADDIE HAD BEEN GOOD ENOUGH TO PERMIT RAY TO SET up a darkroom in one corner of his room in the attic. Enlisting Clyde's help, he constructed the darkroom by nailing a board across the exposed roof joists, then blocking the spaces between each joint, and dropping a double-thick black crinoline drapery from the board as well as down two of the sloping roof joints along either side, making a kind of half tent, half lean-to. He set up a table at the lower end of the roof's pitch, and on this he laid developing trays for developer, toner, and fixing fluids. Along the high end of this makeshift darkroom where he could stand without crouching, he hung two racks, one for his negatives (either glass plates or film) and another for his paper prints. Upon his solemn promise that no leaks would occur, Maddie allowed him to take up to the attic a large steel sink on a metal stand, which served as his print washer, and a seventy-gallon sealed drum that, in order to refill, he had to haul water in two-gallon buckets up the back stairs once a week. (Clyde had said he would help him rig up a hose and drainage system, but they still hadn't gotten to it.) On a smaller table, Ray made his prints using an oil-burning ruby lamp that had a lens to focus the light and a hinged front for when he was ready to expose the sensitized paper. On the door at the top of the back stair that led up to the attic (his room to the left and Clyde's to the right), he hung a sign – "Dark Room in Use" – to keep anyone, mainly Clyde (although the housegirl, Ada, as well), from entering his room and pulling back the crinoline drapery and ruining his work.

Once the darkroom was fully equipped, Ray spent more time behind the drapery with the ruby light on, testing different exposure times, dabbling his fingers in the different chemical washes, watching as his images magically presented themselves in one tray and were fixed in another, than he spent on the street taking photographs. He quickly came to realize that a high-quality photograph resulted as much from the work he did in the darkroom as it did from the work he performed with his camera. Just the same, even with this understanding, it pained him that so few of his photographs – maybe one or two out of every dozen – combined both interesting composition with quality printing. What's more, ever since he'd switched from film to plates with his new camera and began developing those plates and making his own prints, the costs of this whole photography undertaking had increased exponentially. Even though he displayed several of his better photographs on the walls of two downtown studios and occasionally even sold one, he knew he had to make an important decision soon: Would he attempt to become a professional photographer or would he continue in the mode of a hobbyist?

It was around this time that Ray asked Maddie about the two photographs she had in the den. They were each in 10-by-8 brushed-metal frames on a shelf along with several knickknacks (seashells, a Waterford teacup and saucer, a porcelain figurine of a milk maiden) and Clyde's set of Charles Dickens, which was still several volumes short of being complete. Ray had never before taken the trouble to examine the photos closely. From the chair in the den where he smoked his nightly cigar, he had always taken them to be standard depictions of the Gold Rush, the kind that for so many years had filled newspaper pages and covered the walls of photography studios. But when he'd heard, a full year after his arrival at Madison House, that Maddie herself had been in the Yukon, he took each photograph in hand to inspect them more carefully, and to his utter astonishment, Maddie appeared in both. In the first, she stood along the rail of a steamship in her heavy gray coat beside a younger, scared-looking woman who wore a large fur cap. The second photograph showed a group of four people pulling sleds up a rather steep, snowy trail. The two men each pulled a separate sled, their backs to the camera, while behind the men, a third sled was pulled jointly by two women. One of these women was Maddie, who turned around just as the shot was taken, and the other, her face not visible, was the woman in the fur cap.

"Asahel Curtis took those," Maddie told Ray when he at last asked her about them. "He gave them to me back in … I don't really remember now … a year or so after I returned from the Northland. I ran into him on a street, having never thought – it simply wouldn't occur to me – to look him up. On the boat to Skagway, we'd become something of friends. That's my dear friend Laurette beside me."

Ray didn't know how to respond. He felt the fool for never having inquired about the photos prior to this point. He looked at Maddie, confounded that she spoke so familiarly of one of the city's – correct that, one of the country's – greatest photographers, Asahel Curtis. While Asahel Curtis had not quite kept pace with his brother Edward's growing national renown (since after the Gold Rush, Asahel had chosen to center his work in the Northwest while Edward went farther afield), to Ray's estimation, of the two brothers, Asahel remained the superior photographer. Locally he was recognized – somewhat to Ray's chagrin – as a leading commercial photographer. Ray, though, preferred to think of him as a documentarian of the city. One of his favorite Asahel Curtis photographs was an end-of-the-century shot looking up Marion Street from Second Avenue between two matching ten-story buildings as pedestrians, men and women, all nicely attired, crossed the intersection in front of a cable car waiting to proceed down the hill. It is the perfect moment-ness of the photograph, the captured momentum of each person toward the right or left of the frame, the balanced symmetry of the buildings and the macadam, with the two parallel sets of rail tracks down the center, the absolute unawareness of all the people in regard to the camera, except for one who gives it a quick sidewise glance mid-stride … it's this photo, its composition, its values, its historical significance, that led Ray to buy his first camera, his old Kodak Brownie box. Even today, whenever Ray passed W. P. Romans's studio, out of which Asahel Curtis now worked, he would peer through the window to see if any new photographs by the master photographer had been hung for display.

After Ray tried to express to Maddie his admiration for Asahel Curtis's work, Maddie, without a second's hesitation, offered to write him a letter of introduction. "I don't know why I didn't think of it sooner," she said. "It only makes sense that the two of you meet. I trust he'll remember me fondly."

The next day Ray packed up his camera equipment and, wondering at Maddie's past acquaintance with Asahel Curtis (if that's all it was), went down to the W. P. Romans studio with her letter of introduction in hand. Unfortunately, Asahel Curtis was not in at the time, so he lugged his camera and tripod down to the former tideflats, south of Connecticut Street, to photograph the construction that had recently begun on the new landfill there. Large brick warehouses, three stories high and half a block square, were going up. He recalled Clyde telling him how he and his father used to fish from the train trellis that ran along Front Street and out into the tideflats and across the Duwamish head to the westside of Seattle. Now Front Street was First Avenue South, and the tideflats were so many empty lots. Ray focused his camera on a couple of men on scaffolding laying brick, then at three other men milling about below, smoking. After the incident in the alley a couple of weeks ago, he had become much more forward about asking people to let him take their picture. While the people he asked almost always consented, he quickly discovered that his next challenge was to convince them to ignore the camera and go about their business as if he wasn't there.

When he returned to the Romans studio a couple of hours later, he was told by someone up front that Asahel Curtis was in the back. When the photographer came forward after being summoned, Ray introduced himself and handed him Maddie's letter. Curtis scanned the letter and then looked at the Graflex camera that Ray held under his arm.

"Do you like that piece of equipment?" the photographer asked him.

"Yes, sir, I like it just fine," Ray replied. "It's a workhorse of a camera."

"Do you always carry it with you like that?"

Asahel Curtis reminded Ray of his former high school principal: stern and inquisitive. Curtis was a clean-shaven man beginning to go bald. He stood a couple inches shorter than Ray and wore a field jacket with multiple pockets, and beneath this jacket he was dressed like a businessman in a well-pressed shirt and matching vest and pants.

By the nature of the question, Ray figured he might be carrying his camera wrong. "Yes," he answered, anticipating a correction, "I do."

"That's good," Curtis said. "You should always take your camera with you wherever you go. That's the only way you'll get good photographs."

Curtis then invited Ray into the back, telling him that Miss Ingram was a good woman and recounting to him, in brief, the same story Maddie had told him of their meeting on the *S.S. Rosalie* bound for Alaska. "She found gold," he remarked. "I did not."

Ray didn't know if the photographer was genuinely dejected by this fact or simply making fun of his own futile efforts at prospecting. So avoiding the question of who found gold and who didn't, he said, "You took many fine photographs up there."

"Almost as many as my brother, Edward," Curtis replied with a note of sarcasm.

Ray asked Asahel if his brother had gone to the Klondike as well, since he did not remember Maddie having mentioned him.

"No," Curtis said abruptly, "he stayed here," and said nothing more on the matter, leaving Ray somewhat confused over this turn in the conversation.

From that point on, Asahel Curtis wanted only to talk about Seattle, not a single word more about photography. They talked about the construction on the south-end landfill where Ray had just been, an area that Curtis referred to as South Seattle. He asked Ray where he thought the Puget Sound/Lake Washington canal ought to go, through the south-end near Rainier Valley or through the north end near Salmon Bay. Ray said he favored the north-end. Then Curtis brought up the regradings and how they were transforming the city and turning it into a first-class metropolis, and Ray, mildly surprised by Curtis's unflinching support of the projects, discreetly avoided mentioning Maddie's opposition to the Denny Hill regrading. Then, almost as if he'd read Ray's mind, Curtis added that he'd taken a few photographs of the regrading of Denny Hill and that someday people would look upon these images in sheer amazement at what had been achieved in Seattle. Finally, changing the subject, he asked Ray if he liked mountain climbing.

"I don't know," Ray replied. "I've never climbed a mountain before."

"Well, maybe I should take you up to Rainier with me sometime," said Curtis. "We can take pictures." And with that he more or less concluded the conversation, announcing that he had an appointment with a manufacturer to do a product shoot, and escorted Ray back out to the front gallery.

At the door Ray shook the great photographer's hand and said how honored he was to make his acquaintance. Then, as Asahel Curtis closed the door and retreated to the back, Ray gripped his camera, slung his tripod over his shoulder, and began the long walk back uptown, regretting that he and Asahel Curtis had not exchanged one word about photographic art or craftsmanship. While he appreciated the man's enthusiasm for Seattle and supposed it contributed greatly to his photography of the city, he remained puzzled by this omission. And with no small degree of disappointment, Ray had to admit to himself that the introduction had left him feeling less than inspired about his own career in photography – and he resolved to hold off asking his brother to front him the capital to open a studio.

12. Holding Out (1907)

THE NEWS THAT THE WASHINGTON HOTEL WOULD BE destroyed demoralized Maddie—but only temporarily. James A. Moore, who had originally insisted on preserving the first hump of Denny Hill, on which his hotel sat, was now arranging with the city and its assessors to turn a sizeable profit by tearing the existing hotel down and building a new one two blocks east on a freshly regraded site. This meant that the gates were open and the way clear for Reginald H. Thomson to push the steam shovels and hydraulic hoses (or "giants," as the newspapers called them) past the first hump and up the main portion of Denny Hill to begin washing it into the bay.

When another petition came around, this time carried by an assistant to the city engineer, Maddie saw the precise scope and scale of the planned project, and all her fears and suspicions were confirmed. The city engineer's assistant—whom Maddie refused to invite into the front foyer and instead spoke to on the porch despite the blustery wet wind that was blowing that day—seemed more deliberate and assured in his purpose. He commenced his pitch by handing Maddie a copy of the official ordinance (No. 13776), which had been authenticated by the city council president, D. M. Bowen, and the mayor of Seattle, William Hickman Moore, upon its passage several weeks earlier. The petition, explained the assistant, was not a petition *per se*, since the city council had already approved the ordinance; rather it was a contract whereby the signee (or property owner) agreed to all the terms laid out in the ordinance.

Maddie listened, nodded, and tried to follow as best she could while also scanning the document she held in her hands. She had to read various lines more than once to comprehend them. "Whereas, public necessity demands..." (That must be the eminent domain part, she figured.) "...that Third Avenue, between Pike Street and Denny Way; Fourth Avenue, between Pike Street and Denny Way; and Fifth Avenue, between Westlake Avenue and Denny Way..." (Basically all of Denny Hill!) "... be laid off, widened, extended, altered, and established as public streets and highways, the City of Seattle warrants that such streets, avenues, alleys, and approaches thereto be graded in conformity to such established grades.... " (Meaning, presumably, the hill must come down!)

Maddie shook her head in dismay and confusion. She was no lawyer, but the language in the ordinance sounded so overwrought it was barely decipherable. As she read on, the section that really snagged her attention said, "All those lots, blocks, tracts, and parcels of land lying thereto would be graded in conformity to public grades at the sole expense of the property owner." She looked up from the document at the assistant standing before her. "Does this mean we all pay for our own property to be removed?" she asked him. She knew she was being somewhat sarcastic with the hapless assistant, but she doubted he noticed.

The assistant to the city engineer scrutinized the ordinance over Maddie's shoulder to double-check where she had been reading and said straight out, "Yes, it does, ma'am. Each property owner will contract individually with the engineering firm contracted by the city. The city will pay for the regrading of the streets, alleys, approaches, and so forth, while each property owner will assume responsibility for his lot." He gave her a studied look to see that she clearly understood these terms, and added, "So yes, ma'am, you read the section correctly."

Maddie had a slate of questions – some genuine, others not – that she wanted to hurl at the young man, but she had no notion of where to begin, which of her questions were most pertinent (they all seemed pertinent) or how to articulate them. Basic questions such as: *What will become of my house if the ground beneath it is removed? Where will my boarders go? Where will I go? Would I even want to remain in my boardinghouse, if such were possible, if there were no Denny Hill? How can I have worked so hard for all of this to come to naught?* She knew the assistant would likely attempt answers to most of these questions, but as with his earlier response, she also knew that all of his answers would ultimately fall short – that they could never account for what the regrading project threatened to do to her life, her past, her dreams.

She took a deep breath and read to the end of the ordinance: "... just compensation to be made for the property and property rights to be taken or damaged for the laying off, widening, extending, altering, and establishing of said Third Avenue, Fourth Avenue, and Fifth Avenue as public streets, to be ascertained by a jury or by the court in case a jury be waived." When she pointed to this passage and asked if it meant she would be compensated for the loss of her home and business, the assistant leaned forward again, read the passage, and, seeming to hesitate, replied, "In effect," and quickly added, "What this means is, if a property owner opts not to accept the award granted by the assessment committee appointed by the mayor, the city attorney, and the city engineer – a qualified committee of realtors and professional assessors – and an award that takes into account the property's existing value against its augmented value once it has been fully regraded – then the property owner may sue before the court for 'just compensation.'"

Maddie sensed from the assistant's convoluted explanation that he did not favor this clause in the ordinance since it could slow the project down as well as throw a kink into the city's budget for it. However, the clause did not give property owners the option of refusing outright to participate in the regrading project – although it did, for the moment at least, give Maddie something to think about. In the end, it seemed that whether one accepted the assessment committee's award or sued for compensation, one's property was going to be regraded.

Finally, a half dozen sheets attached to the ordinance identified each lot on Denny Hill, its owner, its square footage, and the total number of feet that each lot would have to be lowered to conform to the city's regrading of the adjacent streets and alleys. Maddie located her lot, on the corner of Blanchard and Fourth, with her name beside it, and ran her finger across the page to the total number of feet that the city wanted her to lower her lot by. The number stunned her: 129 feet! She scanned the total number of feet for several other properties on the hill, and the figures proved that Madison House, which stood nearly on the crown of Denny Hill, along with three other properties on Fourth Avenue, was expected to be regraded more than any other property in the neighborhood.

She decided she had seen enough. Yet when she asked the assistant if she might keep the copy of the ordinance she held in her hands, he told her she would have to write to city hall in care of the city engineer's office, to obtain a copy. As he extended his fountain pen to her, she handed the ordinance back to him, again refusing to sign, and wished him good day.

WHEN MADDIE DID FINALLY RECEIVE HER COPY OF THE ordinance in the mail, she showed it right away to Ray, her law clerk boarder, who read it slowly and deliberately and then confirmed to Maddie her initial understanding of the document. She asked what he thought she should do.

"I can't accept the one dollar verdict from the assessment committee," she said, seeing herself increasingly without options in face of the city's unwavering determination to proceed with the regrading project, "because I would have to borrow from the bank against the property's value to rebuild, and I won't do that. Plus I don't believe the property value will increase as they keep promising. Why would it?"

The city's argument about the "natural northerly expansion of business" from the present downtown to Smith Cove and Lake Union seemed too dogmatic. Maddie didn't buy it. And what if she did? What if Thomson's estimates were borne out? The neighborhood would still be sacrificed. In its place, Maddie could envision a flattened, concrete expanse of manufacturing plants, warehouses, and wholesale distributors where now there was a splendid, albeit modest, hillside neighborhood. The prospect of this vision – soon to be a reality if she and other property owners relented to the pressure from city hall – made her fearful.

Ray expressed his sympathy for her, but said flat out that he didn't know what she should do. "You could sue, but there's no guarantee a jury would award you damages . . ."

"I don't want to sue," Maddie said. "Nor do I want to pay to regrade my own property." She dropped her head in her hands. Her exhaustion these days seemed both moral and physical, as well as chronic. Just getting out of bed some mornings seemed as much as she could manage. "It's impossible," she let out.

Scrutinizing the ordinance and the attached list of lots and property owners more closely, Ray said finally, "There must be others on the list who don't want to regrade either. It can't be that every single one of these property owners in the sixty-block radius of Denny Hill consents to this matter."

Maddie raised her head from her hands as he said this. He was right, she thought. There must be others out there who felt as she did, who feared being stripped of what they held most dear – their homes, their livelihoods, and everything attendant on these. Maybe it was just a matter of going door-to-door to seek them out, to bring them to one another's attention, to organize them, just as the two assistants for the city attorney and the city engineer had done for the reverse purpose of driving the project through the city council. Maddie thanked Ray for his help, and with a new sense of optimism went into the kitchen to begin putting supper on the stove.

The next morning, a Saturday, Maddie put on her coat directly after clearing the breakfast table and began canvassing the neighborhood, trying to poll her Denny Hill neighbors, many of whom were the owners of boardinghouses just like her own, though typically much larger than hers. More often than not, the owners of these boardinghouses didn't live on the premises but kept separate quarters elsewhere, which meant the upkeep on their boardinghouses were often lacking, the structures' paint peeling, the porches rotting, the yards unkempt. Usually a manager answered the door at these boardinghouses and was unable, or unwilling, to say where the owner stood on the regrading matter, and when asked what he thought on the matter himself, replied that he wasn't interested in it, and closed the door. Finally, at a single-family residence on Bell Street and Third Avenue, Maddie met Mr. Jules Redelsheimer, who as soon as she announced her purpose launched into a vociferous protest against the Denny Hill regrading. A thin, rough-looking man with large facial features and large hands, Mr. Redelsheimer came to the door after Maddie had knocked twice and did not look particularly pleased at the interruption – perhaps, Maddie later conjectured, he'd expected another city-circulated, pro-regrading petition to be thrust in his face. When Maddie identified herself and stated her purpose, he shook her hand and said hello, and in the next breath cursed the city engineer, Reginald H. Thomson, as a cold-hearted technocrat. "That Thomson needs to be reined in," he spat out. After a few more invectives against the regraders, he invited

Maddie into his front foyer and after taking her coat led her to an armchair in his parlor.

"Will you join me?" he asked her, standing beside a sidetable and holding up a crystal decanter of brandy.

"No thank you," she replied. Had it not been morning still, even just a little closer to eleven than to ten, she might have accepted his offer. Then she wondered if Redelsheimer was legitimately angry at the regrading project or just a bitter old dissipater.

He sat down in the armchair facing hers, took a sip of brandy from his snifter glass, and looked sternly at Maddie. "I built this house with my own hands," he told her. "Right after my wife and I wed back in '87. Two years before the Great Fire."

Maddie had only ever heard stories of Seattle's Great Fire, how it had wiped out nearly all of downtown, leaving a wasteland of ashes and smoldering foundations in and around Pioneer Place. Then, during one of the initial regrading projects, workers raised the street level significantly by filling in the burnt ruins and began building anew on top of them. Within just a few short years, starting almost immediately after the last burning embers were extinguished, the entire district was miraculously restored. All agreed it was an impressive example of civic pride and rejuvenation.

"Back then people told me buying this far north of the city was damned foolishness," Mr. Redelsheimer declared. Maddie expected him to excuse himself for his cussing, but he didn't bother. "And now with this regrading business about to tear down the whole damn hill, I'm starting to think that maybe they were right. This city doesn't know if it's coming or going half the time. Boom, bust, boom, bust, that's all it seems to be about. Down there in Portland they have more sense about these things. They're not so excitable."

"What do you expect to do?" Maddie asked tentatively, hoping he might be able to offer a course of action she could emulate, and in turn give her a small measure of hope that the situation could be resolved without further upset, since this was all she wanted, all she longed for… for her and Clyde and her boarders at Madison House to be able to carry on with their peaceable, well-meaning lives.

"I'm not going to do a blessed thing," he nearly shouted at her. "I'm going to hold out until they make me move, then maybe I'll take them to court. If worse comes to worse, I'll move onto my boat. It's just a small purse seiner, but it's been how I've made my living these past twenty-odd years."

Maddie then hazarded to ask Redelsheimer if he knew of any other property owners on the hill who opposed the regrading, and he said that he did not, that he kept pretty much to himself, but that he thought she might check with the Redemptorist fathers on Fifth Avenue and Vine Street. "They have the whole rectory and library and school over there ... been there for as long as I can remember. Where are they going to go, I'd like to know."

Maddie said she would most certainly check in on them, and thanked Mr. Redelsheimer for his hospitality as well as his mutual opposition to the regrading, and rose from her chair and proceeded to make her way to the front door. He said she could call on him at any time, that he wasn't going anywhere, at least not until he was forced to, and waved goodbye to her from his front porch.

Maddie headed north on the hill, continuing door-to-door, making her way toward the Congregation of the Most Holy Redeemer Monastery. For the most part during her canvassing of the hill, when she was able to speak to one property owner or another, she was dejected to learn how many had already signed on to the ordinance and were ready to pay 25 cents per square foot to have the Hawley Engineering Company, the city's contractor, demolish their home or place of business and then hose away their property. One man even showed her an advertisement from last week's *Post-Intelligencer* for house moving services – *L.B. Gullett/ Experienced House Mover/ House Moving, Raising, Lowering, and Wrecking/ Brick or Concrete Foundations, Retaining Walls, Sidewalks, Etc. / I Can Move Anything* – and said he was going to give them a call that afternoon. The advertisement included a photo of a house similar in size and shape to Madison House that was elevated two or three stories off the ground on a series of wooden crib piles in preparation for being lowered to the new street level. Around the base of the crib piles lay mud and debris from the regrading. The image appalled Maddie. To think of such violence being done to her own house, to invite the removal of the very ground upon which it stood, to accept the loss of the geographic prominence so intrinsic to everything the house meant to her was beyond comprehension. It was enough to make her want to move to the country, somewhere far from the headstrong drive of city people, and start a chicken farm.

Making her way down the north slope of Denny Hill, she knew the Redemptorist fathers were located somewhere over here, but because she rarely ventured in this direction, she wasn't sure exactly where. In the seven, going on eight years that she had lived on the hill, she believed she had passed the monastery maybe three or four times. Add to that the fact that her parents had been Methodist, a faith to which she still laid a distant claim (though she only attended services on the day of the Lord's birth and the day of His resurrection and that's all), and the fact that she had no reason to have anything to do with the Catholic order on this side of the hill, given all of this, it was no wonder that she now had to stray down several wrong streets before finding the monastery. As she finally approached the four buildings that made up the monastery – each structure built of sandstone, darkened by the coal and wood smoke that often clogged the city's air, and cross-sectioned with trusses and supports made of large redwood beams – the compound made her think of a medieval village one might encounter in central Europe. She let herself through the cast-iron gate at the waist-high, brown-painted fence that enclosed the compound and walked up the short path to what appeared to be the main entrance. In the small alcove of the entrance was placed a three-foot painted wood statue of St. Alphonsus de Liguori in his black tunic and white collar, and to the right, a statue of the Holy Mother in her flowing blue garments. Meanwhile, above the thick wood door, there was an intricately carved trefoil representing the Holy Trinity.

After Maddie rapped three times on the door using the cast-iron knocker, the door opened and a somewhat elderly man appeared in a long black tunic identical to the one painted on the wooden statue of St. Alphonsus. The man folded his hands before him, and Maddie could tell that, in sharp contrast to Redelsheimer, he was a gentle-mannered sort.

"Good afternoon," he intoned. "How may we help you?" He looked and spoke just as Maddie expected a Redemptorist father to look and speak, calm and clear and with an air of scholasticism about him.

Maddie explained her purpose to the priest and asked if the fathers had been following the developments surrounding the regrading project or had considered the implications of it for their monastery. Forestalling his answer to Maddie's questions with a raised hand, the monk signaled her to enter the monastery and proceeded to lead her down a dim hallway into a small conferring room. Before stepping into this room, Maddie glanced into the room just opposite, a library with bookcases lining the walls to the high ceiling and a series of long wooden tables in the center. The conferring room, on the other hand, was far more simple: four straight-back wood chairs around a single square wood table. Maddie sat on one side of the table and the priest on the other.

"My name is Father Tromboldt," he began, "and yes, we've heard all about the regrading project, and are deeply concerned."

Then, trusting the priest's sympathetic demeanor, Maddie repeated her own fears about the regrading, articulating them to a degree that she hadn't yet done with anyone else – except perhaps to Clyde that evening after the city council meeting when he had consoled and comforted her. Yet on this occasion, unlike the last, the more she spoke, the greater her apprehension and alarm grew, and by the time she had finished explaining how devastating the loss of her house, her livelihood, her home would be to her, tears filled her eyes and she lowered her head in shame. The priest simply looked down upon her from across the table in consoling silence.

"I'm sorry to behave this way," Maddie said, wiping her eyes with the heal of her palm. "But how can they do this?"

"We'll have to see what comes of it," was all the priest said, and then, more sternly, added, "Indeed, this whole regrading puts me in mind of Matthew, who reminds us, 'Wide is the gate, and broad is the way, that leadeth to destruction.' We risk losing our students just as you do your boarders. We're a scholastic order and without them we cannot sustain ourselves." He paused just then as if to collect himself before making a carefully weighed avowal. "But we recognize that we must be realistic. The city seems determined to carry out this project, and so the fathers have begun to seek a new location where we might fulfill our mission. When we built the monastery here, Denny Hill was still relatively uninhabited, even wild, yet now businesses and industry are edging their way farther north from the city – what you've no doubt heard boasted as the New Seattle – whether we wish it or not. And now the order – the Redemptorist fathers, that is – is coming to the opinion that this might be an opportunity for us to return to our pastoral origins. After much prayer and deliberation on the matter, however, we have also elected to bide our time and not make any hasty decisions. Being as we're on the far north end of the proposed regrading, it will take some time – a year or more at least – for the project to reach us."

Maddie listened to the priest, taking in what he had to say, with neither hope nor despair, and realized that each and every property owner on the hill – as well as each leasee and lettor – would have to make his or her decision about how to respond to the regrading crisis. It would likely come down to a matter of personal conscience rather than collective action. And while it appeared that many had already committed themselves to going along with the regrading, or were on the brink of doing so, a handful of Denny Hill residents seemed set on holding out against it.

"Well," Maddie decided to ask outright, "have the Redemptorist fathers signed the ordinance?"

The priest appeared to know immediately what she was referring to, and said flatly, "No, we have not. It seemed coercive and unjust, and we rejected it out of hand."

Maddie took this condemnation of the regrading ordinance by the Redemptorists for what it was worth, given the priest's earlier comments about biding their time and returning to their pastoral origins, and thanked him for speaking to her so openly about the matter. They both rose from their chairs.

"We pray for an equitable and peaceful resolution to this problem," he said, as they stood across the table from each other. Maddie said that she did, too, and hoped that it would come about soon. Then the priest escorted her back down the hallway to the entrance and remained standing in the doorway inside the front alcove as she let herself out the gate.

SEVERAL DAYS AFTER MADDIE CANVASSED THE NEIGHBOR-
hood, Ada failed to appear at Madison House for two straight days, setting
Maddie to worrying to no end about her house girl. She was accustomed
to Ada occasionally not showing up to the house until later in the morning or even sometime in the afternoon, and once or twice missing the
day entirely. She understood that the child did not enjoy a stable home
life. The father was an odd-jobs man – like Clyde in this respect, though
with a wife and daughter to support – while the taciturn mother seemed
to suffer under a perpetual cloud of despondency. Whenever Maddie had
occasion to speak to her, it was as if she were speaking to a thick, bare
wall. The woman's face indicated no response to what she said, even when
the conversation referred to the woman's own daughter, as it almost
always did. When Maddie had tried, for instance, to speak to the mother
about their house on Second Avenue and the encroaching regrading after
she had seen the perilous state it was in, the only response she received
from the woman was that her husband was looking for a new place for
them. That was all she said on the matter. Other than that, she only
wanted to hear that her daughter was doing her job and would not be
dismissed from it. So it did not surprise Maddie that Ada, now thirteen
years old, often behaved withdrawn and distant herself, while at other
times, in response to the least stimulation, she exhibited an exuberance
that far exceeded what was appropriate or warranted. As far as Maddie
knew, neither the father nor the mother drank, nor did the father beat his
wife or child. Rather, the family seemed to suffer from a general morose-
ness brought on by their circumstances. They were the living embodi-
ment of the fact that, despite Seattle's halcyon days proceeding the Gold
Rush, a substantial portion of the city's citizenry still lived with a measure
of poverty that most people, those who had neither experienced nor witnessed it for themselves, would find deplorable. It made Maddie wonder
if she shouldn't take Ada in after all.

The fact that the small farmhouse that Ada and her parents inhabited
on Second Avenue had been officially condemned by the city (according
to what Clyde had learned) could only worsen their plight. On one of the
mother's more talkative days, when she had actually accompanied Ada

in the morning to Madison House, they had sat on the front porch and the mother had explained how Ezra, the husband, paid the bank $15 a month on the house, which was more than half of what he earned in the same period, and that this was why the four bits that Ada brought home each day from the boardinghouse made such a difference to the family.

Beginning several months back, Maddie (and sometimes Clyde, too) had begun to walk Ada down the hill to her house, especially during the winter months when it was well past nightfall by the time the supper dishes were cleared, cleaned, and put away. (With the exception of Sundays, Ada took her lunch and supper in the boardinghouse kitchen.) The farmhouse, especially at night, had such a bleak cast to it – the paint weathered away long ago, the front porch sagging, the window shutters off their hinges – that Maddie hated to see little Ada enter it, and genuinely feared for her welfare. It was a narrow, single-story house, and although Maddie had never been inside, she had entered similar houses on Denny Hill and knew the floor plan: small front parlor, hallway to the right, two bedrooms to the left, kitchen with a pump sink, and an enclosed back stoop. The only toilet was a smelly old outhouse with a slop bucket out back.

So when two whole days passed without Ada appearing as she usually did in the mudroom at the back of the kitchen, ready to assist Maddie in preparing the day's meals and cleaning the house, Maddie's first impulse was to summon Clyde to walk down the hill to look for her. But this particular morning, she decided she would go see for herself. Perhaps the family had moved, she speculated as she cleared the plates from the breakfast table and set them in the sink. She hoped they had. And it would be just like the mother and father, preoccupied with their own daily hardship, to relocate without informing Maddie that Ada now lived too far away to return to work. On the other hand, they were not likely to give up so readily the four bits a day the girl earned for the family.

Maddie took the poker from its stand, opened the stove door, and pushed the larger coal embers into a pile in the center of the grill to maintain a slow burn during the day, allowing her to add fresh coals just before suppertime. She hung her apron on the backdoor, tidied her hair using a shiny pie tin to catch her reflection, and went to the front foyer for her coat and hat. Although she had errands to run in town, making this little detour to Ada's house had become far more pressing. In the two and a half years that Ada had been working for her, Maddie had grown more than just a little fond of the child. She had to admit to herself now that she adored the dear thing, and found her much more engaging mentally than any school official had ever judged her to be. Maddie enjoyed Ada's presence and looked forward to her company. She never worked her too hard, knowing how much Ada endured already. If anything, she pampered her. And how could she not? The shy, hardworking girl stirred in her the maternal longings that, she now acknowledged to herself, would likely remain unfulfilled now that, husbandless, she had reached the mature age of thirty-seven years. Plus there was no denying the child was just a sweet, darling, little creature that had won over Maddie's heart – as well as the hearts of all her boarders.

As Maddie walked out of the house, she didn't hear the usual chug of the steam engines powering up down the hill to commence the day's regrading. The last time she had walked down to Second and First Avenues, nearly half the houses in the vicinity had already been vacated prior to being razed. Ada's family's house had been one of the few that remained occupied, or even standing.

Now, because of the increased regrading efforts, Maddie first had to walk north two blocks to Battery Street and then turn left and begin down the hill that way. When she reached Third Avenue and looked ahead of her, she wondered if she had not gone too far, or perhaps not far enough, or else had taken a wrong turn at some point. She didn't recognize the terrain anymore. Instead of the apartment building that had once stood on the corner of Wall and Second, a crater of dirt opened before her. For almost the entire length of the avenue, the hill just dropped off into a ravine of mud, dirt, boulders, and debris. Maddie angled down to the next block, to Bell Street, where Ada's house was. Yet when she reached the intersection, or what she thought was the intersection, there was no house to be found. Bell Street, and Blanchard and Lenora just south of it, ceased abruptly at the cut made by the regrading.

Still disoriented, she walked to the edge of the cut and looked down. There, at the bottom of the ravine, she saw the collapsed form of a small farmhouse that, to her horror, resembled the house that Ada's family had lived in. The front half of the structure was caved in, with the roof collapsed forward, crushing the porch. The back end of the house left a trail of rough-sawed timbers down the cut. The house appeared to have buckled and then collapsed, folding in on itself as it slid down the hill, leaving a mound of timbers and shingles that looked like a photograph of a house that someone had shredded and tossed into the air. There was no telling how long ago it had come down. It must have been in the last day or two, at least since Maddie had seen Ada last. She didn't know what to make of the sight. She tried to keep herself from becoming too alarmed, and prayed that Ada was safe.

Two men in Wellington boots appeared poking about the debris of the house with crowbars. Maddie was almost certain now that it was Ada's house, but she wanted confirmation before she decided what to do next. She hurried back up to the next block, where the cut was not quite as sharp and a plank walkway—a series of parallel two-by-eights—made a cutback down the slope and across the mud. She hiked up her skirts and began the tenuous walk down to the new grade to what used to be Second Avenue, then backtracked to the collapsed house. The two men she had spotted moments before were prying boards away from the destroyed house, drawing out the nails, and tossing the boards onto a pile off to the side. As she neared, Maddie could see what looked like a chair and a chest of drawers buried beneath the rubble. She stepped off the two-by-eight planks, trudged through the doughy earth straight up to the house, and waved to the two men to get their attention. The larger man wore only pants and an undershirt, despite the chill morning, while the other man, the one who seemed to be in charge, wore a canvas work jacket, a crumpled felt hat, and a tool belt about his waist. Maddie had seen such two-men work crews before. They were the ones subcontracted by the engineering firm in charge of the regrading to salvage the lumber from collapsed houses. They then sold the lumber by the wagonload as part of their commission.

Maddie continued to signal to the two men. "Where's the family that lived in this house?" she called out to them finally.

"Ma'am?" said the large man in the undershirt just as he was about to drag a section of roof away from the house.

"The family that lived here. Where have they gone?"

The smaller man, after prying apart two floorboards with his crowbar, came up to her and removed his hat.

"Ma'am," he said politely, holding his hat to his chest, "you don't know?"

"Don't know what?" she answered back, a flash of panic racing through her.

He rubbed his whiskered chin and looking at the ground replied, "Then I'm terribly sorry to be the one to tell you, ma'am." The other man had stopped his work and was now watching this exchange. "The house came down of its own early yesterday morning. The earth just gave out from underneath it and she came down."

"Do you mean the house was not supposed to come down?"

"Not yet, I don't suppose," he said. "Not like that."

"Sir," Maddie said to him rather forcefully, to get his full attention. "How do you mean, *Not like that*?"

The man scuffed his feet, looked back at his partner, then said without making eye contact with Maddie, "With them in it."

Maddie's hand came up to her mouth. Did she hear him right? Had he said what she thought he'd said? If nothing else, the way he said it left little doubt. "Dear God, no," she murmured, and thought, *The poor child*.

The man repeated himself, "I'm terribly sorry, ma'am," and added, "Did you know the people?"

Maddie nodded, her hand still cupped over her mouth, and looked off at the mound of rubble that had once been the farmhouse where Ada and her parents had lived. Their home, their lives.

The man watched her. "Well," he began to explain, "they'd been told to vacate long ago. That's what I'm told. But they wouldn't go, and the sluicing just kept getting closer and closer until finally there were only a few yards of earth 'tween the house and the cut. And then we had that big rain two days ago, and, well … I guess no one saw it happen, which meant it probably came down at night when they was asleep. It wouldn't take much, not once that earth gave way. It's a sad way to go. A man and his wife, they say."

Maddie looked up at him. "And a girl too?"

"There was no girl," he replied.

Maddie then turned to the man and insisted he explain to her, as best he could, precisely who had died in the collapsed house.

The man seemed taken aback by her insistence. "I'm only hired to collect the wood, ma'am, so I can only tell you what I've heard."

"So there was no girl found in the house? Just a man and woman?"

"Yes, ma'am. That's what I've heard. The folks residing in the house were supposed to've left it, like I said, some weeks ago, is what the site foreman told us this morning. But they didn't leave, and that's what got 'em killed. A man and a woman." He went on to explain how when the regrading crew showed up yesterday morning the house was already down and one of the workmen, noticing there was the furniture still in it, came up to inspect it and saw a woman's leg beneath the rubble. Several of the crew extracted her body and soon found the man's body as well. "But no child, ma'am. There's been some children's things, like a small bed, but we're pretty certain it was only the two of them in the house, the man and woman, when it came down."

Grief and rage swelled in Maddie. It all seemed so heedless, so senseless, so utterly unnecessary and cruel. The regrading project not only possessed the power to devastate people's lives by stealing their homes from them ... it could now destroy families and take people's lives with impunity. From what this man was telling her, at least Ada had escaped the fate visited upon her parents, and though she was still missing, she had apparently survived. Maddie would now have to find her. She had to save that poor girl from any more suffering. And once she did find her, she would give Ada a new home, a place where she would be safe and well looked after and loved, and never have to be afraid again.

Maddie asked the workman where she could find the site supervisor, thinking he might be able to give her more information about what had happened. The man pointed toward Western Avenue where the engineering firm had set up its largest pump to pull water from harbor and into the hoses used to sluice away the hill. The man reiterated how sorry he was about what had happened, and Maddie thanked him and began walking toward Western Avenue. About half way there, however, she heard a steam engine cough and sputter and start to chug, and within moments she could hear the first gush of water from the hoses, almost like an explosion, and looking north from where she stood she saw the fat white spray being turned on the hillside and ripping into the earth like a giant fang. She knew right then that she would be too beside herself, too enraged by it all, to talk to anyone in charge of such devastation. She would have to return to the boardinghouse and enlist Clyde to help her find Ada. Knowing that she could count on him, she began slogging her way back up the scarred hillside.

She hurried back to the boardinghouse forcing herself to hold back her tears. Now wasn't the time, she knew, not until Ada was found. She reached the house, barely containing her panic. Yet as she rounded the back of the house, there, before her, she saw instantly that she needn't hold back her tears any longer. Sitting on the old milking stool just outside the mudroom door, just as she did many a morning when Maddie sent her outside to shuck corn or snap string beans, was Ada. She sat there quietly explaining something to Clyde, who stood beside her patiently listening. Maddie's tears flooded over her as she rushed up to the thirteen-year-old girl, dropped to her knees, and hugged the child to her. When Maddie pulled away to take a good look at her and make sure she wasn't hurt, Ada was crying too. She was also sucking on a root beer barrel candy that Clyde had given her and that she swiftly popped out of her mouth and dropped into the pocket of her dress.

Once Maddie was certain Ada was unhurt, and had hugged her again several times, she took her inside and fed her oatmeal with brown sugar, raisins, and heavy cream in the kitchen. She didn't try to elicit from the child any explanation of what she had been through. Rather, she simply stroked her hair and in a soothing tone told her that she was going to stay at Madison House that night, and wouldn't that be fun?

"We'll go upstairs, the two of us, and get your room ready as soon as you've had a good breakfast," she told her.

"Yes, ma'am," Ada replied, and took a large spoonful of steaming oatmeal into her mouth. With her mouth full, she asked Maddie, "Won't Miss Chiridah and Loye mind my being upstairs with them?"

Maddie felt herself begin to cry again at the heartfeltness of the question, and answered, "No, dear, they won't mind. They'll be very happy that you're there," and then leaned over Ada and kissed her on the forehead with all the attention and adoration of a loving mother.

13. Modern Seattle (1907)

CLYDE DIDN'T MIND WORKING FOR NED JAMES. HE RAN errands between downtown offices and was usually very leisurely about it. Ned James paid him a flat rate for his day's work and never kept track of his time, so if Clyde wished to dally along the waterfront to watch the ships come and go or to duck into Beck's Cafe to drink a Tannhaeuser or two, he felt perfectly at liberty to do so. In fact, even with his campaign to become the next state senator from the 36th District, Ned James never had an overtaxing amount of work for Clyde to do. Nevertheless, Ned seemed to relish knowing he had Clyde on retainer and could call upon him at a moment's notice. For this reason, Clyde spent most of his morning hours milling about the offices in the Colman Building, doing mundane tasks for James's secretary (filing court documents, taking inventory of office supplies, emptying waste baskets), or else talking the morning away with Erasmo, the other law clerk – who, Clyde learned, had received his secondary education from the raft of school teachers America had sent to the Philippine Islands after the Spanish-American War and who, he also learned, had recently begun taking classes at the University of Washington's new law school. Indeed, Erasmo was an ambitious young man, yet not so ambitious that he wouldn't put his feet up on his desk and chat away the morning with Clyde. He told Clyde that he wanted to be Seattle's first pinoy lawyer, to organize the Filipino farm and cannery workers in the state, and eventually run for the same state senate seat that his boss, Edward Holton James, was running for.

"Imagine, Ned becomes the new state senator," Erasmo said, with a slightly devious gleam in his brown eyes, "and somewhere down the line I have to run against him. If that happened, who would you support?"

Clyde did not hesitate. "I'd support you, Erasmo. I would campaign tirelessly on your behalf." Clyde put his feet up on the other side of Erasmo's desk. "Then, after you won the election, you could bring me to Olympia to help run your office."

"You would be my legislative assistant," Erasmo vowed. "My *aide-de-camp*."

Ray continued to work for Ned James during this same period – the three of them only ever called their boss "Ned" outside his presence; otherwise it was strictly "Mr. James" or "sir." Ray, even more than Clyde, had mastered the means of keeping his distance from the office and still getting his work done, which left him ample time for his photography. Since Clyde had helped his friend set up the darkroom in his attic room, Ray had become ever more serious about photography. He'd recently printed up business cards that read: *Professional Photographer / Available for Events, Portraiture, and Product Photography / Since 1904 / Phone: Seattle 316.* The phone number was Maddie's house phone, and the "Since 1904" referred back to when Ray first began taking pictures with his little Kodak Brownie box camera. Just the same, Ray seemed on his way to making something of himself as a professional photographer. He sold several photographs to the newspapers in recent months and had even had a series of his alley photographs published in *American Amateur Photographer* magazine, edited by his hero Alfred Stieglitz. Yet his main goal, the one that kept him so busy that Clyde rarely saw him anymore, either in the office or at the boardinghouse, was to open his own photography studio.

Ray would do okay for himself, Clyde knew. His concern these days was mostly for Maddie and Ada. The death of Ada's mother and father – to the regrading, no less – struck Maddie a blow that seemed both to scare and rile her. Clyde had found the child the day after she was orphaned, two days after she'd gone missing from Madison House, wandering down on the waterfront. She understood that both her parents had perished. She'd gone out in the middle of the night during the rainstorm to use the outhouse when the house had collapsed. Clyde later found out that the site foreman had come upon her the next day squatting beside the rubble of her family's house but when he'd tried to approach her, she'd scurried away like a frightened woodland animal. When Clyde chanced upon her on the waterfront staring down at the greenish oily water, she was composed enough to tell him what had happened, and she let him walk her back to the boardinghouse. Maddie, who came upon them at the back of the house, took her in without hesitating, putting her in the second-floor bedroom next to hers on the back side of the house, and then arranged for there to be a proper burial of her parents in Lakeview Cemetery on Capitol Hill. However, the manner in which they had died – crushed in their own home – had upset Maddie terribly and she began to fear this might be the end that was in store for anyone who dared resist the regradings. The options seemed to be either settle with the city on its terms or have your house razed with you and your loved ones inside it.

Moreover, though Clyde did not dare articulate it to himself, much less to anyone else, he now knew, undeniably, that he loved Maddie – that he had fallen impossibly in love with her. And yet with everything that was occurring in their lives right now, he could never so much as even consider imposing his feeling upon her at this time – if ever. He knew that Maddie was fond of him, that their friendship meant something to her...yet to what extent, he had no way of judging. At the very least, he knew she appreciated him. She was always telling him so, always expressing how grateful she was for all that he'd done around the house. He knew that expecting anything more, such as embracing her again as he had done that afternoon in the carriage house more than a year ago, was improvident. The circumstances – their histories, their age difference, their appearance (*his*, that is) – excluded any likelihood of his advancing his feelings for Maddie beyond simply taking care of the house, eating meals with her, and reading to her in the evening, a pastime they had happily continued after finishing *Our Mutual Friend* so that now they were well into their third Dickens novel.

All of these people in Clyde's life (including his father, whose garden had grown considerably and who now sold his fruits and vegetables at the city's new farmer's market) occupied his thoughts as he walked back toward Denny Hill after putting in his morning hours at Ned James's office. He had gotten into the habit – unlike Maddie, who avoided the devastation as much as possible – of walking past the spot of the most current regrading and with a helplessness that bordered almost on being pleasurable, inspecting how much more of Denny Hill had been carved away each day. The progress, to be certain, was steady as she goes. With the new ordinance in effect, the regrading crews were going full bore at the hill, slashing in a northeasterly direction from the axis point of

Second and Third Avenues and Stewart and Virginia Streets. Getting one's orientation could only be an approximation at best now since buildings that formerly served as landmarks had been torn down and familiar streets leveled.

No building served this landmark purpose more than the Washington Hotel. Clyde knew that it was slated for demolition; he had watched for the past several months as workmen removed first its furnishings and then all the decorative appointments such as the lavish chandeliers and ornately carved stairway railings, and finally the many marble surfaces and brass fixtures from the men's and ladies' washrooms. Yet witnessing the gutting of the building day after day could not prepare him for his approach to it on the day when he discovered that one entire half of the grand old hotel had been sheered off, like the severing of someone's lower torso, leaving the remaining half ragged and exposed. Several weeks ago the half dozen or so houses that had stood just below the hotel on the southern slope had been razed, and the funicular tracks upon which guests were formerly trundled up to the hotel's front entrance had been removed, after which the steam shovels and hoses had begun working their magic toward the base of the hotel and undermining its foundation. Now the entire western half of the great Gothic building lay in rubble at the bottom of the regrading cut. The two fifth-story cupolas, including the massive center tower, rested on their sides like toppled bandstands among the debris, which a crew of ten or more men now worked over with crow bars and hammers, salvaging what they could of the lumber. Among the rubble, Clyde spotted the outstretched neck and head of one of the four concrete gargoyles that had adorned the four corners of the hotel's center tower.

Far more startling than the sight of the debris from the hotel at the base of the cut was the sheered half that remained standing atop the cut. It seemed like a child's doll house, sawed in two, the five floors, hallways, staircases, and assorted rooms all open to plain view, open to the elements, waiting for some child to come along and fill the rooms with wooden toy furniture and porcelain dolls. Clyde could not take his eyes off the sight of the gaping structure, and for the first time since the regrading of Denny Hill had begun more than eighteen months ago, the monumental nature of the destruction that would accompany the project, apart from the human suffering he'd already witnessed, registered with him. What gain could possibly justify such loss? Without the Washington Hotel, the city would never be the same. How could such an absence ever be reconciled? The city, it seemed, was devouring itself, a starved gorgon feasting on its own limbs.

His answer, he quickly realized, was located just two blocks west, where James Moore had already begun constructing the New Washington Hotel, a simple square structure already four stories high and planned for twelve, made of steel girders and light-colored brick and tile – the emblem of modern Seattle.

THE MUD. EVER THE MUD, MOUNTAINS AND RIVERS OF MUD. One learned to live with it or one didn't. Either way, it remained elemental to life in Seattle since the regrading had begun. Grainy brown sludge, slick blue clay, boulders and debris – all washed from the mooring of the hillside and forever sluiced into the bay. It was one week later, when returning home late at night after working with Erasmo to promote a series of stump speeches Ned James planned to make in coming weeks, that Clyde was halted four blocks short by the expanse of the new cut from that day's regrading of Denny Hill. He tried to go around it, yet the gash in the hillside opening like a maw before him, offered no clear detour. Frustrated, and yet too tired to backtrack, he resolved to abandon the road's firm macadam and angle his way straight up the center of the wedge.

Within moments, he was slogging deep into the mud, sinking to his ankles, then his calves, heaving forward with one knee, then the other, until he nearly crawled through the thick muck. It was no help that the night was so dark, primeval dark – the streetlamps removed weeks ago, the gas lines disconnected and torn from the ground where the Seattle Gas Company had laid them only ten years earlier, and where Seattle City Light planned to replace them with overhead electrical wires (and lights probably too) once the hill was leveled. Eventually, exhausted by his efforts to scale the cut – and exhausted yet further by his daily confrontations with the regrading project – Clyde imagined himself simply lying down in the mud, surrendering to it, and letting it reclaim him. He would become unformed and rudimentary again. Amphibian. Reversing the evolutionary transition from sea to land, he would claw at the lumpy mud, flap through its wetness, gasp for breath with soggy lungs. Instead, though, he simply staggered forward, up the slippery incline, one foot plunging into the thick ooze and then the other. Then, reaching forward suddenly to keep his balance, he felt a form – a body, fur – and looking down made out the bloated carcass of a mongrel dog half submerged in the mud, the creature's teeth exposed in a snarl at the mud's ungiving clutch – a version of himself, he imagined, if he didn't, or couldn't, toil on.

So he pushed ahead, his feet and calves weighted with mud, grown heavy and thick as pachyderm legs. He set his sights on the top of the cut where, perched on either side of the cliff that had been carved out by the powerful hoses, the dark shape of two abandoned houses leered down at him, their bulk floating above the skeletal supports of their partial crib piles, windows boarded, the owners having weeks ago pocketed their one-dollar verdict from the gang of city-appointed assessors before moving into more secure wards on First Hill or else slinking down past the Deadline into the unrestricted zone of taverns, flophouses, brothels, and dance halls.

Clyde plunged onward into the mud and just ahead spotted a long plank – leverage if he could reach it. That very same morning he had scrambled down this side of Denny Hill before the hoses were set to it and the wide wedge had been blasted out by the 1,000-pound jets generated by the two steam-powered pumphouses at the base of the cut. The regrading taking place throughout the city constituted progress, or so city officials told first the residents of Jackson Street, then Second Avenue, and now Denny Hill for the past five years as each successive project was launched. And progress, they said, came at a cost.

Clyde reached for the plank, but as he bent forward to take hold of it his right leg shot out sideways from under him and he felt his hamstring go taut. The sudden and gripping pain in his leg flipped him onto his side, bodylength into the mud. He reached for the back of his thigh and plied his fingers into the muscle, pounding the back of his leg to relieve the tight knot there. His backside was soaked, and he could feel a trickle of silt run beneath his collar and down his back. As the cramp in his leg loosened, he reached again and grasped the plank and, bracing it behind and beneath him, slowly, hand over hand, pulled himself upright.

Yet as he came to his feet and steadied himself, a section of cliff collapsed fifty feet above him and sent a mud slide toward him that nearly took both his legs out from under him again. Leaning into the slide with all his weight he managed to remain standing, using the plank like a rudder, and yet could only watch helplessly as the mud rose toward his groin. Another slide and he knew he might be buried alive, and in the morning the hoses would uncover his young, bloated, alabaster body like some enormous slug right alongside the old dead mongrel's. Or perhaps if the hoses were left unmanned, as they often were, left propped up and aimed full blast at the hillside as the men working them slouched off to a nearby tavern, his body would be sluiced into the flumes and washed out to the bay where the afternoon tides would eventually carry his carcass out through the straits and into the rough Pacific.

Either way, it would be an ugly means by which to exit this life. So rather than persist in his hopeless struggle against the relentless mud, and aiming instead to turn the momentary inertia of the slide to his advantage, he extricated first one leg, then the other, and after making a full about-face, began his retreat from the cut and back to solid ground to find another way home.

HE MADE IT BACK TO THE BOARDINGHOUSE THAT NIGHT exhausted after backtracking four entire blocks, circling the amputated remains of the Washington Hotel, and approaching the house from the eastern side of Denny Hill. Fortunately it was well past midnight and no one was about – not even Maddie, who typically stayed up late and rose early – so he was able to shuck off his mud-caked jacket, shirt, pants, and brogans and conceal them behind a heather shrub along the side of the house and climb up the backstairs in his underpants, telling himself he would find a bucket in the morning, fill it with water from the tap at the back of the house, and wash the mud out of his clothes then. He didn't want Maddie or any one else to know of his ordeal in the cut. It was too humiliating.

He slept late the next morning, missing breakfast, and then, after donning fresh clothes and saying good-morning to Maddie in the kitchen, ducked out the back and retraced the exact same route he'd walked the night before, leaving his clothes from the night before behind the shrub. He wanted to see in broad daylight the cut that had defeated him. When he reached the spot, he discovered along its lower perimeter a dozen sidewalk engineers already gathered to watch the work going on. Sometimes as many as thirty spectators, almost always men, gathered around the most recent section of the hill being regraded and gave a running commentary on the work taking place. For the past seven years, one section of the city or another had been systematically washed into the tideflats or bay. With the exception of a moderate regrading along First Avenue North in the 1890s, the initial regradings began down on Jackson Street and Dearborn and progressively moved north until they reached the base of Denny Hill. Clyde wondered when, if ever, they would cease. Would Thomson try to regrade Queen Anne Hill into Lake Union, Capitol Hill into Lake Washington? How far up the Cascades would he push? San Francisco had never felt compelled to wash its hills into its bay, nor had Rome, whose seven hills Seattle's own had often been compared to. So why should Seattle sluice away its hills? Business was why. Everyone knew that. Commerce was king. It was the engine that drove this great money-mad country, the altar upon which all else – family, friendship, community – would be sacrificed.

Last night's thrashing in the mud had been a nightmare for Clyde. It had left him aching and sore this morning. The odds had been against him in fighting a wounded hill. He scanned the gully he'd tried to trudge up and looked for the carcass of the mongrel dog. Had it been washed away already? Or was it buried deep beneath the mud being churned up by the hoses. In all, there were three of the giant hoses working the cut this day: one positioned along either side working the right and left slopes, and a third at the top of the cut where there were still traces of a street between the partially pyloned houses that Clyde remembered as dark shadows looming above him the night before. The top hose worked one side for a time, then pivoted and worked the other side. Beneath the jets of water from above and below, the earth succumbed, sliding away into the center of the gully where a torrent of water and dirt washed down toward the long, snaking flumes that carried it all out to the bay. The process was basically the same as that used by the large prospecting outfits in the Yukon and Alaska to sluice the hillsides for gold. In great part, the regradings were the result of the wealth that had poured into the city from those gold fields. Seattle had become the undisputed capital of the region – the Great Pacific Northwest – that stretched from northern California to the Bering Straits. The Queen City. Ruler of all it purveyed. And to live up to this station, it needed to ensure accessibility, ease of movement, free ingress and egress … and leveling the hills, city leaders were convinced, would achieve this very goal.

All three hoses were now directed toward the upper right edge of the cut where one of the houses – a two-story clapboard with a pillared front porch and second-story dormers – clung to what remained of the hillside, half of its foundation resting precariously upon crib piles. Some owners spent considerable money to save their houses by having them propped on top of crib piles as the ground beneath their foundations was sluiced away, and then, like pulling cards from the bottom of a deck, the crib piles were removed and the houses lowered 50 to 100 feet – with any luck, still intact. Apparently the owner of this particular house had initially wanted to lower his house but had since abandoned the effort, and now the order had come down to the men manning the hoses that the house could be brought down. One hose riveted the ground directly beneath the crib piles while the other two hoses worked the ground at the base of the house toward the rear. More people gathered along the plank walkway where Clyde stood to watch as it became evident what was about to transpire.

"That was Thomas Bremer's place," a man in a plug hat said, and checked his pocket watch. "A nickel says it comes down in under five minutes."

"You're on," another man replied. "I say ten at least. They haven't reckoned on the pipes holding it fast."

"What pipes?" another asked.

"Those boys had better watch themselves when she tumbles," a tall elderly man said, pulling at the gray beard that reached down to the middle of his greatcoat. "It's likely to land right on their heads if they're not careful."

Another man in only his shirt sleeves and a vest, standing off to the side of these wagering sidewalk engineers, who looked to be one of the site supervisors, cupped his hands over his mouth and began yelling at the man working the hose nearest the walkway. "To the right, Buddy, to the right. Ply that rock out from under there."

Over the rush of water blasting from the hoses, the impact of the jets on the cliff, and the torrent of runoff, the worker couldn't hear his supervisor's command. The man at the top of the cut aimed his hose at a second-story window and broke out the glass. One of the workmen below waved up to him and then pointed to a spot beneath the house where the earth seemed to be giving way. All three hoses were then aimed on this weak spot. Suddenly the house lurched back as if to catch itself from going over the edge, notched forward a few feet and began to tilt, and then in one slow, dramatic motion pitched over the lip of the cut, flipped onto its front side and roof, and crashed thunderously down the embankment, breaking apart instantly at all four corners and crumbling into a mound of rubble at the bottom of the cut.

From the walkway the spectators applauded and cheered as each of the three men on the giant hoses turned to the crowd, lifted his sou'wester from his head, and waved back to acknowledge the applause. Meanwhile Clyde kept his hands in his pockets and, dejected by the clamor of the spectators over the sight of the house coming down, sidled away from the scene and began walking downtown.

14. Tutor Love (1907)

LOYE HAD BEGUN TUTORING ADA SOON AFTER SHE CAME up from Tacoma and moved into Madison House. She helped her write out her letters in her writing tablet (Ada had already been taught her alphabet by Maddie) and to sound out words from her reader. She also helped Ada rehearse her multiplication table, carry numbers, and add and subtract with decimals and fractions; to learn important historical dates such as October 1492 (Christopher Columbus discovering America), July 1776 (signing of the Declaration of Independence), and November 1851 (Seattle's founding pioneers landing at Alki Point); to memorize all the American presidents and at least one important fact about each; and finally, to study maps of the United States and the world and match states and countries to their capitals and major geographical features. Loye liked to view the child as a kind of test case for her future success as a teacher, and of course Maddie, who regarded Ada as her own daughter now, fully endorsed Loye's efforts.

As time went on, the tutoring became more regular and more structured. Loye's schedule of classes at the university permitting, and depending on whether she had to substitute teach at Denny School or not, she and Ada would sit down in the den for two hours either in the morning or the afternoon, every day except for Saturday and Sunday, and devote one hour every other day to each subject, so that Mondays and Wednesdays would be for English and geography, Tuesdays and Thursdays for math and history, and Fridays for review. On Saturdays, Loye showed Ada basic fingering techniques on Maddie's upright piano or let Ada draw for her on large sheets of blank newsprint that James donated. When Loye couldn't be there to guide Ada's lessons, Maddie filled in for her.

Maddie told Loye that she eventually wanted to place Ada in school again, which Loye agreed was the proper course to take. Loye couldn't comprehend how any well-trained physician or school official who cared one scintilla for children could have given up on a girl like Ada so quickly. Shrinkage of the brain, indeed! While Ada had fallen behind for her age group, as far as Loye could discern, it was only because she had been kept out of school. And contrary to the official determination that the girl was slow, Ada had a precocity that was undeniable. She proved particularly facile with numbers and was soon working through calculations much more adroitly (and with fewer pencil scratchings) than Loye herself, who finally had to telephone her mother to send her her old high school math textbooks and notes so she could review before each lesson with Ada just to keep one step ahead of the child.

When Ada's parents were horrifically killed in their own house, Maddie took the girl in and gave her a home. Right away, Loye noticed how Ada became even more determined, and keener, in her studies. Clearly, under Maddie's care and protection, she now had the conditions to become the bright young student that Maddie and Loye knew she could be. Soon, Loye began borrowing textbooks from the Denny School where she occasionally taught and brought them back to the house for Ada's use. With financial help from Maddie, she purchased school supplies for Ada: writing tablets, a small abacus, a wood ruler, a pocket-sized atlas, pencils, erasers, a pencil sharpener, and a pencil bag. She wanted Ada to feel as much like a real student as possible. For their reading material, Loye gave Ada either the books from her own childhood or books that she checked out from the public library. It was a celebratory occasion when she escorted Ada all the way downtown on the streetcar to the immense public library and guided her in procuring her first ever library card. On Ada's thirteenth birthday in June, Loye gave her a present of Louisa May Alcott's *Little Women*. Even though the small print and long sentences challenged Ada at first, forcing her to have to read along with Loye for the first several chapters, eventually she was reading the novel on her own and as soon as she finished it she went back to Chapter One and starting reading it again.

Ada apparently had no relatives other than her parents – at least not in Seattle. So when Maddie and Loye asked the girl about her grandparents and uncles and aunts and cousins, she simply gave them a blank stare. What's more, Maddie never could find out where the parents originally came from. Eight out of ten people in Seattle were from elsewhere, Loye had read in the newspaper recently. The city's population had doubled nearly every year for the past ten years, making it impossible to know where anyone came from anymore. Ada's father had owned the lot on which the family's house had formerly rested, but as Ray learned at the tax assessor's office down at Kutzenjammer Kastle, the city had repossessed it several months earlier for unpaid taxes going back several years. Therefore, since Ada had no relatives and no inheritance, Maddie and Loye considered whether they (meaning Maddie, really) should pursue formally and legally adopting the child. Yet other than themselves, it seemed that no one even knew of the child's existence. So after much discussion on the matter, they decided that a common-law adoption would best suit all involved and simplify matters considerably. And understandably, Maddie didn't want any more wrangling with the city courts than she had already over the regrading project.

All this while, through all this commotion, Loye remained committed to her studies at the university. From September to June of each year, with only the standard breaks between academic terms for the holidays, she faithfully took the streetcar to the University District each day and from University Avenue where the streetcar dropped her off, diligently walked to her classes on campus. After the first year of general education courses, she began her course of study for the Normal Degree in the Department of Education, headed by Professor Edward Octavius Sisson. Because she felt that a well-rounded liberal arts education would serve her just as well as courses in educational psychology and the comparative study of school systems, which were required for the Normal Degree, she also took as many classes outside of the Department of Education as Professor Sisson would allow. She especially enjoyed the humanities and arts and had heard that Professor Frederick Padelford's class on the world's great classics was a must if she ever hoped to teach Homer's *Odyssey* or Dante's *Inferno* at the high school level. Yet when she looked the course up in the university catalogue and saw that it was open only to men, she vowed never to enroll in a course offered by Professor Padelford, period. She would study the classics on her own, she determined, and instead enrolled in Mrs. Ida Geenlee's normal course for students preparing to teach high school English.

When Chiridah would listen to Loye debate with herself over which classes to take each term, she would try to persuade Loye to take drama so they could read lines together and practice scenes. "I hear the university has a wonderful dramatic club," Chiridah said enthusiastically. "It's called the Hammer and Tongs, can you imagine?" Loye had to disappoint Chiridah, though, and replied that unlike her friend, she was never meant to stride the boards. While she enjoyed her oratory class, and could be moved by a fine speech, it was the rhetoric of oratory rather than the delivery that fascinated her. She especially admired one classmate in particular, an intelligent and deliberate young lady named Bertha Oldes, who could make ordinary campus issues, such as whether there should be coed classes and clubs, seem to carry as much political import as whether America should enter the Sino-Russian War. Needless to say, Bertha was also a staunch advocate for women's suffrage, as was Loye after hearing Bertha's end-of-term oration on the issue.

For eight weeks in January, February, and March, Loye also played basketball on the new ladies' basketball team at the university. The team began conditioning sessions and light practices in December, and beginning in the middle of January, played ten scheduled games over the following eight weeks. At first, Loye feared that basketball would be too demanding on top of all her course work, but it took no more time than if she belonged to one of the many service organizations or social clubs on campus – the same ones, such as the Homecoming Gala Committee and Alliance Francaise, that classmates and friends were always cajoling her join. Yet she loved basketball, and that was enough for her. Although she never said this to anyone, she hoped one day to coach the girls' team at a local high school. She loved the way the game combined dexterity with quickness, teamwork with individual skills. She also loved the camaraderie with her teammates. The only aspect of the game that she was not so fond of was the uniform the girls had to wear. The floppy white collar over the black blouse made them look like pilgrims. The puffy bloomers that reached just below the knees were not so terrible since they were loose and airy around the hips and thighs and provided ease of movement, yet the mandatory full-length black stockings and thin black flats that went with them were sinister implements of torture. The UW ladies' team did not do well Loye's first year. They won only two games, and even lost to the Seattle High School senior girls team, and worse still, later in the season lost to Loye's former team, the Tacoma Y W C A. The next year, they showed improvement, though, winning half of their games, and this year already they had beaten both the Snohomish Academy team and the Pacific Lutheran College team, with seven games still left in the season. Unfortunately, unlike men's athletics, there was not yet an official league or end-of-the-season tournament to determine a champion each year. The girls on the team played simply to best their own record from the previous year.

Not only was Loye too busy for campus clubs and organizations, she also felt that she was too busy – most of the time at least – for boys and dating. She would occasionally participate in campus-wide events such as the Plug Scrap, whereby each upperclass tried to smash the hats of the underclass immediately below it, or the Cane Rush, whereby two classes vied for supremacy by getting the most hands on the coveted oak stick placed in the middle of the Commons. Unfortunately, after two hundred students piled onto one another during last year's Cane Rush, causing several injuries, it was decided to replace the oak stick with a gigantic push ball, which many students didn't like. Some people, the less progressive-minded among the campus community, also complained that it was inappropriate for ladies to participate in such roughhouse activities ... yet Loye ignored them. As for the activity of dating, there was the boy from her botany class, Roger Whittlesey, with whom, after an afternoon of combing the campus grounds to identify and describe varieties of fern, she had nestled down beneath a Douglas fir and spent the next hour "queening." He'd asked to take her to a dance in the field house later that week, but she declined. Since he wanted to be a scientist and had no appreciation for literature or the arts, Loye quickly recognized that, as good a cuddler as he was, they ultimately would not be right for each other. Then there was the very handsome literary fellow, Brendan Coffey – who had told her about Professor Padelford's course on the classics – with bright brown eyes, bushy eyebrows, and lush auburn hair that fell in a swooping wave over his brow. She had allowed him to court her for nearly an entire quarter term, one of their favorite pastimes being to take out one of the small rowboats from the A S U W boathouse down on the lake and row over to Webster Point for a picnic lunch. They did this four times before Brendan told her that he felt they should no longer keep each other's company, and the following week Loye spotted him with pretty Laurel Anderson going up into the campus observatory at three o'clock in the afternoon on a cloudy day when, she felt fairly certain, few astronomical bodies would be visible in the sky.

So it came about that Ray Gruhlki, who slept under the same roof as she at Madison House, began increasingly to inhabit the sphere of her notice. Although they usually missed each other at the breakfast table (since Ray was a late sleeper, having usually stayed up late the night before developing his photographs), she encountered him nearly every evening at the supper table. Her initial, somewhat contradictory impression of him held true – that he was both the nervous and forward type. Yet as they became better acquainted, she could see that these characteristics resulted from an awkward combination of shyness and exuberance in him. This combination often made him come across as ill mannered, though Loye knew this was not truly the case. In nearly every respect, once initial impressions were gotten past, he was a perfect gentleman. Loye admired his commitment to photography and believed that his consuming preoccupation with it boded well for his eventual success in the field. At the supper table, he would express his discontent with working for a hack like Ned James – "The man is far overrated in his own mind," Loye remembered him saying once – and would then bemoan not having more time for his photography. But once he got past grumbling about his job and started speaking about his photography, he grew animated, telling Loye about the different shots he had gotten that day, after which there was almost no quieting him on the subject.

To his credit, he was not so self-centered that he spoke only about himself. He regularly asked Loye how her university studies were going. He also showed particular interest in her basketball activities and said he would like very much like to photograph one of her games before the season ended. He said he thought sports photography would be the next big thing in the field. "I've been working on a panning technique that allows me to photograph athletes in motion quite distinctively," he declared.

"Our team prides itself on its speed," Loye said, teasing him some, but also enjoying the boast. "So you had better practice that technique of yours thoroughly unless you want a blur of black bloomers in your photograph."

It was this kind of friendly, casual banter around the table that made Loye feel so at home at the boardinghouse and so at ease with Ray Gruhlki.

"I'll buy a high-speed lens for the bloomer shots," he retorted, and then, blushing slightly, changed the subject by asking Loye how her tutoring of Ada was coming along.

IT WAS A PREDAWN MORNING IN FEBRUARY THAT SEEMED TO mark a sure but subtle shift in Loye's acquaintanceship with Ray. Since the side window in his attic room faced south, he was the first one – up all hours of the night, as was his custom – to notice the light from the flames ferociously burning the half of the Washington Hotel that remained standing. Although the men were prohibited from going on the second floor where the ladies roomed, he notified Maddie in her bedroom, and Maddie in turn woke up Loye, Chiridah, and Ada. In robes and overcoats they all hurried outside and stood by the railing on the south end of the front porch and peered at the flames consuming the old hotel. Initially there was a small panic among the boarders, fearing the fire might spread up the hill. Yet just as they were discussing evacuating the premises, Clyde, who had already run down to the scene of the fire and was just now returning, allayed their fears by reporting that the fire trucks and water wagons were already on the hotel grounds and that the firemen, who had the blaze contained, were going to let it burn itself out.

"It's under control," he told everyone gathered on the porch. "Since there's no threat of its spreading to neighboring buildings, they're going let it bring down the rest of the hotel."

Loye stood at the porch railing with her arm around Chiridah's waist and watched the bright orange flames lap at the hulking old hotel and turn the night sky into a reddish glow. With the view of the city spread out below Denny Hill in the background, one could easily imagine that the whole city were ablaze. Carthage, she thought. As the clanging of fire trucks arriving on the scene continued to reverberate up the hill, the boarders stood silently, and solemnly, watching as if the fire were a warning to them, along with the death of Ada's parents, that Denny Hill had become an uncertain and dangerous place to live. As Loye mulled over this notion, the large turret on the back corner of the hotel crashed to the ground in a brilliant burst of flames and cinders. Soon after this, the sharply pitched, cathedral-like roof caved in on itself even more dramatically.

Throughout the early morning hours, no one dared return to their room as long as the fire continued to burn. Every half hour or so the flames would bring down another portion of the hotel until it appeared that only a large pyre burned on the smaller of the two Denny Hill humps. Finally, near dawn, a misty drizzle started to fall as a heavy fog rolled in from the Sound, and as the sky gradually softened into morning grayness, the worst of the fire burned itself out and the flames were no longer visible. Instead, a dense curtain of sooty smoke rose from the grounds where the glorious Washington Hotel had once stood so stately and ornate, now just a heap of smoldering ashes.

By this time, Chiridah and Ada had retreated into the sitting room and fallen asleep on the davenport and sofa, while Maddie had gone into the kitchen and begun preparing breakfast. Clyde and James decided to walk back down to the site to see the damage up close, talk to people on the scene, and get a story for the *Sentry* – which left Loye and Ray alone on the front porch. When Ray asked if he could bring her an overcoat to put over her robe, since the fog had also made the morning air quite chill, Loye simply wrapped her arms about herself and said, No, she was all right as she was. She remained seated on the porch rail staring out at the now unobstructed view of downtown Seattle as the city woke to a new day, and even though she and Ray did not speak another word to each other, she was grateful for his presence beside her.

15. Regrading (1907)

CLYDE WENT ALMOST DAILY TO WATCH THE ADVANCING regrading work. He would stop at one of the cuts on his way down the hill in the morning and again on his way back up the hill in the evening. With fascination – and no small measure of stealthy guilt – he observed the sheer enormity of the project, as did most of the sidewalk engineers, and tried to estimate how long it would take the giant hydraulics and steam shovels to reach Fourth and Blanchard. Most of the houses that had been near the Washington Hotel had been narrow row houses, while the houses along First and Second Avenues had been old one-story farmhouses, most of which had been leased by property owners who readily vacated them once the regrading ordinance had been passed and who now looked forward to constructing apartment buildings on their leveled lots. It was the larger private homes and boardinghouses farther up the hill that threatened to pose the more significant delay in the progress of the regrading – although, as Maddie had informed Clyde, most of the property owners to whom she had spoken were all too eager to demolish their structures and pay the 10 cents per cubic yard to Lewis & Wiley to lower their lots.

Lewis & Wiley, Inc., of Seattle, was the engineering firm that had won the latest city contract to regrade Denny Hill, combining forces with Hawley Engineering. From his frequent forays to the pits and cuts around the southwest rim of Denny Hill, Clyde came to recognize many of the men who worked for the firm. He was in Staten's Tavern, located on the crest of the hill at Battery and Fourth, a corner joint made up of three rickety tables, a beer-warped wooden bar, and an unvarnished floor with sawdust strewn across it, when a broad-chested fellow with a full beard, whom Clyde had seen manning one of the hoses, entered the tavern and sat on the barstool next to his. It seemed odd that one of the men hired to bring the hill down would patronize a tavern on the very same hill. In fact, as Rooster Staten, the tavern's owner, had told Clyde, he was shutting down in three months time and taking his business to Ballard. "Who needs all this mess and trouble," was how he put it. "By the time the regrading reaches Ballard, I'll be dead."

The bearded hose operator ordered a pitcher of Rainier beer from Rooster, and just as he was about to take his first sip he turned to Clyde and raised his glass and said, "*Helse.*"

Clyde raised his glass in kind and returned the Norwegian salutation, "*Helse,*" and then took a long swig from his beer and turned back to the man and asked, "Haven't I seen you down there working one of the hoses?"

The man swiveled on his stool mid-swallow and replied, "That's right. You one of those fellows got nothing better to do than watch us make mud?"

"I've got plenty to do," Clyde said, not appreciating the big lug's snub. "It's just that I've seen you down there is all."

Clyde was about to take his beer to one of the tables when the man said, "It's a helluvu job, I'll tell you that," and downed his beer. "That's more'an a thousand pounds a pressure coming out of that nozzle. I've been knocked on my arse more than a few times."

Clyde kept his beer on the bar, sensing the man might be trying to make up for his brusqueness, and said to him, "And you're no small man to be knocked on his arse."

The man raised his glass at this, and they both laughed.

"Come to think of it," the man went on, looking Clyde over more closely now, "I think I've seen ya down there as well."

Clyde let him look, and said, "People tell me I stand out in a crowd." He then put his hand out and introduced himself, and the man took Clyde's hand in his big paw and said his name was Ove Jensen.

"Let me fill yer beer for ya," Ove said, and reached over with his pitcher and filled Clyde's glass.

"So how do those hoses work?" asked Clyde, settling into a kind of camaraderie with the big Swede, telling himself that the man seemed friendly enough and surely couldn't be blamed for doing his job. For him, after all, it was just a job, a way to put food on the table and keep a roof over his head. Ove Jensen didn't know Maddie Ingram from Reginald H. Thomson. Lewis & Wiley probably paid him pretty well, and in keeping with the Seattle Spirit, he probably thought he was doing good by his adopted city.

"It's a marvel of engineering," Ove said, clearly honored to explain the mechanics of his job. "They have a 'giant' – that's what we call 'em for short – mounted on a ball-and-socket joint so it can rotate a full circle and the operator – that would be me – can lock it into whatever position he sets it at. There's twenty-two-inch wood stave pipe for the branch line feeding two giants with water from the bay. Whoever is manning the other giant – and myself, of course – we make the wall of the cut as vertical as we can and then undermine it from below. Most of the conglomerate comes right down of its own weight and goes straight into the flumes and out to the bay. If there's boulders, we'll cut the hoses and set a charge beneath 'em to bust 'em loose."

With this explanation, Ove finished his beer and declared he had to get back to the job site. He stood from the bar stool, faced Clyde, and said, "Why don't you come back with me and I'll show you the pumping station."

The invitation surprised Clyde – he was both alarmed and tempted by it – and yet putting his glass down on the bar, he said he would be most interested to see the pumping station. He had a momentary notion of Maddie spotting him down in the pit of the cut being escorted about by one of the regrade men and later condemning him for his betrayal of her, but he quickly realized such a notion was ridiculous. He didn't condone the project, he was just going to look around, out of curiosity, and because the Swede had invited him. Besides, Maddie would never see him since she never ventured down to the regrading sites. The visit to the site would be his secret.

Ove Jensen loped down the hill with big gulping strides with Clyde at his side. When they came to the cut between Second and Third Avenues, they paused. A house about the size of Maddie's stood at the corner with thirty-foot retaining walls on the two sides of its lot where the hoses had blasted away the dirt along the property line. Clyde didn't say anything, but knew this was the house of a holdout, someone not yet willing to regrade his property, someone perhaps holding out for a court settlement, or just on principle. The two retaining walls were little more than sheets of plywood wedged against the exposed dirt with a series of two-by-eight supports. A good solid rain would bring them down in no time.

The Swede circumvented this lot and walked to where a makeshift ramp at the north end of the cut led down into the pit where two hydraulic giants stood unmanned on their ball-and-socket joint mounts. "They're waiting to hear what to do about that house there," he said by way of explanation for both the house with the retaining walls and the stalled work of the giant hoses. He guided Clyde through the pit and down to First Avenue, which had been regraded long ago and was already smoothed out for carriage and motorcar traffic, with new plank sidewalks and even several new buildings going up. At Western Avenue they walked down a steep wooden staircase and crossed the railroad tracks along Railroad Avenue to get to the waterfront.

"This one pumping station," the Swede announced, beginning his tour by pointing ahead to a large square clapboard shed situated at the end of one of the piers along the waterfront, "pumps 7,000 gallons of water a minute, and each day about 12 million gallons." His pride in reciting these figures showed in his serious demeanor.

They walked out onto the pier, just south of which a narrow trestle extended several dozen yards into the bay. Clyde knew already that this trestle supported the main flume that carried the run-off from the sluicing into the bay. At the shed located at the end of the pier, the Swede knocked once on the door and then opened it and walked inside. The interior of the shed was damp and steamy, and until Clyde's eyes could adjust, very dark.

"Heya," Ove said to the three men inside, whom Clyde began to make out through the shadows. Two men in dark wool suits, bow ties, and derbies sat on overturned wood crates around a round cable spindle they used as a table. They were sweating profusely and slapping down cards. One of the men looked up, saw the Swede in the doorway, and shouted, "Come here, Ove, and sit your butt down. You're our fourth. We can play a real hand now." Behind these two, farther back in the shed, a tall man in glasses wearing a long blue work coat, heavy work gloves, and a brakeman's cap held a kerosene lantern up to a glass pressure gauge on a large boiler tank, took the reading, and then turned a tiller-sized valve attached to a shaft that extended down into the floorboards and beneath the shed.

He took his glasses off and wiped the condensation from them with his neckerchief.

"Hey, boss," Ove said to the man, whom Clyde assumed was the operating engineer for the pumping station. "I bringed along a pal to show him the station."

"You know we don't take to havin' visitors just droppin' in on us," the engineer said, reprimanding him.

"What about these two jakes here then?" the Swede answered back, indicating the two men playing cards.

"Alright then," the engineer said, "show him about ... and then out with yas." The engineer pulled a corncob pipe from the pocket of his jacket and stepped past the Swede and Clyde without any acknowledgment of Clyde's presence, and at the door announced over his shoulder, "I'm stepping out for a smoke."

Ove took Clyde by the sleeve of his jacket and guided him farther back into the shed.

"Come on, Ove," one of the cardplayers summoned. "The both of you ... a quick hand while the boss is outside."

"Ya, sure," Ove told them. "After." He then explained to Clyde how the pump station worked. There were two engines, steam and electric power – though he was most keen on showing off the electric engine. "The transformer is outside," he said. "About 25,000 volts comes into the station and the transformer steps that down to an operating voltage of 2,000. Still enough to kill a man." He then went into detail on the 1,000-horsepower Westinghouse induction motor that was direct-connected to a twelve-inch, four-stage Ogdensburg turbine pump. "It runs at 550 rpm. That's rotations per minute. It takes that much power to deliver the water pressure up the hill to the hydraulics."

Clyde indicated that he was duly impressed by nodding to everything Ove told him and asking occasional questions about conduction and voltage and such – although in truth he was only moderately interested. It was clear to Clyde that the Swede was tired of working the hoses and was booking for an engineer's position since, as he told Clyde, "They plan to build two more pump stations to finish the job on the hill." Mostly,

Clyde was strangely intrigued to be standing, in effect, at the heart of the operation that threatened to take his and Maddie's home from them. It was like traipsing behind enemy lines to discover the enemy lived ordinary work-a-day lives – worked jobs, drank beer, played cards, smoked pipes – and hadn't a clue really about the people they were engaged in pitch battle with, or even that they were engaged in a battle with anyone at all ... that is, until one of the cardplayers looked up and asked the Swede about the house that was holding up that day's work.

"They should just bring it down," the other cardplayer spat out, and slapped a card down on the cable spindle. "Wouldn't take long t'all."

Ove seemed embarrassed by this talk, and his embarrassment made Clyde think – as did the Swede's reticence when they had walked past the holdout house – that perhaps he was more sensitive to the antagonisms being stirred up by the regrading than the average regrade worker, which might be why he wanted off the frontlines of the project and assigned to one of the pump stations.

A FEW WEEKS LATER, WHEN CLYDE HEARD THAT EQUIPMENT along the Denny Hill regrading had been sabotaged, the Swede momentarily crossed his mind. But when Clyde ran into him again in Staten's Tavern, he informed Clyde that he had been taken off the giants and made an assistant to the operating engineer at one of the new pump stations along the waterfront. Clyde concluded that not only would Ove not have risked his promotion by tampering with the equipment, but it was his respect and knowledge of that very equipment that had gotten him promoted. In fact, he turned angrier than a baited bear when Clyde mentioned the sabotaging incident, how someone had put large rocks down the flumes to clog them up and slashed the hoses between the giants and the sluicing pumps, which served as the transfer stations between the main pumping stations and the hydraulics.

"I'd like to be first in line at that fellow," Ove snarled into his beer.

Everyone else – the newspapers, the sidewalk engineers, even residents of the hill – said the saboteur was probably one of the Denny Hill holdouts. This scattering of people – those who had refused to sign the ordinance, had refused to abandon their property and get off the hill, had refused to pay L.B. Gullett, House Mover, to lower their house or business to the new grade, and had refused to pay Lewis & Wiley to sluice away the ground beneath their house or business so that the regrading could proceed smoothly – were becoming well known to everyone involved with the project. Most people were already moving off Denny Hill, turning the neighborhood into a ghost town. Those who remained were generally counted among the holdouts, although not all were: some were simply waiting for the right time and price to leave. It saddened Clyde to see the once crowded and active neighborhood become a gloomy vacant place where an ever-present sense of doom seemed to stalk the streets. One day a team of surveyors crisscrossed Denny Hill setting stakes with strips of red cloth flying from them at all four corners of lots that were not to be regraded, unmistakably marking the holdouts. Yet when Clyde suggested yanking the stakes from the ground so Madison House wouldn't have to endure the stigma, Ray pointed out that without them the regraders wouldn't know where to stop sluicing and Maddie could lose untold yardage from her property before they could be stopped. Maddie then announced to all the boarders that she would let the stakes with their red flags stand, that to her they marked her protest against the regrading and were a badge of honor.

Regrettably, there were no organized protests against the regrading. Clyde and Maddie circulated a petition of their own opposing the project, but when almost no one agreed to sign it, they figured people on the hill had had enough of petitions, and moreover, that when it came right down to it, more people, deluded into believing Reginald H. Thomson's promises of augmented property values, favored the regrading than opposed it. Clyde counted eleven lots on the hill, including Jules Redelsheimer's lot and the Redemptorists' square-block compound, that had been *staked* – the term he and Maddie used wryly, knowing it had once promised the riches of a gold claim. They tried to imagine what the hill – if they would still be able to call it that once the project was completed – would look like with these eleven islands. Could such a bizarre landscape work, whereby Madison House and the ten other lots remained elevated (in

Maddie's case by more than 100 feet) above the rest of the neighborhood, including the streets and alleys that led up to the elevated lots? Neither one of them could imagine it. Yet neither could they imagine the neighborhood without the hill, regraded to a barren plain.

When he walked about what remained of the neighborhood or tarried around the regrading sites, Clyde sympathized with whoever was sabotaging the regrading equipment – and in his heart urged the saboteur on. He even had a good hunch about who this saboteur might be. His hunch arose the day he encountered a small stooped man with pale, frantic eyes, weathered forehead and cheeks, and a coarse overgrown beard at the Third Avenue cut near Lenora Street. The man appeared beside him suddenly when no one else was around. Clyde neither saw nor heard him approach; he was just suddenly there, like a phantom. He was dirty and looked like he might have been an old miner hard on his luck. He stood next to Clyde without speaking a word, making Clyde uneasy as he watched the workmen below standing about the rail tracks on which the waste cars were hauled up next to the cut to be loaded by the steam shovels.

"That track needs repairin'," the man mumbled through his beard and without looking up at Clyde.

Although the man was barely audible, Clyde detected a note of bemusement in his voice. When he looked sidewise at the man, the man looked up at him with a smirk on his parched, peeling lips.

"You know that for a fact?" Clyde asked, in half question, half statement.

"They're probably wondering where all the spikes went to," the man mumbled, and looked back down toward the tracks.

Clyde looked down at the six or seven workmen huddled about the tracks. The rails were laid on heavy crossties and partial trellises to keep them from sinking into the soft earth. Two additional men were walking down the track coming toward the group of workmen. They had apparently been counting because one called out, "Twelve missing on my side," followed by the other who shouted, "Fifteen on mine." One of the men in the group, the site supervisor, pulled his hat off his head and seemed about to throw it in the mud. He shouted at the other men to go find spikes and get the rails secured so they could bring the waste cars in and get back to work. When the crew scattered, leaving the site supervisor to himself to contemplate the despiked rails, he did so only briefly before raising his head and looking about the regrading site. When he turned in the direction of Clyde and the stooped, haggard man standing at the top of the cut, the site supervisor paused long enough to take notice of them and then walked away from where he stood, heading down the rails to where the waste cars were lined up with a small steam engine idling behind them.

The old man beside Clyde took his left hand from the pocket of his tattered coat and held out his palm with something in it for Clyde to see. Clyde looked down and realized it was a rail spike. The man snickered and slid the spike back into his coat pocket.

"A souvenir," he said, "for what they done to my house on Jackson Street ... and what they done again to my house on the hill here. Ya can't stop 'em, I'll tell ya that. All a soul can do is slow 'em down." The man eyed Clyde more seriously now, scrutinizing him. "You live up here on the hill, don't ya?"

Clyde nodded.

"I knowed I'd seen ya around. Aren't ya gonna move out, take off, sell out, whatever it is ya have to do to get clear of this mess."

Clyde nodded in the negative this time.

"That's what I thought too," the man went on, "that you're one of the holdout people ..." He paused and squinted at Clyde. "That's why I showed you the spike. I'm not stupid, ya know."

Clyde had kept quiet this whole while, but knowing that he ought to say something, he asked, "Where did you used to live?"

The man then told him how he had once owned a small house on Jackson Street, and how that had been regraded, and then how he'd moved up to lower Denny Hill, just east of the hotel that came down not long ago, and was renting one of the row houses over there until they regraded that side of the hill as well. Twice in two years he'd lost his home and now he didn't live anywhere. He slept sometimes in the train tunnel they were digging at the south end of town or in the alleys downtown or anywhere he could find shelter. At night, he said with a raised eyebrow at Clyde, he had plenty of opportunity for mischief.

Clyde felt sorry for the man in his displacement, and wondered if Maddie and he would eventually share the same plight – be made to wander the city streets, intent on retaliation, feebly and desperately seeking some kind of revenge on those who had cast them out.

"I trust you," the man said to Clyde, with a poke at Clyde's ribs with the rail spike.

Clyde stepped back from the man and stood looking at him for several long moments. "Be careful," he warned him, looking straight into the man's pale eyes, and without saying anything further walked away.

He understood the man might be looking for a cohort in his mischief. Yet, angry as Clyde was at the injustice of the regrading and at the people who so readily complied with the project, he wasn't inclined toward the sort of resistance (if you could call it that) that the old man had taken up. Ultimately, it seemed futile. And far too dangerous. So if anything, Clyde pitied the poor fellow, and realized he ought to steer clear of him in the future.

OVER THE NEXT SEVERAL MONTHS, THE SABOTAGING CONtinued at the rate of one or two incidents a week. Clyde would occasionally spot the haggard old man lingering about one of the regrading sites, mixing in with the other spectators, even betting on a house about to be brought down. He would also see him regularly pulling a bottle out from underneath his coat and taking long pulls from it. As the weeks went by, the man appeared more worn-down and wane, and on several occasions Clyde would break his vow to steer clear of him and bring the old man a ham sandwich or several salmon biscuits from Maddie's kitchen.

One day, while Clyde was at Third and Wall checking out how far the regrading had advanced up the northeast side of the hill, a man dressed in a worsted wool suit and wearing a bowler came up to him where he stood. Clyde vaguely recognized the man but couldn't quite place him. He had with him another fellow who, from the look of his mud-splattered overalls, Clyde gathered was one of the workmen on the regrading crew. They approached him, it seemed, with a clear purpose in mind, which instantly put Clyde on his guard.

The first man, whom Clyde now recognized as the site supervisor he'd seen the day the spikes went missing from the rail tracks, gave Clyde a shove on the shoulder to get his attention.

"What's your problem, Mack," Clyde barked at him, ready to slug him if he tried that again.

"Nothing with me," the man said. "Just wanted to see if you were the ape jack I thought you were."

The second man stepped forward now. "You're one a those who won't let us do our jobs, ain't that right? One a that gang of holdouts up on the hill," he said, spraying Clyde with his tobacco-stained spittle as he spoke.

Clyde wasn't going to say a word to this. He knew better – knew that whatever he said these mud lubbers would turn it against him. He looked from one to the other and back, letting them know that he wasn't about to take his eyes off them so they could sucker punch him.

"You also know who's been having their fun with our equipment, ain't that right," the second one went one. "Maybe you've even had a hand in it."

The man in the suit took a step closer to Clyde then, and in a low, threatening voice said, "You look funny all right, but you don't look *that* stupid. I'm going to tell you this, though. It's awfully odd how you happen to always be around watching us like you're looking for your chance and then being one of the obstinate sumsabitches that won't regrade like the rest. Don't you think that's odd? You can see, can't you, why we might get a little suspicious."

Clyde was still not saying anything. He wondered how he had gotten tagged as one of the holdouts? They knew where he lived and probably took him as one of the owners of Madison House – and in effect, since everything he cherished and hoped for was at stake in the house, including Maddie, wasn't that the case? Couldn't he rightfully lay claim to the house after so many years? Certainly, if not the legal owner of the house, he was its keeper. And as such, he most certainly opposed the regrading. They were right about that.

"I don't give a mule's ass what you think," Clyde said. "Maybe you oughtta find different work if you can't take care of your own equipment." He looked at both men and stood his ground.

The workman took a step closer and Clyde clenched up, ready to flail on them both if it came to that. He had only been in two fights in his life – once in Neah Bay, when he had to prove himself to the rest of the Makah kids by taking on an older and stronger boy who'd been bullying him, and a few years later, when a young tough tried to push him off his spot at the sorting tables at the Cle Elum mines and he had to push right back. It didn't matter how many fights he'd been in, though. He knew that. Rather, what really mattered had everything to do with whether you could turn brutal and vicious enough at the right moment. Whether you were willing to take your life for granted to the degree that it no longer meant anything to you. It didn't matter how many fights you had been in then, because at that point it wasn't fighting at all. It was survival, ruthless and absolute. And a willingness to die. Understanding this, not in your head but in your blood, was also the best incentive for avoiding fights.

Apparently the two men could see that Clyde wasn't going to be cowered by them.

The first one said, "It's only a matter of time for you," and put his arm around the workman and pulled him away from his face-off with Clyde. "Just a matter of time," he repeated over his shoulder, as the two of them headed back down the edge of the cut to the work site below.

Clyde stayed where he was as the two men retreated. He wasn't about to just run scared, and as they walked back down the plank walkway they both turned a couple of times to see Clyde looking down at them from the top of the cut. When they reached the pit, the second one climbed behind one of the two giant hoses set up at the base of the cut while the first one walked over to a nearby sluicing pump. Moments later they were aiming the 1,000-pound spray at Clyde, trying to chase him away, yet the spray couldn't reach where he stood, and after several minutes of watching it fall short even as the workman behind the nozzle tried to maneuver it higher, Clyde decided he'd had enough of the cat-and-mouse game and ambled back up the hill.

The encounter with the two men had the benefit of snapping Clyde out of the hypnotic interest he'd been under in visiting the work sites almost daily to watch the regrading. From then on he stayed away. Like Maddie, he came and went along Sixth Avenue where the work crews had not yet begun to gnaw away at the hill. About this same time, he also noticed, the incidents of sabotage became more infrequent and then ceased altogether. Since Clyde no longer visited the work sites, he didn't know if the stooped little man was still around, had just gone elsewhere, or perhaps had been arrested. One clue was that the newspapers reported that Pinkerton Security guards had been brought in to watch the work sites at night. So maybe the old man had just wised up and stopped his mischief. Clyde hoped so.

However, during this same period, there was a reprieve from the regrading, or at least a slowing of its advance up the hill, as the work was suspended by court order to allow for the hearings and trials that were being scheduled as various property owners opted to sue the city for damages rather than settle for the terms presented in the regrading ordinance. During this time, it almost felt to Clyde as if life were returning to normal on Denny Hill, returning to the peaceful way it been before all the regrading commotion.

Although Maddie expressed feeling more tired than usual, and seemed more downcast than ever, Clyde attributed her fatigue and melancholy to her ongoing worry about Madison House and figured that she simply needed a break from thinking about it so much. To give her a chance to rest during the day, he arranged to do her daily errands for her. He also enlisted Ada to run down the hill on a moment's notice in case something came up that Maddie needed that he'd not gotten on his rounds. Though Maddie said she missed her daily walk down the hill, she also commented on how good it felt to just lounge about the house and not worry about this and that. Eventually Clyde could see some of her vitality returning, and only wished that he could join her now and then in lounging about the house. Yet as the November elections neared and everyone in Ned James's office anticipated their boss's defeat in his race for the state senate, Ray tipped Clyde off that the attorney planned to close his Seattle law office as soon as the election was over and embark on an extended European tour—which meant Clyde would have to get on the stick and find a new job.

16. Gold and Loss (1897–1899)

MADDIE ENTERED THE DARK KITCHEN FROM THE BACK stairway and sensed Laurette already there. She lit the three-way gas lamp that hung from the center of the ceiling ... and still she felt Laurette's presence in the chair beside the stove where Maddie had placed it so her friend would not catch chill, knowing how the back pantry let in such a terrible draft. What became of Laurette, where she went when she wasn't in her chair by the stove, Maddie dared not fathom. Laurette was not the kind of spirit to stray through the big boardinghouse. She only haunted – if *haunt* was the proper word for such a gentle soul – the simple straight-back chair with barley-twist legs, the only piece of furniture to survive the fire set by Laurette's husband that destroyed their home in Dawson City and took her life so many years ago.

Maddie picked up the scoop from the tin coal bucket beside the cast-iron stove and shook several lumps of coal into the furnace compartment through the side hatch. The brand-new gas stove with embossed nickel trimming that Loye was after her to order from the Sears, Roebuck catalog could never heat the house as well as this old half-ton Wehrle stove did. She was content with her old stove and wouldn't trade it in for another even if it were given to her... although there were certainly plenty of other items from the big "wish book" that she coveted, such as the deluxe talking machine or the Beckwith organ, items which, if she could only afford them, she would place in the front parlor for the evening entertainment of her boarders.

She closed the stove's hatch and studied the chair. No proof positive of Laurette's presence existed – except for the way the chair pronounced itself in the room, immune from the shadows the lamp cast throughout the rest of the large kitchen. As the stove heated, Maddie waited, and wondered to herself if spirits actually feel such damp chill – the kind of bone-quivering chill she endured throughout Seattle's tedious wet winters, a chill in many ways far worse than the unthinkable cold she'd survived in the Yukon during her two long years there. She supposed the damp, even more so than the cold, would prove inimical to a spirit, clinging, encumbering, enervating its essential vapors ... though really she knew nothing of such matters. She was not even wholly convinced there was an afterlife, what with Loye with her college education having talked up Mr. Thomas Huxley's *a*-gnosticism to her so much lately. So she still waited for the perceptual evidences to present themselves. Dear as Laurette was to her, and as tragic as her death had been, Maddie feared it might all be, as Chester would have told her, the product of her far-flung female imagination. If only she had genuine proof, a sign, then she could take the situation in hand, she could consult an expert (of which there were plenty in the city), and she could learn the proper procedures for the care and sustenance of a house spirit – or in this case, a chair spirit – and thereby do right by her friend.

IT TOOK THE MEN TWO DAYS AFTER THEIR PARTY ARRIVED in Dawson City to find the agent who could contract them out to work along the Eldorado Creek. The man warned them that both the Eldorado and the Bonanza Creek had been already staked their entire length and that if Chester and Morris wanted to stake their own claim they would have to look elsewhere. The man then offered to sell them a map that identified several areas between the Indian River to the south and the Klondike River to the north where a miner might still stake a claim. "There's gold out there," the agent assured them. "Plenty of it too. Fields as big as the Eldorado and Bonanza. But you have to find them and stake your claim to them."

Chester purchased the map and he and Morris agreed to contract out to the Eldorado gold fields and after they'd earned enough, they would stake their own claim along one of the creeks indicated on the map.

"That's about the best way to go about it," said the man, preparing the paperwork that would send them out to Eldorado Creek.

Chester reported all this to Maddie and Laurette when he and Morris caught up with them that afternoon of their first full day in Dawson City. The four of them had taken a room at the Martony Hotel on Front Street. It was nothing more than a two-story clapboard building that had been put up within the last eight months along with most every other building in town. The clatter of hammering and the whir of sawing were a constant amidst the general clamor from the street that rose to their second-floor room. The city was building itself up as fast as it could. Walking about the streets yesterday, through the crowds of men clustered on the sidewalks in front of saloons and dance halls and gambling joints, Maddie could see that about half the city was still made up mostly of tents. Many folks had hauled their flat-bottomed boat up onto some empty lot or another, pitched their tent on top of it, and then used the boat as the foundation for the wooden shack they were constructing around the tent. A good many buildings were simply rough-hewn logs chinked with mud. Others had high, ornate facades, giving the appearance of a palatial interior, but when Maddie stepped inside these buildings she could see they were nothing more than big one-room sheds. Even though the men had told their wives to stay in the room at the Martony, Maddie and Laurette were restless, and curious, and wanted to look around. Besides, Maddie knew well enough that Chester and Morris weren't just heading off to church when they left them in the hotel room that first night in Dawson. One of them, Chester had explained, would have to stand watch through the night over their outfit that was still piled out on the small pier; but the other, he failed to say, was free to roam the Dawson City streets.

The raucousness of the town astounded Maddie and Laurette; it almost made Seattle's Tenderloin district look tame by comparison. Half the men were drunk and the other half well on their way to being drunk. Piano music and laughter poured out of the dance halls and theaters, and shouting and occasional gunfire sounded from every saloon. From Front Street, where more than a dozen steamers and paddlewheelers were docked and where most of the hotels were situated to accommodate prospectors coming off the boats, a tide of people spread out through the side streets. King Street, where the Palace Grand Theater was located, seemed the most raucous street of all. Maddie and Laurette looked inside the front entrance of the Palace Grand and as they did a man called to them, "Come on in, ladies. Show's about to begin," and they backed away from the theater entrance and continued down the plank sidewalk. At the Stampede Dance Hall, they could see more young women inside at this single location than they had seen yet in the entire city, where the ratio of men to women seemed about fifty-to-one. The women, with their hair done up in high buns about their head, corsages pinned to their blouses, tousled and flung their flowing skirts and petticoats about, beckoning the men to come dance with them. There were plenty of takers, too, as men streamed into the dance hall from the street, strode right up to the women, escorted them to the bar for a glass of champagne or hauled them out onto the dance floor for a twirl or two before they both drifted off to the row of private booths in the far back corner of the dance hall.

At Madame Tremblay's General Store on King Street, Maddie and Laurette treated themselves each to a soft drink, then began their walk back to the hotel along Queen Street. Between Second Avenue and Front Street, they passed a narrow row of one-story alley houses that in the lengthening night were dimly light by kerosene lanterns hung outside every other doorway. Men slinked in and out of the alley, and standing in several doorways or leaning out the front windows, half-dressed women in nothing more than their underskirts and corset covers lounged about making small talk to one another and flirtatiously addressing each man that walked past. A dog lay curled up in front of one doorway and paid no mind as men stepped over it to enter the house. Maddie looked down the length of the street and at the farthest end of the alley suddenly spotted the figure of a man she thought she recognized – Chester, no less – exit a house with a fast step and swiftly turn the corner at the next block. Yet because she saw only the figure's back and it was so dark and at such a distance, she dismissed the idea that the figure was her husband and assured herself that it could have been anybody – though the image of the figure, and an accompanying doubt, lingered in her mind.

"There're too many men in this town," Maddie said to Laurette, who was peering down the alley with a look of curiosity on her face, and then followed Maddie as she moved on.

The next afternoon when Chester came up to the room to tell them about contracting to work Eldorado Creek, he also informed them that women weren't permitted in the camps and so Maddie and Laurette would have to remain in Dawson. "We're going to haul our outfit to camp," he told them, "and then one of us, me or Morris, will come back to town every month or so to cash in our gold and make sure you two girls are all right." He then handed Maddie one hundred dollars – money he hadn't divulged having the day before – and told them this should tide them over for the first month at least.

Morris came by a short while later to speak to Laurette, and the next morning the two women said their goodbyes to their husbands as the two men headed off into the wilderness. As soon as they were gone, Maddie quickly calculated that one hundred dollars would not stretch very far if she and Laurette had to stay in the Martony Hotel all month and remembered seeing a "For Let" sign in a window above an outfitting store on Duke Street. She suggested to Laurette that they look into it without further delay, and by that afternoon they were moved into their two-room apartment above the store – with a double bed, washstand, and dresser and mirror in the one room, and a two-plate stove and a table with four matching straight-back chairs with barley-twist legs in the second room. She then went back to the Martony Hotel and left a note for Chester at the front desk saying where she and Laurette had gone to.

Maddie didn't know what to make of the arrangements they had made with their husbands. In one respect she was relieved not to have to venture into the wilderness, but in another respect she was frustrated at being stranded in Dawson City for one month, two months, six months, who knew how long? For the first two weeks after the men's departure, Laurette pined for her husband, crying nearly every night in her loneliness until Maddie held her in her arms in the double bed they shared and cradled her to sleep. Maddie was grateful to have a friend like Laurette by her side, especially as the cold and dark of winter came on and they spent more hours each day cooped up in their small apartment. After the first week, Maddie, already growing restless, entered the outfitters store below to offer her talents as a seamstress and was put to work on the spot by E. W. Blayton, the store's proprietor, sewing pelts and furs into hats, gloves and boot linings at a rate of one dollar for each item, which E. W. Blayton then sold for five to ten dollars apiece. When Laurette finally began to get past her pining for her absent husband, she got up one morning, unpacked a dress pattern and various fabrics from her trunk, and just like that began cutting, sewing, and trimming a new dress for herself. Maddie was amazed.

"I had no idea you were such a dressmaker," she exclaimed to Laurette over the tea they made each morning on their small cookstove. "I can't wait to see the finished dress."

"It's just something to pass the time," Laurette said in her diffident manner. "My mother showed me how when I was a little girl." She unrolled several yards of checkered tan chiffon and several more yards of striped poplin cloth. "I could make you one if you like," she said, glancing up at Maddie. "I would just need to take your measurements."

Maddie said she would be thrilled to have a new dress, especially one that Laurette made for her, and then suggested that E. W. Blayton might let Laurette use the sewing machine in the back room of the outfitting store downstairs. Laurette agreed that that would make her task a whole lot easier.

When Chester, instead of Morris, returned to Dawson in December, Laurette cried even harder than she had when her husband first left for the gold fields five weeks earlier. While Laurette was downstairs sewing her dresses, Chester brought Maddie up to the bed in the apartment. He was rough with her, not just hungry for her, but forceful and almost angry seeming … and she did not like it. After his first day back, he mostly stayed away, stumbling back to the apartment drunk well after Maddie and Laurette had fallen asleep, and then waking them up with his fumbling drunkenness. Once, when he had undressed and tried to climb into the bed with them, Maddie had to drive him into the next room where she'd laid a pallet and bedroll on the floor next to the stove for him. In the morning, Chester revealed to her that he and Morris had earned just enough working the mines for the company that owned most of the Eldorado stake to resupply themselves for another month, and so it was a good thing that she was working for the outfitters because there was little to spare from that month's take. He told her, too, that he and Morris had made only one expedition, with a few other men and their dog teams, to the places on the map that supposedly remained to be staked, yet everywhere they looked either claims had already been staked or else there wasn't a mite of gold dust to be found and they ended up returning to the Eldorado camp. He assured Maddie that he and Morris would eventually stake a claim and that when they did, they would strike paydirt in no time, and all of them would go back to Seattle filthy rich. "There're a lot of men out there right now is all," he said. "The cold is driving a good many back to town, and that's when we'll have our chance."

The next day, the same morning on which Chester left Dawson to return to the Eldorado camp, was the coldest day yet. Snow had covered the ground since the second week after their arrival in Dawson, but the temperature until now had remained relatively mild, hovering just below the freezing point. This day, though, was suddenly and dramatically different. Every chimney in the city bellowed smoke, and every windowpane was coated in frost on the outside and, if the inhabitants had any wits about them, covered with broadcloth on the inside to try to keep out the drafts as best as possible. Maddie sewed herself and Laurette extra thick fur hats and gloves from beaver pelts and also made them each bear fur slippers to wear about the apartment. Laurette, meanwhile, bargained to make a dress for the lady friend of a man who'd come into the outfitting store in exchange for the two wool blankets he'd just purchased from E. W. Blayton. The two blankets went straight onto her and Maddie's bed that night and warmed their bodies and lifted their spirits considerably.

Yet when the women received word from someone who'd come to town from the Eldorado camp that neither Chester nor Morris would be returning to Dawson for the next three months on account of having to wait out the worst of the winter in camp, Laurette grew despondent. Maddie tried to cheer her up by bringing several fir sprigs into the apartment and decorating them with red and white ribbons for Christmas, and giving her a tailored silk belt for a present on Christmas morning and a splash of whiskey in her tea, but nothing seemed to hearten her. Then on the eve of the New Year, Maddie suggested that they go to a dance hall.

"We won't tell anyone," Maddie said when Laurette gave her a concerned look, and added, "We deserve a little amusement, don't we? How long can we stay cooped up in these rooms without going stir-crazy?"

The Klondyke Dance Emporium was one of a dozen dance halls in Dawson City. As best as Maddie could tell, and as far as was even possible in Dawson, it seemed to be a semi-respectable establishment. Even though women were not typically allowed into dance halls unaccompanied, unless it was understood that they were good-time girls, Maddie didn't care, she wanted to drink champagne with Laurette and dance with a man or two. Besides, it was still early by Dawson standards, only ten o'clock, when the two of them entered the dance hall and found a table not far from the piano, where a man in shirt sleeves, a bowtie, and a bowler sat mechanically running his fingers over the keys. The Emporium had not even gotten busy yet by any stretch. So when the piano man began playing an upbeat waltz, Maddie and Laurette stood up, stepped onto the dance floor, and commenced guiding each other about in their best rendition of a waltz step. The piano man smiled over his shoulder at them and they laughed at themselves and when the number was over they scurried back to their seats. When a handsome young man in a striped suit with a pressed collar came up to their table and politely asked Laurette for the next dance, she looked to Maddie, who appreciated the young man's appearance and manners, and nodded to her friend to go ahead. That night, Laurette danced with three other men and Maddie with two. They were both more than a little tipsy on champagne – which the gentlemen they danced with kept buying them – when they agreed they'd had enough amusement for one night, declined all further invitations to dance, and after retrieving their coats, hats, and gloves from the coatcheck girl, wove their way arm in arm through the cold streets and back to their apartment above the outfitting store.

The next week, Laurette made two new dresses after buying extra fabric from a well-stocked dry goods store in town. Also that week, as she confessed to Maddie only after she'd returned to the apartment late one night, she'd gone dancing again, this time at the Floradora Dance Hall. Maddie didn't know how to respond to this revelation, and was even more shocked when, the following week, Laurette told her that she planned to work at the Floradora to earn a little extra money.

"I can make thirty-five dollars a week just for dancing with the fellas," she explained to Maddie, "on top of a quarter for every drink I sell."

Maddie made sure that Laurette could plainly see what was on her mind when Laurette told her this so casually. Though she looked sternly at Laurette, inside Maddie wanted to cry. They both knew well enough that most dance hall girls provided services to men above and beyond simply keeping them company at their table or letting them lead them across the dance floor. Many of the same girls who worked in the dance halls resided in Paradise Alley, which Maddie had learned was what the locals called the long row of alley houses that she and Laurette had walked past their first night in Dawson City. Now Maddie felt responsible for bringing Laurette to the Klondyke Dance Emporium on that New Year's Eve night and, far worse, worried what would become of her friend if she couldn't talk her out of becoming a dance hall girl at the Floradora.

"It's okay," Laurette reassured her. "I'm still waiting for my gold king to come home. It's just that we need the money. And it's something I can do, somewhere I can go … " She looked about the apartment in which the cold had kept them penned up every night and most days, and then came up to Maddie and hugged her. "When Morris returns and we have more money, I'll quit it for sure."

Maddie could not counter her friend's reasoning. She enjoyed the dance halls herself, and in a way she envied Laurette's adventuresomeness – though she also knew of the perils involved. Of course Laurette was lonely, as was she, and no doubt longed for the companionship and diversion of the dance hall even more than the money she would make. Perhaps, Maddie wondered, if she were as attractive as Laurette – whose soft, almost babyish features and abundant brown hair gave her such a gentle, becoming beauty – maybe then she herself would venture out just as Laurette was doing. The notion had more than a little appeal. She missed having a man's body beside her, and on top of her – and in her. She missed his rank smell and salty sweetness. She missed giving him his pleasure, and she missed having her own. Yet, beyond just how a girl looked, Maddie knew she also lacked the bold spirit for such audacious adventures, just as she also knew she would worry for her friend and would try to make sure Laurette did not get into any trouble. She would miss her friend's company upon an evening as well, especially now that darkness presided over most of the daytime hours as well as the long nights.

THE MEN REMAINED IN CAMP ALL WINTER. THOUGH SHE didn't like it, Maddie knew that's just how it was – that the banks of the creeks were mined during the winter months and when the spring thaw came the pay gravel was sluiced with the runoff from the snow melt. Come spring, when Chester and Morris returned to Dawson, she and Laurette would know whether their husbands had struck paydirt or not. Even if they never managed to stake a claim of their own, if the claim they'd contracted to work came through in a big way, they'd still do all right. The prospect gave her hope. Hope that Chester would find his long-sought-after riches, that Laurette and Morris would be reunited, and that she would finally get to return to Seattle. Sometimes, though, sustaining this sliver of hope in the long darkness and severe cold of the Far North seemed to challenge Maddie beyond what she thought she could endure. Sometimes, she thought that if the Yukon and Klondike Rivers weren't both frozen over solid, she might jump into one or another of those rivers and have an end to all this misery.

By February, Laurette was spending every night at the Floradora Dance Hall and returning to their rooms above the outfitting store well past midnight. She slept most of the day in the double bed, and Maddie would only see her up and about as she drank a cup of tea in the early evening and dressed to go back to the dance hall. With her extra money, she bought herself two new dresses, since she no longer had time to make them herself. Maddie thought the store-bought dresses were not nearly as pretty or well made as Laurette's own. She also bought long silk evening gloves and two new hats with taffeta flowers bursting from them, which Maddie thought a bit extravagant for life in the Yukon. Then one night Laurette did not return to their rooms at all, and in the bitter, lifeless cold of the morning Maddie went out looking for her. An hour later, when Maddie came back, Laurette was in the bed sleeping soundly, her store-bought dress thrown on the floor in the corner of the room. Maddie put several lumps of coal into the small stove and went downstairs to sew several pairs of gloves – relieved that Laurette had returned safely, but angry at having been made to worry so over her.

Later that afternoon, when she came back upstairs, she came right out and accused Laurette of being a good-time girl. Still in bed, Laurette simply rolled over with a grumble and faced the wall as if she hadn't heard Maddie's charges. When Maddie said the words again, this time loud and clear, Laurette sat up abruptly and said to Maddie sternly, "What of it? What if I am? I don't need you mollycoddling me. I can take care of myself," and slid back down into the bed and pulled the covers up over her head.

"There are men out there who will hurt you," Maddie said, fighting back the tears gathering in her eyes. "I don't want my wonderful sweet Laurette to get hurt." Maddie knew she was contradicting her own longings in reproaching Laurette, in taking on the tone of righteous guardian with her friend. But she also knew that what she said was true. Many girls in Dawson City were beaten and abused, chewed up and discarded, like so much dog meat.

Laurette then sat up again and looked at Maddie standing in the corner across the room from the bed. "I won't get hurt," she said. "I promise." She looked so sweetly at Maddie that Maddie felt she would give anything to deliver Laurette from this wretched town and these horrid circumstances. "The girls take care of one another. That's how they make it."

Maddie looked kindly, sorrowfully on Laurette, and heard the sincerity in her voice. She would not, she decided, speak Morris's name to her right now, even though she'd planned to. That would just be too cruel. In many ways, Laurette was right about a girl trying to make it in Dawson. There were few other options. Unless a girl was already married to a miner – which often didn't work out, as she seemed to be discovering for herself – then being a good-time girl was about a girl's only chance at some of the gold that passed through the town. And even if Maddie had her mounting doubts about Chester, she still believed that Morris would come through for Laurette. And this belief, in great part, spurred her concern for her friend.

"I know," she said, "I know," and then came across the room, sat down on the side of the bed, and hugged Laurette and didn't want to let her go. When she did finally pull away, she put a hand to her friend's hair and said, "You're like my very own dear little sister. That's how I think of you. And I couldn't forgive myself if something happened to you."

Laurette took Maddie's other hand and held it to her heart. "Thank you," she said, and kissed Maddie's palm. "You're a wonderful sister to have. You truly are."

As the winter months dragged on, Maddie saw less and less of Laurette. If Laurette came back to the rooms, it was usually in the morning in order to sleep – a heavy, unmoving sleep – until she returned to the Floradora in the evening. When they did share a cup of tea, or on one occasion a bottle of champagne that Laurette brought back to the rooms with her, Laurette seemed tired but generally animated and in good spirits. They did not hear any more from either Chester or Morris after a couple of letters were delivered to them in January from the gold fields, and neither woman any longer spoke of her husband. Laurette, Maddie noticed, had long ago stopped wearing her wedding band. It was beginning to seem as if the two men had never existed in their lives and that Maddie and Laurette had just magically arrived in Dawson City by themselves and were presented with this spare and routine life that they now dragged themselves through.

Then one day in early April, when several feet of snow remained banked along the side of every building in Dawson and the streets remained long sheets of ice, Maddie came upstairs to their apartment to find Laurette with her dress patterns, bolts of fabric, and sewing shears laid out across the floor.

"I'm making a dress for one of the girls," she announced, attired in just her petticoats and corset cover and with her bear fur slippers on her feet. "Gracie is my same exact size, so I can use these old patterns for her."

In the two weeks following, Laurette made two more dresses for girls who also worked at the Floradora. She even reported to Maddie that two of the girls she made dresses for offered to pay her if she would customize the dresses to their exact specifications – one wanted a wider neckline to show off her attractive collarbone; the other wanted a fancy collar to conceal her sagging neck – and if they could pick out the material for themselves. Laurette accepted their offer and went busily to work on the two dresses. Then, at the end of April, and out of the blue, she asked Maddie if she would help her open a dress shop, and then produced from her trunk a roll of bills that amounted to over a thousand dollars, which she had been saving since January when she started working at the Floradora.

Maddie was both shocked and delighted. She readily consented to the venture, and the next day she arranged with E. W. Blayton, the proprietor of the outfitting store, to rent the two back rooms of his store to use as their dress shop. E. W. agreed and even offered to have a sign made up — "The L & M Dress Shop" — a name that was Laurette's idea.

"Like the railroad," said Maddie, ever the railroad worker's daughter.

"Precisely," Laurette replied, and the next week, after stocking the back room with sample fabrics (which they secured in larger swaths from the dry goods store) and drawings and patterns for several different dress styles, Laurette quit the Floradora Dance Hall, Maddie quit making gloves and hats for Blayton's Outfitting, and they opened the L & M Dress Shop for business. To get the word out, they placed a small announcement in the *Dawson Daily Nugget* and posted hand-printed flyers backstage at all the theaters and dance halls in town for the girls to see. For the first time in all their many long months in Dawson City, Maddie felt as if she and Laurette might honestly make it, that they would not only persevere but prosper.

Right away young and old ladies alike, many from the town's demi-monde, but also some from the more respectable south end near the courthouse, were entering the shop. At first Laurette would do all of the fittings in the first room, since she was acquainted with many of the girls and would chat them up as they considered styles and sizes, while Maddie did much of the cutting and sewing on the old Belmont sewing machine in the second room. When they did not have standing orders, they made simple housedresses and nightgowns, which they sold off a rack in the first room. E. M. Blayton, seeing that their shop attracted more business than his own store (the gold stampede having already begun to peter out), gave them the whole front window on the left side of the door to display their goods and raised their rent by two dollars a week.

Laurette did not seem to miss the good-time life she'd had while working at the Floradora, and Maddie was proud of her for having made the change in professions — and ceased worrying about her. It wasn't until June that they received the letter from Morris saying only that he would be returning to Dawson at the end of the month. His reticence, combined with the letter's general lack of information and not a single mention of Chester, gave the single page of scrawled lettering an ominous feel. Laurette appeared both elated and apprehensive about her husband's announced return, while also trying to allay Maddie's growing concern that some harm had perhaps befallen Chester. "Morris never was a very good letter writer," she told her. Throughout the winter both women had sent letters with the men who delivered supplies periodically to the Eldorado Creek camps by dogsled, but they never knew if their husbands received the letters. In their most recent correspondence, they had both conveyed the news about the dress shop. Yet they were both left wondering why Morris had made no mention of the shop in his return letter to them.

MORRIS SHOWED UP – WITHOUT CHESTER – AT THE END OF THE first week in July. Laurette had wanted to celebrate the Fourth of July by hanging red-white-and-blue banners across the storefront, but Maddie had to remind her that they were in Canada, a fact easily forgotten given that four out of five gold seekers in Dawson were indeed American. Morris, just another one of these American gold seekers, was hardly recognizable when he stepped into the dress shop. He was gaunt and haggard with a starved glassiness to his eyes. His beard came down to his chest and was splattered with mud, as was the rest of him from his soggy formless boots to his drooping slouch hat. Laurette ran up and embraced him the instant she saw him standing in the doorway, while Maddie stood back and watched as he received her embrace by slowly lifting his arms and putting them around his wife. When Laurette finally let go, Maddie greeted him, and they looked across the room at each other, but all he said to her was, "Hello, Maddie. Good to see ya again." He wasn't going to say anything about Chester yet, this was clear. And Maddie could not help but suspect that Chester was dead, yet she held her heart in abeyance until Morris could muster the nerve to tell her and she could grieve in earnest. Then Laurette told Morris that she was going to take him straight upstairs and into the big metal washtub that she and Maddie had purchased from the dry goods store back in March, because what he needed most was a hot bath and a good night's sleep.

"It seems you two ladies are doing just fine by your lonesomes," he said, looking over his shoulder again at Maddie as Laurette took his arm and led him up the back staircase.

Maddie, meanwhile, stayed downstairs in the dress shop and let Laurette and Morris have the rest of the day to themselves in the upstairs apartment. She kept the shop open an hour later than usual that evening, until eight, at which time Laurette came down and told her that Morris had washed and slept and was now putting on some clean clothes.

"He lost two toes to the cold," Laurette said quietly to Maddie. "They had to cut them off right there in the camp ... to keep the gangrene from setting in."

"That's horrible," Maddie said, again thinking of Chester and trying to fathom carrying on with her life without him. She wondered at herself for not feeling more upset than she did at the prospective loss of her husband. Was she that cold-hearted? Had she been such an insensitive wife when he was alive? Or perhaps it was just the shock of coming to terms with his death, and the fact that she'd been deprived of the chance to be in his company again, as Laurette was with Morris right now.

Shortly after this brief exchange with Laurette, Morris came down the stairs in a clean shirt (no collar) and clean worsted pants and a long coat, all of which he'd left with Laurette when he took off for the mining camps. His beard was freshly trimmed, and perhaps because he had bathed and the months of dirt and grime no longer clung to his skin, his face looked more sallow than ever. Maddie hurriedly closed the shop and the three of them headed down Duke Street to a chop suey joint run by a couple of Chinamen who had come up from Seattle not long ago. Over their fried eggrolls and bowls of Chinese noodles, Morris related to Laurette and Maddie the details of his and Chester's brutal winter in the Yukon wilderness, working as mere wage laborers in the gold mines with never an opportunity to get into town, living in a shack no bigger than a toolshed, never having enough to eat, and always being so cold you knew that at any time you could fall asleep and never wake up.

"Your letters came telling about the shop," he said at last to Laurette. "I was happy to hear about it and to know you were okay." Then he bowed his head, seemingly ashamed of what he was going to say next. "I'm sorry I didn't write back, Laurette. I didn't have anything to send you, money-wise that is, so I didn't feel proper sending just an old letter with nothin' in it. I didn't want to lie to you either and make that everything was going fine when it wasn't and set you all to worryin'."

Laurette put her arm across his shoulder and said that it was all right, she was just glad he was back with her now, safe and sound. Maddie knew Laurette was scared that he would find out what she'd been doing those few months before they opened the dress shop, and knew that this reunion could not be easy for her friend. After Morris composed himself a little more, he turned to Maddie.

"He ain't dead," were the first words out his mouth to her, "in case that's what you were wondering." Maddie was both relieved and startled by this announcement. Morris then looked up at her and held her eyes with his and said angrily, "The sonuvabitch's run off to Nome," and then paused and added, "That is, if he makes it alive. He's got the gold fever bad, Maddie, and it about killed me and a couple of other fellas going out with him to look for claims to stake. Then he run off with more'an his rightful share of our two's take from the Eldorado operation – that is, the bonus they gave when one of us would strike a good vein. All in all, that Chester of yours has got some people damn mad at him, and they're likely to kill 'im if they ever see him again. And for my part, I might help 'em at it." Morris stopped there and diverted his eyes from Maddie. He slurped several fork-fuls of chop suey and ordered a whiskey from the Chinaman waiter. Then he looked at Maddie again. "He ain't coming back, Maddie. I'm afraid that's the honest truth of the matter. He might as well be dead."

Maddie could only stare at Morris, not fully grasping what he was telling her, though faintly understanding that Chester had done a lot of people wrong – including herself. Despite herself, she began to cry, at first softly, out of relief that her husband was not dead, then more fully from the grievousness expanding in her chest over the realization of his heart-less abandonment of her.

When Morris said that he regretted having to be the bearer of bad news, Maddie asked him to tell her the whole story. Morris agreed and ordered a bottle of whiskey to be brought to the table, with two more glasses, and then after pouring Maddie and Laurette each a glass of the liquor, he began to elaborate on his ordeal with Chester. From the time they had arrived at Eldorado Creek, he said, Chester was sore at having to mine for someone else and kept himself busy making plans to explore the surrounding territory and stake his own claim. As it turned out, in some ways he was right to be sore, because he and Morris worked the Eldorado site all winter and spring and only ever came away with enough to resupply themselves for the next month, even when they did get a bonus. As of right now, Morris told them, he had only a few hundred dollars in gold dust from the entire year's venture. So Chester soon saw that this was how it was going to be and became more and more desperate, believing that every day that passed meant someone else was staking a claim somewhere that by all due rights and obligations should be his. Yet it was when they would venture out from the Eldorado camp to scout other creek beds, some identified on the map and others not, that he became most reckless. Ill-equipped and not reckoning adequately with the heavy snow and severe cold, they were lucky to get back to camp most times, and it was on one of these scouting trips that Morris got the frostbite on his toes. Meanwhile, when they were back at camp, Chester made life hell, complaining that they were slagging more pay gravel than the claim managers were letting on and that they were being shorted their fair share. He didn't like going into the drifting tunnels either, and a couple times got panicky and brought the whole operation to a standstill. That's when rumors starting going around the camp that Alaska was opening up and there was gold to be panned right on the beach in Nome. Chester came to realize the map the contract agent had sold them was bunk and that the Klondike was already played out – and that it was time to move on. One night in their shack, back in April, he told Morris he wasn't going to be caught behind the eight ball this time around. He was going to get a jump on the Alaska rush and stake his claim in Nome.

Here Morris deliberately looked away from Maddie. "When I asked him about you," he said, and sheepishly glanced back at her, "that is, if he wasn't going to bring you with him, he said flat out No, he couldn't be slowed down none, and that you should go back to Seattle, or New Jersey, or wherever it was you wanted to go, without him. Then him and another fellow who was just as gold-mad broke camp in May when the thaw came and struck out for Nome on a little old flatboat they got hold of somewhere."

Sitting in the chop suey joint that night, listening to this tale of her abandonment by her husband and how he'd chosen a reckless chance at gold over his life with her, Maddie got drunk drinking whiskey, and Laurette and Morris had to carry her between them back to the apartment and put her to bed. In the morning, as she lay in the bed with her head throbbing, massaging her temples with her fingers, she cursed Chester for getting so gold crazy and running off like he did, blamed herself for ever having gone along with his half-mad adventures after riches he'd never find, and then swore him from her life forever. Eventually, after several more hours of tearful, exhausted sleep, when she finally managed to lift herself from the bed, she fetched several pails of water from the tank out back, heated the water on the stove, poured it into the washtub, and then climbed in, sank down, and lay there for the rest of the afternoon.

Morris stayed in town for ten more days – eating, drinking, and sleeping, and putting some weight back on his bones and some color back into his face – and then contracted himself out to several commissioned claims and returned to the creeks to work the company mines again. Now that Laurette was set up with the dress shop, she and Morris had decided to try for one more year to see if he might be able to find his paydirt in the Far North, and if not, then the two of them would head back down to Seattle. As for herself, Maddie didn't know what she would do next. She and Laurette had spoken a few times about moving the shop to Seattle, and maybe they would still do that, but right now that wouldn't be for at least another year. And also right now, Maddie didn't have enough savings even to book passage back to Seattle, much less get herself situated once she arrived. So she didn't know what she would do. Remaining in Dawson City, surrounded by desperate, broken miners and the handful of lucky gold kings who showboated about, only made her think more about Chester and his forsaking her. She could always go to work in the dance halls to try to take her mind off him, she thought, but quickly talked herself out of such an absurd notion.

It was in late August, when Maddie knew that if she were going to leave Dawson she would need to do so before the freeze came, that an Indian woman came into the shop asking to be fitted for an evening gown. She was maybe Maddie's age, a bit shorter but not by much, with the strong full body, roundish features, and ruddy complexion of other Tagish women Maddie had observed about town. Many of these women accompanied their husbands who worked in the mines, some were married to white men, and others were on their own working as housemaids in the bigger hotels in town. The woman who came into the shop on this particular day seemed better off than most. Most Indian women didn't go into dress shops to be fitted for custom-made evening gowns.

When Maddie stood the woman on the footstool and circled around her with the tape measure to take her measurements, they got to talking. The woman asked Maddie how she'd come to Dawson and Maddie told her, leaving out the part about Chester going off to Nome without her. Then the woman said her name was Aage Wilson and that she was Kate Cormack's sister. As Maddie and probably everyone else in Dawson well knew, Kate Cormack was the wife of George Washington Cormack, who along with Skookum Jim Mason stacked the first big claims along Bonanza Creek several years ago. George Cormack was now one of the richest men in town, and Kate, word about town had it, currently resided in Seattle where she'd been sent by her husband to escape the drinking and general debauchery of Dawson City.

Though Maddie was fascinated by this personal connection to the people who had more or less kicked off the Gold Rush, she politely refrained from pressing Aage Wilson for further details. Maddie also knew that, given recent events in her life, she was harboring a sizeable measure of resentment toward the whole gold-seeking enterprise. Besides, she recognized that a good shopkeeper always exercises discretion with her clientele. However, two days later, Aage Wilson returned for the final fitting for her evening gown, and while Maddie pinned up her sleeves and chalked her skirts, Aage pressed Maddie for more particulars on how she'd come to run the dress shop. Maddie told her about Laurette, whom Aage had not yet met, and how it was her dressmaking skills that got them started, and that the shop was a way for them to keep themselves occupied while their husbands where out in the gold fields.

"So is your husband rich yet then?" Aage asked her. "Or is he still snuffling around for his paydirt?"

Maddie got off her one knee then, took the pins from mouth, and stood before Aage Wilson and said sternly to her, "No, Mrs. Wilson, I'm afraid my Chester is not rich. In fact, you see, my husband's abandoned me to seek his riches elsewhere. He's run off to Nome and left me to do as I please. Which for the time being, given the other opportunities for a lady like myself in this town, happens to be dressmaking."

Maddie was instantly abashed at the brusque tone she'd taken, yet before she could apologize, Aage Wilson put her hand on Maddie's shoulder and said, "The bastard. He shouldn't'a done you that way." She then expressed how sorry she was for Maddie's misfortune and then, after mumbling "bastard" under her breath a couple more times, let the topic drop and kept quiet for the remainder of her fitting.

When she returned three days later to collect her evening gown, she paid Maddie in full for the dress, and as she was leaving she placed an envelope on the front table and said modestly, "This is for you," and departed from the dress shop.

Maddie picked up the envelope thinking it was a tip, a sympathy gesture for the pitiful account she'd given of herself at their last meeting. Yet inside the envelope, instead of money, she found a one-page letter and a crude hand-drawn map. Maddie unfolded the letter and read it:

Dear Madame,

Your Chester should have been more patient. Enclosed you will find a map to Rock Ledge Creek. It lies ten miles below Bear and Hunker Creeks, near Forty Mile, which two mines were abandoned after my brother Jim and his friend George Cormack staked out Rabbit Creek. A rock cairn marks where Mr. Wilson and I first panned. I make no assurances, but do urge you to stake a claim as soon as possible. I thank you for the dress, which is most elegant and well made.

Yours Truly,
Aage Wilson

Maddie grew shaky as she read the letter again. She could hardly be expected to take it seriously, she told herself, especially after the manner in which Chester and Morris had been led astray with their fraudulent map. How was she to put any faith in this small dark-skinned woman who had just strayed off the street into her shop? Maddie couldn't explain it – and maybe she didn't need to – but by the second and third time she'd read the note and looked at the map, she began, perhaps out of her own desperation, to believe there might be something to this Aage Wilson. This offer seemed far different from the scam Chester and Morris had fallen for their first day in town. This was an unsolicited invitation. A gesture of sympathy and understanding, from one woman to another. And wouldn't someone such as Aage Wilson, who'd been born and reared in the Far North, who had undoubtedly tracked the region for many years with her husband, who herself was obviously enjoying the advantages of newly found wealth … wouldn't such a person merit some measure of trust? Especially on a matter that potentially held forth such promise, that could turn their fates around and answer all their dreams and wishes? On the other hand, Maddie feared, perhaps in her own desperation to escape Dawson, she herself was now becoming gold-mad. What was she willing to risk, she knew she would have to ask herself, to pursue this unsought-after opportunity?

LATER THAT EVENING SHE DISCUSSED THE MATTER THROUGH and through with Laurette, and together they came to the decision that, at least for now, they would trust the letter and the accompanying map. How could they not? To ignore them and be left wondering for the rest of their lives whether they'd made the right decision …No, they had to pursue this lead and see what came of it. It was decided that Laurette would write to Morris at the Eldorado camp insisting that he return immediately to Dawson; then he and Maddie and E. W. Blayton, by now their good and trusted friend, would venture out to Rock Ledge Creek. If the site looked promising, they would stake the claim, and if they then struck paydirt … well, they would all rejoice and happily share in the returns, big or small.

The expedition to Rock Ledge Creek, with the aid of the map that Aage

Wilson had hand-drawn, was an arduous one for Maddie, equal to the journey to Dawson City. At first, E. W. tried to talk Maddie out of going, but she wouldn't hear of it. The letter and map had been given to her, and she would be the one to see if they were bunk or not. For the ten days it took them to locate Rock Ledge Creek, survey and plot their claim, and return to Dawson, Maddie worked hard not to let her spirits flag, pursuing the claim with something of a vengeance, as if in retaliation for Chester's despicable treatment of her. Yet by early October, the task—all except striking paydirt—was accomplished. The claim was theirs, filed and sealed, and Morris and E.W., both of whom thought it was a promising claim, quickly put together a crew of five miners, all men Morris knew from the Eldorado camp, and then returned to Rock Ledge Creek fully supplied and outfitted with the help of Blayton Outfitters.

Throughout October, November, and December, two men from the crew were sent back to Dawson every three weeks to update Maddie and Laurette on the work at the creek and to resupply the camp. Reaching Rock Ledge Creek was a difficult trek, especially as the fierce winter storms arrived with regularity and temperatures dropped to 60 and 70 degrees below zero. By mid-December the seven men had built two log cabins, dug their tunnels into the embankment above the creek, and were settled into the camp for the duration, while Maddie and Laurette stayed in Dawson, tended to their shop, and even took over operating E.W.'s store in his absence. Though the two women tried not to speculate too much on the outcome of their new enterprise, Maddie couldn't help but feel something good would come of it. At times she would have to check her own giddy optimism and put her mind to the task at hand, whether it was trimming a skirt or lining a pair of gloves with otter fur.

In March, when Morris and one of the other men returned to town for the first time since the holiday season, Morris, too, seemed optimistic, though he didn't give them many details of the work crew's progress. Yet he did invite them to come out to the claim with him to see the operation for themselves. Even though the river remained clogged with ice and the trails were banked several feet high with snow, the days were again beginning to lengthen, warming the air to around zero at night and to the teens in the afternoon. Maddie and Laurette accepted the invitation and locked up the shop and the outfitting store and headed out with Morris and the other man for their Rock Ledge Creek claim.

It took them two full days on the Yukon River to reach Forty Mile, which was north of Dawson by about 100 miles, then another day by dogsled along various trails through the wilderness to reach Rock Ledge Creek, and another half day winding their way up the creek to reach their claim. Several other claims had been staked along the creek since last autumn, but theirs was the most established. It also appeared to be the most productive. The men in the camp greeted Maddie as if she were Queen Victoria come to tour one of her kingdom's colonies. The claim was a sizeable one, almost 500 feet along the creek bed and 600 feet up the embankment from the creek. High up on the embankment the men had dug two mine shafts. Smoke drifted out of the window-sized mouth of one of the shafts, coming from the fire that was kept smoldering down in the shaft to thaw the frozen ground. At the mouth of the second shaft, two men from the work crew cranked a windlass, drawing forth buckets of half-thawed gravelly sludge which they dumped onto a six-foot-high, ten-foot-wide drifting pile. A second, even larger, tailing pile lay farther off to the left of this one.

Morris walked up to the drifting pile with a tin pan, put a fistful of the sludge in the pan and poured some water into it from his canteen, then he slowly sloshed the mixture around in the pan, studying its contents and occasionally tipping the pan to pour out some of the muddy water. After a couple of minutes of this, he showed Maddie and Laurette what was left in the pan. Coarse shimmers of gold lay mixed in with the remains of the sludge on the bottom of the pan, some just fine specks, but a few larger pieces as well – reminding Maddie of the first piece of gold she had ever seen, the one Chester revealed to her in their room in the Seattle flophouse. Aage was right, Maddie thought suddenly upon seeing the gold at the bottom of the pan: Chester had been too impatient. And as for herself, it looked as though she had been right to pursue the Indian woman's generous tip.

E. W. Blayton stood beside Maddie and said, "I don't know that we'll find a vein, but the bed's giving us some mighty fine placer deposits."

Three other men were busy building sluice boxes down along the icy bank of the creek. They used planks that they had cut and planed from trees felled on the claim, leaving tree stumps everywhere Maddie looked. Trees from the claim had also been used to build the two small cabins on a narrow clearing farther up the creek about forty yards. The sluice boxes, Morris explained, would eventually run up the embankment to just below the mouths of the two shafts. Then the drifting piles would be sluiced through rocker boxes and the gold recovered. It was that simple.

That night Maddie was happy as she sat in the cold air facing the enormous bonfire the men had built in honor of their lady visitors. Everyone seemed to agree that, even if they didn't strike the vein that E. W. spoke of, the claim was going to be a profitable one, and handsomely so. While one of the men cooked a bear stew with the potatoes, cabbages, and rutabagas that the visitors had brought along, another broke out the two jugs of whiskey and three bottles of champagne that they'd also hauled back with them from Dawson. Everyone felt good in the warmth of the fire, the glow of the spirits, and the nourishment of the stew. At one point, Morris raised one of the champagne bottles and with his arm around Laurette gave a toast. "To paydirt," he shouted, and everyone shouted the toast back to him and drank to it. Everyone seemed to understand that they would be squared away, and maybe even rich, by summertime. And a sweet summertime it would be. Getting a little more drunk than the rest, E. W. began singing his favorite Stephen Foster songs, and then after several of those, he started in on his all-time favorite Far North ditty, "When the Ice Worms Nest Again":

> There's a husky dusky maiden in the Arctic;
> In her igloo she is waiting there in vain,
> But someday I'll put my mukluks on and ask her
> If she'll wed me when the ice worms nest again.

He then jumped to his feet and asked Maddie to dance with him, and then Morris got up and danced with Laurette. The crew cheered the two couples as they do-si-doe'd before the fire, and eventually every man on the five-man crew took a turn at twirling the two women about on the frozen ground that served as their dance floor. As the fire and good cheer blazed on through the night, Maddie felt a new confidence come upon her, a recognition that she could see her way through anything and make good on her faith in herself. More than just the champagne and the dancing, and even more than the gold itself, Maddie knew that something had come over her that would help her carry on with her life in the manner of her own choosing from this point on.

ONE WEEK LATER, MADDIE AND LAURETTE, ACCOMPANIED by two men from the work crew, trekked back to Dawson carrying with them the first gold from their claim, two small pouches of half an ounce each, which they each carried on their persons. E. W. had outfitted the entire crew and paid for their supplies through fall, winter, and spring, so it was understood that he would be duly reimbursed for this outlay. After that, in accordance with the written contract that everyone had signed, the take from the claim would be split four ways between Maddie, E. W., Morris and Laurette, and the five men on the work crew, who would then split their share five ways. When she and Laurette had returned from the camp and were back in their two rooms above the dress shop and outfitting store, Maddie expressed her nagging feeling that maybe her distribution was unfair to the rest, that perhaps it was too great a portion of the overall take, yet Laurette hastened to disabuse her of this notion.

"You're the most deserving of all," she told her. "There'd be no claim at all without you. And besides, none of us will be going poor from our individual takes."

In April and May, Morris and E. W. began transporting the gold into Dawson in earnest, and Maddie accepted the fact that from now on life would be different. By June, the crew had sluiced the drifting piles they had mined during the winter months and were now just doing some clean-up panning. One day, when the two men were still in town, a representative from the Canadian Klondike Mining Company came into the outfitting store and inquired if they would be interested in selling their claim, because his company was prepared to make them a fair and speedy settlement for it. Later that evening, Maddie, E. W., Morris, and Laurette had a sit-down in the back of the store and discussed their options. Estimating that they had already hauled in about $140,000 worth (American dollars) and that the claim was pretty near exhausted unless they brought in hydraulic equipment (to say nothing of the increased fees the government was going to charge them to renew their claim), and realizing they all wanted out of the wilderness and to get back to civilization, they soon determined to sell their claim. A week later, the deal with the mining company was made, landing them another $32,000.

By the Fourth of July, they had pulled out from the Rock Ledge Creek claim, all their accounts were settled, and the money was evenly split. Two of the men from the work crew got on with the Canadian Klondike Mining Company to supervise work at the claim for the following year, while two others took their earnings and boarded a steamer for San Francisco and the fifth headed off to Nome to try to find even more riches. E. W. asked Maddie to marry him, and though she was flattered by his honest and heart-felt proposal, she declined, and shortly after he opened his own dance hall in Dawson. In all, the events of those early summer months left Maddie almost dizzy. There was never as much time to spend with Laurette as she wished, and in some ways she missed the old days when she and her friend had had only each other. Although she sometimes thought of Chester and even imagined herself sharing her new riches with him, she also knew that if he were there he would somehow manage to turn her good fortune into something to regret. Such thoughts, along with the lonesomeness she suffered during the interminable summer twilights, soon spurred her on to plan her next move. And while the prospect of change brought trepidation, and even more sleeplessness, her eagerness for such change helped keep her going.

It was when Maddie was packing to return to Seattle, and when Morris and Laurette were themselves trying to figure out what to do next, whether to keep the dress shop in Dawson or move back to the States, when the worst thing that could have happened did happen. Morris found out that Laurette had spent several months working in the Floradora the previous year. And what's more – news that startled even Maddie – that she'd had a room in Madame Tourant's house on Queen Street. It soon became clear that he had learned about Laurette's activities – or at least this was how E. W. told it – when he himself began frequenting Madame Tourant's house after returning to Dawson so proud and pleased with himself as a newly crowned gold king.

Maddie was upstairs in their apartment the evening she heard Morris storm into the dress shop to confront Laurette, who was finishing two standing dress orders from May, the last orders she had accepted before the gold began coming in. Maddie heard a crash, which she later discovered was the sewing machine stand that Morris had kicked over as soon as he saw Laurette sitting at it, tending to her task. Then the shouting started – mostly his, punctuated by desperate pleas from Laurette for him to forgive her.

"You're nothing but a poke-hunting whore," Morris yelled at her, as Maddie hurried down the back stairs. "Whoring around when my back's turned."

Laurette was sobbing when Maddie entered the back door of the shop and came upon the two of them: Laurette bent over in the straight-back chair where she had sat moments before contentedly sewing, her arms now cradling her head, and Morris raging about the room, charging at her with his body and his curses until she cowered before him. Maddie could instantly smell the heavy fumes of his drinking. The small back room reeked from his whiskey breath and the cigar smoke that still clung to his coat.

"How could you," he shouted, and spat at her feet. "How can I go back home and have a respectable life knowing that my wife is a cheap dance hall whore! Ain't all the gold in the world goin'ta make that right."

"We had no money," Laurette screamed back at him, her face streaked with tears, her soft cheeks and forehead blotched red, her fine auburn hair in disarray about her head and face. "You left me here and never came back and never wrote and just abandoned me."

Morris charged at her again, biting hard on his lower lip in his fury, and bent his scowling bearded face down at hers. "It don't make it right," he said harshly under his breath, pulling back a fist yet restraining himself from striking her. "Once a whore, always a whore. How many were there?

Fifty? A hundred? Did every goddamn gold miner in the Yukon Territory rooster my wife?"

"Stop it," Laurette shouted back at him. "How do you think I could open this dress shop? So as I could feed myself when you were god-knows-where, so I could take care of you whenever you wanted to come back into town?"

"That's it, is it?" he shot back. "That's how you come to be such a high-and-mighty shopkeeper, is it? I shoulda figured as much." He then smacked the side of his head with his own hand in exaggerated recognition of this revelation. "So that's how you come to have yourself such a nice, dainty little dress shop." And with this he snatched off the floor the dress Laurette had been working on and began shredding it in his rough hands. Laurette jumped up from her chair and tried to save the dress by pulling it away from him, but as she did so he thrust his arm out and backhanded her across the face. Laurette fell back across the room and crumpled into the corner. And while Morris continued to tear the dress into shreds, Maddie, who had witnessed all this, bolted past him and into the outfitting store and an instant later came back holding the Winchester repeating shotgun that she knew E. W. kept on the shelf above the supply room door. She slid the forearm on the shotgun, an action that dropped a cartridge in the breech box, and cocked the hammer simultaneously, and then aimed the barrel straight at Morris's chest.

"You bastard!" she shouted at him, and wanted to blast him right then and there – and knew she could, too, both in her heart and in the eyes of the law.

Morris saw the shotgun in Maddie's arms and aimed straight at him and raised his eyes to glare back at her. If he took a single step toward her, Maddie told herself, she would pull the trigger. But instead of coming toward her, he stood right where he was and said, "You a whore too, Maddie? Laurette I can figure all right, but not you." He then turned on his heels, threw the torn dress at Laurette in the corner, and kicking the sewing stand out of his way, ran off out the back door.

Maddie waited a moment and then cautiously stepped toward the door with the shotgun still at the ready, and looked out to check that he had gone for sure. Seeing that he had, she closed the door, threw the deadbolt to lock it, and then went over to Laurette who sat huddled in the corner with her arms around her knees and sobbing. Maddie held her in her arms, yet when she finally stopped crying, she just looked blankly at the torn dress that Morris had thrown at her and didn't say a word. The side of her face was red and beginning to swell where Morris had struck her. Without a word, Maddie helped Laurette to her feet, still holding the shotgun in one hand in case Morris returned, and guided her friend upstairs to their rooms, where she loosened the ties of her blouse, removed her shoes, and laid her in the bed with the covers over her.

For the rest of the night she sat in one of the straight-back chairs and kept guard with the shotgun, watching her companion of the past two years sleep fitfully, and hoping the whole while that Morris would pass out in some alley and in the morning come to his senses. With the light in the sky never fully fading into darkness during these summer months, she was able to fight off falling asleep herself. As she waited out the night, she decided that in the morning she would go to E. W.'s house and ask him to find Morris and speak to him, to make him see his error and apologize to Laurette. She just hoped that after blowing his top last night, he would wake up remorseful and treat his wife the way she deserved to be treated – with sympathy, respect, and kindness. The way any woman deserved to be treated by the man who proclaimed to love her.

By early morning it had begun to rain, so putting on her raincoat, rubber boots, and fur hat, Maddie left Laurette sleeping in the room and went out. E. W. had a small house on Craig Street, right at the confluence of the Klondike and Yukon Rivers. To rouse him from bed, Maddie had to pound at his front door until eventually he came to the door in a silk robe over his longjohns. He invited her inside and, as he brewed a pot of coffee in the kitchen, heard her relate what had happened the night before back at his store. Then he went back upstairs, got dressed, and within a few minutes he and Maddie were striding back into the center of town.

"He might have gone back to Madame Tourant's house," E. W. suggested. "That is, if she'd let him back in if he was as drunk as you say he was. Or he might be in any one of the saloons somewhere."

While Maddie stayed out on the sidewalk in the rain, E. W. entered a few of these saloons as they made their way through the dim morning streets of Dawson. As they neared the center of town, they heard fire bells begin to clang and, looking about trying to figure out where the fire might be, they saw smoke rising into the sky several blocks away. It seemed to occur to both of them simultaneously that the smoke was coming from the direction of the outfitting store and dress shop. They hurried toward it and when they turned the corner onto Duke Street, they could see that the building was ablaze. Two fire wagons had already arrived and were spraying water from their hoses into the busted-out windows and onto the roof. Yet the flames had already engulfed the second floor and were now climbing onto the roof. Upon seeing the flames, Maddie screamed out Laurette's name and rushed toward the burning building, but before she could get even close, E. W. caught her and held her back. Maddie struggled against his grip for several moments and then collapsed into the muddy street, knowing Laurette was gone and that all the gold in the world would not bring her back.

While the firemen were still trying to put out the fire, E. W. brought Maddie, in shock and unresponsive to his entreaties, back to his house on Craig Street. He put her in one of the upstairs bedrooms and ordered a doctor to come and give her a dosage of laudanum so she could sleep. The next day, at Maddie's insistence, despite his protests that she stay in bed and rest, he escorted her back to the building on Duke Street in his barouche. From the street it was plain to see that the second floor was entirely burned out, with the roof partially collapsed on the back side – which, E. W. told her, was where the fire had started – and the entire bottom floor was either charred black by the fire or flooded from the fire hoses. As they got out of the barouche and started walking around the parameter of the building, Maddie's grief kept overwhelming her, and she would have to pause and sob while E. W. held her.

"I should never have left her there alone," she cried out several times, as E. W. tried his best to console her, repeating how it was not her fault.

When they reached the back of the building, she made him let go of her arm so she could approach the burned-out remains of the building. The back door hung open and Maddie stepped up to the threshold, water dripping down from the exposed and still smoldering ceiling timbers, and when she leaned in and looked about the room, there she saw Laurette, seated in the straight-back chair with barley-twist legs, clutching in both hands the dress she had been working on the previous night, before Morris had struck her and stormed out of the shop. She neither cried nor stirred, but simply leaned forward in the chair staring at the rent fabric in her hands. Yet as Maddie's joy overcame her at the sight of her precious friend and she called out to her—"Laurette"—her friend was no longer there. The chair was empty.

Maddie then felt E.W. place his hands on her shoulders and draw her away from the door.

"I saw her," she cried out as he led her to the barouche to take her back to his house. "She was there."

Later in the afternoon, when E.W. told Maddie that he was going to drive his wagon down to the store and try to recover anything that had not been destroyed by the fire and put it in storage in the shed behind his house, Maddie implored him to rescue the straight-back chair for her, and from then on she never again mentioned having seen Laurette seated in the chair in the burned-out room of the dress shop.

Within a matter of days, the Mounted Police apprehended Morris holed up in one of the shallow and already abandoned mine shafts on the slope of a hill just outside of town and charged him with arson and murder. Even after he confessed his crimes to the Mounties and begged E.W. to bring Maddie to the territorial jail, Maddie refused to visit him. Instead she arranged for a proper burial for Laurette in the churchyard of St. Paul's Anglican Church in town and grieved for her friend in private while continuing to stay at E.W.'s house. She did not once think about what she would do next, since plans toward her own future seemed like an outright disgrace to her memories of her friend—which were hardly yet memories at all, but rather the felt presence of Laurette in her life, still there.

Two small purse bags of gold were recovered from the charred building, and fortunately E.W. had been wise enough to deposit most the gold from their claim in the safe at the British Bank on Queen Street. Upon the advice of a barrister in town, he and Maddie agreed to split Morris and Laurette's take evenly between themselves and the five men from their Rock Ledge Creek work crew. Maddie remained at E.W.'s house while she replaced the clothes she had lost in the fire and bought a new trunk. By the end of July, having come to terms with the tragedy and its utter senselessness, she booked her passage for the all-water route down the Yukon River to the Bering Sea, then through the Gulf of Alaska, and back down the coastal passage to Seattle.

MADDIE STUDIED THE CHAIR IN HER KITCHEN A MOMENT longer, then opened the hatch on the stove again, dispensing with the use of oven mitts or dishrags (her fingers long ago callused from handling the hot iron), and reaching into the stove's firebox with the scoop, stirred in the lumps of shiny black anthracite with their red-glowing cousins, which she'd tossed into the stove the previous night before retiring to bed. She pulled her arm out and reached for the bellows that hung from a nail above the stove and gave the bed of coals three long blasts. The coals flared and a wave of heat blew back into her face.

"I wonder," she said aloud, backing away from the stove, thinking of Laurette. Fire genuinely frightened her – from the fire that killed Laurette in Dawson, to the Great Seattle Fire that people still remembered and spoke of, to the fire that destroyed most of San Francisco last year after the earth-quake, to the fire just three weeks ago that brought down the remains of the Washington Hotel. Even her stove fires made her nervous, she realized, as she stared into the firebox transfixed by the bright red mound of coals burning like Nebuchadnezzar's fiery furnace, and then hastily shut the hatch, closed the damper, and hung the bellows back on the wall.

She was reaching for the enameled teapot on the back of the stove when the straight-back chair skidded on the linoleum – abruptly and just once – almost as if she had bumped it herself, though she knew she hadn't. She stared at the chair for a long moment, teapot in hand.

"Laurette," she said. "Laurette, is that you?" One of the chair legs abutted the thick iron floor plate on which the stove rested – which was not right, not right at all, since she vigilantly kept the chair clear from direct contact with the floor plate and the hot stove for fear they might combust.

She set the teapot on the stove lid and making a wide circle in front of the chair – just in case – took hold of the chair from the side and slid it back away from the stove and the iron floor plate. "It's the cold, I know," she said, and wondered if the chair were not trying to join the fate of its companion pieces lost in the Dawson fire, or if perhaps Laurette herself wished the chair to burn so her own wandering soul could come to rest, the table and chair set restored to her complete in the great everlasting.

It was all too much for Maddie to ponder just now. Her morning blurriness, she knew, made her susceptible to such fanciful thinking, and indeed the whole business of the afterlife was really no business of hers. She had enough cares in this world – presented to her in the likes of Thomson and Calhoun and their cohorts in city hall trying to take from her all she'd worked so hard for: a house full of boarders about to rise hungry for their breakfast and morning coffee and a thirteen-year-old girl to get dressed and packed off to school ... and she not even having gotten the water on yet.

So with the faint gray light of dawn beginning to brighten the two kitchen windows, she turned her attention away from the chair – with or without Laurette in it – and set about her morning chores.

Three

17. Durka in Pioneer Place (1907)

CLYDE CAME WALKING DOWN WASHINGTON STREET ALONG
the elevated plank walkway, which had been constructed the week before
to accommodate the ongoing regrading that extended northward from
Jackson Street at the south end of the city. One block ahead, he could see
Robert Patten, his father's drinking buddy and gardening nemesis, resting
on a make-shift bench of bricks stacked along the street, the leftovers from
construction of the Hapworth Insurance Building. The old man surveyed
the low cloud movement, sniffed the moist air, and, with raised chin and
face directed skyward, closed his eyes as if dozing off to sleep. Clyde knew
exactly what the crusty old codger was up to: he was taking a read of the
weather, a faculty he'd become famous for throughout the city.

According to Clyde's father, even before Robert Patten came to Seattle
from Milwaukee on James J. Hill's Great Northern railroad twelve years
ago, he could read the weather in his bones and sinews and on his flesh
and through the whiskers on his cheek and the prickly hairs in his nose
and ears. He was, as a newspaperman from the *Seattle Times* had dubbed
him, a "human barometer." The word about town had it that he would
give a report only if all indications were perfectly aligned. If a single joint
signaled rain and the rest of his physiology called for drought, he would
hedge his prediction or withhold it altogether. Robert Patten was, after
all, a man of integrity. Only after he arrived in Seattle did he begin to refine
his gift, calling out weather conditions (an extended squall or prolonged
sun, an anomalous snowfall or just more rain) as much as a fortnight in
advance. And as the years went by – or so Clyde's father told him, and
Clyde believed every word – Mr. Patten's forecasts grew ever more precise,
sometimes right down to the hour, degree, and quarter-inch of precipita-
tion. He could even tell you tomorrow's barometric pressure.

At the White Pine Tavern just south of Yesler Way, where Clyde dropped in now and then, patrons placed bets on Mr. Patten's forecasts. If accu-
rate, his drinks were free all day – a reward that sometimes had the unfor-
tunate effect of clouding his "long-range vaticinations," as he referred to
them. Yet even the morning after a heavy drinking day, his knack for

sensing shifts in weather seemed to retain a subtly that even the wildest animals did not possess.

"Robby," an Irish carpenter yammered at Mr. Patten from the opposite end of the bar last week, "keep it dry till me crew finishes roofing the Smitson house, will ya do that for me?"

Or, as a farmer in town for seed on Wednesday told him: "A good week's worth of rain, a real soakin', then lots of sun, Robert. That would do fine."

Or, a kid just off the boat from San Francisco who quickly caught on: "Hey, Umbrella Man, steady winds from the south due north, got it. I'm going to Alaska and coming back rich and I won't forget you."

It was plain to see that people mistook his gift to read the weather for the power to determine it. Yet Robert Patten, overall, was an honest man, and he never exploited this false notion for his own gain. As he told Clyde one day, weather was too fickle and too dangerous to take chances with, especially in such a rough region, between coast and mountains where the inland sea made for uncertainty from one inlet to the next, one island to the next, and where lives and livelihoods hung in the balance of the weather's whims. So he paid close attention to the signals and never took them for granted. Clyde thought he resembled a cat in this way, turning agitated and achy if a rainstorm approached, soporific if a warm spell was setting in. And, not a bit to Clyde's surprise, Mr. Patten even admitted once to having taken readings from the two feline companions that shared his houseboat with him on Lake Union.

It was in this manner that Robert Patten's renown grew. He became a fixture downtown, making his way by foot everyday from Lake Union over the broad rise of Denny Hill and into the downtown where he meandered from tavern to cafe, park bench to street corner, and knew the local workmen and merchants like they were his very own family. Clyde was one of the few in town who still addressed him by his surname, while most others had long ago adopted his nickname, Umbrella Man. The moniker, Mr. Patten would grant, was a fitting one, given the hand-fashioned umbrella hat he'd taken to wearing on his head day in and day out, rain or shine.

Mr. Patten, who readily confided in Clyde, had made the hat from wax-rubbed canvas stretched across a round, wire frame. A separate metal band wrapped in leather and suspended below the canvas and wire frame allowed him to set the whole contraption snugly upon his head. And instead of carrying an awkward bumbershoot about with him all day, opening and closing, closing and opening it, and causing untold havoc on the busy city streets, he donned his simple umbrella hat. And the hat seemed to serve him just fine.

The idea had come to him apparently from seeing a broad woven reed hat of the kind Chinese rice harvesters wore. He saw it one day on a back shelf at Ye Olde Curiosity Shoppe on the Colman Dock, where sailors and merchants brought in curios from around the world so "Daddy" Standley, the shop's owner, could sell them to the public: Alaska Indian relics, shells and corals, stuffed marine mammals, native agates, mineral specimens, moccasins, furs, baskets, and everything from a flea in uniform to a whale's jaw of fourteen feet in length. Robert Patten told Clyde that years ago when he was in the shop he purchased a shrunken head that, according to the hand-scripted card beside it, had been spirited out of a village inhabited by tribal cannibals on the South Pacific island of New Guinea by a brave American sailor. The head, no larger than a man's fist, was a hideously shriveled, dark leathery thing with sealed eyes and a pursed mouth and a long hank of pitch black hair drawn up from its scalp into a ponytail at the crown of the skull. He paid two dollars for the thing because he thought he detected in its scrunched, coarsened features a slight resemblance to himself – a recognition, of sorts – and also because he happened to have two dollars in his pocket that day. He said he knew he probably should have bought the rice harvester's hat instead, it plainly being the more practical purchase, except that the hat cost fifty cents more than he'd been able to muster from his two forecasts that morning – one to the captain of a small ketch anchored in Elliott Bay, the other to a street sweeper who hoped for rain so he could find a tavern with a warm fire to retreat to.

At first Mr. Patten wore his umbrella hat only on rainy days. But in Seattle, that might be any day of the week, even if it appeared sunny in the morning. So after being caught bareheaded in several downpours, he started to don the hat each morning as he left his houseboat. It was the *Seattle Times* cartoon artist who several weeks later dubbed him "The Umbrella Man" when he started sketching Robert as the model for his Umbrella Man character in a series of weekly weather forecasts in the newspaper. And soon everyone on the street was greeting him as "Umbrella Man." Within the year a local hat hawker began producing umbrella hats, which were a joke hat, of course, and which no adult man or woman would actually wear, although every now and then Clyde would spy a young lad of nine or ten walking down the street with one on his head.

In a city of eccentrics, Clyde was proud to be acquainted with one of the city's most noted eccentrics. At the spry age of seventy-eight, he had no intention of being anyone other than himself. He did no harm to others, and at times perhaps even did some good. To Clyde, at least, Mr. Patten always seemed generally happy, and of course he always managed to get enough to eat and drink, especially as his renown grew and people treated him to meals and drinks and pressed change into his hand without his even having to ask.

On this particular day and occasion, Clyde was running his usual errands when he spotted Mr. Patten sitting on the bricks in the morning's cool grayness. Clyde descended the hill with a plodding lope, the hill's pitch augmenting his momentum and yet his mud-caked shoes weighting him down like anchors strapped to his feet. Mr. Patten waved at Clyde as he reached the corner, and Clyde waved back and ambled up to where he sat.

"Good morning, Mr. Patten, sir." Clyde was genuinely pleased to see the old man. They'd been friends for many years now – since Clyde's father first introduced them when Clyde was just a young lad of twelve. Yet he had especially come to know Mr. Patten after he himself began to make his daily forays into the city and would encounter his Lake Union neighbor on various street corners, just as he was doing right now. For many years now, whenever he and Mr. Patten chanced to meet each other like this, it was their custom to stop and talk for a spell.

"Good morning to you, Master Hunssler," Robert returned, and gestured to the stack of bricks upon which he sat. "Please, take a seat. You look as if you've been trudging down around the mudflats again."

"Just doing my business about town is all," Clyde said, taking the invitation to join Robert on the bricks and rest his weary legs. "I don't know how others do it … the finely dressed folks, that is. I can't keep out of the mud. It swallows me whole every time." Clyde said this knowing very well that unless you exclusively rode the trolleys or had the luxury of a carriage (or perhaps even a motorcar), indeed if a person had to walk the streets to get anywhere, as he did, even so little as a square block and especially in and around the areas being regraded, then your shoes, socks, and the cuffs of your pants (or the hem of your skirt) would have to be surrendered to the mud. Men prosperous enough to own more than one pair of shoes tended to wear their heavy brogans outside and preserve their dress shoes for inside. Women likewise. He unfortunately did not have the luxury of an extra pair of shoes and therefore had to scrape and pound and rub the accumulated mud from his feet every time he entered a store or cafe. Back at the boardinghouse, Maddie allowed him to remove his shoes in the back mudroom and walk about in his bare socks, although this meant he needed to keep a supply of clean socks on hand, which in itself was difficult enough.

"You're working too hard," Robert told him.

"I work only as much as I need to," Clyde replied, and took off his wool cap and slapped it against his knee to shake off the morning mist, then set it back on his head.

"It's going to rain like locusts this afternoon," said Robert. "So be ye prepared."

"Thanks for the tip," Clyde said, and reached into his pants pocket for a couple of coins to give Robert.

"Ah, ah, ah," Robert muttered and put his hand on Clyde's forearm. "This one's on me."

Clyde took his hand from his pocket and patted Robert on the back. "You're all right, Mr. Patten," and changing the subject said, "How's your garden? My father says your pole beans put his to shame last year."

Robert grinned, tickled no doubt by the report that his pole beans had stirred envy in Clyde's father, and put a thumb through a buttonhole in his gabardine overcoat. Clyde's father also had the highest regard for

Robert's jack cider. Every couple of months or so, he walked the shoreline from his house on Lake Union to Robert's houseboat moored at the northernmost end of the lake and the two men would climb up onto the houseboat's flat roof and drink the fermented and strained apple (or pear) cider. His father called this being neighborly. The two men sometimes stayed neighborly for three or four days, or until the cider was gone, at which time Clyde's father trudged back to his end of the lake and slept for a day or two.

"It was a good summer for my beans all right," Robert said. "I even sold some at the market and then went and bought Ferguson's old apple press from him ... you know, to boost my annual yield."

The rain picked up, turning from mist to drizzle (or "mizzle," as Clyde once heard Robert call it), and after a few moments of quiet between them, Clyde turned to Robert and said, "Let me buy you breakfast, Mr. Patten. Percival's has the best sausage gravy west of the Palouse."

"They do indeed," said Robert. "And I should know why, too, since I made that sausage gravy and the biscuits and flapjacks and corned beef hash they also serve up when I was still working there in the kitchen. That was before all the world knew how good Percival's sausage gravy was. Who do you think made it so good? I put the paprika in, and it's been in ever since."

Clyde accepted this boast without comment, knowing from experience Robert's penchant for exaggeration, and stood up from his seat on the stacked bricks and said, "So let's get a move-on then."

"Let's indeed," Robert said, and more slowly than Clyde rose to his feet with the aid of his cane. Once he was standing, Robert still had the self-assured gait of a man who walked perhaps a dozen miles a day – a trek that took him from Lake Union to Pioneer Place and back again, plus all his perambulations in between. Clyde sometimes fancied that he himself walked the avenues and alleys of Seattle more than anyone else – beat cops and street sweepers included – but in his heart of hearts he knew Robert Patten could best him for distance *and* endurance any day of the week. The pace of Robert's gait only confirmed this as they made their way around the block heading to Percival's Cafe.

They rounded the corner of Washington Street and First Avenue, walking north, and crossed the street just as Clyde saw his friend Ray coming out of the cafe. Ray paused on the sidewalk outside the cafe entrance and lit a thin cigar he withdrew from his inside jacket pocket. His small box camera rested against his chest, slung from his neck by a leather strap. Ray tugged on the cigar once, twice, and a third time to make sure it had a good burn going, and then looked up to see Clyde and Robert walking toward him.

They greeted one another and there were handshakes all around, and then Ray stepped back from the other two and said he wanted to take a snapshot of them. Clyde was reluctant—because frankly Ray took his photograph so often that Clyde was growing tired of it. Robert, on the other hand, stepped forward with a broad grin flashing through his white beard, pouching out his cheeks and revealing his brown teeth, said he'd be honored to have his picture taken. So while Clyde stepped into a doorway to get out of view of the camera, Ray positioned Robert in the middle of the brick sidewalk and told him to stand very still. Robert did exactly as he was told. He leaned against his cane with one hand, hooked his thumb into the buttonhole of his coat with the other, and held steady while Ray rolled the film on his old Kodak Brownie, tested several angles, peered down into the viewfinder, and at last called out, "Ready, steady now, steady ... Got it." Ray got the shot and walking up to Robert shook his hand and slid a dollar bill into his palm. "That was a fine photograph," he said.

"Happy to oblige," said Robert.

Clyde stepped forward from the doorway now. "Are you going to join us for breakfast?" he asked Ray.

"I'm not so sure I'm hungry anymore myself," Robert said a bit sheepishly to Clyde before Ray could answer.

"What do you mean?" Clyde turned to him. "I said I'd buy you breakfast, Mr. Patten."

"Well, with all this picture-taking excitement, I guess I'm just not that hungry anymore," Robert said, and tilted back his umbrella hat. "A man's stomach can have a change of mind, can't it?"

"Not usually," Clyde replied, with a pretty good idea what Robert was up to. He had Ray's dollar in his pocket and wanted to get a drink.

"But listen, son," Robert came back, "I want you two young men to come visit me over at the lake. I mean it. Just come by anytime and I'll cook you up some grub … better than anything you'll eat in here," and with this he indicated the entrance to Percival's and retreated down the street the way Clyde and he had just come, heading, Clyde knew very well, to the sailor's tavern with nickel schooners just around the corner.

Ray was fidgeting with his camera and said to Clyde, "I'll have that breakfast with you, if you're still buying."

"Didn't you just eat?"

"Just coffee and a bearclaw," Ray replied.

"Oh, in that case," Clyde said, and saying nothing more he walked straight up to the entrance to Percival's and held the door open for his friend.

They took a table toward the rear of the cafe and waited for a waiter to serve them. It had been several months since Clyde had last been in Percival's and from the looks of it, the place was trying to spruce itself up and improve its clientele. Once a hash-slinging, smoke-clogged cafe where gold seekers found the cheapest meal in town while waiting for their passage north, there wasn't a sailor or stevedore or prospector to be found in the place anymore. Times had changed that fast. The cafe looked like it was now trying to cater to the merchant and business class instead. The card tables in back had been removed; the counter stools all had backs and upholstered seats on them; the tables were draped with white tablecloths; and the two waiters who worked the dining area wore clean white shirts and black bowties to match their black suspenders. In place of the chalkboard listing the menu and prices that used to be above the front counter, paper menus were now laid between the salt and pepper shakers and ketchup bottle on each table.

"I suppose the prices have gone up too," Clyde said, after noting all the changes to Ray.

Ray had picked up one of the menus and was studying it. "They may not have let the Umbrella Man in," he said. "Too fancy now." He put the menu back. "You're right about the prices. That's why I only had a bearclaw, though I'm fixin' to have the corned beef hash and biscuits this time around. But don't worry," he added, "we'll split the ticket."

The waiter finally came around and they each ordered the corned beef hash and biscuits with sausage gravy and coffee. Ray set his camera on the table and looked at Clyde.

"How come you won't let me take your picture anymore?" Ray asked.

"You have enough already," Clyde said. "I'm trying to get you to branch out, find new subjects."

"You think I photograph you too much?"

"I'm just saying," Clyde went on, "I don't want my picture taken anymore."

"I don't know what you're afraid of. If I were Edward Curtis, I bet you'd let me take your picture."

Clyde didn't want to squabble about it, and he was relieved when the waiter brought them their food. Having skipped Maddie's breakfast back at the boardinghouse and having already run around town to deliver the *Sentry* to its various drop-off points, he was plenty hungry. He and Ray ate in silence for several minutes, until, with half his plate finished, Ray put his fork down, looked up at Clyde, and asked, "What do you hear about the regrading? What's the latest?"

Clyde finished chewing and wiped his mouth with a napkin. "It's not good," he said. "They're still trying to settle with everyone and in the meanwhile the hoses are going full blast. We don't know what we're going to do." He knew that Ray would understand he was referring to Maddie and himself.

"Most people think it's a good idea," Ray went on.

Clyde glared at his friend a moment, then took a calculated sip of coffee. He knew that Ray was not as staunchly opposed to the regrading as he was, that he'd bought into the city's argument about the natural northerly progress of the business district, about being able to connect the downtown with the outlying districts, about the augmented property values once Denny Hill was leveled. Clyde also knew, based on what Ray himself had said to him, that he believed Maddie should mortgage her house to the bank, pay for the regrading of her property, and have the house lowered to the new grade. To him, it was a simple matter. He didn't understand why Maddie didn't trust the city's promises. He just didn't understand what the house, the neighborhood, and the hill – all together, as a whole – meant to her. Or to him.

Then Ray let drop that he was thinking of starting a new series of photographs about Denny Hill and the regrading, which caught Clyde off guard. He knew that in the end Ray was a very a talented photographer, yet he was surprised that Ray was even interested enough in what was happening to the hill to invest his time in photographing it. He wanted Ray to tell him more about this new project of his, but he didn't want to seem overly eager or to ask him about it outright. Clyde watched him a moment longer, and then Ray said, "Asahel Curtis has been shooting the regrading off and on. He's a big backer of it. Men at work, the progress of a great city, and all that. But I thought I might take a different tack. No one's photographing the neighborhood itself, making sure there's a record of what it was like before the regrading. Everyone's just shooting the regrading. I'm thinking I'll do a kind of *then* and *now* series." He hesitated, as if he'd said something he shouldn't have, and added, "That's what it'll turn into at least if the city keeps at it. I was thinking maybe one of the newspapers would be interested in such a series. What do you think?"

Clyde just nodded and said, "It wouldn't hurt to try." He didn't know what to say in response to Ray's new project. It was a good idea, he figured, though he wasn't sure what was really motivating it. Clyde doubted the photographs would have any bearing on the outcome of the regrading project. But on the other hand ... one never knew. At the very least, Ray might bring some attention to what was happening to the residents and neighborhood of Denny Hill. Attention to what was being lost.

Ray finished eating and signaled the waiter for more coffee. "I don't think these biscuits or gravy are as good as they used to be."

Clyde was still thinking about Ray's comments about photographing Denny Hill and was annoyed by his casual "*then* and *now*" remark. He was thinking of Maddie, how utterly aggrieved she was at the prospect of losing her house, how she remained agitated all day fretting about it, how at night she often couldn't sleep, leading to their staying up reading Charles Dickens some nights almost to dawn. He wondered if any photograph could possibly capture this prolonged uncertainty and anguish.

"What about these break-ins that have been happening about town?" Ray asked, again changing the subject. "Have you been reading about those?"

Clyde pushed his plate away, his food half eaten. He tried to believe Maddie would be okay. "You're right," he said. "The biscuits and gravy aren't as good."

"They say they might be connected to the regradings."

"How's that?" asked Clyde. He'd read about the house break-ins in the *Seattle Post-Intelligencer* that Ada fetched for Maddie each morning and brought back to the house. Already three break-ins in two weeks at the homes of prominent city figures. It wasn't until the third break-in that a reporter for the *P-I* noted that each homeowner had some connection to the regradings: City Attorney Scott Calhoun, who drafted the ordinance that Maddie refused to sign; Judge Creighton, who oversaw the assessors committee; and H. W. Hawley, one of the main contractors for the Denny Hill project. The same reporter had also noted that the break-ins had begun shortly after Pinkerton guards had been hired and the sabotaging of the regrading sites had stopped. The reporter's speculations, in the end, all made sense to Clyde.

"It sounds like it could be trouble," Ray remarked. Clyde thought Ray was cautioning him, which he didn't appreciate.

"Do you think I have something to do with them just because I don't want Madison House torn down? Do you think I might be the one breaking into people's houses?" He didn't try to conceal his aggravation with Ray. Sometimes he wondered about their friendship. It seemed too often that Ray wanted life's affairs all bundled up into a neat, tidy package. Yet as hard experience had taught Clyde, sometimes you had to put yourself, as well as life's comforts, on the line. It's what a Japanese acquaintance of his, a Buddhist man, once told him was called *durka*, the fact of life's everyday hardships. And although Clyde knew he wasn't about to become an outlaw in the fight against the regrading of Denny Hill, he also knew he couldn't condone it as Ray seemed implicitly to be doing – photo series or not.

Clyde pushed away from the table.

"Look," Ray said to him, "I didn't mean it that way. Let me pay for this." Ray signaled the waiter, and after checking the total on the bill the waiter handed him, gave him two dollars and some change and told him, "Keep it."

"It's all right," Clyde said. He didn't want to part with sour feelings between them either. He knew Ray meant well. This latest development regarding the break-ins was indeed troubling. Upon reading the reports in the newspaper, Clyde had automatically thought of the stooped and pale-eyed man who'd shown him the rail spike six months ago.

"Listen," Ray said, clearly trying to make amends. "Let's you and me, with Loye and Maddie, go out to Luna Park someday soon. Whatdaya say? We'll take the trolley, bring our swimsuits, the whole deal."

Clyde wasn't readily comfortable with this idea. It sounded like fun. But what would it be like, all four of them, all the way over to West Seattle...? "How much would it cost?" he asked.

"Hardly a ha'penny," Ray shot back, always ready with some quip or another. "We'll get the girls to pack a lunch, and I have a pal at the park who'll get us in for free."

"Why not then," Clyde said, changing his mind on a dime. Since he didn't like to swim all that much, maybe he and Maddie could beg out of that part of the excursion. Otherwise, it could be a good time for all. Since Luna Park had opened last summer, the public excitement about it had been high. A lot of Seattleites said it put the popular amusement park at Coney Island in New York to shame. "Let's plan on it," he said more definitively. "I'll talk to Maddie. It'll be a good break from all these worries of late."

"Thatta boy," Ray said, and picked up his camera from the table and slung it around his neck as Clyde led the way through the cafe and back out onto First Avenue.

18. Stage Fright (1907)

"MR. CONSIDINE HAS BIG PLANS FOR YOU. HE'S SEEN YOU act and he likes your stuff. He told me himself."

Lewis Pittman leaned over Chiridah from behind her and kissed the side of her face. In the stuffy backstage of the Castle Garden Theater, he'd removed his coat and now strutted about in a starched white shirt and black silk vest. He still wore his bowler. No matter how hot it became backstage, he never removed his bowler, which became a running gag with the girls he managed.

"But I haven't even met him," Chiridah complained, looking at herself in the dressing room mirror. She had gotten thinner since she'd begun performing regularly in Considine's theaters – the ones managed by Lewis Pittman. She was thinner and yet somehow puffier too, and she didn't get nearly enough sleep.

"He's a shy man," Lewis said. "That's why you haven't met him yet. Plus he's a very busy man. If he went around to every girl that worked in one of his theaters, they'd hound him to death. That's why he hires me. I'm the intermediary, you see." Standing above Chiridah, his hands on her shoulders, he made eye contact with her in the mirror. "Now let me bring you something to drink. I know I need one." He kissed the top of her head through the feather sprigs she wore in her hair as part of her act, and walked out of the dressing room.

Chiridah continued removing her makeup. The show had gone well, but it wasn't the high-class dramatic stock that she'd expected to become active in when she first started working for Lewis after meeting him on the Lake Washington excursion boat that day last summer. Instead, she was doing strictly variety material, mostly dancing, occasionally a skit or two. Nickel and dime admission. Drinks being served during the performance and people getting looped. When she learned that the Third Avenue Theater had been torn down because of the regrading, her dream of appearing on its stage was destroyed too. However, Lewis kept promising her that there would be lots of leads available once the new Moore Theater was built. "Choice roles, too," he told her.

Lewis came back into the dressing room with a bucket of beer and two schooner glasses. He poured a glass for Chiridah and set it on the dressing table, but she just let it sit there untouched as she removed her costume, a cheap and risqué imitation of an eighteenth-century cotillion gown. Leaning with one hand on the corner of the dressing table, Lewis watched her pull the hoop skirt off and unbutton her petticoat underneath. She removed her blouse and corset covering and asked him to unlace her corset for her.

"Listen here, Chiridah," he said, after finishing off the first glass of beer and pouring himself another. "There's a friend of mine I would like you to entertain this evening. He's in town from San Francisco and I told him one of the girls from the show would be happy to give him a little company. Now I've already asked all the other girls, but they have this or that or the other thing and can't do me this one small favor. So I'm asking you. What d'ya say?"

Chiridah pulled over her head the dress she had borrowed from Loye last month, the one with the houndstooth trim around the sleeves and waist. Loye had been kind enough not to ask for it back yet, since it was one of the few good dresses Chiridah had to wear. "I don't know, Lewis. I'm awfully tired tonight. And I told my friend Loye I would play cards with her and Maddie and Ada tonight."

Lewis stepped in front of Chiridah, took hold of her by the shoulders, and looked directly into her face. "Chiridah," he said to her, "I've done a lot to get you on your feet in this town and help your acting career come along and all. So I'm asking you to do this one favor for me. You'll like ol' H.T. The two of you will have a grand ol' time. And like I said, it would be doing me a big, big favor." Then he reached into his pants pocket and pulled out his billfold and handed her a ten dollar bill. "I want you to take this, just 'cause you deserve it for how hard you work."

Chiridah looked at the ten spot in his hand. It more than doubled a single night's wages, and she could certainly use it after having gotten more than a couple of weeks behind in paying Maddie for her room and board, borrowing clothes from Loye all the time, and generally being dead broke Sunday through Saturday. She took the ten dollars and smiled softly and thanked Lewis for it. Then she took a drink from the beer he'd poured her and asked him where she was supposed to meet his friend from San Francisco.

CHIRIDAH ENTERED THE SALOON MORE THAN A LITTLE APPRE-
hensive about meeting a complete stranger, much less keeping him company for however long before she could go home. Although she regularly performed in several of the smaller (and more raucous) theaters that Lewis managed about town, she didn't like frequenting establishments below the Deadline during her off-hours. She knew that a girl, especially a stage actress, could acquire a reputation as easily as catching a cold. From the front entrance of the saloon, she had to step down to enter the main barroom. The ceiling was low and the air was tight with cigar smoke. She had just come down the three short steps when a small roundish man came up to her and introduced himself as Harvey Tutweiler. "You must be Lew Pittman's girl."

"How do you do," Chiridah said, and introduced herself. Because she stood almost a head taller than the man, for a moment she thought she might still be standing on one of the steps leading down into the barroom. Yet as he took her hand and led her across the expanse of the barroom to a small table in the back, he seemed not to be bothered at all by the difference in their height. Chiridah told herself that's just how it was going to be, since he was the guest and she the hostess. It was only for the one evening after all, and she already had the ten dollars tucked away in her change purse.

Harvey Tutweiler – "People call me H.T.," he informed her – pulled a chair out for Chiridah and then sat down right beside her, rather than across the table, and signaled to the barmaid. He ordered a double bourbon for himself and asked Chiridah what she was drinking.

"Nothing for me, thank you."

"None of that now," H.T. exclaimed. "Jackie," he said to the barmaid, "bring the lady a sherry," and held three fingers up and winked at her.

When the drinks came, H.T. raised his glass. "To the evening," he toasted, and Chiridah went along with the toast and took a sip of the sherry, her first ever. It tasted both sweet and bitter. Although she now and then took a taste of beer with one of the other girls after the show, she never ordered drinks and rarely finished a full glass of anything. She'd gotten drunk only twice, both times almost by accident, the first time when she was drinking wine at a dinner party and the second time when she was hanging around in the dressing room late one night with the other girls. In general, neither the taste nor the effects of drink appealed to her.

"I've heard San Francisco is a lovely town," Chiridah chimed in, wanting to be the good hostess. "I've always thought I'd take my stage career there after Seattle. Do you like San Francisco?"

"I should say it's all right," H.T. remarked, not really paying attention to what she said, and instead sipped his drink and looked about the room at the other patrons. "Haven't been there but once or twice and both times was rattled senseless by those damn earthquakes."

"You mean you're not from San Francisco?" Chiridah asked.

"Hell no, miss," he shot back – Chiridah didn't like his swearing at her, and also began to suspect he'd already forgotten her name – "I'm in town from Grand Falls, Montana. I supervise a copper mining operation out there. Did Pittman tell you I was from San Francisco? Well then he must have me confused with some other fella he provides services for."

The way Lewis had described Harvey Tutweiler to her, Chiridah figured they were old school chums, or perhaps business associates from the Considine-Sullivan theaters, which were beginning to expand into other cities. That's why she'd made the comment about trying her luck in San Francisco, thinking H.T. might provide a future contact for her. Yet it seemed that she'd misunderstood Lewis. In any case, she was here now and could clear it up tomorrow with Lewis back at the Castle Garden … yet from now on, she told herself, no more such favors for him or his "friends."

H.T. continued to ignore Chiridah as he finished his drink and signaled the barmaid to bring them both another. He was not a particularly attractive man, Chiridah mused. His thin dark hair was parted in the middle and slicked down straight along either side of his overlarge head. His stubby fingers had grime beneath the nails. And the wool suit he wore seemed rather rumpled and worn, as if he hadn't had a change of clothes in several days.

"Drink up, miss," he told her, and to avoid coming across as discourteous she obliged him, sipping from the brimful glass of sherry. "We'll go when you finish your drink," he said, but didn't indicate where they would go. Chiridah imagined he might take her to a show, probably at one of the dance halls since they were the only shows that went on this late at night. She tried to think of what she might buy with the ten dollars Lewis had given her.

Harvey Tutweiler had two more drinks, though Chiridah had yet to finish her first, when he said they should be going. Chiridah looked forward to escaping the smoky saloon and breathing some fresh air out on the street. She wondered still where it was he was going to take her, yet didn't have the nerve to ask. As he pushed his chair back and stood up from the table, he took Chiridah's wrist, pulling her to her feet, and then wobbled some as he guided her to the back of the saloon and suddenly up the back stairs. When she asked where they were going, all he said was, "To the room," and Chiridah, a little unnerved by this detour, assumed he needed to get something, his hat perhaps, before they made their way to wherever it was they would go for the rest of the evening.

The hallway to the rooming house above the saloon was dark, the wood floors creaky, and the air stale and closed in. Chiridah had stayed in a similar place when she'd first arrived in Seattle from Tacoma right after graduating high school, before she discovered the old man who owned the house on Denny Hill that Maddie had eventually taken over. H.T. still held her wrist rather tightly, which she was about to object to when they reached a door at the end of the hallway and he let go in order to work the key into the lock. He opened the door and signaled Chiridah to enter ahead of him. Her initial thought was to decline and wait for him out in the hallway – because a lady simply did not enter a man's room – but when he continued to stare at her and said, "Please, I'm in a hurry," she relented and stepped into the room.

Chiridah felt instantly uncomfortable the moment she crossed the threshold. The room was terribly dreary: an iron bed with a beaded brown covering, a wicker chair with an open leather suitcase on it, a washstand with filthy water standing in the bowl, and long yellowish drapery pulled across the narrow window. As soon as they were inside the room, H.T. closed and locked the door behind Chiridah and removed his jacket and threw it onto the wicker chair. He then loosened his tie and undid the button on his collar.

"Undress," he ordered her.

Chiridah turned and looked at him. Was he actually speaking to her? "Sir!" she said, making her astonishment plain. "Please behave yourself."

"I told you miss, I ain't got much time. You've been paid, ain't ya?"

"Mr. Tutweiler," Chiridah began. "I beg your pardon ... but I believe there's been a misunderstanding. I shall be leaving now." Chiridah moved toward the door.

As she reached for the door knob, however, Harvey Tutweiler grabbed her wrist, yanked her away from the door, and pushed her onto the bed.

"Here," he said, flashing a ten dollar bill in front of her, and then snatched her cloth handbag from her hand and stuffed the bill into it. "Maybe he paid you and maybe he didn't. But you ain't leaving without your doing what you've been paid for." When Chiridah tried to get up from the bed, he pushed her back down and then fell on top of her. As she began to object, he pressed his face into her neck. When she struggled, trying to push his weight off and free herself, he drew back and struck her with his open hand across her left temple. Then he dug his fingers sharply into the neckline of her dress and tore it down off her shoulders to her waist and buried his face in her bosom. When she continued to struggle, he bit her breast and she screamed. He raised up and hit her again to quiet her and then climbed onto her chest and pinned her arms with his knees. He reached back and grabbed between her legs with one hand while with the other he unfastened his pants. He then held Chiridah by the back of the head and pushed himself toward her face, and every time she tried to scream, he slapped her harder until finally, pinned by his weight and nearly blinded by his blows, she relented.

When he rolled off her, she pulled her dress about her as best she could and ran from the room, spitting his filth from her mouth all the way down the hallway. She ran down the back stairs, through the crowded barroom, out the front entrance of the saloon, and rushed around the corner and into the alley. She stepped out of the light from the street lamp, and in the alley's dark seclusion keeled over and vomited. She clutched the neckline of her torn dress – Loye's dress – and held onto it as the convulsions came in waves, and each time wiped her mouth with the back of her hand. When the convulsing had stopped and she became composed enough to stand upright again, she found two safety pins in her handbag and pinned up her dress. From the shadows of the alley, she looked out into the street – a trolley scraping up the hill on its tracks, a horse and wagon clattering past, a scattering of men walking in different directions, some accompanied by women – and was fearful of throwing herself out among it all. Two men in overcoats and derbies walked past and spotting her in the alley paused briefly to peer at her, and then walked on.

Her face felt bruised, and as she raised a hand to her cheek she feared suddenly she would not be able to go on stage the next day. She thought of finding a telephone and trying to phone Loye, or just taking the trolley back uptown to Maddie's. But both options terrified her. She didn't want either Loye or Maddie to see her like this, or to ever find out what had happened. They would think she had brought it on herself, especially by taking up with Lewis Pittman. After all, Loye was such a good wholesome girl who knew everyone who was anyone in Tacoma, and Chiridah didn't dare risk Loye's bad opinion of her. So when the way was clear, she ducked back out of the alley and, keeping close to the walls of the buildings adjacent the plank sidewalks, made her way as quickly as she could back to the Castle Garden Theater.

Luckily for her, the backstage door was unlocked and she slipped in and went straight to the dressing room. She didn't want to encounter Lewis, in case he was still lurking about the building, so she kept as quiet as possible. She couldn't tell how much of what had happened had been his doing, though she knew he was not blameless. She closed the dressing room door behind her and, leaving the electric light off and the room dark, lay down on one of the two sofas provided for the girls to take naps on between shows. A billowy taffeta costume lay at her feet at one end of the sofa and Chiridah pulled this over herself and curled up beneath it. When the dark filled the room and all seemed still again, she began quietly to weep. She didn't know how long she wept until she finally fell asleep.

BESSIE NIVENS FOUND HER IN THE DRESSING ROOM THE NEXT morning. Chiridah had been only half asleep when Bessie came in and gasped upon seeing her lying on the couch. "Oh Chi, what did he do to you?" And she sat down beside Chiridah and took her in her arms.

Chiridah tried to stand, to go to the mirror to look at the bruises on her face, but Bessie held her back and told her not to stir, to just lie still and rest. She then left the dressing room to retrieve a bowl of ice from the front bar and wet washcloths to use as compresses. While Bessie was out of the room, Chiridah stood, steadied herself against the dizziness that swept over her, and stumbled to the dressing table to look at herself in the mirror. Her left cheek was swollen and red, and a yellowish-purple bruise darkened her left eye and spread across the left side of her face. As she fingered each area to test its tenderness and winced in doing so, she knew she was lucky not to have been cut. Her upper lip, though twice its normal size, was not split, and her left eye, though mean and ugly, was not swollen shut. She returned to the sofa just as Bessie returned with ice and washcloths. Bessie immediately wrapped ice in one washcloth and told Chiridah to hold it to the side of her face and her lip. She then dampened and folded the other washcloth and laid it across Chiridah's forehead.

When Chiridah began to tell Bessie what had happened, how Lewis had arranged for her to entertain a friend of his, how the friend turned out not to be a friend at all but just a small nasty man who hit her and violated her, Bessie shook her head in sympathy and indignation. Yet, rather than express outrage at Lewis, as Chiridah expected her to, she only repeated how sorry she was this had happened to her. Then she said, "Lewis should know better than to put you in a situation like that."

Chiridah did not understand what Bessie meant by this and only wanted to feel better so she could go home. When she expressed her wish to Bessie, though, Bessie advised her to stay where she was, that she shouldn't go out like this – "Not until the swelling goes down at least," she said – and that later in the evening she would help her back to her own place on Jefferson Street, where she could stay for as long as she liked.

"But what about the show tonight?" Chiridah asked, afraid she would lose her slot in the show's rotation, and just as Bessie seemed to be searching for a way to respond, a knock came at the door and Lewis walked in.

He looked at the two women on the sofa and then leaned over Chiridah, took her chin in his hand, and inspected her injuries.

"What happened?" he wanted to know.

Chiridah removed the ice and wet compress from her face and sat up. "Shouldn't you know already? Your friend H.T. did this to me – and worse. You lied to me." Despite her anger, Chiridah felt her tears coming back and tried to stave them off.

Lewis stepped back from the couch and lit the cigar he'd been carrying in his hand. Between puffs, he said, "Well, you must of done something, little girl. H.T.'s an all right customer in most cases."

"I was just trying to protect myself," Chiridah said, and now cried in earnest.

Lewis nodded at Bessie to leave the room, and she did so without hesitation. Then he stepped over to the sofa and looked down at Chiridah. "I'll tell you how it is," he said, "and I'll tell you just this once – because I don't like my friends or my girls getting upset, especially with one another. I like to run a smooth operation, understand?" He sat down on the opposite end of the sofa, and Chiridah retracted from him by curling up at her end. "You give him what he wants and you never *ever* fight back. If you do, you only got yourself to blame for what's coming. Got that? And remember, I asked you to do this favor for me and you said you would. But now look at the mess you made of it. Wouldn't surprise me if I never heard hide nor hair of H.T. again."

Chiridah felt like she might be sick again as she glared up at him. "That was no favor," she said, returning the washcloth with the ice in it to her cheek. "You're nothing but a whoremonger."

Lewis jumped to his feet and pointed a finger at Chiridah. "That's right," he said. "And you're nothing but a whore! All you goddamn mabs are alike. Think you're some damn starlet, dontcha?"

Chiridah pulled her knees up to her chest and wrapped her arms around her legs. What was happening to her? Where was Bessie? Why was Lewis suddenly behaving this way? She knew she would be safe if she could just get back to Maddie's. "How am I going to go on stage like this?" she asked tentatively, ignoring the words Lewis had just shouted at her—but then adding, "I don't want to meet anymore of your 'friends.'"

That's when Lewis sidled up to her on the sofa, making her flinch and pull back even more. He leaned into her, his harsh breath on her face, and said, "I'm not asking you anymore, Miss Chiridah. I'm telling you. You'll see my friends when I want you to. Just like the other girls in the show. Or else you won't work here, and you won't work anywhere in this town again. The whole West Coast. Your acting career, Miss Sarah Bernhardt, is over. If you don't like our arrangement, you can forget opening night at the Opera House or the Moore Theater." He stood again and put his cigar back in his mouth and puffed on it several times, then looked back at Chiridah. "On the other hand, if you don't make a fuss—like you did last night by the looks of you—you'll do all right. You keep doing the show, Mr. Considine will still be happy and maybe move you up. There's also the extra dough-ray-me in it for you. So you can treat yourself to some nice things when you want to."

He didn't wait for Chiridah to reply to this last bit, but stepped over to the door and looked back at her. "It's simple, girlie. Don't ditch a good thing," he said, his tone more composed, sounding like a theater manager again. "Talk to Bessie. She'll set you straight." He blew cigar smoke out the side of his mouth and left the dressing room, closing the door behind him.

Chiridah knew what it all meant. Only she couldn't fathom why it was happening to her. Had her aspirations been her downfall? Surely Sarah Bernhardt had not had to prostitute herself, or Jane Oaker, who appeared last year in *Babette of the Nest* at the Grand Opera House, or May Irwin, who'd been in *Mrs. Black Is Back* at the Grand Opera House that same season. They were artists, dedicated and true to their craft. She only wanted to be like them. Yet here was precisely what her mother from the start had warned her about in becoming an actress: It was a sinful profession. Lewis Pittman, who was no more than a pimp posing as a theater manager, proved this point.

Stiff and frightened, she rose from the sofa, determined to make her way back to Maddie's, just as Bessie stepped back into the room. Seeing how Chiridah tottered on her feet, she guided her back to the sofa and said, "Here, I brought you something. It'll help you calm down and rest. Then when you're feeling better, we can put some makeup on over those bruises. I'm sure you'll be able to go back on in a day or two."

She handed Chiridah a small soft wad of something waxy and told her to chew on it. "Slowly," Bessie instructed her, "and swallow every now and then. It's just a tinge of morphine that the doctor gives me. I mix it in with the bees wax so it's like chewing gum. You'll feel better in a wee bit, I promise."

Chiridah did as Bessie told her and put the gumdrop-sized piece of wax in her mouth and began slowly chewing it. It was tasteless as first, then a little bitter, but gradually she felt her mouth begin to numb, then a tingling rise up her neck and a lightness fill her head. Her injuries ceased throbbing, and she smiled softly at Bessie and thanked her for being so kind to her. Soon she wanted only to sleep.

19. The Great Author (1907)

CLYDE BEGAN READING THE GREAT AMERICAN AUTHOR – "our international novelist," the *Post-Intelligencer* dubbed him – when Edward Holton James, Clyde's employer and Henry James's nephew, confirmed to Clyde that his uncle Henry would be visiting him in Seattle. Clyde even reread *The Portrait of a Lady* and *Daisy Miller* aloud to Maddie. He both admired and puzzled over the works. Their literary mastery was unquestionable, in his estimation. Yet was this mastery – of prose style and portraiture – being put to its best use in the author's tireless treatment of society's upper crust? He would have liked to have seen the great writer take on mankind in its shirtsleeves, as Stephen Crane and Jack London had ... even though these two authors plainly lacked Henry James's acute sensitivity and selectiveness, qualities which Clyde appreciated and admired in Mr. James's lengthy, often challenging sentences. It had taken him and Maddie two weeks to get through *Daisy Miller*, the shorter of the two novels they read together, and more than two months to finish *The Portrait of a Lady*. Yet Maddie still quoted to him from her favorite passages – the infinitely perceptive narrator observing how Isabel's "originality was that she gave one an impression of having intentions of her own," or the irrepressible heroine exclaiming to Lord Warburton, "I adore a moat ... Goodbye."

Ned James had agreed to arrange an audience for Clyde with the great author. Yet as Clyde came to discover, Ned had a chameleon streak in him when dealing with people, so Clyde was cautious and hedged his expectations for the meeting. In his campaign for the state senate, Ned James had stumped for the workingman, directly opposing the titans of industry, such giants as President Baer of the Philadelphia & Reading Railroad who in response to a recent coal strike had declared, "The rights and interests of the laboring man will be protected and cared for – not by the labor agitators, but by the Christian men and women to whom God in his infinite wisdom has given control of the property interests of this country." Ned was also stalwart in his opposition to America's imperialist expansion, and to prove it he had hired a Filipino man, Erasmo Marcos, as one of his law clerks. On the other hand, Ned could turn quite imperial himself. His intolerance of those who on occasion took a drink was confounding. In his public talks, as he did before the newly founded Rotary Club of Seattle, a branch of the Chicago group, Ned stumped for temperance as fiercely as he did for corporate reform.

Clyde now walked down Fifth Avenue. Ned had instructed him to meet him at the Pioneer Building, where, after losing the election in November, he now leased smaller, less costly offices. From there, Ned had promised, he would take Clyde to meet his uncle at the author's hotel. From Denny Hill, Clyde could look out across the burgeoning city below. Rising above it all, the guardian presence of Mount Rainier. A streetcar scraped and rattled past, leaving the smell of heated steel from the car's breaking to slow its descent down the hill. The overhead wire crackled where it met with the car's connecting rod. The streetcar, which was one of the last routes running on Denny Hill since the regrading had commenced, was nearly empty. Clyde considered flagging it down, to save his best energy for later, but then decided not to and let the streetcar pass.

He took a deep breath before reaching the bottom of the hill. He knew that as soon as he was down the hill and past Pike Street, the fresh breezes blew less freely. The streets downtown were far more congested, and where they had been newly regraded, the air tended to stagnate along the straight and leveled avenues, filling with the stench of horse dung, sweaty pedestrians, and the exhaust from combustion engines. It was odd that in this age of vim and vigor people wanted to deprive themselves of the kind of invigorating fresh air, brisk exercise, and sweeping views afforded by the inclines of the city's hills. They would rather wash those hills into the sea and board a streetcar. With this in mind, Clyde broke into a loping trot for the two steep blocks from Lenora to Stewart, loving the pound of the macadam reverberating up through his calves and thighs, his lungs sucking in the wind that rushed against his face in his downward momentum. His trot turned into a nearly out of control gallop and he pictured himself, as if in a movie reel at the nickelodeon, plummeting forward, then tripping and tumbling, in a blur of flailing limbs.

Another streetcar, this one slowly trudging uphill, passed him, or rather he passed it, and as he raced through the intersection of Fifth and

Pine where the street leveled out, he slowed to a trot again and eventually settled back to merely walking. He was perspiring by now and worried that he might not be presentable to Henry James. Normally he would remove his wool jacket, but decorum on the Seattle streets in recent years had become mandatory, as if people needed to compensate for the unaccountable upheaval of their city by the incessant regradings. Plus, the city was growing at an unprecedented rate – far faster than Clyde could keep up with. To someone like his father, who had settled on Lake Union when most of the city was still forest and who now only occasionally rode his wagon into the downtown to bring his produce to the farmer's market, the rapid changes were beyond comprehension.

Sometimes Clyde wondered if he lacked the demonic ambition or wherewithal that seemed so necessary to make a go of it in this twentieth-century metropolis. He was still a young man, so why couldn't he find his opportunity and exploit it, carve out his niche and secure his fortune? Perhaps his reformist sympathies were just the residue of his perennial lack of self-confidence. Then he began to wonder if such thinking – this unrelenting self-scrutiny that led only to self-doubt and inaction – was not the kind of thinking a Henry James character might wallow in. He needed to shake it off. To think more positively. Certainly Mr. James had not written his great novels under the onus of such thinking. Achievement of that magnitude took ambition, drive, determination. One need only apply oneself. Wasn't that today's creed?

The street clock in front of Rivkin Jewelers read 12:09. He had less than an hour to reach the Pioneer Building, and to cool down and dry off. The next block over was Beatty Booksellers, one of his favorite businesses in the entire city ... after Madison House, of course, which he rarely thought of as a business *per se*. At least once a week he stopped in at Beatty Booksellers, usually just to browse, a luxury he felt he had earned by faithfully purchasing the complete set of Charles Dickens's novels over the past twelve months. Beatty's was where he had also purchased the two Henry James tomes.

Clyde pushed open the door, setting the bell attached to the door frame jangling. Mrs. Beatty, serene and attentive as usual, sat behind the front counter while Mr. Beatty, agitated and distracted as usual, hurried about the various rooms of the store with a stack of books in his arms. The main room was large and spacious, with a high formed-tin ceiling from which hung gas lamps recently converted to electric. The back and side rooms were like a catacomb, connected by low doorways from which the doors and hinges had been removed. Throughout the store, shelves that bowed with the weight of books reached to within a few feet of the ceiling. Stepladders were scattered about on the oak floors to assist patrons in reaching the higher shelves. Books were also arranged spine up on two center tables, most of these being resale volumes. The Beattys' trade increasingly inclined toward used books, which suited Clyde just fine since he could rarely afford to buy a new, uncut volume at full price.

"Good morning," he called out to Mrs. Beatty.

"Good afternoon, young man," she returned. She smiled at him through her spectacles, a book in her lap. "Morning ended eleven minutes ago."

"So right you are," Clyde said. "Good afternoon, then. How's business?"

"Business is business," said Mrs. Beatty flatly, sounding like the Jewish tailor down on Union Street rather than the gentile booklady she was. Between the two of them – Mrs. Beatty and Mr. Beatty – Clyde always believed her to be the more knowledgeable reader. Mr. Beatty refused to read female authors, but not Mrs. Beatty. She recommended to him the novels of Edith Wharton and of this newer authoress, Willa Cather, which he put on his *to-read* list, while Mr. Beatty continued to dismiss them all as lady scribblers.

"Did you know the great Henry James is in town?" he asked Mrs. Beatty.

"Is 'great' his first name? By your manner of speaking, I should think so."

"No, ma'am, I only meant – "

"No apologies," she said. "He's still just a man. And yes, I've heard."

Clyde lifted the cover of a book lying on the nearest table: an anthology of verse. He was an irreclaimable prose man himself, though he enjoyed a well-turned poem now and then.

"I'm on my way to meet him," Clyde said, without looking up from the anthology.

"You don't say," was Mrs. Beatty's reply.

Mr. Beatty, a storm of white hair on his head, his eyes red-rimmed and wide, came forward from one of the back rooms with an armload of books and set them on the counter next to the large oak cash register. "By special order," he said, "of Mr. Edward Holton James. To be delivered to the Seattle Hotel."

Clyde looked up.

Mr. Beatty's manner was even more curt, though less clever, than his wife's. Mrs. Beatty took each of the books he had set down and one at a time examined it front and back, carefully opened the cloth cover to the frontispiece, and then jotted down the title, author, and price on a piece of scrap paper with a pencil stub. There were half a dozen books at least.

"They go to the *great* Henry James," said Mr. Beatty, who must have been listening to his and Mrs. Beatty's conversation all along, and proceeded to say that it was a good thing Clyde had stopped in or else he would have had to backtrack to the store from the Pioneer Building. He explained how Mr. James – Edward Holton, that is – had phoned in the order, per his uncle's request, and was going to send Clyde around to pick it up and deliver it to the Seattle Hotel, where Mr. James – Henry, that is – was staying.

"So here you are," Mr. Beatty announced.

"How fortuitous," Mrs. Beatty chimed in.

"He said for you to bring them straight up to Mr. James's room," Mr. Beatty went on, "where Mr. James would introduce you to the *great* Mr. James."

"Perfectly novelistic," said Mrs. Beatty.

Clyde put down the verse anthology. "Thank you," was all he could think to add to this bizarre exchange. Mr. and Mrs. Beatty were kindly people, he knew, but at times could be quite peculiar.

Mrs. Beatty then bundled the books in brown wrapping paper with a string around them. She then handed the package across the counter to Clyde.

Mr. Beatty stood aside, and as Clyde was about to walk out the door, he said, "Give my best regards to Mr. James."

"Don't let him turn supercilious with you," Mrs. Beatty added.

"No," said Clyde, "I won't," making a note to himself to look the word up later, and left the store with the bundle under his arm.

As he walked down the block he became increasingly curious as to which titles Henry James had ordered. He could untie the string and take a look, he thought, but to do so would be a lot of trouble and time, so he decided to let the mystery be and inquire of the Beattys next time he visited the store.

He had just over half an hour to deliver the books to the Seattle Hotel. Behind him he heard the clang of a streetcar, and since he now had to go straight to the hotel he trotted up to the next car stop to wait for it. The car rocked on its tracks as it rattled toward him and glided to a stop right where he stood. The doors folded back, a step dropped down, and Clyde boarded. The green car had wood trim along its windows and wood floorboards and reversible wood benches. Before he could seat himself, the driver cranked the handle to close the doors, clanged the bells, and set the car rolling down the tracks. Though several seats were vacant near the front, Clyde stepped to the rear and took a seat near the car man, who approached Clyde for his fare. Clyde fished into his pants for the nickel, handed it to the car man, and then pushed open the window so he could take in the breeze.

At Yesler Way, when the streetcar turned left, about to head up over the hill to Lake Washington, Clyde and two other passengers got off. The streets in Pioneer Place were clogged with horsedrawn wagons and streetcars, a few automobiles, an occasional motor-powered omnibus, and people going about in every direction at once. Clyde could recall being brought down here by his father when he was still a kid. They would get off the streetcar on Front Street – now called First Avenue – and around Dearborn Street start walking the trestles that traversed the tideflats straight across to Seattle's westside. Clyde remembered standing along the railing on the Front Street trestle, looking down into the brackish wash as his father baited a hook for each of them and dropped their lines into the water. They would fish until dusk and then head back to the lake. That was before the fire of '89 destroyed much of the old city around Pioneer Place, before the hordes of gold seekers poured into the city on their way north – both events having changed the city forever. Back then, Seattle seemed like a much simpler place, a place where it was okay to take an afternoon to go fishing.

From the corner of Third and Yesler, Clyde walked the block and a half to the Seattle Hotel, the wedge-shaped building that reminded him of a large slice of cake. The five-story building hugged the slope of the street in such a manner that it gained an extra floor as Clyde strolled down the hill. He turned beneath the cast-iron and maroon-canvas awning that stretched out from the building's south face and approached the ornate entrance. Above the door, where the transom would be, thick leading imbedded in red and blue stained glass spelled out *Seattle Hotel*. Parked in front of the hotel, at the curb, was the hotel's omnibus, with round headlamps in front and gold-plated postlamps on all four corners of the carriage. Having just returned from a run to the King Street train station, the driver was still sitting up behind the wheel of the vehicle as his assistant helped the newly arrived guests negotiate the step down from the carriage to the sidewalk. A liveried doorman signaled to several bellboys to retrieve the baggage from the rear of the bus and carry it all into the hotel lobby.

Clyde skirted the commotion and, taking the service door adjacent to the main entrance, entered the hotel. He attracted immediate stares from guests milling about the lobby, lounging in the reading chairs, loitering near the cigar and newspaper stand. A man in a wing-backed leather chair looked up from his newspaper and tracked Clyde crossing the lobby floor on his way to the concierge's desk. Clyde could feel the man's eyes on him. He then heard a rambunctious boy, a child of eight or nine, say to his mother, "Look, Mummy, look. He glows." Such attention, like moths drawn to a flame, was part of his daily existence, and he paid no special attention to it. Except that, knowing he was out of place in the posh hotel, he was reluctant to look about the well-appointed lobby as he wanted to. Finally, he ventured to scan the spacious room, forcing the man who had tracked him to withdraw his gaze and resume reading his newspaper. The lobby was one of the more splendid in the city, right up there with the old Washington Hotel on Denny Hill and the Lincoln Hotel on Fourth Avenue. Like those, the interior of the Seattle Hotel was lavish, yet being a smaller building, demanded more discretion in the selection and placement of its furnishings, which made the lobby seem more refined than those of the bigger hotels. In the two farthest corners were two sets of leather wing-backed reading chairs, each with a matching ottoman and a mahogany drink and ashtray stand. Toward the center of the lobby were placed a lengthy sofa, a satin-covered divan, a reverse-facing loveseat, an overstuffed lounge chair, and on the floor three large oriental rugs and three potted sword ferns, the whole creating an island oasis apart from the bustle of the bellboys and the guests who scurried to and fro between the main entrance, the front desk, and the brass-door elevators. To the right of the entrance stood the cigar and newspaper stand, behind which an elderly attendant in his rolled shirtsleeves and black braces sat perched on a stool, looking blankly out at the lobby. Two wire racks stood on either side of the glass cigar case, one for Seattle's many newspapers, the other for national periodicals such as *McClure's, Ladies Home Journal, The Saturday Evening Post,* and *Atlantic Monthly.*

Clyde thought of buying a cigar, perhaps several, as an offering to Ned and his uncle. He walked over to the cigar stand and looked down through the glass counter at the wooden boxes with their lids open to display the rows of cigars that each contained. The cheapest cigars were a dime apiece, more than he'd bargained for, and he let the notion pass. He looked up and saw the concierge watching him closely from across the lobby, preparing to intercept him should he try to stray beyond the public confines of the lobby.

Clyde approached the tall podium at which the concierge stood, one hand cupped placidly over the other, the telephone placed at the ready on the slanted corner of the podium.

"A delivery for Mr. Henry James," Clyde enunciated. "From Beatty Booksellers."

The concierge was impeccably dressed in a coat, waist-jacket, and cravat, the right arm of his coat adorned with three gold chevrons. He peered over the top of the podium and eyed Clyde head to foot, then with a lift of his chin indicated the package in Clyde's arms. "Are those the books?"

"The very same," said Clyde.

"You can leave them. I'll see that they're delivered to Mr. James."

Clyde held onto the package. "I was told by Mr. Edward Holton James, Mr. James's nephew, *and* my employer, that *I* was to deliver the books. That's my commission."

The concierge, perhaps ten years older than Clyde, squinted at this rebuke, but remained composed, hands cupped.

"Mr. James may not wish to be disturbed right now," he answered. "He may very well be in the act of composition as we speak."

Clyde was growing annoyed. He didn't want to disturb the great Henry James as he wrote. On the other hand, he'd been directed by Ned to deliver the books – and furthermore, he'd been looking forward to the introduction to Henry James for the past four months. He then remembered something Ray had told him about the novelist: that he wrote standing up, at a lectern, and often wrote through the night. It was now 12:45, and Clyde calculated that if Mr. James had been up all night writing, he would surely have rested and begun the day by now. He held his ground.

"Mr. James only writes at night," he declared to the concierge. "Besides, as I said, Mr. James's nephew, Edward Holton James, commissioned me to deliver the books." Clyde enjoyed using such an imperious tone with the obstinate concierge.

"All right then," the concierge said, and picked up the telephone receiver, pressed it to his ear, and asked the hotel operator to ring Mr. James's suite. Clyde assumed it was Ned who answered when the concierge murmured into the mouthpiece and then put the receiver back down. "All right then," he said. "I'll have a bellboy accompany you," and raising his arm with the gold chevrons on the sleeve, snapped his fingers, bringing a bellboy in a tight maroon uniform and pillbox hat promptly to Clyde's side. "Stuart, escort this gentleman ... sir, what is your name?"

"Clyde Hunssler,"

"Escort Mr. Hunssler to Mr. James's suite. Five-O-Seven."

The bellboy sneaked a glance at Clyde, then looked away. "This way, sir."

Clyde followed, traversing the marble lobby floor and stepping into the brass-plated elevator. Then it was up to the fifth floor and down the carpeted hallway to the corner apartment in the flatiron building. Neither said a word. The bellboy sneaked several more glances at Clyde, his face, hair, hands, but Clyde, who would normally ward off such looks with a sharp counterstare, ignored him, preoccupied with what he would say to Henry James when the author opened the door.

At Suite 507, the bellboy leaned in close to listen, then rapped his knuckles on the door, and called out, "Delivery for Mr. James."

A moment passed and the door opened and Ned James stood before them. His hair had been cut and pomaded since Clyde had seen him last, two days ago, and traces of talcum powder from his morning shave dusted his neck around the stiff collar. He wore a white shirt, burgundy bow tie, and a double-breasted, pin-striped, woolen jacket buttoned military-style from his collarbone right down past his waist. He looked more starched and pressed than Clyde had ever seen him.

"Clyde," Ned James said, "Good, you made it," and without tipping the bellboy, took Clyde by the elbow and led him into the room and closed the door. The suite's interior was not quite as lavish as Clyde had imagined – no chandeliers, no Louis Quatorze furnishings – yet it had a stateliness to it nonetheless. The walls were painted a pale yellow, the trim and ceiling white. The heavy, ceiling-to-floor curtains were drawn back and tied, leaving a diaphanous white lace over the three windows that made up the baylike section of the corner room. Clyde could see through the lace straight out over the waterfront and piers to the Sound, where the late-morning sun dappled the wide expanse of water. The furniture included a long couch upholstered in pale yellow chintz, three plush armchairs, and in the center, a two-foot high marble-topped table. At the very end of the couch sat a man Clyde did not recognize, in a brown suit and slightly muddied spats. The man was about the same age as Ned James, in his mid-thirties, yet more at ease in both his clothing and his manner than Ned. He intently read yesterday's edition of the *Seattle Argus*, the city's progressive paper, the reformer Harry Chadwick's mouthpiece.

"Oliver," Ned called to the man, "this is my other office assistant, Clyde Hunssler. The one albino, the other Filipino." Ned paused at his own rhymed wisecrack in reference to Clyde and his Filipino officemate, Erasmo – a crack Clyde heard him spout more than once to office visitors.

"This fine gentleman, Clyde, is Mr. Oliver La Farge, co-founder of Bond and La Farge, one of our leading real estate and insurance firms. The La Farges are old family friends of the Jameses."

Oliver La Farge rose from the long yellow couch and leaned forward across the marble-topped table to shake Clyde's hand. He nodded his greeting and, unfazed by Clyde's appearance, sat back down to resume reading the newspaper.

"Uncle Henry is still getting ready," Ned James whispered to Clyde. "Take a seat and we'll wait for him. I'll introduce you."

Clyde understood how this introduction served less as a courtesy to him than as an opportunity for Ned James to show off his albino office clerk to his famous uncle. Yet for the chance to shake hands with the renowned novelist, Clyde would submit to his employer's carnival sideshow.

He sat down and heard, coming from the back sleeping room, a phlegmy cough and knew it must be Henry James. There was silence for several minutes between the three men in the front room, Clyde staring down at his mud-caked brogans, Ned James fidgeting with his pocketwatch, and Oliver La Farge reading the *Argus*, when from the back room entered a round-visaged, bald-pated, fleshy-jowled gentleman whom Clyde recognized instantly from newspaper photographs as Henry James. Clyde stared at the personage as he approached one of the armchairs and rested both hands upon its curved back.

"Good day, gentlemen," he said.

Ned James was first to his feet, then Clyde, followed more leisurely by Oliver La Farge, who carefully laid his paper on the table. Henry James smiled benignly, and, it seemed to Clyde, rather tiredly. Clyde thought the man had an appealing face, the assurance of a banker's face and yet with something at once both alert and introspective about it, a person on whom nothing was lost, for which every observation counted. Bluish shadows ringed his eyes – Clyde imagined from his having stood at his writing lectern all night – shadows that the light from his attentive eyes helped dispel. The author was shorter than his nephew, more approximately Clyde's own height, which was shorter than Clyde had expected in a man who had penned such statuesque novels.

Mr. James, as Clyde referred to him even to himself, greeted Oliver La Farge first. "Your father would never have suffered so late a start in our Newport days. A waste of good light, he would declare. I'm afraid I've become a regular sluggard."

"It's our cursed and blessed climate," Oliver La Farge said. "It makes slugs of us all."

Henry James laughed. "You may be right, Oliver."

To Clyde, it was plain that the great Henry James had been pouring himself onto the page all night while the rest of the world slumbered and snored, and this was why the author was starting his day so late. Clyde watched him carefully, scrutinized his attire: a black woolen jacket over a tight black waistcoat that restrained the sixty-year-old author's mid-section, a gold watch fob looped across the left side of the waistcoat, gray pin-striped trousers, wing collar, and a blue and silver striped silk cravat. A banker, thought Clyde again, yet a demeanor that thoroughly defied austerity – fiscal, literary, or otherwise.

Ned James stepped around the armchair where he'd been seated and, taking his uncle's elbow much as he had Clyde's a few minutes earlier, though with far more deference, turned Mr. James's attention toward Clyde. The author looked at Clyde as if he had only just then, for the first time upon entering the room, been made aware of his presence. Freeing his arm from his officious nephew, he stepped forward and extended his hand to Clyde.

"A pleasure to meet you, young sir. And what is your name?"

"Clyde Hunssler, your honor." Clyde took the author's hand, but was utterly mortified. Where had he come up with such a stiff and inappropriate address? Probably from hanging around the law offices too much, hearing Ray and Erasmo refer sarcastically to the judges this way.

"German is it?" Henry James asked.

Clyde blinked, trying to figure the question.

Henry James asked again, "Hunssler is German, is it not?"

Clyde glanced over the author's shoulder to his employer, who stood erect and stolid, without expression.

"Yes, sir," Clyde answered. "My father. He was born in Hamburg."

"Ah yes, in the north," the author said, and asked, "And what else?"

"Sir?"

"Your mother."

"Oh. Indian, sir. Makah Indian. From Neah Bay."

Ned James stepped forward at this point and inserted himself into the conversation. "It's out on the Olympic Peninsula, Uncle, the farthest inhabited point in the contiguous United States. Quite untamed." He stood beside his uncle and faced Clyde. "Clyde's a half-breed, Uncle, but bright to a tee. Self-educated. Quite a reader, and speaks the Chinook jargon as well as any fur trader. Go ahead, Clyde, say something in Chinook."

Henry James looked away from his nephew and watched Clyde, not with the awe-struck freak show gaze he was accustomed to, but with calm, steady interest. Why was his employer putting him on the spot like this? What could he possibly say? He looked at Henry James, met his eyes, and said, "*Maika tzum pepah, yaka kahkwa pot-latch. Mahsie, sihks.*"

Henry James turned to his nephew, who shrugged, open-mouthed, and looked back at Clyde. There was silence in the room until Oliver La Farge spoke up from the couch, where he once again sat. "He says your writing is as a gift. Thank you, friend."

Henry James put a hand on Clyde's shoulder. "Thank you. I admire a person, any person, who can, and does in fact, read my books. I take a lot of care with them, you understand, yet I'm afraid the populace prefers Bret Harte or that Crane fellow, bless his rough soul, to my drawing room dramas."

"No sir," Clyde said. "I've not read them all, but what I've read, I've enjoyed. I even read them aloud to Maddie ... she's my landlady."

"How about that, Oliver?" The author, appearing genuinely amused, turned to Oliver La Farge. "The young man has read more of my work than my own family members." The pointedness of this remark, aimed as it was at Ned James, was not lost on Clyde, and he instantly knew he would be the one to pay the price for it, no doubt with a swift banishment from the author's presence. "Except that is," Henry James went on, "for my niece Peg. She's the most avid reader of all the Jameses, and would, I dare say, admire this young man. Wouldn't you agree, Ned?"

"I'm afraid, Uncle," Ned James said, "that our young friend, Mr. Hunssler, must fetch himself back to the office. Business, you know, waits on no man." Ned James took from Clyde the package of books, which he'd been carrying all morning, and placed it on the small secretary stand near the door. "He came only to deliver the volumes you requested, Uncle ... and must be on his way."

As Clyde had predicted, his petulant employer was nipping the interview in its bud.

Ned James sidled up to Clyde to escort him out.

"I hope you enjoy your stay," Clyde said to Henry James, who himself advanced toward the door and, from the umbrella stand, retrieved a brass-handled, brass-tipped walking stick.

He faced Clyde. "Your city is one of the real flowers of geography. Already I take away the exquisite impression of the mystic lake in the hills, with the woods overhanging it, to which Oliver so benevolently escorted me yesterday. Such wondrous moist, ethereal wildness ..."

Clyde heard this praise and knew that the author had probably not yet toured the city proper, at least not past the Deadline, in among the taverns and flophouses, brothels and dance halls.

"I'm afraid, however," Henry James continued, "that I will have to cut my visit to a couple of days. It saddens me to stint myself so."

"Yes, sir," was all Clyde could think to say, sensing the impatience of his employer.

"Here," said Henry James, and handed him the walking stick. "A token of my visit. I shall remember you in my *American Scene*."

Clyde received the walking stick – a fine piece of red mahogany, the brass handle worn smooth with use – but felt odd doing so. What retribution would Ned James extract for this unsolicited kindness bestowed upon him? He gripped the handle and planted the brass tip into the wood floor. "Thank you," he said, and again shook hands with the author, whose grip was gentle in his, and then parted without a single further glance at Ned James, who stood holding the door.

Clyde stepped into the hallway and the door closed behind him. He walked halfway to the elevators, stopped, and leaning on the walking stick, looked back at Suite 507. He suddenly, and desperately, wished to inquire about this *American Scene* that he would be remembered in. Was it the author's next novel? An essay? When would it appear? Without a single clue as to how to pursue these questions, Clyde decided to skip out on the office and rush back to Beatty Booksellers to inform Mr. and Mrs. Beatty that he would be named in the next volume penned by the *great* Henry James.

20. Journalism (1907)

JAMES COLTER UNDERSTOOD, AT THE SAME TIME HE WAS
publishing profiles in the *Sentry* of people and businesses affected by the
regradings – including a blacksmith, a shoe-shine stand, a clock and pocketwatch repair shop, and, because he was a tenant, Madison House – that
he would eventually have to find a new building for the press and new
lodgings for himself. The regrading of Denny Hill, in its entirety, seemed
inevitable. He ran editorials objecting to it as a chamber of commerce land
grab from ordinary, hard-working people duped into believing the value
of their modest property holdings would be augmented tenfold and their
lives vastly improved by the razing of half the city's hills and the leveling
of its streets. The propaganda campaign behind the project made any opposition to it seem downright anti-Seattle and very nearly un-American.
No wonder so many residents of the hill went along so readily with it. James
knew better, though. He knew that once city and business leaders determined to "redevelop" a part of the city, the people who could least afford
to relocate, could least afford a "hiatus" in their businesses, people in
situations like his own (and very often black people and Chinese), were
left high and dry. And always with the reassurance that the redevelopment
was for their own good. So in contrast to his polemical editorials, the
profiles in the *Sentry* – such as the one of the Negro owner of the shoe-shine
stand who had been at his corner of Fourth and Stewart for the past fifteen
years and would now have to reestablish himself elsewhere – were James's
protest to the regradings from the purely human angle. No other newspaper in Seattle gave the issue the kind of attention the *Sentry* did. Several
papers, such as Alden Blethen's *Times* and Harry Chadwick's *Argus*, railed
against the mayor and the city engineer for the expense and boondoggled-
ness of the regrading project. Yet crass political backbiting motivated this
opposition far more than any social concern for the Denny Hill residents.
With the exception of a few vocal holdout property owners on the hill, the
public opposition to the regradings was, in James' estimation, limited to
the *Sentry*. And being a realist about the influence his small newspaper
brought to bear on popular opinion and civic policy, he knew this lack

of opposition did not bode well for Denny Hill. How much did the majority of Seattle citizens, even those living in the neighborhood, really care about an old Negro shoeshine anyways? The answer was in the roar of the hoses blasting away at the hill each and every day.

The one issue that did stir up controversy for the *Sentry* was its reporting on the rampant lynchings of black folks in the Southern states. At considerable risk to himself and his family, a friend of James's from their college days at Colbert College in St. Louis, who now ran a small bank in Nashville, Tennessee, mailed James clippings of articles about the lynchings from local Southern newspapers, occasionally accompanied by photographs of the gruesome acts. The images of the contorted, mutilated, often burned bodies of the black men filled James with anguish and disgust ... and a swelling sense of vengeance. Only vengeance seemed capable of quailing the despair such images instilled in him. This desire for vengeance was compounded by the images of white people milling about the lynched body, backslapping one another, grinning triumphantly, strutting about, showing off their prize, their morbid trophy. James wrote a front-page editorial on the lynchings every week for a month. The first editorial grieved over the plight of the black man in the Southern states and throughout the nation, the struggle he faced just to preserve his own life and that of his family, not only from vigilante mobs but from the immoral and debilitating discrimination in employment, housing, education, health care, transportation, and democratic representation. The second front-page editorial excoriated white people for their misguided *laissez-faire* policies toward race, their hypocritical religious posturing, and their historical and persistent cruelty toward all nonwhite races. The next editorial retraced the history of the Negro in America, the contributions the race had made to the establishment and preservation of the Union of States, citing the all-Negro regiments of the Federal Army and asking what had been the return for the Negro's valor and sacrifice in battle. In the fourth editorial, he told of his own encounters with hatred and prejudice, from being beaten up in St. Louis by four white store clerks after he opened a department store door for a white lady and tipped his hat to her, to being charged twice the cost of a ham sandwich at a Seattle lunch counter. (People in Seattle seemed to believe such discrimination existed only elsewhere, or that Jim Crow practices were simply an export from the South, but James knew better.) In each editorial, his line of thought always connected back to the epidemic of lynchings taking place in the country, the logic behind these most grisly violations against his people being essentially the same as that behind the most mundane violations – race hatred and bigotry.

The four editorials prompted more letters to the publisher than the *Sentry* had received over the course of its entire six-year existence. Black people, who proudly identified themselves in their letters as such, praised James for his courage and forthrightness in telling it how it was. White people, who never identified themselves as such in their letters, castigated James for his African-bred ingratitude and, as the final salutation, either insulted his character or threatened bodily injury to his person. From then on, James took extra care when picking up his mail at the P.O. box he kept downtown as the *Sentry's* business address. For several weeks the circulation jumped and he printed an extra 400 papers each week, with warnings to Clyde and his newsboys to be careful when distributing the paper and to walk away from any uncomfortable or threatening situations. Although Seattle did not enforce the harsh Jim Crow laws the Southern states did, it had its share of unabashed bigots who participated in their own subtle, or not so subtle, methods of racial violence and discrimination.

James confronted this discrimination head-on when he organized the Negro Swimming Club of Seattle. At first he had thought to call it the African Swimming Club, but knew that few black men in America, no matter how progressive their politics, were inclined to identify themselves as African. The racial stigmas were difficult enough to overcome without the added weight of nationalist designations. He put an announcement on the back page of the *Sentry* each week inviting men (and only men) to Madison Park on Lake Washington for instructional, recreational, and competitive swimming. James did not know if the Negro Swimming Club would succeed, but he wanted to give it a try. He was tired of swimming by himself the two times each week he ventured out to the lake during the summer months.

He liked to think of himself as an avid swimmer. He had learned to swim as a boy wading out from the muddy banks of the Mississippi, and yet had given the pastime up during his school years and college. But when he came to Seattle a decade ago and discovered the crystal-clear, mountain-fed, bone-chilling waters of Lake Washington, he rediscovered his love of the water and resumed swimming as part of his weekly exercise regime. He enjoyed the freedom of the water, the total ease of movement it allowed, how he could be both immersed in it and buoyed by it simultaneously. He especially enjoyed the invigorating waters of Lake Washington. From as early as the second week in May to the second week in September, he took the streetcar to Madison Park and, just north of the resort where he had discovered a small, apparently unused bathing beach, he swam for a full hour twice a week. A few times Clyde had accompanied him, and to see their four arms and four legs splashing about, like stalks of ebony and ivory, when the two of them were in the water was something to behold.

The first meeting of the Negro Swimming Club of Seattle drew only two men: James himself and a young streetcar mechanic named Kerwin who did not know how to swim. James agreed to instruct Kerwin and together they walked to the secluded beach that James's had discovered, changed behind some trees, and then entered the water. James first showed Kerwin how to tread water by waving his arms in a circular motion while scissor-kicking with his legs. Unlike most novice adult swimmers, Kerwin had no fear of the water and followed James out to a depth above his head where he readily began moving his arms and legs to keep his mouth and nose bobbing just above the surface. After that, and closer in toward the shore, James held Kerwin's outstretched hands for support as Kerwin extended his body out and practiced freestyle kicking, with James count-ing out loud: one, two, one, two, one, two. He then had Kerwin stand up in chest-high water, lean forward, and practice his stroke by reaching forward into the water and pulling back with cupped hands, fingers slightly splayed. By the end of the day's lesson, Kerwin was happily thrashing through the freestyle stroke for several yards at a time before gulping a mouthful of water and having to stop to catch his breath. After more than an hour in the water, they dried off and dressed and on their way back to the streetcar stop agreed to meet again the following week, when perhaps others might join them as well.

Sure enough, the next week two more men showed up at the meeting place at Madison Park. One was a cafe owner in the expanding Central District, the other a teamster for a lumber yard. James welcomed the two men and introduced them to young Kerwin, and announced that the Negro Swimming Club of Seattle now had enough members to officially grant itself a charter.

"What's that?" the teamster asked, as James led the way to the beach.

"It means that we're a corporate body with guiding principles, functions, and elected officials," James said, and when there was only silence following this pronouncement, he added, "It means we can do whatever we like."

"That's my kind of club," the teamster shot back.

James went on to say that his goal for the club was to enjoy the physical invigoration of the water and the athletic exercise of swimming, but that also, as a long-range goal, he hoped that by the end of the summer the members might attempt to swim across the width of Lake Washington.

"How far's that?" the cafe owner wanted to know, looking across the lake to the opposite shore.

"It's a mile and three quarters," James answered, having consulted two maps when this idea first occurred to him.

Kerwin looked a bit frightened at the proposition, yet James reassured him that as a novice swimmer he wouldn't be expected to swim the full distance. "We'll have one man in a skiff alongside the others, so everyone can swim as much or as little as he wants," he elaborated, adding, "And damn if I'm going to swim back too!"– getting a laugh out of the others.

"I just want to see if I remember how to swim at all," the cafe owner said.

They changed into their swimsuits, and of the four of them, only the teamster didn't have the standard tank top and knee-length suit and instead pulled off his shirt and cinched his belt and rolled his pants up above his knees.

"Whoever heard of a Negro swimming club anyway?" he asked, as they all walked to the water's edge. "What is this, Princeton University? Next thing you know he'll have us playing lawn tennis."

James was the first to plunge in and come up with a hoot and holler, followed by Kerwin, and then the two new club members shivering and tiptoeing their way in until the cafe owner slipped on a rock, toppled under, and came up splashing water at the cursing and laughing teamster.

By the next meeting of the Negro Swimming Club of Seattle, word had gotten around and three more men joined; all three were temporarily unemployed scullerymen waiting consignment aboard cargo ships. This brought the total membership to seven, exceeding James's expectations for the club. The cafe owner brought sandwiches for everyone, and the teamster had with him two milk canisters filled with beer – which it was agreed they would partake of only after their swim, James having voiced ample warnings about the agony and danger of cramps. It was also agreed that the club would now meet twice a week, on Wednesday evenings and Sunday afternoons. The three new members, who like James had grown up swimming, were more comfortable in the water than the first three members. Kerwin continued to practice the freestyle stroke, learning to keep his head down and exhale underwater and tilt his body to the side on every other stroke to take a new breath. James also showed him the side stroke. "It's like picking apples and putting them in the basket," he said, demonstrating the arm motion. "This is a good stroke to do when you get tired because you're basically just lying on your side in the water." The cafe owner and teamster mostly splashed about with each other near the shore, while farther out the three new members and James raced one another, with Kerwin treading water and serving as the starter judge.

It was the next week, during the first Wednesday evening meeting of the Negro Swimming Club, that a policeman found his way to their secluded beach and, after calling them all into shore, began questioning them about their activities.

"Swimming," James answered, standing before the uniformed policeman dripping wet. "For exercise, recreation, and competition," he went on, quoting his own announcement in the *Sentry*. "This is the Negro Swimming Club of Seattle."

The policeman looked at James, at the cafe owner sitting against a tree with a sandwich in his hand, and then at the five other club members standing about starting to shiver in the cool evening air. "Let's go," he told James. "You're going to have to find somewhere else to swim. This is private property and the owner wants you off."

"But I've never seen a single person down here," James dissented. "Are you sure this is privately owned?"

The policeman cocked his head at James. "Are you questioning me now, mister? How do you think I knew you were down here? The owner told me he'd seen a bunch of naked niggers on his property and he wanted them off. Now let's go." He placed his hand on the nightstick that was slung through his belt.

"What if I talked to the owner," James suggested. "We'll pay him a fee for the use of his property. You know we're only down here because they don't want us over near the resort."

"I don't think so," the policeman said. "He said if you wanted to swim you could all go to a pier down on the bay. He wants you off his property, or else I'm going to have to charge the lot of you with trespassing."

James kicked the ground. The idea of swimming in Puget Sound, which was much colder than Lake Washington, was out of the question. He looked at the policeman and saw that he was growing impatient with them. He said, "All right," and signaled to the others to dry off and get dressed, they were moving over to Madison Park.

"I wouldn't do that either," the policeman told him.

James pulled his pants on over his swimsuit. "Are you telling me that's not a public beach either?" James knew for a fact that it was a public beach. He also knew that he had never seen a black person there unless he was wearing a white waiter's jacket and serving drinks at the resort. The few times he had used the beach, all the white people would leave the water until he had finished his swim and only then would they return.

"I'm saying," the policeman reprimanded him, "that you and your club aren't welcome there. This is my beat, you hear me, and I don't want to see any of you around here again or I'll call in the wagon next time. Like the man said, find yourselves a nice pier downtown to go swimming from."

After this incident, the Negro Swimming Club was forced to skip its next two meetings. But by the following Sunday, with the help of the teamster driving him up and down the Lake Washington shoreline in his two-seater buckboard wagon, James determined that the Mount Baker Bathing Beach, five miles south of Madison Park, would be where the club would meet for the remainder of the season. Though white people were beginning to build houses in the neighborhood, the area leading up from the beach remained fairly wooded and the beach mostly unused. James put a notice in that week's *Sentry* notifying prospective members of the club's change of venue, and wrote an editorial criticizing Seattle's citizenry for promoting a *de facto* Jim Crow segregation of the city's public beaches by using law enforcement to prohibit certain segments of the public from exercising their freedom to use those beaches. "Good Negro boys and girls," he wrote, "should be able to enjoy – and, by those freedoms that America stands for, have the right to enjoy – a cool swim on a warm summer's days, just as good Caucasian boys and girls do."

SEVERAL WEEKS AFTER THE FOURTH EDITORIAL ON THE lynchings appeared in the *Seattle Sentry*, James received a note, hand delivered by a small boy identifying himself as Horace R. Cayton, Jr., stating that the publisher of the *Seattle Republican*, the highly respected Horace R. Cayton, would like James to join him for dinner at his home on Capitol Hill that Thursday evening. James wrote his R S V P accepting the invitation on the back of the note and handed it back to Horace R., Jr. He thanked the boy and then invited him into the carriage house to show him the press.

"Do you go to school?" he asked the boy, who wore knickers and a matching coat and seemed about ten or eleven years old.

"Of course I do," the boy shot back. "I go to the Broadway School."

James was amused by the boy's feistiness. "Are you going to be a newspaperman like your father?"

The boy shook his head no, and said, "I want to be a United States Senator like my granddaddy."

James, somewhat startled by such an idea from the boy and not sure where he'd gotten it, received it as boyhood exuberance and said, "Why stop there? Why not President of the United States?"

The boy looked up at him, the two standing beside the big press, and said, "Maybe," and that was all.

On Thursday, James walked up Capitol Hill an hour before the appointed time for dinner. The invitation had come as a surprise to him. Although he had met Horace Cayton once before, at a conference of Seattle newspapermen held downtown at the Rainier Club, he felt their meeting had been overly formal, despite the fact that they were the only two black men in attendance. He left the conference with little hope of an eventual warming between the older man and himself. Perhaps, James speculated, the more established, more respected newspaper publisher felt threatened by someone he perceived as a young upstart. After all, they competed for the same readership. Cayton was highly respected among the city's white establishment, especially within the Republican Party, and the *Seattle Republican* maintained a sizable white readership for a colored-owned newspaper. This respectability, however, had weakened Cayton's credibility among many colored people, whose numbers in Seattle had increased threefold in the past decade. James doubted that this weakening of confidence in the *Seattle Republican* among colored Seattleites was justified. Cayton often ran profiles of successful Negro businessmen, churchmen, and politicians. On the question of whether the *Seattle Sentry* was more committed editorially to the issues concerning colored Seattleites, James was convinced it was. Recently, to Cayton's credit, he had also run front-page articles condemning the lynchings in the South, for which he incurred criticism from white boosters who objected to such faraway and unsavory subjects being raised in their Northwest sanctuary. He had also published a review of Booker T. Washington's autobiography *Up from Slavery* side by side with a review of W. E. B. Dubois's book *The Souls of Black Folk*, delineating the still raging debate between the two important thinkers. James found this a bold move on Cayton's part and wished he had thought of doing it himself in the pages of the *Sentry*.

So in all, he was apprehensive about the dinner with Horace Cayton, though he knew it would be cordial and well-mannered. As the hour neared, he walked down Broadway Avenue into the Capitol Hill neighborhood. Set on a residential corner, the Cayton home was a square, Italianate manse painted light yellow with white trim. The property had an iron fence around its well-manicured grounds and a carriage house twice the size of the one he occupied at Maddie's. At first he thought he might be expected to go to the back door, but he said bunk to that notion and unlatched the gate and walked straight up the pathway to the large front door. He rapped twice with the brass knocker and stepped back, standing straight, shoulders square, chin up, just as his mother had taught him. The door was opened by a Japanese houseboy who made a partial bow and signaled James to enter. In the front foyer, where a small chandelier hung from the twelve-foot ceiling, James removed his hat and handed it to the houseboy. He was then led into the front parlor and told he could sit wherever he wished. He chose a large leather chair with brass upholstery tacks, which he fingered nervously.

"I will tell them you are here," the houseboy said, and left the room.

Moments later, Mr. and Mrs. Cayton entered the parlor together and welcomed James, who rose from his chair to greet them. Horace Cayton was a distinguished-looking man with trimmed hair around the sides of his head where he had not yet gone bald and a clean-shaven face, with the exception of a closely trimmed moustache. He was about the same height as James, with a physique that, for a man in his fifties, seemed both trim and robust—a swimmer's physique, James thought. He wore a smartly tailored long jacket, silk vest, and pin-striped pants. Mrs. Cayton, whose straightened hair was perfectly coifed, was a fairly short woman and was elegantly appareled in a lavender silk evening gown with a broad, trailing hem. Horace Cayton extended his hand to James, saying how good it was to see him again, and then introduced him to his wife, Susie Cayton.

"And I believe you've met my son," Cayton said, peering about the room in a parent's exaggerated search for the boy, "who at present is nowhere to be found."

"He's a smart one," James replied.

Mrs. Cayton then signaled James to resume his seat, while she and her husband seated themselves side by side on the facing sofa. For the next half hour, they mixed small talk about the weather and various events about the city with discreet forays onto more serious topics concerning local and national politics (Cayton was a Taft supporter, James for Roosevelt) and the business of running a newspaper. Cayton invited James to visit the *Seattle Republican* offices, and in reply James said he did not feel he could reciprocate the invitation given his offices were the two rooms above the carriage house where he kept his press. "As your son who's had the full tour will tell you," he added, "there's not much to see."

"You do an outstanding job nevertheless," Cayton complimented him.

After aperitifs served by the houseboy, Horace, Jr., appeared and was again introduced to James. He seemed much more shy around his parents than James remembered him from the afternoon he delivered the dinner invitation. After telling Horace, Jr., to go wash his hands, Susie Cayton announced that dinner was ready and proceeded to lead the way into the dining room. A cut-glass gas chandelier hung above the center of the table, around which four place settings with rose-spray china dinnerware and polished sterling silverware had been precisely laid. James waited beside his chair as Mr. Cayton pulled Mrs. Cayton's chair out from the table for her. After everyone was seated and Mr. Cayton had blessed the food they were about to eat, the houseboy brought out a tureen of zucchini soup as the first course. This was followed by oysters on the half shell with lemon wedges in cheesecloth aprons for squeezing over them. Then came the main course, a roasted pork loin with roasted carrots and potatoes. Horace Cayton stood from his seat at the end of the table and leaned over the platter to cut the meat and deliver portions to the plates that Susie Cayton passed to him. Throughout the meal, which was unquestionably one of the best James had ever eaten, the same level of discussion as that in the front parlor was resumed at the dining table. Mr. Cayton asked James about his Negro Swimming Club, which perked the interest of young Horace, who asked if he could join, prompting Mrs. Cayton to say flatly, "When you're older, you may." In all, James remained perplexed as to why Horace Cayton had extended this invitation to him – and solely to him – for a private dinner at his home. When the dessert of blackberry tart with whipped cream was finished, Mrs. Cayton suggested returning to the parlor with their coffee and perhaps, if the gentlemen wished, a taste of brandy.

In the front parlor again, James took his same seat and Mr. Cayton took the matching leather chair adjacent to his. After sitting on the sofa and sipping her coffee as the men exclaimed and sighed over the meal just consumed, with all due compliments to the mistress of the house, Mrs. Cayton excused herself and went back through the dining room and disappeared into the kitchen. Cayton then got up and asked, "Brandy?"

"Yes," James answered, sensing they were going to get down to business now.

When Cayton returned from the liquor stand and handed James his snifter of aromatic brandy, he sat back down, looked at James, and said, "Those were powerful pieces you published on the front page several weeks ago."

James knew he was talking about the editorials on the lynchings, and thanked Cayton for his recognition of them. "A difficult subject," he replied, "and not always a popular one."

"Indeed," Cayton returned. "You no doubt saw the pieces we ran on the issue."

James nodded. He had read them, but had also felt that they were too restrained—which he deemed inadequate in light of the increasing frequency and horror of the lynchings.

"The *Republican's* circulation has gone down as a result," Cayton went on, "yet if I can trust my sources on the street, the *Sentry's* has gone up."

James nodded again. Cayton had summoned him here, he decided, so he was going to let the older man play out his line a little farther so he could get a good look at the bait.

Which became apparent to James with the next words out of Cayton's mouth. "I want you to come work for the *Seattle Republican*. I'm certain that I can offer you more than what you're making now. In fact I'm prepared to buy out your whole operation and we can announce a merger of sorts. You'll be city editor, with a biweekly column on page two." Cayton took a long drink from his brandy, smacked his lips, and said, "What do you say, Mr. Colter?"

There it was, James thought to himself. He held his brandy snifter to his lips but did not drink. The offer astounded him. He knew it would be lucrative to work for Cayton, and quite possibly his big break as a newspaperman. After all, how long could he continue with the *Sentry*, which through its ups and downs over the past six years had basically remained unchanged? Didn't he deserve more? Plus, he admired Horace Cayton – genuinely admired him – as both a newspaperman and a respected representative of their race. They did not see eye to eye on many issues, but here was one of the country's most accomplished black newspaper publishers. That in itself stood for something!

"And editorial oversight of my columns would remain with me?" he asked Cayton. He could see the older man balking, ever so slightly, as he smoothed out a wrinkle in his pants leg.

"The newspaper business, James, is still a business, as you know, and as such..."

"So the publisher of the *Seattle Republican* would have to approve each piece I wrote?" James interrupted him.

"Compromises...," Cayton began, and then changed his tone, "I trust you, James. I think you are a very promising newspaperman, with a sharp eye and sound judgment. You're also a remarkable writer. However, to answer your question: Yes, I read everything that's to be published in my newspaper and I give it my final approval... or, in some cases, not."

James appreciated the older man's directness, and told him so. He also thanked him for the generous offer to join the staff of the *Seattle Republican*. "The offer alone is an honor," he said. Yet knowing that he should neither accept nor decline such an offer without careful consideration, he asked Cayton if he could take two or three days to think it over.

"Of course," Cayton said, rising heavily from his chair and, James quickly surmised, concluding the dinner and the momentous conversation that had followed. "Let me know when you've decided."

James rose and shook Horace Cayton's hand and as they walked to the front door asked him to extend his gratitude once more to Mrs. Cayton.

James took his hat and left the house still rather breathless from what had just transpired – although in his heart he already knew he would probably decline Cayton's offer. There was too much variance in their views of the world and of newspaper publishing. Furthermore, James liked to think that the *Seattle Sentry* still had some life in it. All the same, he enjoyed the walk down Capitol Hill and back up Denny Hill just knowing that he had been so genuinely courted by the owner and publisher of the *Seattle Republican*. He also appreciated the veteran newspaperman's admissions about his paper's circulation. Maybe, James fancied as he looked out at Elliott Bay, the *Sentry* might someday surpass the *Republican*. Just maybe.

The very next morning, with just such thoughts going through his mind, James sent word thanking Horace R. Cayton for his generous offer but graciously declining it.

One week later, he read in the *Seattle Republican* that Booker T. Washington would be visiting Seattle, giving a lecture at the YMCA, and, in a side note, dining with Mr. and Mrs. Horace R. Cayton at their residence on Capitol Hill. While James planned to attend the lecture at the YMCA, he did not anticipate an invitation from Horace R. Cayton to meet the esteemed and influential Booker T. – and indeed none arrived.

At the end of the summer, on August 31, four members of the Negro Swimming Club of Seattle – James and the three unemployed scullery-men – swam from the Mount Baker bathing beach to Calkins Landing on Mercer Island in the middle of Lake Washington, a distance of approximately three-quarters of a mile, while the three other members of the club rowed in two separate skiffs beside the swimmers. Upon reaching Mercer Island, they all rowed triumphantly back to Seattle.

21. Luna Park (1907)

CLYDE KNEW MADDIE WAS HAVING TROUBLE MAKING ENDS meet. It was an old house and as such required considerable and often costly upkeep. Every week something new needed repairing, from a window casement shaken loose during the most recent storm to a rotting eave, from a clogged sewer drainage pipe to trouble with the newfangled electrical wiring that Maddie had asked Clyde to install in the downstairs last year. Lately it was the boiler in the side shed that had been acting up. And every time something new broke down, more often than not the repair job cost money, try as Clyde might to rig things without having to spend any. But if the threads on the steam valve on the boiler were worn down, as he'd discovered last week, it was best to replace the whole valve rather than risk a boiler explosion. In each of these cases, he was reluctant to ask Maddie for money for the repairs, given what he knew of her diminished house funds. So without telling her, he began an expense account at Nelson's Hardware nearby and with his odd jobs elsewhere paid the bill down as best he could, when he could.

Unfortunately, the last time he went into the hardware store and asked for a bag of nails and a roll of tar paper to patch the roof, the storekeeper told him he had to pay in cash from now on, that his tab was already too long and overdue. To pay for the supplies Clyde forked over the last of what he'd been paid the day before by Ned James, who had told him he was cutting back his hours – all of which left him broke for the foreseeable future.

So the next day Clyde walked down to the Kutzenjammer Kastle and applied for one of the new street sweeper positions being made available under the city's recent Good Roads initiative. Until then, street cleaning had been left up to local residents and business owners, and for the most part they had done a shabby job of it. So as part of the civic self-improvement drive that regrettably also included the regradings, the city levied a new sales tax and took over the maintenance and improvement of all its roads.

The new supervisor for city streets, a fat man with a walrus moustache and an unbuttoned vest, eyeballed Clyde's application. "It pays a dollar a day," were the first words out of his mouth. "Take it or leave it."

Clyde said he'd take it. A dollar a day, with Sundays off, came to six dollars a week, which meant he could have the tab at the hardware store paid off in three weeks … and then start contributing to Maddie's house fund. Over the years nothing had changed from their original arrangement of his paying five dollars a month for room and board and doing maintenance to supplement this rate. He knew that in many ways she was far too lenient a businesswoman, regularly letting boarders slide on their weekly payments and often preparing overly lavish meals. For instance, he knew for a fact that Ray was in arrears to her, and probably Chiridah too, and that James and Loye were the only two who paid on time every week. Maddie was just too kind-hearted for her own good, and didn't know how to demand payment the way the hardware store owner had demanded it of him.

In the initial weeks of his new job, Clyde took great pleasure in being a street sweeper. It got him up early – 4:30 a.m. – and out and about the city at the time of day he enjoyed most: when night opened onto dawn, when the morning quiet welcomed the first clatter of workmen going about their jobs, when the light was dim and soft and the air moist and still. At first, to save on streetcar fare, he walked all the way to the Sanitation Department wagon barn in the downtown warehouse district where all the equipment was kept. But since the job required him to be walking all day already, this soon became more walking than even he preferred, and he started flagging down the streetcar in the morning. It was the northside car's first run of the day that he usually caught, and most days he was the only passenger that early. After the first week on the streetcar, the driver, a black-haired Irishman, dropped his hand over the fare box when Clyde boarded and waved him on. "Forget it," he said.

Clyde stood beside the fare box at the head of the car looking down at the driver, who looked straight ahead.

"You're holding me up," the driver said in his rounded Irish brogue. "Now take your seat or get off."

Clyde did as he was told and sat down on one of the wood-slatted seats as the driver pulled the rope above his head to ring the bell, released the handbrake, and slid the car along the track.

Clyde was one of a dozen street sweepers the city had recently hired.

With his cart – a wooden bin between two wagon wheels and two handles like a handtruck – and his rake, shovel, and hay-bristle broom, he was assigned the entire Pioneer Place area, plus First, Second, Third, and Fourth Avenues between Yesler and Pike, including the alleys – all of which constituted some of the city's filthiest streets. At least ten times each day, between five in the morning and three in the afternoon, he had to cover his assigned area like a cop walking his beat. His work pace varied depending on how much he stopped to talk to shop owners and barkeeps, street vendors and wagon drivers, window cleaners and doormen, and the various other downtown denizens whom he quickly came to know. He passed Robert Patten in his umbrella hat almost every day, which meant a ten-minute break on each occasion to discuss gardening or the weather.

By the end of the first week, Clyde felt perfectly at ease in his new job. On Saturday evening, the last day of his first week, he was heaving his bin over the high sideboards of the wagon that each night hauled the day's accumulated waste to a barge on the waterfront, which eventually hauled it out into the bay, when one of the other street sweepers came up beside him and started talking to him as if the two of them were old chums. Clyde recognized the fellow from around the wagon barn but had never said more than a how-do to him. So he was surprised by his sudden forwardness, his sudden garrulity.

"I swear on my dear dead mother's grave that since I've taken this here job I can tell the fine and subtle differences between horse manure, mule manure, donkey manure, and in those rare instances, people manure. Not only that, I can tell what kind of feed the animal has been given, if the animal is healthy or ill, and the weight of the load the animal is pulling."

Clyde looked over his shoulder at the fellow speaking, unsure whether he was addressing him directly or was just holding forth to the general surroundings. He wore the same dirty brown canvas coat that all the sweepers wore, which they had been assigned their first day on the job. He seemed about Clyde's same age, maybe a few years older.

"It's all just manure to me," Clyde replied. "I try not to think about it."

"Well, that's where you're wrong, my friend." The fellow stepped forward.

Clyde righted his cart and tossed his rake, shovel, and broom into the bin. "Is that so?" He wasn't sure he wanted to have this conversation.

"Manure is like a Sanskrit scroll." The fellow pulled the bin off his cart and dumped it over the wagon's sideboard as Clyde had just done, and kept talking the whole while. "Learn to read it and it reveals the most materialistic workings of our metropolis. For example, how come the streets have twice as much traffic as the alleys and yet the streets have far less waste? In addition to which we're made to clean the streets far more diligently? Have you noticed that?"

Clyde certainly knew what wretched, rat-infested areas the alleys could be. They were used more for waste disposal than for waste removal. Restaurants and hotels dumped their discarded foodstuffs in the alleys, creating a stew of rotting vegetables and the offal from slaughtered cattle, horses, pigs, and chickens. The fishhouses offended worst of all, discarding whole schools of fish heads and entrails into the alleys in square wood bins. Many hotels without commode facilities on every floor looked the other way when residents tossed their commode buckets out an alley-facing window – the thinking among most people being that the rain would wash it away. The reality was that many Seattle alleys were more filthy and festering than those of medieval cities. His friend Ray's interest in them stupefied Clyde. All the same, Clyde didn't quite follow this particular fellow's reasoning. Did he have a point to make, or was he just pulling Clyde's leg? Perhaps he should be talking to Ray instead, since they shared this keen interest in alleys.

"You see," he went on, "the business elite and city sycophants demand clean streets. Who do you think's behind this whole Good Roads scheme? Even though it's in the alleys where the real work of the city gets done. You won't find any of your finer stallion manure there. It's all the heavy, steamy product of dray horses." He finished dumping his bin and set it back on his cart. He then wiped his right hand on his overalls and stuck it out for Clyde to shake. "I've seen you around but never had the pleasure. The name's Russell Bowles. Or Russ. Street sweeper and proud of it."

Clyde shook Russ Bowles's hand and introduced himself. "Those are very interesting theories on manure you've got," he said.

"Just theories," Russ replied. "Yet a man can learn a lot from just observing and thinking. It's a simple process that can lead to remarkable deducements."

Clyde said he reckoned so, and then commented that what got his ire up about the city, far more than its policies on manure, which after all was just part of the job, were the damn regradings. "How's a person supposed to keep a street clean if they keep tearing it up? To say nothing of everyone being kicked out of their homes!"

Russ looked at Clyde contemplatively for a moment, and then said, "The regrading, my friend, is a land grab of the highest order. Our beloved pioneers took the land from the Injuns – just like they done out in the Indian Territory in Oklahoma – and now the city's rich and powerful land grabbers want to take it from the regular folks like you and me who worked to make it what it is. It's not hard to calculate who wins and who loses. It's grab as grab can."

Apart from the stooped little man whom Clyde suspected of being the saboteur at the various regrading sites, this was the first time he'd heard anyone outside of Maddie's house voice such unequivocal condemnation of the regradings. If people had anything to say about them, it was more often than not to complain about the inconvenience of the muddy streets and discontinued streetcar lines. But here was this Russ fellow condemning the regradings, no bones about it, as outright wrong, an injustice of the highest order – which Clyde found quite refreshing.

"Do you think James Moore lost anything by tearing down his big hotel and building this new one he's putting up?" Russ took Clyde by the elbow and guided him to the side of the waste wagon. He took a piece of paper from his coat pocket and with a pencil stub wrote down an address, then handed it to Clyde. "Listen, my friend, we're having a meeting at this here place on Thursday night. You need to bring yourself to it. I'll introduce you to some people, you'll learn something."

Clyde took the piece of paper, glanced at the address – Plummer Street, below the line, down near Maynard Avenue – and looked at Russ. "What kind of meeting?" he asked, and slipped the paper into his coat pocket.

"Now don't lose that," Russ said, and in response to Clyde's question, added, "It's a meeting of people like you and me who don't think so highly 'bout the way the government protects the few wealthy and well-fed big-wigs who run this city at the same time that they're disadvantaging folks like you and me and most of the other poor slobs like us you see inhabiting this sorry town. It's a meeting about fair and equitable distribution of resources, and about power and who controls the means of production." He put his hand on Clyde's shoulder and leaned in toward him. "And it's a meeting of people brave enough to bring about the necessary changes. Which includes this regrading business you're so upset about."

Russ walked back over to his cart. "Remember what I said about the manure," he called to Clyde, as he pushed his cart out of the yard. "It's good to meet ya, Clyde Hunssler."

Clyde watched Russ return to the barn with his cart. He wondered about this meeting he'd invited him to and fingered the piece of paper in his coat pocket. He knew Russ's talk had some unpopular politics behind it, radical politics even – he was not so naive as to not know that much – and hence Russ's conspiratorial hushedness in urging Clyde to attend the meeting. But maybe, Clyde thought, he had ought to look into it anyway. Just maybe it was time to start doing something more forthrightly to oppose the regradings. Something more bold and more direct. And finding like-minded people would be the logical first step.

THE MEETING WAS HELD IN THE BOTTOM FLOOR OF A PRINT shop in the Blackchapel area bounded by Fifth and Sixth Avenues, and Jackson and Lane Streets. It was the same area to which the city had tried several years ago to relocate the brothels and honkytonks from the Tenderloin to make room for more wholesale and jobbing houses in that district. The plan didn't work and the Blackchapel area, not far from the new train station, remained a collection of low-slung brick buildings and warehouses with a few corner taverns thrown in where the workmen could get breakfast or lunch and a pail of beer to bring back to work. The bottom floor of the building that housed the print shop was, in actuality, the building's basement, since the true first floor, where the offices and presses were, was entered from the street while the bottom floor was entered from the alley, lower down the hill. Seattle being the hilly city that it was, most buildings had more than one ground floor depending on where the entrances were situated.

Russ was waiting outside the alley entrance smoking and jawing to another man when Clyde turned the corner and entered the alley. Russ stomped out his cigarette when he saw Clyde approaching and clapped him on the shoulder to welcome him into his and the other man's company.

"My street-sweeping pal," he said to Clyde, and with his arm about his shoulder turned him to face the other man. "Clyde, let me introduce you to one of our members. This is Billy Kovitz. He works down on the docks. That's why he's got that he-man build on him."

Clyde and Billy shook hands, and both men nodded to each other. The man indeed was big and had an overly firm handshake that caught Clyde off guard. Then Russ put his hand back on Clyde's shoulder and led him through the doorway and to the inside where palettes piled high with cartons of paper formed a narrow aisle that the two could barely fit through without walking single file. They passed through another doorway and into a room that was being used as a makeshift boxing gym. A ring was set up in the middle of the room, ropes looped around four iron poles planted in concrete blocks, while along the far wall a heavy bag and a speed bag hung side by side from the rafters. Along the near wall, a medicine ball, several jump ropes, and a collection of dumbbells lay on the floor.

"Do you box, Clyde?"

The question surprised Clyde. "Not me," he said. "Not interested."

"You should try it sometime. Every Wednesday night and Sunday morning some of the guys, instead of going to church, come around and we'll do a little sparring. Nothing serious. Purely recreational."

"Maybe I'll just come by and look in," Clyde replied, though he thought he'd really rather not, since he didn't want someone trying to talk him into the ring with some guy like Billy.

Once past the boxing gym, they walked through yet another doorway and entered a much larger room set up for the meeting. Eight or so short rows of folding chairs and benches were lined up in front of a foot-high platform on which a podium was planted dead center. About half the seats were already occupied, maybe twenty men scattered about in twos and threes and then four women sitting together on a bench off to one side of the room. Four bare electric lightbulbs at the end of thread-wrapped wires dangled from the rafters of the low ceiling, leaving the room with a dim, murky light. Many of the men smoked, as did two of the women. Along the walls, printed banners proclaimed various slogans: *Live Free or Die*; *No Government Is the Best Government*; *6/60 Work Week*; *Universal Suffrage*; *Union Forever.*

Russ saw Clyde reading the banners and offered an explanation: "We're more of a coalition than a single organization, you see. Some of us are socialists, some anarchists, some syndacalists, some communists, others just plain union men – it's a delicate balance, you might say. But we all recognize one important truth: that the capitalist hierarchy is anti-worker, anti-individual, and oppressive to basic rights. You've heard of Emma Goldman, haven't you?"

Clyde was only half listening. "Who?"

"Emma Goldman?"

"No," he said, and thought maybe he had, he wasn't sure.

"Well, maybe you'll have a chance to meet her if you keep coming to meetings. We're trying to bring her to Seattle for our May Day rally. That is, if the coppers don't have her sitting in a jail cell at that particular time, as they usually do."

Clyde and Russ stood in the back of the room while more people entered and took seats. Some seemed to be arguing with one another, others laughing. A few came in by themselves and sat quietly toward the back; others went right up to the front. When Billy Kovitz came in, he walked forward and took a seat directly in front of the podium. Russ tried to escort Clyde to the front of the room as well, but Clyde balked, held back, and told Russ he'd just stand in the back and watch for tonight. "To get a feel of things," he said.

"That's fine," Russ said. "Just make sure you don't make yourself look too much like a snoop. Some of the fellas get a little nervous seeing someone lurking around the edges, if you know what I mean." He slapped Clyde on the shoulder again and moved up front and took a seat next to

Billy. When Russ leaned over and said something to him, Billy turned around and peered back at Clyde standing in the rear.

Not wanting to draw more attention than his translucent skin and white hair already did, he took a seat in the second to last row and waited for the meeting to start. Although he didn't know much about politics, he knew that fraternizing with anarchists and socialists could get a person in trouble if he wasn't careful. Ever since McKinley was gunned down by the self-proclaimed anarchist assassin Leon Czolgosz at the Pan-American Exposition in Buffalo, the general population, stirred up by yellow journalists, had become fiercely intolerant of any politics that didn't fit neatly within the mainstream parties. Yet as Clyde reminded himself, he was here to see what people had to say about the regradings, to see if there were an organized – and legal – means of putting pressure on city officials, slowing down the sluicing crews, and perhaps, just perhaps, saving Denny Hill.

When the room was about two-thirds full, Russ hopped up onto the platform, stood behind the podium, and called the meeting to order. He told everyone that the agenda for that night's meeting would be the organizing taking place down on the wharves and that to speak to that issue they were going to hear first from Billy Kovitz, from the International Longshoremen's Association and, he added, "One of the bravest men I know, a man solely responsible for the dangerous efforts being made to unionize the waterfront and thereby bring respectable wages and safe working conditions to our docks."

Without any applause from the people in the room, Billy Kovitz stepped up to the podium and Russ resumed his seat down front. In a deep and slurry voice, Billy proceeded to recount for his audience what organizers on the waterfront, led by himself, had been up to for the past two weeks since their last meeting. His voice rose as he told of repeated incidents of men being beaten or threatened by hired thugs. A man's dog, which accompanied him to the docks each morning, had been impaled by a cargo hook and its carcass latched to a piling. Then he recited the names of the half dozen men who had been fired in the past month for their union activity – a lot of men were now afraid to be seen even talking to him for this reason – and taking up from there he elaborated on the hardships the fired workers and their families now faced. He said a fund was being gotten up for their benefit and warned that if a strike was called and there was a lockout, the situation would get a lot worse before it got better. Someone from the middle of the room yelled out, "We'll stand with ya, Billy."

"Just 'cause times is flush don't mean a man don't need to work and make an honest wage so he can put bread on the table and a roof over his head," Billy answered back, his voice growing more hoarse and raspy.

Someone else from the audience called out, "What will ya do if ya get fired, Billy?"

"I'll keep right on organizin' and fightin', that's what I'll do," he shouted back, thumping his fist on the podium, and with this demonstration of defiance and commitment, the room erupted into applause and cheers. Billy glared out at the room, yet in the pause to let the cheering subside, he also looked tired. Then he went on. "We've talked to Big Bill Haywood, who you all know has been out organizin' in the fields near Yakima and Ellensburg and Ephrata on behalf of the IWW. We're talking to Big Bill about leading us in a march on the Seattle waterfront and closing down the docks, the rail lines, and keeping the ships out in the harbor. Won't Big Bill strike the fear of god and union into some of these damn bosses!"

The cheers and applause doubled.

Wrapping up his address to the meeting, Billy Kovitz called on people to sign a pledge of support to the longshoremen and dockworkers and for everyone to contribute one dollar to the strike fund he'd mentioned earlier. He thanked the roomful of supporters and stepped down from the platform and resumed his seat.

Russ stood up and applauded Billy and shook his hand. He applauded Billy a moment longer and then hop-skipped back up to the podium and exhorted everyone at the meeting to recognize what was at stake if the efforts of people like Billy Kovitz did not succeed. He started pointing to various people in the room, calling out the name of each person and his or her trade – Niles, boilermaker; Clem, tannery worker; Ernie, machinist; Carl, tugboat hand; Alice and Janie, seamstresses in the textile factory – and then he pointed to the back of the room and called out, "Even you, Clyde, a plain old street sweeper like me, but the best damn street sweeper there is. You should see this man go to work with his broom and shovel. What's at stake for Billy here is what's at stake for ol' Clyde back there. It's all of a piece."

All heads turned around to get a look at the person Russ was pointing to. Everyone seemed to pause a moment in their looking as they realized he was pointing at the albino seated in the second to last row.

Abashed at being called out, Clyde remained still, staring at the back of the chair in front of him until the room's attention gradually turned back to the front. Russ now began holding forth about the precepts of true anarcho-communalism, in which a balance is struck between man as a social being who must cooperate with his fellows against the overwhelming odds of nature and man as an independent agent who must resist oppression by the arcane laws and regulations of an illegitimate body politic. He invoked the names of Bakunin and Proudhon and referred to a stack of literature available to all interested members at the back. "It's all there in black and white," he said, and went on to announce that a retreat on Vashon Island was being planned and that once the time and exact location were determined, all would be invited to attend.

By now Clyde was growing discouraged that nothing had yet been said about the regradings. Russ kept on about the retreat commune and the establishment of dues, and Clyde just didn't see that it had much to do with fighting city hall, or keeping the city from confiscating people's property or preventing the hoses from washing Denny Hill into Elliott Bay. As several people asked Russ for details about the retreat commune, Clyde took his chances and raised his hand from the back. When Russ finally called on him, he stood up and, speaking as clearly as he could, said, "I'm interested in the fight against the mayor and the city engineer who aim to bring down Denny Hill. A lot of people are losing their homes and businesses because of the regradings. Where do people here stand on this question?"

For a moment following Clyde's statement and question, near total silence filled the room, as if no one knew what he was talking about. Then from the middle of the room, a thin young man wearing a longcoat and tiny round spectacles rose to his feet and declared, "It's a struggle between the propertied classes, that's where we stand. Let them bloody one another over their deeds and titles. Who in this room ever owned so much as a scrap of property that he should care about your petit-bourgeois property owners on Denny Hill?" He turned to face Clyde. "Let their little fiefdom fall. We're fighting here for jobs and a living wage." The young man's posture straightened at his own vehemence, and his face turned red with assumed outrage. He scanned the room sternly, apparently looking for anyone who might hold a dissenting opinion.

Clyde heard him out and knew that anyone in the room who had ever owned "a scrap a property" – and some probably had, and did still, while others certainly wished to – would not dare speak out after such a strident declaration.

"See," he said, looking at Clyde again. "When you lose your property, then you'll be one of us, the proletariat. In the meanwhile, let them regrade the whole damn city for all I care. Tax dollars of the poor raising the property values of the rich, that's all it is." He shook his head in disgust at Clyde and sat back down.

"Bullshit," Clyde muttered, not bothering to stand – but then, letting his own outrage show, repeated much louder, with greater emphasis … "*Bull*-shit."

The young man in the wire-rimmed spectacles was back on his feet, staring Clyde down. Clyde acknowledged the challenge and rose to his feet. Everyone in the room, including Russ, watched the two face off.

Not to be shouted down by some hot-headed radical, Clyde went right about saying what he had to say. "I let a room in the attic of a boarding-house owned by a lady who bought her house and fixed it up with every red cent she had. She works hard and lets rooms to all sorts – workers, students, journalists – at a good price too, and some don't ever pay up, but she lets them stay. But now you're telling me she deserves to lose her house, that all these *unpropertied* people in that house of hers, which means me too, deserve to end up without a roof over our heads or a place to find a decent a meal. I'll say it again, mister … *Bullshit*."

"Whatever it takes to seize the property from the elite and redistribute it …," the young radical began, scowling back at Clyde.

"Maddie is not the elite!" Clyde shouted at him. "She doesn't want to lose her house. It's her livelihood, just as Billy's job on the docks is his."

"Your landlady functions under the same principles as every other property owner – theft!"

With this denouncement of Maddie and calling her a thief, Clyde had had enough. He could tell that everyone in the room expected him to lunge at the outspoken radical as he made his way from his seat to the side of the room. But that's not what he had in mind. He'd had enough of Russ's meeting, period, and without so much as looking back at the offensive fellow in the longcoat, he walked out of the meeting room with everyone's eyes riveted on his back. He walked through the building the same way he'd entered and stopped at the heavy bag in the makeshift gym and delivered a flurry of hard jabs and several hooks to the coarse canvas. Maybe he'd come back and do a little boxing after all, he thought, as he left the bag swinging from its chain and made his way out into the alley.

LUNA PARK HAD BEEN OPEN SINCE JUNE. THE OUTING OVER to the westside of Seattle – which had come to be called West Seattle following its official annexation to the city – had been Ray's great enthusiasm for the past several weeks. The amusement park had garnered a lot of attention in the local newspapers – some praising it for the excitement it generated in the city, for the diversion it provided to work-weary citizens on weekends; others condemning it for the corruptive element they saw it attracting, for the seed of sin it disseminated. When Ray first suggested the outing, Clyde thought the idea would pass and Ray would eventually forget about it. He himself wasn't much interested in it. Then one day Ray took the trolley over to West Seattle on his own and like an ancient mariner returning from an exotic and distant land, he carried with him the next morning to the breakfast table fantastic tales of the twelve-acre "entertainment emporium." It was truly "the White City," he announced, paraphrasing a recent newspaper article, supplying every modern appliance and equipment possessed by an up-to-date seaside pleasure resort.

"It's the best thing to happen to this city since gold was discovered on the Klondike," he exclaimed, a comparison that made Clyde even more skeptical.

Yet, in truth, it was not Ray's exuberance for the park so much that led to Clyde's reluctance to go as it was the prospect of the oddball four-some – Ray, Loye, Maddie, and himself – trooping over there as a group. He didn't wish to embarrass his friends by making them endure, by associa-tion, the incessant stares that in public were always directed his way. Fur-thermore, he didn't know how Maddie would receive the notion of the outing. While Ray and Loye were openly courting each other these days, he and Maddie, despite their apparent closeness, did not acknowledge their feelings to either the Madison House boarders or, more important, to them-selves. Despite their fondness for each other, despite their many evenings spent together reading until neither could stay awake, they maintained the veneer of proprietress and handyman. Clyde forthrightly admitted – to him-self at least – that he feared jeopardizing the fondness they shared for each other should he try to advance his truer feelings for Maddie. He persuaded himself he could be content with simple proximity to Maddie, her com-pany, their mutual quiet as they occupied the same room, her smiles when he said something that amused her, her willingness to have him near.

All the same, none of this delicate balance between Clyde and Maddie occurred to Ray, who remained persistent in urging the outing to Luna Park and eventually convinced Clyde to broach the subject with Maddie. Clyde asked her several days later if she might like to join him and Ray and Loye for an afternoon at the new amusement park … and if not, well, he understood perfectly. To his surprise, delight, and mild alarm, she was thrilled by the idea, readily accepted his invitation, and after several min-utes even divulged to Clyde that she had already spoken to Loye about the outing two days prior.

When the day came, Ray and Clyde both wore their best stepping-out suits – though Clyde had to borrow Erasmo's since he didn't have one of his own. Clyde also borrowed from Ray one of the two new sporting straw hats with silk bands that he'd recently picked up at Schwabacher's on his brother's discount. Meanwhile, the ladies dressed in their Saturday-best skirts and blouses, and while Maddie wore a simple straw leghorn hat, Loye donned atop her head a summer-style chapeau stacked high with silk bows and a white ribbon that trailed down the middle of her back. Indeed, she wore it boldly – if there were any other way to wear such a hat – seeming to know full well that it grabbed far more attention than the typical lady's hat. Clyde quietly commended her for that.

Initially Ray suggested they hire a car to drive them to West Seattle, but Loye and Maddie – the former with the student's frugality, the latter with the landlady's practicality – vetoed the idea and said they could quite easily take the no. 5 trolley that went right up to the Luna Park entrance. So at five o'clock on Saturday afternoon they all four emerged from the house and onto the front porch in a flurry of excitement. It was the only time of the week, from Saturday afternoon to Monday morning, when the steam shovels and hydraulic hoses could not be heard on Denny Hill.

Wasting no time, they trundled down the south slope along Fourth Avenue to Pike Street and took the streetcar to Pioneer Place, and after a short wait there they boarded the no. 5 trolley which carried them over the complex of trestles traversing the tideflats and around the curve where the Duwamish River let into the bay and then along the West Seattle peninsula heading straight to the amusement park entrance.

The trolley was filled with people, young people mostly, in small and not so small groups, but also several older couples, married most likely, who had probably secured a nanny to watch over the children so they could have a summer's evening out. Everyone seemed in high spirits, eager to reach Luna Park and happily lay out their hard-earned money for the sake of a little diversion. Everyone had heard of the wonders of Coney Island in New York, and now citizens felt, at last, that they had an attraction to rival any amusement park back east. Times were relatively prosperous again, people worked hard to get ahead, and by god if a city could not reward its hard-working citizenry with the simple and exuberant pleasures of a place like Luna Park. This seemed to be the general mood aboard the trolley.

Clyde soon shed his reserve and became charged by this spirit as the trolley stopped at the arching white gate leading into the amusement park. Ray leapt off the trolley first and helped Loye down, and then Clyde followed suit and helped Maddie. They quickly fell in with the crowd streaming toward the gate to purchase tickets and push its way through the turnstiles. Even while waiting in line, Clyde could hear the racket and commotion from inside the park: bells and whistles and calliope organ music from the rides, yells and squeals from people on those same rides, and a general clamor of folks giving themselves over to the thrill of it all. The smell of briny air from the bay was much sharper out here than in the middle of the city. It mixed pleasantly with the warm odors of grilled meat, fried dough, and burnt sugar.

Ray purchased tickets for them all – his treat, he said, since the friend who'd promised to get him in for free wasn't working that day – and after handing the tickets out to the other three, took Clyde's elbow and whispered that he could buy the first round of beers in exchange for the tickets. In single file, they entered the park, emerging through the gate onto the expansive boardwalk plaza that served as the park's central staging area.

"There's the natatorium," Ray exclaimed, and then in a more dejected tone, "And look here, we all forgot our bathing suits. Wouldn't ya know it."

"Maybe they have suits inside," Loye suggested.

"There's an idea," he came back. "You know, dontcha, the water's heated? That's what makes it so great, Maddie."

Clyde could not figure why he'd addressed this comment to Maddie.

"Really," she answered him, apparently not as interested in the natatorium as Ray was, which came as a relief to Clyde, who wasn't interested in it either.

"Look," Ray said. "Why don't we go over and see if they have suits so we can all take a swim."

Maddie continued to look about the park grounds at the various rides and stands and people, seemingly wonder-struck by it all. Clyde watched her and then turned to Ray and said, "Maybe we should split up and meet later at the Summer Garden for sandwiches. That way you and Loye can go swimming and Maddie and I can look around."

"I think I want to go on the carousel," said Maddie out of the blue, getting everyone's attention.

"The carousel!" Ray said. "You've got to be kidding."

"It sounds like fun," Loye put in.

"Okay, okay," Ray relented, and to Loye said, "You and I will go see about the suits at the natatorium and afterwards I'll take you on the carousel. And we'll meet up with Clyde and Maddie at the bar in two hours. What do you say to that, Clyde?"

Having gotten his wish to be by himself with Maddie, Clyde agreed to Ray's plan of meeting at the bar – touted as "the longest bar on the bay," according to the sign at the entrance – rather than at the Summer Garden restaurant. "And I'll buy the first round," he threw in for Ray's benefit.

"Damn right you will," Ray said, and knocked the back of Clyde's straw hat so that the front brim fell over his eyes. "And you'll be sorry you didn't go swimming. Right, Loye?"

Loye just smiled and pulled Ray off in the direction of the natatorium. "See you two in a couple of hours," she said. "Have a good time."

Like a little kid with only one purpose in mind, Maddie darted off in the direction of the carousel as soon as Loye and Ray were gone. Clyde had to trot to catch up to her and, before he even knew he'd done so, had hooked his arm through hers. Just as they were approaching the large open structure that looked like an Arabian tent and under which the carousel whirled, two clowns in bright billowing silk suits with stripes and patches passed in front of them, one blowing loudly on a trombone and the other covering his ears in mock agony. Clyde and Maddie side-stepped them, paused to let them pass, and watched as a cluster of children ran after them looking for handouts of saltwater taffy.

Clyde bought their tickets and they waited for the carousel to slow to a stop. When it did, everyone on the carousel climbed off and everyone on the perimeter climbed on. Maddie made for an elegant white-red-and-green horse with a flowing mane and bejeweled bridle while Clyde mounted a saddled and snarling tiger right beside her. When the carousel started up, they gripped the poles and bobbed up and down as the whirligig music played and the big carousel went around. Maddie rode sidesaddle and when Clyde reached over and seized one of her ankles, she let out a squeal and kicked his hand away. He had never seen her laugh so freely. Over the five and a half years they had known each other, he had mostly watched her struggle – first putting her house in order to let the rooms, then keeping up with repairs, and now worrying about the Denny Hill regrading. During this brief respite, though, none of that seemed to matter.

On the third go-round, she reached out and snagged one of the brass rings from the hook, and then another the next time around, putting one on each thumb. Clyde was delighted just watching her, and as the ride slowed and their turn came to an end, he wanted to stay on the carousel and maybe ask Maddie to sit in one of the ornate carriages with him. But as soon as the carousel came to a stop, she hopped off before he could say anything and stood off to the side of the ride waiting for him to join her.

"I haven't done that since I was a child," she said, "when mother and father brought me to the beach at Wildwood and we rode the carousel and afterward waded in the Atlantic Ocean." She adjusted her hat and straightened her blouse and skirt. "This one, though, was even better. I'll always remember it."

Clyde was happy for her and asked, "Where to now?"

Maddie scanned the grounds, took in a deep breath, and said, "Let's just walk, shall we?"

They hooked arms again and began strolling about the park's broad open plaza. They entered the ice cream parlor and each ordered a cone of strawberry parfait. As they sat on a bench outside the ice cream parlor, a barker began shouting that the next daredevil high-diving act was about to commence and to step right up to witness this breath-taking, death-defying feat of derring-do. The bench they sat on gave them the perfect vantage point to view the act, and as they licked their cones, a man in black tights climbed the perpendicular ladder that rose a hundred feet or more straight up into the air. The ladder was secured by guidewires on all four sides and topped with a platform no bigger than what a man could stand on. Below the ladder lay a tub of water that closely resembled a horse trough. The diver reached the top of the ladder, stepped onto the platform, and paused as the barker again summoned everyone's attention. Then he about-faced so that his back was to the pool below him, eliciting oohs and aahs from the crowd, then raised both hands above his head, held them there an instant, and let himself fall backwards. Maddie gasped and turned her head away from the sight as he fell head first. Yet Clyde kept his eyes on the diver as he tucked his limbs in, somersaulted, and finally plunged feet-first into the pool of water. A split-second later he sprang to the surface and, to wild applause from everyone milling about, waved to the crowd.

At the sound of the applause, Maddie looked up again, embarrassed by her own silly fright, and Clyde remarked how he believed the pool must be cut into the boards so that it was actually much deeper than it appeared.

A few moments later, a pair of men wearing leather jackets and racing goggles climbed to a second platform on the opposite side of the plaza. Atop this larger and less elevated platform were parked two vehicles that looked like miniature automobiles, both pointed down a narrow, sharply angled track that ended in a loop-de-loop on the plaza boardwalk. Each of the two daredevil drivers climbed onto one of the two vehicles and stood up in it as if to steer with his feet. Then, like the diver before them, each raised a hand high above his head to hold the audience's attention, and when the driver in front brought his hand down, he quickly squatted into the tiny vehicle and went sailing down the track and up and through the loop-de-loop. Then the second driver dropped his hand, and he performed the same maneuver in his vehicle. This time Maddie watched the daredevils without batting an eye and politely clapped with the rest of the crowd when the stunt was over.

"Let's ride the coaster," she said, again out of the blue, as Clyde finished crunching on his cone.

For you, Maddie, Clyde mused to himself, *I'll go anywhere.* Yet, moments later, on the ride, the loud rattling of the steep wooden coaster as their small car crept up the track had Clyde feeling more than a little worried, even as Maddie sat at his side wide-eyed and giddy with anticipation. As the car slowly ascended, they could view all of Luna Park, and for the three or four seconds when the car crested the top of the track and seemed to pause there, Clyde could look out past the park and see all the way across Elliott Bay to Seattle. But then the car plummeted and hurled him and Maddie back against their seats, abruptly banked and slung them against each other, then banked in the opposite direction, furiously shaking them with each turn, and after several more stomach-churning twists and dips and turns finally coasted back to level ground and was finished rattling them senseless.

As they wobbled back to the open plaza, they agreed that after the rollercoaster all the other rides would be perfectly tame. So they rode the

Chutes, the giant water slide that nearly soaked them both, and then the Circle Swing, which was Maddie's favorite, and then just for the heck of it took another go on the rollercoaster. When they had finished this circuit of rides, they walked through the dark and scary, but ultimately very silly, Cave of Mystery and afterward decided to pass on viewing the Infant Electrobator, which Maddie said sounded just too creepy. Finally, not knowing the exact time but guessing that two hours must have passed, they made their way to the bar, but not before stopping off at the Summer Garden lunch counter for a quick ham sandwich.

Ray and Loye were already standing at the bar when Clyde and Maddie arrived. Carved from a single straight Douglas fir, with a brass foot railing, the bar faced out onto the plaza and extended the length of the shed-like structure under which it sat.

"Where've you two been all this time?" Ray said, and signaled the man behind the bar to bring all four of them a mug of beer just like the one he now brought to his lips.

"How was the swimming?" Clyde asked.

"Wonderful," Loye said. "The water was like a tropical ocean, and Ray even talked me into going off the high dive."

"Well," Ray said, as the bartender brought the four foaming mugs and set them down on the bar, "let's drink."

They took a table and Ray ordered a plate of Limburger cheese, saltwater crackers, and hot mustard. Clyde and Maddie recounted to Loye and Ray the rides they'd gone on, the daredevil acts they'd seen, and the Cave of Mystery they'd walked through. Ray told them how after swimming – the natatorium, by the way, did have bathing suits – they also rode the roller coaster and then had gone in to see the Electrobator babies.

"It was terribly sad," Loye said. "There were babies, tiny, tiny babies, some no bigger than a man's fist, all in little glass ovens heated by electrical coils. Some were blue and shriveled and some were as pink as piglets, almost as if they were being singed by the hot wires. To tell you the truth, I'm not even sure they were real babies. They didn't move at all."

"Oh, they were real all right," said Ray, but with such a smirk that Clyde didn't know if he was yanking Loye's chain or not.

When the first round was finished, Clyde ordered another beer for himself to put out the fire the hot mustard ignited in his mouth. The electrical lights in the park gradually came on and sparkled across the plaza. Across the way, the Joy Wheel lit up, a giant funnel of hundreds of light bulbs through which people strolled, letting the brilliant illumination surround them. Maddie was beginning to look tired and Clyde thought he might suggest they leave shortly when, before he could speak, a band started playing beneath a canvas awning right next to the bar. Almost instantly people strolled from the bar to the area in front of the bar and began dancing.

"The night's young," Ray exclaimed. "The evening's fair, and … " Here he took Loye's hand in his. "We're in the company of two charming and lovely ladies." He rose from his chair and offered his hand to Loye, and the two sidled away from the table, stepped out onto the dance area, and began dancing.

Clyde and Maddie got up too and moved themselves over to the side of the crowd to watch the dancers. When it eventually became too darn awkward to simply be standing there in silence watching, Clyde said to Maddie, "I've never danced before and wouldn't know how."

"It's not hard," she replied.

"Would you show me?" he asked, and looked at her.

She gave him her arm and said, "Gladly."

Clyde led Maddie out among the other dancers and then faced her and placed his free hand on her shoulder. He tried to lead but was not sure what that role entailed. He watched his feet to avoid stepping on hers, and eventually they found a mutual rhythm. As one dance number ended and the next started up, they remained among the crowd of dancers. By the third dance, Clyde had placed his hand in the middle of Maddie's back and they moved much more smoothly.

As night came on, the young families that had come out to Luna Park began to disappear. While a few of the older married couples remained, the crowd became mostly young couples and small groups of working folks – men and women just now arriving at the park to commence their revelries after a long week's work on the docks and in the mills and factories. When the band finally took a break, Ray and Loye joined back up with Clyde and Maddie, and then as the two women walked over to the lemonade stand, Ray tugged on Clyde's elbow and revealed a silver flask he'd been carrying in his inside jacket pocket all evening.

"I've been saving this for when we need a little pick-me-up," he said conspiratorially. "And I do believe that time has come." He put the flask in Clyde's hand, the cap already screwed off. "Go ahead ... "

Clyde typically stayed away from the hard stuff, having seen what it had done to his father and to more than a few people in the tribe out at Neeah. Yet Ray was waiting for him to take a swig, and the girls would be back any moment now ... and besides that, it was their big night out, a time to relax and enjoy themselves ... so he took a pull from the flask and handed it quickly back to Ray. Ray looked about to make sure no one was watching, then took a long pull from the flask himself. He smacked his lips, recapped the flask, and put it back in his jacket pocket.

"How's that feel?" he asked Clyde.

Clyde nodded, already feeling a mild swoon coming over him. At first the whiskey had made him shiver, and now it was making him perspire. It made him feel more glad than ever to be out and about with Ray and Loye and especially Maddie on such a beautiful night. He was a lucky man. "It feels all right," he answered.

As Ray laughed at his delayed response and told Clyde he could have more anytime, two men approached them and bookended them where they stood. They both wore canvas work coats and dungarees and heavy work boots. They smelled of engine grease, and the caps they wore were smudged with it. Without speaking, they simply stood next to Clyde and Ray and looked at them with disgust on their faces. Clyde looked from one to the other and thought he recognized the bigger of the two. Then he was sure of it. Here was the big lout who had tried to intimidate him above the regrading cut several months ago, the one who had tried to spray him with the hose afterwards.

"What can we do for you fellas?" Ray said to them, looking unconcerned by their sudden presence.

"It's your friend here we're interested in," the big one said. "We know what he's up to."

Clyde started to say something, but the second man interrupted him.

"We hear you were making a big stink at one of those anarchist meetings in town. Tryin' to rile up some of those bomb throwers to get behind you now that we've got the Pinkerton men keeping you from doing your dirty work to our equipment. Ain't that right? Well, we're telling you, you better keep a sharp look out."

Clyde was growing damn tired of these idiots' routine threats, and worse, with their stupidity in thinking he had anything to do with their equipment being sabotaged. What's more, the whiskey had him feeling a bit bold, if not downright pissed off, so he was going to let them know just what he thought of their idiocy.

"What the hell are you talking about?" he spat back at them and turned to face the bigger of the two. Even though the bigger man hadn't been the one to make the threat, he was the one Clyde recognized, so he addressed him. "I don't like the way you're talking to me while I'm out enjoying my evening. So why don't you just step away now."

"And your lady friend, the one who's holding out, she better watch herself too," the other man said.

Clyde heard this threat against Maddie and whipped around and got right up into the face of the smaller man. "I'll kill you first," he said.

Ray grabbed Clyde's jacket, pulled him back, and tried to steer him away from the two men.

"What're you anyway?" the bigger one now chimed in, trying to antagonize him. "You a Siwash? 'Cause you sure do stand out there. A bit pale for an Injun, ain't it? Maybe your papa went and peckered a squaw. By god, you damn well make me look like a darky."

Clyde strained against Ray's hold on his arm and glared back at the two men.

"Tell your foreigner anarchist pals we're ready for them," the smaller man said. "Damn half-breed albino – or whatever the hell you are. They'll get as good as they're giving out."

Ray continued to push Clyde away. "Listen ... " he said, "it's not worth it, Clyde. They want to rile you up. So just cool down."

With that, Clyde heeded Ray's words. He turned away from the two men and veered off with Ray still gripping his arm. The moment they had gotten out of earshot of the two men, he turned to Ray and held his hand out for the whiskey flask. He took a quick pull and handed it back. Ray took one too and returned the flask to his jacket pocket.

"What was that all about?" Maddie asked, as she and Loye came up to them a few moments later.

"Just a couple of roughs," Ray said.

"What did they want?" Loye asked him.

"Just looking for trouble, you know how it is," he answered, and left it at that.

Clyde said nothing.

"They thought we were some fellas they had a scrap with last week. And then they wanted a little taste of my whiskey ... "

"You didn't tell me you had whiskey," Loye said, sounding indignant.

"But I told them to go buy their own, this wee bit was for Clyde and me." He patted his jacket where the flask lay in the inside pocket. "And for you two ladies, if you'd like a little taste."

"You're a pesky little sneak, Ray Gruhlki," Loye said, smiling at him now. "Look at the trouble you caused. Almost getting into a fight with those two men." Then she paused and looked at Ray more slyly. "I believe I'll need a nip of that whiskey just to calm my nerves now that you've gotten me so rattled. How about you Maddie?"

Maddie declined Loye's invitation and said she was just glad there wasn't any more serious trouble than that. "I think we should go home now," she added.

Clyde nodded his consent, and Ray and Loye agreed it was time to call it a night. So as the dance band returned to their instruments and began playing again, the four friends walked across the planked plaza and exited the Luna Park grounds through the large white gate. Across the road at the trolley stop, the trolley car was already filled with revelers waiting for the return ride back to Seattle.

22. Imogen (1907)

THE IMAGE OF LOYE SITTING ON THE PORCH RAILING IN her nightgown on that drizzly morning of the Washington Hotel fire remained with Ray. He still regretted not having run up to his room for his camera. He knew the trouble and attention attendant on setting up the camera would have spoiled the moment. And good photography was so much about moments and half moments. This moment was about Loye's inattention to him, her sleepless languor, the balanced curve of her neck, back, and legs against the symmetry of the porch rail, the near diaphanous quality of her nightgown, the misty, smoke-laden air giving the scene an uncanny softness – these compositional elements had con-verged in this one moment, and then, when he'd looked at her again after asking if he could bring her a coat, they were gone: the air had more light in it, Loye shifted her back against the porch post, she asked him what time it was. Even in its fleeting momentariness, however, the image had revealed something about Loye. Here was a soul in the world, a self-con-tained being, a caring person, a beautiful woman. He counted this moment as the one when he began to fall in love with Loye.

Their outing to Luna Park with Clyde and Maddie three months later was as important a milestone in what, love aside, Ray recognized as his evolving interest in Loye. They had great fun together at the natatorium, buying bathing suits right there on the spot, and splashing about the enormous pool with its heated, Puget Sound-fed water, the echoing clamor of kids and young adults like themselves, the physical display of everyone in their partial nakedness, the steaminess of everything under the steel and glass roof. It delighted him how willing Loye was, once in the water, to splash and tussle and dunk and be dunked and play tag and jump off the high dive. She was a surprisingly strong girl, too. And with quite a fetching figure in the wet mohair swimsuit she wore. The little incident later that evening with the two roughs was certainly unpleasant business, but it did nothing to detract from the pleasure he had taken in dancing with Loye for several numbers prior to it ... and it absolutely charmed him when she so cleverly finagled a nip of his whiskey from him.

So it was with the intention of seeing Loye play basketball, of all things, that he found himself riding the streetcar one day in July to the University of Washington campus clear across Portage Bay in the far north end of the city. Although the game was a winter sport, a summer tournament had been organized, Loye had explained to him, to help maintain the girls' conditioning and keep their individual and teamwork skills honed. This time he brought his camera, having promised Loye that he would photograph the team in action. Because he had never ventured out this way before, having generally confined himself to the city proper, he arrived at the campus with a case full of glass plates three hours before the game was scheduled to start. He wanted to tour the grounds to see if any opportunities for photographs presented themselves to him.

It was a mildly warm summer day, a faint dewiness still in the air as he walked onto the campus, which hardly seemed like a campus at all but more like what he remembered Golden Gate Park in San Francisco looking like: large cleared spaces for laying out a picnic, copses of cedar and spruce and some young big-leaf maples, paths meandering through the rolling landscape – all quite sylvan in its way. He hadn't really done any nature photography, but several vistas and certain hidden recesses on the campus led him to recognize how one might be inspired to such photographic work. He had heard a rumor (perhaps Asahel Curtis had mentioned it to him) that the city hoped to host a major exposition, on the scale of Chicago's and St. Louis's, on these very grounds in the near future. Such an event would change the campus forever, certainly, but he could think of no more attractive site for showing off the natural splendors that were so much a part of the city and distinguished it from any other world-class city he knew of, save perhaps Geneva, Switzerland.

After walking about a bit, he took a photograph of the administrative building – a very stock Webster and Stevens type shot, he thought. He then entered the building and, after asking the gentleman's permission, photographed a mathematics professor at his desk in posed concentration over a particularly obstinate problem.

"Are you a scientific photographer?" the professor asked him when he was done.

"Pardon?" Ray replied.

"Science," the professor adamantly returned. "Have you studied the chemistry of your profession?"

"Yes, sir," Ray answered. "Not formally, mind you, but I know what chemicals to use."

"Well," the professor said, "that's good. Though formal instruction is always preferred."

"I'm sure," was all Ray could offer.

"That's all," the professor added, and with that went back to work on his problem. Ray quickly packed his camera, collapsed his tripod, and exited the building.

He then headed toward the most wooded area of the campus, off to the right of the administration building, an area that appeared to lead down to the marshy lakeshore. He was thinking sympathetically of Loye and how she must have to endure her professors' haughtiness, when he came to a grassy opening and at its farthest edge spotted a camera on a tripod. Then, stepping out from the grass where she had apparently been lying, sprang a young woman, thoroughly nude, without a scrap of clothing on her – something, honestly, he had never seen before – who scurried back to the camera, threw a kimono-type robe about herself, and then rapidly removed a glass plate from the camera and set it in the case on the ground. Ray watched this take place, then stepped quietly back in among the trees and out of plain view. As he walked around the perimeter of the field, he began whistling, and as he neared where the woman had been with her camera, he emerged again into the opening, appeared surprised when the woman looked up and spotted him, and, tipping his hat, approached her.

"A fellow photographer, I see."

The woman pulled her kimono more tightly about her neck. Closer up, Ray thought, she appeared to be a somewhat plain-looking maiden, noting her hair twirled and pinned into a tidy bun, her gentle roundish face, her generous nose, and her clear eyes made wide by the large round eyeglasses she donned as he neared. She seemed hardly alarmed by his sudden presence, or that he might have seen her as she lay naked in the grass just moments before.

"Excuse me, sir," she called out to him. She had a clear, direct voice – like her eyes.

"Have I interrupted you?" Ray asked her.

"In a manner," she said.

"It's just that I saw your camera and became interested. What sort is it?"

"It's a Graflex standard format camera," she said flatly. "Same as yours basically, though I believe you have a more updated model, with the rectilinear lens."

"That's correct," Ray said, impressed by her ready knowledge of cameras. "I'm Ray Gruhlki."

"Pleased to meet you, Ray Gruhlki. I'm Imogen. Now if you'll excuse me, I need to dress." She bent down and picked up a housedress that lay at her bare feet. "If you turn around, we can speak further about cameras and photography after I'm properly attired."

Ray did as requested, saying, "I don't like to turn my back on a lady … but in this case an exception to the rule seems warranted."

"Done," she said, just that fast, and Ray turned around and looked at her now in a flower-print dress with frilly shoulders, while on her feet she wore what looked like simple house slippers. She stepped up to Ray and extended her hand. "It's good to meet you, Ray. What kind of photographs do you like to take?"

Unlike Asahel Curtis, Imogen wanted to talk *only* about photography. After he told her about his street photographs, mostly of people on the streets, and of his alley photographs, and even mentioned the Denny Hill regrade series he'd half-heartedly begun six weeks ago, she came straight out and told him that she had just now been experimenting with taking her very first nude photographs. "And I thought I would make as good a subject as any," she said.

"Certainly," Ray affirmed.

As they spoke, Imogen packed up her camera. "It's getting warmer," she said. "Would you like to walk down to the lake with me?"

As they followed a path that led through the trees to the lake, Ray learned that Imogen was also a student at the university, and when he asked if she knew Loye, she replied, "I believe she was in my botany class with Professor Frye last year." He also learned that like him, she developed her own negatives and made her own prints, using a darkroom her father had rigged for her in his woodshed. "Mine is in the attic," he told her. It also came out that she knew Edward Curtis, brother of Asahel, and had even begun working in his studio last month. "The man himself is never there," she commented. Ray then recounted his conversation with Asahel Curtis and the connection with his landlady. "Still," he said, "I think he takes great photographs." When Ray bragged that he had recently had three of his alley photographs accepted for publication by Alfred Stieglitz in *American Amateur Photographer*, she seemed duly impressed.

By the time they reached the marsh that opened onto Lake Washington's Union Bay – a cool, shady glen with big leafy skunk cabbages growing in the squashy ground and hundreds of round waterlily pads with an occasional white-petaled flower in the more watery areas – the conversation was already the most informed and engaging discussion about photography that Ray had ever had. It ranged from techniques for retouching negatives to the debate over photography's indebtedness to painting. "If it's really its own art," Imogen contended, as she reclined against a large alder, "then there is no indebtedness. Only misguided imitation." Ray, who was standing at the water's edge tossing bark chips into the water, concurred and added, "Print quality is paramount, sure, but darkroom manipulations should only be used to enhance what the photographer has seen with his eye and composed through the lens. Otherwise you're just painting." Ray made this declaration knowing full well his darkroom technique needed much improvement. Then, when Imogen asked him if he had done any nudes himself or whether he would ever consider modeling – "The lines of the human form are unequaled, don't you think?" she said – he didn't know how to respond. The answer, of course, was No, and again, No – but he didn't want to sound like a prudish Nelly in front of this woman who, no less than an hour earlier, he had witnessed photographing herself bare naked – qualifying her as both nude photographer and nude model in one fell swoop.

"I haven't," he said, pausing in his boyish tossing, and wishing that he might have the moxie to say, *But I would be interested,* or that she might ask,

Would you be interested? and he might say, *Absolutely!* Yet he didn't have the moxie, and she didn't ask, and the conversation on the topic of nudes ended there.

Imogen then abruptly stood up and, like a practiced professional, had her tripod set up and her camera ready within moments. "I like that shadow on the water," she said, leading Ray to try to find where she was looking. "Then I want a photograph of you tossing the bark into the lake. But you'll have to hold that movement. I'm not very good at panning"

Ray obliged. Then he reciprocated by setting up his own camera and asking Imogen to sit back down beneath the alder, with her arms around her knees as she had been sitting moments before.

"How pastoral," she said, and then asked, "Have you tried double exposures yet?"

WHEN RAY AND IMOGEN FINALLY PARTED COMPANY, RAY knew that if he hadn't already missed Loye's basketball game, then he would most certainly be arriving very late to it. He and Imogen had exchanged phone numbers and addresses and agreed to get together again soon, perhaps downtown, to continue their conversation. His thoughts were still racing from the initial conversation with her, as well as from the two mental images of Imogen that he kept coming back to – of her rising nude from the tall grass and of her seated beneath the alder – when he finally found the campus field house where the basketball tournament was being held.

The building looked like a hollow, unfinished train station inside. Fifty or more spectators cheered from the low-rise bleachers. As he made his way to those bleachers to take a seat, he heard several men and women who were waving purple-and-gold pennants shout in unison:

U of W Hiah! Hiah!
U of W Siah! Siah!
Skookum! Skookum!
Washington!

Apparently, from what he could decipher from the crowd's enthusiasm and from the scoreboard on the wall at the other end of the gymnasium (beside which the scorekeeper stoically stood), the game with the University of Washington team had just begun several minutes ago. The ten young women scrambled around the polished hardwood floor in their bloomers, white collars, black stockings, and flat shoes. The University of Washington women were distinguishable by the gold W woven into the upper left side of their blouses. The Washington coach – a fairly shrimpy man for a basketball coach, Ray thought – shouted at his players incessantly. When they were at one end of the court on offense, it was, "Pass the ball! Run the play, girls, run the play! Lillian, you stay low!" Then, when his team was on defense at the other end of the court, just as emphatically it became, "Keep your arms up, girls! UP! UP! UP!" – demonstrating by raising his own short arms high and wide – and then, "Rotate, rotate!" followed by "Rebound, girls! Get in there and rebound, for gimmineysake!"

Loye was easy to pick out because the ball kept going to her. From what Ray could tell, she seemed to be playing exceptionally well. She scooted back and forth underneath the basket from one corner of the court to the other until she shed her defender, and then when one of her teammates invariably passed the ball to her, she planted her feet, eyed the rim in the fraction of a second available to her as the defender ran to catch up with her, and launched her high-arching set shot. As the first half of the game wound down, she had missed only twice. Ray decided he would finish watching the first half to get a sense of the game and then set up his camera at the end of the court where Loye's team would be shooting in the second half.

When the ladies resumed the game after a short intermission, the opposing team – from the Tacoma YWCA, which Ray knew was Loye's former team – played with far more energy than they had in the first half. Although they played a zone defense, one girl seemed to have been assigned exclusively to chasing after Loye. It seemed to frustrate the girl to no end that Loye would not stop moving or even slow down. From his vantage point on the floor, Ray could see clearly how Loye played the situation to her advantage. Twice he photographed her taking her shot from the corner and once dribbling the ball to the basket – though he knew both shots would be blurry, since he was no good at panning either. Loye, well aware that this Tacoma girl was going to keep pestering her, saw one of her teammates, the biggest girl on the UW team, standing just below the basket and, using her like a wall to block her opponent, ran past her fast and close, grazing shoulders with the bigger girl, and sent the Tacoma player colliding into her teammate. Momentarily freed, Loye received a pass from another teammate, planted her feet, and shot. The ball fell through the netting as the Tacoma girl slowly got up after bouncing off Loye's teammate and onto her backside.

As the UW team trotted down the court, Ray heard Loye say to her teammate, "Let's try that again, Hazel," and Hazel nodded, clearly pleased with her contribution.

The next play, the YWCA girls came down the court, passed the ball around the horn two or three times, and then took a shot and missed. A big-boned, dark-haired girl grabbed the rebound for UW and dribbled the ball back down the court toward where Ray stood with his camera at the ready. Loye waited for Hazel to lumber down and take her position down low again. Then, with the same Tacoma girl on her tail, Loye began zigzagging back and forth from one corner to the next. This time, however, when she tried to use Hazel as a screen, the Tacoma girl sidestepped around her and continued after Loye. Loye took the pass from her dark-haired teammate, yet as she set to release the ball, the Tacoma girl sprinted toward her, and just as Loye let the ball sail from her hands, the Tacoma girl plowed headlong into her. Loye had no chance to turn away or even lower her arms to protect herself. The girl collided with Loye and the two of them fell violently to the floor, with the Tacoma girl landing with all her weight directly on top of Loye.

The crowd jeered this rough play as Loye's teammates ran to her aid, pushing the Tacoma girl aside and bending down to check on Loye, who lay on the floor trying to catch her breath. As her teammates tried to help her to her feet, it seemed as if she would be okay, but as she tried to stand, her right knee appeared to crumple beneath her and she fell back to the floor shrieking in pain. The coach ran over and ordered the other girls to stand back and give Loye some room. Loye clutched her knee in both hands and grimaced from the pain when, on the coach's advice, she tried to flex it. Eventually, the coach and Hazel gently helped Loye to her one good leg and half-carried her off the playing floor.

Ray held back all the while that this scene unfolded, yet once Loye was safely back on her team's bench, he hurried over to where she sat with her coach and teammates encircling her.

"Did the ball go in?" she asked him, clenching her teeth against the pain in her knee and forcing a smile in his direction.

"It went in," he assured her. "You're some player."

"Did you get good pictures?"

"You bet."

It was then resolved by the referee that the game had gotten too rough and should not be continued. "These girls need to learn to play like ladies or not play at all. It's disgraceful," Ray heard the referee telling Loye's coach. Neither team was awarded the victory, even though the UW team had been in the lead the entire game.

Loye was then carried into the ladies locker room by her teammates, and the coach's assistant was sent to fetch a doctor to come examine her leg. Meanwhile Ray packed up his camera and left the field house to wait outside until he learned if Loye would be okay. If her leg was broken, he determined, he would accompany her to the doctor's office and be with her when she had it set and a cast put on; then he would hire a car and have her driven back to Madison House, where he and Maddie could tend to her. Almost an hour passed before he saw the coach's assistant return carrying a pair of wood crutches and trailed by a tall, elderly man carrying a black leather doctor's case. It was nearly another hour before the assistant came out and told him her leg was not broken, but that her knee was severely sprained. "It's swollen to the size of a melon," he said. "The doctor's wrapping it up tight right now."

Ray waited until Loye came out of the field house, having changed out of her playing clothes and into a dress and hobbling along on the crutches, her knee slightly bent and her foot elevated off the ground. She smiled at him and he smiled back, relieved to see that she was okay. After a short exchange, it was agreed that Hazel would take Loye back to the ladies dormitory to spend the night. Then, the next day at noon, Ray would come by with a car to bring her back to Madison House.

"We'll get everything set up for you back at the house," Ray assured her as she hobbled off toward the ladies dormitory escorted by her hovering teammates. Loye blew him a kiss, and satisfied that he'd done all he could do, he headed back across campus with his camera, tripod, and plate case in hand. How could anyone be so sweet and courageous? he thought, pledging himself to her care once she returned to the boardinghouse. It wasn't until he reached the streetcar stop that he even remembered the intriguing encounter he'd had with Imogen earlier in the day.

23. Home Colony (1907)

CLYDE ARRIVED AT THE DOCK TO MEET RUSS CARRYING the brass-handled walking stick that Henry James had bestowed upon him. Russ wore a soft, broad-brimmed slouch hat, similar to the kind worn by the colorful new president of the city council, Hiram C. Gill, or Hi Gill as most people called him – which led Clyde to call his work friend Hi Russ. The morning was still gray and damp, though the waterfront was already quite busy. Ships docked and were unloaded by longshore-man. Teamsters pulled their wagons up to the warehouses and loaded or unloaded their goods. The passenger ferry to West Seattle departed. Negro men walked up and down the waterfront looking for pick-up work. Loaf-ers leaned over the pier railings and smoked, waiting for a windfall. And gulls squawked for scraps from the handful of stevedores eating their breakfasts out of lunch pails on a nearby bench.

It had been several months since the rather disappointing meeting that Clyde had attended in the basement of the printing company, the one at which he'd faced off with the bespeckled radical. The following day at work, Russ had apologized to Clyde for the confrontation, explain-ing how Stewart was just plain hot-headed and Clyde shouldn't take his remarks personally. "For what it's worth, I'm with you on this regrading thing," he told Clyde. For the next few months they remained friendly but rarely talked politics. Then three nights ago, Clyde ran into Russ at Charles D. Raymer's Bookstore, which, as Russ had once told him, was where anyone with a political conscience gathered for lively discussion and the free exchange of ideas. Russ was in the back of the store reading a broadsheet called *Demonstrator* when Clyde wandered in. When Clyde saw Russ and asked what he was reading, Russ gave him the full account of his reading material – how it was an anarchist sheet put out by James F. Morton from his base at Home Colony, how its name had been changed from *Discontent* because the postmaster general had barred it from the mails as subversive, and went on to explain that Home Colony was an anarcharist-communitarianist-syndicalist commune located at Joe's Bay on the Key Peninsula in the south end of Puget Sound. Then he informed

Clyde that he planned to take an excursion there in the next few days and would Clyde like to come along—just to see what it was all about. Clyde decided to let bygones be bygones and, feeling adventuresome, feeling as if he could do with a jaunt outside of the city for a couple of days, told Russ sure, he'd be happy to visit this Home Colony with him.

"Hey," Russ called out, as Clyde walked down the dock swinging his walking stick. "If it's not Kid Alabaster himself, world champion street sweeper and by the looks of the stick he's swinging, man about town."

"So to Home Sweet Home Colony we go," Clyde called back.

Russ removed a pouch of tobacco from his coat pocket and carefully rolled a cigarette. Clyde stood beside him and looked about at the heavy mist that hung in the air thick with coal smoke and pungent with the briny smell of low tide and creosote from the dock pilings. From somewhere in the distance the smell of coffee came toward him, and he wished he could have a cup. For several moments after their initial greeting, he and Russ did not speak. Russ smoked his cigarette and Clyde shuffled his feet in the cold.

"Whaddaya say, pal," Russ spoke up finally, tossing his cigarette over the dock railing and into the green water that lapped at the barnacle-encrusted pilings. "Shall we board?"

The *Flyer*, the steamboat that made four roundtrips a day between Seattle and Tacoma, was in its slip at the dock already taking on passengers for its 6:20 run. Russ and Clyde walked to the ticket booth beside the gangplank that led up onto the ship's deck. Looking up at the single-stack steamboat with its long sleek hull, Clyde recalled that back in '05 the boat had rammed the Albert Oyster Company dock, sending dozens of crates of oysters crashing onto its decks and nearly burying several passengers. Other than that one incident, the boat was known for being one of the fastest and most reliable excursion boats on the Sound. Above the ticket window hung a banner reading "Fly on the *Flyer*," below which were listed the ticket prices. Clyde purchased a two-dollar roundtrip ticket and followed Russ up the gangplank.

Clyde was excited about the trip as much for having the chance to take two boat rides to reach Home Colony as for visiting the renowned commune of radical thinkers and free-love advocates. He was also a little apprehensive about spending three days in Russ's company. In the half year they'd known each other, Clyde had never gotten totally comfortable around Russ. He liked to pal around with him on the job, since Russ generally had a playful nature, and at times he was genuinely interested in Russ's ideas, crazy as some of them were, but there remained something about him that kept Clyde from ever completely letting his guard down around him, the way he could with Ray. He felt Russ was not always being above-aboard with him. Instead he often felt Russ was stringing him along, humoring him, usually in order to get something from him, his attendance at a union meeting or his signature on a petition or his nickel for a copy of *Challenge*, to which Russ had contributed an article called "Congregating Versus Agitating: To Act en Masse or Solo." It seemed to Clyde that he never got the whole story from Russ, that something was always being left out or overlooked. At the same time, he appreciated Russ's enthusiasm (verbal and otherwise), his commitment to his political positions, and his willingness to take jabs at the powers that be.

Once aboard the *Flyer*, Clyde could feel the gentle rocking of the boat even as it remained tied to the dock. Several gulls cavorted overhead, screeching and squawking, as a young girl about Ada's age, fourteen or so, stood along the ship's railing tossing bread crust into the air. The gulls let the bread fall into the water before dropping down and snatching it up. Twice she laid a piece of bread on the railing and one of the bigger gulls, its gray and white chest boldly extended, balanced itself on the railing and waddled over to retrieve it. The display amused Clyde and, settling his mind about Russ, he decided to take the whole trip in stride and let things happen as they may. He was just happy to escape the city for a few days, to not have to worry about the house and Maddie and the regrading that was advancing ever farther up Denny Hill. He turned to Russ and suggested they find the galley to see about getting a cup of coffee.

As they waited in line at the galley counter, the steamboat blew its piercing whistle and several moments later gently pulled away from the dock. By the time Clyde and Russ reemerged onto the deck, the *Flyer* was aiming straight across Elliott Bay toward the tip of West Seattle. Clyde was surprised at how fast the ship moved, how smoothly it rode the swell, how effortlessly its prow sliced through the water leaving an even wake along either side. From the stern, Clyde looked back at the city. Its buildings rose dark and varied along the wet slopes of its many hills. To the left, the long and prominent rise of Denny Hill continued to define that portion of the city's skyline, though he could plainly see the raw and ragged cut along the hill's western slope where the buildings stopped and the hillside became a sheer cliff, a palisades of sorts. Clyde tried to imagine the city's topography without the hill and its neighborhood – an indistinguishable flatness – but found the notion impossible to entertain. As the steamship put more distance between itself and the waterfront, the city's features became less distinguishable and Clyde found himself almost elated when it finally rounded Duwamish Head and cruised toward Alki Point, cutting off his view of the city entirely.

For the next hour and a half, the *Flyer* steered a steady course southward through Puget Sound. While Russ went inside, Clyde remained on deck and studied the shoreline, the long, uninterrupted swaths of Douglas firs rising up from the pebbly beaches, a couple of fishermen standing knee deep in the water and pulling a drag seine to shore, the occasional homestead set back from a narrow dock where a skiff was tied. The sight of such homesteads made Clyde imagine himself and Maddie and Ada settling on some remote stretch of shoreline, far from the city, where they could dig razor clams at low tide, gather salmonberries and thimbleberries in the woods, fish from the dock (as he often had with the Makah), maybe raise a few chickens, and at night sit near the fire inside their snug cabin and read to each other. On holidays they would go to Seattle and visit Ray and Loye, who would be married by then, or else their city friends would come visit them for a stay in the country.

When the large black dorsal fins from a pod of orcas broke the water's surface a dozen yards off the boat's starboard side, Clyde ran inside to alert Russ, who was fast asleep in one of the wooden chairs in the ship's lounge area. He decided not to wake him and returned to the deck to watch the whales breach the surface, showing their white undersides and blowing spray from their spouts before submerging again. Several other passengers came to the railing to watch the orcas as well, including the young girl who had been feeding the gulls. When the girl seemed to be looking as much at Clyde as she was the orcas, Clyde turned to her and asked her her name. "Annie," she told him, and when Clyde told her his name, she replied that it was a pleasure to meet him. Eventually the ship passed the pod of orcas and Annie went on her way. Clyde then returned to the lounge where he removed his wool cap and slapped it against his thigh, brushed the mist droplets off his canvas coat as he sat down next to Russ, and closed his eyes.

He was roused by the steamship's whistle blowing again, this time to announce the *Flyer's* entry into Commencement Bay. Clyde elbowed Russ until he stirred, and together they followed the rest of the passengers onto the aft deck to watch as the steamship glided toward the terminus. This was Clyde's first time in Tacoma, a city that had remained approximately the same size in the past decade while Seattle had grown tenfold. Nevertheless, it seemed like a busy city. Several cargo ships, mostly schooners loaded with timber, had dropped anchor in the bay; the clang of ships' bells and the shouts of stevedores could be heard echoing across the water from the docks; several smelter stacks bellowed smoke into the sky, giving the air, Clyde suspected, its acrid tinge. To the right of the waterfront, along its waterways, the downtown with its tall brick buildings stretched along the base of a bluff that rose up from the bay, commencing at the domed and rotund railroad station just past where the *Flyer* eased into dock.

In the short time it took to get from Seattle to Tacoma, the day had grown brighter and warmer. The sun now illuminated the last of the morning fog that clung to the hills rising behind Tacoma. Its warmth seemed to energize the waterfront. Russ was suddenly alert and raring to go. He hustled Clyde along so that they were at the front of the line when the *Flyer's* crew dropped the gangplank and released the restraint lines to let the passengers disembark.

"Do you know where we're going?"

"We have to find where Ed Lorenz docks," Russ said, as they shuffled down the gangplank. He then collared one of the *Flyer's* crew who was on the dock and asked him where to go.

The crewman pointed down the row of piers and said that Lorenz had his boats down at Pier 12. "Where you boys headed?" he asked.

"Home Colony," said Russ.

The man shook his head in derision. "Goin' ta get naked and make some bombs are ya?"

Russ stepped up to the man to challenge him and Clyde moved between them and shouldered Russ aside.

"Now go on with ya," the man said, and threw up his hand at them. "Your type belong with one another anyhow."

Clyde put an arm around Russ and walked him toward the end of the dock. "Never mind him."

Russ relented to Clyde's coaxing, smiled at him, and put his arm around his shoulder so that the two of them strode down the dock like old shipmates. "I wasn't going to rough him up too much," he said. "He's just a capitalist stooge and most of 'em scare pretty easy. Let me tell you about this Ed Lorenz fella, though. He's the one knows how to handle thugs like that back there." Russ went on to tell Clyde how in '01, on the day President McKinley finally succumbed to the assassin's bullet, a gang of vigilantes — the Loyal League of the Grand Army of the Republic, they called themselves — got up a posse of vigilantes seeking revenge on the people at Home Colony, and it was brave Ed Lorenz who talked the thugs out of their rampage when they tried to charter his boat to ferry them over to Joe's Bay. Lorenz knew the colonists for what they were: sober, industrious, peace-loving people who had nothing to do with assassinations or bomb-making or any other kind of violence. And that's exactly what he told them. It settled them down and that was the end of the incident.

When they reached Pier 12 where Ed Lorenz's small steamers, the *Typhoon* and the *Queenie*, were docked, they learned that the legendary Ed Lorenz was captaining a third steamer to Olympia that morning. Clyde and Russ introduced themselves to the captain of the *Queenie* and, after paying the firstmate for passage, they boarded the boat that would take them to Joe's Bay. A dozen more people boarded before the small steamer blew its whistle and pulled away from the dock.

Mount Rainier, visible now through the morning fog, loomed even more magnificently over Tacoma than it did Seattle, appearing almost to crowd the city into the bay. Clyde and Russ sat on wooden deck chairs and took in the scenery as the *Queenie* steered past Point Defiance and into the narrow, winding channels of the south end of Puget Sound. The boat first stopped at Fircrest, then Steilacoom, then McNeil Island (where a new state penitentiary had been built), and then at Fox Island. When the trip from Tacoma to Joe's Bay began to take as long as the one from Seattle to Tacoma, Russ griped that it was turning into a regular milk run, and because of the loading and unloading of goods at each stop, Clyde figured his complaint wasn't far from the truth. Eventually the *Queenie* eased up to a long pier that jutted out from the shore nearly a third of the way into the narrow inlet. A sign on a post at the end of the pier read *Joe's Bay*.

"Home Colony," someone shouted from the window of the pilot's house.

Most of the passengers who had boarded the *Queenie* in Tacoma had already disembarked at previous stops, but a few remained who now prepared to get off at Joe's Bay. As the boat bumped into the dock, a tall muscular man in a white cotton shirt and coveralls, with a shock of black hair and a black walrus moustache that hung over his entire mouth, stood beside Clyde and Russ on the deck and asked them if they were visiting or coming to stay.

"Visiting," Russ said.

"Who with?" the man inquired.

"Carl Lermond," answered Russ. "He's the fella I met at one of our organizing meetings in Seattle, who a couple of months ago invited us down. Perhaps you could direct us to where he lives."

The boat settled against the wood pilings, and a man came out of the small hut at the end of the pier and one of the crew from the *Queenie* threw him a guide rope from the bow which he quickly tied around one of the endposts on the pier, then did the same at the stern of the boat.

"Well," the man said, running his hand over his moustache, "if it's the same Carl Lermond I'm thinking of, then you're out of luck, 'cause he up and left three weeks ago."

Russ scrutinized the man to see if he might be pulling his leg, but it didn't seem that way, and finally Russ said, "Ah hell," and kicked the boat's railing and turned to Clyde. "What do we do now?"

Clyde wasn't surprised by this sudden turn of events. It was just like Russ to lead him all the way down here on nothing more than a two-month-old invitation from some fella he'd probably met only once at one of his disorganized organizational meetings. Maybe he even knew before-hand that this Carl had left Home Colony already, and was just using the invitation as a pretense to lead him down here to see what they could find. This was most likely the case. Russ was just that kind of fly-by-the-seat-of-your-pants guy, without much regard for the cost or inconvenience his approach imposed on others.

"Hold on there," the man said. He picked up the large duffel bag that lay at his feet. "We always welcome visitors. You two gentlemen just follow me and we'll find you a place to stay."

Russ looked at Clyde with a shrug, as if to say, *See, it all worked out*, and as they all three walked down the gangplank to the pier, the man looked over his shoulder and introduced himself. "Cyrus Benton," he said. "I do much of the carpentry work around here." He set his duffelbag on the pier and greeted the man who'd tied the boat to the dock. Then, together, the two men walked back up the gangplank and began carrying several large crates from the boat deck to the pier.

"Can we lend a hand?" Clyde called up to them.

"Certainly can," Cyrus called back.

Clyde and Russ hustled up the gangplank and, each taking the end of a large steamer trunk, lugged it down onto the pier. In two more trips the four men had everything destined for Home Colony off the boat and onto the pier. Only then did Clyde remember to introduce himself, and Russ followed suit. When Clyde asked if they should carry the items to the hut at the other end of the pier, Cyrus told him no, the rightful owners would be coming along in due time to claim their own. "I just wanted to lend Arthur a hand unloading is all. You boys follow me and we'll find you lodging, probably over there in Liberty Hall." He pointed to a large barn-like building made of clapboard that was situated about halfway up the small hill that sloped up from the shore.

"We really do appreciate this," Russ said.

Cyrus waved off this expression of appreciation and said that as long as they were willing to help with chores, then they were welcome to stay as long as they liked. "Like I said, we get visitors all the time. It's what keeps the place interesting."

Cyrus then led them along a dirt track toward Liberty Hall. From what Clyde could see, the colony of reputed bomb-making anarchists and free-lovers looked like any other community of homesteaders a person might find almost anywhere along the Puget Sound coastline. The hillside had been clear cut, and between the occasional massive fir or cedar stump that remained in the ground, a couple dozen one- and two-story houses were scattered across the acreage, usually with an outhouse and shed of some sort out back. Some of the houses had fences around the half to full acre on which they sat, usually with a sizeable garden off to the side of the house and several young apple trees just beyond that – very much like his father's homestead, thought Clyde. Women were out hanging laundry on clothes-lines, and here and there a man was on a roof hammering down shingles or in a yard chopping firewood or in a garden working the rows with a hoe.

Cyrus showed them a backroom in the large meeting hall where they could stay. There were several cots set up already with a bedroll laid at the foot of each. Cyrus told them about the communal kitchen where they could get supper and the commissary where they could pick up some other foodstuffs and coffee in the morning. There were usually meetings in the hall every night, but he didn't always attend and didn't know who might be speaking that particular night. He told them if they needed anything, they could find his house about a quarter of a mile down the track at the very edge of the colony. When Cyrus was about to part, Russ asked him what he knew about Carl Lermond's leaving.

"I'm afraid I don't know anything unusual about it," Cyrus admitted. "For some the life here is just rougher than they expected or they just get lonesome, or maybe it just wasn't his cup of tea. Philosophically, I mean. Carl was all right from what I knew of him, and I wish him well."

Clyde felt impelled to ask Cyrus if he were either an anarchist or a free-lover, but he knew such a question would sound utterly foolish. The answer didn't really matter. He appreciated that Cyrus Benton took no special notice of his albinism and had already been so welcoming to them, two strangers fresh off the boat. So Clyde simply thanked him for his hospitality, and they all shook hands again before Cyrus wandered back to his own house.

Although it wasn't even noon, Clyde and Russ both agreed they were bushed, even after dozing on the *Flyer*, and decided to choose theirs cots and take a nap. About an hour later when Clyde woke up, he went back out to the front hall area to look around and found a large table strewn with copies of the various broadsheets that were published at the colony, along with various other tracts and pamphlets written by current or one-time members of the colony. Clyde picked up a copy of *My Century Plant* by Lois Waisbrooker, one of the more famous advocates of free love, a woman now well into her seventies. Clyde had heard someone at Raymer's Bookstore call the pamphlet "the perfect encyclopedia on the sex question," but as Clyde perused its pages it appeared to be nothing more than a harmless book of manners. Specific acts were neither named nor, to his disappointment, described. He put the pamphlet down and looked over the small bookcase beside the table. In among the titles by William Morris, Pyotr Kropotkin, Mikhail Bakunin, Karl Marx, and Pierre-Joseph Proudhon, he also found a slew of dime-store novels, a copy of *Raggedy Andy*, and Benjamin Franklin's *Poor Richard's Almanac*. There were also several manuals on architectural drawing, carpentry, plumbing, masonry, and printmaking.

For the rest of the afternoon, Clyde and Russ walked about exploring the grounds of the colony. There were few people around, which rather surprised them. Occasionally they would meet someone along their path who would introduce himself to them. One young woman hanging linens on a line in front of her house, with two small children at her apron strings, invited them into her kitchen for cookies and milk and then left them with the children to play pick-up sticks while she went down the road to visit with a neighbor. This took nearly an hour of their afternoon. When the woman returned, they went over to the commissary and perused its shelves, which were stacked like any other country general store with dry goods and canned goods, bolts of cloth, and hardware and tack. The clerk was a fellow about Clyde's age, in his mid-twenties, who sat in the back twisting wire into the shape of circus figures. Clyde placed a nickel on the counter by the cash register and fished a pickle from the pickle barrel. On their way back to Liberty Hall, they passed the one-room schoolhouse and could hear children singing inside. In all, the colony seemed like a very quiet and ordinary, if somewhat quirky, community. It certainly didn't strike one as place where revolution was being fomented.

By late afternoon more people began to appear. Another steamboat arrived at the pier and dropped off a dozen or so men in greasy coveralls who looked as though they might have been working in Tacoma on the docks or in one of the pulp mills. The clerk from the commissary showed up at the pier driving a buckboard wagon and took away several of the crates that Clyde and Russ had unloaded earlier in the day. Another wagon loaded with firewood and coal made rounds to the dozen or more houses in the immediate vicinity of Liberty Hall. Clyde could smell cooking, which stirred his hunger, and so he and Russ set out to find the common dining hall and see about getting some supper in their bellies.

The dining hall turned out to be in a building of the same design as the meeting hall but about half its size. It had a slope-roofed kitchen at the back from which a stovepipe bellowed smoke. Clyde and Russ removed their hats upon entering the hall and looked up and down the four rows of tables and benches that filled the main room. Maybe twenty or more men, women and children were already seated and eating. A young woman in what looked to be her petticoats approached them and asked if they were visiting, and when they said yes, she escorted them to a table at the end of the middle row and told them she'd be right back. Within minutes, she and another woman were carrying out to each of them a tray loaded with a bowl of fish stew, a slab of cornbread, a large slice of apple pie, and a tall glass of milk. Since Clyde had observed that nearly every house had a cow in its fenced area, it didn't surprise him that the people at Home Colony seemed to drink so much milk.

They thanked the two women, and then the first one, the young one in her petticoats, sat down across from them and introduced herself as Emily – or Emi, as most folks there called her. "Cyrus told me I might see you two coming around. I'm sorry your friend Carl has left. I sorta remember him. I believe he's the one who said he was going off to San Francisco to unionize the newspapers."

"That sounds like Carl," Russ said, between spoonfuls of fish stew. "Always organizing."

The young woman asked Russ if he'd like more cornbread, and when he said certainly, she turned to Clyde to ask if he would like some more too. Clyde nodded, and as she walked back to the kitchen he had the distinct sense that she had taken a shine to Russ. He had seen Russ attract the flirtations of women on more than one occasion. Even in his dirty street sweeper clothes, leaning against his broom, Russ could say howdy to a young well-dressed lady on the street corner and she would pause to smile and chat with him. When Emi returned with more cornbread, she sat back down at their table again. Although she conversed mostly with Russ, wanting to know what had brought him to Home Colony and so forth, she turned to Clyde at one point and said, "You certainly are fair-complected, aren't you?"

Of all the responses to his albinism that he'd grown accustomed to over the years, this one, perhaps the simplest, the most plainly spoken one he'd ever heard, rather endeared Emi to him. At least she wasn't calling him a specter or an angel or comparing him to baby powder or snow or mother's milk or the pages in a book. She was simply making what sounded like an objective and what seemed to be a thoroughly nonjudgmental observation.

"And such beautiful brown eyes," she went on. "They're quite sensual, really."

So much for objectivity, Clyde thought. Though he had trained himself to be nonresponsive to people's remarks about his appearance, to show neither by word nor gesture that he acknowledged their comments, he nonetheless had to smile at the enticing way in which Emi said this. He raised his glass of milk to her, engaging in the banter, and said, "Your own ebony oculi are quite becoming."

While Russ looked blankly at Clyde, dumbfounded by his diction, Emi laughed good-naturedly at the compliment and called Clyde a flirt.

She then turned to Russ and looking in his eyes said, "And you, sir, have the ocean bottom's beryl stones."

"Is that so," said Russ, and seemed to have no comeback for Emi's lyric praise of him.

"Indeed it is," she said. "You also have the hairy arms of an old randy goat."

More alert to the game now, Russ gazed up to the ceiling and bayed liked a Billy goat, drawing the attention of several people sitting nearby. They carried on this banter through a second piece of pie and another glass of milk, until, just as people started to leave the hall, a man at the opposite end from where they sat stood up on his chair to announce that there would be two speakers in Liberty Hall that evening, one to address the question of anarchism and ecology, the other a follower of Dr. C. R. Teed from Koreshan Unity Settlement in Estero, Florida.

Clyde asked Emi if she would be attending and she replied that she would, but that first she had to do kitchen duty by helping to clean up after dinner. "It's how I earn my keep," she explained. "I may have to cook and clean just as I did when I was a house girl in Olympia, but at least I'm somewhere where I can think as I wish, believe as I wish, and live as I wish."

Clyde wondered if Russ was as impressed by this heartfelt declaration as he was. When Emi carried off their plates rather than letting them bus their table for themselves, as seemed to be the protocol, Russ turned to Clyde and with a slight ogle back in Emi's direction said, "Home Sweet Home indeed."

Outside the dining hall, the mid-June evening was stretching into night. The eastern sky across the inlet had deepened to a radiant azure, a scattering of stars dotting it, while above the line of fir trees marking the crest of the hill, the sky retained a faint orange cast. Clyde and Russ walked down to the water and soon were met by Cyrus, who had changed from his overalls into clean pants and a white cotton shirt, although he still wore the same heavy work boots. He asked them if they cared to share a cigar with him.

"Most people here frown on such," he said, "and they won't sell them in the commissary. But I walked over the hill to Lake Bay and bought a dozen just this afternoon."

Clyde and Russ said they would be happy to join him in a smoke, and the three men sat on a large piece of driftwood on the shore and lit their cigars. By the time Clyde's cigar was down to a soggy stub, the full night was upon the small inlet and kerosene lamps were lighting the windows of the houses behind them.

"Will you be attending the talk," Russ asked Cyrus, who answered that he would probably skip tonight's program and hit the hay early.

After a little while longer down on the beach, the three men wished one another goodnight, and while Cyrus headed back to his house, Clyde and Russ walked back to Liberty Hall. To Clyde's astonishment, the hall was crowded with close to a hundred people. He wondered where they all had come from, figuring there must be numerous homesteads beyond the colony proper. Chairs previously stacked in the back room were now set out in rows in the meeting hall, but still there weren't enough seats and people had to stand along the walls. When Clyde and Russ arrived, the first speaker was already at the podium and seemed to be finishing his talk. He was a lanky man with an angular face and intense eyes who spoke very calmly and deliberately.

"Anarchism," he was stating when Clyde and Russ entered, "is that political philosophy that most coincides with nature. The institutions of concentrated power, be they regal, dictatorial, parliamentary, or legislative, are human contrivances that aim to limit individual responsibility. Whereas nature, as with anarchism, seeks to maximize individual responsibility by loosening – nay, abolishing – the shackles imposed by government, corporation, church, and, dare I say, even family."

The man paused long enough to wipe his brow with a kerchief, then continued. "The individual chooses his own means of self-regulation in order to maximize his responsibility – which in the end is true freedom, is it not? However, lest pride precede the fall, such self-regulation means practicing self-abnegation. We cannot rightly ask the monarch to abdicate unless we ourselves are willing to abnegate. Hence the lone wolf in the wilderness survives by remaining strong, lean, and efficient. This is the ecology of anarchism."

Clyde found the man intriguing, if somewhat verbose. He seemed genuine in his statements, even if they were rather convoluted.

"This, my friends, is the reason why Home Colony is such an ideal of anarchism. Not because we are a pact of bomb-throwing radicals, as so many in the press would have the general public believe, but because we do not deign to proscribe the community I envisage for us here tonight. Do I contradict myself, you may ask. How can one speak of maximizing individualism and creating community in the same breath? Very well then, I say, to paraphrase the great anarchist poet Walt Whitman, I contradict myself. Yet such contradiction curtails the concentration of power and itself becomes the exercise of nature's highest calling for man: responsibility."

With that, the man abruptly stepped away from the podium and a round of applause followed him as he walked back to an empty chair in the middle of the room and quietly sat down, preparing to turn his attention to the next speaker. The same man who had gotten up in the dining hall to announce the speakers at supper now came to the podium to introduce the next speaker, a young follower of Koresh, he explained, the Biblical name assumed by Dr. C. R. Teed, who had built a community in rural Florida based on certain mathematical precepts according to which everything must unite to form a center of spiritual force. In welcoming the Koresh representative to the podium, the audience seemed a bit tentative in its applause, perhaps unsure of what to expect from this unusual sect.

The speaker, a young man with a long beard and shoulder-length hair and vibrant eyes – a young man with an Old Testament appearance, Clyde thought – walked to the podium slowly and before saying anything, bowed his head with closed eyes, then raised his head with his eyes still closed and recited a prayer in a language Clyde had never heard before – although it sounded remotely like the Makah tongue. The young man opened his eyes and thanked the assembly for welcoming him, and then explained how his prayer was an ancient Hebrew call for community and harmony.

He went on to inform everyone of the similarities he had found, since his arrival at Joe's Bay last week, between the Koreshan Unity Settlement in Florida and Home Colony. Both settlements, he said, sustained themselves with industry, self-sufficiency, and devotion to the communal good. (At this remark, however, a snicker could be heard from the back of the room.) The speaker went on to say that the Koreshan Unity Settlement would be the New Jerusalem, to which, in time, ten million people would flock, and that – and here he raised his voice in declamation – this shiny new city would be laid out in accordance with the mathematical principles revealed to their founder, Koresh, replicating the seven wills of God that bind man to the Holy One.

Hearing all of this, and once more not fully comprehending its import, Clyde wished that Ray, the ardent agnostic, could be there to hear it for himself. He knew Ray would be able to explain it to him – or at least denounce it for him. Clyde looked at Russ standing beside him, yet Russ paid the speaker no mind whatsoever. He was instead watching the door, waiting, Clyde suspected, for Emi to enter, and a few moments later, sure enough, she did enter and Russ immediately signaled to her.

Meanwhile, the speaker's manner was turning more animated as his talk became more confusing. He leaned over the podium and stared out at the audience with eyes as wide and bright as reflector lamps. "Koresh commissioned the construction of a rectilineator by the Pullman Works Company to demonstrate the earth's concavity," he expounded. "We know now, based on the apparatus's equations, that the earth is a hollow sphere which contains the universe, confirming Koresh's illuminations prior to these proofs." He paused here to catch his breath. "I know," he said more calmly, leaning back from the podium, "I know such a cosmology seems strange, perhaps even ludicrous, yet unless it had not been mathematically proven through the rectilineation process, I dare say I would have doubted it myself and would not be standing here before you this instant." The man then went into an elaborate explanation of the role that squares, diagonals, circles, and diameters played within the Koreshan cosmology.

Clyde, after standing now for more than an hour against the back wall, could not keep his mind from drifting and wondered when the talk would end so he could step outside for some fresh air and the nearest outhouse. At one point he heard the speaker say something about the "Koreshanity promulgation of celibacy," but after that his attention blanked entirely. When finally the speaker concluded his remarks and asked if there were any questions, the earlier speaker raised his hand and inquired if the

Koreshanity division of its governing council upon a hierarchical structure based on the number seven was not contrary to the anarchistic anti-hierarchical, anti-government mission. The Koreshan speaker shook his head as if nothing he had said during the past hour had been heard by the questioner and replied by saying, "Unity, sir, not chaos, is the Koreshanity guiding principle."

The man from the dining hall stepped to the front and thanked the speaker for coming to Home Colony as an emissary from the Koreshan settlement. "I believe our guest has brought with him several publications from the settlement press, which I am sure he will be happy to distribute. Thank you again." He then led the applause that escorted the Koreshanity speaker away from the podium. The man then rapped his knuckles on the podium to get everyone's attention and made several announcements about the next evening's speakers, a petition and defense fund being circulated on behalf of one of their residents currently facing obscenity charges in a Pierce County court, and a skiff that was for sale by a Mr. Edgerton. He then stepped away from the podium and the crowd in the hall began to disperse.

As soon as he, Russ, and Emi were outside again, Clyde took in several deep breaths of the night air and let them out with pleasure in the capacity of his own lungs.

"Sure was hot in there," said Russ.

"I don't believe my fifth-grade education allowed me to follow more than two sentences of what I just heard," Clyde said.

"People sometimes like to hear themselves talk around here," commented Emi. "But usually we're a fairly hard-working bunch and try not to spout off too much."

Russ put his arm around Emi's shoulder. "Clyde, my friend," he said, "Emily and I are going to take a walk down to the beach. I'll catch up with you later, if that's all right with you."

Clyde looked at them and said that was fine by him, he welcomed the opportunity to go relieve himself. Emi then pointed him in the right direction, and she and Russ turned to go down to the beach. After using the outhouse, Clyde fished the stub from the cigar he'd smoked earlier from his jacket pocket and sat down on a tree stump and relit it. It was a fine night, he thought. A good night to clear one's head, though he couldn't help but wonder what Maddie was doing right then and if she missed him at all.

Early the next morning, when he awoke on the cot in the back room of Liberty Hall, he felt as if he'd had one of the best night's sleep of his life. Yet when he looked around to see which of the cots Russ was on, his friend was not to be found. Across the room the man from the Koreshanity settlement slumbered away on another cot. Clyde was afraid of waking him and having him start up again with his numbers and geometry. As quietly as he could, he slid off his cot, put his shirt and pants back on, folded his bedroll, and stepped outside. After stopping in the commissary for a cup of coffee and a half loaf of sourdough bread with thick creamery butter and loganberry jam on it, he wandered down to the beach. The tide was out and at a bend in the shoreline, where the tideflats widened out, several people, children among them, were busy clamming. Clyde joined them and when he offered to help was told to remove his shoes and roll up his pants and was promptly handed a bucket and spade. He spent the next couple of hours in the tideflats, bending over to stare at the mud, pitching his spade into it when he spotted air bubbles coming up, and then plying through the thick muck with his fingers to retrieve the stone-sized clam and drop it into his bucket. When the clam digging was done for the morning, one of the families invited him to share in the lunch basket they had brought with them down to the beach, and afterward he accompanied the husband to the colony's shingle mill and, using an old wooden wheelbarrow, helped him haul several dozen bundles of shingles back to his house to begin siding the clapboard. It wasn't until late afternoon, as Clyde lay under an apple sapling, that he finally spotted Russ, who was walking toward him with his jacket hooked on his finger and slung over his shoulder.

"That Emi is some girl," he said, sitting himself down next to Clyde. "I'll tell you what."

Though Russ clearly seemed to want to go on, Clyde was too tired from the work he'd done all day to inquire after more details. Russ seemed mildly disappointed, and then said, "She's got me thinking of staying on. At least for a little while anyway. She's the kind of independent woman I really admire."

Although he was very nearly dozing off with fatigue and the comforting warmth of the afternoon sun, Clyde mustered up the strength to say, "If it's all the same to you then, I believe I'll take the next boat back to Tacoma. It's been a nice visit and all, but I'm starting to worry about Maddie and how she's getting on back at the house."

Russ patted Clyde's knee. "I understand, pal, and I hope you don't mind this little change in plans."

"Not at all," Clyde said, relieved to think he could be back at Madison House that very night, sleeping again in his own attic room.

Two hours later, he boarded the *Queenie* for the return trip to Tacoma, and as the steamship pulled away from the Home Colony pier and made its way back out of the narrow inlet, Clyde could see six or seven people along the beach bathing in the nude. Among them were Russ and Emi. He leaned on the deck railing watching the bathers and thought that if Maddie lost the house to the regrading, they could always move to Home Colony.

24. System (1908)

ON FEBRUARY 3, 1908, HER FORTIETH BIRTHDAY, MADDIE resolved to run a more systematic household.

The boardinghouse, after all, was a business – *her* business – and therefore ought to be run as one. In the past, she knew all too well, she had not been such a good business lady. She did not keep her books in the best order and she could rarely reconcile her monthly intake against her monthly expenditures. This probably accounted for why, after seven years as proprietress of Madison House, the money she had come back with from the Yukon was almost depleted and she had to rely increasingly on the room and board she collected each week from her four boarders – not counting Clyde of course. Unfortunately, as she soon discovered, this weekly income was inadequate to the actual cost of running the house. So her reserve funds (her Yukon take) continued steadily to diminish.

In some far-hidden chamber of her heart, she felt that if she could run Madison House more efficiently, then somehow it might be spared from the threat of the regrading. The city would recognize what a high-class, affordable, and efficient boardinghouse she ran, and conscientious city officials would intercede to save it. Using her best mathematical calculations, she had determined last month that she could not afford to have the house lowered to the new grade, especially since her lot was one of the highest on Denny Hill. The city expected property owners – all of them save James A. Moore – to incur the cost of both lowering their structures and regrading their own lots, promising tenfold returns in property values once the project was completed. Yet even if she trusted these odds, she could not afford to make the wager. So finally, on advice from Clyde and Ray, she retained Erasmo Marcos, the former clerk in Edward Holton James's law office and now a practicing attorney himself, to look into the prospect of filing for damages with the city on her behalf. Being a cautious attorney, however, Erasmo made no promises. Besides, Maddie asked herself, what did suing for damages really mean? What were the implications for Madison House? Accepting damages from the city would mean that she would also have to accept the loss of the boardinghouse – and she was just not prepared to do that.

Every day the ravaging cuts made by the hoses and steam shovels advanced farther up the hill and closer to the house. At times the floorboards shuddered and the windowpanes rattled when the work crews used blasting caps to remove a particularly stubborn portion of the hillside. Pedestrian and wagon traffic along the streets on Denny Hill had diminished significantly. The neighborhood was emptying out, as if everyone were going on holiday – though Maddie knew the reason for the evacuation was far more portentous. The engineering firm in charge of the project had recently begun to attack the hill from the southeast side as well as from the west. Every day the wrecking crews brought down more houses and apartment buildings and businesses. The neighborhood was being carved away, lot by lot.

Many property owners had sold their lots, some quite lucratively, or so the newspapers reported. The *Post-Intelligencer* regularly printed notices of "heavy sales of property" in the area north of Pike Street, which was currently being regraded. These sales figures invariably proved the "big appreciation" on the property, as promised by City Engineer Reginald H. Thomson. But Maddie was deeply skeptical about these reports. She noticed that more often than not, the sales involved only the largest property owners. James A. Moore, for example, was reported to have sold a corner lot on Third Avenue, the exact site of the west wing of the old Washington Hotel, for $120,000. According to the buyer, R. W. Hill, "The lots adjacent on all sides are to be improved handsomely." The purchase price even included the cost of completing the excavation of the lot to the new grade, nearly 100 feet. Of all the property owners affected by the regrading of Denny Hill, Mr. Moore seemed to be the greatest beneficiary. The newspapers held him forth as a model of the profits to be had by every Denny Hill property owner, even the smallest. His name was invoked as evidence that the leveling of Denny Hill was the most profitable civic improvement project ever undertaken by the city of Seattle. In fitting with the era of national boosterism, Moore's profits proved that the Seattle Spirit was alive and well and making money for everyone hand over fist.

Since the start of the regrading, real estate companies had been buying out individual property owners and amassing large portions of Denny

Hill for themselves. As completion of the regrading project became just a matter of time, the real estate companies began a campaign to resell these properties to developers at enormously inflated prices. Disheartening notices of these property sales appeared in the newspaper, touting the inevitability of augmented property values:

$85,000

Corner. 120 × 108, AT BLANCHARD AND SECOND AVENUE — This is little more than the price of First Hill double corners; as an investment in ground value, we believe this is cheaper at $85,000 than any corner on the hill at $70,000. Now, as to income, the Washington Annex pays better rent per room than any First Hill property, and in a few years the ground floor on Second Avenue at this point will pay ten times more rent than the ground floor on the hill.

$100,000

60 × 108, ON THE WEST SIDE OF THIRD AVENUE — North of Stewart. All property on Third Avenue that we advertise today will double in value in the next three years; in that time improvements that will be built in this district will more than likely amount to more in value than any other part of this or any other city of this size ever constructed.

As for herself, Maddie didn't know of a single property owner other than Moore and a few other major landholders on the hill who had seen such enormous windfalls. It seemed to her, clearly, that right now it was the high-stakes property dealers who were reaping the greatest benefits from the devastation being inflicted upon her Denny Hill neighborhood. Nevertheless, as buildings continued to come down and sections of the hill continued to be washed into Elliott Bay, the city kept reassuring nervous residents that, whether they sold their lots outright or subsidized their excavation, they would inevitably come out ahead. Which, as far as Maddie could tell, was all bunk.

Nearly half of Denny Hill had disappeared over the past six months. Along the southwest side of the hill, several small property owners who had refused to abide by the regrading ordinance now found the earth surrounding their lots carved away, leaving their houses and yards elevated on tall, precipitous towers of dirt, which they had to climb by a series of cut-back ladders. The situation was appalling, and Maddie feared it portended what was in store for Madison House. If she let it, the horrific sounds and sights of the regrading project could set her to whimpering.

In the midst of this devastation to her neighborhood – and the accompanying despondency she managed to keep at bay – Maddie read of the city's plan to stage a major exposition in 1909 – the Alaska-Yukon-Pacific Exposition, they were dubbing it – the likes of which had never been witnessed west of the Mississippi. The event would showcase Seattle as a modern twentieth-century metropolis, highlighting the city's rapid progress while also honoring its pioneer past. It would also showcase Seattle as the city best situated to serve the needs of what forecasters deemed to be the Pacific Era. The long coastline from Alaska to California, the vast farmlands from the Dakotas to Oregon, the great mainland of China and Russia, the Oriental island nations of Japan and the Philippines ... the great city of Seattle, boosters claimed, would link all of these rich regions and serve as their primary terminus. The Alaska-Yukon-Pacific Exposition, which would include delegations and displays from each region, would inaugurate this new era. The vital areas of industry, invention, agriculture, forestry, animal husbandry, and fisheries would be highlighted for the benefit of participants and attendees alike. The A-Y-P Exposition's mission would be primarily educational. Though with the brightest and liveliest midway of any previous exposition in the world, it would also have an important recreational component. The newspapers reported that the Olmstead brothers, the famous landscape architects from Massachusetts, would design the site for the Exposition on the grounds of the University of Washington and that the president of the United States (whom everyone assumed would be William Howard Taft, come the November elections) would attend the opening ceremony. It was predicted that the Exposition would become the proud focal point of Seattle life over the course of the next year.

Maddie's response to the news of the Exposition was mixed. Her enthusiasm for seeing her cherished city and its splendors put on display for the rest the world to behold was, frankly, tainted by her outrage at the city for threatening to rend her home and livelihood from her. She loved Seattle. Yet how could she abide by what it was doing to her, her hill, her neighborhood, the very life she had worked so hard for? How could she celebrate the city under such circumstances?

Dwelling this way on the tragedy of the regrading always left her in a stupor, feeling weak and lethargic – as it did this very morning, when all she was able to accomplish was to sit in one of the armchairs in the parlor and read about the A-Y-P Exposition in the newspaper and then stare at the fading wallpaper. The house during the day was exceptionally still now that Ada was enrolled at Denny School. Loye had arranged with the school's administrators to place Ada in the fifth grade, two years behind her age group, with the understanding that if she proved a fast learner (as both Maddie and Loye knew she would), she would be allowed to skip ahead in order to catch up with her classmates. Although Ada had always been a quiet girl prior to the tragedy that took her parents' lives, she gradually opened up more while living under Maddie's care and in the company of her boarders, especially now that she was growing into a young lady. In either case, quiet or loquacious, Ada could always be counted on to make her presence in the house felt. Whether she was in the den studying her maps, at the kitchen table doing her arithmetic, or lying on the rag rug in the parlor reading another novel, Maddie was always coming upon her as Ada was preparing for her next day's lessons. When she was not doing her homework, she would be in the kitchen clanging about at whatever task Maddie assigned her to help put supper on the table. Occasionally, the young girl still displayed a bit of mischievousness and would sneak up into Chiridah's or Loye's bedroom and dream over the dresses hanging in her closet or the jewelry on her dressing table. Upon discovering Ada snooping about her room one time, Chiridah, instead of scolding the girl, gave her a necklace with a small rhinestone pendant that Chiridah herself had worn as a young girl. Ada now wore the necklace to school every day beneath her school uniform. Maddie could not be more pleased with the child's progress... yet she worried about her too. Denny School was located just blocks from Madison House on the eastern slope of Denny Hill. Would Ada lose not only her home again once the regrading reached the boardinghouse, but her school as well? What would such a loss mean to a child who had already seen both parents taken from her, murdered in effect, as a kind of sacrifice to the gods of progress and their efforts to reshape the good earth to their whims? How would Maddie ever quell the trepidation – the terror even – that these events might instill in such a young soul? Every night, when she saw Ada to bed, tucking her in beneath the heavy covers and kissing her forehead and wishing her sweet dreams, these questions plagued Maddie.

To combat her worry, Maddie called up the resolution she had made on her birthday the week before (for which there had been a small celebration: a bakery-bought cake with candles, and Clyde, Ada, Loye, and Ray singing "Happy Birthday" to her) to run a more systematic household. One important aspect involved managing her money better, but another, equally important aspect entailed keeping better house and providing superior meals for her boarders.

To this end, she now dropped the newspaper on the floor, rose from the armchair she had been languishing in most of the morning, and marched into the kitchen. She set straight to inspecting the larder to take inventory of her provisions, jotting on a small notepad the items she needed to restock. She told herself she ought to arrange everything better: grains and flours and baking ingredients to one side, dried beans to the other, boxed goods below, canned goods above. There ought to be a system. If the homemaker maintained a thorough and comprehensive system, a columnist in the *P-I's* women's section had admonished readers last week, then she could better economize on time, money, and exertion in keeping house! For inspiration, Maddie now retrieved this column, which she'd clipped and placed on the shelf above Laurette's chair, and reread it: "System – by which I mean a sagacious and economical apportionment of duty to the hour and the minute; an avoidance of needless waste of working hours; a courageous putting forth of the hand to the plow, instead of talking over the labors to be performed while the cool morning moments are flying – SYSTEM, then, is not a talent. It is a dedication!" Indeed, Maddie thought, chagrined at having wasted her most productive morning hours. One must practice dedication! She folded the newspaper clipping and placed it in the pocket of her apron, vowing to commit it to memory by reading it twice every morning and twice every afternoon. System, she resolved, would be her salvation.

It was already late in the day and she could not take the long, circuitous route necessary to avoid the regrading and still make her rounds to the butcher, the fishmonger, the greengrocer, and the dry goods store, so she decided to test her innovativeness and concoct a "toss-up" for her boarders' supper – the kind of meal Frenchwomen were so renowned for making. With the remains of yesterday's roast, a few tablespoons of gravy stretched to a full cup with water and bouillon, assorted vegetable scraps, half a dozen eggs, the heel of a dried-out cheese, and several handfuls of bread crusts, she began assembling a dish that she knew would at least fill her boarders' stomachs.

With the dish in the oven, her next assignment toward system (which included superior meals) was to chart out the next week's menu. This being Thursday, she would make do for Friday and Saturday and commence the new menu in a grand way on Sunday, when she knew she would have Ada to help her. She took down her three cookbooks from the shelf above Laurette's chair and, with a new sheet of notepad paper at the ready, began leafing through the cookbooks and logging the exact menu for each day of the week:

Sunday Breakfast: Hominy boiled in milk, breaded mussels, toast, tea and coffee.
Sunday Supper: Beef loaf, scalloped beets, baked potatoes, crackers and cheese, prune pudding with whipped cream, black coffee.

Monday Breakfast: Cereal with cream, fried breakfast bacon, poached eggs on toast, hot biscuits, tea and coffee.
Monday Supper: Chicken Gumbo soup, baked beefsteak, spaghetti, cherry pie, black coffee.

Tuesday Breakfast: Oatmeal with berries and cream, corn bread and jelly, tea and coffee.
Tuesday Supper: Fried oysters, tomato and lettuce salad, baked potatoes, meringue pudding, black coffee.

Wednesday Breakfast: Indian meal mush, muffins, fruit (honeydew melon), tea and coffee.

Wednesday Supper: Boiled corned beef, stewed potatoes, stewed beets, rice pudding with raisins, black coffee.

By the time she finished Wednesday's menu, she was already thinking that the meals might be more ambitious (and costly) than she would be able to pull off. Still, she thought, she couldn't give up. She had to try. She could do it, she knew, if she only implemented and maintained the proper system. She returned to the cookbooks to finish composing the week's meals:

Thursday Breakfast: Clam fritters, graham muffins, apple slices with honey, tea and coffee.

Thursday Supper: Black bean soup (based on stock from Wednesday's boiled corned beef), roast chicken, boiled potatoes, green peas, cherry roly-poly, black coffee.

Friday Breakfast: Oatmeal with berries and cream, graham muffins (from Thursday's breakfast), tea and coffee.

Friday Supper: Halibut steaks, mashed potatoes, cucumber and lettuce salad, queen of puddings, black coffee.

Saturday Breakfast: Omelets, bacon, biscuits, tea and coffee.

Saturday Supper: Vegetable soup, salmon loaf, string beans, young beets, lemon meringue pie, black coffee.

She put her pencil down and looked at the two sheets of notepad paper on which she'd scrawled the menu. "That's a prodigious menu, Laurette," she said, turning to the empty chair beside the stove, "and without Ada's help, I just don't know if I'm capable of it." She returned the cookbooks to the shelf and studied the menu again. It made Maddie tired just to reread it. She would also have to shop for it each week. She told herself she would have to trust that it would simply become easier over time, once she grew more accustomed to preparing such superior meals. She knew that as one week followed another she might better utilize leftovers into various and tasty combinations. The thought crossed her mind that she might even buy a second dining room table and open the house to nonlodgers for their supper. She could advertise in the *P-I*, and once business picked up she might even hire another kitchen girl or two to relieve her of the peeling and chopping and clean-up work that would be required.

THREE WEEKS LATER MADDIE SAT IN THE SITTING ROOM IN HER favorite old armchair, its damask upholstery wearing thinner every year, and found herself very nearly catatonic with fatigue. The house chores, the shopping, the cooking, the endless worry about the regrading, all of it had left her exhausted. She had managed to keep up with the daily menu for two full weeks, but by the third week it had become too much and she had begun modifying it with more modest dishes such as shepherd's pie and creamed chipped beef on toast. Her systematic household was proving anything but.

Most afternoons now, she let herself rest. Every once in a while during the late afternoon, Clyde would come through the house, usually on his way to the next task, and they would talk, which always proved to be a refreshing respite in her day. Something about Clyde, perhaps simply the fact that they had now known each other for so long, longer than Maddie had known anyone else presently in her life, that made his company such a solace to her. Since becoming a street sweeper for the city – something she told him he didn't need to do since he could live at the house for free – he did all of the house maintenance in the late afternoon and evening and on Sunday, his one day off. She admired his ability to carry on so steadfastly – unhurriedly, assuredly, without any of the worry that seemed to prostrate her for hours, and sometimes whole days at a time. Every day there were chores to do, errands to run, meals to prepare. The afternoon sunlight through the front windows warmed the room and made her drowsy until her head rolled back and she snapped to again. The house was generally quiet except for the *chug-chug-chug* of the steam engines now only a block and a half away at the closest regrading site. She knew she would have to say something soon to her boarders, inform them that they had probably best seek new lodging, that the future of Madison House was uncertain at best. Only Clyde and Ray had ever discussed openly with her the regrading project and what it meant to them. The others were too discreet to bring it up with her.

As for Clyde, she knew he could take care of himself, though she could not imagine her own life without him close at hand. Ray also would do okay. He was earning money now as a photographer and making plans to open his own studio downtown. Loye would finish college in the fall, half a year early, and become a schoolteacher as she'd always planned. James would either move his press to another location – though he insisted the present arrangement suited his needs perfectly – or begin working for one of the city's daily newspapers, as he had once spoken of doing.

Aside from Ada of course, it was Chiridah whom Maddie worried about the most. Since going to work for this theater manager named Pittman, which Loye one day told her about, Chiridah was at the house less and less. She slept past breakfast and around noon would drink some coffee, which Maddie warmed for her on the stove, and then she would head downtown to the theater. Maddie would not see her again until the next day, and several nights each week she would not return to the house at all. When Maddie asked after her, she said she had done an extra show and stayed the night with Betsy, her friend from the theater. She even spoke of moving in with Betsy, which did not console Maddie much. When she did see Chiridah, she appeared thin and wane, with grayish blue shadows under her eyes. She also took less care with the way she dressed and no longer spoke of working to get into one of John Considine's theaters.

Only last month, Ray had told Loye (who told Maddie) that he had seen Chiridah in one of the gambling houses far below the Deadline when he had gone there to take some photographs for a new series he was starting. It was well after all the theaters had closed and she clung to the arm of a well-dressed fellow he had never seen before, someone laying out a lot of dough on the blackjack table. The next night, when he went back to the same gambling house, he saw Chiridah again, this time sitting in a back booth and drinking with a different fellow. Ray hazarded to guess that these men weren't actors or any other kind of theater people for that matter. "I think they're goons," he told Loye.

After that, Loye and Maddie waited for their chance and then had a sit-down talk with Chiridah. At first she insisted that her life was going just as she had planned, that she was right on course. She even talked of moving to Chicago or New York soon to work in the theater there. Mr. Pittman, she said, was going to help her. But when Loye pressed her further on why she was still working for Lewis Pittman at all, Chiridah explained that he took good care of her, gave her the best parts, and paid her well. "But you're still doing variety shows," Loye came back. Maddie knew that Loye was holding off mentioning what Ray had told her. "I thought you wanted to do drama," she went on, and with that Chiridah, looking at her friend, began slowly to cry. "I did," she said. When Loye asked her if Pittman was really the best person for her to be working for, she answered, "No, he's not the best person," and then began crying in earnest. When she finally composed herself enough, she began telling Loye and Maddie everything that had happened to her over the past nine months: how Pittman threatened to ban her from every theater from Seattle to San Francisco unless she became one of his girls; how she chewed the little wax balls of morphine every night when her shows were done; how she needed them now; how a few of the men that Pittman set her up with had robbed and beaten her; how this whole life she had fallen into made her want to board a ferry some night and throw herself off the back of it into the middle of the Sound.

The story made Loye cry right along with her friend, and of course it reminded Maddie of Laurette and the sad fate she had met with in Dawson. Maddie asked Chiridah to stop working for Pittman immediately and told her she didn't have to worry about paying her room and board. "Maybe you could teach acting at the Egan School," she suggested, when Chiridah said she would have to work somewhere. Yet even with Loye endorsing Maddie's suggestion, Chiridah said she could not just quit the Castle Garden Theater, pleading that it was all she had right now and she couldn't give it up. "Besides," she said, "Mr. Pittman won't let me quit," making Maddie think that Pittman's intimidation of Chiridah – and the morphine – was her real reason.

It was another month before anything definitive changed for Chiridah. Taking turns, Loye and Ray, and then Maddie and Clyde, would go down to the Castle Garden Theater and after the final show of the evening would make their way backstage and insist on taking Chiridah to dinner with

them, and then after dinner they would take her straight back to the boardinghouse. Although Pittman was rarely around, he eventually caught on
to what was happening when on several occasions he discovered that
Chiridah was not available. It was a night after one of these dinners that
Chiridah's friend Betsy brought her back to Madison House so severely
battered about the face that her eyes had nearly swollen shut and she had
difficulty breathing. Seeing Chiridah so badly beaten, Clyde stormed out
of the house on his way to track down Pittman, but Maddie stopped him
on the porch and told him she needed him there with her. "It doesn't matter
anyway," she said to him, "because she's not going back this time."

Chiridah stayed in her room the entire next week, with Maddie, Loye,
and Ada looking after her. During this time, Loye was also on the telephone
frequently with her parents, and the following Sunday, Loye and Chiridah
boarded the *Flyer* going down to Tacoma. It was arranged that Chiridah
would stay with Loye's parents for the next several months to help her steer
clear of the corrupting influences she was susceptible to in Seattle and help
her get back on her feet. Maddie tried to reassure Chiridah that Pittman
had neither the power nor the position to ban her from Seattle theaters
and that once she was ready to get back on the stage there would be a place
for her. In a letter to Maddie from Loye's father, Mr. Atchinson, the suggestion was made that the young lady coming to stay with him and his wife
might be interested in taking classes at the local business college, which
might even lead to a position at his bank. While Maddie did not share Mr.
Atchinson's suggestion with Chiridah, not wanting to put too much on
her so soon, she privately endorsed it and hoped it would come to pass.

Still, she worried about Chiridah for many weeks after she had moved
out of the boardinghouse and back down to Tacoma – she knew what had
happened to Laurette even after she had quit the dance hall – yet Loye
reassured Maddie that her parents and Chiridah were getting along splen-
didly. Chiridah, she said, planned to enroll in the business college after
all. The fact that Madison House had lost a boarder and was unlikely to
find another at this stage of the regrading project was a matter that never
crossed Maddie's mind.

25. Persecution (1908)

CLYDE HAD BEEN WORKING AS A STREET SWEEPER FOR WELL over a year when he started to think of doing something different. It was not a terrible job – shoveling manure, spearing litter, and sweeping trash along the curb, mostly – and he liked the men he worked with. They were whites and Negroes, along with a few Indians. The job was the lowest-paying one on the city's payroll, but the longer he stayed at it, the more latitude he was given in choosing the neighborhoods where he worked. He was also granted more flexible working hours. This enabled him to help Maddie about the house more regularly, continue to distribute the *Sentry* for James, and occasionally lend his father a hand with his ever-expanding garden. The job also let him get out and about the city, his city, which, when it came right down to it, is what he loved doing most. So what if he had to scoop up horse dung during his perambulations? At least he was getting paid for it.

Unfortunately the only person on the job he wasn't getting along with lately was Russell. Russ had very nearly lost his job when he remained at Home Colony for two weeks after their excursion there. On the Sunday evening after Clyde's return to Seattle, he received a telephone call at Madison House from Russ, who was still at Joe's Bay. He asked Clyde to tell their supervisor the next morning that Russ had to rush off to Olympia to see his dying mother; then he asked Clyde to cover his work route for him. For Clyde, this meant doubling the territory he already had to cover – just to save Russ's hide. Russ vowed he would make it up to him, but he didn't say how. Clyde agreed to help Russ out, but just this once, and hung up the telephone. The next day – commencing a period that stretched into nearly two weeks – he worked the territory from King Street to Yesler between Railroad and Sixth, in addition to his regular route from Yesler to Pike. Yet when Russ finally showed up for work again, he didn't offer Clyde a cut of his pay or even so much as buy him lunch. When Clyde asked him about Emily at Home Colony, Russ didn't say anything specific about her either way.

"They can't expect to change the world by retreating from it," was all he said, referring to the Home Colony crowd, while Clyde and he stood on a street corner beside their carts. "It's right here, on the street, that the real revolution's gonna take place."

Clyde had nothing to say to this. He just looked down at his shoes, the soles worn through from all the extra walking he'd done over the past two weeks, and pushed off on his route.

So the following week, when the supervisor asked Clyde if he could handle a team of horses and Clyde told him he could, and then asked Clyde if he wanted to take over driving one of the water wagons, Clyde jumped at the opportunity. His pay would be doubled, he would get to drive up through some of the city's finest neighborhoods along First Hill and Capitol Hill, and the whole while he would get to ride high atop the water wagon. In all, the change would be a most welcome one.

Clyde arrived at the water wagon barn before anyone else the next morning and had to wait for the supervisor to show up with the keys to let him in. Seeing Clyde's eagerness, the supervisor straightaway brought him to the stall where his team of horses was waiting.

"Ya feed 'em and water 'em, ya see to it they're shoed properly, and ya make sure to brush 'em down at the end of every day, and ya put enough hay in their stall at night. They're your responsibility, ya got that? Anything happens to them, it's your arse."

Clyde placed his hand on the forelock of one of the two large mares. They were roan horses, their sorrel coats spotted with white and gray, yet stained darker around their legs and haunches from trudging through the city's muddy streets. Someone, he thought, hadn't been washing them down well enough. Their long, wiry manes were lighter in color, almost tan. Together, they seemed like a solid team, accustomed to being harnessed to each other. Good solid work horses. Clyde gave each horse an apple from the bag of apples he'd brought with him from his father's orchard just for this purpose.

Then the foreman showed Clyde where his water wagon was. It was a basic flatboard wagon with a 5,000-gallon water tank strapped onto its bed. The driver sat in a saddlelike seat atop the tank, like riding an enormous elephant, and at the back of the wagon a hose came down with a brass nozzle on the end of it. The nozzle, suspended a foot above the road, sprayed a jet of water across the road's surface and, when there was one, along the curb. The city had a dozen such wagons, part of its recent City Beautiful initiative.

"There's a pump out back where you fill your tank," the supervisor instructed him. "Now with a new guy usually, I'd send out another man with him on his first day. But I ain't got a man to spare today, so I'm sending you out on your own. You think you can manage it without getting into trouble?"

Clyde assured him he could.

"All right then," the supervisor said. "Now harness your team and fill your tank and I'll give you a map of your route."

By the time the other street washers began to straggle into the barn, Clyde was clicking his tongue at his team of horses, giving their haunches a gentle slap with the reins, and pulling out of the barn while sitting proudly atop his water wagon with its tank filled to the brim. In the past several years, while the city had been regrading so many downtown streets, it had also been busy replacing street planking with brick, concrete, and asphalt roads in the residential neighborhoods on First Hill and Capitol Hill. The city's wealth had concentrated itself in these neighborhoods long before the gold rush, and the city's current prosperity (despite the sudden market crash of '07) served only to further establish these precincts as the exclusive enclave of luxury and privilege. The houses on Denny Hill were quite humble compared to the many-storied, multi-winged mansions in these two fancy neighborhoods. Perched high above the rest of the city, Seattle's businessmen, politicians, attorneys, and judges, those who belonged to the chamber of commerce and the Rainier Club, could peer down upon the city spread out below them like the gods of antiquity gazing down upon their mortal minions, manipulating the traffic of their workaday lives as they saw fit. Their newly built churches reflected their self-made glory. The massive St. Mark's Episcopal Church, with its wide gabled roof and reddish sandstone façade, seemed almost modest compared to St. James Roman Catholic Cathedral, opened six months earlier, with its ornate arched entryway, double cupola-topped campaniles, bulging nave, and center dome. These men clearly worshipped on a scale comparable to their net worth, if not their piety.

It was during his second week driving the water wagon that Clyde decided he had to get down and have a look inside the new cathedral. Since the area surrounding it was always so quiet and serene, especially so early in the morning, Clyde, after spraying the streets around the cathedral grounds, parked the wagon along one of the side streets, climbed down from his seat atop the tank, and walked around the corner and up the white concrete stairs leading to the entrance. He had never entered a Roman Catholic church before. Although his father came from a Lutheran lineage back in the Fatherland, in matters of faith the old man was, if not quite a freethinker, then certainly too damn cantankerous for any organized religion to contain him. As for his mother, he remembered her as being simply disinterested, which probably suited his father just fine. Clyde liked to think that when it came to religion, he shared equally in his father's recalcitrance and his mother's disinterest.

Nevertheless, right now, the prospect of entering the large, monumental structure made his pulse thump. According to a metal sign in the grass near the street, the Cathedral was the See of the Diocese of Nisqually – which to Clyde sounded quite curious in its odd blend of church and Indian terms. Adjacent to the cathedral was the mansard-roofed residence of the bishop. Clyde approached the entrance and pushed on the ten-foot-tall, brass-plated door. The foyer was narrow, but it had six doorways lined up to the right and left, on either side of a large basin of holy water, that led into the cathedral's vast interior. The building was less than a year old, yet the cool marbled walls and dark row of pews gave off a musty air that seemed almost medieval. The stained glass windows, depicting the Stations of the Cross, muted the already dull morning light outside. On rainy days, Clyde thought, it must be almost too dark to see inside. Then he looked up and saw the multiarmed, cast-iron lamps with incandescent bulbs hanging from chains along either side of the center aisle. The church was wired for electricity. Far off at the front stood the ornately carved pulpit, encircled by a series of three-foot-tall wooden saints, and rising gloriously above the pulpit, the white marble figure of Christ, knees bent and torso arched, writhing on a wooden cross. The marble was of such stunning purity, its whiteness emanating like a beacon down the full length of the dark nave. Clyde stared at the figure, entranced by its absolute whiteness, but also appalled by its contortions. It seemed that, beyond its pained face and twisted limbs, the figure's whiteness became an even more profound expression of the figure's unrelenting agony.

Quite honestly, the figure frightened him. He had not anticipated such an encounter so early in the morning, and without proceeding any farther up the center aisle, he turned around and retreated from the cathedral. Pushing past the large entrance doors, going down the front steps, and turning the corner again, he was cheered to see his team of horses waiting patiently on the side street, their wide, alert eyes recognizing him as he approached. He gave each horse an apple and patted their thick muscular necks. He then swung himself up into the seat atop the tank with a great sense of relief in having a job to do, unloosened the reins, released the brake, and clicked his team to move on.

As the horses clopped along through the Capitol Hill neighborhood at a steady pace, Clyde occasionally turned the valve to release the spray and wash the street paving clear of mud or manure. His route took him west on Boren Avenue, east on Madison Street, and then down Boylston Avenue. He had rarely walked these streets – except for a few times when he had to run an errand for Ned James. His supervisor had instructed him to be sure to spray in front of all the biggest houses, that important people complained if their streets weren't kept clean. Clyde could not help gazing up at the mansions set so neat and tidy in the well-tended yards behind wrought-iron fences. Each house presented a different style: a Tudor house with heavy timbers, stucco siding, and lofty dormers; a square Italianate house with portico-like eaves and terra-cotta shingles on its roof; a tall Victorian house with window boxes, a wrap-around porch, and decorative trim; a massive stone Greek Revival house with austere pediments over each window and a mansard roof; a sheer-faced Colonial house with shuttered windows and a whitewashed front door. Each house presented a different style and a different set of lives to be imagined behind its exterior. Clyde imagined lives of opulence and luxury, in which house girls cooked and served the meals, French was spoken, piano lessons were taken, and tawdriness of any sort was expertly expunged. He had read enough Henry James to know what kind of people – the cultured and moneyed class, the *haute bourgeoisie* – resided in the estates that lined Boylston and Boren and the other elegant avenues atop First Hill and Capitol Hill. Indeed, he thought, the upstanding Dr. Austin Sloper and his charming daughter, Catherine, could just as readily live here as in their townhouse on Washington Square in New York City. Clyde also believed he understood Henry James's novels well enough not to envy these people their pampered lives.

All the same, he enjoyed the peaceableness of driving his water wagon through the wealthy neighborhoods in the quiet of the early mornings. It was especially still on mornings when a mist lingered in the air and the entire downtown and bay were obscured by the thick grayish blanket that hung over the region. Only the kitchen and yard help stirred at such an early hour. He would wave to the Japanese houseboy who emerged from an alley with a bucket and a wash brush to scrub the outside windows of a house, or to the gardener trimming the hedges that lined the perimeter of a particular property. When he passed the milk wagon or ice wagon, he would greet the driver. They would pause in the middle of the street and from their respective wagon seats – Clyde always seated higher – they would pass a few minutes discussing the weather or their horses, and occasionally share a cigar.

The only aspect of his old street sweeper job that Clyde missed was being on the bustling downtown streets. People knew who he was down there, they greeted him by name, and everything seemed more open and democratic to him. In the affluent neighborhoods, he could sometimes go the entire morning without seeing anyone. And if the person was anyone other than a deliveryman or the house help, he dared not extend a greeting and risk drawing attention to himself. That's just how it was.

CLYDE'S NEW POSITION MEANT THAT HE HAD MORE MONEY to contribute to Maddie's house fund – which she initially objected to, but in time accepted from him. Increasingly, however, it appeared that no amount of money could save the boardinghouse from the final regrading of Denny Hill. The best that could be hoped for now was that Erasmo would use the courts to stall the hoses and maybe convince a judge or jury to award Maddie enough in damages to resettle elsewhere in the city. It was now only a matter of months, half a year at most, before the regrading would reach the boardinghouse. The scenario seemed both inevitable and thoroughly beyond reckoning.

It was this dilemma, this utter irreconcilability, that drove Clyde to break his vow (to Maddie and himself) to steer clear of the regrading sites along Denny Hill. He had to see the worst for himself. He could no longer keep away from the work site. For the past year or more, even as he knew the various cuts in the hillside were creeping ever closer, he had avoided the three main regrading sites along the south and west sides of the sixty-square-block radius of Denny Hill. He had tried to pretend nothing unusual was happening to his neighborhood, that it was as peaceful and secure as ever, that his life upon the hill would proceed according to its uneventful routines. Yet as the sluicing and shoveling work extended now around the clock, and as the blast of the hoses and the churn of the steam shovels forced him awake each night, he became more restive, and angry, and couldn't stay away. He had to go, he told himself. Whether he could do anything about it or not, he had to inspect the regrading site for himself.

The whole civic undertaking of regrading Denny Hill, of removing a neighborhood and sluicing and shoveling the ground beneath it into Elliott Bay, made Clyde grind his teeth at the terrible might of men, magnified as it was by their audacious faith in themselves in moving mountains. City Engineer Reginald H. Thomson seemed destined, like Moses parting the Red Sea, to recast nature in service to himself and the powerful cabal of Seattle boosters who would reap the profits from this venture while hard-working people would be left high and dry, their residences and businesses on Denny Hill done in, sold off, and forgotten. A few holdouts continued to make their stand against the regrading, yet the juggernaut that was the city engineer and the corporate commission seemed more unstoppable than ever. The Bible gave them their motto, their creed, their justification: "If ye have faith, ye can remove mountains." Clyde had spotted the saying painted on one of the big plywood signboards that the engineering firm of Lewis & Wiley had put up at one of their many pump stations. Though not a regular Bible reader, he knew enough Scripture to know the line read "ye can move mountains," not *remove* them.

It was a bright, early September morning, a light gauzy haze still in the air, as he walked to the site along Fourth and Battery, the largest of the three regrading sites on Denny Hill. The week before, news had reached Madison House that a large new steam shovel had been brought in on the tracks along the perimeter of the regrading. When Clyde reached the rim of the vast, bowl-shaped cut, sure enough, there it was, not far from the base of the cut. Far bigger than the donkey-engine shovels that had been used up to now, this new steam shovel presented an ominous sight. Its bucket had the capacity of a small house. From the two-story boiler that powered the engine arose a pair of tall stacks, one blowing steam, the other coal smoke. A flywheel wider than a man's outstretched arms turned a leather belt two feet wide and fifteen feet long. Valves, gauges, and crank handles crowded the machine's inner workings.

Clyde wanted to scuttle down through the mud to get a better look at the thing. But a work crew kept a close watch over it. A more select crew of three manned the steam shovel itself – an oiler, a water tender, and an operator – the whole job overseen by the engineer, a man with a broad jaw enhanced by a well-trimmed beard and wearing a stiff, round-brimmed hat that shaded his eyes. During the course of the morning, as Clyde looked on from above, the engineer came around every hour or so to look up at the steam shovel and its engine, his arms severely crossed, and shout orders at the crew. The operator, pulling the levers that controlled the crane and bucket, seemed mostly to ignore the engineer from his perch atop the engine. It was the oiler and the water tender who came in for the worst abuse. It was their responsibility, it appeared, to kept the behemoth piece of machinery functioning smoothly.

It seemed like some fatalistic impulse on Clyde's part that kept him watching as the operator of the steam shovel dropped the clawed bucket into the hillside and tore away a section of earth deep enough and wide enough to bury a regiment of men. Big plumes of coal smoke and steam blew forth from the dual stacks, and the engine hissed and chugged, loudly and steadily, like some ancient creature that had been disturbed in its lair.

Clyde calculated that it would take only a few hundred such gouges into the hill before the steam shovel reached Maddie's house.

Clyde had asked Ray to accompany him to the site to take photographs of the big new machine. Yet Ray had never been as obsessed with the regrading as Clyde, and declined the invitation. And now, already noon, overlooking the regrading site, Clyde again wondered why he himself had come. Did he believe the onslaught to the hill could still be stopped? Did he think he might still do something to spare Madison House? He could not say why he had come down to the cut to watch the progress of this enormous civic project, perhaps the greatest undertaking in the city's history. He just had to. The fact of the project ate away at him the way the steam shovels and sluicing hoses ate away at the earth that had once made Denny Hill one of most prominent of the city's many hills.

He watched as the operator of the massive steam shovel climbed down from his seat in the controls cab above the engine, slapped the water tender on the back, put his arm around the oiler, and then led the two men off to lunch, leaving the engine running at a slow idle with only a trace of steam coming from one of the dual stacks. By this time, a few other sidewalk engineers had shown up – spectators, like himself, who with nothing better to do gathered around the regrading sites to watch, and remark on, the work being done – and Clyde listened to their commentary on the new steam shovel. One man, who explained that it had been brought up from the Panama Canal, said it was nicknamed the "Yankee Geologist." Another man predicted it would have all of Denny Hill leveled within the next month or two. Clyde kept to himself and only listened. He knew that his presence at the site was more conspicuous than that of the other spectators. He dressed in his usual manner – corduroy pants, blue work shirt, canvas jacket, wool newsboy cap, and the calico neckerchief Maddie had given him years ago tied about his neck – but he realized that most everyone knew him to be the albino handyman who lived at one of the houses on the hill that continued to hold out against the regrading project.

So he kept to himself most of the morning until, as the work crew and spectators alike drifted away from the work site for lunch, a tall, red-headed Irishman approached him and introduced himself as James Carney.

He told Clyde that he'd spent three years in the Yukon working the Eldorado Creek claim for Tom Lippey, the Seattle millionaire. He leaned over
the railing of the sidewalk set up for the spectators and spat down into
the cut. Then he turned his head to scrutinize Clyde and said, "I think
they're looking for gold right here in Seattle." He took a plug of chaw
from his jacket pocket and bit off a corner of it. "All this diggin' and sluicin'
would be well worth the trouble if they struck just one vein. You want to
talk about a pay streak? That's for sure what the whole gang running this
operation is after. I heard Thomson hired geologists, one from each of
the fancy Ivy League schools back East, to come out here and test the
hills ... and they determined there's gold right here beneath our feet! And
plenty of it too!" He cocked his head to look at Clyde and then turned
and spat again. He then did an about-face and leaned the small of his back
against the railing and crossed his arms. "Why go all the way to Alaska
when you can find what you're looking for right here. I'm telling you this
because you look like the trustworthy type to me. But I don't want to hear
it getting around, you understand?"

Clyde said that was fine by him and looked down along the base of the
cut to see if the work crew was returning to the site. Although Jim Carney
seemed to be dead serious in his ideas about gold beneath Denny Hill,
Clyde figured he was just a crazy Irishman talking a load of blarney.

"I'll tell you what's more," Carney went on. "The reason I come around
here is to watch and see. To wait my chance. If you watch carefully, you'll
see the engineer or one of those Harvard or Princeton geologists come
around every once in a while and talk to the crew and look at the cut real
closely. I want to be here when they find that vein. They won't make a big
fuss of it, you can be sure of that. But if I keep watching close enough, I'll
know when it happens. And that, lad, is when I'll spring into action and
claim my share. What was denied me by Tom Lippey in the Yukon, by
God, I'll get back in spades."

Clyde didn't try to follow the Irishman's story. Maybe this Carney
fella only wanted to see if he could get a rise out of Clyde, or maybe he
wanted to recruit him to help him claim his so-called share. Whatever
the case, Clyde had to admit that it enticed him to think that perhaps, just

perhaps, if there was gold underneath Denny Hill and Maddie still hadn't sold her house and property off, then by god she would be the one claiming a share of it. She would be gold rich for the second time in her life, and if anyone deserved such an uncommon stroke of good fortune, it was Maddie.

Listening to Carney go on about how he would spend his riches, Clyde became convinced the man was just plain nuts. He'd gone bust in the Yukon, like most of the gold grubbers, and had never gotten over it. The notion of Denny Hill gold was another pipe dream he was selling himself, and so Clyde decided to humor the big redhead. "That would be quite a strike," he said flatly, and looked again for the work crew returning from their lunch break. He imagined they'd all gone off to a tavern and that's what was taking them so long. "A man could get rich awfully fast," he added offhandedly.

"You know it," the Irishman said, and spat tobacco juice at the ground and wiped his jacket sleeve across his mouth. Then he looked hard at Clyde. "I'm only telling you because I might need help when the time comes. Once they hit that vein, you can bet they'll have the Wells Fargo boys in here faster than the U.S. Calvary."

Not wanting any part of the Irishman's scheme, Clyde wished now that he hadn't said anything. He replied, "That's kindly of you to include me, but I best stay clear." Clyde wondered how many other sidewalk engineers held the same harebrained notion as this Carney fella. How many were just waiting for their big chance?

Carney shrugged. "I like you, Clyde Hunssler, that's why I offered." And then he turned stern again. "But like I said, I don't want to hear this getting around, or else I'll know who spread it."

Clyde tried to remember if he'd told Carney his name or not – he didn't think so – and then looked him straight in the eye and said, "I wouldn't blame you one bit, Jim," and with that the Irishman seemed satisfied.

Clyde noticed the shovel operator finally walking back to the site just as Carney said he was going to move up to Vine Street and check out the progress at that end. "It's all one man can do to keep up," he said, and walked off. Meanwhile, Clyde kept his eye on the operator as he took a bucket of coal from a big bin near the steam engine and tossed it into the enormous furnace compartment beneath the boiler. He then climbed atop the engine and into the cab and sat down on the metal seat behind the controls. The rest of the crew that worked the steam shovel had not yet returned, though several other men from the general work crew were milling about, leaning on their shovels, one man with a pick ax slung length-wise over his shoulders like a yoke and his two arms hooked over either end of it.

The front stack on the steam shovel suddenly released a gust of black coal smoke as the operator waited for the engine to raise a head of steam. The leather belts on the large flywheel whirred at first and then hummed as the engine torqued up. Clyde watched from his perch along the upper ridge of the cut. He hadn't seen fewer than three men working the steam shovel that morning and wondered how the operator could manage the machine on his own. The operator pulled a lever and the long, jointed arm of the crane reared back. He pulled another lever and the cables that were strung through the crane raised the bucket into the air and back. Clyde had watched the same maneuver a score of times already that day. The operator would drive the bucket into the slope of the earth and then drag it toward him, scooping up the ragged dirt, blue clay, small and large boulders, and anything else that lay in its path; then he would spin the bucket around and dump its contents into a waste car that waited on a second set of tracks directly behind the steam shovel.

This time, though, there was a hitch in the usual sequence. The bucket would not drop. Something, a cable perhaps, had jammed. The operator yelled down to one of the men off to the side, but over the rumble of the engine he couldn't make himself heard. Clyde saw only the man's mouth moving and his angry gesturing. Finally one of the workmen heard him, jabbed his shovel into the ground, and ran up to the steam engine and began looking over its inner workings as if hunting for a particular control. Meanwhile the operator was roughly cranking a lever, apparently the one that maneuvered the bucket, but to no avail: the bucket remained suspended in the air, stuck. He leaned over from his perch in the cab and shouted at the man beside the engine again. Clyde, watching the scene below, took a sly pleasure in the general confusion.

At that moment, the engine let out a low growl, like the giant beast it was, and a sonorous rumble from deep in its cast-iron belly followed, as if it were preparing to belch. The flywheel with the leather belt began to smoke and the operator, spotting this, shouted at the man with the pick ax over his shoulder, who ran up to the flywheel with a water bucket and poured the water onto the smoking belt. The operator returned to cranking the lever even more furiously than before, but the crane remained jammed.

When Clyde looked up from this frantic scene it was just in time to see the oiler and the water tender both running toward the steam shovel and shouting madly. The water tender waved his arms as if to signal the men away from the engine. Then, just as they came within a dozen yards of it, the engine seemed to lock up entirely, followed by a loud, prolonged cracking noise of metal severing. The engine seized up and the flywheel wrenched itself off its axle, sending the leather belt whipping away from the engine and whiplashing the man with the water bucket across the side of the head, nearly decapitating him and sending his body reeling to the ground. Then just as the oiler and the water tender reached the engine, the two-story boiler that powered the great machine erupted and the whole engine exploded.

Clyde recoiled from the blast, but not before seeing the catastrophe rip before his eyes. A parabola of bright red coal cinders burst into the sky. The explosion instantly mowed down the oiler and the water tender, shredding them with sheared metal from the boiler. So great was the force of the explosion that it lifted the massive steam shovel off the ground and tossed it back onto the workman on the other side who had been desperately searching for the right switch to throw. The operator was hurled high into the air where he disappeared into a cloud of white steam and black coal smoke that followed the bloom of coal cinders. The deafening noise from the explosion echoed back and forth between the West Seattle bluffs across the bay and what remained of Denny Hill. Clyde stumbled back from the railing and fell to the ground.

As he raised himself to his feet, the concussiveness of the explosion reverberated in his ears and he could hear nothing, just a dull hollowness in his head. Gray coal ash filled the air. Through it he could see the devastation that lay below him at the base of the cut. The scene looked as if a dozen cases of dynamite had been set off simultaneously. The boiler explosion was so great that it left a crater in the earth at least thirty feet in diameter. The steam engine was a hulk of wreckage lying on its side along one edge of the crater, the crane a tangle of steel and wires, the boiler nothing more than a heap of shredded scrap metal. The damage spread out from the point of the blast. A nearby waste car was knocked off the adjacent tracks. A wagon parked about fifty feet away was shattered, the mutilated carcass of the mule that had pulled it lying beside it. The bodies of the three men who had been nearest the boiler lay evenly spaced out around the crater, twisted limbs and mangled torsos in a heap of tattered and burnt clothing. Even the outhouse some forty yards away had collapsed into a pile of kindling. Not far from the debris field lay another body, whom Clyde guessed was the operator, also a mangled heap. The other man who had been in the vicinity, the one who had been pouring water over the flywheel, Clyde figured, probably lay beneath the remains of the steam engine.

It didn't take long for workmen from adjacent regrading sites to arrive on the scene of the explosion. Clyde looked about and saw that no more spectators remained on the rim of the cut other than himself. As with Jim Carney, they had all wandered away when the crew knocked off for lunch. He thought momentarily of scrambling down the hillside to aid in the rescue, but he could plainly see that there was nothing to be done for the five men who had been nearest the steam shovel. Their jobs were done.

So with the echo of the explosion still in his ears, and moving somewhat unsteadily on his feet, Clyde turned from the wreckage of the blast and began to walk back up the hill to Madison House.

THE NEXT DAY HE COULD STILL HEAR A DULL RING FROM THE explosion in the inner canals of both ears. The image of the event remained vivid in his mind. After the boiler on the steam shovel had exploded, instantly killing the five men nearest it, he'd staggered back to the boardinghouse and slipped up the backstairs to his attic room, avoiding Maddie, who was resting in the sitting room. He didn't leave the house for the remainder of the afternoon, nor did he go downstairs to dinner. At some point deep in the night, he woke up with a wracking headache, thought of going downstairs to find the headache powder, but then recalled what he had witnessed that afternoon and wondered to himself if it were real or simply a wretched dream he needed to shake. His headache grew worse as he tried to sort out the images that remained sharp in his mind, though eventually he was able to drop back to sleep.

Several hours later, the morning light through his dormer window finally woke him. His headache lingered, but he could now remember clearly the events of the day before. He couldn't decide whether to return to the site. He thought that maybe he should tell someone what he'd seen, perhaps one of the regrading engineers, or even the police. But first, he decided, he wanted to see how the morning papers were reporting the explosion.

When he went downstairs, Maddie was surprised to see him there so late in the morning. She was just finishing the breakfast dishes when Clyde stepped into the kitchen, still feeling a bit shaky, and, not thinking, sat down on Laurette's chair near the stove. For an instant Maddie looked at him, alarmed, but then came up to him and asked if he was all right.

"Sure," he said, resting his elbows on his knees, his hands clasped.

"I thought you had left the house long ago," Maddie said. She placed the back of her hand on his forehead. "You don't have a fever, do you?"

"I'm all right," he told her, and yawned. "You don't have any headache powder, do you?"

"Of course," Maddie said, and walked out of the kitchen and a moment later returned with a small tin of Clark's Powder. She looked at Clyde as she mixed a spoonful of the white powder into a glass tumbler of water. "You didn't go out carousing with Ray last night, did you? I thought I heard someone going up the backstairs rather late."

Clyde smiled wanly at her and shook his head. "No, Mother Maddie, that wasn't me. I did not go carousing with Raymond last night," he said, making fun of her despite his tormenting headache.

"Okay then," Maddie said and handed him the glass. "I just don't like to see any of my boarders get sick, is all." She stroked his white hair and returned to putting the cleaned dishes up in the cupboards. When done, she set a place for Clyde at the kitchen table, unwrapped several biscuits, and put them on a plate next to a thick slice of ham steak she took from the ice box.

"I'm not terribly hungry, Maddie. This headache's got the best of me this morning." He knew he was already late for work and, hoping he wouldn't be fired, hoping he was in good enough stead with the supervisor to cover him, he decided to just skip out on the day, something he'd never done before, not even as a street sweeper.

"You should eat something," Maddie replied.

Clyde obliged by getting up from Laurette's chair and seating himself on the bench at the kitchen table. He bit into one of the biscuits and cut a piece of ham with his knife and fork. "Maddie," he said, "why don't you just wrap the rest of this in some parchment paper and I'll take it with me. I need to get my route started."

Maddie sat on the bench next to Clyde and put her hand on his knee. "You go slow today, you hear? I don't know what's wrong, but I don't want you overexerting yourself and getting sick."

She then took his plate to the kitchen counter and wrapped up the biscuits and ham, added an apple, and handed it back to him. As Clyde traversed the kitchen, she trailed behind him, and as he stepped into the mudroom, she asked him if he'd heard the loud explosion yesterday afternoon.

If not for being so tired still, Clyde probably would have explained to Maddie what the noise had been – he didn't like to hide anything from her – but for the moment all he wanted to do was get out of the house and start walking. "I might have," he lied, adding, "I don't know," and then left without so much as a goodbye to Maddie.

His first thought was to stop by the carriage house and talk to James, who better than anyone else, certainly better than any of the big dailies, could give him the scuttlebutt on what was being said about yesterday's disaster. In fact, on Clyde's insistence, James had begun to give the regrading story more of his editorial attention and was now one of the fiercest voices – and one of the few voices in print – opposing the project. Yet, not surprisingly, James wasn't in the carriage house. The *Seattle Sentry* had come out on Thursday and another issue wouldn't appear until Monday, so James was likely out gathering stories for the next issue. Clyde decided he would head down to the Carnegie Public Library on Fourth Avenue, where in the back reading room the librarians hung the half dozen local newspapers every day on long wooden poles.

He walked east, avoiding the regrading wherever possible. From the top of Denny Hill, he could see Lake Union spread out to the north, sparkling blue and clear in the late-morning light. To the right, looking south past where the Washington Hotel had formerly stood, the first knoll having been regraded the previous month, he had an unobstructed view of downtown. He considered changing his course and going out to see his father at the lake, giving himself a respite from the turmoil taking place in the city, but knew he couldn't rest until he found out what was being said about the explosion. At Sixth Avenue he turned south and headed downtown. He passed up buying a paper from several newsboys and made his way to the library between Union and University.

With his headache finally subsiding, Clyde picked up his pace and reached the library in no time. Yet instead of racing up the steps of the large, square sandstone building, he decided he'd better eat the breakfast Maddie had wrapped for him. The library, wedged into the hillside, rested in the center of a squareblock of well-manicured lawn, which is where Clyde sat down. The biscuits and ham tasted good. He swallowed the last of the salty ham and floury biscuits, wishing he'd brought along something to drink, and then took a deep breath. Maybe, he thought, he shouldn't go into the musty old library after all. Maybe he should just give the day over to walking about and enjoying the fine weather. Hadn't he been through enough by simply having witnessed the event? What good would reading about it do? He let himself lie in the grass and, still very tired, was just beginning to doze off when a shamus, swinging his nightstick and letting out a hoary throat-clearing, nudged Clyde in the side with his boot and told him to move it along.

"There'll be no loitering on public property. That means no eating and no sleeping. So get along now."

The copper stood over him, silhouetted against the glare off the bay, and Clyde had to blink several times against the morning brightness.

"Can't ye hear me, I said move along," and with that the shamus gave him a much firmer nudge with his boot. "And pick up your litter there." He pointed to the parchment paper on the grass beside Clyde.

Clyde snatched up the paper, scuffled to his feet, and took several steps back.

"Go on now," the shamus said.

Instead of heading straight to the library entrance, Clyde walked around the building first, losing sight of the copper, and then bounded up the steps and through the heavy front doors into the library's lobby. A mural depicting the Lewis and Clark Expedition, Captain George Vancouver's exploration of Puget Sound, the Oregon Trail wagon trains, and the schooner *Exact* and the landing of Seattle's first pioneers on Alki Point wrapped around the upper portion of the lobby's four walls. Clyde recognized the librarian behind the front desk, Nona Pareil, a woman about Maddie's age who had greeted him from the very first day he'd entered the library after it opened in '04. On many occasions over the years, the library had served as a sanctuary for Clyde, whether as a resource for his reading or simply as shelter from the rain as he made his rounds about the city.

"Good morning," she said, looking up from her own reading.

"Good morning," Clyde returned, glad to see a friendly face.

"If you've come to read the morning papers, I should warn you there's quite a crowd in the periodicals room already." Nona smiled sympathetically.

Clyde hesitated and said, "I'll wait my turn," and smiled back at her.

The librarian nodded and returned to her reading as Clyde walked past the front desk and into the reading room at the back of the library. Indeed it was crowded, far more than usual. Typically there were three or four men at most reading the day's papers. A few of these were regulars, including the old Norwegian who came to read the month-old newspapers from Oslo, or the young fellow with a shaved head who pretended to read but who usually had his eyes closed, fast asleep. Today, though, a score of men crowded around the three tables in the room, some sitting side by side reading the same newspaper. All the papers were off the rack: the *Argus*, the *Municipal News*, the *Post-Intelligencer*, the *Republican*, the *Star*, the *Sun*, the *Times*. Since not a single chair remained unoccupied, Clyde stood along the wall beside the rack and waited for someone to return one of the papers. He assumed the stir had something to do with the steam engine explosion.

He had to wait only a few minutes before he had his answer. A man at one of the tables stood and returned a newspaper to the rack. Clyde quickly took it up – the *Post-Intelligencer*, which he realized he might have read right there in Maddie's parlor – and also took the man's place at the table. Two gentlemen seated across the table stared at him momentarily, then put their heads down when Clyde stared back at them. Clyde spread the front page out before him on the table and sure enough the top headline read: "REGRADE EXPLOSION KILLS FIVE," followed by the subheading, "Investigators Looking into Cause," followed by the second subheading, "Denny Hill Regrading Temporarily Suspended."

The article went on to detail what had happened without any speculation as to the likely cause. It reported how two of the men killed had families, each family now left bereft of a husband and father; how the explosion was heard in all quarters of the city, and as far north as Ballard; and how work at the site would not be resumed until a full investigation into the explosion had been conducted. Simon Lewis, of Lewis & Wiley, was quoted, saying, "The circumstances surrounding this tragedy are highly suspicious." When asked by the reporter if his men operating the steam shovel might have been at fault, Lewis adamantly denied it, reminding the reporter that the steam shovel was top-of-the-line and that his engineers and operators were trained to maximize the safety and efficiency of such valuable equipment. "It wouldn't surprise me if this turned out to be more anarchist sabotage," he declared. "It would be just like the radical cowards who assassinated President McKinley, and just two years ago Governor Steunenberg in Idaho, to try something like this. It's the Leon Czolgoszs and Harry Orchards of this world who hinder the progress of our great country." The article then reported that city detectives, as well as Pinkerton detectives, were investigating the possibility of involvement by "an anarchist element" in the explosion. Lewis was quoted again, saying, "The Denny Hill holdouts have caused enough hardship to our city already and the faster their spite mounds are leveled, the sooner this will all be settled and the sooner the city will have peace restored." He went on to say that the incident would not delay his company's work for more than a day. The full-page article closed by quoting City Engineer Reginald H. Thomson, who commented that the brave and hardworking men who perished did so in the service of making Seattle one of the finest cities in the world. "The future is indebted to them," Thomson said.

Clyde knew that there had been no plot behind the explosion. He knew that such an undertaking would have been far too involved for the rumpled and displaced little man with the rail spike in his coat pocket. It had been a mechanical error, due to negligence, plain and simple. Boilers blew if they weren't tended to properly. Anyone who had noticed that the oiler and the water tender were missing from their posts, that the operator was trying to work the big machine all by himself, and that the flywheel had jammed just moments before the whole thing blew could easily deduce where the fault lay. Clyde knew that he was probably the only person, other than the men who were killed, who had witnessed the accident. He also knew that it was unlikely anyone would give any credence to what he had to say on the matter. He knew as well that if people found out he'd been at the site, he would quickly become a main suspect in the case.

He lingered about the reading room for another hour and read several different newspaper accounts of the explosion. Each one, despite the usual partisan bickering among them, gave essentially the same version of events, including the offhanded conjecture that anarchist saboteurs might be involved.

Clyde knew that city officials and the regrading people already had him pegged as one of the holdouts and that if he tried to explain to a detective what he'd seen, they would no doubt treat him like a suspect in the case. So he decided, instead of talking to anyone, to backtrack to Madison House and see if James had returned, and then head out to the lake to see his father. He would stop at the Lincoln Hotel and call his supervisor at work to apologize for missing his shift, and to make sure someone down at the barn fed his team of horses; then, since he wasn't scheduled to work the following day, he would spend the night at his father's place.

He made his way back up Denny Hill and went straight to the carriage house. He called out for James, expecting him to still be out. A chair scrapped the floorboards above his head and James shouted down to him to come upstairs right away. Clyde stepped around the idle printing press – it wouldn't be cranked up again until Sunday evening – and climbed the short staircase that led to the upstairs portion of the carriage house where James kept his office and living quarters. The arrangement of furniture was spare at best: along one wall, a desk with an Underwood typewriter on it and a stack of typing paper held down with a large horseshoe; then, right beside this desk, a four-drawer wood filing cabinet, and on the other side of it, another desk, with a pen stand and inkwell and a small stack of the *Seattle Sentry* letterhead and envelopes on it. At each desk, there was a chair on casters and a floor stand for an oil lamp. Tacked to the wall above the first desk was a monthly calendar marked with upcoming events and meetings and beside it three large sheets of newsprint on which James budgeted the stories for the next three issues. On the wall above the second desk was a reproduced photograph of a gray-haired Frederick Douglass with a quote handwritten below it that read, "I wished to learn how to write, as I might have occasion to write my own pass," and next to this an original photograph, taken by Ray, of James in his bathing trunks posing with his fists on his hips while standing on the shore of Lake Washington, and just below the photo the inscription, "James Colter, President of the Negro Swimming Club of Seattle." This was the office portion of the room. On the other side, there was an iron bedstead with a thin mattress and a quilt on top, a battered old armoire where James kept his clothes, a reading chair (with another floor stand and oil lamp on one side, a stack of books and magazines on the other), a washstand with a mirror on the wall, and a small stove identical to the one downstairs. It was plain to see that James's home life and work life were one and the same.

"Come over here," James said to Clyde from the second desk where he sat. He looked rather haggard, as if he had been chasing leads all morning, talking to more people than a person could count on two hands, performing the work of an entire staff of reporters. He swiveled about in the chair and looked up at Clyde with as much seriousness on his face as Clyde had ever seen there – and James, he knew, was a serious man. "I heard from someone that you might've been down by the cut yesterday at the time of the explosion. Is this true?"

Clyde was startled to hear that people were already tying him to the disaster. He wasn't going to conceal anything from James, however, and replied, "I was there. I saw the whole thing. It was terrible. The crew went off somewhere, left the goddamned machine idling, and when one of them came back, the boiler blew. That's it. The whole story. You can quote me if you like."

James kept looking at Clyde. He rubbed his hand over the day-old stubble on his chin and shook his head in a worrisome manner. "Sounds about right to me. But this is the thing, Clyde. I'm afraid others will probably see you as involved somehow and start pointing fingers. Some are already talking up the sabotage angle."

"I saw the papers this morning," Clyde said. "It's a great big lying dodge on the part of Lewis & Wiley."

"Be that as it may," James replied, "I'm letting you know that if I were you, I'd lay low for a few days. Give the reporters time to catch up to the rumor mongering." James stood up and clapped Clyde on the shoulder. "You're one of the most footloose guys I've ever known," he said, and laughed. "It's a good time to make yourself scarce."

WALKING DOWN TO LAKE UNION, CLYDE GREW TIRED. IT wasn't the distances he'd covered that day that wore him down so much as all of the worry and commotion that surrounded his going from here to there and back again. He pushed on, though, knowing he could rest once he reached his father's place.

In just the past couple of years, the area extending from the north side of Denny Hill to the south shore of Lake Union had been thoroughly developed into a mix of modest residences and, with more arriving each year, small manufacturing plants and warehouses. A double line of rail tracks running east-west were laid along the south shore where until recently the Brace and Hergert Mill, one of the oldest mills in the city, had operated. When it finally shut down, its shingle mill operations relocated to Ballard and the lumber mill went north to the township of Everett. Earlier in the decade, the mill had contracted with Clyde's father for a good many of its shingles. And now the mill was closed. The massive old mill barn and surrounding buildings, including a wharf where cargo schooners had once docked and a rail trellis that cut across the south shore's marshy inlet, stood abandoned.

Past the deserted mill, the walk along the east shore became more pleasant. Although activity was increasing all around the lake – including the new gas plant built last year on the north shore, the brewery and the rug factory on the southwest shore, and several new houses on the slope of the east shore – sections of the lake remained almost rural, as they had been when Clyde grew up there. A half dozen years ago, when the city won its case to keep the U.S. Navy from turning the entire lake into a storage basin for its decommissioned warships, the lake was spared. Yet Clyde knew that gradually the lake was being given over to industry – and that small property owners along the lake, like his father, were being driven away.

His father's property still resembled the old homestead it had always been. Although his father had sold off portions of his land over the years (the property values along Lake Union having shot up when the canal connecting it to Lake Washington was completed in '06), his father still retained more than a dozen acres surrounding the small three-room house and the shed where the shingle mill had once operated.

Clyde came upon his father working diligently in the full-acre garden that seemed to grow larger each year. They greeted each other, and his father immediately ordered him to start washing off the beets he'd just pulled from the ground.

"I'm going to the market tomorrow morning," he told him. "To sell this produce."

Clyde picked up the bushel of dark purple beets, carried them to the water pump at the side of the house, and rinsed the caked soil off of them, the cold, purplish-brown water washing over his hands. He laid the beets on the weathered table between the water pump and the garden and returned to where he father was crawling on his hands and knees between a row of beets and a row of radishes.

"You can come if you like," his father said, and pointed to the radishes he'd just pulled from the ground. Clyde picked up the radishes and brought them to the water pump. Clyde wanted to tell his father that he shouldn't go into town, that there might be trouble waiting for him, and that he should just stay put at the homestead for a few days and work in the garden. But he didn't have the heart to tell his father he wouldn't help him, or the will to explain why, and resigned himself to going to the market with him in the morning.

The afternoon's work went on like this until Clyde at last said he needed to rest, that he hadn't come out here to work – eliciting a grumph from his father – and retired to the willow tree along the lake's edge on the opposite side of the house, out of view of the garden. Desiring quiet over company, Clyde stayed out of his father's way the rest of the day.

The next morning his father was up before dawn. He had a pot of coffee on the stove, and by the time Clyde rose from his mat in the loft, his father was outside washing off the four dozen heads of lettuce he'd picked that morning. In various-sized cedar crates constructed of left-over shingles from the old mill, he had already packed the radishes, beets, carrots, cucumbers, plums, strawberries, and three tin pails of elderberries. After Clyde drank a cup of coffee and watched his father finish packing the lettuce into a crate, they loaded all the produce onto the buckboard wagon, harnessed the mule, climbed up onto the wagon seat, and headed into town to the farmer's market.

Pike Street Market had opened in June the previous year, and so far it had been a big success, allowing local farmers to bring their produce to town and sell it directly to town folks as well as to hotels and restaurants. Many farmers occupied permanent stalls in the new open-air market building, while others sold their produce directly from their wagons and pushcarts at the north end of the building. When Clyde and his father arrived, the market was already noisy and crowded, though not nearly as crowded as it would become by mid-morning. Most of the commotion came from the farmers unloading their wagons, lining up their produce for display, sweeping away the unsold fruits and vegetables left to rot on the ground from the day before. The sweet, fragrant scent of the fresh produce mingled with a heavy, pungent odor from the rotting produce and pervaded the cramped market area, mixing with the strong smell of sweat-soaked horse flesh, unwashed men, and wet paving stones. There was shouting up and down the row of tin-topped tables, the farmers' boys shouting greetings to one another, warming up their voices to hawk their produce once the buyers arrived.

While Clyde stayed with the wagon, his father, who had been to the market a dozen times that summer already, found the man who managed the stalls and after paying him the daily fee of twenty cents was assigned a table at the farthest end of the row. Father and son then pulled their wagon as near to their stall as they could get and Clyde began handing the cedar crates of vegetables and fruit to his father, who set them on the table and tilted each one up with an eight-inch wood chock for better display. His father then charred a small wedge of fir bark and wrote out the price of each item on a piece of brown wrapping paper – Elderberries, 20¢ a pint; Beets, 10¢ a bundle; Melons, 5¢ apiece; and so on – and laid the paper in front of that item. Forever the crank, his father insisted he was a gardener, not a farmer on the scale of the Japanese and Italian men who drove all the way in from the townships of Kent or Bothell or took the ferry in from Vashon or Bainbridge Island. Although he needed the money that his modest produce brought in, he could sell at fairly low prices compared to the farmers, and this usually meant that he unloaded everything he had by noon and could then leave, never cutting too sharply into the real farmers' profits.

By nine o'clock the market was teeming with people. Something new at the market since mid-summer was a man with an enormous moustache – Clyde's father called him the Armenian – who would bring in a cart with a wood stove on it and a large vat of oil on the stove to make hot doughnuts right there on the spot. Clyde could never resist the aroma of the fried dough and knew that before long he would have to make his way to the cart to buy a half dozen of the golden-brown cakes. Fishmongers had also begun to set up at the market since Clyde had been there last. Large Chinook and sockeye salmon lay on beds of shaved ice in wooden crates like those his father made. The fishmongers also had clams, mussels, and oysters for sale. One vendor had several geoducks laid out, the meaty necks extruding from their razor shells like massive cow udders. Clyde had eaten boiled geoducks meat several times with the Makah during his childhood sojourn at Neah Bay and remembered his jaw muscles growing sore from all the chewing that was required before he could swallow the tough meat.

With the crates lined up, Clyde let his father take over so he could stroll about the market. At nearly every stall, buyers were inspecting the produce, haggling with farmers over prices, and eventually walking off with a bag of new red potatoes or a bushel of young asparagus or some other fresh produce they would serve their diners or family that evening. There seemed to be two kinds of buyers in the market: the ladies of the house in their billowing skirts, waist trusses, and lofty hats, usually accompanied by a house girl tagging behind to carry the purchases; and the restaurant owners and cooks in their white jackets or just their shirts, with the sleeves rolled up to their elbows, and typically a kitchen boy at their side. Then there were the people who just came down to the market to be part of the commotion, mostly men in derbies and worsted suits who loitered about in small clusters smoking cigars and pipes, watching the haggling that took place as if it were a spectator sport, and addressing one another with some comment or another and then laughing out loud and engaging in a fair amount of backslapping.

Clyde bought a dozen hot doughnuts and began eating them straight from the greasy bag, taking his own sweet time, forgetting the events of the past two days – all of which began with the irrefutable impulse, like a drunk returning to the bottle, to revisit the regrading site – when suddenly, from out of nowhere, two sharply dressed men stepped in front of him, bringing him up short. When Clyde tried to sidestep them, the smaller one, the one wearing an imperial hat, said, "I said, are you Clyde Hunssler?" And that's when it all started.

The pummeling and arrest that followed at the hands of the two bull detectives seemed to be proof of the kind of penalties the city could hand out for resisting the regrading project. Here, too, was proof that he'd been tracked all along as a suspect in the series of sabotagings that had taken place at the regrading sites over the past couple of years. And then there were also the break-ins at the homes of city officials associated with the regrading. Word among the small cadre of reporters who congregated in the carriage house with James had it that Reginald H. Thomson now posted two guards at his home and office around the clock. Clyde knew that he'd long been a suspect in the sabotaging, and maybe the break-ins too, which was partly why he'd avoided the regrading sites for so long in the first place.

Though he would have preferred to stay at his father's place back on Lake Union that morning, Clyde never expected that, right there in the open, two detectives would hammer him to the ground, slam a pistol butt upside his head, and drag him off half-conscious to the county jail. He lay in the backseat of the detectives' Studebaker, gasping to recover his breath and unable to see out of one eye, and worrying that his father wouldn't know what had happened to him and that Maddie might need him back at the boardinghouse. When he tried to sit up, the same detective who had walloped him in the gut moments before and had called him an anarchist knocked him back down onto the seat and told him to stay there. Once they reached the county jail and got Clyde into a cell, the two detectives went to work on him in earnest. He lashed back at them, figuring this was his day to die, and could tell by their cussing and the two uniformed coppers they pulled in for extra muscle, that he was giving them more than they'd bargained for. When they finally had him restrained, handcuffed to a metal ring attached to a spike driven into the floor, they begin grilling him, wanting to know why he'd blown up the steam shovel down at the regrading site two days before. He told them to go to hell and they clubbed him about the shoulders and back some more. Then they wanted to know why he'd been sabotaging the regrading equipment for the past two years, and who'd been helping him. Clyde wouldn't say anything on that score, though, even if it meant he'd never see Maddie or his father or the light of day again.

Five or six hours later – he couldn't tell how much time had passed – the two detectives eased up on him. The next day, though, they were back, working him over just as steadily. And the day after that, more of the same. This went on until a full week had passed. Then they let him be for a long stretch, during which time he was allowed to speak to Erasmo, who told him that he was trying to get him released and that Maddie and his father were both all right. As another month passed, Clyde wondered if, when he'd walked down to the regrading site that morning in early September, he could have foreseen being locked in a rancid cell indefinitely with nothing but a bucket and a blanket during some of the coldest nights of the year, beaten once a week when he wouldn't answer the questions the two detectives hurled at him, nearly starved to death on the watery corn mash and moldy bread he was fed, shouted down or else ignored every time he voiced a grievance, deprived of visitors or any company (even cell mates) for most of his incarceration, and ultimately left to believe that he would probably die in these conditions.

26. Impending Nuptials (1908)

AFTER LOYE'S INJURY, RAY MADE AN EFFORT TO SEE A LOT more of her. Her sprained knee healed, though not entirely, and to her great disappointment she was forced to stop playing on the ladies' basketball team. This left her more time for her studies, so she could finish her Normal degree sooner rather than later, and more time, by Ray's calculations, for him. They would ride the trolley to Lake Washington for a picnic and go canoeing at one of the lake resorts, or take the new streetcar line to Green Lake in the city's northern most precinct and go swimming or wander over to nearby Woodland Park to visit the new zoo with its exotic animals from sub-Saharan Africa. On each of these outings, Ray would update Loye on his plans to open his own photography studio downtown. One day he reported excitedly that he had found the perfect location in a storefront in the relatively new Arcade Building on Second Avenue. His brother had agreed to back him with a loan to help him lease the space and buy new equipment, including a portrait camera, since portraits would be his bread and butter in the business. "Everyone wants portraits," he said. "They want to see if the photographer can make them look better than they think they look already. It's rather sad actually."

He never met Imogen Cunningham for lunch as the two of them had planned, although he did bump into her one day on the street when they were both out lugging their cameras about, taking photographs. When he mentioned to Imogen his plans to open a studio, she replied with the news that she had received a scholarship from her sorority to study photochemistry in Dresden, Germany. Neither before nor after this final encounter did Ray ever mention Imogen to Loye, not even to ask if she knew her from the university. One evening, when they were riding back from Green Lake on the streetcar, he did, however, reveal to Loye how he wished he had photographed her that morning on the porch after the Washington Hotel fire. She seemed genuinely touched by this recollection, and said that if he liked, he was welcome to photograph her anytime.

"I'm sorry the basketball shots didn't come out as well as I expected," he said, leaning in toward her. "Of course I would be honored with another opportunity to photograph such a lovely subject as yourself." And at this small bit of flattery, she reached over and squeezed his hand.

A week later, in his attic room at Madison House, in a mock-up of Ray's planned studio, Loye formally sat for her portrait. At first, Ray took several standard portrait photos of her in her lavish hat – the same one she had worn to Luna Park – while she held her silk parasol over her shoulder or her taffetine fan (closed, then open) at her bosom. He then asked her to remove her hat while he took down the portrait screen (a very neutral gray washed with shades of tan) and adjusted the light from the incandescent lamp that he'd had in the attic ever since Clyde finished wiring the entire house. He shined it more directly on Loye's face and asked her to turn her head slightly and cast her gaze toward the corner of the room. Removing the hat, he felt, was removing an enormous distraction. This partial profile, combined with the shadows it created on her face, accentuated her features wonderfully. He was reminded of Julia Margaret Cameron's carefully posed photographs of women. He also asked Loye to lay down the parasol and fan and place her hands in her lap.

Two days later, when he showed Loye the prints, they agreed that the subsequent photographs were far more becoming in their simplicity than the ones that Loye referred to as "portraits with hat and parasol."

When Ray next invited Loye to his "studio," he told her that he wanted to photograph her without any adornment at all – simply for her natural beauty. He tried several different poses: head tilted up, eyes down, head turned sharply away from the camera, or her gaze looking straight at it. In one of these shots, Loye, becoming playful with all of the posing Ray was asking her to do, gave him her cool, sensuous imitation of Evelyn Nesbit, the chorus-girl wife of Harry Thaw, the convicted killer of her millionaire lover, the renowned architect Stanford White. The simultaneous glint of mockery and defiance and come-hitherness brightening her expression startled Ray. He'd never seen such a look on Loye's face before, or even imagined her capable of such a look.

When he asked her to sit on the window seat that was part of his room's dormer, she happily obliged. Because it was such a blustery autumn day, the light kept shifting from full and brilliant to soft and muted, creating unpredictable shadings across Loye's face and body and playing with her expression. When on an impulse he asked to photograph only her hands, it was Loye's turn to be startled.

"Why my hands?"

"Why not your hands?" He took both of Loye's hands in his own. "Look how supple and strong, delicate and defined." He told her to hold them away from her body and cross them at the wrist. Voluntarily, she unbuttoned her cuffs and rolled up her dress sleeves so that only her hands would be in the photograph and nothing else and held them out as instructed.

"Would you like to photograph any other parts of me?" she asked shyly when he was done focusing his camera on her hands and taking the shot. "How about my neck?" she suggested. "I've always been very fond of my neck."

Ray looked at her as she slowly unbuttoned her turnover collar and folded it away from her neck. She leaned back on the window seat as he brought the camera up close and focused the lens on her throat. As with every shot he took, he asked her to be as still as possible, yet through the viewfinder he could see her breath gently lifting her neck away from the cloth of her dress. He took the photo and when he stepped away from the camera, Loye remained watching him.

"You have a beautiful neck," he said to her, and then watched as she raised her hands and undid the next two buttons on her dress, revealing the smooth plane of skin just below her collar bone and above the rise of her breasts.

Ray placed his camera on the floor and came closer, and when Loye put her hand out to him he took it and she gently pulled him toward her. He laid his other hand on the soft pale skin below her neck and felt her breathing. Caressing her neck, he leaned in toward her as she arched herself forward, and on the warm, sunlit window seat they kissed.

BY CHRISTMAS, LOYE HAD FINISHED HER CLASSES AT THE university and in January was hired by the maverick superintendent of Seattle schools, Frank B. Cooper, to teach fifth through eighth grades at Broadway School on Capitol Hill. The following month, Ray opened his photography studio in the Arcade Building downtown. By June, they were secretly engaged to each other, waiting until Ray could make a trip to Tacoma in late summer to formally ask Mr. Atchinson for his daughter's hand in marriage before they made a public announcement.

He and Loye were in his attic room, kissing and fondling each other in the window seat, casually discussing the best tact to take with her father, when the news of Clyde's arrest reached Madison House. It was a full three days after his arrest when Maddie received the telephone call from Erasmo, who had just learned of the arrest himself from a fellow attorney who worked criminal cases from the county jail. Maddie had been worrying ceaselessly about Clyde's absence for those past three days, but now expressed both relief and horror at learning where he was. As she prepared a good, hearty meal for his return to the house that evening and Loye looked after Ada, Ray and James rushed down to the county jail to meet Erasmo, who had filed a motion with a judge to dismiss the charges against Clyde.

The county jail was a square, one-story brick building without windows, except for in the front. It was located directly behind the central police station, where they had to check in before entering the jail. Erasmo met Ray and James out front and came right out and asked both men if either of them could put up the collateral against a bond. Neither hesitated. Ray had his studio and James his newspaper, and both men offered to sign whatever they had to. Erasmo said that, with their combined collateral, that should be plenty and then led them around the corner to a bail bondsmen he had worked with in the past.

To everyone's horror, however, the presiding judge in the case declared Clyde a flight risk, based on the fact that he'd resisted arrest, and refused to accept Erasmo's motion for dismissal or even to set bail for Clyde. Which meant Clyde would stay locked up. Erasmo was incredulous, and James indignant. Erasmo declared that the court was acting unconstitutionally, while James insisted it was outright criminal. Ray didn't know what to make of the situation. He asked if they could visit Clyde in the jail, and Erasmo said no, that the judge feared Clyde might be part of a faction of anti-government saboteurs and anarchists and therefore would not be allowed free communications with persons other than his legal counsel. The judge even warned Erasmo not to overestimate or abuse his attorney-client privilege.

James said he was going to write an editorial and submit it to the *Argus*, as the editor of the paper, Harry Chadwick, had been urging him to do for quite some time. The *Argus*, he said, had a vastly greater circulation than the *Sentry* ever would. James said he would show how Clyde, first harassed and now persecuted, was being made the scapegoat for the debacle that the regrading of Denny Hill had become. He didn't think it would get Clyde out of jail, but he hoped it might shine the spotlight on the judge whom the city engineer and corporate commission obviously had eating out of their hands.

For his part, Ray didn't know how he could help Clyde. He almost wished he had kept with his reading of the law and had become an attorney so he could join legal forces with Erasmo to free their friend. He thought of his photographs of the regrading and determined, once again, to renew his efforts with the series. Aside from this, the very least he could do – and what he knew Clyde would want most – would be to ensure that Maddie and Ada remained safe and comfortable through whatever was to transpire at Madison House over the next several weeks or months.

IT WASN'T UNTIL THE START OF OCTOBER, WHEN CLYDE HAD been in jail going on two weeks, that Ray decided it was time to buy a ticket on the interurban train to Tacoma, the City of Destiny, to make his fateful visit to Loye's father. He knew that Clyde would approve. So a week prior to his planned trip, he sent a telegram to Tacoma stating that he would be in town on Tuesday and could he meet Mr. Atchinson either at his home, in his office at the bank, or at a location of Mr. Atchinson's choosing. Mr. Atchinson sent back a reply telegram that same afternoon instructing Ray to come to his office.

So exactly seven days after the exchange of telegrams, at the appointed time on the appointed day, Ray walked into the Tacoma First National Bank in his best suit and a brand-new chocolate-brown derby, a fresh polish on his shoes from the shoe-shine stand in the Union Station in

Seattle, and the Henry James walking stick that Clyde had told him he could borrow anytime he needed an extra dash of sophistication. Looking about the marble-lined bank with its vaulted ceiling, he was surprised to see Chiridah behind the thin wrought-iron grille of a teller's counter. She appeared more herself, prettier and healthier than he'd seen her in some time prior to her moving out of Madison House. In fact, she looked much as she did – though more confident and knowing – when he'd first met her after arriving at the boardinghouse some four years ago. He approached her counter and instantly she recognized him, delighted by his unexpected appearance.

The first thing they did after their excited greeting was to commiserate with each other over Clyde's unjust incarceration.

"How is Maddie handling it?" Chiridah inquired.

"She's doing all right," Ray answered. "She's not even so worried about the boardinghouse anymore now that there's Clyde's awful situation to upset her to no end. Sometimes it seems she'd almost rather be done with the house. She'd leave tomorrow if it would secure Clyde's release."

"The poor darling," was all Chiridah could say.

Then Ray asked after her. He refrained from saying anything related to acting or the theater but did say that he had heard good tidings about her through Loye.

"I'm taking classes at the business college and working here part time," she told him with pride. "I think I'll stay in Tacoma for the time being," she added. "Seattle has gotten too big and noisy." She then asked Ray what he was doing there at the bank. "Are you opening an account?"

"You might say that," he said. Then, leaning in close to the counter and lowering his voice, he confided to her his mission in coming to see Mr. Atchinson.

Chiridah could hardly contain herself behind the iron grille separating her from Ray. The teller at the counter next to hers cast a disapproving glance in their direction. Ray commented that he took her excitement as an endorsement of the engagement ... that is, should Mr. A. give his approval. Chiridah promptly asked if the wedding would be in Seattle or Tacoma, and Ray answered that he hadn't thought that far ahead. "Let me show you to Mr. Atchinson's office," she offered, and met Ray at the end of the long counter, gave him a restrained embrace, and led him to a row of offices off to the side of the bank's main lobby and pointed to Mr. Atchinson's office at the very end.

Mr. Atchinson was a stolid, well-groomed man with gray muttonchops and a balding crown. He welcomed Ray cordially into his office and had him take a seat in a maroon leather armchair across from his spacious cherrywood desk. Ray felt as if he were applying for a bank loan and tried to reassure himself that all would go well – his credit may not be outstanding, but it was basically sound.

"Well, young sir," Mr. Atchinson said. "What may I do for you?"

Ray launched into the statement he had been preparing for the past two weeks: giving a testimony of his profound and abiding love for Loye; outlining his professional background, current standing, and plans for future security as a photographer; vowing to care for, protect, and guide Mr. Atchinson's daughter as a loyal and caring husband; and forecasting a prosperous and progenitive household for Loye and himself once they were married.

Mr. Atchinson heard him out without comment, and when Ray was finished, asked him several questions about his family history and the business operations of a photography studio. Finally he said, "And how long do you expect to remain in that boardinghouse where, against my original wishes, the two of you mutually reside? I understand there's been some contention surrounding the proprietress of the house and this business of the regradings in Seattle. The circumstances do not seem conducive to beginning a marriage, to say nothing of a family."

The implied criticism of Maddie – and of himself and Loye – cast by these remarks was unsettling to Ray and threw him off his scripted conversation with Loye's father. He had not thought in any concrete terms about the household he and Loye, once wed, would make for themselves. He knew that Maddie could not likely hold out indefinitely against the regrading and that he and everyone else in the boardinghouse would eventually have to find a new place to live. His photographs of the disappearing Denny Hill neighborhood were evidence of this, to say nothing of the troubles that had befallen Clyde. Every few weeks, the neighbor-hood was diminished by another block or two, and so many of the simple, honest residences that he had photographed, with their stoical inhabit-ants out front staring straight at the camera, were now lost forever. So, yes, it was inevitable that he and Loye would soon have to relocate. Yet he also knew that he could not afford to buy a house in any of the city's expanding residential neighborhoods, especially after overextending him-self financially to open his studio.

Mr. Atchinson cleared his throat and when Ray looked up at him, he said, "I believe the Tacoma First National Bank, upon my recommenda-tion, would be willing to offer you and your bride a *very* low-interest loan toward the purchase of a new home. Mrs. Atchinson and myself, in turn, would see to the necessary down payment."

Ray understood this statement to mean not only that Loye's father had approved their engagement but had just offered, more or less, to buy them a house. He rose from his chair to shake his future father-in-law's hand and in the same instant realized he would now have to tell Maddie that he and Loye would be moving out.

27. Love (1908)

JULY AND AUGUST UNFOLDED SLOWLY AND PROVED TO BE especially tiresome months. For Maddie, the cool days and moist nights of September, when they finally arrived, were a release, a palliative to the drawn-out summer months. But then Clyde was arrested and her whole world was thrown into utter distress. She recalled her worry and confusion over Clyde's initial disappearance for three agonizing days and then her alarm at learning he had been arrested and was being held in the King County jail. She tried to keep a brave face when Erasmo told her Clyde would not be released right away. But she was outraged when she was told that Clyde was not being allowed any visitors other than Erasmo, his attorney.

"How is he?" she implored Erasmo every time he returned from one of his visitations during the ensuing weeks.

"He was roughed up pretty good when they first arrested him," Erasmo told her, being forthright with her, "and the conditions in the jailhouse are not the best, you can count on that. But he's holding up."

Erasmo's reports on Clyde's condition only worsened her distress. Until Erasmo explained to her that the detectives kept questioning Clyde not only about the sabotaging of the regrading equipment but also about Madison House and the other Denny Hill holdouts, Maddie had no idea the police had been watching him so closely or that he'd been a suspect in any crimes. She felt ashamed at her own ignorance – it simply wasn't in her to imagine such things – though she wondered if even Clyde had been aware of his being under such tight scrutiny. She became upset thinking about her own culpability in Clyde's predicament. Her resistance to the regrading, passive as it was, had stirred up all of this trouble. She could not help but feel responsible for the brutality that was being inflicted upon him now as he sat battered and alone in that jail cell. None of this would ever have happened, she imagined, if she had only sold the house and property and relocated to another part of the city, as she now believed she should have done long ago. She knew it would be hard, and probably impossible, for her to forgive herself for the harm that had befallen Clyde, and felt that she would do anything to make the harm stop and keep it from ever happening again. Nothing, not even Madison House, was worth the price that Clyde was paying right now.

According to Erasmo, Clyde was being charged with the murder of the five men who had died in the steam shovel explosion, and yet the city prosecutor refused to move forward with the case, was stalling, denying Clyde a speedy trial. Erasmo claimed this was because the police department and the prosecutor's office didn't have a case against him and were dragging their feet in order to keep Clyde jailed longer so they could continue to question him.

"Even though he doesn't know anything about any of this!" Maddie pleaded, sitting in the one-room office that Erasmo leased in the Pioneer Building.

"They must think he does," Erasmo answered from behind his desk. "And," he added, "I suspect they might see holding him as a way of putting pressure on you."

Such a notion appalled Maddie, though at this point nothing seemed out of the realm of possibility. The whole situation was out of hand. Yet the situation did make her recognize – more fully and more honestly – how much Clyde really meant to her.

OFFSETTING ALL THESE TROUBLES AND THEIR ATTENDANT anguish, October brought the heartwarming (and not surprising) announcement that Loye and Ray were engaged to be married. The wedding was set for the first Saturday in November. Loye had wanted to delay the wedding until Clyde was released from jail and all of the charges against him dropped, which Erasmo assured them would eventually happen. Ray wanted to delay the wedding as well, for the same reason, yet joked with everyone about how he didn't want it to upstage the 1908 presidential election between William Howard Taft and William Cullen Bryant. Unfortunately, Mr. and Mrs. Atchinson were adamant that the wedding take place sooner rather than later – while mortgage interest rates were still low, Mr. Atchinson had explained to Ray, though Ray and Loye both understood this to simply be his ploy, that her parents really just wanted them out of Madison House as soon as possible.

Despite the ongoing crisis involving Clyde, a certain subdued elation over the impending nuptials filled the house for the three weeks following the announcement. It was dampened only a little for Maddie when the inevitable took place, when Ray and Loye, sitting her down in the parlor one evening after dinner, revealed that they had made a down payment (courtesy of Loye's father) on one of the new box houses being built on First Hill and that they would be moving into it on their wedding night. Their house would be in the newly developed Madrona neighborhood, halfway between the Madrona Park on Lake Washington and the new Providence Hospital at the crest of the hill. They couldn't wait to show it to her, they said, to which Maddie replied that she would love to see it. Yet, even though she had fully expected this news and knew that the newly-weds could not possibly continue to live in her old boardinghouse, and that they were extremely fortunate to be buying their own home (as she had done almost a decade ago), her sorrow at losing her two beloved boarders was equal to her joy over their betrothal.

"I'm so happy for you," Maddie said from her armchair, unable to hold back the tears that leaked onto her cheek. "You both deserve it so much and are going to be so happy." She then added, "I suppose it'll be time soon for all of us to find a new place to live."

The following week, with the best intentions, Ray asked Maddie if he could photograph her in front of the boardinghouse, and Maddie almost broke down crying again to think how he was documenting the final days of Madison House. When he tried to comfort her by explaining that he had been sporadically photographing the entire neighborhood in an effort to ensure that a record of Denny Hill remained, Maddie did not know if that information made her feel better or worse. After he posed her on the porch, then on the sidewalk, and then along the side of the house and took several photographs each time, he brought her back into the house and showed her the pictures he had taken of the hill over the past several months. Indeed, many of the building were ones she recognized and that no longer existed. The images made her feel as if she were viewing her own future through some strange lens of the past. She also felt that the photographs of her alone in front of Madison House, without Clyde, inaccurately represented the house, which, in her estimation, would not have existed if not for her and Clyde's mutual efforts.

Ray's photographic record aside, there was no denying that the regrading had very nearly reached the doorstep of Madison House, and Maddie, as proprietress, was touched that all her boarders had hung on as long as they had. Residing on what remained of Denny Hill was trying at best, dangerous at worst. The only remaining access to the house was via Blanchard Street going east to Sixth Avenue, where one could still turn right onto Westlake Avenue heading toward Olive, Pine, and Pike Streets and the rest of downtown Seattle. The south, west, and northwest portions of Denny Hill were gone, obliterated. On three sides of Maddie's property – one block south at Lenora Street, half a block east at what was once the alley between Fourth and Third Avenues, and three blocks north at Wall Street – the hoses and steam shovels daily cut away at the once-stately hill, closing in on the boardinghouse like ferocious termites devouring everything in their path. Although the gas line to the house had long ago been disconnected – which Maddie discovered one morning when she entered the kitchen in the dark and was unable to light the gas lamps – Clyde had successfully wired the entire house for electricity a couple of years ago and fortunately Seattle City Light's overhead lines ran straight down Blanchard Street to the transformer at Seventh Avenue. Furthermore, the water main and sewage lines remained intact – though for how long was anyone's guess – and Clyde (and now Ray and James, while Clyde was in jail) kept the boiler in the side shed in good working order to supply hot water for baths and steam heat as the nights turned colder. Everything considered, it was remarkable that Ray and Loye and James had not fled long ago. That they had stayed on so long without complaint was a testament to their loyalty to Maddie, which in turn had made her all the more stalwart in her refusal to concede to the regrading. Why else would they keep enduring such terrible uncertainty – to say nothing of the inconvenience – unless they believed, as she believed, that there was some hope to save what remained of Denny Hill? Indeed, only a handful of residents, stubborn or luckless or perhaps a little of both, remained on the hill, hunkered in their houses along the northeast side of the hill, the one side that had not yet been attacked by the giant hoses and steam shovels.

With Maddie hopeful of getting Ada admitted to the Academy of the Holy Names of Jesus and Mary, where she would board and attend school in the glorious new building on the east side of Capitol Hill, built after the Sisters of Holy Names were driven from their former location on Jackson Street by the regrading project there, she would soon have only James and Clyde to worry about her. James was still waivering about his future, whether to continue publishing the *Seattle Sentry* or to join the staff of one of the large city dailies. She was particularly grateful to him for his firebrand columns in the *Argus* of late, condemning the regrading project as a land grab on the order of Governor Isaac Stevenson's treaties fifty years ago placing all of the Puget Sound Indians onto reservations. Maddie didn't know if the columns had any effect, she doubted they did, yet it did her good to know that the holdouts were not going to go away so quietly. Ultimately, whatever James's final decision with respect to his career, Maddie knew he would prosper.

She knew, too, that if Clyde were not tried and convicted of murder, if he were not condemned to be hanged or sentenced to the state penitentiary on McNeil Island for the rest of his years – all of which Erasmo continued to assure her would never happen, although she'd seen too much of the government's draconian powers to accept these assurances – if Clyde made it through this ordeal and was finally freed, then Maddie knew he would get by just fine once Madison House was gone. That was the kind of person he was. If left to his own devices, he would always get by. With or without her. As the days Clyde spent in the county jail turned into weeks and the weeks into months, and as the fate of Madison House became more precarious as more of Denny Hill was washed into the bay each day, it seemed to Maddie that her attachment to Clyde grew more apparent – to her at least – and more obstinate. Clyde inhabited her thoughts in ways she'd never fully heeded, or even noticed, before. Whether she had been afraid to acknowledge these thoughts before or whether they had just never been as pronounced as they were now, she didn't know. But they were most certainly there. Apart from her deep concern for his welfare while he was jailed, she missed his presence about the house. From one hour to the next, she wondered what he might be doing right then if he were free, what they would say to each other as they crossed paths throughout the day. And during the lengthening nights, she let her mind stray back and linger on that one afternoon when he'd held her in his arms. She could no longer deny to herself that she would welcome such an opportunity again. She longed for those quiet nights when they used to read aloud to each other, and she wished she could visit him in his jail cell and read to him now. In his absence, and probably for the first time in the nearly eight years that they had lived under the same roof, Maddie realized how much she depended on Clyde's company, his physical proximity, and the humor, calm, and caring that were so much a part of everything he did. She realized she depended on this aspect of Clyde far more than she depended on the countless chores he did for her, and that this dependence had gradually been growing into something more, something stronger, with each passing year. For the past three months, since Clyde's incarceration, when she would hear someone enter the kitchen from the mudroom, she expected it to be Clyde. Even as she walked from the parlor to the kitchen, her anticipation in discovering him there would rise so sharply, despite her knowing better, that to find anyone else was a great disappointment. Indeed, it saddened her that she should only recognize this connection to Clyde, this deeper need for him, under the present circumstances.

Four

28. Release from Jail (1909)

JAMES PUT HIS PRINTING PRESS UP AS COLLATERAL AND Ray all of the new equipment in his photography studio, and then the paperwork for the bail bond to secure Clyde's freedom, five months after his arrest, was completed in under an hour. While James and Ray were made to wait outside the county jail on the sidewalk, Erasmo was led inside by a policeman. Twenty minutes later, by James's watch, Erasmo escorted Clyde out the front door of the jail and onto the sidewalk. His eyes were bruised and his lips swollen, and the cuts on his blanched face had barely begun to close and would most certainly leave scars. Blood was clotted in the forelock of pearly white hair that hung over his forehead. He looked even more pale than usual, as if he had become anemic in jail. He also looked thinner, as though he had barely been fed over the course of his incarceration, and he was clearly unsteady on his feet. Erasmo kept an arm around Clyde's back as he led him down the front steps of the jail.

James hurried up the steps to support Clyde from the other side. Almost instinctively, he knew that Clyde wouldn't have been so badly brutalized if he were not a half-breed. That's how it was, whether in the Deep South or way up here in Seattle: there was always a little something extra for you if you weren't white and you stepped out of line. James figured Clyde was just lucky he wasn't a black man or else he'd probably be dead already.

"Jeez, Clyde," Ray let out at the sight of his friend, "those bastards did a number on you." He offered Clyde the flask of whiskey he had concealed in the inside pocket of his coat, but Clyde waved it away.

"I gave back my fair share," Clyde said. "But they had me outnumbered, that's for sure." He winced as he tried to walk without their help, yet when Erasmo suggested bringing his car around, Clyde said he wanted to walk away from the jail on his own two feet. James admired his spirit, so he and Erasmo stood back and let Clyde hobble down the sidewalk, with Ray right behind them, and two blocks from the jail they came to Erasmo's parked automobile – one of the new gas engine models, a sure sign of his success as an attorney, James thought – and they helped Clyde into the front seat.

Since Clyde's arrest, James had published five columns in the *Argus*, one for each month he was in jail, decrying not only the regrading but also the bullying tactics of Reginald H. Thomson and the corporate commission, in addition to the engineering firm that held the main regrading contract, the private security bulls it hired, the city prosecutor's office, and the county and state judges who bent over backwards on the prosecutor's behalf. One of James's pieces went directly after Judge Ethridge Callister, the presiding judge in most of the civil suits brought forth by Denny Hill holdouts against the city. His condemnation of Callister elicited from Colonel Alden J. Blethen, the publisher of the *Seattle Times* and one of the judge's cronies, a swift and fierce rebuttal, lambasting both James and the *Argus*. This row pleased Harry Chadwick, the *Argus's* publisher and sworn nemesis of Colonel Blethen, to no end. Despite his generally less than flattering views of black people, Chadwick wanted to hire James to be a full-time staff writer for the *Argus*. James appreciated the unlimited column space that Chadwick had allowed him in the five pieces he'd written for him, and felt that his words had softened up the prosecutor's office some so that Erasmo could gain some legal leverage to secure Clyde's release on bail. The charge of murder against Clyde had been reduced to "subversion and conspiracy to riot," which carried a ten-year prison sentence if he were convicted – but at least Clyde wouldn't hang.

Back at the boardinghouse, Maddie started crying when she saw what had been done to Clyde. Even though Erasmo had given her regular reports on his condition, this was the first time she'd set eyes on him in five months. He had been arrested in early September and it was now nearly February. Maddie embraced Clyde, still crying, and sat him straight down at the kitchen table and put a plate of warm beef stew and a chunk of fresh-baked soda bread in front of him, and told everyone else to go back into the parlor or den so he could eat in peace.

James, Ray, and Erasmo followed Maddie's order and retreated into the parlor, while Loye and Ada stayed with Maddie in the kitchen. Erasmo explained to James and Ray that he believed he would be able to get the charges against Clyde dropped within the month, at which time the two men would be released from their obligation to the bond.

"The beating those coppers gave him will probably satisfy them," he said. "Of course, it's appalling that they brought any charges at all against him. They were mostly buying time to hold him in the tank for as long as possible. And now this subversion and conspiracy charge is just to keep him on a short leash. They can yank him in at any time, so Clyde's going to have to play it safe. It's all just bullcrap."

James marveled at what a good lawyer Erasmo was. After Clyde was first arrested, Ray had told him that Erasmo had become a sharper attorney than even their old employer, Ned James (who, according to Ray, was now touring Europe after having lost the state senatorial race). Ray even admitted to a tinge of jealousy over Erasmo's success, knowing that the equivalent success for himself as a photographer was still off in the undefined future. James reassured Ray that he'd done the right thing in pursuing his ruling passion, and added that he was a very lucky man to be married to such a sophisticated lady as Loye and to be living in such a nice new house. When it came right down to it, James had always liked Ray Gruhlki well enough and thought him a more than competent photographer, but he sometimes came across to James as downright spoiled. He would have preferred to tell Ray to buck up, shut up, and take care of the business at hand.

Although Maddie wanted Clyde to go upstairs right away so he could get out of his dirty clothes and she could wash his wounds and clean him up, he insisted on coming out to the parlor after he had eaten and talking about his ordeal. He asked Ray if he still had that flask in his coat pocket and Ray said he would get some glasses so they could all have a taste. Clyde sat on the piano bench – telling Maddie he was too dirty to sit in one of the armchairs or on the sofa or davenport – and thanked the three men again for finally springing him from jail. When James offered a toast to Clyde's freedom, they all four raised their glasses and said heartily, "Hear, hear." Clyde then went on to tell them how the two detectives grilled him hard almost weekly about the steam shovel explosion, starting with questions about the equipment that was sabotaged so long ago, the break-ins that had occurred, his association with Russ Bowles, his attendance at the one and only anarchist meeting he'd ever gone to in his life, his overnight visit to Home Colony, and also – and here he looked at Maddie, who stood with her arms crossed near the threshold to the dining room – about why the owner of Madison House had still not arranged for the regrading of her lot. This, he said, is what stewed him the most.

"What business is it of theirs?" he demanded, as if the two detectives were right there in the parlor with them.

Erasmo put down his glass and said, "It's because we have a lawsuit pending against the city, that's why. And because they're damn thugs."

Clyde explained how he told the detectives that if they thought Maddie's holding out against the regrading had anything to do with the explosion, then they should also be questioning Jules Redelsheimer and the Redemptorist fathers, because they hadn't gone along with the regrading either. As for all the other questions, he answered them straight out: no, he had nothing to do with the sabotaged equipment or the break-ins; no, he wasn't an anarchist (and so what if he were?); no, he hadn't been plotting down at Home Colony or learning to make bombs (he ate their food, listened to a crazy mathematician from Florida, and dug for clams); and no, as far as he knew Russell Bowles was nothing more than a street sweeper with a concern for the average workingman but who mostly talked big and got other people to do his work for him.

When he didn't answer the way the detectives wanted him to, Clyde said in a more subdued tone, they would box him about the head. This comment sent Maddie back into the kitchen crying, and Loye followed after her to console her. Ada had already been sent upstairs to do her schoolwork in her room.

But no matter what, Clyde went on, his answers never varied – he remained truthful to the end. "And after a while I think they just got tired of whacking me about."

James leaned against the side wall of the parlor and, listening intently to Clyde's account of his incarceration, occasionally took a sip of the whiskey Ray had poured for everyone. His friend, he mused, was one tough, bleached-out Injun-Kraut. Then he thought about the columns he'd written in the *Argus*. In the end, he thought, journalism enabled the practitioner to inform the public. By writing for the *Argus*, James felt, with its wide circulation and reputation for muckraking, he'd at least been able to really shout at the offender and get his attention, whereas he wasn't sure he could have achieved this by publishing his columns in the *Sentry*. And so maybe, as much as he hated to admit it, this is why he was seriously considering Chadwick's offer to go full time with the *Argus*.

When Maddie came back into the parlor, she announced that she was going to have to insist that Clyde go upstairs so she could clean and dress his wounds. It wasn't right for the men to keep him talking given his condition, she declared, mustering all her authority.

"I think you should let Clyde get some rest," Loye told Ray.

Clyde was just finishing explaining how during his last couple of weeks in jail the first mate of the schooner *Wawona* had come to the jailhouse every day to recruit men to sign up for the ship's next sailing to the Bering Sea Slime banks. It was cold, hard work out on the small dories hauling in codfish with handlines all day, or else pushing fish about the decks of the schooner, getting them sorted to be filleted and packed in salt below. But according to the first mate, the skipper of the ship predicted big profits this season and was promising a generous share for the entire crew. What's more, any man who wasn't a murderer who signed on to the six-month voyage would have his sentence commuted. Clyde said he considered this offer long and hard, especially given he didn't know if he would ever get out. Who knows, he added, if Erasmo hadn't told him two days ago that he was going to be released on bail, he might be headed to Alaska right now.

Maddie let Clyde finish his story and then repeated her insistence that he go upstairs. No one argued with her, and the men rose from their seats to let Maddie assist Clyde back into the kitchen and up the back staircase. James watched as Ray followed behind them, and as Clyde and Maddie climbed up the stairs, Ray asked if he could get a single photograph of Clyde before Maddie cleaned him up. "Just for the record," he said. "It could be important later on."

Maddie turned about and gave Ray a withering look from the top of the stairs, but before she could say anything Clyde told Ray to go fetch his camera. Ray assured Clyde and Maddie that it would only take a minute and followed them into the attic. *That's the stuff*, James thought, noting Ray's insistence.

LATER THAT WEEK WHEN JAMES LEARNED THAT CLYDE HAD, of course, been fired from his job as a water wagon driver two days after his arrest, he offered to help him out by paying him to go door-to-door to Seattle businesses soliciting advertisements for the *Sentry*. When Ray heard of Clyde's predicament, he also came around and offered to pay Clyde to distribute flyers on downtown street corners advertising the Gruhlki Photography Studio. Clyde thanked them for their generous offers but declined them both. James then suggested that if he were interested, Clyde could probably get work on the grounds of the Alaska-Yukon-Pacific Exposition that was getting ready to open in another few months.

"I heard they're taking applications at the Alaska Building downtown," Ray added. "It's going to be a big deal all right. I already bought two dozen shares of stock in it at a quarter apiece. I put in a bid to be the official photographer, but R. H. Nowell landed the assignment – and a good one it'll be for him, too!"

James didn't mention to Clyde that there would be only six more issues of the *Sentry*. The day after Clyde's release from jail, he had gone down to the *Argus* offices and accepted Harry Chadwick's offer to write for his paper full-time. Along with this decision, he was planning to sell his press, end the *Sentry's* seven-year run, and finally, with his increased earnings, buy a house of his own in the Central District. He decided he would tell Maddie the news first, and then Clyde.

29. To the Lake (1909)

FOR THE WEEK IMMEDIATELY FOLLOWING CLYDE'S RELEASE from jail and his return to Madison House, Maddie didn't have the heart to tell him that she was broke and was going to have to move out of the boardinghouse. She had no other recourse but to accept Ray and Loye's generous offer to move into their new house in the Madrona neighborhood. It was her only option, especially since the regrading now nearly reached the doorstep of Madison House and, she'd been warned, the electricity to the house would be cut off any day now. Ray and Loye had moved into their new home in November immediately following their wedding, a simple ceremony at a church near the University; Ada was now enrolled at the Holy Names school on the far side of Capitol Hill, where she also boarded; and James, her last boarder, bless his soul, had given notice, which meant she no longer had any income from the boardinghouse.

When Maddie did tell Clyde, he showed little reaction, other than to apologize to Maddie for not being able to contribute to the household funds over the past six months. He had a job now at the A-Y-P grounds, he told her, doing carpentry and assorted tasks in preparation for the Exposition's big opening day in June, and he would see to it that she had money from now on. She thanked him and told him she was going to sell most of the furniture in the house, which would tide her over.

It was two days later when Maddie, having not seen Clyde since telling him she was moving out of Madison House, pushed through the kitchen door and found him pouring a glass of water for himself at the sink. He wore a pair of coveralls, like an old farmer. She admired how his looks over the years she had known him had matured – how his boyish features had taken on more weight, more firmness, and how across the shoulders and in the waist his comportment was more that of a man. When she'd first met him, nearly eight years ago, he had been hardly more than a boy, a young man in his early twenties, and now he was approaching thirty, nearly her own age when they'd met. As he leaned against the sink counter and gulped down the full glass of water, he saw her from the corner of his eye. "Ah," he let out, placing the empty glass in the sink basin. "Good water."

"You're a hard worker, Clyde Hunssler." Ever since that afternoon more than three years ago when she'd returned so distraught from the city council meeting and Clyde had comforted her in the carriage house, they had shared an ease and familiarity with each other. The excursion to Luna Park last summer had shown them how much they honestly enjoyed each other's company. Their increasingly open, mutual fondness was clearly based on a sense of commonality between them that had slowly taken shape over the years – despite their obvious differences, which to Maddie were no longer so apparent – and this commonality had only been heightened during the trying period of the regrading and, for Maddie at least, during Clyde's incarceration. Neither she nor Clyde seemed inclined to state exactly what it was between them, where the reciprocal interest lay, the mutual attraction. Rather, it was just there – as it was right now, as they stood together in the kitchen, facing each other, clearly pleased to be sharing this unexpected moment together during what they both recognized as their final days in the house.

"I don't know about that," Clyde said, and looked down at his coveralls. "I know I'm a filthy worker." He paused and sniffed at his shirt collar. "And probably a little stinky too."

"Toss those in the hamper and I'll wash them for you," Maddie offered.

"Or," he replied, "you could come with me to my father's place and I could jump in the lake with a bar of soap and scrub them clean right there. I'm heading down that way anyway, so why don't you come along? He's got potatoes and carrots and some spring lettuce and radishes he wants to cart up to the farmer's market tomorrow, and I told him I'd help."

Ever since his arrest there, Maddie worried about Clyde going to the farmer's market. Yet she considered the invitation. With Ada boarding at Holy Names now, Maddie no longer got to greet her darling girl when she came home from school. Ada was now sixteen, no longer the little girl she'd been when she first came to Madison House. Yet more than ever, Maddie regarded her as her very own daughter, and for this reason she missed her dearly. There were also no boarders to prepare supper for. And there was certainly no point in cleaning house any longer. Furthermore, Maddie thought, it would do her good to get away from the house and off of Denny Hill – what remained of it – for a spell. And even more to the point, she knew that it would do her good to spend an afternoon with Clyde before she moved in with Ray and Loye.

"I think I can leave for a little while," she said.

"Great," Clyde replied, and stepped away from the sink and turned toward Maddie. "We'll take the trolley down Westlake and walk from there. It's not too far really."

"I don't mind," Maddie said, and thought how she would enjoy walking in "the seasonal sublime," as Ray last week had termed the afternoon light as it began to linger and the shadows to shorten and the air to turn more fragrant. She liked the sound of the phrase and figured it had something to do with his photography.

"I can't believe I've never brought you to visit the old man before now," Clyde remarked.

Maddie knew that Clyde and his father had not always gotten along so well and that it had been worse when the old man was drinking a lot in the years immediately after he lost his mill. But that was long ago, and once his father had platted his property into half-acre lots and began selling the lots off for extra income and then commenced his ambitious gardening, he seemed to have gotten back on his feet, and father and son seemed to be getting along better than ever. Apparently, too, Clyde's spell in jail (as well as the still pending charges against him) did a lot to renew the father's concern and affection for his son.

Before leaving the house, Maddie persuaded Clyde to change out of his coveralls and into a clean shirt and pants. Once they reached the trolley stop, it seemed like a waste of a fine afternoon not to walk the whole distance, so they pocketed their nickel fare and began hoofing the two and a half miles down to Herr Hunssler's Lake Union homestead. Although Clyde had resumed his habit of making the walk two or three times a week, Maddie had very rarely had any occasion to come out this way and was startled to see how much the lake's shoreline had changed. Like everywhere else in the city, it was rapidly being built up.

The walk was tiring to Maddie – she had gotten out of the habit of making her daily morning rounds down and back up Denny Hill – yet the exercise felt good. The early afternoon sunlight warmed her face at the same time that a cool breeze blew up from the lake as they reached the south shoreline and began walking east. Clyde told Maddie about his work on the Alaska-Yukon-Pacific Exposition grounds, and she was happy to listen. She knew the job kept him from worrying about the prospect of his having to go back to jail. He told her about the Forestry Building he'd been assigned to work on. "The largest log structure ever," he proclaimed. It had 124 columns made from full-grown Douglas fir trees, 50 feet high and 60 inches in diameter, which had been harvested on the Olympic Peninsula. The column trees weighed as much as thirty tons apiece and had to be lifted with a steam crane and set into concrete piers. "A man told me that a single column contained enough board measure to build a five-room house." He remarked that he was glad they'd put him to work on the Forestry Building and not the Good Roads Building. "After my years of street sweeping and then being fired from the water wagon job ... ," he added, and left it at that. He then went on to describe two pools at the center of the Exposition grounds. The first, called the Cascades, was a long series of six short waterfalls and was underlit at night. It flowed into the second pool, the Geyser Basin, which was a large round pool that spouted a splendid fifty-foot fountain of water from its center. Above these two pools was the massive dome of the United States Government Building. A person standing at its entrance looked out over the two pools, down a wide pedestrian boulevard called Rainier Vista, and straight out at Mount Rainier in all its glory – "Provided the weather's agreeable." When he told her that the Exposition's amusement quarter was going to be called the Pay Streak, Maddie got a kick out of that and said, "Maybe I could get lucky twice!" To which Clyde shot back, "I don't see why not."

He said that hundreds of men were working to get the grounds ready in time for the Exposition's opening on June 1, and that the whole operation was something to behold. Then, as he stared out across the lake with a musing look on his face, he said, "Perhaps you'd like to come with me one day and I could show you around the grounds."

Maddie didn't hesitate. She answered that she looked forward to that day and hoped it would come sooner rather than later. With this invitation, she almost felt as if, in that old-fashioned way, Clyde was beginning to court her. Silly as the idea was, given who they were and all that they'd been through together, it nonetheless appealed to her. Not so much the notion of courting, but of her being courted by *Clyde* and receiving *his* attentions. And perhaps of anticipating the spark that might come of it.

Her response clearly pleased him. He smiled at her and said that he would make sure she wouldn't miss a thing on the tour he would give her, and for the rest of the walk along the eastern shoreline of Lake Union they said very little to each other except to comment on the weather and point out a formation of Canada geese flying overhead.

When they reached the place where Clyde had been born and reared for most of his childhood, Herman Hunssler was exactly where Clyde said he was to be found from early March to late November – in among his vegetable beds. When Clyde and Maddie strolled up and stood on the opposite side of the four-foot chicken-wire fence surrounding the square-acre garden, Mr. Hunssler was bent over inspecting the remains of the viney rows of winter squash. He had on a wide-brimmed straw hat, baggy overalls (just like the pair Clyde had been wearing earlier), and a white shirt that seemed permanently yellowed by perspiration. He didn't notice them until they entered the small swing gate and stood within several yards of him.

"Pa," Clyde called out.

The old man pushed his hands against his knees as if he'd been bent over a very long time and straightened himself up. He turned around and looked at Clyde, but didn't say anything to him. Instead, he removed his straw hat and with a blue kerchief wiped his sweaty brow and the back of his neck. The upper portion of his face was creviced and wrinkled and the lower portion grizzled and gray, as if he hadn't shaved in several days. Perhaps, Maddie thought, he was used to his son appearing from out of nowhere at anytime of the day, which explained why he offered them no greeting.

Based on comments Clyde would occasionally drop about him, Maddie was used to thinking of Clyde's father as a cranky old man. And here the father was, proving himself to be precisely that cranky old man right before her eyes.

"I brought Maddie along for you to meet. And to show her the old homestead."

Mr. Hunssler looked at Maddie through his weathered eyes. "Then go ahead," he said to Clyde, "and introduce us properly."

Clyde seemed to smile in exasperation at his father, shook his head, and stepped up between Maddie and his father and said very formally, "Madison Ingram, this is my father, Mr. Herman Hunssler. Father, please meet Miss Madison Ingram, owner and proprietress of Madison House, where I've been privileged to reside for the past . . ." He looked at Maddie. "Seven years?"

"Almost eight," Maddie said, while Mr. Hunssler stepped forward and after brushing his palm on his coveralls, extended his right hand to Maddie. "Pleased to meet you, Miss Ingram." Maddie shook his rough hand and noticed he was missing a couple of fingers.

"We call her Maddie," Clyde said.

"I'll let the lady decide how she'll allow a total stranger to address her," his father retorted, and looked kindly to Maddie to resolve the matter.

"Please, Mr. Hunssler, *Maddie* will be fine," she said. "It's a pleasure to meet you as well."

Mr. Hunssler turned to Clyde. "Well done, son. Now let's sit in the shade and get acquainted."

They all three walked from the freshly turned garden, across a grassy yard of sorts, and toward the house. Weathered remnants of cedar shakes and shingles from Mr. Hunssler's former mill still littered the property after all these years, and sawdust drifts remained at the base of the small frame house that resembled a large shack more than it did an actual house. The tar-papered back of the house faced the road and the front of the house looked out toward the lake. A post-and-beam overhang with sheet metal laid over the top extended from the door. Strewn about under the overhang were several mismatched chairs and a couple of side tables patched together from shingles. From the corner of the house where she stood, Maddie could see two more chairs beneath a weeping willow near the lake's edge, the tree's droopy, sinewy limbs dangling out over the water, its tiny new leaves tinted bright green in the spring light.

"Take hold of another chair, Clyde, and we'll go sit under the tree there," Mr. Hunssler ordered his son. His accent, Maddie thought, sounded both German and English, though it was tempered by his general taciturnity.

Clyde carried an old stick chair, its wicker seat and back coming undone, down to the willow tree, where his father and Maddie had already seated themselves in the more sturdy, though old and weather-worn straight-back chairs. Throughout the afternoon, the breeze off the lake had picked up, yet coming off the sun-drenched water as it did, it felt both warm and cooling at the same time. The abrupt rise of Queen Anne Hill across the lake was almost hazy in the afternoon sunlight. A small steamer, a tug boat, and several skiffs with sails crisscrossed the breeze-rippled waters, and as soon as Maddie and Clyde and his father were seated, a flotilla of ducks and geese began swimming toward them. Maddie found the peaceful scene soothing. Clyde and his father seemed content to simply be still and look out quietly at the water, as if this were their regular routine, and so she fell in with what she assumed was their custom and did the same. At one point she closed her eyes and even nodded off, only to be awoken by Clyde's father shooing away a large gray-and-white Canada goose that had waddled ashore and was coming toward them.

She didn't know how long they had been sitting beneath the willow tree when Mr. Hunssler spoke up and said, "There's a patch of black morels not far up the shore I want to harvest and bring to the market tomorrow."

Maddie blinked her eyes open and sat up in her chair. She looked to Clyde, who apparently understood that his father was asking for help in picking the mushrooms, and looked to Maddie and asked, "What do you say? Not too tired from the walk, are you?"

"No," she said. "I just needed a little catnap, like they say Thomas Edison always takes. I would love to pick mushrooms with you."

They sat a few moments longer, and Clyde asked his father if he'd been feeding the geese to get them so friendly. Mr. Hunssler answered that he'd just begun fattening them up with bread scraps and that in a couple of months they'd be good and plump for eating. His father then stood up from his chair, went over to the small shed beside the house, and came back with three metal pails.

"Follow me," he said, and Maddie and Clyde stood up and followed Clyde's father down a path to a section of the lakeshore that appeared to have been cleared long ago but with many of the logs left on the ground and now covered with moss and sprouting hemlock saplings. Clyde's father explained how an old Finn by the name of Ilke Hästö had owned the property for many years but had sold it to Mr. Hunssler thirty years ago when he gave up on stump farming and became a candlemaker in town. Clyde's father, though, had never gotten around to doing anything with the property and it was now one of the lots he hoped to sell off. Clyde then corrected his father by explaining to Maddie how fifteen years ago the property was thick with alders, which his father had harvested, then stripped, sawed, and planed them, and eventually worked the hardwood into a dozen hutch cabinets that he sold to a furniture dealer downtown.

Mr. Hunssler's only response was to hand Maddie and Clyde each a bucket.

"For whatever reason," Clyde went on, "the property's been sprouting these black morels every spring and Pa figured out last year that he could get top price for them at the market."

With Clyde's help, Maddie began to easily spot the conical-shaped mushrooms. They appeared in small clusters, often partially concealed by an old log or else in an open patch of rotting leaves. Their frilly heads seemed almost charred, as if they'd been in a fire. Their yellowy stems, though, were firm, and it took a bit of effort for her to reach down and snap them off at their base.

As the three of them set about harvesting the mushrooms, they worked in almost complete silence. But Clyde did tell Maddie how in the summer he and his father would also pick salmonberries and elderberries on the property.

Mr. Hunssler was the first to fill his pail. He walked over to where Maddie and Clyde were picking side-by-side, and said, "Not bad for city folks," after looking down into their pails.

"Does Mr. Patten still make his elderberry wine?" Clyde inquired, having told Maddie how good the berries were for jelly and wine.

His father reached down and picked a small cluster of black morels that Clyde had missed. "Of course he does. We'll have a taste back at the house."

Clyde told Maddie how the first time he'd ever gotten drunk it was from drinking Mr. Patten's elderberry wine, the second time was from drinking Mr. Patten's homemade applejack, and the third time from drinking Mr. Patten's blackberry brandy. Clyde said that Mr. Patten picked the elderberries for his wine from this very same spot, since his houseboat was moored down the lakeshore just the other side of this very lot.

"I let him pick them even though they're rightfully my berries," Mr. Hunssler volunteered. "Just as these morels are mine."

"You're not thinking of going into the wine-making business now, are you, Pa?"

"Noooo," Mr. Hunssler said. "That's why I let Robert pick them."

By the time they finished picking the black morels, the sun had gone down, and though the sky still glowed orange over Queen Anne Hill, the lakeshore was quickly becoming dark. They returned to the house and while Maddie and Clyde sat in the chairs beneath the overhang, Mr. Hunssler brought out a smooth cedar shingle stacked high with slabs of smoked halibut and washed and cut carrots and radishes. He set the shingle on one of the makeshift tables, and then lit an oil lamp and hung it from a hook set in one of the overhead beams. He brought them each a small glass tumbler, popped a cork from a bottle, and filled each glass with a full draught of Mr. Patten's dark blue elderberry wine. While Maddie and Clyde nibbled at the halibut, carrots, and radishes and sipped the sour-sweet wine, Mr. Hunssler sorted through the morels they'd picked and dusted the dirt off of each one with a horse-hair paintbrush before setting it gently into a shallow wood crate. He then finished off his tumbler of elderberry wine in three takes, stood up, and looking a bit impatient announced that he was going over to Robert Patten's houseboat to bring him some mushrooms and would be back shortly. And just like that, without so much as a farewell or goodnight, Clyde's father headed away from the house and back down the path.

"Will he be all right?" Maddie asked, as the old man disappeared into the dark.

Clyde broke off a large chunk of halibut. "He'll be all right," he said, and put the halibut into his mouth. "He won't be coming back, though," he said, still chewing, "at least not any time soon," and washed the halibut down with a swig of elderberry wine.

MADDIE AND CLYDE SAT BENEATH THE OVERHANG IN THE quiet of the night for a long time after they finished eating the halibut, carrots, and radishes and drinking the wine. The full tumbler of wine that Maddie drank flushed her cheeks and made her feel snug and just a little bit sleepy. She laughed when Clyde recounted some of the escapades his father and Robert Patten had had over the years, such as the time they tried to row a leaky old punt Mr. Patten wanted to salvage from the abandoned Western Mill on the west shore of the lake, but how it sank before they could reach his father's property in it. "They're lucky they didn't drown," he said, describing for Maddie the two old men thrashing away in the water after the punt went down about fifty yards from the shore.

As the night closed in on them and only a few lights across the dark lake were visible, Maddie turned to Clyde in the lamplight beneath the overhang and watched his profile as he looked out at the water. Her tiredness from all the walking they'd done, combined with the tenderness she'd been feeling toward Clyde all afternoon, soon overtook her, and so when he turned and saw her watching him and slid his chair closer to hers, she let her body lean into his and rested her head on his shoulder. When she raised her head after a few moments to look at him again, he gently placed his hands around her face and leaned down and kissed her. It was what she wanted. His lips felt full and plush and effused with warmth, and she lingered in the kiss as long as she could. When he pulled his face away from hers and looked into her eyes, she smiled sweetly at him and reached her hand around the back of his neck and pulled him to her again.

It seemed suddenly as if the entire past four years – since that afternoon he had held and comforted her in the carriage house – were just a fleeting prelude to this moment. The fullness of their feeling for each other, and the recognition of that feeling, could no longer be restrained.

Except for a brief and unlikely encounter with Asahel Curtis shortly after they had both returned from the Yukon and had happened upon each other on a downtown street, Maddie had not been with a man in nearly a decade, not since her husband had abandoned her. But none of that mattered now, not in comparison to what she felt toward Clyde, the person with whom she'd shared the past eight years of her life, the one person she knew she could always count on, and whom in return she could care for and look after. This man, she now thought to herself, this strange and beautiful man – whom she loved.

Clyde took her hand in his and guided her through the low doorway and into the house. "We'll stay here for the night," he told her, and without saying anything, with just a look, she let him know that she consented. He guided her to a wide, handmade ladder that led up to the loft, and Maddie, gathering her skirt and petticoats in one hand, climbed ahead of Clyde while he held the ladder steady. When she was in the loft, she looked back over the edge at him.

"Aren't you coming up?"

Clyde did not answer except to step up the ladder and tumble into the loft beside her. Maddie laughed as he tickled her beneath the ribs and tugged her onto the goosefeather mattress that was in the corner of the loft. She kissed him lightly on the lips, and then again more firmly, luxuriating in the kiss as he pulled her body to his. She undid the buttons of his flannel shirt and pushed the shirt off his shoulders. His arms and chest seemed almost to glow in the near absolute darkness. His body was lean and solid, and Maddie stroked his chest with her cheeks and lips and breathed in his strong, sweet scent. He rolled her onto her back and she let him unbutton her collar and waistshirt and untie the bow at the top of her lace corset cover. As he did so, she closed her eyes and felt the light touch of his fingers unbinding her from her garments. She ached for the first full touch of his hand to her breasts, for the moist kiss of his lips, and opened her eyes just as he was inclining his head toward her. She stroked the back of his head with one hand, his long white hair, and with the other reached down below his waist and pressed the firmness she discovered there.

They continued to undress each other – the first time Maddie had ever been fully undressed before a man. She lay entirely naked beneath him, inviting the full weight of his body onto hers. Her passion was fed by both the newness and the familiarity of Clyde's body next to hers, his body a part of her own. A combined light seemed to emanate from them, to illuminate the space surrounding them on the mattress, and to guide their reciprocal caresses. They looked into each other's eyes and moved slowly, steadily, and soon Maddie experienced an elation with Clyde that she had never known before, a lingering, exquisite moment that he clearly shared in ... followed by an ease and restfulness into which the two of them simultaneously submerged as into a warm, fragrant pool.

Beneath the weighty wool blanket that Clyde pulled over them, Maddie slept peacefully in Clyde's arms, not stirring once the entire night.

THE NEXT MORNING, THE FAINT GRAYISH LIGHT AND THE steady rhythm of the rain on the roof awakened her. It was raining heavily outside. She sat up from the mattress, pulled the wool blanket to her neck, and looked over the side of the loft to see Clyde putting a block of wood into the stove below. When he looked up and saw Maddie watching him, he climbed the ladder and reached forward and kissed her.

"Good morning," he said.

"Good morning."

He kissed her again.

"I'll have breakfast ready in just a short while."

"Where's your father?"

"He probably stayed at Mr. Patten's once it started to rain. Just as well, too," he said and smiled at Maddie, then started back down the ladder. "I'll let you be now."

Maddie could smell ham sizzling and flapjacks frying and coffee steaming as she dressed in the loft. She felt absolutely no remorse for her decision to stay the night with Clyde. She could no more entertain remorse or reproach herself over what had been the most exquisite, most cherished night of her life than she could wish the night had never happened. It *had* happened. And it was a fine and wondrous thing.

Despite the rain outside, the first real spring showers, the small house was well heated by the wood stove below. It was so warm even that Clyde left the door open, allowing a full view out to the yard. Maddie came down the ladder and looked out through the rain pouring off the overhang. She could see the lake but not the opposite shore, which was obscured in a thick gray cloud that sat on the water. Clyde said that if she were cold he would close the door, but she told him she wasn't cold at all, and that she enjoyed the smell of the rain. He then offered her his father's wool-lined canvas coat to put over her shoulders, which she accepted.

Clyde put two plates on the table next to the stove and on each plate laid a slice of pan-seared ham and a large oval flapjack covered with melting butter and brown sugar. He also filled a tin mug with coffee for each of them. They ate without speaking, occasionally gazing out at the rain before taking another bite of ham or sip of coffee. Maddie could not remember when she had ever felt so contented. Perhaps when she had first arrived back in Seattle from Alaska, though even then a certain loneliness and apprehension had tempered her joy. No, not even that experience could compare to the fullness she felt now. When they finished eating, Clyde retrieved the wool blanket from the loft and they took their coffee out to the chairs under the overhang and sat side by side with the blanket draped over their laps. For a long time they sat like this and watched the rain.

"It's pretty," Maddie said, and put the tin mug on the ground and pulled the blanket up to her shoulders. "Where will you go?" she then asked Clyde after another moment's pause, keeping her gaze on the lake, knowing full well that he had already turned in his seat to look at her. The question just came out, and although she almost wished it hadn't, she knew that it had to. Perhaps she just regretted her poor timing in asking it now. Yet her sudden and full recognition of how thoroughly in love she was with Clyde seemed to require that she ask it.

For several moments he did not respond. "I don't know," he said finally, and hesitated before adding, "There're many places we could go."

Maddie didn't know what to say to this and let the exchange end there, and when Clyde turned forward again, she leaned her shoulder into his and let herself rest there.

By late morning the rain eased up and by noon it had stopped altogether. Though the ground was thoroughly soggy and the trees still dripped heavily, Maddie and Clyde decided it was time to venture back up Denny Hill to the boardinghouse. Of what came next, she was uncertain, but this much she knew: her trust in herself – and in Clyde – was whole.

30. Final Stand (1909)

WHEN CLYDE WAS NOT WORKING AT THE A-Y-P GROUNDS doing carpentry, making plaster-cast statuary, assembling and dismantling scaffolding, clearing woods and brush, or setting fences, he spent as much time as possible with Maddie. Today, however, was an exception. Today he was moving Maddie's few remaining furnishings – after selling most of them – out of Madison House and into a storage facility, and then later, with Ray's help, moving Maddie into Ray and Loye's new house on Twenty-Sixth Avenue between Union and Spring Streets. Maddie, who had been stoic up to the very end but on the morning of the move became suddenly distraught, was spending the entire day with Loye, visiting her parents and Chiridah in Tacoma. The move was also difficult for Clyde, yet the physical task of it kept him from dwelling too much on its significance. He knew that the life he'd known for the past eight years was gone for good, that the future for him and Maddie remained unclear, and that there was very little he could do about it. To himself, however, without consulting with Maddie on the point, he had resolved to remain in Madison House to the very end. It seemed, on principle, the least he could do.

Ray and Loye's house was one of the new box houses being built all over the city, from the University District across the top of Capitol Hill all the way over to Mount Baker. It was a simple yet sizable house, designed for the city's expanding middle class of business owners, office workers, journalists, and lawyers. It sat on a quarter-acre lot raised slightly above the street, a clean, lovely street lined with grass median strips and recently planted maple saplings. Theirs was a rectangular, two-story structure with a hip roof. The entry was located to the right of the first floor and had a small covered porch just wide enough for getting out of the rain and supported by two unadorned wood columns. Above the front door was a glass transom, and set into the wall to the left of the door was an octagonal window about the size of a serving platter. There were three bedrooms and a bath upstairs, and downstairs a parlor, a dining room, and a kitchen. There was also a basement for the boiler, as well as enough room down there for Ray to set up a darkroom. From the back of the house, by either peering out one of the windows or just standing in the yard, one could look out over downtown Seattle and all of Elliott Bay.

Just three weeks earlier, Clyde and Ray had carried a five-piece parlor suite, which included an automatic reclining Morris chair, into the house from the motortruck that had delivered the suite from Schwabacher's Department Store. The golden oak suite, covered in Verona plush, had been a wedding gift from Ray's brother, who was a floor manager now at the store. (Not coincidentally, Ray had recently secured a photo assignment from the department store as well.) That same day, Clyde and Ray had carried a large new rolltop desk into the den and a complete bedroom suite into the upstairs master bedroom, both presents from Loye's parents, who, Clyde suspected, had also made it possible for Ray and Loye to buy their new house.

Today's moving of Maddie's belongings was far easier. She'd sold nearly everything she owned, which hurt Clyde to see. Yet no matter how much he reasoned with her, he couldn't dissuade her from doing so. After moving the piano (saved for Ada), the reading chairs, and a desk into the large new Bekins storage warehouse built recently on the landfill over the old tideflats, he and Ray had only a trunk of clothes and the old straight-back chair with the barley- twist legs to transport to the Twenty-sixth Avenue house. It was Clyde's one day off from work at the A-Y-P grounds, and given the circumstances, about as morose a day as he could imagine. Nonetheless, the moving at last finished, he was relieved when he and Ray could sit down in the Adirondack chairs in Ray's backyard, open a bottle of beer, and watch the sun set behind the Olympic Mountains. By late afternoon, Maddie and Loye had returned from Tacoma, but then Maddie had insisted on making one last run to Madison House to retrieve, as she explained, the English Delft punch bowl that was to be her belated wedding present to the newlyweds and which she'd forgotten to pack. When Clyde told her he would accompany her, she insisted on going by herself.

Tired and sore, Clyde relented. Almost two months since his release from the county jail, his body still remembered the beatings he'd suffered during the interrogations of him. To this day, when he moved the wrong way, twisted too abruptly to one side, he could feel a quiver of pain in his lower ribs where the detectives had pummeled him. When they'd gotten him to the police station that day after sucker-punching him in the market, he was just beginning to get his senses back. As soon as they'd uncuffed him and tried to strip search him, he came to more fully and, deciding it was as good a day as any to die, started flailing at the two detectives, thrashing them both pretty hard before three uniformed coppers stormed into the room and beat him down with their nightsticks. When he came to again, they had him in handcuffs and leg irons in the corner and could wallop him with their boots and fists as they pleased. They let him lie in the barren cell for most of the next two days, feeding him a plate of corn mash at night, and finally, when he was somewhat clear in his head again, but pretty well bloodied and bruised, they started questioning him about the explosion, slapping him upside the head and jabbing him in the ribs with their nightsticks whenever they didn't like his answers. This procedure went on about once a week for the first couple of months, and then either because the dicks and the uniformed men grew bored with beating him or had come to the conclusion he had nothing to tell them, they let up on him. For the next few months he remained isolated in his cell, received visits by Erasmo every other week, and at one point came down with a fever and a case of the shivers that he thought would do him in, but which finally broke several weeks before his release. Then, in the days immediately following Erasmo's news that the murder charges were going to be dropped and new charges of subversion and conspiracy would be filed against him, but that the judge had nonetheless agreed to grant him release on bail, the detectives resumed their once-over of him. This time, their beatings contained more threats than questions.

"We see you anywhere near the regrading equipment and you'll be going to meet the Great Spirit in the sky," the bigger of the two detectives said, and whopped Clyde in the back of the head with a leather-bound police blotter.

Even then, Clyde managed to sneak in a bruising kick or two to the shins of the detectives, which cost him an incisor and a bloody cut on his inner cheek where the second detective swung the blackjack across his face.

When Erasmo, James, and Ray hauled him out of jail two days later and took him home, he was so glad to get out of there that he thought maybe he wasn't so badly hurt. Only when he woke the next day in his bed in the attic in Madison House and could barely move did he realize he was mistaken. If not for Maddie's tending to him for the entire next week, he didn't know if he could have ever gotten out of bed again. It was her tenderness toward him, then and all the times previous, that he recalled when he followed Maddie into the loft at his father's place that night back in early March.

All this Clyde remembered while sitting on the porch with Ray drinking beer, feeling the lingering ache in his side, and anticipating Maddie's return to Ray and Loye's house.

WHEN CLYDE SAW HOW GRIEF-STRICKEN MADDIE WAS UPON her return from Madison House, and as he observed the despondency that descended upon her in the weeks following her moving in with Ray and Loye, he wished he'd joined with the Jackson Street man in trying to stop the regrading through more direct and covert means. Maybe together they could have caused enough damage to make the engineering companies withdraw, to cause the city to cease viewing the project as profitable, to buy time for city leaders to realize that Denny Hill was not an obstacle to progress but a genuine attribute to the city, the way Nob Hill and Russian Hill were to San Francisco. Maybe others would have joined them once if they saw what risks the two men were willing to take to preserve the neighborhood, and what damage they were capable of inflicting. He feared this piercing doubt over his own inaction would remain with him long after Madison House and Denny Hill were gone.

Since the day in March when he first brought Maddie to meet his father, they had made return visits once a week. Although his father's property was increasingly being encroached upon by lakeshore development, it had been a haven from the devastation being visited upon Denny Hill during Maddie's final weeks in Madison House. She and Clyde helped his father plant his beans, cucumbers, beets, squash, and melons. Occasionally, and especially if his father was off on one of his visits to Robert Patten's houseboat, which he did regularly to help Mr. Patten finish off last year's stash of applejack, Clyde and Maddie would stay the night in the loft. During this short period, Maddie had also invited him to share her bed with her at Madison House. But with her living with Ray and Loye's now, all this came to a stop.

Clyde wished they could at least continue to visit his father's homestead every now and then. But whenever he suggested this to Maddie, she always declined, saying she no longer felt right doing so. He remembered their last visit there, about three weeks ago, when she'd asked him to tell her more about his father's shingle mill. They were sitting by the lake's edge, tossing bread crumbs to the ducks and geese. The imminent loss of Madison House made Clyde reflective about the loss of his father's once-prosperous mill. He told Maddie it was now almost six years since the last shingle had been made, four since his father had torn down the large open-air barn in which the saw had been kept. He pointed to the lumber from the barn that was still stacked where the barn had once stood, slowly rotting. Clyde said how he didn't miss the work of the mill operations, but that he sometimes missed the overwhelming smell of the Western red cedar that used to pervade the property. Sometimes there would be a fog of dust in the air around the mill so thick it was difficult to see. The cedar dust would coat his sweaty white skin, giving him a light reddish tint throughout the day. It would get deep into his scalp, around his eyes, in his ears, up his nostrils, on his tongue, until by the end of a day spent hauling bolts of shingles from the barn to the wagon, he could barely see, hear, smell, or taste anything other than cedar dust. After knocking off work for the day, he would jump in the lake to wash it off, but would have to swim a good ways out, past the scrim of oil and dust that coated the water's surface along the lakeshore, if he really wanted to get clean.

Maddie then asked how his father had lost his two fingers, and Clyde said that it was simple: the saw blade was very sharp. He said that after his father lost his first finger to the saw, he rarely let Clyde operate the machine again. Granted, the Caldwell Bros. Shingle Machine was highly effective in cutting the soft but brittle cedar blocks into neatly edged shingles, but it could slice a man's finger off, and sometimes a whole limb, as easily as cutting through a blade of grass.

Clyde recounted to Maddie how he was there when his father lost his second finger to the saw. Although his father was as careful a shingle weaver as ever worked a mill, there wasn't a sawyer in all the Pacific Northwest who wasn't missing one or two digits on either hand. The law of averages didn't favor the shingle weaver. His father, he said, could tell of men with four finger stumps and a thumb, and that's all. A custom-carved hand like that, it turned out, was ideal for pushing a wood block through the saw.

Clyde said his father lost his second finger right after a building spurt in San Francisco had spiked the demand for lumber and shingles to be shipped to California. His father, Clyde, and Lester, a full-blooded Duwamish whom his father had hired on, were working eighteen-hour days to fill the orders coming in. It was late evening and even though the open shed let light in during the day, there was still no electricity out to the property and his father wouldn't allow oil lamps within a hundred feet of the cedar logs or shingles for fear of starting a fire. His father was so accustomed to the saw that he used to say he could operate it blindfolded, but when you're dealing with a blade that's spinning 2,000 rotations per minute, you don't press your luck – which was exactly what he was doing as the night grew darker.

Lester handed the cedar blocks to his father, who milled them, while Clyde stoked the steam-powered engine that turned the belts that kept the blades whirring. His father fed the saw like he was just another cast-iron component of the massive machine. With his left hand, he pushed the cedar block into the blade and sliced the block into roughly even-sized shingles, and then with his right hand passed each shingle through the trimming saw and tossed the finished shingle into a pile next to the machine for Clyde to collect and stack into bolts of twenty shingles apiece.

The whole operation moved along smoothly for a couple of hours until, just when it was nearly too dark to see in the shed, Clyde heard his father cuss fiercely over the noise of the saw and when he looked up saw him holding his right hand at the wrist with his left hand and blood pouring down both forearms.

"Shut it down," his father shouted. "Shut it down, goddammit."

Clyde hustled around to where his father stood and threw the shut-off switch and then hustled to the boiler and opened the release valve. Lester had rushed over to his father and was helping him knot a piece of bundling twine around the stump of his father's missing middle finger. His father didn't fidget, and hardly even winced, but just watched, holding his hand upright at chest level and observing Lester's work. He could have been thinking, *Well, there goes another one*, though most likely he was worrying how he was going to cut the rest of the shingles to fill the order in time.

He looked over at Clyde. "Son, bring me that bottle of whiskey from over there in the corner." The whiskey was kept on a shelf beside the oil can and tools just for emergencies such as this. Clyde brought the bottle over, uncorked it, and held it up to his father's mouth for him to take a slug from it. "Another," his father said, and Clyde tipped the bottle up again.

Although Lester had squeezed off most of the circulation to his father's severed finger, it was still bleeding. Clyde could see the raw bone that had been cut cleanly just above the large, second knuckle. He took his shirt off and wrapped it about the finger stump. With Lester on one side of his father and him on the other, they brought him out to the wagon that was half-loaded with shingles, the mule already harnessed and waiting to go. They set him down on the buckboard and put the bottle of whiskey between his legs. Although fully conscious, he'd stopped cussing and seemed somewhat subdued now, perhaps from the loss of blood.

"I'll finish milling what's left of the cut blocks," Lester said to Clyde.

Hearing this, Clyde's father shouted from the back of the wagon, "It's down for the night, Lester. You hear me? Don't operate that machine by yourself."

Clyde looked at Lester. "You heard him. Just bundle what's there and we'll mill the rest at first light."

"That's right," they heard his father say, though less forcefully than just a moment before.

Clyde climbed onto the wagon seat, released the break, and snapped the reins on the back of the mule. The only doctor in the vicinity, the company doctor for the big Brace and Hergert Mill, who had probably sewn more sawed-off fingers than any doctor in all of Seattle, lived half way around the lake on the west shore.

The very next morning, his father was back at the saw while Lester fed him blocks and Clyde stoked the boiler and bundled the shingles. His stump was bandaged and he worked more carefully, yet by noon they had the wagon loaded and Clyde and Lester were delivering the shingles to the Seattle Lumber Company near Smith's Cove, where they would be loaded on a ship bound for San Francisco.

Clyde told Maddie that, for better or worse, that shipment marked the beginning of the end of his father's shingle mill. Henry Yesler's mill, the biggest in the city, had already shut down almost two decades earlier, and rumor had it that the Brace and Hergert Mill would close soon too. The city was just growing too fast to accommodate small-time mill operators like his father. The big mills were now in Ballard, and after his father sold off his equipment, he went to work in one of the Ballard mills, cutting fir planks for street pavings. When the city stopped using wood planks and started paving its streets, he was laid off. It was about a year later that he took up gardening.

JUST TWO WEEKS PRIOR TO MOVING MADDIE OUT OF MADISON House, Clyde had done the same for James. The final edition of the *Seattle Sentry* had come off the large press the previous Thursday. The press's hand-cranked canisters stopped turning, and for the first time, James accompanied Clyde on his predawn rounds to distribute the paper to the newsboys at their appointed corners throughout the city. James had accepted a city desk position with Harry Chadwick at the *Seattle Argus*, perhaps the city's most progressive (and most contrarian) newspaper. While Chadwick was a notorious crank and even something of a bigot, as James explained to Clyde the morning they made their rounds, he was going to give James the kind of editorial control that Horace Cayton would not, which meant that James would continue to write on issues involving Seattle's colored population in the manner he deemed right and necessary. Plus, Chadwick paid a lot better. Wth the money James made from selling his press to a printing company in West Seattle, he was able to put a down payment on a small bungalow in the Central District. He told Clyde that he was always welcome at his house and that he was a lifetime honorary member of the Negro Swimming Club of Seattle, which was preparing for its fourth season come summer.

Now, with first James and then Maddie gone, only Clyde remained at Madison House. To begin the assault on the highest points of Denny Hill, which entailed roughly a two-block area around Madison House, the regrading crews had mounted the giant hoses onto derricks so that they could blast at the cut either at a level or from above. Two new steam shovels, identical to the one that had blown up last summer, were also brought in. City officials had begun clamoring about the necessity to bring the regrading of the hill to a speedy conclusion, well in time for the throngs of visitors expected to pour into the city for the Alaska-Yukon-Pacific Exposition opening in June. Seattle wanted to put on its best face, and as the mayor declared, having "spite mounds" rising from the street would just not do. Not only would the regrading of Denny Hill need to be completed, but the entire city was going to have to spit and polish itself into a bright shine for the visiting masses. Drunkards and Indians were shuttled off the sidewalks and into designated flophouses; alarmed city officials, spurred by rumors of rats spreading the plague throughout the city, closed off the underground streets in Pioneer Place and put out a dime-a-head bounty on the rodents. Though Clyde anticipated the opening of the Exposition with enthusiasm, the attitude and actions of the city leaders proved to Clyde that they were more concerned with impressing outsiders than with caring for their fellow citizens.

It was around this time, toward the end of the rainy spring season, that Clyde ran into his old friend the Swede in a tavern on First Avenue below Pike Street. Ove Jensen still had his position as a pumphouse supervisor, to which he'd been promoted shortly after he'd given Clyde the tour of the main pumphouse down on the waterfront.

"I heard about your run-in with the law," he said to Clyde, leaning over the bar and picking at a pickled pig's foot. "I was sorry to learn of it." He went on to tell Clyde that a couple of detectives had asked him a lot of questions and that he'd told them Clyde was an alright fellow, just curious is all, with no ill intentions whatsoever. He also said that Lewis & Wiley had been eyeing him with suspicion for a long time, but that eventually everyone on the job vouched for him and they finally backed off. "I knew it was the damn boiler the minute I heard what had happened. Any fool could've told you that. They don't have the right men on half this equipment, that's their problem. They've been hurrying the job from the start."

Clyde told the Swede that he regretted if he were the cause of any trouble to him, and thanked him for backing him up when the detectives came around. "Let me stand you a schooner," he offered, and signaled to the barkeep to bring them both another round.

After the Swede finished the beer he was drinking and started on the one Clyde ordered him, he turned to Clyde and asked him if he'd heard the news about the little man who was killed, the one who'd been sabotaging all the equipment, it turned out, and doing the break-ins.

Clyde looked up, surprised, and said he hadn't, and then remembered the man who held out the rail spike in his hand for Clyde to see that day long ago at the regrading cut. "Killed, you say?"

"That's right," the Swede went on. "By one of our own men. A big galoot named Baxter, used to work one of the giants in the pit. From the way he used to talk about getting all those folks like you that didn't go along with the work we were doing, you might have had your own run-in with him a time or two." The Swede turned his head to look at Clyde, to see if his hunch was correct.

"I might have," Clyde said, and knew right away who the Swede was talking about, the same one who'd tried to rile him up at Luna Park and earlier tried to blast him with the hose.

"Anyway," the Swede went on, "he found out about this fella ... who'd been made to move twice on account of the regrading, you see, once from Jackson Street and again from Denny Hill ... well, somehow Baxter found him out before the police did, maybe from all of the little fellow's snooping around the work sites ... " Here the Swede paused. "Which is why they had you pegged for it."

"There're a lot of sidewalk engineers," Clyde replied.

"They're not all holdouts," the Swede came back.

Maybe Ove held a grudge after all, Clyde thought. "So what happened?"

"Baxter found him in an alley one night and crushed his skull in with a piece of new Hopkirk pipe."

Clyde shook his head in outrage at the brute who'd done the crime and sorrow for the old guy who'd been his victim. When he asked what Hopkirk pipe was, the Swede seemed pleased to explain how it was the new patent wood pipe that had replaced the plain wood stave pipe in the sluice boxes at all the regrading sites. The Hopkirk pipe, he elaborated, went with the grain so it didn't wear down or get holes in it like the old stave pipe. "It means the sluice boxes hold up a lot better." The Swede seemed to think a moment, drank down his schooner of beer, and added, "Baxter's in the pokey now."

RIGHT AFTER MADDIE'S DEPARTURE FROM MADISON HOUSE, the electricity and water were disconnected. The giant hoses were within yards of the property line. Maddie told Clyde he should leave the house, move back to his father's. However, Erasmo, who was still representing Maddie in her lawsuit against the city and still hoping to reach a settlement that would award her damages, advised Clyde to stay in the house, if at all possible, to highlight the urgency of their case. Erasmo, upon learning of Ray's photographic series on the Denny Hill neighborhood, was now pressing Ray to let him have prints of the photos, especially the ones of Madison House, to present to the jurors, feeling certain they would carry more emotional value than any verbal arguments he could make on Maddie's behalf. For his own part, Clyde didn't need any urging from Erasmo to stay on at the boardinghouse. He was determined by his own volition to do so – whether as a last stand or from sheer stubbornness, he wasn't sure. Probably a bit of both. However, even though Clyde didn't have a great need for creature comforts, remaining in the abandoned boardinghouse was not so easy.

He would leave the house in the very early morning to go to work at Exposition City, which was what they were calling the A-Y-P grounds now, before the hoses were manned and the blasting started on what remained of Denny Hill. When he returned to the house in the evening, the access to the property would be narrowed even more. The steam shovels and hoses were closing in from several angles. Then finally, one day in mid-April, he tried to return to the boardinghouse – trudging over the newly regraded earth since the new roads had still not been surveyed – only to find that the house and the property on which it stood had become an island, cut off from the last portion of Denny Hill just east of the house's property line. It was now officially a "spite mound." Madison House was one of ten such mounds scattered across the Denny Hill regrade area – Devil's Tower-like columns of dirt anywhere from forty to a hundred feet high, some with buildings still on them, some just flat-topped mounds of dirt that property owners refused to regrade and, in most cases, were still trying to settle damages on with the city.

At the south end of what the newspapers were now calling the Denny Regrade, in the area of Denny Hill that was the first to be leveled, brick apartment buildings three to six stories high were being constructed among the new cinderblock warehouses that had gone up ahead of them. Several large houses, some former boardinghouses, which owners had paid house movers to lower to the new grade, were scattered across the regrade area like the ruins of an ancient civilization. A few of these were still propped up on crib piles. All of the lowered houses were surrounded by a flat, wide-open wasteland of mud, like a roiling brown sea, that was interspersed with the prominent "spite mounds."

Reaching Madison House now involved a trek through and around the pits where the hoses continued to carve away at the loam and blue clay of Denny Hill and send the hill churning into the sluice boxes that snaked their way toward the bay. At first, enough slope remained for Clyde to clamber up the mound to the house without great difficulty. But with each day that passed and each spring rain that fell, the slope eroded away further until finally he had to nail together a series of steps and ladders, using the lumber from his father's old saw mill barn, to reach the top of the mound where the house remained.

As far as he could tell, he was the only person actually living in the Denny Hill regrade area any longer. Maybe if he stayed long enough, he fancied, the regrading crews might forget about him and he could eventually build a massive retaining wall, first with plywood and later with bricks and masonry, to keep Maddie's property from further erosion. The mound and the house that sat upon it would become not just a curiosity but a monument to the once tall hill and the proud neighborhood that had been perched upon it. Several of the windows in Madison House had been shattered by rocks thrown through them, and the sides of the house were bespattered with clots of mud that had been hurled at the house, no doubt by the workmen on the regrading crews. Early on in his effort to hold down the house, some of the men jeered at him as he wended his way back to the property. After a couple of weeks of this, though, they lost interest in him and began going about their work as if he were simply invisible to them.

Atop the mound that was Maddie's property, Clyde now had a 360-degree view of the regraded plain that stretched out around him in a vista of waste and devastation. He could see straight north beyond Denny Way to lower Queen Anne Hill, northeast past Westlake Avenue to Lake Union (almost to his father's place), south to the Pike Street boundary of the downtown, and west to the waterfront. A small portion of Denny Hill remained standing in the east quadrant of the work area, looking like some kind of berm or levee, yet Clyde had little doubt it would soon go as well. He looked out at these four horizons like a sea captain aboard the only ship adrift in a storm-churned ocean – or perhaps, more appropriately, like Ahab fatally strapped to the leviathan at which he'd hurled his futile obsession.

Inside the empty house, he only became more lonely and forlorn. To combat his weariness at being in the house, he worked as many hours at Exposition City as his supervisor would allow and ate most of his meals at a lunch counter near the university campus. When he returned to the regrade area each evening, it was already dark, and by the time he climbed to the top of the mound and let himself in through the back mudroom as he always had, from the very first night he ever slept in the house, he was weary and exhausted. If he wanted to read, he lit a kerosene lantern, the hurricane glass encasing the flame blackened with use; yet if it were simply a matter of undressing himself and then collapsing onto his mattress, he managed well enough in the dark. He dearly missed the nights when he and Maddie had slept together in her old bedroom on the second floor for that short spell when they were the only two who remained in the house. Initially, after she had moved out, he had tried to sleep in his old room in the attic, but after a couple of nights of this he dragged his bed and mattress down to the parlor, although it didn't feel right to be sleeping there either. All this while, whenever Clyde saw Maddie, which wasn't often these days, she tried to talk him out of remaining at the house, afraid for his safety and reminding him of what had happened to Ada's parents. She told him she no longer cared about the lawsuit against the city, and that she just wanted him to be safe.

Of course it was far more than the lawsuit that kept him at the house, though he never could tell Maddie this. He never could explain to her how he was trying to hold onto something, a life perhaps, that he had commenced eight years ago and that he hadn't yet fully or adequately completed. The house and the property were a place that, even though Maddie legally owned them, belonged to him as well. His mother had returned to Neah Bay, to her people on the Makah reservation, to die and be buried there, and for more than three decades his father had held onto his Lake Union homestead despite the encroachment of industry. When he was a child, his parents had yanked him back and forth between these two poles, the Lake Union homestead and the Neah Bay village, each time tearing him from the place he believed to be his home. So when Maddie invited him into her house on Denny Hill and let him contribute to its improvement and upkeep and care, he had felt as if he'd finally arrived at a home of his own making, and his own choosing. It was now eight years that he had lived in the house. Denny Hill, Blanchard Street, Madison House, the attic room, these were his home – and he could not see himself surrendering them.

31. A House Fallen (1909)

AT FIRST, MADDIE WOKE UP EVERY MORNING IN RAY AND
Loye's house and was unable to shake the feeling of defeat that overtook
her. Her last visit to Madison House, taken on the pretext of picking up
a punch bowl, had been traumatic. She'd entered every room and lingered,
recounting as much of the life of each room as possible. It had been a
self-tormenting farewell, she knew, but one she had to make. Despite
Clyde's quixotic belief that the house might yet be spared, she knew better:
She understood that this was to be her last time in the house, which is
why she had insisted on going alone.

Over the next several weeks, though, her grief seemed to subside. She
began to recognize that living in Madison House with the knowledge
that it was doomed had been more disturbing, in subtle ways, than actually giving up the house for lost. The property had become virtually an
island, and she and Clyde the two morose castaways stranded upon it. It
was no way to live, even as a point of principle. The house had grown
dirtier by the day as Maddie had stopped cleaning. She no longer dared
step out the door or look out a window as the rumble of the steam shovels and the growl of the hoses steadily approached her front door. At night
she could hardly sleep for fear the house would collapse on itself and kill
her and Clyde, as had happened to Ada's parents. She soon regretted not
having made better plans for relocating. She'd made none, in fact, and
this failure, combined with her very limited financial means, forced her
to accept Loye and Ray's offer to stay with them in their new house for
as long as she wished.

Mostly, though, she feared for Clyde, who remained in the vacant and
abandoned house with no water or sewage, gas or electricity, simply
camped out there in what appeared to be a futile effort to bolster their
legal case. And worse yet, as the loss of the house had become inevitable,
a matter of weeks at best, Clyde became ever more brooding on the infrequent occasions when she saw him. He began cursing the regraders openly
to Maddie, behavior that was thoroughly uncharacteristic of him. He
seemed to become obsessed, and though she tried her best to talk him

out of remaining in the house, her reasoning (her plea even that he leave for her sake, if not his own) had no suasion with him – which only left Maddie sad for Clyde, as well as sad for the two of them and any future they might have together. She also continued to worry about the criminal charges that remained hanging over his head. The judge kept delaying setting a trial date, which Erasmo told her was a good thing, yet the charges were so serious and carried such a severe penalty that she couldn't help fear for Clyde every time she thought of him.

It was not long after she moved in with Ray and Loye that Maddie received through Erasmo a summons to testify before the city's condemnation committee regarding her property. The committee consisted of seven city-appointed experts – realtors and contractors primarily, yet not a single Denny Hill resident – who would proffer their own assessment of her property's value and the damages incurred. A recent article in the *P-I* had quoted City Attorney Scott Calhoun, who had appointed the committee members, as saying that "the unmanly insinuations and deliberately juggled figures of those who hold out against the regrading of Denny Hill must be checked by common sense and a concern for the welfare of our fair city." According to Erasmo, after Maddie testified before the condemnation committee, her case would be presented to a twelve-person jury specially impaneled to ascertain fair and just compensation to be made to the remaining Denny Hill holdouts, herself included.

Maddie entertained little hope that, when all was said and done, the proceedings would break in her favor. From the reports Erasmo routinely provided her, she could see the jury verdicts were not favoring the holdouts. Jules Redelsheimer received a verdict of only $300. Ellis and Sarah Closson, who had owned a small dry goods store on the hill and had sold their stock off at severely reduced prices the week before closing shop, had received a verdict "in the sum of no dollars," according to one report she saw. Meanwhile, W. R. and Gertrude Brawley had for whatever reason fared somewhat better than others when the jury awarded them damages in the sum of $3,530. Erasmo said that he couldn't account for the discrepancies in the awards, that they all seemed equally arbitrary. He could only speculate that they were contingent on the recommendations made by the condemnation committee, the testimony of individual property owners, and whatever the jury members happened to ingest for breakfast that morning. He was, however, hopeful of exploiting the photographs Ray had finally handed over to him to help persuade the jury, should it be necessary to appeal the committee's verdict. As he explained to Maddie one day, many of the very people assigned to deciding the fate of the Denny Hill residents had never so much as set foot in the neighborhood, and the photographs would help him show that it had indeed once been a district where decent, hardworking people had lived their lives and conducted their business – and that these people deserved to be compensated for their losses.

The day she was to testify before the condemnation committee, Maddie dressed in her Sunday best. She even put on a corset to make her waist as small and uncomfortable as possible for the assessing committee members. Over her silk dress she wore her long broadcloth coat, since her appointment with the committee fell during one of those rare weeks in Seattle each spring when the weather reverts to winter and the temperature drops to near freezing. She felt as though she were trekking off into the wilderness of Alaska and the Yukon again, once more having to face down the grizzlies and gray wolves that wanted to devour her. Unfortunately, none of her friends and former boarders, including Clyde, was able to accompany her.

Down at the city hall, a medium-sized conference room had been reserved for the hearing. Condensation from the steam heat fogged the inside of the tall windows that lined one wall of the room. Just like at the city council hearing she'd attended years ago at the start of the regrading project, the stout Scott Calhoun was in attendance. Gone was his extremely arrogant assistant, who was replaced by a more dowdy middle-aged man seated quietly at the city attorney's side. Maddie had expected to find the city engineer, Reginald H. Thomson, also in attendance, but he was nowhere to be found. Perhaps at this advanced stage of his glorious undertaking to regrade all of Seattle, he had deemed the hearings a mere formality. The city engineer's attention was likely focused on his next conquest: the controversial ship canal linking Puget Sound to the fresh water ports on Lake Union and Lake Washington. But what then? Maddie wondered. Tunnels beneath Elliott Bay to connect the city to its westernmost district and beyond? Pyramids atop the filled-in mudflats? Elevated streetcars crisscrossing the city? Or perhaps the elimination of *all* neighborhoods – residents pushed out of the city entirely – so as to encourage the "natural" progress of commerce?

In addition to Maddie, three other holdouts were scheduled to testify before the condemnation committee. Before the holdouts were granted their turn to speak, however, a line-up of bankers, realtors, contractors, and property owners who had either sold or brought to grade their Denny Hill lots gave well-rehearsed statements on the unqualified benefits to be had by residents and businesses alike in complying with the original regrading ordinance. The president of Northern Bank and Trust Company stated, "The property at the present time" – no doubt alluding to the "spite mounds" – "was not fit for single-residence use or apartment construction, and clearly has no value for manufacturing or light industry. However, this property will attain a direct and great increase in value as soon as it is opened up as business property, and the current owners will be the direct beneficiaries of such a reclassification." Following the bank president, a Seattle realtor informed the committee that "Little homes in that part of our city were assessed for widening and regrading of their streets and avenues, while their owners, generally people of humble circumstances, were compelled in the past to pay taxes that were extremely burdensome to them. Yet by reason of the improvements to their lots, many sold their holdings at a profit of anywhere from 250 percent to 400 percent over the values that ruled prior to the inauguration of the improvement."

Maddie felt she had heard it all before. What possible effect could her brief yet heartfelt statement have in the face of these overblown and inaccurate avowals of profitability by the city's leading businessmen? To these men, and no doubt to the committee members as well, it was all about business opportunities and property value indices. They recognized no other real or potential value in the properties they spoke of. To them, the regrading did not ultimately concern people's lives, their histories, their dreams, their day-to-day routines and domestic habits. Nevertheless, when it came time for Maddie to take her seat at the table before the panel of committee members and testify on what she perceived to be her property's true value and the damages incurred by the so-called improvements to the neighborhood, she laid out for the committee her entire story.

"I came to Seattle twelve years ago, in 1897, and without even knowing the city or anyone here, fell in love with it. But being the naïve young woman I was, I allowed myself to be whisked off to the frozen Northland by a gold-fevered husband and was eventually abandoned in Dawson City by this very same husband." Maddie could see the impatience in the committee members' expressions, but she refused to pay them any mind. They owed her at least this: the chance to tell her story. "But I was one of the few souls fortunate enough to come out of the Yukon with more change in my pocket than I'd arrived with," she went on. "A fancy Indian woman took pity on me and bestowed upon me a claim that almost immediately struck paydirt. But soon after that, when it looked as if all was going well, my dearest friend Laurette was murdered in an arson fire. Do you know how terrible it is to lose a friend to a murderer? Do you?" Maddie could feel herself begin to break up with grief as she recalled Laurette's death, but quickly took hold of herself. "Through all this," she resumed, "my sights always remained on returning to Seattle." She went on to describe her wagon ride up Denny Hill upon her arrival back in the city after two years in the north, then her continued good fortune in having the opportunity to buy, with her Yukon poke, the boardinghouse where she was lodging, then meeting and hiring Clyde Hunssler as her handyman – "Whom," she digressed momentarily, "has been unjustly imprisoned and persecuted for his right to resist the theft of my home and property" – and then with Clyde's help beginning the long and committed work of repairing the house and modernizing it with electricity and other conveniences, and at last taking in boarders and for most of the past decade running one of the most reputable boardinghouses in all of Seattle. "Madison House," she concluded, her tone becoming more subdued, sadder, "fulfilled a dream for me, one I'd had since first seeing the Washington Hotel atop Denny Hill. I loved the old neighborhood more than any place else, more than my childhood home, and I firmly believed, sirs, that I would spend the rest of my days there. I am a concerned and contributing citizen of Seattle, I always have been, but I tell you right now that I and every one of the Denny Hill holdouts have been wronged by this city."

She looked at the committee lined up before her for several full seconds more, in silence, before adding, "That's all I have to say." Yet as soon as she was done speaking, the chairman of the committee cleared his throat, thanked her for her testimony, and curtly asked her to state in terms of dollars the value of her property.

Whether anything she had said had been heard or not, Maddie did not care. She was glad that she'd made her stand and had her say, and said succinctly, "Thirty thousand dollars, plus ten thousand dollars in damages, sir."

"Thank you," the committee member replied. "You may step down now."

THE NEXT WEEK, WHEN THE WEATHER IMPROVED AND THE days began to hint of summer, Clyde surprised Maddie by coming around to Loye and Ray's house and asking her if she would like to take a special preview tour of the grounds of the Alaska-Yukon-Pacific Exposition. She leapt at the invitation and told him she would love to, not because she was excited about the Exposition *per se*, which indeed was all the talk of the city, bumping the regrading project to the far back pages of the newspapers, but because she welcomed any time she could have to spend with Clyde. At times it seemed to Maddie that the first night they had spent together (as well as subsequent nights) and the emotional union it had confirmed for them had been erased by the incessant drudgery and distress of reckoning with the regrading, which is why she'd initially refused to visit the Lake Union homestead immediately after she had moved. Yet the invitation to spend the afternoon with Clyde at the A-Y-P grounds helped return to her a sense of joy and splendor, apart from the usual chin-up determination with which she mostly lived her life these days. She even had the temerity to hope the afternoon might conclude in some remote and secluded corner of the Exposition grounds where they could, the two of them, lie down together.

Maddie had only been to the campus of the university twice before, both times to bring Ada to watch Loye play basketball. Although that was not so long ago, from the look of the campus those two visits might as well have taken place in another era. The campus had been transformed from the near wilderness that she remembered to a magnificent playland city. She and Clyde entered the A-Y-P grounds beneath the massive, three-arched Japanese gate off of Fifteenth Avenue, with Clyde walking briskly ahead of Maddie in his enthusiasm to serve as her tour guide. Once inside the gate, they stood momentarily beneath several towering totem poles with carved and painted bear, raven, salmon, and eagle faces stacked on top of one another and rising straight into the sky. They walked past the entrance to the Pay Streak, which Clyde explained they would skip today since it was still under construction, and then strolled through Puget Plaza, where, he said, a life-sized statue of George Washington would be unveiled on opening day. Maddie was amused by Clyde's boyish enthusiasm in directing her attention here and there as they made their way next to the center of Exposition City, called the Court of Honor, marked by a 100-foot fluted column with four classical statuary figures at its base and a giant sculpted eagle with raised wings perched atop its capital. The scene before them seemed like a combination of antiquity Rome and the French *ancien regime*. To their left was the United State Government Building, the largest building at the Exposition, crowned by a dome that rose twice as high as the monument column and winged by peristyles leading to two adjacent buildings on either side. Like all of the buildings leading down the length of the Court of Honor, as Clyde pointed out, the U.S. Government Building was designed in the ornate French Renaissance style. Though the façades of all the buildings appeared to be made of carved stone, including those of the Agriculture Building and the Manu-facturing Building that bordered the Geyser Basin farther down the court, they were actually all constructed of wood and plaster. This fact aston-ished Maddie, given the convincing detail work on the facades. Yet she was even further astonished when Clyde divulged that while a few of the newly constructed buildings would be transferred to the university when the Exposition closed in October, the most ornate buildings along the

Court of Honor would be demolished at the end of November. The notion of such blatant waste put her back in mind of the devastation of the regrading, and she fell silent for a good while until Clyde took her arm and led her down along the side of the splendid Cascade pools. Maddie welcomed Clyde's escort and felt like Josephine being led by a proud Napoleon through their new palace grounds.

The pools had not yet been filled with water, yet Clyde vividly described to Maddie how the water would descend all the way from the Geyser Fountain and at night be lit from beneath by air-tight electrical lights. At the bottom of the Cascade pools, they came to what was called Yukon Avenue and turned left toward Nome Circle, and Maddie laughed to herself to think how this configuration replicated the route her husband Chester may have taken when he forsook her in Dawson City. With the exception of workmen here and there pushing handcarts and wheelbarrows between work sites or preparing beds for spring plantings, and then occasionally small formal parties of Exposition officials and visiting delegates wandering about, the grounds were eerily empty. In leading her here and there, pointing out architectural details, explaining the future function of each building and the exhibitions it would house, Clyde took possession of the grounds, guiding Maddie about as if he himself were the director of the A-Y-P Exposition. She was glad that he had such an escape from the dismal life he continued to endure at the abandoned boardinghouse, a subject that Maddie anxiously avoided as they strolled about. She also avoided asking him about the charges against him and whether or not a trial date had been set.

He was especially eager to show her the Forestry Building, which he'd worked on during his first month on the job and which dominated Nome Circle. It was a long two-story structure with a series of massive timbers, with the bark still on them, serving as columns from one end of the building to the other. At either end, the building was topped by a pentagonal cupola with large mullioned windows placed between shorter timber columns on all five sides. Beneath the portico and stretching the entire length of the building was what Clyde, blushing, said the workmen had nicknamed "the big stick," a timber 143-feet long and 18-feet round, one of the biggest ever harvested in the state. Fortunately, since the Forestry Building was one of the first buildings completed, its exhibits were already in place, and so Clyde was able to lead Maddie inside for a look.

Once inside, Maddie declared that she didn't know if she was in a forest or a museum when she looked around at the massive fir trees that had been turned into posts and columns throughout the building. In the center of the building's north end stood the hollowed trunk of a fir tree with a door at its base and on top of it a viewing platform. The forestry exhibit displayed all the products and machinery related to the industry, from five-foot-square wood dice to a complete cottage made of six different kinds of native wood. The south end of the building, curiously, was given over to the fisheries exhibit, which fascinated Maddie even more than the forestry exhibit. A live seal with long spiny whiskers barked at them from a large, open tank. Opposite the seal tank were numerous aquaria containing specimens of all the fish that inhabited the salt and fresh waters of the State of Washington, from spiny rockfish to steelhead trout. Another shallow tank held only crustaceans and other sea-floor life, from clusters of black mussels and heavy geoducks to florid sea anemones and languid starfish in purple and orange hues. At one end of the fisheries exhibit, a rivulet ran down a miniature mountain into a pool inhabited by kaleidoscopic trout and surrounded by a variety of ferns and mosses. Maddie felt that she hadn't been this close to the wilderness since she'd trekked out to her Rock Ledge Creek claim in the Yukon with Laurette and Morris.

After visiting the Forestry Building, they decided simply to amble about the grounds. Clyde pointed out the Mission-style California Building and explained how a subtropical garden of olive, banana, almond, kiwi, orange, and grapefruit trees would eventually be planted in the large tubs surrounding the building. Maddie soon picked up that about a third of the states in the union, and certainly all of the western states, had their own buildings. There were also buildings for the U.S. Territories, Alaska included of course, but also Hawaii and the Philippines. There were buildings for Europe and the Orient, though Canada and Japan were the only foreign countries that sponsored their own buildings. A handful of smaller buildings existed as well for Washington State counties, most notably King County and Yakima County, the former the most populated county in the state and the latter its breadbasket. Although crews were just beginning to prepare the many walkways and bypaths for planting, Clyde assured Maddie that flowers and ornamental shrubbery would reign throughout the grounds. By the time Clyde felt satisfied that he had given Maddie as complete a tour as was possible a full month prior to the Exposition's grand opening, Maddie said that her feet were becoming sore and asked if they could sit on one of the benches along the perimeter of Klondike Circle.

It wasn't the secluded corner she had hoped for, yet it would give them a chance to pause in their ambitious tour of the grounds. As soon as they sat, Maddie freely and boldly swung her legs and feet up onto the bench and leaned back against Clyde's side as if he were a chaise lounge. "How immodest of me, I know," she said, and inclined her head to the side so Clyde could kiss her, which he did without hesitating. Since Maddie had moved in with Loye and Ray, she and Clyde had not spent a single night together. Not only did Maddie miss those nights – the one positive memory she retained from their days alone in the boardinghouse – she most of all missed Clyde, whom she saw now on only those few occasions he stopped by for dinner or to deliver a message on the state of her property and the boardinghouse.

"I think you should leave the house," she told him, sitting up and taking his hand in hers. She had not meant to say anything and risk spoiling this moment they shared, but how could she not? Clyde meant more to her than a single stolen kiss.

Clyde stared down at the ground and looked solemn, his excitement in hosting her at the Exposition grounds clearly deflated by her bringing up the question of the house. Yet he didn't try to withdraw his hand from hers.

"I don't know what to do," he admitted finally.

Maddie sensed he might shed tears, he seemed so distraught over the whole matter, his avowal so genuine. Over the past couple of weeks, she had begun to understand that in some ways the house meant more to him than it ever had to her. She patted the back of his hand, and he returned the gesture with a faint, sympathetic smile. She told him that they should know soon what the verdict in the lawsuit against the city would be, and yet as soon as she said this she knew such information was irrelevant, that there was something more at stake, almost as if the house was all that they retained between them, all that kept them together, seated side by side on this bench, and that without the house they would soon drift apart, become strangers to each other, two people who had never met. The thought frightened Maddie, and she could sense that it frightened Clyde as well. Yet how could they advance beyond it? Maddie feared that if they rose from the bench without resolving whatever it was that was at stake for them, they might never see each other again.

Then Clyde spoke. "My father says Mr. Patten is leaving Seattle." He frowned and looked down again after saying this, but then with a faint laugh, added, "He's throwing away his umbrella hat and moving to Southern California. Says he's going to collect his Union Army pension and lie on the beach beneath a palm tree from now on. Imagine that."

Maddie laughed at this too. Yet she dreaded what Clyde might be suggesting by revealing this stray bit of news to her. Was he considering leaving Seattle as well? Was this his way of letting her know that his departure was a distinct possibility? Perhaps it was the right thing to do. What if, contrary to Erasmo's best legal predictions, the charges against Clyde weren't dropped and he was convicted and sent to prison? She would rather see him jump bail, flee the state, and live the rest of his life on the lam than go back to jail. Yet Maddie also knew in her heart that even more hurtful, more devastating than losing Madison House would be to lose Clyde. With each day that passed since having to abandon the life she knew, despite Clyde's looming legal straits, despite the unencouraging outlook for her claim against the city, despite the transitoriness of her present circumstances … she still felt that somehow, each day, she was gaining more confidence in herself and with this confidence the growing belief that everything would be all right once the upheaval of the Denny Hill regrading was finally over. This was one reason why, aside from his general welfare, she wanted Clyde to leave the house and give up his dogged stand on its behalf. Her confidence, combined with this feeling of renewal, astounded Maddie – so unexpected was it given the trying circumstances, and therefore so impossible to account for – but there it was. And she wanted to share it with Clyde, if only he would allow her to. Her sole hesitation in trusting this feeling entirely, in giving herself over to it and abiding by it unconditionally, came with the uncertainty still surrounding Clyde.

When he squeezed her hand in his and they stood, he kissed her again and concluded the kiss with a long, tender embrace. It seemed to Maddie then, while in his embrace, that the finality of the moment had for now at least been deferred.

AT THE END OF APRIL, START OF MAY, A LINE OF FEROCIOUS storms blew in from the Pacific Ocean and pounded Puget Sound for ten straight days. Contrary to the typically soft, incessant rain that the city was accustomed to, Seattle was deluged by thunderous downpours that lasted hours at a time and made crossing the street hazardous. And the severity of the heavy rains was only compounded by the fierce winds that accompanied them.

It was on the sixth day of this succession of storms that Madison House came down. By loosening and washing away great volumes of dirt from the dozen or so mounds that remained in the Denny Hill regrade area, the storms did much of the regraders' work for them during these days when the crews were unable to work. To Maddie's great relief, Clyde had been staying at his father's house during the worst of the spring storms. Slogging through the mud and trying to climb slippery wet steps and ladders to reach the house had become too perilous, even for him. At the start of the storms, Maddie had been preparing in her mind to simply order Clyde out of her house and off her property. Then he showed up one afternoon at Ray and Loye's and informed her that he had already packed his few belongings and had left, locking the back door to the mudroom on his way out. As he stood on the small front porch of the Twenty-Sixth Avenue house, he seemed genuinely beaten down. He'd refused to come inside, but instead, drenched through and through and muddied from the waist down, he tarried with one foot on the steps and told Maddie that he was worried the boardinghouse would collapse if the rain continued at this rate. Maddie tried to make a joke of his prediction, saying that if that were the case then she wouldn't have to pay for the property to be regraded. Yet Clyde wasn't having any part her levity over this matter. He looked back at her more somberly than ever, and a moment later, when Ray came out to the porch with his shiny pocket flask of whiskey and handed it to Clyde, he slipped the flask into his coat pocket and walked off as if Ray's flask had been a gift. Maddie would have been offended by his brusque behavior if she hadn't already been so worried about him.

Four days later, late in the afternoon, almost evening, he showed up again at Ray and Loye's house and, coming all the way into the front foyer this time, he paused before saying, "The house came down last night," and nothing more. Maddie's response was stolid; she knew she could indulge in tears later. Clyde looked her straight in the eyes this time, not in recrimination but in sympathy, and explained how when he had walked around the property mound the previous afternoon to inspect how it was holding up, he found the ground gone from underneath the front porch and the entire southwest corner of the house sagging. Then, when he returned before first light this morning, the rain still falling, he could see from a good distance off that the house was no longer standing. As he neared the mound on which the house had been perilously perched the day before and saw the debris at its base, he could tell that the house had collapsed forward, that once the front gave way, it had pulled the rest of the house down with it. Oddly enough, the boiler shed had somehow detached from the house and remained standing, as did the carriage house. Yet the main structure, Madison House, was gone.

"I'm sorry," he told her, when he was finished describing the scene.

To Maddie, this report merely confirmed what she'd imagined in her mind's eye time and time again as the regrading had approached the property line. It was a version of the events she'd seen unfold with Ada's parents' house, the old Washington Hotel, and numerous other houses and buildings on the once steep and graceful slopes of Denny Hill. Her boardinghouse was no more. Yet contrary to what she'd once deemed her unimaginable fate upon its loss, she knew her life would go on. Just as her life would go on in respect to Clyde – with or without him.

She could see that it pained him to tell her the news of the house. She wiped away the tears that, despite herself, had seeped into her own eyes, yet she didn't know how else to respond. What was there to say? The loss of the house had been a foregone conclusion, at least for the past several months. All the same, despite her confidence in herself, it was not easy to reconcile the anticipation of its loss with the knowledge that it was finally gone – that Madison House, her dream, her home, was now only a pile of rubble at the bottom of a mound of mud. She could only compare what she was feeling now to how she'd felt upon learning that her parents had died, or when Laurette had perished in the fire in Dawson City... but these comparison didn't quite hold up either. How could they? Those were lives, her loved ones, and this was only a building, made of wood and nails, which she had bought with a sack of rough gold that had more or less fallen into her lap when her claim panned out. Maybe, she even thought, the jury down at city hall would be right in not awarding her anything for her loss of property; perhaps they would recognize the randomness of her good fortune in possessing the house in the first place. Such a notion almost made her laugh through her tears.

Clyde stepped forward and put his arms around Maddie and pulled her to him and held her for a long while. It seemed that he, too, had perhaps broken free from the chains that the house had seemed to shackle him with these past many months. As they remained standing in the front foyer, acceptance that the house was gone settled over her. As when Clyde had first held her, after she'd returned from that hideous public hearing about the Denny Hill regrading so long ago, she again allowed herself to cry openly and let him comfort her with his full embrace. His arms and back, she felt, were stronger and more sturdy than any house.

Loye and Ray, all this while, stood back from them in the parlor, giving them this moment of reprieve and mutual comfort, and when Maddie pulled out of Clyde's embrace and kissed him on the cheek and thanked him, Loye finally stepped forward and guided her into the parlor and had her sit down in one of armchairs there.

"I'll go to Holy Names tomorrow and tell Ada," Maddie said. "She'll be sad, but she's a strong girl. Do you know, Loye, that she told me last week she wants to go to college just like her 'Aunt Loye.' That's what she calls you these days." The thought of seeing Ada heartened Maddie.

"Oh no," Loye exclaimed, "as soon as I'm married I become an old auntie. I prefer 'sister.'"

"A beautiful old auntie," Ray declared, as he carried a tray with a bottle of brandy and four glasses on it into the parlor from the den. He poured everyone a glass and set about lighting a fire in the fireplace.

Loye, meanwhile, took Clyde's wet coat from him and told him he had to go upstairs and put on some of Ray's clothes, perhaps even a nightshirt and robe, because he wasn't leaving the house again that night. "Did you know," she told him, "that the teachers from Broadway School are planning to have an exhibit in the Women's Building at the Exposition? It'll highlight all the latest educational methodologies and show off the most outstanding students' work. I may be called upon to guide visitors through the exhibit. Isn't that exciting? We'll both be working at the Exposition."

Maddie could not be more grateful to two people than she was to Loye and Ray at that moment for all their understanding during this ordeal. "If Ada's learning is any indication of what an outstanding teacher you are," she told Loye, whom she indeed regarded with the fondness and love of a younger sister, "then the Seattle school system should count its lucky stars to have you in its employ."

Loye replied to this compliment as she did to most attention directed her way, by deflecting it, and saying that Ada would always be her most prized pupil.

Clyde, who had remained silent since telling Maddie about the boardinghouse, and whose thoughts, unlike Maddie's own, clearly remained on it, remarked that in the morning he would see about hiring a crew and wagon to salvage the lumber and then give whatever money he could get for the scrap to Maddie. With that, Ray took hold of Clyde's wet shirt, pulled him to the foot of the staircase, told him he'd been out in the weather too long, that it was softening his brain, and led him upstairs to get a change of clothes.

Maddie appreciated Ray's brisk manner with Clyde, even though she could plainly see that in Clyde's view his plan to salvage the scrap from the house was his final task in looking after the house for her – his final gesture, by means of the house, in looking after *her*. Just as in their first months of getting the house ready for boarders almost a decade ago, she knew she could count on him to carry out his plan. Likewise, she knew with the same assuredness that she could count on herself to do whatever she had to do next as well.

32. At Home, Afloat (1909)

CLYDE'S JOB AT THE ALASKA-YUKON-PACIFIC EXPOSITION grounds was steady work that paid well. His supervisor liked his work, and one afternoon around quitting time he asked Clyde if he would stay on to join the maintenance crew once the Exposition opened, mostly working at night after the grounds closed each day to the general public. His supervisor assured him that with 15,000 people expected to pass through the gates every day from the Exposition's opening on June 1 to its closing on October 16, it would be a hectic four and a half months. The maintenance crew would be kept busy around the clock, but especially at night getting ready for the next day. Clyde replied that he was glad to have the work – and he genuinely was. His supervisor knew nothing of Clyde's six months in jail or the charges still outstanding against him, and Clyde wanted to keep it that way. He knew that if word got out he would likely be fired, and though typically such a thing would not disturb him, this was no longer the case. The job seemed to be the only certain thing in his life right now. Not only did it pay good money, but the intensive schedule – seven days a week as Opening Day rapidly approached – kept him from dwelling on the loss of Madison House, the criminal charges still hanging over his head like an axe, and his uncertain relationship with Maddie.

In the weeks following the collapse of the house, Clyde saw even less of Maddie than he had after she'd moved in with Ray and Loye. In the days immediately after the house's coming down and the storm's passing, he brought her the $140 that he'd managed to get for the scrap lumber. Then, at Loye's invitation, he would go by the house every Saturday evening for supper, and afterward smoke a cigar with Ray in their small backyard garden. It wasn't that he didn't want to see Maddie or be with her more if he could. He did. Yet seeing how, in the light of recent events, she seemed so much more eager and confident about carrying on with life than he himself did, he didn't want to be the shadow that darkened her spirit. Instead he would just put in his twelve to sixteen hours a day at the Exposition and trudge back to his father's Lake Union hovel.

Unfortunately, and for whatever reasons, he was more successful at staying away from Maddie than he was at staying away from the Denny Regrade, as the area was now called. Rather than ride the streetcar to Ray and Loye's house to visit Maddie, he used whatever spare time he had to wander over to the regrade area to watch the last of the "spite mounds" being leveled and the newly graded streets and alleys paved and curbed into the checkerboard grid that now crisscrossed the empty plain where Denny Hill had once stood. Clyde kept thinking that when the project was completed, when the last giant hydraulic hoses and the last Yankee Geologist steam shovels were pulled from the site, when all the waste car rails and sluice boxes and flumes were finally pulled up and removed, when there was no more regrading to be done, he might like to see if he could find Ove Jensen, the Swede, and share a pitcher of beer with him.

It was toward the end of May, about a month since the boardinghouse had come down, that Clyde and his father walked over to Robert Patten's houseboat on Lake Union to say farewell to their old friend. In the morning, Mr. Patten, as Clyde still addressed him, would be boarding a train for Los Angeles, California. Clyde carried with him the walking stick Henry James had given him several years earlier, and that he never used, to give to Mr. Patten as a going-away gift. When they arrived, Clyde's father called out to the long-bearded and amiable old man, whom was known citywide now as the Umbrella Man. "Tillikum," his father greeted him from the shore, using the Chinook greeting common among friends who still knew the trading jargon.

Clyde and his father balanced their way across the ten-foot plank that connected the houseboat to the shore as Mr. Patten stepped out of the houseboat's one and only door. They all three shook hands and Clyde handed Mr. Patten the brass-handled walking stick, along with his best wishes for a safe voyage and prosperous future.

"That's very kindly of you, young Clyde," the eighty-year-old gray beard said, as he inspected the stick's shiny brass handle and polished mahogany. "Not that I can't walk on my own steam, mind you."

"Of course not," Clyde replied quickly to dispel any doubt. "It's merely a token of my friendship."

"Indeed, indeed," Robert Patten returned. He brandished the walking stick in the air like a sword. "I think this will come in handy, by God. Let's have a toast." He then led the way inside and retrieved a clay jug of apple-jack off a shelf above his bed, the remains of last fall's batch. He uncorked the jug, took a swig, and passed it to Clyde's father, who took a swig and passed it on to Clyde, who took a swig but found himself gagging on the sharp, acidy liquor the moment it touched his lips.

"That's the stuff," said Mr. Patten, and took the jug from Clyde's hands.

"So you're selling your houseboat?" Clyde asked, and looked about the floating shack. As houseboats went it was a sizeable one, though run-down and in need of maintenance. It was almost the same size as his father's house; it even had an open loft like his father's house, and window casings very much like his father's house as well. Clyde had been on the houseboat only two or three times in all the years he'd known Mr. Patten. For the very first time, however, everything about it seemed very familiar to him, and as he looked about Mr. Patten's houseboat, the realization dawned on him that his father had most likely helped Mr. Patten build it. It made perfect sense. Based on what Clyde knew of Mr. Patten's history and his arrival in Seattle fifteen years ago, and on what he knew of his father's quiet willingness to help others out when called upon, it only figured that his father had had a hand in the houseboat's construction. In all likelihood, his father had been the architect and primary builder. He wanted to step outside that very instant and inspect the cedar shingles on the outside walls for confirmation. His father's shingles would be the telltale sign; they had the distinctive cut of Hunssler Mill, and if Clyde looked at them closely, he could distinguish them anywhere.

"I'm planning to sell, yes I am," Mr. Patten remarked, and looked at Clyde with a coy squint. "Unless you want to take it off my hands."

Clyde looked into Mr. Patten's bright, rheumy eyes and wondered what he was up to. He thought a moment and answered, "I could sell it for you and send you the money, if that's what you mean. How much will you be asking for it?"

Mr. Patten frowned at Clyde. "How old are you, son?" he asked him.

Clyde studied the old man, and then, before he could respond, his father entered the mix by saying, "The lad's almost thirty. Next month's his birthday."

"Is that so," Mr. Patten said, and took a plug of tobacco from his pants pocket, folded back the brown paper wrapper, and pulled a corner off the thick chaw with his long yellow teeth. Mumbling through the mouthful of tobacco, he said, "That's too damn old to be living with your pap. What I'm trying to tell you, young sir, is you should take this floating shithouse for your own. Damn if I want to sell it. Who needs the trouble? I want you to have it."

Clyde cast a look at his father, who appeared as he always did, stubborn and impatient, and then at Mr. Patten, who looked at him with his unflinching squint. Clyde glanced over the insides of the boathouse again and slowly began nodding his approval. The old man was absolutely right, he thought. He needed to get out of his father's house and into some place of his own. And this would do as well as any. Unless he was going to return to Neah Bay – an idea that he occasionally entertained, especially when he thought about having to face a judge and jury in a criminal trial that could cost him ten years in prison – he would have to move on with his life here in Seattle. And maybe this was the first step.

"Well," Mr. Patten said. "I've got a train to catch in the morning."

"Let's make a toast then," Clyde answered, and snatched the applejack jug from Mr. Patten's hand. "To my new houseboat! And to Mr. Robert W. Patten ... whom Seattle will never forget!" He then hefted the jug up and, bracing himself, took a hearty swig from it in honor of his friend.

"Hear, hear," called out Clyde's father and Mr. Patten in unison, as Clyde lowered the jug and passed it along.

The applejack kept going around until the jug was empty. By nightfall, after his father and Mr. Patten had climbed to the roof deck to smoke cigars and gaze at the stars in the night sky, Clyde was feeling right at home in the ramshackle houseboat, slumped in the chair next to the coal-burning stove and dozing off to the sound of the lake gently lapping the float platoons below.

The next morning, Mr. Patten roughly shook Clyde's shoulder to wake him, wished him a hearty farewell, and was out the door. Clyde roused himself from the chair he'd slept in all night and stumbled out onto the misty deck of the houseboat just in time to see Mr. Patten on the lakeshore climbing onto his father's buckboard wagon that had the old mule harnessed to it. Clyde waved to Mr. Patten as his father clicked his tongue and snapped the reins, and the wagon set off rattling down the dirt track to take their friend to the train station and from there to sunny California. Mr. Patten turned around on the wagon seat and seeing Clyde waving to him, began swinging Henry James's walking stick in air. Clyde noticed he no longer wore his umbrella hat.

FROM THAT DAY ON, CLYDE WORKED ON THE HOUSEBOAT every evening after work until one or two in the morning, making it as structurally sound and as domestically pleasing as possible – all in anticipation, he decided, of the day he would invite Maddie to come see it.

The houseboat was not in as dire condition as he'd at first thought. Certainly, it was far from being just another live-aboard or a mere hut plopped atop a retired barge or boat hull, of the sort one could find plenty of in and around Seattle's waterways. Rather than being set afloat upon soggy log rafts as many houseboats were, this particular houseboat had steel pontoons (salvaged, his father told him, from the Moran Shipyard) supporting the large fir plank surface-deck. The deck itself had a double railing on all four sides, which had probably kept his father and Mr. Patten from falling into the drink any number of times. From the deck, there was a four-inch step-up to the house, which had large mullioned windows on all four sides and a mansard roof raised high enough to accommodate the sleeping loft inside, just like at his father's house – which he hoped would appeal to Maddie. The roof deck, set atop the mansard roof, could be reached by a narrow staircase attached to the south wall on the outside of the house. The staircase looked newer than the rest of the houseboat, and Clyde figured it had probably been added a few years ago. Meanwhile, on the north side of the house, a small skiff with oars and oar locks at the ready was tied to the deck rail. This was the same skiff, recovered and repaired, that his father and Mr. Patten had gone down in fifty yards from shore that one time years back.

One of Clyde's first projects after replacing every board that had any rot to it was to build a dormer into the roof so that light could enter the loft and whoever was up there could have a full view of the lake outside. While aspects of the houseboat were fairly makeshift, much of its crafts-manship – along with the now-recognizable cedar shingles that covered all four sides of the house and the roof – confirmed to Clyde that his father had had a major part in constructing it. In some ways, Clyde felt as if the shack that had been his childhood home had been latched onto pontoons and cast out onto the lake. Yet, by the time he would bring Maddie to it – that is, if she agreed to come – he wanted the houseboat to be far more than this.

Clyde planned eventually to extend the deck atop the pontoons and build an addition off of one side of the houseboat that would allow for a separate kitchen. Right now, on the inside, there was essentially one room divided three ways: the cooking and eating section, which included a four-plate coal-and-wood stove, a small cabinet, and a wobbly table with three rickety chairs beneath the window; the den area, which included a small office desk and a reading chair; and the parlor area, which had a frayed armchair, a scuffed sidetable, and a milking stool that Mr. Patten had used as a footrest. As for water and toilet, the occupant (or visitor, for that matter) had to step ashore to use the well pump and outhouse.

In all, it wasn't Madison House ... but neither was it uninhabitable. As houseboats went, Mr. Patten's (now Clyde's own, he often reminded him-self) fell somewhere between the shanty boats inhabited by fishermen and migrant workers that the Seattle Health Department had last year deemed unsanitary and had forced away from the city's waterfront (even-tually relocating them at the head of the Duwamish River) and the resort set's lavish, two-story floating homes along the shores of Lake Washing-ton near Madison Park. Though Clyde was more or less content with the houseboat as it was, he was thinking of Maddie, and knew he would have to make even more improvements to make the structure at all present-able. So one week before the grand opening of the Alaska-Yukon-Pacific Exposition, he made his big move and hired one of the tugboat operators on Lake Union to tow his houseboat around the point, beneath the Uni-versity Bridge, and into Portage Bay. Not only was the bay more protected from bad weather, it also had a moorage site that would allow him to rig the houseboat with running water, proper sewage, and electricity for the monthly moorage fee of $10.

It was at this time that Clyde received notice from Erasmo that he had been summoned to appear before the judge presiding over his case. Clyde telephoned Erasmo in his office in the Pioneer Building to ask him what he thought the summons meant. In his guarded attorney's manner, Erasmo said he didn't know, but bad or good, it probably meant something was going to happen in the case, that it would finally move forward.

"Could he throw me back in jail?" Clyde wanted to know.

"He could," Erasmo answered honestly, "but I doubt that's what will happen."

Clyde could not sleep that night for worrying about his appearance before the judge the next day and wondering if he should bolt now for Neah Bay or perhaps Canada. Ultimately, he decided he couldn't jump bail and cost Ray and James all the collateral they'd put up on his behalf. He also couldn't leave Maddie behind.

Beginning at dawn, he walked all the way from Portage Bay, up and over Capitol Hill, and down into Pioneer Place to Erasmo's office, where Erasmo had ready a wool suit and a fresh shirt and collar for Clyde to wear to the courthouse for his nine o'clock appearance.

The judge, a white-haired man in black judicial robes, never even looked at Clyde. Nor did he look at Erasmo, who stood by Clyde's side. From his bench, his eyes on the papers before him, he asked Clyde to state his name, which Clyde did, and then the judge cleared his throat and said, "Mr Hunssler, the prosecutor has dropped the charges against you. You are released from bail." He then brought down his gavel, rose from his chair, and retired to his chambers.

Confused by the brevity of this appearance, Clyde looked at Erasmo, who just shrugged his shoulders and said, "It's about time." He shook Clyde's hand. "You're a free man, Clyde. If you were in a magnanimous mood, you might say that justice has been served."

A WEEK LATER, ON JUNE 1, CLYDE WAS ALMOST TOO EXHAUSTED from his work at the A-Y-P grounds and his work on the houseboat to enjoy the Exposition's Opening Day. Nevertheless, the houseboat was now fully connected to water, sewage, and electricity, and he felt he could take a break from his work on it and relax. It was also the first chance he had to fully appreciate his restored freedom.

Immediately upon the opening of the Exposition gates at eight o'clock, people began streaming onto the grounds, everyone dressed in their best stepping-out suits. In just the past few months, the fashion among men had turned from derbies to felt fedoras, and Clyde expected that the next time he saw Ray, his friend would be donning one as well. Clyde's work shift did not officially start until noon, which gave him the chance to amble about the grounds and mingle with the crowds. At 9:30, a grand military parade led by Colonel T. C. Woodbury, Grand Marshal, formed at the Military Camp near the south entrance and proceeded through Rainier Circle, Klondike Circle, and Olympic Plaza, then down Cascade Court to Geyser Basin, over to Washington Circle, Nome Circle, and Dome Circle, concluding finally at the Natural Amphitheater. There, the Innes Band of Chicago played the "Americana" overture and the Right Reverend Bishop Edward O'Dea, Catholic Bishop of Seattle, delivered the invocation. (Hearing it, Clyde remembered his visit to the Sacred Heart Cathedral.) Then commenced the endless series of official addresses, interspersed with the Innes Band playing "Gloria Washington" and the National Anthem accompanied by 200 Seattle high school students. The A-Y-P Exposition's director-general spoke, the A-Y-P's President spoke, the railroad magnate James J. Hill spoke, even the A-Y-P's official secretary spoke, making the only statement that actually registered with Clyde as he stood in the far back near the hut-sized Baptists Building. The A-Y-P secretary leaned forward at the bunting-draped podium, looked steadily out over the crowd and, without any of the bluster in his voice that the other speakers had displayed, declared, "This event closes one epoch of this Commonwealth's history, and opens another. The pioneer days, the days of adventure, the days of uncertainty, the days during which we have been practically unknown to the great body of the people of the nation, will, when this Exposition is over, be ended forever. When this Exposition closes we will take our proper place among the great states and great cities of the

republic, and be recognized as such by all of its citizens. Thank you, all."
Perhaps it was because of everything he'd been through with the Denny
Hill regrading, or perhaps it was simply because his father and Mr. Patten
had ribbed him about his turning thirty, yet whatever the reason, Clyde
found himself appreciating the prospect that the days of uncertainty were
over, that something more settled, more established lay ahead for him.

The secretary's simple address was followed by the A-Y-P president
ceremoniously touching a button to notify President William Howard
Taft in Washington, D.C., that the Exposition was ready for its official
opening. President Taft, as the crowd had earlier been informed he would,
then turned a special key 3,000 miles away in the nation's capital that set
the machinery moving that ran the flags of the United States, Washington
State, and the Alaska-Yukon-Pacific Exposition up three tall flagstaffs
simultaneously, hence signaling a squadron of United States infantrymen
to fire a three-round rifle salute over the heads of the crowd. And with this,
the Alaska-Yukon-Pacific Exposition was officially open to the public.

By the time the midday fireworks were being set off, Clyde had to
report to work. Yet work meant he still got to go around the grounds:
checking in with each building manager, making rounds to the various
boiler rooms, and being on hand at a moment's notice to repair water
leaks, replace broken benches and railings, adjust lighting fixtures, or
perform any number of handyman tasks. Generally, he was assigned to
keep everything running smoothly during the day so that there would
be minimal maintenance to do by day's end, at the strike of midnight,
when the last person left the grounds and the gates closed.

After the first full week of the Exposition – which Clyde reached from
his houseboat by rowing his skiff across Portage Bay to a small dock beside
the U.S. Life Saving Station at the lower end of the grounds – he stopped
going in until it was time for his shift to begin. He spent his mornings
instead working on the houseboat, mostly constructing the kitchen addition, and finally at the end of July, as a final touch, he placed flower boxes
beneath the bayside window and the shoreside window and filled each
box with primroses and marigolds. Then, through Ray, whose downtown
photography studio he stopped into once or twice a week, Clyde extended

an invitation to Maddie to visit the Exposition again with him on his next day off. He said nothing about the houseboat.

Early on the appointed morning in mid-August, he took the streetcar to Ray and Loye's house, which took two transfers, the first on Broadway and the second at Pine Street. He was nervous, not knowing whether Maddie was privy to what he'd been up to or not, and worse, fearing that she would not be interested, at any rate, since she had probably moved on with her own life and was now only indulging him by accepting his silly invitation to the Exposition again. He had not even had the courtesy to extend the invitation in person, but had used Ray as his proxy.

However, when he finally arrived at Ray and Loye's house, Maddie was ready and waiting for him—though also, it seemed, behaving rather shyly—and they wasted no time in setting off. In the four months since the boardinghouse had come down, he had seen Maddie once a week or less, yet during those visits, they had seemed to enjoy each other's company with few, if any, expectations—almost as when they'd first met so long ago on the front lawn of Madison House. To Clyde, the past several months had been a necessary respite from the turmoil leading up to and immediately following the loss of the boardinghouse. In May, Maddie had received the verdict from the condemnation committee—a mere $2,000 in damages. However, using Ray's photographs, Erasmo appealed this verdict and convinced a jury to raise the damages award to an astounding $8,000. Soon after this, Maddie, after declining several earlier (and lower) bids, sold the lot where the house once stood to an eager local developer for another $17,000. She said she was satisfied now, seeing how the total amount, though not equal to what she'd returned to Seattle with from the Yukon nine years earlier, still felt like a windfall. Fate had again turned disadvantage into good fortune for her. She spoke of buying a new house, something small, and perhaps using the rest of her money to buy an apartment building, someplace where she could still give people a home and yet no longer have to cook for them. In all, she seemed very happy, and was forever thanking Erasmo for his tireless lawyering on her behalf (for which he received a third of her jury award), Ray for his ever-so-persuasive photographs, and James for his unrelenting commentaries in the *Argus*. According to Ray,

Erasmo was now planning to use the photographs to leverage higher settlements from the city on behalf of a number of former Denny Hill holdouts, just as he had for Maddie. The relief Maddie felt at Clyde's criminal charges being dismissed had been overwhelming, and she continuously expressed her deep gratitude to him for everything he had done.

All of these developments made Clyde wonder if Maddie would still be interested in him, much less his quaint, little houseboat. Since Clyde's plan was to tell Maddie about the houseboat while they walked about the A-Y-P grounds and then take her to it via the most scenic route – straight across Portage Bay – he had tied his skiff up at the Life Saving Station dock the day before and had walked back home across the University Bridge. He wanted to make a full day of it with Maddie, first by touring the Exposition (which Maddie still hadn't been to since her visit prior to the opening) and then by rowing across the bay to the boathouse. As they walked from Twenty-Sixth Avenue to Madison Avenue, Clyde spotted the cable car coming up the hill and hurried Maddie along so they could catch it. At the corner, the cable car stopped for them and they rode it all the way down the other side of the hill to Madison Park. From there, among the local crowd also making its way to the Exposition, they boarded the *Fortuna*, one of several steamboats that ferried people to the A-Y-P boat landing in Lake Washington's Union Bay, near the Exposition's Wild Animal Park. It was a sunny late-summer morning, and Maddie and Clyde stood together at the prow of the steamboat as it plied its way out into the lake, rounded Webster Point, and headed into Union Bay. So far, he thought, she seemed to be enjoying herself.

There was not a single calendar day during the Exposition that was not specially designated as this or that honorary day. Sometimes the same day was specially designated four or five times over, with special events and exhibits honoring each official designee – Sailors Day, Dairy Day, Norway Day, San Francisco Day, Sportsmen's Day, Alaska Children's Day, Christian Church Day, Toppenish Day. Anyone, it seemed, could have a day designated to their organization, affiliation, or interest. This particular day, September 6, was Seattle Day, expected to be the biggest day yet at the Alaska-Yukon-Pacific Exposition, which was why Clyde had chosen it.

As the steamboat approached the landing, a group of forty or so school-children sang out the official Seattle Day song to the arriving visitors:

You must wake and call me early, call me early, mother, dear,
For today's the biggest day of all days at the Fair.
Of all the celebrations, there's one beyond compare,

And that's Seattle Day, mother, and, believe me, I'll Be There!
We've had the Eisteddfodders, the German Saengerfests,
We've had the Welshmen, Scotchmen, and Dutchmen as our guests,
We've had the Norway vikings – and the viking lassies fair,
But Seattle's due today, mother – it's a cinch that I'll Be There!

The boat docked and the crew let down the gangplank while the children carried on with their song.

"Will those poor children sing that all day," Maddie asked, as she and Clyde walked down the gangplank to the landing and past the schoolchildren.

Clyde had seen enough of the Exposition to suppose the children might very well have to sing the same song all day, and told Maddie so.

"The poor souls," was all she said, and took Clyde's arm as he guided her toward the entrance to the Exposition. Clyde nodded to his buddy working the gate, the one who said he would let Clyde and his friends in for free, and with a nod back from the friend he and Maddie pushed through the turnstiles, walked beneath the large Japanese Torii gate, and entered the A-Y-P grounds. While walking around the perimeter of Wild Animal Park and over the rustic trestle that crossed the Northern Pacific railroad tracks, they decided to just stroll through the grounds rather than set off on any planned course. Maddie said she wanted to see all of the people as much as any exhibits – and Clyde was more than happy to oblige her – so they made their way up Union Vista to Union Circle and from there to Arctic Circle and around the Geyser Basin. At this central location, scores of people ambled about, especially near the large round pool – younger couples arm in arm, stately older gentlemen with matronly ladies, new families with the mothers pushing baby strollers – all taken by the massive fountain at the center of the pool, the rainbow that appeared in its spray, and the lavish beds of begonias that encircled the entire pool.

The many large pots that had been empty in April were now filled with spiky palm ferns and dwarf cedar trees. The lampposts stuck Maddie as most peculiar, each one a single round globe atop a column with a score of perfectly round white bulbs attached to the globe, reminding her of bath bubbles. After strolling about the Geyser Basin three times, Maddie asked Clyde to take her to the Education Building, where the Broadway School was displaying the exhibit that Loye had helped assemble. She also wanted to see inside the King County Building, she said, but when Clyde informed her that there was an exhibit there on the regrading of Seattle, she said that the two of them had already seen enough of that exhibit first hand, and asked if they might instead just sit on a bench near the descending pools of the Cascades. This time they sat side by side, and Clyde could sense the mild awkwardness of the moment, remembering how Maddie had leaned into him and invited his kiss and then laid his hand on top of hers that first time they had sat on a bench at the Exposition grounds. He also remembered how she'd asked him on that day where he would be going next.

"I've missed you, Maddie," he said softly, without looking up, his eyes on his hands.

She reached over and took his hands in hers and squeezed them. "I've missed you, too."

This seemed to be all that either of them could say, or wanted to say. It was enough for now. Clyde didn't want to press the matter further, or even tell Maddie about the houseboat yet.

After a moment of sitting still and watching the passersby, Clyde laughed to himself, and Maddie released his hands, nudged him with her shoulder, and asked him what was so funny.

"I was thinking how the regrading exhibit makes no mention of Madison House or Jules Redelsheimer or the Redemptorists or any of the folks that didn't want their property cut away from beneath them. Wouldn't you just know it?" He looked up and saw Maddie looking at him, a somewhat vacant look on her face, and wondered if he'd misspoken and possibly upset her.

Then a smile seemed to creep across one corner of her mouth. "They really should have consulted us for the exhibit," she said, amused now as well, and then rested her cheek against Clyde's shoulder. "We're experts on the subject, aren't we?"

Neither said anything else on the matter, and it seemed to Clyde that the brief exchange had set them both to musing on the simple fact of their many years together on Denny Hill. They watched the crowds strolling past, some folks pausing alongside the Cascades and tossing in a penny to make a wish, others entering or exiting the decorative buildings on either side of the pools, and still others just sitting on benches, resting their feet and watching the show of activity.

Clyde remarked that, to the dismay of many of the Exposition's planners, the exhibition buildings were not proving to be nearly as popular as the Pay Streak. When it came right down to it, people were just more inclined toward amusing themselves than educating themselves.

"How about feeding themselves? Are they inclined that way too?" Maddie asked, and sat up straight with renewed enthusiasm, looking eager to move on. "Sir," she announced to Clyde, "I would like you to take me to the Japanese Tea House, if you don't mind."

"Then take you I shall," Clyde replied, and sprang to his feet and offered Maddie his hand.

On their way to the Nikko Cafe and Tea House, which Clyde knew was on the other side of the Cascade pools behind the Manufacturing Building, they had to stop short for a procession of the small, dark-skinned Igorots from the simulated Philippines tribal village on the Pay Streak, the men of the village clad in nothing more than leather G-strings and grass skirts and the few women among them in colorful striped sheets wrapped about their waists and over one shoulder. They paraded barefoot across the grounds carrying a United States flag and long banners that read, "We Igorots Have the Seattle Spirit!" and "We Celebrate Seattle Day!" Several of the men carried steel-tipped spears and carved-wood shields. In no particular ranks that Clyde could discern, they walked past the ogling onlookers, who readily stepped aside for them, and made their way to the U.S. Government Building. Clyde and Maddie watched them go by and Clyde told Maddie how the A-Y-P president, Arthur Chilberg, had been pleading with the Igorots to make themselves more decent by putting on pants – the Exposition was, after all, for families – but apparently his efforts had fallen on deaf ears.

At the Nikko Cafe, housed inside the Nikko Pavilion, two Japanese geisha-style hostesses invited Maddie and Clyde to remove their shoes and then led them to a two-foot-high table and sat them on the floor. A few moments later they served them green tea and tempura. The hostesses were extraordinarily solicitous toward Clyde, a sharp contrast to the familiar stares and outright snubs he was accustomed to receiving. Yet the attention that these smiling, bowing, powder-faced women gave him embarrassed him in ways the stares and snubs never had, and he could feel his face turn florid with his own blushing whenever one of them returned to their table to pour them more tea. Meanwhile Maddie contentedly drank her green tea and seemed amused at Clyde's discomfort in being so looked after by the hostesses. They finished their meal with ginger ice cream, and then one of the women brought them each a moist, steaming hot hand towel to freshen themselves with. Throughout their time in the Nikko Cafe, they spoke mostly of Ada, of Ray and Loye, and also of James and Chiridah – but not at all of themselves.

It was mid-afternoon by the time they walked out of the Nikko Cafe and back into the day's sunlight and mutually agreed that it was time to see the Pay Streak. As the afternoon continued to pass, though, Clyde grew more anxious about broaching the topic of the houseboat with Maddie. He knew that asking her to row across Portage Bay with him to visit it was not something he should spring on her at the very last minute. To do so would not be good manners. Yet he also didn't want to risk spoiling their outing by asking her too soon and placing her in the awkward position of having to decline his invitation. When they reached the entrance at the top of the long, loud boulevard that constituted the Pay Streak and that sloped down the hill toward Lake Union, Clyde purchased from a vendor an A-Y-P Seattle Day pennant attached to a stick and handed it to Maddie, who readily began waving it.

"That's the Seattle Spirit," he kidded her, as she waved it some more and sang, *"That's Seattle Day, mother, and, believe me, I'll Be There!"*

From the top of the Pay Streak, all that either of them could see was a swarm of humanity on the boardwalk heading down to the water. Maddie seized Clyde's arm as if not to lose him, and thus linked they ventured forth into the crowd. In the center of the boardwalk were a series of Oriental pagodas that functioned as novelty stands and food concessions. At the first pagoda they purchased a booklet of twenty tickets, which would allow them to go into any ten of the forty or more attractions along the Pay Streak. Maddie said she simply wanted to walk about first to see what there was before deciding what to enter, and again Clyde was happy to oblige her. He loved walking with Maddie, their arms locked, as they jostled their way through the crowd. Amidst the shouting from the barkers and the general clamor from the masses, they became, at different moments, like a raft, moving with the current of the crowd as it shifted, or like an island, standing firm against the tide and letting the crowd ebb and flow past them. Occasionally, a jinricksha pulled by a Japanese man in native costume, and with a man and woman seated on its cushioned bench, would scurry past them.

They walked past the two-story straw hut that led into the Igorot Village. Its steeply pitched thatched roof was topped with two American flags, and on either side of the hut a fifteen-foot bamboo screen prevented nonpaying onlookers from peering into the tribal compound. They walked past the Igorot Village and then paused in front of the Dixieland Concert Hall as a score of colored men in maroon band uniforms trimmed out in bright yellow marched onto the steps of the concert hall carrying their assorted brass instruments. The band leader, in an all-white uniform and white shoes, stepped forward once all the band members had assembled, raised his baton, and then swung the band into a rousing Dixieland number that left Maddie smiling and strumming her fingers on Clyde's forearm. Their next stop was in front of Namy Salih's Streets of Cairo, with the two towering obelisks covered in Egyptian hieroglyphics and a miniature Sphinx at the base of each. Outside the entrance, taking tickets, stood a dark, whiskered man wearing a yellow pongee toga with a cream-colored sash, a white turban, and red Moroccan shoes. He nodded to Clyde as if he recognized him, and Clyde, admitting to Maddie that he had seen the show twice already, explained how inside, the famous Princess Lala performed Cleopatra's Death Dance with a live asp, followed by La Belle Fatima doing the Danse du Ventre and La Belle Zamora doing her Salome dance. Maddie tugged on Clyde's arm and remarked how impressed she was by his interest and expertise in exotic dance.

Shortly after moving on from the Streets of Cairo, they were forced to stop at a ring of people in the center of the boardwalk blocking the flow of the crowd. Uproarious laughter rose from the crowd, and when Clyde and Maddie edged in closer they could see why. George "The Cardiff Giant" Auger, the tallest man on earth at eight feet two inches, was being chased in circles around a milk bottle by Ernest "The Giant Killer" Rommell, the shortest man on earth at four feet one inch. It was a promotional skit for their production of *Jack, the Giant Killer,* which was playing that week downtown at the Orpheum Theater. Once the skit concluded and the ring of people dispersed, Clyde and Maddie moved on to the Eskimo Village, where they looked in on Caribou Bill and his dog team. Even though the a-y-p Exposition was intended in part as a celebration of Alaska's great contribution to America, Maddie had no interest in any exhibit having anything to do with the territory – including the Eskimo Village, the Alaska Theater of Sensations, the Land of the Midnight Sun, the Gold Camps of Alaska (featuring Alkali Bill's Wild West and Injun Show), or the Klondyke Saloon and Dance Hall – remarking to Clyde that it all reminded her too much of her friend Laurette and everything she'd gone through in the Northland, even as she recognized the shows were all good wholesome fun for visitors from back East who'd only ever read Jack London novels. For her, the Alaska and Yukon shows and exhibits were like the regrading exhibit. There was nothing new for her to see.

They strolled past the halls housing the Battle of Gettysburg and the Monitor and Merrimack cycloramas and could hear the rifle pops and rebel yells coming from the first hall and the boom of cannons coming from the second. They passed the Spanish Theater, the Chinese Theater, the Jardin de Paris, the Temple of Palmistry, the Temple of Mirth, the Japanese Village, the stables of Prince Albert the Educated Horse, the Hunting in the Cascades Shooting Gallery, the Haunted Swing (where an unsmiling man in a billowy red and white polka dot clown suit leaned forlornly against the ticket window), the Tickler, the Flip-Flap, the Bridge of Sighs, the Trip to the Moon, Ezra Meeker's Pioneers Restaurant, the Baby Incubator Exhibit (and Cafe), the Upside-Down House, Pain's Fall of Port Arthur, the Vacuum Tube Railway, the Creation Diorama, the Wild Animal Show, the Flying Automobile and Fighting the Flames rides, and the Scenic Railway rollercoaster. Not until they reached the Ferris wheel at the very end of the Pay Streak, where a signboard announced this to be the "Largest Ferris Wheel in All the World," did Maddie express a genuine desire to partake of one of the amusements or rides.

She hurriedly pulled Clyde toward the entrance, whispering in his ear, "We can get away from the crowd."

Clyde thought that maybe this would be his chance. Their day at the Exposition, after all, was coming to an end.

The line of people waiting for a ride on the Ferris wheel surprisingly was not very long, and when their turn came, the operator opened the door to the semi-enclosed, egg-shaped car and had Maddie sit on one side and Clyde on the other to keep the car balanced. Yet as soon as the Ferris wheel turned, lifting their car into the sky, Maddie made a panicked reach across the space between them and clasped both of Clyde's hands in hers. He knew she wasn't genuinely afraid, yet he appreciated her playful gesture at being so.

"You're not really afraid, are you?" Clyde asked, remembering how enthusiastically Maddie had gone on the rides at Luna Park.

"No," she said, and gave him a mischievous smile. "Are you?"

Clyde shook his head no.

When their car reached the very top of the Ferris wheel and came to stop, Maddie scooted over to one side of her bench and tugged on Clyde's hands to pull him to her. He looked at her, surprised at her audacity, and then, as gently as he could, transferred his weight over to her side, tipping and rocking the car as he did so. When they were both seated again and the car had stilled itself, Maddie put her arms around Clyde and pulled him to her. This forwardness on her part came very unexpectedly for Clyde, and he wasn't sure how to respond to it. What of his inviting her to his houseboat? Yet this much was certain: he was happy to return Maddie's embrace. He even kissed her cheek as he wrapped both arms about her shoulders and pulled her body into his.

They held each other tightly for several moments, and then their car lurched and the Ferris wheel began moving again, and like youngsters caught behind the shed, they hastily released each other from their embrace. As the Ferris wheel rotated around several more times, they sat back, holding hands, and, with the car gently rocking them like a porch swing, looked out over the Pay Streak boulevard all the way up to the main Exposition grounds. On their second go-round to the top, Clyde turned to Maddie and kissed her on the forehead and cheek, and then on their third and final turn, she seized his face in her hands and kissed him firmly on the lips.

By the time the ride was over and they'd climbed out of their car and were back on solid ground, the bright afternoon was dimming into blue evening and the thousands of lights that illuminated the Alaska-Yukon-Pacific Exposition at night were beginning to make the grounds glow like a large torch flame. Not wanting to preempt Maddie's visit to the Exposition but also knowing that he didn't have a lamp on his skiff, Clyde realized he had to speak up now. So trying to sound as nonchalant as possible, but struggling for breath as he spoke, he suggested to Maddie that she might like to see the houseboat he'd recently come into possession of and that, for the past two months, had been hard at work improving.

"I believe," Maddie replied in a rather bemused tone, "that I heard Raymond say something about this houseboat of yours."

Clyde watched her face for a sign, was uncertain whether he saw one or not in her kind eyes, the slight part of her lips, the gentle curve of her cheek, the subtle tilt of her chin ... and then explained how the houseboat was located on the other side of Portage Bay, almost directly across the water from where they stood, and that he could row them there before nightfall if she wished.

Maddie did not respond immediately, but stood watching him, studying him, much as he had been watching and studying her just moments before. The delay in her response seemed very deliberate, though in no way malicious. "I think I would like that," she at last answered.

It was agreed then, and when they handed their booklet of Pay Streak tickets to a youngster tarrying outside the Ferris wheel entrance, the boy leapt with excitement, thanked them profusely, and sprinted to the nearby ice cream stand waving the tickets above his head and hollering out to his friends.

Clyde led Maddie along the shoreline the short distance from the base of the Pay Streak to the Life Saving Station where he had secured his skiff the day before. For the first time since Madison House had collapsed into a pile of rubble during the week of storms in May, leaving them both without a proper home and indefinitely separated from each other, Clyde felt as if their lives were about to dramatically change once more. It seemed that everything they had endured during the past decade – as the city scraped, hosed, and blasted Denny Hill from its skyline and in doing so erased the neighborhood that had once thrived there – was behind them now for good. All of the conflict, strife, heartache, pain, and worry of those years were no more, just as the boardinghouse and the hill upon which it had stood were no more. And what remained was just this – the two of them together.

As they approached the Life Saving Station, Clyde waved to one of the uniformed men atop the station tower, a buddy of his since he'd begun rowing to the A-Y-P grounds each day. He then escorted Maddie down the short dock. However, when they came to where the skiff was tied, Maddie paused, stepped back, and asked him, "What now for us, Clyde?"

He looked at her and also paused. He wasn't sure what answer she expected to hear – maybe she had no expectation of one – but he knew what he wanted to say to her.

"You'll come live with me on the houseboat," he said. "It'll be our home, and Ada's home. We'll be together there." There was more he could say, he knew, but for now, this was enough.

Maddie did not say anything. Instead, she gave him her hand, they glanced at each other, and without another word between them, he helped her step from the dock into the small skiff. He then untied the mooring rope, stepped into the skiff himself, and pushed it away from the dock. With Maddie seated facing him, he took hold of the oars, dropped them into the water, and began rowing them across the bay.

Acknowledgements

EXTENSIVE PRIMARY RESEARCH WENT INTO THE WRITING of *Madison House*. I am indebted to the following institutions for their assistance in this research: The Museum of History and Industry in Seattle, the Central Branch of the Seattle Public Library, the University of Washington Library (including the Pacific Northwest Special Collections), the Washington State History Museum in Tacoma, the Makah Cultural and Research Center in Neah Bay, the Northwest Seaport and Maritime Museum in Seattle, the Seattle Municipal Archives, and the National Park Service's Klondike Gold Rush Center in Seattle. In addition, I consulted numerous secondary sources. In respect to Seattle history, key among these were Cornelius H. Hanford's *Seattle and Environs 1852–1924*, Clarence B. Bagley's *History of Seattle from the Earliest Settlement to the Present Time*, Richard C. Berner's *Seattle 1900-1920: From Boomtown, Urban Turbulence, to Restoration*, Roger Sale's *Seattle, Past and Present*, Jeffrey Karl Ochsner's *Shaping Seattle Architecture: A Historical Guide to the Architects*, and Howard Draker's *Seattle's Unsinkable Houseboats*. For information on Puget Sound's utopian communities, I referred to Charles Pierce Lewarne's *Utopias on Puget Sound, 1885-1915*, while for Dawson City history, I relied on Lael Morgan's *Good Time Girls of the Alaska-Yukon Gold Rush*. For pertinent background on Asahel Curtis, Imogen Cunningham, and Henry James, I am obliged to David Sucher's *The Asahel Curtis Sampler: Photographs of Puget Sound Past*, Richard Lorenz's *Imogen Cunningham, Ideas without End: A Life in Photographs*, and Milton A. Mays's "Henry James in Seattle," among other works. In all, the list of titles that went into the research for the novel is long. A portion of Chapter 4 first appeared in the *Washington English Journal*, the annual literary publication of the Washington State Council of Teachers of English. I am grateful to Birmingham-Southern College for its financial and staff support during the writing of this work. For their astute editorial advice, I thank Val Clark and Emma Sweeney, and for his help with the Chinook jargon, I thank artist Duane Pasco. For their continued friendship and Northwest satori, I graciously bow to John Trombold and Philip Heldrich. For their instant belief in and enthusiasm for this novel, as well as for their editorial savvy, I owe a mammoth debt of gratitude to Kate Sage and Rhonda Hughes of Hawthorne Books and Literary Arts. And finally, for her unflagging love and support throughout the long journey that was the writing of this novel, I kiss my darling wife, Susan.

Titles available from Hawthorne Books

AT YOUR LOCAL BOOKSELLER OR FROM OUR WEBSITE : *hawthornebooks.com*

Core: A Romance
BY KASSTEN ALONSO

This intense and compact novel crackles with obsession, betrayal, and madness. As the narrator becomes fixated on his best friend's girlfriend, his precarious hold on sanity rapidly deteriorates into delusion and violence. This story can be read as the classic myth of Hades and Persephone (Core) rewritten for a twenty-first century audience as well as a dark tale of unrequited love and loneliness.

Alonso skillfully uses language to imitate memory and psychosis, putting the reader squarely inside the narrator's head ; deliberate misuse of standard punctuation blurs the distinction between the narrator's internal and external worlds. Alienation and Faulknerian grotesquerie permeate this landscape, where desire is borne in the bloom of a daffodil and sanity lies toppled like an applecart in the mud.

JUMP THROUGH THIS GOTHIC STAINED GLASS WINDOW *and you are in for some serious investigation of darkness and all of its deadly sins. But take heart, brave traveler, the adventure will prove thrilling. For you are in the beautiful hands of Kassten Alonso.*

—TOM SPANBAUER
Author of In the City of Shy Hunters

Decline of the Lawrence Welk Empire
BY POE BALLANTINE

"It's impossible not to be charmed by Edgar Donahoe [Publishers Weekly]," and he's back for another misguided adventure. When Edgar is expelled from college for drunkenly bellowing expletives from a dorm window at 3:00 am, he hitchhikes to Colorado and trains as a cook. A postcard arrives from Edgar's college buddy, Mountain Moses, inviting him to a Caribbean island. Once there Edgar cooks at the local tourist resort and falls in love with Mountain's girl, Kate. He becomes embroiled in a love triangle and his troubles multiply as he is stalked by murderous island native, Chollie Legion. Even Cinnamon Jim, the medicine man, is no help. Ultimately it takes a hurricane to blow Edgar out of this mess.

God Clobbers Us All

BY POE BALLANTINE

Set against the dilapidated halls of a San Diego rest home in the 1970s, *God Clobbers Us All* is the shimmering, hysterical, and melancholy story of eighteen-year-old surfer-boy orderly Edgar Donahoe's struggles with friendship, death, and an ill-advised affair with the wife of a maladjusted war veteran. All of Edgar's problems become mundane, however, when he and his lesbian Blackfoot nurse's aide best friend, Pat Fillmore, become responsible for the disappearance of their fellow worker after an LSD party gone awry. *God Clobbers Us All* is guaranteed to satisfy longtime Ballantine fans as well as convert those lucky enough to be discovering his work for the first time.

A SURFER DUDE TRANSFORMS *into someone captivatingly fragile, and Ballantine's novel becomes something tender, vulnerable, even sweet without that icky, cloying literary aftertaste. This vulnerability separates Ballantine's work from his chosen peers. Calmer than Bukowski, less portentous than Kerouac, more hopeful than West, Poe Ballantine may not be sitting at the table of his mentors, but perhaps he deserves his own after all.* —SETH TAYLOR
San Diego *Union-Tribune*

Things I Like About America

BY POE BALLANTINE

Best American Short Story Award Winner 1998

These risky, personal essays are populated with odd jobs, eccentric characters, boarding houses, buses, and beer. Ballantine takes us along on his Greyhound journey through small-town America, exploring what it means to be human. Written with piercing intimacy and self-effacing humor, Ballantine's writings provide entertainment, social commentary, and completely compelling slices of life.

IN HIS SEARCH *for the real America, Poe Ballantine reminds me of the legendary musk deer, who wanders from valley to valley and hilltop to hilltop searching for the source of the intoxicating musk fragrance that actually comes from him. Along the way, he writes some of the best prose I've ever read.* —SY SAFRANSKY
Editor, *The Sun*

 HAWTHORNE BOOKS & LITERARY ARTS :: *Portland, Oregon*

Madison House

BY PETER DONAHUE

Peter Donahue's debut novel *Madison House* chronicles turn-of-the-century Seattle's explosive transformation from frontier outpost to major metropolis. Maddie Ingram, owner of Madison House, and her quirky and endearing boarders find their lives inextricably linked when the city decides to regrade Denny Hill and the fate of Madison House hangs in the balance. Clyde Hunssler, Maddie's albino handyman and furtive love interest; James Colter, a muckraking black journalist who owns and publishes the Seattle *Sentry* newspaper; and Chiridah Simpson, an aspiring stage actress forced into prostitution and morphine addiction while working in the city's corrupt vaudeville theater, all call Madison House home. Had E.L. Doctorow and Charles Dickens met on the streets of Seattle, they couldn't have created a better book.

PETER DONAHUE *seems to have a map of old Seattle in his head. No novel extant is nearly as thorough in its presentation of the early city, and all future attempts in its historical vein will be made in light of this book.* —DAVID GUTERSON
Author of *Snow Falling on Cedars* and *Our Lady of the Forest*

So Late, So Soon

BY D'ARCY FALLON

This memoir offers an irreverent, fly-on-the-wall view of the Lighthouse Ranch, the Christian commune D'Arcy Fallon called home for three years in the mid-1970s. At eighteen years old, when life's questions overwhelmed her and reconciling her family past with her future seemed impossible, she accidentally came upon the Ranch during a hitchhike gone awry. Perched on a windswept bluff in Loleta, a dozen miles from anywhere in Northern California, this community of lost and found twenty-somethings lured her in with promises of abounding love, spiritual serenity, and a hardy, pioneer existence. What she didn't count on was the fog.

I FOUND FALLON'S STORY *fascinating, as will anyone who has ever wondered about the role women play in fundamental religious sects. What would draw an otherwise independent woman to a life of menial labor and subservience? Fallon's answer is this story, both an inside look at 70s commune life and a funny, irreverent, poignant coming of age.* —JUDY BLUNT
author of *Breaking Clean*

www.hawthornebooks.com

Dastgah: Diary of a Headtrip
BY MARK MORDUE

Australian journalist Mark Mordue invites you on a journey that ranges from a Rolling Stones concert in Istanbul to talking with mullahs and junkies in Tehran, from a cricket match in Calcutta to an S&M bar in New York, and to many points in between, exploring countries most Americans never see as well as issues of world citizenship in the 21st century. Written in the tradition of literary journalism, *Dastgah* will take you to all kinds of places, across the world ... and inside yourself.

I JUST TOOK A TRIP AROUND THE WORLD IN ONE GO, *first zigzagging my way through this incredible book, and finally, almost feverishly, making sure I hadn't missed out on a chapter along the way. I'm not sure what I'd call it now: A road movie of the mind, a diary, a love story, a new version of the subterranean homesick and wanderlust blues – anyway, it's a great ride. Paul Bowles and Kerouac are in the back, and Mark Mordue has taken over the wheel of that pickup truck from Bruce Chatwin, who's dozing in the passenger seat.*

—WIM WENDERS
Director of *Paris, Texas; Wings of Desire;*
and *The Buena Vista Social Club*

The Cantor's Daughter
Stories
BY SCOTT NADELSON

The Cantor's Daughter is the compelling new collection from Oregon Book Award Winner and recipient of the GLCA's New Writers Award for 2005, Scott Nadelson. In his follow-up to *Saving Stanley: The Brickman Stories*, these new stories capture Jewish New Jersey suburbanites in moments of crucial transition, when they have the opportunity to connect with those closest to them or forever miss their chance for true intimacy. In the title story, Noa Nechemia and her father have immigrated from Israel to Chatwin, New Jersey, following a tragic car accident her mother did not survive. In one stunning moment of insight following a disastrous prom night, Noa discovers her ability to transcend grief and determine the direction of her own life. Nadelson's stories are sympathetic, heartbreaking, and funny as they investigate the characters' fragile emotional bonds and the fears that often cause those bonds to falter or fail.

HAWTHORNE BOOKS & LITERARY ARTS :: Portland, Oregon

Saving Stanley: The Brickman Stories

BY SCOTT NADELSON

Oregon Book Award Winner 2004
GLCA's New Writers Award for 2005

Scott Nadelson's interrelated short stories are graceful, vivid narratives that bring into sudden focus the spirit and the stubborn resilience of the Brickmans, a Jewish family of four living in suburban New Jersey. The central character, Daniel Brickman, forges obstinately through his own plots and desires as he struggles to balance his sense of identity with his longing to gain acceptance from his family and peers. This fierce collection provides an unblinking examination of family life and the human instinct for attachment.

SCOTT NADELSON PLAYFULLY INTRODUCES *us to a fascinating family of characters with sharp and entertaining psychological observations in gracefully beautiful language, reminiscent of young Updike. I wish I could write such sentences. There is a lot of eros and humor here – a perfectly enjoyable book.* —JOSIP NOVAKOVICH
author of *April Fool's Day: A Novel*

The Greening of Ben Brown

BY MICHAEL STRELOW

Michael Strelow weaves the story of a town and its mysteries in his debut novel. Ben Brown becomes a citizen of East Leven, Oregon, after he recovers from an electrocution that has not left him dead but has turned him green. He befriends 22 year-old Andrew James and together they unearth a chemical spill cover-up that forces the town to confront its demons and its citizens to choose sides. Strelow's lyrical prose and his talent for storytelling come together in this poetic and important first work that looks at how a town and the natural environment are inextricably linked. *The Greening of Ben Brown* will find itself in good company on the shelves between Winesburg, Ohio and To Kill a Mockingbird; readers of both will have a new story to cherish.

MICHAEL STRELOW HAS GIVEN NORTHWEST READERS *an amazing fable for our time and place featuring Ben Brown, a utility lineman who transforms into the Green Man following an industrial accident. Eco-Hero and prophet, the Green Man heads a cast of wonderful and zany characters who fixate over sundry items from filberts to hubcaps. A timely raid on a company producing heavy metals galvanizes Strelow's mythical East Leven as much as the Boston Tea Party rallied Boston. Fascinating, humorous and wise,* The Greening of Ben Brown *deserves its place on bookshelves along with other Northwest classics.*

—CRAIG LESLEY
Author of *Storm Riders*

September 11:
West Coast Writers Approach Ground Zero
EDITED BY JEFF MEYERS

The myriad repercussions and varied and often contradictory responses to the acts of terrorism perpetuated on September 11, 2001 have inspired thirty-four West Coast writers to come together in their attempts to make meaning from chaos. By virtue of history and geography, the West Coast has developed a community different from that of the East, but ultimately shared experiences bridge the distinctions in provocative and heartening ways. Jeff Meyers anthologizes the voices of American writers as history unfolds and the country braces, mourns, and rebuilds.

CONTRIBUTORS INCLUDE: *Diana Abu-Jaber, T. C. Boyle, Michael Byers, Tom Clark, Joshua Clover, Peter Coyote, John Daniel, Harlan Ellison, Lawrence Ferlinghetti, Amy Gerstler, Lawrence Grobel, Ehud Havazelet, Ken Kesey, Maxine Hong Kingston, Stacey Levine, Tom Spanbauer, Primus St. John, Sallie Tisdale, Alice Walker, and many others.*

 HAWTHORNE BOOKS & LITERARY ARTS :: *Portland, Oregon*